RELIC OF THE DAMNED

Thomas A. Bradley

For John and Ruth, forever with me.

PART ONE

The Coming

CHAPTER 1

Patricia O'Donnell stood against the wall of the EasyMart with her fingers interlaced behind her head. In front of her, the man in the ski mask was waving a 9mm Beretta around and barking orders she could hardly understand. Tears streamed freely down her face and her knees were visibly shaking.

"C'mon! c'mon, I ain't got all damned day! Open the fuckin' cash register or I'll splash your pretty brains all over that wall behind ya." The robber's voice was almost whiny. Most of what he said came out sounding like a '50s AM disc jockey monologue.

"C'mon, girl ... git movin'," he barked. He grabbed her by the shoulder and shoved her over to the register. "Open it! Now!"

Patricia was twenty-six and scared to death that she wouldn't make twenty-seven. Her hands shook as she fumbled for the drawer's master key. Without a sale, there was no other way to open it. She was whimpering out loud as she turned the key and the drawer popped open.

The man in the mask grabbed her by the hair and flung her up against the wall. After he had cleaned out the register, collecting all of two hundred and twenty-eight dollars, he turned and faced her. He stuck the barrel of the semi-automatic up against her forehead and with his free hand, grabbed her left breast and squeezed.

"If I had the time," he growled, "I'd do you. I bet you'd be real fine, too ... but I ain't got that kinda time ... so just get on your knees ... and hurry up about it." He reached up and put his free hand on top of her head. He eased her to the floor and made her unzip his pants.

Before she sank to her knees behind the counter, Patricia saw Sheriff Dougherty's patrol car slow, then a yellow car shot by him and he went after it. For the briefest of moments she thought she had been saved – but just as quickly that safety raced off in pursuit of a speeder.

"Gaw'head, baby...get it *all* the way in there. The man held on tightly to the back of her head. When she finished, he pushed her backwards, laughed and pulled the trigger on the Beretta.

Bang! The sound echoed around the empty store. Its volume even startled the robber. Patricia slumped backward and lay there like a broken mannequin. Blood and brain matter were stuck to the white tile wall and a pool of blood widened beneath her.

The man in the ski mask pulled up his zipper and left. When he got outside he took a quick look around, pulled off his mask, filled his Camry with premium and drove off.

Five minutes after Patricia lost her life, a State Police car rolled in. The officer inside pulled out his report log and started writing. In ten more minutes he'd go in for a cup of coffee, and thirteen minutes after that, Jack Dougherty would be looking at the first murder victim Banderman Falls had ever had.

***

Jack Dougherty was the sheriff of Banderman Falls and if anyone knew that town inside and out it was Jack. He was on a first-name basis with most of the residents, some for reasons he'd rather not be. Most of the time his job was fairly routine; the big crimes were primarily confined to the Falls's neighbor, Philadelphia. There had never been a crime, involving a weapon. The most frequent call to action for Jack centered on speeding or collisions. Occasionally he got to assist in an arrest when a fleeing suspect crossed the border from Philadelphia to Banderman Falls. Jack was always willing to cooperate with the Philly police, and it went the other way, too. There had been a few times when Jack required their assistance with a suspect that "perped" in the Falls and then ran back to his home in Philly. In such cases, arrest warrants were served jointly and the suspect handed over to Jack. It was a good cooperative working arrangement and benefited both departments.

Jack was sitting in his Lincoln Town Car with the 482 Interceptor engine, struggling with a crossword puzzle. The cruiser, sitting just off the road where Ridge Avenue turned to Ridge Pike, was obscured by a small stand of trees. This was the place most likely to catch any speeders as they zoomed in from Andorra, the Philadelphia suburb that butted up against Banderman Falls.

A burst of static cut the silence preceding Audrey Archibald's voice. Audrey was one of two radio dispatchers; the other was her sister, Gwen. They alternated shifts and manned the station desk.

When Jack or the deputies were out on patrol, they were the only ones there to mind the store.

"Jack," crackled Audrey, "there's about six people here with their applications for part-time holiday patrol duty. Did you want to come on back in and talk to them?"

Jack stuck a pen in the crossword book to hold the page and tossed it on the passenger seat. The idea of having to hire part-time help didn't sit well with him. It could all too easily lead to trouble. Screening for the right people was imperative; otherwise, Jack was afraid he'd end up with someone who thought he was "Dirty Harry."

"No! I don't," sighed Jack. "But I guess I'd better. Have they already finished filling out the apps?"

"Yep! Sure have; and they're milling about like flies caught in a mason jar."

Jack chuckled to himself. Audrey had a way of putting things that could bring a smile to your face, even when it wasn't appropriate. She called them as she saw them and never held back. Tact was *not* her strong point.

"Ok, tell them I'm on my way. "Who've I got there, anyway?"

"Well, there's Frank Mowery; Sam Twilling, if you can believe that ... Sam Crowley, another winner; Ethan Kennedy, probably your best choice; Matt O'Donnell, and the best of the best – the one I saved for last – the one you won't believe – the one-"

Jack cut her off. "Ok, I get the picture, Audrey. Who is this mystery gem, already?"

"Ok, you ready? Here goes?"

Jack knew Audrey loved getting under his skin. It was always in fun, but it tickled her no end to exasperate him, just a little.

"It's ... drum roll please ... Rachel Parker."

"Oh Christ, no! You've got to be kidding. *She's* got to be kidding! That's perfect."

"Yeah," chortled Audrey. "Can't you just see her now, running down the street after a pickpocket in her stiletto heels and fishnets, with her boobs slapping her in the chin? Lovely sight for families on the Fourth, don't you think?" Audrey was laughing boisterously now, totally unconstrained.

"Give me liberty...or give me death ... by 38Ds," she roared, in the deepest voice she could manage. She was on a roll and Jack knew it was unlikely to end anytime soon.

"Audrey, is she there? Can she hear you?"

"Of course, to both questions. I'm already getting the iceberg stare, but who cares. Hey, you gonna give her a nightstick? God, and the rest of the town, knows where she'll stick that."

"Enough, Audrey. I'm on my way in. Just settle down and leave it alone till I get there. Christ, I'm gonna have to listen to her, you know. I'll be there in fifteen minutes. Out!"

"Well, so much for you, my friend," Jack said, stuffing the crossword puzzle book into the glove box. "Maybe later." He eased the unmarked gray cruiser out onto Ridge Pike and headed back toward the center of town. His thumbs tapped out the conga beat from *Sympathy for the Devil* on the top of the steering wheel as he tried to figure out exactly how he was going to appease Rachel when he got there. She'd be furious and probably demand some sort of disciplinary action against Audrey. *God, I wish that woman would learn when NOT to talk out loud*, Jack thought.

On the way in, Jack passed the EasyMart and considered stopping to grab a fresh cup of coffee but was afraid that if he left Audrey to her own devices with Rachel there'd be a fistfight by the time he got back. He slowed but didn't stop. As he did, a yellow Mustang shot by him on the left, which barely missed taking his side-view mirror with it. Jack hit the reds and blues and accelerated. Had he stopped, he might have prevented Banderman Falls's first murder.

CHAPTER 2

On the morning that would change his life forever, Carlton Wedgemore trotted down the steps to the basement of his antique shop. Coffee cup in hand, he threaded the maze of eclectic odds and ends – furniture pieces, paintings, statuettes and the like – that awaited restoration and relocation to the shop above.

For the most part, Wedgemore's Antique Shop was a one-man operation, except on Thursdays and Fridays. On those days, Evelyn Ramsey would mind the shop upstairs while Carlton unpacked and cataloged his new acquisitions.

Carlton set his cup on the edge of a roll-top desk that he had been meaning for months to move upstairs. Leaning against its edge, he ripped open the envelope tab, sighed in disgust and dropped its contents on the desk. There was nothing in the envelope of any immediate interest. He pushed away from the desk, stopped to brush the dust off the seat of his pants, and grumbled about the mark it had probably left on his newly tailored Armani.

Carlton was one of the wealthier residents of Banderman Falls, but not because of his antique shop's success. No, it barely made a profit. His money had come from his parents on their death. He inherited a sprawling estate, complete with tended gardens and servant's quarters. But Carlton had no servants; he couldn't stand the thought of anyone going through his house or his things.

As he began inventorying his new arrivals, he could hear Evelyn clomping back and forth across the solid oak floors above. Having her in his shop was a necessity but an annoyance, nonetheless. She had an eye for detail and a thorough knowledge of what was and what was *not* truly antique. What Carlton resented was her appearance, feeling it detracted from the finery of his business. She was what was euphemistically called a big-boned child, although not *everyone* in Banderman Falls was that kind to her. She had suffered her share of insults: *fatty, look at the whale on the beach, shouldn't you have a license plate on your ass,* and *I'll bet they can see you from space.* Carlton never knew, nor would he have cared if he had, that at night, alone in the dark and quiet of her room, she'd cry herself to sleep, wishing she could be thin.

Carlton had sorted through most of the boxes when the corner of a wooden crate jutting out from under a pile of packing peanuts drew his attention. He stared at it with the curiosity of a child on Christmas morning. He stooped down (being very careful not to let the knee of his suit trousers touch the dirty concrete floor) and brushed the peanuts aside. Most of them went flying, but a few were tenacious. Static electricity is a powerful anchoring tool if you're a packing peanut. They clung to the back of his hand and decorated the lapel and sleeve of his dark gray suit jacket.

Beneath the pesky packing material sat a solidly constructed shipping crate about the size of a military footlocker. The outside was stamped in several different languages, none of which Carlton spoke. It was like nothing he'd ever seen before. But at this moment, he was only interested in the English, and the delivery address it was printed in.

He leaned in closer to read the label in the dim illumination of the naked 60w bulbs that severed as basement lighting. It read:

Antiquities Service
1411 Ridgemans Pike
Benderick Falls, AZ 86449

"Terrific," he muttered, "another damned glitch in the morning." He gave it a tug with his fingertips but it didn't budge. It was much heavier than it looked. Using both hands and grunting, he slid it out into the middle of the floor. The lid was fastened tight with heavy-duty packing staples, and there were a ton of them – one almost every inch all the way around.

"That's a little overkill, I think." He worked himself upright and was rewarded with the familiar pins-and-needles effect you experience when you've cut off the circulation to your extremities too long. He stamped his feet, hoping to force it into remission, but it rebuked his efforts. Such things have a will of their own.

Carlton pulled off his suit jacket and looked around for a suitable place to hang it. The shop's foundation was stone and mortar, a lot of which was crumbling. The walls were damp, and the open rafters above shed tiny clouds of dust wherever someone upstairs was walking. Long abandoned webs, hanging down like forgotten party streamers, held the decaying remains of unused prey.

"Have to get that cow down here and clean up," he muttered, as he gave up the search for a clean place to hang his suit jacket and laid it carefully across the antique desk. While rolling up his sleeves, he set about finding a crowbar. His starched white cuffs crackled in protest as he curled them back. His curiosity had gotten the best of him and he decided to open the box – his or not.

The metallic sound of metal tools being unceremoniously tossed aside echoed throughout the basement as he dug through the rusted tool chest drawers. The rollers squeaked and stuck as he yanked one draw open after another. At last, at the very bottom, he hit pay dirt. He found an old molding lifter.

"This'll do very nicely." The corners of his mouth curled upwards in a victory grin. A few more minutes and he'd see what, exactly, was in the misguided crate. He strode over to it and stood there.

One must take their time when opening a surprise gift, he thought, *the thrill is in the discovery.* Completely out of character, he knelt on the cold hard floor, no longer concerned with the care of his suit, and began prying open the crate. Something inside him was driving him. It didn't matter that the crate wasn't his; it was calling to him and he had to know what was inside. More than that, he had to hold it; he could feel it deep inside, an overwhelming lust to hold the object, whatever it was, in his hand – to caress it – to make it his own.

***

Carlton worked himself into a sweat, a smile breaking across his lips as he pried the last of the ninety-five packing staples out. When the lid popped up, he let the molding lifter bang down on the floor. It made a clanging ring that bounced around the walls. He flipped the wooden lid off in his excitement to find out what treasure he had received. He didn't even realize that he was now thinking of it as *his* treasure.

Inside the crate, covered in pounds of excelsior, were three smaller wooden boxes, neatly packed side-by-side with just enough material between them to keep them from bumping up against one another.

Unable to constrain himself, he reached in and yanked the center box out. He placed it carefully on the floor before searching for the dropped molding lifter. His palms were sweaty with exhilaration, and his tongue wagged between his teeth.

He jammed the blade of the lifter under the lid and was about to push down when he suddenly stopped. From some hidden, dusty recess of his mind, a voice called to him – instructed him – demanded of him – that he choose another box to open first.

Carlton withdrew the molding lifter from the edge of the box, laid it on top and wiped the sweat from his palms on his pants. He rubbed them briskly up and down, ensuring that they were clean and dry, and ready to lift the *right* box – *the one that counted* – from the crate in front of him.

Everything else around Carlton but the box faded to insignificance. His mind was fixated on only one thing, and everything else around him suddenly became meaningless. He *had* to open the box. He had to have what was inside; he had to have what was calling to him. He pulled out heaps of excelsior, tossing them everywhere. When he was sure he could get a good grip on it and lift it out safely, he tugged it up and over the lip of its shipping crate, gently placing it on the floor in front of him.

"Deep breath, Carlton ... deep breath ... take it nice and slow. It's going to be grand, isn't it?

You *know* it is. And it's yours ... all yours. Your gift for having to put up with these idiots that surround you in this dumpy town. These low-life's that are just waiting for you to die so that they can divvy up your property among themselves. But, we'll show them, won't we? Oh yes! We'll show them now."

His words echoed through the basement and came back to him, but the voice was unrecognizable. It was as if someone else were down there speaking to him. *We're not sharing this little gem, are we, Carlton? Oh no! No sharing here.*

Carlton grabbed up the molding lifter again, ready to free his prize, when he heard it. It was soft, but commanding. A hissing voice. It sounded as if someone were calling to him through a leaky steam pipe. It's what he had always imagined a snake would sound like if it could speak.

"Not yet, Carlton," it hissed. "Not until tonight. Tonight, when the shop is closed and dark. When the light of day has given up its life to the velvety blackness of night and all the inquisitive, intrusive, busybodies of the town are lying lazily in their beds. That's when you shall open me, and not before."

Carlton should have been frightened. He should have backed away from the box like a man backing away from an unexpectedly discovered hornet's nest. But he didn't. He couldn't. He wasn't frightened at all. He was elated, excited, overcome with desire. He had no idea what was in the box, but he sensed it was power. It was a kind of power that Carlton Wedgemore had only dreamed of having; a power beyond wealth. And now – now the power was here, and it would be his. Tonight!

CHAPTER 3

Jasper Collins cut the engine to the power mower, drew a dirty, sweat-soaked, paisley handkerchief from his back pocket and mopped the beads of sweat from his brow and cheeks. The Briggs and Stratton engine clunked a few times, expelling a small cloud of blue smoke from the exhaust before falling silent. Jasper's face was red from the heat and the exertion of pushing the mower up and down the cemetery hills. Beneath the red, his face was already starting to turn a rich bronze. An early tan was one of the benefits of working outdoors every day.

Working in the quiet of the cemetery suited Jasper. He wasn't much of a people person. His tours in Vietnam, and the subsequent treatment he'd received from the general populace at large when he'd arrived home, turned him inside himself. And he was happy living there. He avoided people as much as possible and rarely spoke when he did encounter them. Tending to the dead was, to his way of thinking, the best job you could have. Not one of his *customers* ever asked more from him than a blanket of dirt and a trim of the weeds above his head.

Jasper leaned against the Richland monument and lit a Marlboro. The granite monument towered above him; it was the carved likeness of Michael the Archangel, perched on a mountain-top-shaped bolder. He was bent over in his descent to earth, one leg outstretched for landing, the other leg trailing behind. His wings were spread out full and folded inward on the edges; his right arm crossed in front of him holding the sword with which he had driven Lucifer from heaven. In his left hand was a large tablet on which were carved the names of all the Richlands that resided below him. Patches of moss and algae had invaded the crevices of his wing feathers giving a shadowy texture to the weathering granite. He was frozen there, standing eternal sentry duty over the Richlands.

Jasper drew in deeply on the cigarette and exhaled slowly. The smoke drifted lazily upward in the still air, splitting into two gray columns as it hit the edge of Michael's blade. Somewhere in the distance he could hear a dog barking, and just over the next hill, the sound of the backhoe opening another grave – the ultimate storage facility. *This way to the great egress.* He looked up, watching the smoke dissipate into the late morning sky. Catching sight of Michael's stern and resolute visage, he smiled to himself. He always thought: *One of these days ol' Michael here is going to jump off this marker and do battle with the two gargoyles perched atop the Langer's stone, two rows up and to the left.* In fact, on more than one occasion, Jasper had come into the cemetery at night and sat beneath

Michael smoking a joint or two, waiting for the cataclysmic battle to begin. It never did.

Stubbing out the butt of his cigarette on the Richland's stone, he tossed it over into the weeds that lined the drive. He looked down at the sleeping mower, thought about firing it up again, then thought better of it and lit another cigarette. *One can never be too cautious in the heat,* he reasoned. *Take things nice an' easy - that's ol' Jasper's motto. No sense pushing for heatstroke.*

The sky above was clear except for the few wispy clouds that drifted by occasionally. The sun was high overhead, a bright orange-white globe surrounded by that certain kind of limpid halo that rings it on the hottest days. The asphalt and stone roadway that snaked through the cemetery fought desperately to fend off the heat it couldn't absorb, creating a kind of fluid motion above its surface.

Peaceful Haven was, by today's standards, a small cemetery, but it was old. The first plot laid had been that of Myra Banderman, wife of the town founder, Aloysius Banderman. Myra died in 1851 of tuberculosis – called consumption in those days. Banderman had interred her himself in the lower end of his back field. At some point, a fence had been erected and the plot of land became the unofficial cemetery for the burgeoning town. Every family living in the town at the time was connected to Banderman or his mill in some capacity; so it was only natural that, when the inevitable occurred, they'd be laid to rest on his property.

As time passed and the town grew, so did the cemetery. And at some point it had been sanctioned by the Catholic Church. Saint Agnes was built in the early twentieth century, and it seemed only fitting to finally consecrate the ground where so many souls were already at rest.

Jasper dropped the butt that was now burned down to the filter and mashed it out with the ball of his foot. He glanced at his Timex, rubbed a smudge of dirt off the crystal with his thumb and pushed away from the marker. Taking a few steps forward, he stopped, turned around and bowed to the statue.

"If you'll excuse me, Mr. Archangel, it's twelve-ten, time for ol' Jasper's lunch. Can I bring you anything back?" Jasper looked into the cold, rounded stone eyes that burned downward, warding off any possible return to heaven by Lucifer. "No? Oh well, have it your way."

As he turned to go, a grating sound, like someone dragging a heavy stone across the road, filled the air. He whirled around, but no one was there. When he started to turn back he stopped dead in his tracks. The head on the statue of Michael was now angled to the left and the eyes seemed to have closed to near squints. If it had been a human being, the expression on its face would have been described as intense anger. Jasper could almost feel the fury emanating from the granite. The hairs on the back of his neck rose up in bristly patches and goosebumps broke out on his arms.

The statue seemed to be looking somewhere beyond Jasper – somewhere over his shoulder. He wanted to turn to look but was afraid of what he might see. Instinctively, defensively, the way we do when we know that what we're seeing cannot possibly be real, he pinched his eyes shut with his thumb and forefinger. He squeezed hard enough to make them ache for a moment and then released his grip, believing that when he opened them the statue would be as it had always been, and that it was only the heat that had played his mind a trick. Warily, he raised a single eyelid.

As the cascade of flashing lights from having put too much pressure on the eyeballs cleared, he staggered backwards, tripping over a ground marker and went sprawling out onto the grass. He pushed himself up on one elbow, and as he moved, the statue's head did also – following him with its cold, dead eyes. The wings folded back behind it with a scraping noise and the arm with the sword unfolded at the elbow - straightening, pointing the tip of the blade at Jasper.

Jasper fell back whimpering, not believing. He closed his eyes, covering them with both hands in hopes that if he couldn't see it anymore it couldn't see him. The terror inside him welled out of his eyes and rolled down his cheeks in the form of tears. He never ever remembered being as frightened as he was at that moment – not even in the worst firefight he'd been in in "The Nam."

He wanted to holler – to scream out for help, but his throat would not cooperate. It was dry – cotton-filled and useless. The best he was able to manage was tiny squeaks, like those of a child whimpering under his blankets because of the bogeyman in the closet. Despite the day's heat, he was shivering and clammy.

A horrible sound filled his ears. It sounded like someone raking the surface off stone blocks with the claw end of a hammer, while simultaneously churning cinders in a steel drum. Jasper pulled his hands from in front of his eyes and covered his ears but the sound persisted, growing louder until it became coherent, raspy words.

"Prepare!" it said. "It is here. He will come! Many will fall while others will rise. Darkness and decay shall walk in the light. Prepare!"

As suddenly as it began, all fell silent. The only sounds that Jasper could hear were the birds singing in the trees and the backhoe over the hill pounding its bucket on the freshly refilled grave.

With more apprehension than he'd ever experienced, Jasper opened his eyes. He turned his head so that he was not looking directly at the winged statue. The first thing he saw was the waves of heat wiggling up from the hot roadway. The sight seemed to settle him a little. It was something normal – something anyone would expect to see.

Mustering every ounce of will he had left in him, he swiveled his head around to face the granite archangel. There it stood, alighting on the marker as before, arm bent across the front of it holding the sword, and the wings were once again folded forward, bent in at the edges. All was as it should be.

Jasper worked himself to his feet and stood there staring. Inching forward, one step at a time, his legs feeling rubbery, he made his way to the base of the stone figure. He reached out his hand a

placed it on its foot. The toes were smooth and cool
to the touch. He was relieved. He had been sure
that it would have been body-temperature warm –
alive warm. It wasn't. It was just cold stone. He
slowly raised his eyes to its.

Nothing! No anger, just determination; the
determination the sculptor had given it when he
chiseled it into existence. Whatever Jasper Collins,
humble cemetery worker, had seen or heard (or
thought he had seen or heard) was gone. All that
remained in front of him was an enormous
visualization of a mythic being, brought to life by
the hand of the sculptor's mental image of what an
angel, an *archangel*, should look like.

"I'll be God-" Jasper caught himself, too
shaken to continue with the full – blasphemy? -
cuss. "Must be the heat. Has to be! Yep, that's it.
Ol' Jasper's been out in the sun too long. That's all.
Think I'll call it a day." He nodded his head up and
down agreeing with himself. "Yep, that's it for sure.
Has to be the heat. Ol' Jasper's goin home for the
day."

The sounds of the distant backhoe had died
away and the air was calm. An intermittent light
breeze rustled the leaves of the trees and blades of
grass that had not yet been shortened by Jasper's
mower. A chipmunk darted across the road and
disappeared into the brush on the far side, tail raised
straight up like an empty flagpole.

Jasper walked over to one of the headstones
where he'd left his water bottle and retrieved it.
Grabbing the mower handle by one hand, he
dragged it behind him across the roadway and

parked it unceremoniously amidst the shrubbery on the shoulder. The possibility of any sudden rainstorm was remote, so he concluded it would keep there safely until tomorrow morning. Besides, at this point, he didn't really care all that much about the mower. All he wanted to do was put some distance between him and the cemetery – between him and the statue. *All would be right with the world*, he told himself – *tomorrow*.

CHAPTER 4

There's a certain kind of smell that permeates the air when the day is hot and sticky. It's a smell that clings to your clothes and works its way into your hair. You carry it with you, like the unseen dust mites that make their living off your decay. It's that familiar mixture of baked asphalt and concrete, blended with over- and under-watered lawns, auto exhaust, and perspiration – a kind of warmed staleness that pervades your daily routines. Banderman Falls had that smell.

The radio reported that they were going to hit an unprecedented one hundred and two degrees, agreed by all as being much too hot for the beginning of July. In two days the town would be celebrating the two hundred and thirty-fourth birth of its nation. Parades and backyard cookouts would be in full swing, and the pops and bangs of fireworks (illegal, but covertly purchased and detonated nonetheless) would sound throughout the neighborhoods.

Grady Peters had landed a temporary job helping to put up the town's Fourth of July decorations. It was only three days' work, but it was better than nothing. He'd lost his former job when the Sanitation Department was privatized. Since then, he and his family had been struggling along as best they could.

His wife, Tamika, had taken on part-time work at the dry cleaners and supplemented this by a work-from-home job stuffing envelopes. It barely paid the bills. Their son, Willie, was in Catholic School, and the tuition and clothing bills were killing them. But they made all the payments – on time – even if it meant cutting back on groceries here and there.

Grady settled the hardhat onto his head and climbed into the bucket. He waved his readiness to Eric Baxter and then grabbed the levers, hoisting the bucket into the air. The hydraulic pump of the cherry-picker made a whiney noise as it extended its silver arm. When he eased the levers to the stop position, the bucket bobbed up and down until it reached its equilibrium.

"That gonna do it?" shouted Eric.

"Yep! It won't take too long. Just gotta tie off the ends," Grady shouted back. The rope he was tying was connected to the large celebration banner that would span Ridge Pike. It was the same banner that went up year after year, a deep blue background with red and white stripes. One end sported a cluster of white stars, and sprawled across the length of the banner, in twenty-four-inch characters read the message:

Banderman Falls Celebrates Our Nation's Birth
July 4, 1776

The blue T-shirt with cut off sleeves that Grady wore was already plastered to his chest and back. The sweat ran down his muscular arms, giving his black skin a reflective sheen. He balanced himself carefully as he leaned out of the swaying fiberglass bucket to wrap the rope around the pole. When he had cinched it up and knotted the ends to his satisfaction, he motioned to Eric that he was going to lower the bucket.

***

By late morning Eric and Grady had worked themselves around the town.

"Ok then, that'll 'bout put the wrappins on that," said Eric. "Last a-the decs to go up on this street, anyhows. You 'bout ready for lunch, big feller?"

Grady looked at Eric, not knowing exactly what to say. He was famished, but he couldn't afford to spend any money on lunch. No sireee Bob's yer uncle, lunch was not a necessity in Grady's world.

Eric picked up on it right away. Eric Baxter was one of those people who get to wander through this world with a heart five times his own size. He wasn't a wealthy man. Hell, probably never would be, either. But he was comfortable. He lived alone, except for his dog, Ruby, and did just fine on the

salary the Township paid him. He had no mortgage
debt, the trailer he lived in he owned free and clear.
He was fond of telling people how it had all the
room, *and more*, he'd ever need for him and old
Ruby. "It's set on a nice sized plot a-ground, and
the little stream that runs by the back a-the place ...
well ... always fuller trout. And, by God, these days
... free fish were free fish."

"I think I'm gonna just sit here on the curb
and relax a bit," said Grady. "You go on and eat
and I'll be right here when you get back."

Eric laughed. "I don't think so, big feller.
You's gonna come right 'long with me and git
sumpin really nur'shin for that heap-a-frame you
carry 'round." Eric held up a quick hand. "Don't
want no scuses, don't want no falderal ... we're goin
over t'the diner and eat us up a lunch that'll put the
steam back in our pipes. And don't you be worried
'bout paying me back, neither. I know what it's like
when yer down on yer luck. Been there a time er
two m'self."

"I really appreciate what you're saying, Eric,
but I'm not quite ready for charity yet."

"Char'ty – shmar'ty. T'ain't char'ty. It's one
feller buyin his friend a lunch. You done that afore,
ain't cha? I *know* you c'nt stan' there an' tell me you
ain't never bought no friend a-yours no lunch ...
never."

"I guess I have-" started Grady, but Eric cut
him off again.

"You guess? You guess? I know ya has,
ev'n if I don't *know* it. We all done things like that
in'r lifetimes." Eric wagged a finger in his face.

"An' don't you deny it none, neither. Now just shut up and let's go. I'm starvin' ... an' tir'd a-arguing wit-cha."

Grady realized he was outmatched. He had known Eric a long time, and once the man made up his mind about something, there was no turning him back. And in truth, on a day like today, Grady could use a nice cold glass of ice tea, if nothing else.

When they got to the diner, Grady stopped at the front door and gave a quick sniff under each armpit. He didn't want to go inside with other people if he smelled like a bag of apples that had been sitting too long in the sun. When he was content that he was ok, he opened the door for Eric and then walked in behind him.

The place was fairly crowded, but there was an open booth in the back. Eric nodded a hello to Sally Potter, the waitress behind the counter, and pointed to the back, letting her know where they'd be. Sally flashed a smile in answer, then grabbed up an armload of dirty plates and backed into the kitchen through the swinging doors.

Grady slid into the booth, banging his knees on the end of the table as he went. When he was settled in, he pulled out two menus from behind the napkin dispenser and handed one to Eric. They were the kind of menus you'd find in any diner anywhere across the country. Bordered in black cloth and laminated – the pages held in by a thick piece of black ribbon. There was a mustard thumbprint on the corner of the one Grady was reading, obscuring the *A* and *L* of "SPECIALS."

This made Grady chuckle; if pronounced with a little license, it now read: DAILY SPECI(e)S.

"So whutcha thinkin on havin, big feller?"

"Dunno yet. Maybe just a slice of apple pie and a big tea."

"That it? That all ya want? That ain't gonna fill a big feller the likes-a you up. No way, dad-blamed Jo-se, it ain't. Un-huh! Gotta git sumpin better an' that in yer tum-tum 'fore we start the decs in the town hall. Me, I'm a-starin at *The Biggie Burger* here. Load it up with everythin and add a handful or two-a tater chips ... now that's a lunch."

"Ok, then," hedged Gray, "how abou-t ... the turkey club. That sounds pretty good to me."

"Now that there's a lunch. See, I knew ya could do it if ya tried." Eric shot Grady a great big smile that seemed to almost swallow his entire face. His blue eyes sparkled beneath the bushy gray eyebrows. The white cotton T-shirt he was wearing was stained with sweat around the collar to about halfway down his chest, but other than that it was clean. Eric had always prided himself on keeping his appearance as neat as he could, although he was nowhere near as fastidious – or uppity, as he would call it – as Carlton Wedgemore.

When Sally came by, they placed their orders and settled in to await their arrival. Neither of them was in a particular hurry, they had the rest of the day to get the town hall decorated for the festivities, and it probably wouldn't take them any more than two hours at the most to do it.

By the time they had finished eating, the diner was nearly empty. Joe Torres and Andy

Michelson were still sitting at the counter sipping on their ice teas. Sally had disappeared into the back, presumably washing dishes and defrosting steaks for the dinner rush.

Eric pushed his plate aside and leaned in across the table, arms folded in front of him.

"So tell me, Grady-" It wasn't often that Eric used Grady's name. And when he did, it meant that he was about to say something important. "-you and the misses doin ok? Now ... I mean really and honest t'God ok? I know it's been rough on ya an' all ... what with losin your job an' all. But I want a straight answer; an' I'll tell ya why after ya gimme one."

Grady slumped back in the booth and let out a long sigh. He liked Eric well enough, but he was never one for carrying tales, especially when it concerned his family and his private life. Still, there was something in the way that Eric had asked this time that made him feel that he should tell him.

Watching the emotions play across Grady's face while he decided what he was going to say, Eric reached out his hand and laid it on top of Grady's.

"Listen son ... I ain't tryin t'pry. I ain't! But I kin feel it in m'bones. Sumpin awful's 'bout t'happen 'roun' here, and ... God-as-my-judge ... I kin feel it's gonna suck you in somehow." He paused for a long moment. "An' the misses, too. I seen it in a dream I had last night."

"Of course, we're struggling a bit," began Grady. "Tamika's doing the best she can, trying to pick up the ends-" He stopped and looked down at his hands, for no particular reason other than he needed a moment before continuing. "-but if things don't break loose soon, we'll probably have to take Willie out of Catholic school and put him in the public system. And that'll break Tamika's heart."

"Now you listen to me, Grady Peters. I ain't never been no clairvoyager ... or whatever ya call it ... person. My great aunt used t'tell me she'd see things in her dreams ... things that'd come ture ... but I ain't never been like that. No sir. Never!"

Eric reached into the back of his pants and pulled out his pocket watch. He held it out flat on the table without opening it. "Ya see this here? This watch was gived t'me by my granddaddy. It ain't never run right. Too old I 'spect. But here's the thing. Last night I dreamed about this watch. It was a right doozie of a dream, too. What it was 'bout ... well, I ain't ready t'say yet. Lookie here-"

Eric pushed in on the release and the cover of the watch popped open. He turned it around so Grady could read it.

"Now ... don't touch it ... but look at it. What time does it say?"

Grady looked at the hands on the watch. "It's 1:47."

"Right. Rightchoo-are. Now watch *this*." Eric pulled out the stem of the watch and wound the hands so that the time read 6:30. Still holding the stem, he set the watch back on the table in front of Grady. "Ok ... you ready?" He let go of the stem. For a moment, the watch just sat there. Then it began to shimmy around, like a cell phone set on vibrate. When it stopped, the hands began to twirl backwards, spinning faster and faster. They went around the face at least seven or eight complete times before coming to rest. When they did, both hands were straight up.

"Holy cow," cried Grady, and Eric held a hand up to stop him from saying anything else.

"That ain't the half of it. But like I said ... I ain't ready fer that part yet. Now ... here's the thing. I think ... I think, accordin to m'dream, if it kin be believed, you're gonna be offered some money soon. Real soon. An' here's the thing. This is whut I need t'tell ya. Don't take it, Grady. Please, God ... don't take it er sumpin really bad's gonna happen. You understand me? Ya gotta trust me. Don't take it."

Grady didn't know what to say. He knew Eric was a straight shooter, and he also knew that he wasn't given to preaching about dreams or visitations or any of that. He was a level headed, down to earth man. But there was something so earnest in his face ... so serious that Grady almost thought that maybe he *did* know something. But almost wasn't quite enough for Grady. He was well-grounded too, and being able to see the future was something you only got when you watched the *Twilight Zone* or *Night Gallery*.

"I know whut-cher thinkin, big feller. I really do. So I'll just ask ya this. For the sake of an old friend ... don't let yer sitcheayshun *now* make ya do sumpin ya norm'lly wouldn't. That's all I'm askin. That's all. If'n ya get an offer smells like a rat, it prob'ly is; so don't let it in the house...smack it with a broom handle."

CHAPTER 5

As it wound through the west end of Philadelphia, the main thoroughfare was known as Ridge Avenue. At the Philadelphia-Banderman Falls border it became Ridge Pike, eventually thinning from three lanes to one. Main Street (nobody called it the pike) was lined with small shops and boutiques, most of them still privately owned. Banderman Falls seemed to be stuck in a time warp. The flavor of life there was more late 50s and 60s than 2000s. In some places, the sidewalks remained red brick, though these areas had dwindled over the years.

Pyle's Bookstore was no rival to the bigger chains. In fact, it was very much in danger of going extinct because of the new Barnes & Nobel that just opened in the mall. It held its head above water, so far, because it was the town's book exchange. You could go in and trade books or sell your old ones. The new releases, the ones with the bright shiny dust jackets, all occupied a place in the front. But it was in the back, among the older shelves of tattered and thumb-stained books, where most of the townies shopped. Back there, amidst the dusty-edged novels, poetry, and biographies, the air was different – more "down-home." A permanent musty smell saturated the walls and floorboards, which creaked and groaned underfoot. Walking through the maze of tall shelves, there was a sense of familiarity - of comfort - like walking through the hallway of your old high school.

The worn brass bell above the door jingled as Gwen Archibald stepped across the threshold. Ernie Johnson looked up over the top of the book cart he was wheeling down the aisle.

"Morning, Gwen," he hollered.   "How's everything today?"

"Pretty good so far, Ernie. 'Cept for this blasted heat. Can you believe it? Not even hardly into July yet and we're broilin'."

"Know   whutcha   mean,   Gwen.   Air conditioner ain't stopped cycling since I kicked it on this mornin'. Can hardly wait t'see my electric bill at the end of *this* month." Ernie set a stack of books precariously on top of the cart and wormed his way around. Wiping his hands on his pants, he asked, "Anything in particular you're lookin for today, Gwen?"

"Naa, not really, Ernie.   Just snoopin' around," said Gwen. "I got me the graveyard shift tonight and need something to read." Gwen was digging in her handbag for her glasses. "O'course, that all depends on how quiet it is," she added, finally seating the glasses on her nose. "Nor'mlly it'd be pretty tame, bein' a Thursday an' all, but with the holiday, who can tell?"

"Know ex-*act*-ly what you mean, Gwen." Ernie smiled; it was a broad smile, showing lots of teeth, teeth that had been well cared for over the years. "You goin to the town picnic on Saturday?" he asked.

"Maybe! Not really sure yet. Audrey's workin, and our mom'll be in from Seattle. She'll be eighty-eight this year; can you believe that, eighty-eight? Just don't know where the time goes. But she's doin good. Gets around on her own; uses a walker sometimes, but goes where she pleases. No stopping *that* gal."

"Well that's good, Gwen. That's real good." Ernie nodded in approval, his brown bangs flapping against his forehead. He was an outgoing fellow, always willing to please. At thirty-seven he was one of the few "older" bachelors around. But it wasn't for lack of trying; he just couldn't seem to find the right woman. Oh, he'd enjoyed plenty of dates in his time, a few with Rachel Parker, and boy could she turn it on. He'd dated Laura Sweeny too, but that didn't pan out. Laura ended up marrying some guy in the Air Force and moved to Texas. So Ernie contented himself with the book store and the occasional dance that they threw at the town hall.

"Well, if you won't be needin' my help, guess I'll get back to shelvin' these books."

"You go right ahead, Ernie. I'm just gonna browse a bit and see if I can find anything interesting."

"Ok. Let me know if you need anything, and I'll be right here when you're ready to check out."

Gwen shot Ernie a big smile. She secretly had a thing for Ernie, but she figured that, at her age, 48, he'd never be interested. So she kept her secret to herself, but she never failed to take a good look at his ass when he wasn't looking. She considered it her reward for suffering in silence.

Packing her glasses back into her purse, only to have to drag them out again once she reached the back, she headed down the aisle. When she got to the cart where Ernie was, she turned sideways and squeezed through, purposely rubbing butts with him. She nodded at him when she was past, as if to say, *Sorry...but there just wasn't enough room.* There had been, but she'd never admit that to Ernie.

Gwen never noticed Ernie turn and watch her walk to the back of the store – never noticed that he licked his lips unconsciously as his eyes played up and down her shapely legs. And she would have been surprised to know what he was secretly thinking: *Sure wouldn't mind takin her out on a date one night. Too bad, too. She probably thinks I'm too young for her.*

CHAPTER 6

Sheriff Jack Dougherty arrived back at the station after having issued a one hundred and seventy-five dollar speeding ticket to the owner of the yellow Mustang. Jack was also going to hit him with a reckless driving ticket as well for almost tearing off his side-view mirror, but the kid was pleasant and cooperative, so Jack let him off on that one.

When he arrived, Rachel Parker was still shooting evil glances in Audrey's direction but was seated quietly on the bench by the wall. Matt O'Donnell had already left, entrusting his application to Audrey. Ethan Kennedy sat reading a book, as far removed from Rachel as he could get. Sam Twilling, on the other hand, was seated as close to her as *he* could get, eyeing her legs and taking a quick peek down the front of her blouse at every opportunity.

Jack was about to begin the interview process when the call came in from the state police about the EasyMart shooting. Without explanation or hesitation, Jack jumped in his car and headed over there. On the way, he radioed in, telling Audrey to get Tyler and Bill up and rolling. He'd check back in after he had assessed the situation.

When he arrived on scene there were two State cars already there, and Doc Robertson was standing beside his dark blue Grand Cherokee. The Staties had cordoned off the lot with the familiar yellow crime scene tape. He eased the cruiser in beside one of the State cars and cut the ignition. Before he'd even had time to grab the door handle, Doc Robertson pulled his door open.

"This is a helluva thing, Jack."

Jack just shook his head. It sure was. Nobody had ever died of intentional violence in this town since the late eighteen hundreds.

"You been inside yet, Doc?" he asked.

"No. Just got here myself. I knew you'd be here pretty quick, so I figured I'd wait and we could go in together. From what I've been told ... nothing I could do medically anyway. At least, that is, not palliatively. From a medical standpoint, all I can do is the autopsy."

"C'mon, Doc. Let's go."

The two men entered the EasyMart. Behind the counter, one of the State Patrol officers was standing over Patricia O'Donnell's body. The blood smear on the wall behind her was beginning to dry and cake. It looked surreal, as if someone had painted a misshapen arrow in dark red paint – an arrow pointing down toward Patricia. Her body was leaning partially against the wall, slumped to one side with her left cheek on her shoulder. Her eyes were wide and staring vacantly at the stacks of hot-cups that were kept under the counter for the coffee bar. Those eyes hadn't yet begun to glaze over, giving her the appearance of someone completely lost in thought. A large flap of scalp hung down the right side of her face where the bullet had torn through the upper back of her skull and embedded itself and bits of her brain in the wall.

"Hey Jack," Alex Kerrigan said, as he approached the two men. Alex was the supervising State Police officer on scene. He and Jack went back a long way. They had worked successfully together on a number of inter-township operations; they knew and respected each other's ability and dedication.

"Alex. Can you believe this mess? Who in the world would want to kill a young woman for a few lousy dollars? I can't imagine there was more than two or three hundred in the till at the time ... if that."

"You know as well as I, Jack ... some people in this world are just downright mean."

While Jack and Alex spoke, Robertson examined the body from head to toe. He checked for the usual signs of rigor, as well as body temp to determine the exact time of death. When he completed his exam, he stood up and faced Jack and Alex.

"Not much else I can do here. And I don't think the autopsy's gonna tell us any more than we already know. C-O-D. was a gunshot to the head. Less than an hour ago, I'd estimate."

Robertson went outside to greet the ambulance that had been summoned. Banderman Falls did not have a full-time coroner, so the ambulance was the transport vehicle for both the living and the dead. Robertson explained to the attendants how he wanted the body handled and where to take it. In the Falls, all sudden death victims went to Twilling's Mortuary. It would be there that the final post would be conducted in the basement embalming room; then Patricia would be attended to by Sam and moved upstairs for her final public appearance.

After giving specific instructions to the ambulance attendants, Robertson walked back into the EasyMart and over to Jack. He moved slowly, not really wanting to admit to himself that there had been nothing he could do for Patty. As he approached the two officers, he was thinking about the last time he had seen Patty in his office, two months ago. She had been in for her annual exam, required before Robertson could refill her birth control pills.

"I don't envy you, Jack," said Robertson, "I can't imagine what you're going to say to her parents, Matt and Carla."

"No place is immune anymore," said Alex. "It seems to be getting worse all the time; and the state of the economy surely isn't helping."

"Yeah," broke in Jack, "but there was no reason for this. The register drawer's open ... the key's still in the lock, which means Pat opened it for whoever did this. They could have taken the money and gone. What in the world possessed them to pull the trigger?"

"Sometimes, unfortunately, it's just for the thrill, Jack," said Alex. He then shook his head. "I wish it were different. I wish I could tell you that there was some kind of rhyme and reason for this ... but I can't. And I think the worst part is ... you already know that as well as I ... and for the same reasons. The business we're in ... can really suck sometimes."

An empty, hollow pit formed in Jack's stomach as he thought about how frightened Patty must have been – how helpless and alone. A mixture of anger and sorrow swept over him as he visualized Patty, standing there against the wall pleading for her life – hoping someone would come and save her. And someone *should* have come to save her – *he*, Jack Dougherty, Sheriff of Banderman Falls, the man responsible for the safety of the town and its residents – *he* should have been able to save her.

"Where'd you go, Jack?" asked Robertson. "You have the look of a man miles away from himself."

"Nowhere I really wanted to have to be, Doc."

"I'm going to head over to Twilling's and start the post right after I take care of what's left of my morning office hours. If I find anything more than we already know, I'll get in touch. Barring that, I'll send the final report to your office. That ok?"

"Yeah, that'll be fine, Doc." Jack looked over at the body again. The ambulance attendants were just getting ready to bag her up and move her into the ambulance. As they lifted her, her head fell limply backward. From that angle, it seemed to Jack as if her open, empty eyes were staring at him – questioning him: *Where were you? Why weren't you here when I needed you? Look at me now! How am I ever going to get my hair done for Saturday night's dance with this big hole in my head? Why didn't you save me?*

Jack turned away. It wasn't the body – no, he'd seen death before, and some more grizzly than this; it was the stare – the pleading, questioning stare that got to him. He hung his head, like a child being caught in a lie. *Why weren't you here, Sheriff? I depended on you ... we all do. Why weren't you able to save me?*

When he heard the tinny *zzhippp* of the zipper on the body bag, he looked up. There was nothing more to see; a dark vinyl bag being carted to a waiting truck; that was all. He watched as the attendants maneuvered the bag around the counter and out the front door. The bang of the ambulance doors made him shudder. Is that what it sounded like? Is that what a passer-by might have heard when the fatal shot rang out? *Why didn't you save me, Jack? Why?*

CHAPTER 7

It was eleven forty-seven when Colleen Slater was led into the exam room. She had been waiting since 10:45 precisely for her 11:00 appointment. Colleen was not the most patient of people and was grumbling vociferously about the wait. Once in the exam room she quieted down some but was still hurling snide remarks at the nurse.

"You know, you people should respect the fact that others have a life, too. We all can't just sit around here waiting forever for an appointment that-" she glanced at her watch "-should have been forty-seven minutes ago. I have a schedule too, you know."

"I know, Mrs. Slater. I'm sorry for the delay, but Dr. Robertson had an emergency this morning, he's extremely busy today."

"Oh hell, he's always busy. That's no excuse for wasting my time. If you couldn't see me until near noon then you shouldn't have made the appointment for eleven."

"I'll see if we can do a little better next time," appeased Jillian Culligan. "Now, temperature and blood pressure!"

Colleen stuck out her right arm and opened her mouth. She was fifty-eight years old and thought she could pass for forty. She was wrong. Her worst habit was buying clothes one size too small and secretly trying to out-look Rachel Parker. She envisioned younger men wanting her for her body and experience. She did have a nice body and she tried her best to keep it fit, but age is age and she was fighting an opponent that had timeless years of experience.

"Blood pressure's good; temp normal. Dr. Robertson will be in shortly," said Jillian.

"He damned well better be," snapped Colleen, "and it better be *damned shortly* too."

Jillian closed the door behind her when she left and stuck Mrs. Slater's chart in the door rack. She smiled to herself on her way back to the front desk after sticking her tongue out at the closed door, certain that by the time Doc Robertson entered the exam room Mrs. Slater would be less than half-dressed.

The office had that typical disinfectant smell, the smell of alcohol mixed with floor cleaner. It was illuminated by rows of fluorescent fixtures that were recessed into the drop ceiling. The walls were painted a neutral beige, except for the waiting room, which was paneled in solid oak. Not the cheap paneling you could buy at any home improvement store, but the real thing. The boards were laid out on a diagonal and capped with real cherry wood molding. The carpeting was a tan, ninety-ounce double-twist, beautifully and tastefully accenting the paneling.

Jillian was filing when Doc Robertson came around the corner. Michael was a tall man, and at the age of fifty-eight, his partially silver hair was starting to thin. He wore tortoiseshell glasses (didn't need bifocals yet) which he kept pushed up tight against the bridge of his nose. His white starched lab coat stood in contrast to his T-shirt and jeans. He had never believed in pretense and had always been a jeans kind of fellow, so that's what he wore. None of his patients seemed to mind. Or if they did, they never mentioned it to him. It wouldn't have mattered anyway – it was who he was.

"I see Mrs. Slater is here and ready to go," he said to Jillian. "I almost dread going in there. Have any idea what it is today?"

"Nope, she just said she needed to see you and made the appointment." Jillian rolled her eyes. "And you know as well as I, with Mrs. Slater ... you only get what she wants to give you."

"Un-huh! Well, wish me luck. If I'm not back in a reasonable time ... send the cavalry." He raised his arm and blew his invisible bugle, then walked down the hall and pulled the Slater chart from the rack. Taking a deep breath, he opened the door and stepped in.

"Morning Mrs. Slater. What seems to be the trouble?" He knew better than to open a conversation with the Slater woman with, "How are you today?" because, invariably, he'd get, "If I were good, I wouldn't be in your office, would I?" as a response.

"No problem, Doc," answered Colleen. "I just have a few questions about these." She palmed the lower edges of her breasts and bounced them up and down. "I've been thinking of having them augmented and wondered if you knew a really good plastic surgeon. You know me, don't do anything halfway; so before I go trotting off to some strange doctor I want an opinion on him ... *or her* ... from somebody I trust."

"Well, of course, my first opinion would be to forget it. But I don't guess that's the opinion you really want, is it?"

"No! It absolutely is *not* the opinion I want. I'm going to have these puppies upgraded ... you know, like a computer. I'm adding more mammary-" She winked and let out a hiccup of a laugh. "-and I need the name of a reliable, top of the line, doctor to do it."

"In that case, Mrs. Slater, I'm afraid I can't help you. I am not personally familiar with any plastic surgeons. As much as I disagree with your decision - and I do - I would still furnish a reference if I had one to furnish. But I don't."

"You sure you're not just saying that to change my mind."

"No, I'm not, Mrs. Slater. I really don't know any plastic surgeons. We don't really get that much call for them around here. I ... sup-pose ... Philadelphia would be the best place to start your search, at least the closest. Assuming you're determined to do this. Frankly, I don't see why you feel you need it. Your breasts appear healthy enough, medically speaking of course, as confirmed by your last mammogram a month ago. And as to size, I can't see that going from a C to a D cup is going to make that much difference in your life."

"Huh! A lot you know. Have you seen that Parker woman? My God! And she lets 'em hang out all over the place. I notice *she's* not short on dating material around this town. And I want my fair share of the looks."

Doc Robertson scratched his head. It was clear that he wasn't going to dissuade her from her destiny no matter what he said, but he thought he'd try a different angle.

"You've discussed this with Paul, I assume?"

"Oh, Paul-schmall." Colleen was scowling. "What does he know anyway? If he'd spend more time lookin at me instead of the damned computer screen of his, who knows, maybe I wouldn't want more. But hell, Doc, a woman don't live by movie rentals alone."

"Well Mrs. Slater, the best I can do at this point is tell you I'll look into it. I'll see what I can find out for you."

"Yeah ... sure you will," she said sarcastically. "Never mind. I'll find one myself."

"That's certainly your prerogative, Mrs. Slater. If you change your mind though, don't hesitate to call." Robertson drew a pen from his breast pocket and scribbled on the chart. "You can get dressed now, Mrs. Slater. And good luck in your search."

When he left the room, he fell back against the wall and shook his head, letting out a long, slow sigh. Nothing was ever easy where Colleen Slater was concerned. And having escaped relatively intact was one for the books.

"Where Shakespeare said 'Frailty,' I say ... '*Vanity*,' thy name is woman." Robertson pushed himself away from the wall and pulled the chart out of the rack next door. He took a deep breath and went in.

"Morning, Mr. Cavanaugh."

CHAPTER 8

Banderman Falls had two religions, Catholic and Baptist. At least, they were the only two churches within the town's limits. If you practiced anything else you had to drive across the border into Philadelphia. There had been talk of building an Episcopal church several years back, but it never materialized. Some speculated that it was *those damned Catholics* that put a stop to it, while others thought that it was due to lack of funds. The truth be told, it was neither. It was decided at a higher ecclesiastical level that there would not be enough parishioners in such a small community to support it.

In the end, the land that had been earmarked for the church sat vacant and overgrown with vegetation. Some of the kids used it to play in, but for the most part it was just considered an eyesore by the general populace.

Nellie Cash and Penny Bishop often discussed the "horrendousness" of it during their weekly bingo games at Saint Agnes's. They were convinced that even a parking lot would be better than *that old degenerated lot.* Of course, Nellie and Penny had opinions on everything that went on in Banderman Falls. Trash pick-ups came too early in the morning, making far too much noise; mail delivery came too late; in the winter one found herself walking to the mailbox in the dark – *not safe for older folks like us.* The library had bad hours; the supermarket was laid out all wrong, and the cable company charged way too much with no other way to get your shows. Nellie and Penny both agreed: Banderman Falls was going to hell in a handbasket.

The two women sat at the bistro table outside The Falls Café. Nellie was sipping on a cup of Earl Gray and Penny was in the middle of her fifth cup of coffee for the morning.

"I swear, Nellie, these kids today!" she shook her head in disapproval. "They think the world owes 'em something, you know? It's not like when we were growing up. Back then you had to *earn* whatever it was you wanted from your own sweat. Nothing was handed to you. These kids today ... spoiled, spoiled, spoiled!"

"Well, you know what it is, don't you?" replied Nellie. "It's the parents. No family anymore. Everyone's out making a career. No time for the kids ... pass 'em off to the schools and the nannies or daycare centers. No structured home life."

"Yes ... oh my yes," agreed Penny. "But that's not all. These days ... well, it's kids havin' kids. Not even old enough to take care of themselves and they're out there poppin' 'em out left and right. And what's the upshot? I'll tell you ... the grandparents get stuck with 'em ... or they get ignored. *You* know what I'm talkin' about."

"I most *certainly* do," answered Nellie, bobbing her head up and down in agreement. "As long as the kids ain't botherin' the parents ... well ... whatever they get into ... that's what they get into. No discipline! That's the crux of the matter. There's no discipline anymore. And you know why not? I'll tell you. It's this goddamned namby-pamby, kiss-the-kids'-asses system we got goin. To hit your kids, that's child abuse − and I'll tell ya, some of 'em deserve a really good smackin'. Don't yell at 'em, you'll give 'em a complex. You can't do anything without thinking you'll wind up in jail"

"Oh, you're so right, Penny. But it wasn't like that for us, was it? Oh no! When you stepped outta line ... wham, the hammer fell and you didn't do it again. Am I right or am I right?"

Nellie nodded affirmatively, sipping on her tea. At sixty-eight years old her hands shook from the Parkinson's, so she needed both to steady the cup. Every so often she'd push her index finger into her mouth and reseat her upper dentures; when she did, the teacup she held with her free hand would set to clinking against the china saucer, sounding like distant wind chimes. It was the constant sound of her summer ritual. Down to the Café on Thursdays to meet with Penny; walk to the post office and mail her bills for the week; head over to the bookstore for a new romance novel (if she could find one she hadn't already read), and then back home. She called it her *outing day*, and in the last five years she hadn't missed but one day – and that was because of the flu.

Penny Bishop was sixty-five. She had just buried her husband Oliver two months ago. He had been on his way home from The Falls Bait & Tackle when he suffered a stroke and fell facedown dead into the middle of Main Street. The plastic tub of night crawlers he was carrying broke open and the inhabitants made their best attempt at *The Great Escape*. Most were fried on the hot asphalt before reaching a safe haven. Oliver had retired from the railroad as a conductor not five days before and had been planning a fishing trip. As so often happens, irony played its part and Oliver became a full-time resident of the worm domain.

"Well, Penny," said Nellie, struggling to push her chair back and stand up. "I'd best be gettin' along with my Thursday chores." Once on her feet, she tottered beside the table for a moment or two until she had her cane firmly planted beside her. She reached down and smoothed out her gingham dress, both front and back, making particularly sure (as best she could) that there were no waffle lines on her rear from the bistro chair.

As she shuffled down the street, she raised a hand and waved goodbye over her shoulder without turning or looking around. She had no idea that that would be the last time that she would see Penny Bishop alive.

CHAPTER 9

Father Gabriel Jacobs peered over the top of his glasses at the man sitting across from him. He was a quick study, displaying an uncanny ability to size up any man or situation quickly and correctly. It was this ability that had led to his early appointment as Pastor of Saint Agnes, a privilege not often accorded to one as young as he. At the ripe old age of thirty-nine, he had assumed the responsibilities associated with keeping the parish up and running smoothly – which is exactly what he intended to do, at the least amount of cost to the diocese and the parishioners.

"So what you're telling me, Mr. Ballario," said Jacobs leaning back in his leather chair, "is that it will cost me over forty-five thousand dollars to replace one section of the roof. Is that essentially correct?" Jacobs glared at Ballario.

"Yes, Father," replied Ballario, swallowing hard and speaking in the softest tone he could manage while still being heard. "You see-"

"Oh yes, I *do* see," snapped Jacobs. "Actually, I see more than you think I do. As it turns out, you're the third contractor to give me an estimate ... not the first like I had intimated ... a little game I like to play to get to God's truth, if you will. And wouldn't you know it, but it seems your estimate is three times higher than the highest I've received so far. Can you explain to me, please, why you're work is *so* much better than anyone else's that it commands such an outrageous price?" Jacobs leaned forward, pulled off his glasses and fixed his eyes directly on those of Ballario. His gaze was intense and relentless – never blinking.

Ballario leaned forward just the slightest bit.

"Father-" began Ballario, but Jacobs held up a hand. Ballario sat there with his mouth hanging open, not knowing what to say or do next.

"I'll tell you what," said Jacobs, "let's say ... oh, I don't know ... how about ... fifteen-five, and that will include re-patching the concrete steps in front of the rectory and mending the chain-link fence around the parking lot. What do you say?"

"Father-" Jacobs raised his hand, stopping him again. "Think carefully, Mr. Ballario, there's always a lot of work that needs doing in a parish. The wrong answer now ... well...
I think you know what I mean."

Ballario sank back in his chair, drawing the fingers and thumb of his left hand across his mouth, considering his options. If he balked now, future work here would surely pass him by, and lord knows that a lock with the church could be very lucrative in the long run. But Ballario wasn't a man who liked to be beaten at anything, and it stuck in his craw to have to give in. He was stalled at a mental railroad crossing and he knew the time was short before the train arrived. Oh yes, he knew *that* from the look on Jacobs's face.

At last, he slid all the way forward. "Ok Father, why don't I go run some numbers and let you know by tomorrow. How would that be?"

Jacobs smiled and leaned back in his chair. "That would be just fine, Mr. Ballario. Just fine indeed ... if you want Carlin Contracting doing my work." A kind of sinister grin spread across the priest's face, knowing he had forced Ballario into making a decision the man didn't want to make. Would it be yes – or no? Checkmate or stalemate? He waited with hands folded on his lap, his thumbs tapping against each other.

Ballario squirmed in his seat and grumbled audibly. The man was caught between the proverbial rock and hard spot and there was nowhere to turn. That he would have to capitulate to win in the long run was reading like a signpost on his features. Jacobs could see how much Ballario hated the idea of losing in the short.

Father Jacobs unlaced his fingers and made a point of overtly looking at his watch. He then laid the palms of his hands flat on his desk and pushed himself to a standing position. His five foot-eleven inch frame loomed over Ballario from the opposite side of the desk, casting a shadow across Ballario's face as he obstructed the sunlight coming in the window behind him.

"Well," said Jacobs, matter-of-factly, "I have a great many things I need to accomplish today. I thank you for coming, Mr. Ballario." Jacobs reached out across the desk, offering Ballario his hand.

"Now wait a minute, Father. I haven't answered yet. I think-" Ballario forced the words unwillingly from his mouth. "-I think we can certainly do business." Thinking as fast as he could to come up with a compromise that would allow him to save face, he continued. "What would you say to ... Twenty-two thousand, which of course would include the fence and steps." Ballario paused briefly. "And-" he continued, "a fresh coat of paint for the nun's residence. How would that suit you Father? Do we have a deal?"

Jacobs smiled, and his whole face seemed to soften. The lines around his eyes smoothed and disappeared. He had the look of a man congratulating a family on the arrival of their first child.

"Yes, Mr. Ballario. I believe that would be totally acceptable. Provided the final price was eighteen. Would you like to draw up the contract, or should I have our attorney do it?"

Ballario grumbled. "All right, Father. I'll have it all spelled out and on your desk by close of business tomorrow. Would that be alright?"

"That would be just perfect." Jacobs stepped around his desk and almost literally pulled Ballario from his chair. Gently, but with purpose, Jacobs guided Ballario to the door and nodded just before he closed it behind him.

"Well," Jacobs said aloud, "that's that, isn't it? So let's see what's next on the agenda." He strode over to his desk, plopped himself down in the chair and pulled out a file drawer from the cabinet beneath the window behind him. "Basketball uniforms."

Jacobs reached up on a shelf, pulled down the yellow pages and started his search for the best and least expensive uniform manufacturer he could find. As he searched the crinkly pages of the book, he ran potential lines of argument through his head

– lines designed to get the manufacturer to practically *donate* the uniforms.

"I bet I'd have made a *helluva* lawyer," he chuckled as he dialed the first number.

CHAPTER 10

Two hours (his time) after Carlton Wedgemore discovered his newfound treasure, Arliss Peterson discovered a misdirected shipment of her own. As the curator of the Antiquities Service in Benderick Falls, Arizona, she was responsible for overseeing, cataloging, preserving and displaying all foreign treasures that were on loan to her museum. The box she was staring at now was not for her. It was addressed to someplace she'd never heard of in Pennsylvania.

Arliss was a practical person with an inordinate amount of patience, which is what made her so good at her job. She could spend weeks cleaning a museum piece without getting frustrated that the job was taking too long.

"Well now," she said softly. "Just what are we supposed to do with this?" She laughed out loud. "Strike one up for the delivery service again." She bent down and lifted the crate, carrying it carefully over to a staging table.

"Bill," she called. "Got another shipper here. We got it by mistake. Can you be sure it gets out and on its way to its proper destination this afternoon?"

"Will do, Dr. Peterson," came a voice from around a corner. "I'll make sure it gets out on the three-thirty pickup."

"Thanks Bill. Oh, and when you get a chance, check the incoming manifest and be sure it was just a misdelivery and not a switcheraroo."

"I'll be sure to do that, Doc. Let you know how it turns out."

"Thanks Bill. I'll be up in my office. Lots of customs stuff to finish off today." Arliss grabbed up the stack of papers that had arrived with the other shipments and made her way up to her office. It wouldn't be until much later that she found out about the switch – that she found out a priceless, and as yet unidentified, artifact had gone missing from the Ural Mountains' shipment.

CHAPTER 11

Linda Killerman ran the Killerman Bed & Breakfast. It sat on nearly four acres of secluded, wooded lot at the far end of the Falls. Originally, it had been a storage facility for the Banderman Grist Mill but the Killermans had converted it into a beautiful, rustic vacation spot. Linda ran the place by herself. Her husband, Harvey, had died two years ago in a motorcycle accident. He had been on his way home at one-thirty in the morning after having one too many Michelob lites. By the time he had seen the deer, it was too late. After the breaks locked up, the Sportster fishtailed into the deer's hindquarters. Harvey was flipped through the air like a bottle top, landing in the middle of the street on the back of his head. The impact shattered his helmet, which he always promised Linda to wear, and snapped his neck. The deer limped off into the woods.

Remodeling the mill had taken thirty-six months; everything was redone to specification. The interior had been completely gutted and rebuilt. The stone face exterior had been sandblasted to a pristine manila colored finish. A huge white door with a half-moon window at the top, split with radial mullions, hung invitingly within the finely detailed maroon trim that surrounded it. The semi-circular driveway, at one time only dirt, had been covered in white stone and bordered with a low stone wall. The wall curved all the way around on both sides of the drive. A gap, flanked by concrete lions, permitted entrance to a flagstone walkway that led to the front door and was adorned on either side with marigolds.

Linda was stooped over one of the large flower pots that guarded the front of the B & B when the dark green Jaguar XK-E pulled up. She turned, listening to the sound of the stone grumble under the weight of the moving vehicle. It was a sound she always enjoyed, like crinkling a big ball of paper or writing on a theme tablet that gotten wet and then dried.

"Good morning," called the man who stepped from the car. As he made his way around the front and up the walkway, Linda noticed that he walked with a slight limp on the right side. He was wearing blue jeans, black biker-boots and a T-shirt with the Grateful Dead skull and lightning bolt on it.

Linda pushed herself up from the kneepad she was kneeling on and brushed away the dirt from her knees. She was wearing cutoffs, sneakers and an old T-shirt of Harvey's emblazoned with a faded picture of John Fogerty and CCR. She had yard gloves on and was holding a garden spade in one hand.

"Good morning," she replied, a smile spreading across her face. "Can I help you?"

"Perhaps," answered the man. "Perhaps you can, indeed." When he got to the top of the steps he reached out his hand and grabbed hers, glove and all. He seemed to Linda to be a pleasant little man with lots of energy. His hair was silvery, as if he was in his late sixties, but his face was that of a forty-year-old.

As they were shaking hands, he continued. "I'm looking for a quiet little place to stay for a while, and this looks like it would be absolutely ... *absolutely* perfect. Can you tell me ... are there any rooms still available for say ... oh ... two weeks ... maybe three?"

"I can *certainly* tell you," said Linda. The little man was still furiously pumping her arm up and down in greeting. His eyes were a bright blue, and when she looked into them they seemed to go on forever, like staring into an infinity mirror. "We still have two rooms left, and they're both available for a stay of that length." Something about the man in front of her made her feel relaxed – open.

"Actually, we could probably accommodate you for a lot longer than that, if you wished."

"Well that's just *absolutely* splendid. Splendid! You know, the minute I entered your tiny little town I said to myself, Hertzog Witherstone ... I did, I said it right out loud ... Hertzog Witherstone, you've come to the right place. Yes you did, you've come to the *absolute* right place. And then-" He reached out and gently folded his fingers around Linda's upper right arm and started to lead her inside. "-then I came across your ad. You know, the one in the little PLACES FOR RENT booklet down at the diner. I stopped for a quick bite, you see ... and there it was. Just staring me in the face ... tempting me. So who could resist? I ask you, who could resist such a charming little place?" He shrugged his shoulders on this sentence as if it were common knowledge that anyone reading that line would beat a path to Killerman's Bed & Breakfast. Do not stop, do not pass go, go straight to Killerman's.

Before she knew it, Linda was standing behind the front desk opening the registry. She flipped it around to face the customer. She was about to hand him a pen when he reached into his back pocket.

"No need, dear. I have one here." He leaned in across the counter so closely that they were almost touching noses. "I always carry my own, you see. Never know when you're going to have to write something down. And pens are so personal, aren't they? Think about it. They are the instruments of our elusive thoughts ... usurpers of time, they are. They're the only thing in the world we can possess that can truly make us ... and our intangible thoughts ... immortal. Isn't that simply an *absolutely* incredible ability? I ask you, isn't it?"

Witherstone gently pulled the shiny black cap with the gold trim off the top of the pen and held it up so Linda could see it. It reflected the light streaming in the window, its rich onyx color showing Linda a tiny curved image of herself. The pen itself was a throwback. A fountain pen, something Linda had not seen in a long, long time.

Quickly, the little man scrawled out his signature with a flourish, repeating the words out loud as he wrote them. "Hert-zog Wi-ther-stone." He then recapped the pen and pushed it back down into his hip pocket.

"There," he said, "*now* ... I'm an *official* guest of this *absolutely* beautiful establishment." He flashed a big smile, and when he did, for the briefest of moments, Linda thought that all his teeth looked pointed – piranha teeth – but the image faded quickly and she could see he had perfectly white, perfectly maintained teeth.

"Well now," said Linda, running a hand through her long black hair, "let's see if we can't get you settled." She reached around behind her and pulled a key out of one of the slots in the guest board. "Here you go, Mr. Witherstone. Room 227. If you'll give me a moment, I'll show you upstairs."

The little man leaned in close again. "Ordinarily, I'd say not to bother. I'd say that I could certainly find my way. But then, who would turn down a chance to be accompanied upstairs by such a lovely woman as yourself? Who? Who in their right mind would do such a thing?" He reached across the desktop and ran the back of his fingers down her cheek. His touch was light, and at the same time charged. Linda felt as if she had just been caressed by an electric eel. The feeling spread all the way down her body, and she could feel goosebumps rising on her arms. A quick shudder ran through her and she actually shook briefly from the sensation. There was something more in it, too ... it was almost erotic. She felt her nipples stiffen when his fingers first touched the flesh of her face, and the area between her legs tingled.

Hertzog Witherstone wrapped his arm in hers and they headed off toward the stairs. When they reached his room, Linda opened the door and stood to one side so Witherstone could enter. As she stood watching him take in the room, she realized what an odd sensation had befallen her downstairs. Looking at him confused her even more. He was not a particularly handsome man. He was what she would consider average. And now that he was no longer facing her, he seemed somehow older than he had at first. From the back he appeared to be hunched a bit, like her father had looked when he was in his late seventies. She also noticed that he seemed to shuffle into the room – a gait that stood in stark contrast to the way he spryly climbed the front steps to greet her, limp and all.

When he turned to face her again, he smiled. He was standing straight and tall – as tall as he could for a man of five-seven. He had a big grin painted across his face and his eyes were open as wide as a frightened cat's.

"That's alright, dear," he said. "No need to fret about such things. We all see what we want to see, you know. Oh yes, we *absolutely* see what we want to." The grin on his face slowly melted to a plain smile, and his eyes narrowed – softened. He stood there looking at her as one might look at a child who had scraped a knee. It was a kind and gentle look. But somewhere beneath it, somewhere hidden in the darkest corners of that look was something menacing. Linda couldn't really see it, but she could feel it. She could feel it with the whole of her being.

"Well," said Linda rather abruptly. "Why don't I let you get settled in. Dinner is served at six in the dining hall, downstairs to the left of the foyer. If there's anything you need in the meantime, please let me know. We do our best to keep everyone happy here."

"I will certainly do that. I will *absolutely* do that. In fact, there just might be something you'll be able to help me with later on. But we'll worry about that when the time comes. For now, I'll bid you ado, and thank you for the wonderful service and the beautiful room." He spread his arms out wide, sweeping one in front of him the way a model might show the grand prize on a quiz show.

"Now, you run along," he smiled, "and I'll see you at dinner. I'm certain you must have lots of things you want to accomplish today. Don't you worry about me. I'll be just fine." The whole time he was saying this he had been moving forward and

Linda had been slowly back peddling. She only realized it when he closed the door and she was looking at the numbers 2-2-7.

CHAPTER 12

Gwen Archibald had not found anything that she had really wanted at the bookstore and had decided to check out the magazine rack at the CVS. Ernie had secretly watched her walk down the street and disappear around the corner. When she was gone, he went back to shelving the last of the books that remained on the cart. Two more boxes of new releases had been delivered and sat waiting for him at the counter. Of all the jobs he did, restacking and displaying the new releases was the one he hated most. It always required tearing all three of the shelves apart and rearranging them from top to bottom.

Ernie pushed the empty book cart to the back room and rolled it up against the far wall. On the wall by the door was an old Black Forest Cuckoo clock. It had belonged to old man Pyle's father and hadn't worked for years. But Pyle insisted that it stay. When the doors flew open and the little blue bird shot out – *cuckoo, cuckoo, cuckoo*, Ernie whirled around. He couldn't remember ever hearing it go off. In fact, it didn't even keep time at all. He walked over to it, laying a hand lightly on one of the pinecone pendulums. The bird, still sticking out of the front of the clock, but now silent, cocked its head and looked down at him. Ernie jumped back. He rubbed his eyes with the heels of his hands and then looked up again. The doors to the clock were closed, and the hands still frozen a 7:10, as they always had been.

"Wow, Ernie," he said to himself, "too much time in the stacks this morning. Now you're seeing things." He started to cross the threshold of the door to the inner store, stopped, backed up and took another look at the clock. No bird, no ticking. He shook his head and moved into the store and down the aisle to the front.

Getting from the front to the back or visa versa required navigating quite a few little turns between the tall shelves. On his way, he stooped to pick up a book that had fallen on the floor and re-shelve it. As he pushed it into its niche, he noticed the title: *Paradise Lost*, by Milton. He slipped it into its slot between the other books and continued his trek to the front of the store.

He had just rounded the last of the bookcases when he heard a thump behind him. He turned and looked, but no one was there – at least – no one that he could see.

"Hello," he called. "Is there someone back here?" He waited, thinking that a customer had come in while he was hallucinating in the back with the clock. There was no response. He took a few steps back the way he came and peered down one of the long aisles.

Nothing!

Curious, he wandered down the aisle listening for the sound of footsteps or books rustling

– anything that might tell him a potential customer was rummaging through the stacks.

When he got to the end of the aisle, he turned right and ambled down the final row of books. Halfway down, he saw it. There on the floor, right where it had been when he'd picked it up the first time, was *Paradise Lost*.

"What in the name of blue heaven is going on here?"

Ernie stepped over the book and went around to the other side of the huge shelf, thinking that maybe someone had replaced a book and knocked *Paradise Lost* off from the other side. But that did not turn out to be the case. On the other side, all the books were neatly stacked with the spines perfectly aligned. Not one of them was pushed in farther than it should be. *And besides*, he recalled, *there's a small lip that runs along the center of the shelves to prevent exactly that kind of thing.*

Ernie Johnson was just as jumpy and superstitious as he was pleasant and outgoing. He believed in ghosts, magic, and witchcraft, and always carried his lucky quarter in his left hip pocket to ward off anything evil. The coin had professed its power to Ernie down in Atlantic City. He had dropped it into one of the one-armed bandits and then yanked the handle. Nothing had happened, so he pressed the coin release. The quarter clinked and clanked its way back down into the return slot, and the machine's icons flipped around to three stars, winning Ernie $2700. Testing fate, he dropped the same quarter into another bandit two rows down with exactly the same results – quarter returned, winnings: $1000. Ever since then the coin remained in his back pocket.

Ernie stood in the dingy light of the store, staring down at the book that lay at his feet. Something deep inside him was preventing him from picking it up a second time, although he knew he had to. After a long deliberation with his conscience, he decided that the coin would decide his course of action. He plucked it from his hip and tossed it into the air.

"Heads I pick it up, tails it stays there for some customer to find." He watched the coin turn end over end – first up – then down. It flopped into the palm of his outstretched hand with a soft thwap. Ernie hesitated, keeping his fingers closed tightly around the magical object, not too anxious to see if he'd have to pick up the book. At last, he closed his eyes and opened his fist.

Ernie shrieked and shook the coin out of his hand. It fluttered to the floor, silvery metallic wings beating furiously. The eagle's talons descended from the obverse side, gripping the floorboards as it landed. The wings folded up and the legs shrank back into the coin as it came to rest. George Washington lay there staring up at Ernie. The face was full-on not profile, and his eyes followed every movement Ernie made.

Ernie started to back away, trying to put some distance between him and the thing looking up at him. He did it one step at a time, running his hand along the bookshelf to tell him where he was. But getting away was not going to be that easy. The quarter stood on end, pushed upward by the eagle's legs, and began to roll toward Ernie.

"Where are you going, Ernie?" asked George, in a voice that sounded like he was talking through a copper pipe. "I thought we were friends. Buds! Pals and all that? Where are you going?" Washington started to laugh, causing the coin to wobble from side to side as it rolled its way down the aisle toward Ernie.

That was it. Ernie couldn't take any more. Screaming in terror, he turned and ran toward the front of the store. He made it around two lanes of shelves before he stopped and looked back.

"I'm coming; I'm coming," the coin called.

His heart pounding in his chest and unable to catch his breath, Ernie turned the last corner looking over his shoulder for the approaching coin. *Whap*! He ran headlong into a customer who had just come into the store. The force of the impact knocked Ernie to the floor. Before he even thought of looking up at the customer, he looked down the aisle, certain the coin would be on top of him. But it wasn't. There was nothing there.

"Let me help you, my friend."

"No ... no, stay away," Ernie shouted, and then realized it wasn't the quarter talking, it was the stranger standing over him.

"I'm sorry," he said. "I just wanted to help you up. But I guess there's something to be said for wanting to do things yourself." The man smiled down at Ernie – a broad and toothy, smile.

Ernie pushed himself up on his elbows, giving a quick glance behind before pulling himself to his feet. Standing there, now with another human being in front of him, made the whole thing seem surreal – an event that could never have happened – except maybe in his mind. *Too many goddamned King, Koontz and McCammon books*, he thought. Hesitantly, he reached back and slid his fingers down into his hip pocket. They came to rest on a solid round object. He drew it out and looked at it. It was the coin, and it looked exactly as it should. He slid it back in and turned his attention to the man standing there.

"Did I hurt you?" asked Ernie apologetically.

"Hurt *me*? No! No, of course you didn't. But I seem to have given *you* quite a start. And for that-" the man bowed at the waist sweeping his arm in front of him "-I'm humbly sorry."

The stranger was an older man; he looked to Ernie to be in his late eighties. His movements were slow and deliberate, almost practiced. He was wearing a starched white button-down shirt, open at the neck, and dark blue khaki trousers. His belt sported a large buckle with a relief of a howling wolf's head in the center. What Ernie could see of the man's hair beneath the wide-brimmed Stetson hat was silver-gray. The skin on his face was grayish in color and reminded Ernie of a moldy prune. He wore dark sunglasses that wrapped around the corners of his eyes, and in his left hand was the signature white cane of the blind.

"No," said Ernie, "I'm sorry. I should have been watching where I was going."

"Well, it's all water under the bridge now." The man flashed another smile, and for a brief instant, before they disappeared behind the saggy lips, his teeth seemed to be chiseled to fine points. "So, now that we have that all straightened out ... perhaps you can help me find the Braille section."

Ernie smiled, then realized it was a wasted gesture.

"I'm afraid what we have in that line is not too extensive. We do have some audiobooks though, but again, I'm afraid they're not the most recent releases."

"Oh, that doesn't matter at all. I just enjoy reading. I'll pass on the audio books, though. Just let me browse what you have in Braille and I'm sure I'll come up with something worth taking home."

"I have that section kind of all lumped together by title. I never really bothered dividing it into genre since we don't really sell that many of them. I hope that won't be too inconvenient for you."

"It won't at all. I enjoy books – all kinds. I like touching them, don't you? There's something very special about the printed word, don't you agree? If you'd just be kind enough to guide me in the right direction-" he held out his arm, bent at the elbow, "-I'll begin my treasure hunt."

Ernie reached out and took the man's arm. As soon as he touched it he wanted to draw his hand away. It felt as if a thousand worms had been dumped down inside the man's clothes, and it was cold; very cold. He fought the feeling, and the impulse to draw back, not wanting to insult his customer, but he could barely stand it. He led him through the maze of floor-to-ceiling shelves, the man's feet scuffing along the floor as they went. They reached the Braille section not a minute too soon for Ernie, and he let go of the man's arm.

"Here we are," said Ernie, as politely as he could, still trying to shake off the wormy feeling. "A to Z in Braille, such as it is. It takes up this entire stack of shelves and half the one to the right of this."

"That's wonderful. I *do* believe I'm going to thoroughly enjoy myself here." The man reached out his hand and ran it along the spines of the books. Then he leaned forward and inhaled deeply. "Ahh ... such a pleasant smell: binding and leather, don't you agree?" The man gave a quick, forced cough. "And dust," he added, letting out a little snort of a laugh.

Ernie stood there, not quite sure whether or not to leave him on his own. There was something about him that gave Ernie the creeps. And yet, the man looked so fragile. It appeared to Ernie that if the man sneezed too hard he would fall to pieces on the floor like a broken marionette.

"Well sir," Ernie finally said, "If there'll be-"

"Sir? Oh my goodness, yes. I haven't introduced myself properly. Please do forgive my lapse of common courtesy. My name is Witherby ... Zachariah Witherby." He held out his hand.

Ernie reached out to take it, and thought of the last time he had touched ... Mr. Witherby. He closed his eyes and took the man's hand, fully expecting to be worm-swarmed again, but the only sensation was that of skin touching skin.

"I'm Ernie Johnson, Mr. Witherby. Glad to meet you."

"More than likewise, Ernie. May I call you Ernie; would that be too improper of me?"

"Ernie it is, Mr. Wither-"

"Zach. Please, Zach will do just fine. Now, you run along about your business. I'll be quite fine back here, and if I *do* feel I need any help, I'll not hesitate to call. Deal?"

"Deal," agreed Ernie. "I'll be up front doing some unpacking, but don't worry, I'll be able to hear if you call."

"I'm not worried. Not worried at all, Ernie. I have every confidence in you. And besides-" Witherby leaned in closer to Ernie, "-I'm really quite self-sufficient. Can't get to my age without being that."

"No, I guess not. Anyway, I'll be up front. Happy hunting."

Ernie stepped around Witherby and made his way to the end of the shelving. He was about to turn the corner when Witherby called out.

"Ernie? You still there?"

"Yes, I am, Zach."

"I believe you've forgotten something."

"Have I? What?"

"This," said Witherby, tossing a book up the length of aisle. Ernie caught it in both hands. It was *Paradise Lost*.

The blood drained from his face and he could feel himself losing ground to the blackness.

Placing a hand on the shelves, he steadied himself, closing his eyes and hoping the dizziness would pass. Somewhere outside of himself, outside of the swimming feeling he had, he could hear laughter. It was a deep raucous laugh, coarse and gravelly, and malicious. It sounded far away and close at the same time. It sounded like the kind of sick laughter you'd hear from a psychotic killer on TV or in the movies: a demented, grating cackling. It filled his ears and his mind until the darkness took him, and he slid to the floor.

CHAPTER 13

After Nellie had waved goodbye and disappeared into the FALLS CLEANERS- *We'll Remove the SPOT or Pay You'll NOT!,* Penny Bishop finished her last cup of coffee for the morning and decided it was time to do some shopping. She thought about making a quick stop at DSW to pick up a new pair of bedroom slippers, but then suddenly felt an urge to buy a new book. It felt kind of silly to her because she had such a hard time reading, what with her glaucoma and cataracts and all – but she felt she just *had* to have a book, or maybe one of those talkie ones.

She pushed away from the table; struggled to her feet; dug in her purse for a pair of quarters (her idea of a big tip) and plunked them down on the table. One of them landed on edge, and rolled in a circle around the other, which was lying heads down. She watched it for a moment, mesmerized –

the same way you might stare at an object without really seeing it, but unable to pull your eyes away.

Penny watched it roll around and around, wondering whether it would fall over to heads or tails. Then she reached up and rubbed her eyes hard with both hands. For a moment, she thought she had seen the eagle on the quarter that was lying flat reach out with its head and poke the circling quarter, knocking it out of its orbit. It fell over, wobbling around on its rim with a metallic whirring sound – heads up.

Better get my eyes examined, she thought, *instead of buying shoes.* The idea of buying a book had completely evaporated from her mind. She shook her head and turned to make her way to DSW.

"Don't forget your book," came a voice from behind her.

She whirled about as fast as was possible for someone her age, startled by the voice. She expected to see the waiter or someone behind her. There was no one.

"Great," she muttered, "now you're hearing things too."

"No you're not," came the voice again. She looked down at the table, bending in closer and trying to focus. What she saw just couldn't be. Not possible – and yet – there it was.

On the table, the quarter that had fallen face up had a head sticking up out of it. When she first looked, it had been George Washington's head. But as she looked closer, it changed, slowly dissolving and reforming. The head now looking up at her was her dead husband's – Oliver's.   It smiled, then laughed, then spoke again.

"Don't forget to get your book, I said.   I know you were always hard of hearing, and most times didn't pay any attention to what I said, but really ... don't forget your *goddamned* book."

After issuing its reminder/command, it shrank back down into the quarter and was once again, good old George.   Penny unfolded, straightening up in a shot.   She stood so quickly that she lost her balance and stumble back a few steps before regaining it.   When she had managed to steady herself, she edged forward and looked at the coins again, but there was nothing unusual to see.   Two quarters lay on the checkered table cloth next to her empty coffee cup.   One was face up, George Washington in profile and the other was face down, the American eagle.

Penny shook her head, wondering why her mind could have played such a trick on her.   She had been around the block in her life way too many times to start hallucinating such nonsense.   Such things were not common in her family, and certainly not within the realm of *Penny Bishop's* psyche.   No sir!   No ghosts, goblins, witches or paranormal crap for rock-solid, get-your-hands-dirty-and-get-the-job-done, as grounded as they come, Penny Bishop.   We're not having any of that.

She wiped her hands together, pushed the chair into the table, turned and strode off down the street, determined the whole thing had never happened.   The denial of the event was forced and exacting, commanded by strength of will alone.   But beneath it, hidden in the corners of the mind where no one likes to shine a light, it lived on, waiting to be revisited at a more convenient time.

Without realizing it, Penny walked right past the DSW store, rounded the corner and laid her thinning, arthritic hand on the doorknob of Pyle's bookstore. She was just about to turn it when the door opened, pushing her backwards. The force caused her to lose her balance and she started to tumble. She tottered momentarily on the backs of her heels, waiting for the impending fall and stomach-turning crack of bone as she hit the pavement.

A moment later she was standing upright again, safe, sound, and balanced, and the sound of crunching bones on concrete that she expected to hear was replaced with the clatter of wood on cement. The grip that had pulled her from the brink of catastrophe still had hold of her upper arms. It held her securely, tight enough to have kept her from cracking her skull, and yet soft enough for her to realize that she wouldn't even show a bruise, and that was saying something. At her age, she bruised easily.

"I'm terribly, terribly sorry," said the man who had snatched her from a certain trip to the emergency room. "How terribly clumsy of me."

The man who had come through the door let go of her arms, unwrapping his fingers in the same way a pianist might finish a glissando. He was obviously blind, the sunglasses and the straight-ahead stare told Penny that much. Not to mention the white cane lying on the sidewalk at her feet.

But there was something more – something about him that put her instantly at ease. Something about him that made her momentarily feel as giddy inside as a schoolgirl watching a boy she had a crush on try to find the words to ask her out.

"I certainly hope that you're all right, and that you'll forgive me for not paying more attention to what I was doing."

"I'm fi ... fine," Penny stuttered. "You just caught me by surprise. That's all. No harm done." She couldn't explain it, not even to herself, but she could feel the warmth fill her cheeks as she blushed. "I'm quit fine, really."

"Well thank the stars for that," said the man. "For a moment there ... I thought you were a goner. How rude would that have been of me? Just arriving in this lovely town and *wham*, what's the first thing I do? I send some poor, unsuspecting lovely lady to the hospital. Unconscionable ... totally unconscionable."

The man smiled a broad, warm smile, and it reminded Penny of someone she once knew; although, for the life of her, she couldn't place who at the moment. She watched him as he stooped down to retrieve his cane, and for some reason just had to look at his ass. She couldn't help herself. And although she felt half ashamed for doing so, she also felt excited – sexually excited – a feeling she hadn't had in years.

"Please," asked the man, "let me buy you a cup of coffee to make up for this horrible incident. I *absolutely* couldn't live with myself if I thought I couldn't redeem myself. What do you say?"

Penny thought for a moment. Her mind was telling her to pass on the invitation, that she didn't know this guy from a rat's rump, and that there was something about him she should avoid. But her emotions were telling her something completely different. She felt young inside again, and she liked the feeling. It overwhelmed her. She almost couldn't believe the words she heard coming out of her mouth as she spoke them.

"I'll pass on the coffee. But if you'd care to buy me a nice glass of wine ... well *that* I'd agree to."

"It would be my pleasure," said the man. His voice was soft and reassuring. "My absolute pleasure."

Penny blushed again when the man reached out and entwined his arm with hers. It was as if he were escorting her into a grand ballroom. It felt good; it felt refined; it felt – youthful.

"I'm afraid that you'll have to lead the way," he said, "I'm at a distinct handicap here." He paused. "I don't know your lovely town yet, or where to take you." Then he laughed. It was a gentle laugh, almost a giggle. It reminded Penny of the boy who had lived next door to her when she was growing up, and how he used to laugh every time Penny's puppy would lick his face. She had had a very bad school girl crush on him, but he was too young to be interested in girls at the time.

Nick. Nicholas Maloney, she thought. *Yes, that was his name. Nicholas Maloney.* Her mind shot across the decades, she could smell the lilacs that bloomed in her back yard, and feel the grass on her bare feet as they raced around the yard chasing the puppy and then having the puppy chase them. The memory swallowed her the way a fish swallows a worm – whole.

They walked along, arm in arm, Penny lost in her own thoughts and memories. They didn't speak. They didn't have to. Everything was right with the world.

When they reached what Penny thought was D'Anjollel's Italian Restaurant, she waited while her new gentleman friend opened and held the door for her. Stepping inside, the contrast of outside light to inside dark deepened the daydream Penny was having.

They sat at a quiet booth in the far corner. A black and red checkered cloth covered the booth's table and there was an empty bottle of wine, now in use as a candle holder. It sat up against the window rail, the sides coated with multicolored wax drippings.

When Penny looked down, she didn't see a table. What she saw was a checkered blanket spread out on the greenest grass she'd ever seen. The corner was held down in place against the gentle breeze with a hand-crafted picnic basket – the kind that opened like a doctor's bag and had everything inside you could possibly need for a good time outdoors. Plates in a pocket on one side of the basket, glasses tethered gently to the other side and silverware nestled down among the salad makings and aluminum foil-covered plate of bar-b-cue chicken.

"Now-," said the man, who looked to Penny to be in his mid-twenties. "Isn't this much better than some stuffy old bookstore?"

"Oh my yes," answered Penny, reaching over and running the back of her hand down the man's cheek. "Oh yes. So, so much better, Nicholas."

"I can't tell you how long I've waited for this, Penelope Bishop. It almost seems like I've waited forever." The man took Penny's hand from his cheek and kissed it softly. She could feel the warmth of his lips and breath on her fingers. He then filled two wine glasses with the richest red wine Penny had ever seen.

"To you," he said, passing her a glass and raising his own in salute, "The most beautiful woman I've ever met."

These were the words that Penelope Bishop had always wanted to hear from Nicholas – the words she had dreamed of so many times while lying next to Oliver.

"There's something about you, Penny. A kind of strength; a kind of evil strength. You've spent your life getting what you want – a perfect manipulator." The man smiled again. "Don't get me wrong, I'm not deriding you. No, not at all; on the contrary, I admire you. You've always had a way of using that little evil corner of your soul to assure your success."

The words angered Penny, but at the same time, somewhere inside her, they pleased her because she knew them to be true. She had always manipulated her situations to come out on top.

The man finished his wine in one large gulp, letting some slip from the corner of his mouth, run down his cheek and drip off his chin. Penny watched the drops splash down, one after another, onto the checkered cloth. The rhythmic *tap*, *tap*, *tap* memorized her, and she lost herself inside that rhythm, and the sound of the man's voice.

"-really do admire you." Penny had not heard what he had said before that, only the cadence of his speech. "-And I'm more than sure that I'll find a way to use those tenacious, willful attributes to their best advantage."

Her mind kept telling her that this was all wrong – that her youth had long since passed. But her eyes were telling her that her mind was lying. His skin was soft and supple. She could see its smoothness as she watched Nicholas kiss her hand. She could feel the silkiness of her hair lying against her cheek; it was light and wispy, not the brittle hair of someone who has weathered sixty-eight years of Banderman Falls winters.

Outside, a motorcycle roared by, its tailpipe belching and coughing out the heated exhaust. Penny turned to look out the window, startled at the sudden sound. When she did, her mind snapped fully awake. The window frame was broken and rotted; the plaster walls were decayed and yellow stained from water damage, and the table where she was seated was standing on two legs, supported only by the bench it was laying against. Across the room, a pair of rats scurried along the wall and disappeared into a hole chewed into the baseboard.

Penny had never been terrified in her life –
until that moment. She was alone and had no idea
where she was or how she got there. Panic took
her. Her chest began to feel tight and it became
hard for her to catch her breath. Somewhere in the
distance she could hear laughter. A demonic
cackling that filled her ears and made her temples
throb. It bellowed through the darkness of the
abandoned building, circling the walls like a
windstorm in a cul-de-sac.

Penny Bishop awakened to the fact that she
was *not* twenty-eight, not at a picnic with Nicholas
Maloney – and, worst of all, not at D'Anjollel's with
a kind man who had kept her from falling. She was
alone in a dark, dank abandoned building – she
knew not where, sitting at a broken down, dust
covered table. A table that had but two items on it:
a picture of Oliver Bishop and the wedding ring that
had been buried with him two months ago.

Penny tried to scream but it got stuck in her
throat – like a lump of peanut butter too large to
swallow. She clawed frantically at the base of her
neck trying to dislodge the phantom bolus; trying to
give voice to her terror. She could feel her tongue
beginning to swell, and the pounding in her ears
told her that her blood pressure was dangerously
high.

Get a grip, Penny, she tried to tell herself.
*Calm down and think. You're just hyperventilating,
that's all. Settle yourself and everything will be all
right.*

"Oh yes, do calm down, dear," said the
picture of Oliver on the table. "No sense in having

your face all screwed into a knot. It'd take Sam Twilling hours to undo *that*. And I certainly want you looking your best when you come to join me."

The image of her dead husband glared up at her. Its eyes darted from side to side watching her as she struggled to breathe.

"I'd like to help," it said, "but, unfortunately, I'm just a headshot. No arms, I fear. Not much use to you without arms. But it's all ok. You'll be here with me soon now. *Very* soon now. In fact, from the lovely blue color of your lips, I'd say ... minutes."

CHAPTER 14

Father Jacobs had wangled a good deal from ProSports, Inc. He'd not only gotten the basketball uniforms at less than half price, but he'd also managed to talk them into throwing in a half a dozen balls and two new carrier bags.

He was just coming down the steps of the nun's quarters, having given it a quick inspection with an eye toward the new paint job, when the phone rang in his office. As he spent most of the time working around the church and school, he'd had multiple remote bells installed throughout the buildings. He had always meant to have a few extra lines installed as well but never got around to it.

Jacobs quickened his pace, but refused to run. He knew he'd never get there in time to answer it anyway. But that didn't matter. Whoever it was would leave a message, and their number would be on the Caller ID if they didn't.

He pushed open the back door that led to the passageway between the nun's quarters and the rectory and padded briskly down the steps. His rubber soles made a muted tapping sound on the concrete and his cassock rustled about his feet as he passed the Day Lilly border-garden and the sycamore trees, and strode through the pillared alcove that led to his office.

Before he went in he stopped and took in a long deep breath. The sweet smell of the garden hung heavy in the hot July air. On the opposite side of the garden, dandelions were gaining a foothold in the grass. Here and there, the long-stemmed seed pods shot upward in clumps, looking like cotton lollipops. Father Jacobs watched the honey bees buzzing around and crawling over the yellow flower heads, bumping into and climbing over one another. He loved summer; more than any other season, Father Jacobs *loved* summer.

Jacobs's office would have been the envy of any scholar or book lover. Two of the four walls were solid oak, floor-to-ceiling bookshelves filled to capacity. The third wall, the one immediately to the right of the corner entrance, was paneled in teak. A large silver crucifix held the center position and was flanked on either side with portraits of the Pope, cardinals, and bishops that Gabriel Jacobs knew personally. Behind his desk, a large bay window looked out over the front lawn of the school.

Jacobs pushed the REVIEW button on the Caller ID as he dropped into his leather, high-backed desk chair. The number that came up was unknown to him, but he recognized the area code as belonging to New York. He hit the talk button and heard the familiar stutter buzz that indicated he had a message. Deftly punching in his mailbox number and passcode, he waited.

"You have one new message," intoned the mechanical female voice. "To listen to your-"

Jacobs knew what he had to do and didn't need to be told by some machine. He pressed down on the number 1.

"Gabriel, this is Geoffrey Dunsmore; I'm in New York. Just arrived from Heathrow. I think we need to sit down together. I'm on the move, so I'll give you a call when I get into Philadelphia, probably sometime around seven tonight. Please be waiting. Thanks." The phone clicked, and the lifeless female voice began to give Jacobs options as to what to do next with the call. He didn't listen. He dropped the phone down into its charger and sat back in his chair to think.

Gabriel Jacobs had neither seen nor heard from Geoffrey Dunsmore in more than fifteen years. The last time they were together was in London in the fall of '94. Gabriel had just vacated his post at Saint Peter's and was getting ready to return to the U.S. He had run into Geoffrey accidentally at the post office. The two men shared beers (pints, as they were called there) and stories of old times together. They had met for the first time when Jacobs was posted in Africa at an Ethiopian

Mission. Geoffrey was there as a representative of some world syndication that helped provide relief to impoverished areas. Jacobs never could pin Geoffrey down as to what he did, *exactly*. The best he ever got out of him was that he was an advisor to a special group within the organization, and coordinated all initial contacts that his company would make.

"That's a bit elusive, wouldn't you say," Father Jacobs had said.

"No," answered Geoffrey, in his British accent, making the word no sound like *now*. "I just go in with my lads, assess the situation, see what kind of help is needed and how it can best be utilized ... and then we draw up our recommendation to the board. No cloak and dagger here, Father. I can assure you of that. Nothing so grandiose for this lad." But Jacobs had never quite swallowed that story whole. There was definitely something more to Geoffrey Dunsmore than he would let anyone see.

At first, Jacobs thought that it might just be the man's natural self-confidence, but there was something deeper than that that the priest recognized – something evasive in his mannerism and speech. One of the first things Jacobs learned about Dunsmore, the man, was that he chose his words carefully and well. He was one of those people who *always* thought before they spoke, and said only what was necessary and germane to the conversation at the time. Jacobs had always thought that Dunsmore would have made a good spy. But he didn't truly believe that that *was* his line of work.

Jacobs sat back in his chair thinking about Dunsmore – assessing him all over again. He came to no solid conclusions, but two facts he was sure of: Dunsmore was not a man to be trifled with, and whatever it was he *really* did for a living probably made James Bond look like a vacuum cleaner salesman. He just had that aura about him.

Gabriel Jacobs looked over at his desk clock. It was a miniature Big Ben and had been given to him by Dunsmore the last time they'd been together. Staring at the clock opened a gateway in Jacobs's mind. He recalled the odd thing that Dunsmore had said when he gave it to him.

They had been sitting in the bar, coughing on the smoke and dodging stray darts. Dunsmore had taken a very large swallow of his Guinness, plunked the mug on the bar with a bang and looked Jacobs's right in the eyes.

"Father, listen to me," he'd said. His voice was strong, almost commanding Jacobs's compliance. "I have something here for you. A kind of a gift. I've been carrying it around now for a couple of days. I knew ... I mean ... I'd hoped I'd get a chance to give it to you before you left for the States." There was a seriousness in Dunsmore's eyes that Jacobs had never seen before, and he'd seen Dunsmore get more than serious on a few occasions.

Jacobs remembered missing it at the time, but now, sitting here reflecting on it, he was sure that Dunsmore had said exactly what he'd meant.

He "knew" he'd see him before he left. But that wasn't what had captured Jacobs's attention at the time. It was what he did next that sent a chill up his spine, and Father Jacobs could count on a leper's hand how many times he'd experienced the chills.

Dunsmore had taken the Big Ben replica from his raincoat pocket and placed it on the bar. With his index finger, he'd slid it over in front of Jacobs.

"*This*," he'd said, pointing to the timepiece, "is a very special clock. Let's call it our friendship clock. It'll keep perfect time of our friendship ... no matter where we are." He reached into his other pocket and produced another replica of the clock. "Now, this one's mine ... and it'll keep track of you. Yours, needless to say, will keep track of me." He stopped talking and had stared the priest right in the eyes.

"I'm dead serious, Father" he continued. (He never called him Gabe; that would have been disrespectful in his eyes.) "Don't laugh, I'm not joking. Think what you want when I'm gone, but don't laugh."

Jacobs had tried to assure Dunsmore that he'd had no intention of laughing, but Dunsmore had cut him short with a wave of the hand.

"Now, do me a favor first, would you, Father? Before I go on."

"Sure," Jacobs had replied, even though he was a bit skeptical.

"Bless the two clocks, Father. Lock them together in spirit, as we're locked together in friendship."

Jacobs thought for a moment, saw no harm in it, as common things were blessed every day. He raised his hand, made the benediction while making the sign of the cross over the clocks and finished with: "Amen", which Dunsmore had echoed.

"Ok. Watch carefully, Father." Dunsmore picked up his version of Big Ben, checked his watch and then set the hands on the clock to the correct time if he'd been in the U.S. When he did, the hands on Jacobs's clock began winding forward, coming to rest on exactly the correct time in London. The clocks were, to the minute, six hours apart.

"What in-," began Jacobs.

"Don't ask, Father. Don't ask! I just want you to take it on a bit of faith."

"How in the world can you expect me *not* to ask about something like this?"

"Well, I guess I can't. But here's how I'll handle that question." Dunsmore picked up his mug, drained the last bit down, patted the priest on the back and left, calling over his shoulder, "Stay well, Father. And don't lose that clock, whatever you do."

By the time Jacobs slid off his stool, made his way through the crowded pub and out into the street, Dunsmore was gone. He'd disappeared into the evening throng of Londoners, and that was the last time Jacobs had seen or heard from him – until now.

He looked at the clock, wondering if Dunsmore still had his – wondering, if he did, was it set at the same time as the one he was looking at; if

Dunsmore was in New York, both clocks should read the same time. Jacobs folded his hands together, steepled his index fingers and laid them against his lips. There was nothing to do now but wait until seven o'clock and see what was up with Geoffrey Dunsmore, and what had brought him to the U.S.

CHAPTER 15

Witherby (Witherstone to Linda Killerman) sat at the round, wrought-iron bistro table at the Falls Café, drawing his lemonade up through a flexible, red and white striped straw. When he reached the bottom, he stirred the ice cubes around and took one last, long draw, making that gurgling vacuum sound that children were so fond of.

Instantly, the waiter appeared at the front door and rushed over to him.

"Would you like another, Mr. Smith," he said, winking. "I'd really like to get your autograph if you wouldn't mind. I promise I won't tell anyone you're here in town. I promise."

Witherby took his sunglasses off and smiled at the boy.

"So, you've figured out who I am, did you? Well, I guess I can't blame you. But we have a deal, right? If I give you an autograph ... you'll keep my secret safe, right?"

"Oh absolutely, Mr. Mas-er-Smith. We've never had a real, live, movie star in this town

before.   Never.   I promise, promise, promise, I
won't say a word to anyone that you're here."
     "Very well, then said Witherby, looking
very similar to James Mason, "get me something to
write on, my boy."
     After he had signed the napkin, Witherby
requested a second lemonade, which the waiter got
him on the house. While drinking it, Witherby took
in the town and its residents. Cars and trucks,
motorcycles and bicycles, pedestrians and bus
riders. He watched them all pass by.
     Witherby started to laugh – a long, low
laugh, like someone who had just gotten a mildly
funny joke they'd been told an hour ago.
     "My, my, my," said Witherby, "this is my
kind of town. I do believe I could put down some
productive roots *here*. And with that, he broke into
a raucous peel of satanic laughter.

CHAPTER 16

     Banderman Falls was certainly a small and
rural community, but it was not, by any stretch of
the imagination, a wilderness community. It was
true that it was bordered by a vast acreage of
undisturbed, uninhabited forest, most of which
belonged to the National Park System and
designated as Fairmount Park, but the fiercest wild
creature roaming those woods would be the
occasional Black Bear. For the most part, the
woods' residents were made up mostly of White
Tailed-Deer, groundhogs, raccoons, opossums,

snakes, salamanders, wild turkey and pheasant; and, of course, the state bird, the grouse. For those who enjoyed their leisure time hiking, biking or playing in the woods, there was little danger of encountering a dangerous wild animal, the occasional case of rabies notwithstanding.

Anyone wishing a true, back-to-nature experience would have to travel to someplace like Yosemite. The only way one would encounter grizzly bears, wolves, moose, caribou and the like in Banderman Falls would be to subscribe to *National Geographic* or the Discovery Channel.

With the holiday just around the corner, Frank Mowery and Charlie Maloney decided to take the afternoon off from fixing mufflers, changing batteries and performing State Inspections at Alderman's Tire and Battery, and get in a little fishing.

Charlie Maloney had just bought himself a new *Thomas and Thomas AX908S-4*, $750 fly rod and was anxious to put it to the test. The quarry of the day would be trout – Rainbow, Brook or Brown, it didn't matter to Charlie, as long as it was trout.

Frank Mowery, on the other hand, was a bit more particular. He loved fishing and enjoyed catching most anything, but he only took home the Rainbows – and an occasional catfish. He had never been a big fish eater, except for fresh Rainbow trout, but he found the occupation of catching them relaxing.

After making a quick change at work, grabbing their gear from their lockers (and the two six packs from the fridge), and punching out, Frank and Charlie climbed into Frank's old CJ-7. The jeep was twenty-three years old, now a classic, and it was Frank's pride and joy. Yuppie machines is what he called all the newer models. "Stupid yuppie machines with plastic dashboards and useless air-conditionin' ... on a vehicle that was meant to be driven top-down." They ripped out of the parking lot, almost making the turn on two wheels, and shot down "the pike" (Charlie and Frank were the only two residents of Banderman Falls that called it that.)

Making a quick left onto Bells Mill Road, the yellow jeep bounced over the little rise that gave way to the downward-sloping road that lead to the entrance of the creek area. At the very bottom there was a one-lane bridge that spanned the Wissahickon Creek, allowing through-traffic to reach the other side of Philadelphia, the affluent Chestnut Hill area. Just after the bridge was a gravel turn-off that emptied into a small parking area. It could only hold ten cars at most, but it was a convenient entrance to the park and its recreational amenities.

Frank skidded the jeep to a stop, kicking up dust and gravel that pinged off the undercarriage. There were only two other cars parked there, so there was a good chance that their favorite fishing spot was free and clear. With any luck, they'd be bringing home the limit.

Frank jumped out, went around to the back and started yanking on his green waders. He cinched the straps up as tight as he could get them and still be comfortable. He exchanged his red ball cap with the big P on it (Frank was a faithful

Phillies fan) for his good luck fishing hat and was
ready to go.

Charlie had undergone a similar ritual,
minus the hat exchange.   Charlie was not a hat
wearer. He kept his lures in a small plastic box that
just fit into his shirt pocket, always making sure that
the pocket flap was buttoned so that he wouldn't
lose them while bending over to net his catch.

Snagging the cooler with the six-packs, they
headed across the lot to the dirt path that led down
to the creek.   The mosquitoes took note of them
immediately and set about enjoying their newly
arrived smorgasbord.   But it wasn't the mosquitoes
that annoyed Charlie and Frank the most, it was the
horseflies.   When they bit – it hurt.   There were
plenty of gnats, too. But they were just a nuisance,
and could easily be ignored. For everything, there
was *OFF!*

When they got to the edge of the water, they
turned left and made their way up a narrow strip of
dirt that ran along the embankment.   Some parts
rose up more steeply than others, threatening to
dump them into the creek if they took a single
misstep. Low shrubs and brambles did their best to
keep them from getting to their desired location. At
some points, the branches crossed out over the
water too far for them to get around, so they had to
fight their way through them, climbing over or
ducking under.

The air was much cooler down by the water,
maybe even by ten whole degrees.   In spots,
sunlight filtered through the overhead canopy of
trees making the water shimmer like there was one

of those cut-glass disco balls hanging above it. Thrushes hunted through the remnant leaves of last year looking for something tasty, while robins, cardinals, finches and crows competed in the avian version of American Idol.

The two men finally reached their hallowed hunting ground and settled in. Frank twisted the tops off of two Yuenglings, handed one to Charlie and then set his carefully on the ground, digging the bottom of the bottle into the mud to keep it upright.

Taking several paces to his right, Charlie whipped the rod back and forth and let the lure sail. It floated lightly through the air and dropped, just where Charlie had aimed. Frank copied the motion but was not quite as accurate as Charlie. It didn't matter. They were fishing, not changing tires, and *anything* was better than that.

By late afternoon, Charlie had caught two Browns, and Frank had snagged two Brook, a Rainbow and one sorry looking catfish. The Brook he gave to Charlie and the cat he threw back. The creek was completely in shadow now, as the sun was too low to penetrate the trees, even though there were still several hours of daylight left. Forest sounds began to pick up and mix together as the change-over-time approached – that time of afternoon when the diurnals prepare to give way to the nocturnals.

Earlier, while Charlie had been trying to change his vantage point, he'd slipped on a moss-covered rock and went down in the creek. He'd cut up his left arm, but that didn't bother him nearly as much as the fact that his waders flooded. For the rest of the afternoon he'd slogged around, sounding like an under-filled water balloon. *Slosh-g'blunk, slosh-g'blunk.*

Charlie glanced at his watch; it was still running, but there was water lapping back and forth underneath the crystal.

"Hey Frank," he called, "whudda ya say we call it a day?"

"What time ya got, Chal?"

"Goin on for five."

"Yeah, guess so then. By the time we get packed up and back to the jeep we'll be hittin' rush'our traffic."

"Think it'll be that bad?" asked Charlie as he sloshed his way back to the bank. "I'd think most folks woulda got t'go home early t'day 'cause o'the holiday commin an' all."

"Maybe, but I'll bet it's still pretty jammed at the top of the hill there at the Pike. Got all the Philly folks trying to get home."

Snap! Crunch-snap! The distinctive sound of twigs snapping beneath leaves came from behind them, just out of view. It was a crisp sound – the kind of sound only the larger branches could make. The two men froze to listen. It was most likely a deer coming in for a drink.

They stood there, still in the water just shy of the bank. Neither one moved a muscle. When there were no follow-up cracking sounds, they moved to the bank and climbed out of the water.

"That gave me a start for a minute there," said Charlie.

"Yeah ... me too. Musta been deer, I guess," replied Frank as he gathered his stuff together. "I'm just glad it wasn't a bear. Don't need no fight over my fish ... cause I'll tell ya ... I'd win. Ain't no bear takin my dinner."

The two men laughed, but it was a hollow, forced laughter. Not because they had really thought it had been a bear, or that they'd really been in any kind of danger, but mostly because they were tired and it seemed like the thing to do.

They edged along the water, working their way back to the parking lot. It was still a ways off from sundown, but the light had faded significantly in the thick woods. Sounds came at them from all directions. Rustlings beneath the leaves were accompanied by the chirpings of crickets and click beetles, which, in turn, were joined by the rustling of branches and brush. Nightfall came early in the woods, without regard to what held sway over the sky – sun or moon.

Frank and Charlie had just managed to fight their way through the section of branches that overhung the creek when they heard the distinctive sound of a low growl. Both men came to an abrupt halt, Charlie standing with one foot in the water.

"Did you hear that?" whispered Frank, but he already knew the answer.

"Yeah, I did," Charlie whispered back. "Whadda ya think it was?"

"Sounded like a dog, if ya wanna know the truth," answered Frank.

"Maybe," said Charlie. "But it must be a big one."

"Shhh! I'm tryin t'listen." Frank held his index finger up in front of his lips.

To their right and slightly behind, they could hear the unmistakable sound of a large, four-legged animal padding along in the dried leaves just beyond their sight. As they stood listening, the sound died abruptly.

"Whatever it is," said Frank in a hushed voice, "It's stopped. But it's still out there. Ya c'n be sure-a that."

"Probably just somebody's mutt that got loose. That's all," said Charlie, trying more to convince himself than Frank. "That's gotta be it, don't ya think?"

Suddenly, the sound started up again. A quick crinkling of leaves, and this time there was no mistaking the fact that – whatever it was – there was more of them than just one.

"How many?" asked Charlie

"I make it three, maybe four."

"Four what, though?"

"Dunno for sure, but I'd guess large dogs. Maybe some wild ones." Frank was still whispering, his voice as soft and low as he could make it. "You know, ya hear tell of em every now'n'then ... strays that pack up together."

"Ya think that's what it really is?"

"Dunno, I *said*. Just guessin."

The two of them scanned the brush line intently, trying to pick out a shape or movement, but saw nothing. A light breeze began to pick up, the early sign of an impending thunderstorm, not uncommon on unusually hot days. But the breeze wasn't any comfort. It only added to the problem. It stirred the leaves around on the ground and waggled the arched brambles and branches of the lower shrubs, making it impossible to hear anything, or detect any movement that wasn't wind caused.

Charlie was the first to spot it. A pair of eyes glaring at them through the brush to their immediate right, not more than ten yards off. He squinted his eyes to sharpen his focus and was able to make out a set of pointed ears above the eyes. They were bent forward, listening - listening for Charlie and Frank.

The attack came swiftly, and from multiple directions, including the water. There were not, as they had guessed, three or four of them out there, there were eight, and no time to react. Frank brought his fishing rod up like a swordsman raises his blade before slashing, but it was a useless gesture. In one quick *snap*, the hand holding the rod was gone.

Further down the stream, two teenagers were walking the trail and heard the screams. They were horrible, high-pitched sounds that came in waves. But they faded as quickly as they'd begun, and the teenagers chalked it up to Barn Owls getting an early start to the evening. They headed home, never knowing that two men had just been torn apart not more than sixty yards from where they were walking.

The last car pulled out of the tiny, gravel parking lot at seven-twenty. By eight fifty-two,

Frank's yellow jeep was swallowed by the night, awaiting a driver that would never return.

CHAPTER 17

Evening settled over the Falls like drowsiness settles over a late night reader. It came in stages, but the stages blended so well together they went unnoticed. The last remnants of the sun-splashed wispy bands of pink and orange across the western sky just above the tree line. The aerial changing of the guard was underway; sparrows shared the sky with a few bats that had already left their roosts, and fireflies were flashing in the grass as they emerged from their underground havens. The melodies of the songbirds were supplanted by the imitative whistlings of the mockingbirds and the ghostly calls of owls.

Unlike big cities that continue to hustle and bustle through the night, small towns have their own rhythm. Things slow down as dusk settles; lights begin to wink on throughout the neighborhoods; shops shut their doors, leaving only the hazy glow of their security lights behind; cars idle at traffic lights waiting for non-existent cross-traffic; and the tumult of the day fades to a hushed sleepiness.

Jack Dougherty sat in the living room of his small bungalow home, a mile and a half away from his office. The ceiling fan above his head limped around in endless circles, creating a small breeze that ruffled the open newspaper that was lying on the coffee table. Rivulets of condensation trickled down the sides of the brown Michelob bottle he held in his left hand, its bottom resting on the arm of his blue wing-back chair. The receiver of his cordless phone lay face up on the table portion of the floor lamp he'd bought for $42.50 at K-Mart.

Jack sat there drumming the fingers of his right hand on the arm of the chair, occasionally glancing at the receiver beside him, waiting for the reports from Doc Robertson and the Forensics Division of the Pennsylvania State Police. He could get neither the image of Patty's staring, lifeless eyes, nor the haunting questions she kept asking from his mind. *Why didn't you save me, Jack? Where WERE you? Why, Jack? Why weren't you there for me?*

As soon as the phone rang, he snapped it up and hit the "talk" button. A sales call! He didn't even wait for the poor guy to finish his spiel before hanging up on him. He leaned forward and set the half-empty beer on the coffee table, stood up and began pacing around the room. Every so often he'd finger the edge of the drapes aside to look out the front window. He didn't expect to see anything out there, and wasn't looking for anything in particular – he was just moving – doing meaningless things to occupy the time.

Jack thought about taking a shower but didn't want to miss the call. True, he could take the phone into the bathroom with him, but water and electronics were never a match made in heaven. And on top of that, he didn't want to be caught with his pants down, literally, if he was needed at either of the two places whose calls he awaited.

Dinner was out of the question. When the image of a young girl's dead body is the only thing floating around in your head, your appetite gets drastically reduced. That thought made Jack half-smile. *A new diet plan: hop on down to your local morgue or undertaker right before dinner and scope out the corpses of the day. Guaranteed to trim those unsightly pounds or your money back.*

Jack picked up the phone on the second ring. He'd crossed the fifteen-foot space of his living room in a dead run.

"Yeah what do you have for me," he snapped.

"Jack? Sheriff Dougherty?" came a shaky female voice.

"Yes, this is Sheriff Dougherty."

"Jack, it's Lillian Mowery. I hate to bother you, but I'm getting concerned. Frank isn't home yet. I already called Piggly's, but Mitch said he hadn't been in; Shirley Maloney called me and said Charlie wasn't home yet either. I know they like to-"

"Slow down, Lil, you're chattering away like a magpie. Take a breath and slow down."

"Sorry. It's just that it's not like Frank to be this late ... not without calling. He's always been real good about that - and not hearing from him has me-"

"You're racing again, Lil. Just slow down. Besides, I got the picture. I'll have Tyler swing by Frank's usual haunts. I'm sure he'll turn up.

Probably just got side-tracked. You know, holiday spirit and all. I *promise* I'll be back in touch with you shortly.   In the meantime, just try to stay relaxed and figure out how you're gonna brain 'im when he comes strutting in." This got the expected giggle from Lil that Jack had hoped for. "Now just stay calm, we'll get this all straightened out".

"Well, if you find him first, Jack Dougherty, cuff him and put him right in the cell. It'll be a lot safer for him than comin home." It was Lil's best attempt at taking it easy.   Her voice was still trembling as she'd said the words, but, somehow, making that small joke made her feel a little better.

"Ok. You hang tight, Lil," advised Jack. "I'll let you know."

There was a soft click as the call was disconnected. *Great!* thought Jack, *I don't have enough going on, and now I got Frank and Charlie off somewhere playing hooky from home.* Even before the thought had passed, an uneasiness settled into Jack's stomach. He knew Frank and Charlie well. Not the brightest bulbs in the attic, but not run-arounds either. If they weren't home and hadn't bothered to call their wives, something was wrong. And that thought – that uneasiness – spurned another thought. Something was not quite right in Banderman Falls today. There was something very wrong happening in Jack's quiet little town. First a murder, virtually unheard of here, now two men missing. It didn't sit right with Jack. He knew this community inside and out – all of its goings-on. He knew its rhythm – and its rhythm was changing - had changed.

Jack decided he'd waited long enough. He grabbed up the phone, dialed Twilling's Mortuary and waited while it rang.

"Hello, Sam?" he said, when the voice picked up, but then realized it was the answering machine. He thought about leaving a message to have Robertson call him immediately but decided against it. He tossed the phone onto the blue wingback and headed out the door. No more waiting. He'd drive over to Twillings and find out just what the story was and where the situation stood.

Two minutes after he'd backed out of the driveway, tires squealing, Jack's phone rang.

CHAPTER 18

After the incident at the cemetery, Jasper Collins had beaten a quick retreat home and tried to forget the whole thing with the help of Old Crow. He had huddled in a corner of his room, bottle in hand with WYSP blaring Classic Rock. He only crawled out of the corner once, and that was to fetch another bottle of bourbon. As the afternoon had worn into evening and then into night, the room was slowly swallowed in shadow. But it didn't matter to Jasper. He wasn't about to leave the safety of his little corner to turn on a light.

Having gone through about a quarter of the second bottle, Jasper was feeling no pain. But he couldn't shake the vivid memory of the winged statue in the cemetery. He couldn't escape its grinding movements and raspy voice. He couldn't escape its ominous warning. Swallow after swallow, gulp after gulp had numbed him, made his head ache and his legs rubbery, but it hadn't erased the blackboard of his mind and the images that were drawn on it.

"Prepare!" it had said. "It is here. He will come! Many will fall while others will rise. Darkness and decay shall walk in the light. Prepare!"

Jasper sat hunched in the corner, knees pulled up to his chest and arms wrapped tightly around them, releasing his grip only long enough to take another swig from the bottle. A steady stream of tears oozed from the corners of his eyes, and he whimpered like a child who had had a candy bar taken from him so he wouldn't spoil his dinner.

The trailer that Jasper owned sat on a 3-acre plot of wooded ground just outside the Banderman Falls limits. Jasper's father had acquired the land in a poker game from Sam Twilling's father. Three queens had taken the acreage from Twilling's three jacks' hands, so to speak. Over the years, Sam had tried on several occasions to convince Jasper to sell it back but was never successful. Jasper appreciated and relished the quiet of the area. His only neighbor was Harold Wilcox, whose property butted up against Jasper's. Wilcox had a rancher that sat fifty yards in from the property line. Each could see the other's place, but they weren't on top of each other, so both were satisfied.

Wilcox lived alone except for his border collie, Rascal. Both Wilcox and the dog were getting up there in years. Jasper often wondered which would go first. The dog limped, its back legs dragging from time to time, and Wilcox needed a cane to get around. The two men rarely interacted, but had an unwritten, unspoken agreement to look out for each other's land. Anyone snooping around would find out fast that a pair of twelve gaugers on either side of them was not the place they wanted to be.

Except for an occasional thumping, created by a pine branch that refused to stop swiping at the side of the trailer, and Jasper's whimpering, the trailer was dead silent. Not even the sound of crickets disturbed the silence, which was unusual in itself. Darkness had a way of magnifying sound, but tonight, it only seemed to magnify its lacking.

Jasper drained the last of the bourbon and tossed the plastic empty across the room. It hit the edge of his bureau and rolled across the uneven, uncarpeted plywood floor, clacking along as it bumped around on its indented handgrips. When it came to rest is when Jasper first heard the shrill scream. It was a cross between a yelp and howl. There were two more, just like the first; then everything was silent again.

Jasper pulled himself to his feet, wobbled there a moment or two, hoping the room would at least slow down, if not stop spinning completely. With a hand against the wall to steady himself, he made his way around to the window, turned the rod and opened the blinds. Blackness was all he could see.

He stood there peering out into the darkness, hoping his eyes would adjust. Then he realized that it was *too* dark outside. No light at all. Wilcox usually kept a back porch light on so that he could let Rascal out at night to do his business, but it was pitch black – no light on at Wilcox's.

There should have been enough light from the moon to see as far as the Wilcox place, but there was no moonlight. Jasper stumbled to his closet and took out his shotgun, cracked the barrel to check that it was loaded, snapped it shut and teetered his way to the front door. The screen door's hinges squealed as he pushed it open and stepped out into the darkness. He stood there listening and straining his eyes to focus. Across the way, something was moving around the back of Wilcox's place. From where he was, Jasper couldn't be sure what it was, but it looked like a large dog. It padded around in circles with something unrecognizable in its mouth.

Jasper took a few steps forward, shotgun leveled on the object and finger on the double triggers. He looked up to find the moon, but there was nothing but a carpet of black above him. No stars, no moon, no light. He lowered his gaze and tried to refocus on the area where he'd seen - (the dog?). When he finally spotted it, it was no longer one, but two. Two large dogs were playing tug of war with something that he couldn't quite make out. But deep inside he knew exactly what it was. It was Rascal. The two beasts were tugging and pulling in opposite directions on what was left of the old dog's carcass. The sound of the rending flesh was brittle as if someone were ripping an old, dried-out leather sofa into strips.

Jasper pulled the shotgun up under his chin and sighted along the barrel. From this distance, he might even be able to hit both of them as the shot spread out. As he started to put pressure on the triggers, intending to let both barrels rip at the same time, a hand touched his shoulder. The unexpected touch made him jump, and he dropped the shotgun.

"Certainly you're not intending on shooting my children, are you, Jasper Collins?" questioned the stranger that had a tight grip on Jasper's shoulder and neck. The hold reminded Jasper of the way Mr. Spock put people to sleep on the old *Star Trek* show. In fact, Jasper was sure that if the man squeezed his fingers together *just* a little tighter, he *would* pass out.

The figure that had Jasper by the neck spun him around to face him. He was tall and lanky. There was a skeleton thinness to him that did not do justice to the strength he exhibited. Jasper tried to see the man's face but the darkness obscured it, held it deep in shadow. Sensing Jasper's curiosity, the man laughed. He placed his other hand on Jasper's opposite shoulder and drew him in.

"My but you're a curious fellow, aren't you? Way too curious for a man in your position, but I suppose I can understand that." The man paused. His breath was foul; it had the odor of garbage that had been rotting in an August sun. Jasper couldn't see the man's teeth, but he was positive they were more yellow than a fresh piss stain on a white carpet.

"You know what?" asked the man, rhetorically. "I think we're kindred spirits, you and

I, Jasper. I really do. So, as one spirit to the next, I'm inclined to grant your wish." He let go of Jasper with one hand, raised it skyward and waved it back and forth as if he were clearing smoke from his face. When he did, the clouds that had covered the night sky wisped away and disappeared. The moon and stars were back, and Jasper could see the face of what was holding him. It was a skeleton face. Not thin *like* a skeleton face – it was an actual skeleton face. No flesh clung to the features, and the eyes sat like globular balls in the sockets.

Jasper opened his mouth to scream, but before any sound came out, the thing holding him raised his hand and rolled his fingers into his palm, as if grabbing a coin. As he did so, Jasper could feel his throat close up.

"Can't have that, Jasper, my friend," said the man. "Not that there's anyone around to hear, but it's awfully annoying, don't you agree?" The man shrugged his shoulders and then shuddered. "Ghastly sound ... just ghastly. Now ... I'm going to open my hand, you're going to be able to breathe again, and you're *not* going to scream. Deal?"

Jasper nodded his agreement, acquiescing to the stranger's will. The terror he had felt when he first saw the man's face was somehow strangely dissipating. There was no reason for him to feel comfort; no reason for Jasper to feel anything but sheer terror, and yet, he was beginning to relax; beginning to understand that nothing was going to hurt him, even though he had no idea why he should feel that way.

The man let go of Jasper completely, and then rubbed both of his hands across Jasper's shoulder, as if smoothing out a wrinkled suit. He was wearing a wide-brimmed hat that hung down in front, but the skeletal features of his face were clearly visible.

"Oh my," he said, "Pardon me. I'm so absent-minded sometimes. How rude of me to be frightening you like this." He pulled off his hat and passed a hand in front of his face. Instantly, muscle, tendon, ligament and flesh and hair formed over the face and skull. It was like watching the "dripping paint" effects of a screen saver as the image changed from one picture to another.

"There, that's better I'm sure. Now, we have a lot to discuss, Jasper ... an awful lot to discuss. And a helluva lot more to do." Having said that, the man broke out into thunderous peals of laughter, slapping Jasper on the back. "Helluva ... get it? *Hell* of a lot to do. I kill myself sometimes." He stopped laughing and looked Jasper dead in the eyes. "You and me, we're gonna be great pals. *Great* pals." The man frowned. "But I have the feeling I've forgotten something. Dear me ... what could I have forgotten?" He raised a finger to his lips and squinted his eyes closed in thought.

"Oh yes," he said at last, snapping his finger. "I've got it. I've completely forgotten to introduce myself, haven't I? How rude of me."

"Don't bother," said Jasper, suddenly feeling a bit stronger. He also noticed that he wasn't feeling drunk anymore either. "I think I've already got the picture."

"Yes ... yes, I'm sure you do. But you'll have to call me something when we speak, won't you? I mean really, how rude would it be for you to always be calling me, 'Hey you!'?" The man laughed again, a kind of lighthearted, self-serving laugh.

"Let's see," he pondered, "how about-"

Jasper cut him off. "Master?" Jasper asked, sarcastically.

The man began to laugh again, this time it was a genuine, deep from the innards laugh.

"You *are* a card, Jasper Collins. A true card. And such a sarcastic wit. Yep, we're going to get along famously. But, that aside, how about you just call me ... Zach. Yes, that'll do very nicely." He held out his hand. "Oh take it, Jasper. It won't bite." He paused again. "Hmmm ... bite? That reminds me."

The man turned to face the Wilcox place. "Children, children," he called. "Play time's over. Finish up with the mutt and dispose of the old man's carcass ... but mind now ... don't tear it up too badly, we'll be using it again. Chop-chop. Moonlight's a-wastin."

Jasper looked at his new, unwanted friend. "Are *they* ... wolves?" he asked, surprised. "Wolves? Here in Pennsylvania? Where the hell did they come from?"

"Exactly," replied Zach, "exactly."

CHAPTER 19

As Jasper Collins hid in the safety of his room, Carlton Wedgemore sat in an antique rocker with a cane-laced back. He was initially going to have it reconditioned and sell it for twice what he paid. But he made the mistake of sitting in it one day, and after that, any thoughts of selling it had evaporated from his mind like morning dew in sunshine. His office was tiny but serviceable. Rows of filing cabinets rimmed the walls, paper trails of all the purchases and sales he'd made over the years.

All day, he sat there alone in the office and waited. He rocked back and forth, the runners creaking against the floorboards. Evelyn Ramsey had long since departed for places unknown. At least, for places unknown or un-cared about to Carlton. All he cared about was that she was gone, and the sun was beginning to set. Soon it would be full dark. The time he'd been waiting for since finding his treasure box this morning.

Carlton drummed his fingers on the arms of the rocker, impatiently staring out the window and willing the sun to drop below the horizon. In his excitement he had, uncharacteristically, closed the shop two hours ahead of time, thanked Evelyn for a good day's work and hustled her out the door, closing it behind her so fast that he actually bumped her in the ass with it. He just shrugged, flipped the sign from OPEN to CLOSED and pulled down the shade. From there, he'd retreated to his office to sit in silence and count the minutes until he could open his new, as yet unknown, acquisition.

Cereeeek-crick.   Careeeek-crick.   All afternoon the sound of the rocker had reverberated around the walls and bounced off the metal filing cabinets. Ordinarily, Carlton would have found the sound relaxing – soothing. Today, he only found it irritating, because it meant he was in limbo. So close to his prize and so far away, as the saying goes.

"C'mon, c'mon," he murmured, still peering out the window at the horizon. "How much longer you gonna keep me waiting?" He was talking to a star that burned ninety-three million miles away ... a ball of gas that had no concept of time, or if it did, it certainly wasn't on the same scale as Carlton's. He was talking out loud to an inanimate object – and didn't care. "C'mon already," he repeated through gritted teeth, his impatience growing exponentially in indirect proportion to the amount of sunlight left in the sky.

Finally, the last sliver of daylight was vanquished by the encroaching blue-black of twilight, and in the heart of the summer, twilight was short-lived. It lingered briefly, staying long enough to announce the nightfall, as an old town crier might ring his bell furiously, announce a bit of news, and then move on. It was merely a transition period. A caution light on the street corner of time and space that heralded the stirrings of those things that preferred shadow to light.

Carlton stopped rocking and just sat there, absolutely still. The darkness had wrapped itself around him like a favorite old coat that had hung too long in the closet without use. All the impatient moments he had suffered faded away like the closing shot of an old black and white movie. He was relaxed. His time was at hand. He had but to seize it; but not too quickly. No, that would ruin the whole flavor of it.

Placing his palms on his knees he pushed himself up out of the rocker. It rolled back on its runners, then forward again, bumping him lightly. Carlton breathed in; the air was heavy with the smell of antique wood and varnish. The rich scent of the finely crafted pieces that populated his shop pleased him, like the smell of wood smoke rising from a fireplace on a chilly morning.

He moved through the darkness of the room with ease, avoiding the end of a desk here and the edge of a filing cabinet there. He swung open his office door and had to throw his hands up in front of his face. The shop lights were still burning and they stabbed at his dark-adjusted eyes with a savage intensity. When his vision finally cleared, he made his way to the cellar, down the steps and over to the box he had singled out from the crate. The box, his prize, sat there on the floor waiting for him.

Carlton reached over for the molding lifter, then stopped. It was lying right where he had left it, but beside it were all the staples from the box he intended to open. Someone had removed them already. Anger swept over him like a tornado sweeps through a town. Who had dared to open his box? Who had dared to invade his privacy? Who wanted his box? Each of these thoughts swirled around inside his head as he searched the basement for signs that someone had been there.

Tossing boxes and packages aside haphazardly, he scanned the floor for footprints in the dust and flaking plaster. He found none. The rage inside him was building. He felt he was going to explode. His temples throbbed; he thought he might even have a stroke, but he didn't care. All he cared about was finding out who had opened his box. Who had done it, and how he'd make them pay for it.

"Sss-ettle down." The voice came from fathoms inside his head, but he recognized it. It was the voice from the box that had commanded him to wait so many hours ago. It was soft and hissing – and it was in his head. "No one'sss been down here, Carlton. It'sss all right. It'sss all yoursss."

"Yes, mine. All mine; and I'm not sharing it."

"No Carlton," hissed the voice, "you won't have to share it with a living soul. Not one. It'sss all yoursss."

Carlton stopped his searching and returned to the box on the floor. He stood over it, looking down at it like an owner looking down on a beloved pet. He knelt beside it and laid his hands on it, his fingers gently wrapping around the edges of the lid. He could feel the rough texture of the unfinished pine that held his prize within it. Carefully lifting, he pulled the lid straight up, swung it to the side and placed it gently on the concrete floor. He leaned forward and peered into the box. His mouth and lips were dry, the latter he kept licking with his tongue in a nervous fashion.

The item he sought, still unknown to him, lay buried somewhere within the excelsior packaging material. Straightening his fingers, he slipped his hands carefully into the curls of bedding. He could barely contain himself. He lifted out a large lump of the protective stuff and tossed it to the side. Still nothing visible. Reaching in again with a single hand he felt around until his fingers bumped into something hard – something round, cold and metallic. At last, it was in his grasp. He closed his fingers around it, closing his eyes at the same time, and drew it up and out of the box. It was heavy. Heavier than he had expected it to be.

Carlton held it up in front of his face with one hand, eyes still closed. He ran his other hand over it slowly, feeling its contour, its texture. His mind tried to form a picture of what it was his fingers were feeling. It was globe-like and metal at one end and then extended downward about ten inches in a straight line. This part was rough but not as metallic, like leather. His fingers slid down slowly until they reached an uneven, angled edge. The edge itself was jagged and worn.

Slowly, as slowly as he possibly could, Carlton opened his eyes. The object he held looked like the broken handle of a sword, the globe-like structure he'd felt – the pommel. He turned it over and over in his hand, admiring its beauty – its weight – its design. He was amazed to find that the pommel was not metal at all. It was as clear as glass, as clean and clear as crystal, but extremely hard.

The pommel was rimmed with an extraordinarily detailed snake in relief, whose curled tail wrapped several times around the circumference like one of those hypnotizing black and white spinning wheels. At the center was a misshapen skull with two large, recurved prominences protruding from either side of its forehead, looking very much like small ram's horns. To the right and left of the skull were inverted Ankhs and beneath its jawbone were the words: Cado Infirmis. The letters were in angular print, almost like sticks laid together. Carlton recognized the script as runic, and, although his Latin was fairly rusty, he was sure the inscription read: Perish the Weak. There was no mistaking that what he held in his hand had once been the handle of a very large, very heavy sword.

In the dampness of the antique shop's basement, everything was still and quiet. Nothing moved, not even Carlton. He knelt there holding the sword handle, staring at it, absorbing its detail – being absorbed *by* it. A feeling of completeness and power coursed through his body. His whole body tingled. His mind raced with ever-shifting images and discursive voices. Images and tauntings of all the people and all the wrongs those people had done to him over the years. Schoolyard bullies merged with his father's beratings, blending with his mother's drunken insults and the ignominies he had suffered in college before he'd dropped out. They all clattered around inside his head, shifting from one to the other and back again. And beneath it all was a powerful voice. It was his voice, only not his voice. And it kept repeating one thing over and over and over. Beneath every image that solidified in his mind were the words: *They'll pay. They'll pay now, and the price will be heavy*."

Carlton started to laugh. The laugh turned into a cackle and he slumped down onto the cool, concrete floor, caressing and hugging the precious find to his chest. He laid there, knees curled up and sword handle beneath him murmuring. "They'll pay. Every single one of them. They'll pay."

From somewhere deep in the darkness in that basement, his vow of revenge was punctuated with a hissing laughter. It floated through the darkness and settled in Carlton's ears. It wrapped him in a sense of warmth and security. It told him he would not be alone in his quest for revenge, and that he, little Carlton Wedgemore, would have the last and the *best* laugh on all the stupid, mean people that had treated him like dirt all his life. It told him that he was now, somehow, more powerful than all of those toads put together, and he would exact a revenge that would be sweeter than even he could imagine.

"They'll pay. I'll make them, and they'll pay. Every ... single ... one of them."

CHAPTER 20

After arriving at Philadelphia International, Geoffrey Dunsmore took a cab to the Marriot in

Conshohocken.   His strong features and British accent titillated the desk clerk who had checked him in.   She had made a point of touching his fingers when she'd handed him his room key.   And there had been a certain sultriness to the way she had reminded him that, "if there's *anything* you need, please don't hesitate to call. We're always willing to go that extra mile for our guests."   Geoffrey had smiled warmly at her, taken his key and headed to the elevator.   Halfway there, he stopped, turned around and walked back to the desk.

The clerk had been watching him the whole time.   When she saw him stop, she quickly pulled the barrette out of her hair.   As he approached the counter, she gave her head a quick shake to ensure that her locks were laying just the way she wanted them to.   The action also served as a come-on, a tactic as second nature to women as leaning forward at the right time in the right blouse.

"Can you tell me," said Geoffrey, as he stepped up to the counter, "what time the hotel's pub opens?"   The accent and the use of the word pub actually made the clerk, Alicia Davis, blush from desire.

"It ... it's already o-open. Opens at n-noon every day," she stuttered.

"Thanks," smiled Geoffrey. "You're a doll." He then made his way to the elevator, got off at the seventh floor and found his room, 702. It took him a moment or two to get the swipe card to function properly and let him in. Once inside, he tossed the two bags he was carrying onto the bed, checked his watch and decided he had time to take a quick shower before making his call to Father Jacobs.

He could feel his muscles relaxing as the steam from the shower swirled around him. He stood there, letting the hot water beat down on his neck and shoulders. One nice thing about most hotels these days was the shower's massager head. There were several different pulsing options, virtually guaranteeing a setting that would do the job.

Sliding the glass door back, Geoffrey stepped out and toweled himself off. The foggy image in the mirror told him he could probably use a shave as well, but he decided to skip that. There were several elongated, bleached-out scars on his chest, back and thighs; as well as two circular ones with puckered edges just below his right shoulder. Anyone looking at him with his shirt off would have no trouble guessing that Geoffrey Dunsmore had not led a sedentary life.

Geoffrey unzipped one of the leather bags, grabbed out a blue shirt, underwear – rooted around until he found a pair of socks – and a pair of dress pants. As he dressed, he realized that he was hungry. He hadn't eaten in almost fourteen hours. The thoughts of a big juicy steak and a pint of Guinness sounded really good, but he knew he didn't have the time.

Reaching into the bag again, he pulled out the Big Ben clock and set it on the night table next to the bed. Five more minutes and he'd make his call to Jacobs. He then dragged the second bag, a leather carry-on the size of a gym bag, off the bed, knelt down and shoved it underneath, working it as far back under the bed as he could get it.

He walked over, sat at the desk beside the clothes cabinet and plucked the receiver from the phone. At first, he thought about calling the front desk to have them connect his number, in hopes that the redhead might pick up. But he decided against that. As much as he would have liked to, he just didn't have the time right now. He pushed 9 for an outside line and then dialed the number.

Geoffrey didn't have long to wait. Father Jacobs picked up on the second ring.

"Geoffrey, that you?" asked Jacobs.

"You bloody well bet it's me," Geoffrey said, his tone warm, friendly and relaxed. "How the hel- how have you been, Father?"

"I've been doing very well, my old friend. I hope the same can be said for you? I have to say that I was surprised to hear from you after all this time ... but it was a *pleasant* surprise."

There was a long pause, then Geoffrey said, "To be honest with you Father, I'm not sure how pleasant this is going to turn out to be. Don't get me wrong, lad, I'm happier than a Frenchman in a whorehouse about getting together with you, but there's a bit of nasty business that needs looking into, and *that's* what I'm not sure is going to be so pleasant."

"What kind of nasty business are we talking about ... exactly?"

"It's probably better if we do this face to face. What do you say I meet you somewhere for a bite to eat? I'm starving. I'm staying at the Marriot in a little bloody town called Conshohocken. Do you know where that is?"

"Yes. You're about fifteen minutes from me."

"Bloody wonderful! I've got to rent a car, so why don't you give me an address of some nice little restaurant, and I'll meet you there in – oh - say forty, forty-five minutes?"

Jacobs thought for a moment. "I've got just the place. Do you like Italian?"

"Right now, I'd pretty much eat just about anything. Give me an address, and I'll be there."

Jacobs gave Dunsmore directions to the restaurant. He also suggested Enterprise as the rental company. "They'll pick you up. A lot easier that way," he'd said.

After hanging up, Geoffrey went into the bathroom, brushed his teeth and combed his sandy brown hair. He then called down to the desk, spoke for a few minutes to the infatuated redhead, and had her call the rental company. So far, things were going swimmingly as far as Geoffrey was concerned. But this was the easy part, and he knew it. Things would get a whole lot more complicated before long. He could feel it. He wasn't in the habit of chasing down ghosts, so when he believed things warranted a trip from London to Philadelphia, it was almost a sure bet that the situation was far from simple.

Geoffrey decided to wait downstairs in the lobby for the rental to arrive. He found a quiet corner near the coffee bar, grabbed a local paper and started absently thumbing through it. He had a lot to think about. Explaining his visit to Jacobs wasn't going to be a walk in the park. That was a certainty. He'd learned over the years that when people got the kind of news that he usually carried, overcoming their skepticism and disbelief made talking a one-armed man into buying a rowboat seem like child's play.

When Enterprise finally arrived, Geoffrey shot a quick wink at Alicia as he followed the little man out through the automatic doors of the hotel. They had to go back to the rental office to square away the paperwork, and then it would be on to the restaurant.   The eating part, as well as the reconnecting with an old friend part, he was looking forward to. The rest ... well, work was work, and he'd done this too many times not to know that you enjoyed what you could, and then dealt with what you had to.

***

When he'd hung up the phone, Jacobs pushed back in his chair and sank into the leather cushions. Knowing Geoffrey as he did, at least, knowing he was a serious man, gave the priest pause. Of course, on reflection, Jacobs realized that he actually knew very little about Dunsmore. True they had formed a friendship, and true he knew – or at least, believed he knew – the man's character. But beyond that, the truth of the matter was that Geoffrey Dunsmore was a bit of a mystery. Still, there *was* a certain sense of pleasure that Jacobs felt about seeing him again.   But there was also something underneath that. Something that made the priest's stomach knot up; some unknown, intangible quality about Geoffrey's arrival that made him feel that, whatever he might think was going on was bad, it was probably quite a few times worse.

Jacobs stirred himself from his reverie, leaned forward far enough to grab the receiver from its cradle and then sank back again. When he'd made the reservations (not difficult to do when you're a priest, even if the place is packed), he dropped the receiver back down and closed his eyes. Whatever was going on, for whatever reason Geoffrey Dunsmore had shown up, Jacobs was sure of this much, a couple of Our Fathers wasn't going to make it go away.

CHAPTER 21

Grady Peters walked through the door at 6:35, gave a great big bear hug to his son, Willie, and a tender kiss to his wife, Tamika. Her lips were dried and chapped from licking envelopes all day. She had been meaning to buy one of those spongy things to do the job, but the money always seemed to be earmarked for other things.

The house smelled wonderful to Grady – a mixture of garlic, onion and fried ground beef. The aroma made his mouth water, and he made his way to the kitchen. Looking over his shoulder to see if Tamika was watching, he lifted the lid on the beef and snatched out a bit. He blew on it to cool it - still a bit too hot.

"Don't think I don't know what *you're* up to, Grady Peters. You'd best be keepin those fat fingers ayours outta my pots an' pans ifin you want to be keeping all of em." Tamika laughed, stepping into the kitchen behind him. Grady looked sheepish. He wrapped his arms around her and gave her a big kiss. Not a peck, but a proper, "I love you more than anything", kiss. He then flipped on the tap to let the water run. You had to do that if you wanted it even close to cold. He filled a glass, drank it down and then filled another.

"I got time to take a quick shower, baby?" he asked.

"You go right on an' get the day's smell offa ya. We got at least 'nother twenty minutes. Twenty minutes that is, if you c'n keep yer paws outta the pans."

Grady went into their bedroom, took of his clothes and laid them neatly on a towel by the dresser. He'd have to wear them again tomorrow, and he didn't want his work grime getting all over their furniture.

Willie followed him into the bathroom, his legs stretching as far out as possible to imitate his father's big steps. He almost lost his balance at one point but managed to right himself before he went down.

"So wutch you plannin on doin little man? You ready t'jump in here with me an git all cleaned up?"

"Sure am. You ain't gonna make it cold again, are ya, pop?"

"No," said Grady. "I'll make it nice an' warm for ya. But-" he paused and looked down at his son.

"But what pop?"

"But ... there ain't no word as ain't. It's *aren't*."

"But I hear you say it all the time, an' so does mama."

"Maybe. May-be ... but we *aren't* the ones in school, are we? You is." He said the word *is* with a flair, letting the boy know that he knew it was wrong, and they both started laughing and giggling.

"Oh pop. Stop messin with me." Their laughter continued until they heard Tamika calling.

"You two better quitcher foolin an' git washed up. Supper's almost ready."

When they finished, Grady helped Willie get all toweled off and dressed for bed. He'd still have to brush his teeth after dinner, but other than that, he'd be ready to sit down and watch some television. In the summer, Willie was allowed to stay up until nine-thirty. For a nine-year-old, that was all night. Sometimes Grady and Willie would watch a basketball game together (if they were lucky enough for Tamika to have fallen asleep on the couch, Grady would let Willie stay up till the end of the game.) At other times Grady would sit through a cartoon show or two, laughing just as hard as Willie did.

Grady Peters loved his family. He adored his wife, and it broke his heart that he could not provide for them like he wanted to. He had wanted desperately to get Willie a new baseball glove for his birthday, but the prices were not only outrageous, but way out of reach for Grady.

At supper, they each talked about their day. It was a law in the Peters' household. Everyone took turns and there was no such thing as "nothing happened". No matter how trivial it might have been each one explained what had happened or not happened to them that day. It was also a law that they ate at the table. No meals in front of the TV for the Peters.

"Guess what?" asked Tamika, wearing a grin from ear to ear.

"What?" Grady asked, swallowing the last bit of his mashed potatoes.

"Un-unh. I ain't tellin. I tol' ya t'guess."

"Dunno. Let's see ... you're smilin, so it's gotta be somthin good. Umm ... they found a cure for your mama's diabetes."

"I wish! Nope!"

"Uhh ... Miss Applewhite give ya a full-time job at the cleaners."

"Nope, but tha'd be nice. Go on. One more guess."

"Hmm ... It ain't a job, it ain't a cure for your mama ... must be-"

Grady was interrupted by the doorbell. Immediately, Willie dropped his fork on his plate and started to slide off the chair.

"You just sit yourself right back down again, young man," admonished his mother. "Ain't no children a-mine runnin off t'answer no doors at night."

By this time, Grady was out of his seat. He pulled off the napkin that he always tucked under his chin for dinner and tossed it on his chair. A drop of gravy clung to the collar of his T-shirt, having stealthily avoided the corner of the napkin.

"Dunno who that could be, but I guess I'll find out quick 'nough." He gave Tamika a kiss on the top of her head and briskly ruffled Willie's hair. "Y'all finish up, don't be waitin on me and don't let it go cold on ya. I'll be right back."

The house the Peters lived in was small but comfortable. It was a straight through twin, so Tamika could see the front door from where she was sitting. She watched Grady open it, say something she couldn't quite make out, and step outside.

***

"I promise I won't take much of your time, Mr. Peters, and I also promise that I'm not selling anything." The man Grady was listening to looked to be in his early fifties. He was wearing a dark blue suit and his yellow-blond hair was perfectly combed. He had a stick pin just below the knot of his tie that Grady couldn't seem to pull his eyes away from. At first glance it looked like a diamond, but it seemed to change size and shape as the man spoke.

"I certainly hope you'll pardon my evening intrusion, but I'd heard that you've recently lost your job." The man held up a hand to prevent Grady from responding. He then touched his index finger to the stickpin and it seemed to crawl around in a circle like a beetle and then settle back down into place, once more looking like a diamond.

"My name is Jedadiah Witherspoon," the man said, extending his hand. His voice was rhythmic and mesmerizing; the sound of it made Grady's whole body seem to relax. When he shook hands with the man, there was a tingling sensation that worked its way up his arm and into his shoulder. Instantly, the soreness Grady had from having his arms above his head most of the day hanging banners dissolved.

"As I said, I won't take much of your time, but if you're interested in full-time work-" the man grinned, "-all legal, I assure you, I'm opening a new store in town, and I believe you'd be just the right man for me. Now, there's no need to make any snap decisions you're not comfortable with. I'll give you my card-" He produced a small red card and handed it to Grady. "-and you go talk it over with the Missus. If you're interested, be at the address on the card at ten o'clock tomorrow morning. That's ten o'clock sharp. I'm a fair employer, but I just can't stand tardiness."

Grady looked at the card, but couldn't quite read the black letters printed on it in the evening's light.

"Now, before I take my leave and let you good folks get back to your supper, I'll tell you this much. The job pays well. I'd say, for a man as responsible as you-" He let another greasy smile slip across his face. "-I confess, I asked around bout your character ... but as I was saying ... for a man as responsible as you, I'd be willing to start you off at ... oh ... let's say fifteen dollars an hour. Now, you go back and do all the mulling and discussing you need. Hopefully, I'll see you tomorrow at ten."

The man didn't wait for a reply. He gave a quick nod of his head and turned to go. The stickpin on his tie seemed to grow legs. It stood up, opened what looked like wings, refolded them and sat back down. It reminded Grady of one of those scarab beetles he'd seen in the *Mummy* with Brandon Frazer.

Grady watched silently as the man made his way down the walkway, cut left onto the sidewalk and slowly disappeared down the street. It took several minutes for Grady to regain himself and walk, trancelike, back to the kitchen.

***

"What was that all 'bout, baby?" asked Tamika, as Grady sat back down."

"Um ... I'm not really sure yet. Some guy wants to give me a job at his new store." Grady passed the card over to Tamika without even looking at it again. "Said he'd pay me fifteen dollars an hour." There was a blank, emotionless look on Grady's face, and the words came out in a monotone, reminding Tamika of how those women in *The Stepford Wives* spoke. She looked down at the red card Grady had passed to her. Printed on it in black Edwardian Script was:

Witherspoon Enterprises

The World's Largest Broker of Dream Vacations
The Thrill of a Lifetime is Guaranteed
Bring Your Fantasies, Dreams & Desires
110 Maple Street N.W.
Banderman Falls, PA 19428

Across the bottom of the card, in much smaller, Times Roman was written:

No phone calls – No Personal Checks – All Major Credit Cards Accepted

"You all right?" asked Tamika. "Ya look like a man that's just been hit in the head with a foul ball."

Grady blinked, his brain sending a RESET impulse through him.

"Yeah. Sorry. Just kinda took me by surprise, that's all. What's the card say?"

Tamika read him the card, then handed it back to him. He stared blankly down at it. His eyes locked on the printing, but only seeing the stickpin on Witherspoon's tie.

"Lemme see. Lemme see," shouted Willie. "I wanna see it too."

"Finish yer peas, young man. Then git yerself t'brushin yer teeth s'we c'n watch some TV before bedtime." Grady's voice was flat again. Sometimes, you have to flip the RESET button more than once to get all the circuits back online.

After Willie shoved the last of his peas down his throat and went to brush his teeth, Tamika reached out and put a hand over Grady's

"What do you make of it?" she asked. "Do you think it's fer real?"

"I dunno. Dunno what t'make of it. Whudda you think?"

"Well ... I guess it couldn't hurt t'go see what it's all about. Do you?"

"No ... I guess not. I'll see if Eric'll let me slip off a bit tomorrow t'go over and check it out."

A stern look spread across Tamika's face, like rain clouds on a sunny afternoon. "Don't you go do nothin foolish. An' don't you say yea or nay till we talk about it. You hear, Grady Peters? We ain't jumpin from the fryin pan t'the fire just t'make a few extra bucks."

"Extra?" questioned Grady, more sternly than he had wanted to. "Extra? There ain't no *extra* here, babe. We're just barely makin it. Maybe not even that. It ain't extra; it's a lifeline."

"It might be. An' it might not. All I'm sayin is before you go committin yerself t'somethin, we should talk about it. Git all the details an' then we'll see. If it's good, ok. If it ain't, well, it ain't."

Grady smiled, reached across and ran the backs of his fingers down Tamika's cheek. "I promise, baby. I won't do nothin till we talk about it. Sorry for soundin so gruff; just feelin the pinch, you know?"

Tamika took his hand and squeezed it. "I know, sugar. And on that note, to add insult to injury, I don't think we c'n afford the cable no more. It's just getting too darned expensive."

Grady pinched his eyes shut as if he were in deep pain. "Well, we'll worry 'bout that next month when the bill's due. Now tell me what the good news is that you were tryin t'get me t'guess when we got interrupted."

"You know Mr. Wasko, down t'the EasyMart? Well he says that if I come by on Thursday afternoons, he'll let me have whatever premade sandwiches are left over. Says he can't sell em after a certain time and that he hates t'throw em out."

"That's terrific," said Grady. He leaned across the table on his elbows and gave Tamika a peck on the cheek. "That's absolutely terrific."

***

Grady and Willie played checkers until it was Willie's bedtime. Grady had let Willie win three straight games and the boy was beaming from ear to ear. At nine o'clock, they packed up the board and Willie made a last trip to the bathroom before climbing into bed. Tamika and Grady each gave their son a goodnight kiss, and Tamika flipped the switch, killing the light as she left. The faint glow of the Star Wars nightlight spilled softly out into the hallway.

Grady and Tamika waited until they were sure Willie was sound asleep and then made love. When they finished, Grady rolled over, totally spent. His eyes fluttered shut and he drifted off. The clock in the hall had just chimed eleven. Tamika leaned over and turned off the lamp on her bedside table. She rolled over on her back and laid there thinking about the red card, and what it might mean for them if it was legitimate.

CHAPTER 22

Night was not the only thing that had settled over Banderman Falls. An insidious malevolence descended upon the town like an unexpected snow that falls during the dark hours. Its morbid fingers stretched out, scratching at the minds of the residents, clawing at their souls and digging into their unconscious thoughts. It hid in shadows of darkened bedrooms or underneath the pillows of those still awake. For those already asleep, it usurped the projection room of their minds, presenting to them, in living color, the embodiment of their darkest longings, desires, lusts, and terrors.

Tamika lay there in the dark listening to the sound of her own breathing and that of her husband's. Her mind drifted from one subject to the next and back again as she slowly succumbed to sleep. Even as she faded, she could feel the dream coming on.

The house at the top of the hill had a familiar outline. She recognized it, but couldn't place it. An eerie feeling closed in around her. It frightened her to think of going up there – of going inside. A sliver of moon cut through the clouds, lighting the steep steps that climbed to the front door. All the windows, except one on the second floor were dark. A pale yellow light shone through that one. She knew that she should turn and run. But the light – that light - was calling to her, and it was a call she had to answer.

A chill washed over her as she started up the steps. She noticed that she was wearing only a man's T-shirt that barely covered her, leaving most of her thighs exposed. Her feet were bare and she could feel the lightest of breezes ruffling her hair. One step at a time – she climbed to the front door.

The air on the porch of the house was musty and stale. She still could not place where she'd seen this house before, but she was sure she knew it from somewhere. And she was sure she knew it to be a place to be avoided. Yet, she also knew she had to go in. She had no choice.

Her heart was pounding in her chest as she twisted the brass knob and the door creaked open on its rusted hinges. Just inside was a large staircase. Around the room, various animals had been mounted on the walls. A framed, Home Sweet Home, needlepoint hung over the unlit fireplace. The room was cold and dank as if nothing living had moved through it in many years.

Tamika placed her hand on the curved banister head and lifted a foot up onto the first step. The room on the second floor with the yellow glow was calling to her, and she could hear its voice in her head. It was soft yet demanding. It beckoned her, commanded her, desired her. She made her way up the steps and across the landing. Standing in front of the bedroom door, she paused. Every nerve inside her was alive and tingling. She knew, in a vague way, what was on the other side of that door. She knew what would happen to her if she went in there. She knew she didn't want it to happen, and she knew she did.

As she turned the knob on the door, she could feel the wetness between her legs. Her body ached to be taken by what awaited her, even though her mind rebuffed it. She stepped through the doorway, every ounce of her sexuality alive and burning.

In front of the four-poster bed stood a tall man. His face was in shadow and he was wearing a long black bathrobe. On the table to the left of the bed was a bottle of wine and two glasses, already filled. Tamika stood in the doorway, shivering with fear and excitement. The man raised a hand and beckoned her forward. His fingers were long and thick and seemed to move independently of the hand. Tamika advanced. A voice called to her from the basement of her memory, urging her to turn around and leave now; telling her that this is not what she really wanted. But every single step she took toward the man in front of her diminished the power and volume of her warning voice.

Standing in front of him, she stopped and looked up. The face that leered down at her was drawn as if the skin belonged to a skull two sizes larger. His eyes were deep pools of swirling red, and gazing into them, she lost herself.

He reached out his hand and laid it gently on her ass. It was cold, but the minute he touched her she could feel herself orgasm. The fingers were moving over her cheeks in a way that felt like they were growing, elongating. She could feel them slipping up under the edge of the T-shirt, searching her, probing her.

He pulled her in closer to him and placed his other hand on her shoulder. Out of the corner of her eye, because she could not stop staring into the red liquid of his pupils, she saw that his fingers were snakes. They hissed and curled around each other, and when he laid them on her they began to wrap themselves around her. One twined around her neck, tightening just enough to make her start to pant for air. Another coursed over her shoulder and down between her breasts, wrapping around her waist. She could feel it squeezing her, making it even harder for her to breathe. The other fingers on that hand began to encircle her arms, pulling them up and out, as if she were tied to an invisible St. Andrew's cross. Her legs were also splayed in the same fashion, the snakes wriggling and slithering over her flesh.

The man lifted her up in the air, his arms lengthening so that she was held horizontal above the floor. His robe seemed to collapse in on him, as if it was black, scaly skin, and he took her, again and again. And she wanted it, again and again and again.

***

Grady's dream was not so erotic. He also found himself in a house that was familiar, but unknown.

He stood in the middle of an empty room, devoid of rugs and furniture, except for the clocks. There were hundreds of them, all shapes, makes and sizes, all ticking loudly, beating their rhythm into his head. He clapped his hands over his ears, but the clocks only seemed to tick louder, pummeling their way through his hands. He turned wildly in circles, desperately searching for an exit, but there were no doors.

The clocks read a variety of times, yet all had one thing in common. They were all moments away from being straight up on the hour. In only moments, each clock would begin to chime, ring, gong or clang, and the sound would be deafening. He had to get out of there. Frantically, hands still clamped over his ears, he searched the room for a way out and found none.

With a tremendous click, every clock snapped to the hour. The clanging cacophony began. Grady fell to the floor screaming in agony. He could feel the blood begin to leak from his ears and ooze through his fingers. The room began to swim and wisps of blacks and blues, like party streamers, swirled around behind his eyes. He thought he was going to lose consciousness, but as suddenly as it began, it stopped. All the clocks fell silent. Grady lay on the floor, tears streaming from his eyes, thankful that it was over. He looked at his hands and was surprised to see there was no blood on them. He ran a finger through the inside of each ear, but there was no blood there either. Through sheer will, he pulled himself to his feet. And as soon as he was standing, the clocks all began ticking again, and were all set to go off in less than a minute.

The pattern repeated itself, time after time. Ticking to ringing. Ringing to bleeding. Bleeding to falling. Falling to getting up. Getting up to ticking. Grady was trapped in a Mobius loop of horror.

***

All across Banderman Falls, sleepers were drawn into their darkest nightmares or their darkest pleasures. Men were tortured in various ways, depending on what lay buried beneath their consciousness. Some were caught in bank vaults that would not open but filled mysteriously with snakes from an unseen source. Others were trapped on busses that wouldn't stop and kept driving in circles past fountains of water, while the men on the busses gazed from the windows, parched from thirst. A few men were forced to watch their wives making love to other men and enjoying it.

Women were taken sexually according to their most secret fantasies. Some were man-handled, some had multiple partners, some were immersed in their most dreamed-of romantic fantasy. And all from the same dark man. Even when there was more than one – they all wore the same face and had the same snake-like fingers.

Those who were not yet asleep had only to lay their heads on their pillows. Only two people within the whole town, aside from the children, were spared the dreams that night. And the purveyor of the dreams, the author of the nocturnal mental plays, the cinematographer of the nightmares, wailed in anguish and anger that he could not touch these two. Stretching his dark powers to their limits, he could not enter the minds of these two men. His rage burst forth, making the flavor of the dreams that he *could* inspire more violent, more sadistic and more physically real.

CHAPTER 23

While others were tossing in their beds, drowning in their unspoken hells and heavens, Curtis Lattimore sat in his basement drinking beer and smoking a joint. He was debating whether he could make it over to the fridge for another beer when he heard the click of the pull-handle on the old FridgiKing. He looked up and saw a man reaching into the fridge. He was bent over, searching through the bottles, apparently looking for a particular brand. The jeans he was wearing had a sixties bellbottom cut, the bottom edges of which clung to the heels of his Converse sneakers.

"Who the hell are you?" Curtis yelled, struggling to get up off the couch that had swallowed him. "And what the hell are you doing in my house?"

The man straightened, turned, raised his hand palm outward, and smiled.

"If I were you, I'd just shut up and-" he tossed a fresh beer across the room to Curtis "-drink your beer. Who I am, we'll get to. Right now, just drink your beer, finish your joint and listen. I'm about to make you a very happy man. A very happy man, indeed."

Curtis got to his feet. He started to charge across the room at the man, but suddenly found himself unable to move. He was frozen in mid-stride, looking like a statue that was made for a beer commercial. One leg was stuck out behind him and his right hand held the beer out in front.

"You know," said the man, his face looking strikingly like Jerry Garcia, "you're just the kind of soul I've been looking for." He walked around Curtis in a continual circle. "Yes. You're *exactly* the kind of person I could use. You're hired." The man burst out laughing. It was a high pitched, squealing sound that pierced Curtis' ears like an ice pick.

Curtis tried to speak but couldn't move his lips. The bottle of beer in his hand was beginning to slip. Despite his efforts, he couldn't close his fingers any tighter and the bottle dropped from his hands. An inch from the floor it stopped, holding its position in mid-air.

"My goodness. I hope you can hold on to a gun better than a beer bottle. But then, we know you can do *that*, don't we? I mean, you didn't have any trouble decorating the wall of the EasyMart with Pat O'Donnell's brains, did you? No. None whatsoever." The man laughed again. "Well, I suppose I should release you. I'm pretty sure by now that you'll not try any of the nonsense that was in your head when I arrived, will you?"

Curtis tried to answer but couldn't.

"Oh, dear me. Have I forgotten something?" The man walked over and touched Curtis on the shoulder. Instantly, the momentum he'd had when he was frozen pitched him forward. He lost his balance and fell, catching himself with his hands before his face hit the tile floor. When he managed to get to his feet he turned to face the man in the bellbottoms. As he did, he noticed that the beer bottle he'd dropped was still floating above the floor.

"My name is Jordan Witherleaf. You're Curtis Lattimore. We're pleased to meet each other, I'm sure. Now ... why don't you have a seat over there where you were and we'll get down to business. And don't worry, I'll answer all your questions. And probably a few you'd never dare to ask in the bargain." Again, the man laughed, only this one was deep and sonorous and reverberated off the walls, rattling the few posters that Curtis had stuck there with tac.

Witherleaf looked at his watch. "Hmm. Eleven thirty-five," he said, "you'll have to pardon me if I seem a bit distracted as we speak, but I'm a little busier at present than I appear to be. Many fronts, so to speak."

"What is it, *exactly*, that you want?" asked Curtis "And why do you want it from me? And who told you about the EasyMart?"

"You are a dense one, aren't you, Curtis? Oh well, no matter. You still suit my purposes. Yes, I can definitely use a man of your talents, even if you aren't particularly bright." He held up a hand, signaling Curtis to keep his mouth shut. Curtis complied.

"I have a miniature problem, Curtis, that, as it so happens, is right up your alley for fixing. Now, naturally, I wouldn't expect you to work for free. But I'll bet there's something you've always wanted that's worth more to you than a few dollars. Am I right?"

There was a confused look on Curtis' face. Witherleaf could see he was struggling to think of something that he wanted more than money.

Witherleaf exhaled loudly and slowly, somewhat exasperated. He clapped his hands together and began rubbing the palms against each other like someone about to cash in on the winning lottery ticket. Then he held them out toward Curtis, patting them in the air.

"Ok. Let me spell it out for you, then. You do me a teensy-weensy, itsy-bitsy favor, and I'll grant your most depraved wish. And believe me, I know what that is. Actually, it kind of makes me a little randy, too. But that's of no consequence, it's your wish, not mine." He looked at Curtis with his head cocked to the side. Curtis thought he looked like a dog that had just heard a whistle and couldn't figure out where it came from.

"Ok," said Curtis, "I'll bite, what's my wish? What do you think is more important to me than cold hard cash?"

"Well, let me see here," said Witherleaf, reaching into his front pants pocket. He drew out a key and held it up. It was an old fashioned skeleton key. He then dipped into his other pocket and pulled out what looked to Curtis to be two photographs. "Wait, I'm not done yet ... not done at all." Dipping back into the same pocket he pulled out two sets of handcuffs, two ball gags, two blindfolds, a tube of lubricant, a bottle of baby oil, a pocket knife and ten feet of steel chain. He tossed the stuff on the couch beside Curtis; all except the two photographs. Those he held up in the air, the faces turned toward himself.

"Do you know who these are?" He grinned. "Can't you guess which two women in this town you've always wanted to do ... at the same time ... and without their permission? Oh, yes, without their permission for sure. That makes it so much juicer, doesn't it? Well, the key will get you in to them, I'll make sure they're together when you come to call. The rest-" he swept his arm out over the items lying on the sofa, "-the rest is up to you."

Curtis looked at the things beside him, then back at Witherleaf. His mind was racing, trying to figure out which two women Witherleaf was talking about. As far as Curtis was concerned, he'd do all the women in stupid Banderman Falls at the same time. Except that fat Ramsey woman, of course. But then he reconsidered and thought that she might even be fun.

"So what is it you want me to do, and who's the pictures of?

"Who *are* the pictures of?" Witherleaf corrected, "my word, you're grammar's as lacking as your intellect. But again, no matter. You'll still do very nicely."

"Do *what*?" Curtis yelled, his minimal patience strained to the limit.

"I'm coming to that. You are a rascal, aren't you? Why don't you relax and enjoy your beer." Witherleaf turned and swept his hand over the bottle that was still hanging above the floor. It disappeared, only to reappear in Curtis' hand. "Now drink up and listen. That's all you have to do at this point. And for pity's sake, please, no more interruptions. I'll explain everything you'll need to know."

Witherleaf walked over, swept the toys he'd given Curtis off the couch and sat down. He laid a hand on Curtis' knee. The feeling was cold but electric. Curtis could feel the muscles in his leg tense and then relax. His leg felt like someone had dumped a block of dry ice on it.

CHAPTER 24

By nine thirty-five, D'Anjollel's was starting to thin out. It had taken Geoffrey longer at the rental office than he had anticipated. When he finally arrived at eight forty, Father Jacobs was already seated at a table by the large picture window in the front. The two men had shaken hands and hugged. There was the usual background hum of conversations, rattling china and clinking silverware and glasses that pervades all successful restaurants. All accompanied by the heavy smell of oregano and garlic. The mood during dinner was jovial and lighthearted – surface stuff that old friends exchange before delving into the more serious issues.

Jacobs had related the ups and downs of his present assignment, and Dunsmore of his most recent travels, although he gave no real specifics about the whys and wherefores. The laughter they shared was genuine, yet there was also a sense of foreboding that ran beneath it like an underground stream. Both men could sense it.

Geoffrey pushed his plate aside. "What do you say we go grab a nightcap at the bar?" asked Geoffrey. "Seems to be quiet enough over there."

Father Jacobs just nodded and pushed back from the table. He was wearing the standard black suit and white collar for which all priests are famous. As he reached behind to pull out his wallet, Geoffrey snagged him by the wrist.

"Not on your life, Padre." He was wearing a broad and somewhat iconic grin. "This one's on me. And no argument about that. I wouldn't want to have to hurt a member of the cloth in public." He squinted his eyes to near slits, giving Jacobs the same stare Clint Eastwood would give the poor slob he was about to gun down.

Jacobs pulled his hand away from his hip. "Ok. Who am I to insult a foreign guest?"

Geoffrey slid his MasterCard into the little slot at the top of the billing pouch and carried it over to the bar, as the men took two stools at the far corner. He handed it to the bartender and ordered a Chivas for himself and a Beefeaters martini for Jacobs.

"So," began Jacobs, "what is it that brings you all the way to the U S of A?" His tone was informal, and though it sounded it on the surface, the question was anything but lighthearted.

Geoffrey took a last look around the restaurant. A man wearing a dark green suit was just taking a stool at the opposite end of the bar. A young couple was sitting at a table near the middle with their hands clasped together across their empty plates and their eyes locked on each other. In the middle of the bar, between the man in the green suit and Jacobs and Geoffrey, was a man waiting to pay his bill. From what Geoffrey could see of him from a side view, he appeared to be an elderly gentleman. His powder-blue sports shirt was neatly tucked into his burnished orange khaki trousers. He steadied himself with a polished ebony walking stick that was capped with a silver snakehead. When he'd received his change, he turned and faced Jacobs and Dunsmore. His eyes looked like two lumps of coal stuffed into a Halloween skull. Greasy straggles of thinning black hair hung down both sides of his face and a thick tuft stuck up from the back of his head in a very Alfalfa-ish style.

The man lingered for a long time, eyeing them. With one hand on the bar rail and the other on his stick, he sidled down the bar toward them, stopping about three feet away. Very slowly, he dipped his chin to his chest and brought it back up again in an exaggerated nod. He then turned and made his way to the front door. When he got there, he turned back to them and smiled. As he did, the skin on his cheeks seemed to shrivel up like bacon on a hot griddle. The lips drew back into a snarl; the teeth were yellow and pointed. The sound that issued from his throat as his mouth gaped open sent a shiver down Geoffrey's spine. It was a horrid wailing accompanied by a thick grayish-black mist that blew outward in great cloudlike puffs.

The other patrons seemed to be oblivious to the whole thing. They sat perfectly still, portraits of people at a restaurant. The bartender held a silver metal shaker over a Manhattan glass, but the golden liquid hung on its rim, ignoring the pull of gravity.

As the piercing cry faded, the man turned and left. The restaurant resumed its activity; the bourbon-vermouth spilled neatly into the glass beneath the shaker, the couple continued staring into each other's eyes, and the man at the other end of the bar took a big swallow of his Lowenbrau while waiting for his Manhattan to arrive. Geoffrey looked at Jacobs but said nothing, and Jacobs knew better than to speak first.

Geoffrey pushed his drink back, dropped a twenty on the counter and slid off his stool.

"Come on, Father. I think the best place for our discussion is back at the rectory."

"After that display, I'm not inclined to argue with you. My car's in the lot. Yours?"

"Out front, in the street." Geoffrey reached out and took Jacobs by the arm, pulling him in. "I think it's best if we ride together. I have a feeling it'll be a bloody lot safer that way. Your car or mine doesn't matter."

"Let's take mine. If anything goes wrong, you won't have to explain to the rental company what happened to their car."

Dunsmore looked solemnly at the priest. "If anything goes wrong, I doubt I'd be *able* to explain it. At least, not in any credible fashion that they'd be willing to buy if I told them the truth."

It was a little past ten and the street was nearly empty, except for a single car, a Chevy Nova. It rumbled and sputtered past them. It bucked its way up Main Street, stopped at the corner and then made a right, its lone signal winking briefly at them before disappearing behind the brick façade of Carla's Ice Cream Parlour.

Jacobs and Dunsmore walked briskly to Jacobs's Marquis, constantly aware of their surroundings. They pulled out of the lot and made a left onto Main Street. Jacobs was driving a bit faster than usual (and usual was always well over the speed limit.) He managed to cut a ten-minute drive to the church parking lot down to seven and a half. The Marquis rolled to a stop just in front of the rectory door.

All the lights in the nun's residence were out, and only a single ray of yellow shone through the rectory window where Jacobs's office was located. Geoffrey climbed out of the car and looked around, his eyes and ears straining to see or hear anything, but there was nothing to be heard. Not a sound.

When they'd made their way through the little portico that fronted the rectory they froze. On the oak door, just above the circular wrought iron knocker hung a dead animal. It was the body of a cat, still fully furred except for the head, which hung grotesquely down on its chest like the head of a broken puppet. The belly was cut open and the flesh had been peeled off the skull. On the front stoop, the entrails had been chopped up and laid out in a message that looked like it had been written with sausages.

C U R I O S I T Y !
A B A N D O N   A L L   H O P E

Geoffrey started to remove the cat from the door when its head swiveled upward with the crackling sound of shattered, misarticulated bone. It spat out a low growl from its dead mouth, its tongue flicking in and out and its eyes rolling from side to side in convulsive, jerky movements. Finally settling into place, the glazed eyes glared at the two men. Geoffrey had backed away the moment it moved, yanking his hand off it as swiftly as if he'd laid it on a lit burner.

"Go hence, from where you've come, keeper of the light," it spat at Geoffrey, more howling than speaking. "There is no light here to keep and it cannot be restored." Raising its tail, it pointed at Jacobs. "Thou art lost, priest, the battle has already been won, and the souls you seek to save shall come to claim yours." The thing's head sank back down to its open chest as it spoke the final word, its tail dropped and swung like the pendulum of a run-down clock until it once again hung limp and still.

A steeliness washed over Geoffrey and he approached the cat a second time. As he reached for it, it burst into flames. With one swift motion, he grabbed the carcass, pulled it free from the door and tossed it out into the parking lot where it fizzled and smoked until it was nothing more than ash. The intestinal message followed suit and burned away before their eyes. No trace of either remained; the door and steps were as pristine as the day they'd been built.

Geoffrey and Jacobs just looked at each other for the longest time, saying nothing. Then

Jacobs opened the door and they went in, straight to the priest's study and locked the door behind them. Jacobs was wearing a look of shocked disbelief, although there was no doubt in his mind that what he'd just seen was real. He went directly over to his desk, pulled out the bottom right-hand drawer and poured out two glasses of scotch, which both men drank down in a single swallow. He then refilled the glasses and slumped down into his leather chair. Geoffrey pulled up one of the guest seats and sat. With a glass of scotch in one hand, he stared blankly at the floor, considering where he should begin his tale, now that the difficult part was definitely out of the way. Getting his friend, a respected priest, to believe what he was about to say just got a whole lot simpler.

CHAPTER 25

Jack pulled the Town Car into his driveway, stopping just in front of the garage. After throwing it in PARK and cutting the engine, he bent forward and banged his forehead a couple of times on the top of the steering wheel in frustration. By the time he'd arrived at the mortuary, Robertson was just finishing up the post. There wasn't a whole lot to report that Jack didn't already know, except for the semen evidence found in Pat O'Donnell's mouth. The final conclusion was that she had been raped then shot in the head. Other than that, there was no new information that would be of any use in tracking down her killer. If a suspect could be found, the DNA from the semen would help – *if* a suspect could be found.

Jack popped the door and slid out, grabbing the manila envelope off the passenger's seat as he did. Lost in thought, he ambled up the walk, stuck the key in the door and went inside. His mind was swimming. Pat O'Donnell murdered, Frank Mowery and Charlie Maloney off somewhere. A feeling of foreboding crawled around inside him like a rat seeking a way out of its cage, a feeling that told him that Banderman Falls was on the verge of coming apart.

Jack plopped himself down on the couch. He hadn't heard anything from Tyler yet, which might be a good thing. Doubtful at best.

Feeling utterly burned out and lacking any concrete idea of what he should do – what he *could* do – next, he snagged the warm beer off the table and finished it in a single gulp. When he placed the empty back on the table, he noticed the blinking light on the phone out of the corner of his eye. A new message. The light bulb in the psychic room flashed on again, and before he even dialed the voicemail number he knew it was going to be bad news.

Jack recognized the gruff, three-pack-a-day voice of Harold Wilcox. He'd been out to the Wilcox place a few times, mostly on harmless trespass complaints. Kids would cut across the back part of Wilcox's garden to get into the woods, inevitably trampling the old man's vegetables in the process. On a number of occasions, Wilcox had threatened to "shotgun 'em down and let Rascal eat the remains". But of course, he never did. He'd just call Jack and have him come out to inspect the damage.

"Dougherty," coughed Wilcox, on the crackly recording, "better git yerself out here. Got a might big problem. C'n hardly believe it m'self, but I'm starin at it. Got me a pack-a wolves here in the yard, an' they tore up m'Rascal. I'm goin out an' shoot 'em. Mind, I know there ain't no wolves 'round here, but they're here. Sure as cows shit in the field. Better git on over here." There was no goodbye, just the click of the disconnect.

"Short and to the point," Jack said. *Wolves? Wilcox must be into the grain again. Wild dogs, maybe ... but wolves?* Jack dropped the phone back into the charger. He thought about heading over to Wilcox's place, but decided that it could wait until tomorrow. There was no real point to going now. The message had been left hours ago and there was no second, so whatever was done was done. Tomorrow would be soon enough to go out and inspect the damage.

Jack thought about grabbing another beer from the fridge, but he was just too tired to get up. He settled back on the couch, half sitting, half lying, and picked up the remote. He looked at it for a minute then tossed it on the cushion beside him. He reached down, unbuckled the leather pistol belt and clumped the whole thing down on the coffee table in front of him.

He sat there tired, very tired. It was one of those wiped out feelings where your body is exhausted but your mind is still whirling around.

He decided that the beer really might be the way to go.

When he came back from the kitchen, cold Michelob in hand, he flicked the switch and the lamp quietly died. The room went dark, except for the faint pale light that stretched its way in from the kitchen. A single car motored by outside, temporarily breaking the silence and then was gone. Jack slid himself over to the corner of the couch and laid back, stretching his left leg out and leaving the right knee dangling over the side. He slid down so that his back was nestled between the seat and back cushions and his head was on the small square pillow that rested against the couch's padded arm.

He closed his eyes, hoping to let the day fall away. Almost asleep, but not quite, in that limbo land that straddles wakefulness and dreams, where your leg jerks out suddenly just enough to bring you back to consciousness, he heard it. A soft tinkling sound. His eyes snapped open just in time to see the light from the kitchen grow brighter and then dim. He swung his leg off the couch and sat up. He kept still, trying to hear anything that didn't sound like it belonged. A soft metallic pop punctured the silence.

Jack stood up, slipped the Ruger .357 from its holster and padded softly toward the sound. As he got to the doorway he could see a figure standing with its back toward him. He recognized her instantly. There was a gaping hole in the back of her head and her hair hung down in stringy, matted clumps. The blue and white EasyMart smock was covered in dried blood from the top collar all the way down the left shoulder and back to the waist.

"Pat?" asked Jack, his voice shaky with disbelief.

She turned in slow motion to face him, almost whirling in place without lifting her feet. Her face was a pallid grayish-white and her eyes looked like cracked glass marbles. Above her left eye was a black hole and her lips were a dusky blue. She lifted her arm and held out the Michelob she was holding, tilting her head to the left questioningly.

"Want a beer, Jack?" she asked. Her voice was empty, devoid of emotion, like a bad recording made from a distant room. "Where were you, Jack?"

Everything inside him turned to ice. In his years as a police officer, he'd seen a lot of strange and nasty things, but nothing like this. He was dreaming, of course. He had to be. Jack absently lowered the gun to his side, letting it hang there limply. He couldn't take his eyes off hers. It was like looking into the face of a Henry Keen picture that had been retouched by H.R. Giger. The kitchen was ice cold and he could see his breath hanging in the air in front of him.

"Look at me, Jack. Look what happened to my pretty hair." She pivoted around and lifted a hand to point to the back of her head. With the tip of her finger, she waggled a flap of loose scalp up and down. "Look what that man did to my pretty hair, Jack. Why didn't you stop him? Why weren't you there?" She revolved back around to face him.

"Pat, I-" he started to say, but his mind was telling him that the whole situation was ridiculous. Corpses of young girls don't show up in your kitchen. And if he needed any further proof, there was the beer. *Do you really think the dead stop by for a quick beer and some accusatory conversation? Maybe they do on TV or in the movies, but this ain't either of them, pal.*

The thing in front of him glided forward a few feet, the beer still held in her outstretched hand. The sorrowful expression she had been wearing was melting into something more sinister. The blue lips curled back exposing stunningly white pointed teeth. Her lids dropped halfway down across the black-marble eyes in a menacing squint, and the upper half of her body pitched forward. Abruptly, she drew her arm back and launched the beer bottle. It struck the doorway beside Jack's head, splintering into various sizes of glass shrapnel. A triangular piece buried itself in Jack's temple, and foamy liquid slid down the door frame and puddled on the floor.

Jack took a step back and instinctively raised the .357. *What, exactly, are you planning to do with this?* Jack asked himself, even as he drew the hammer back. *Think you're going to stop a ghost with a hollow point?* The idea that people respond to irrational situations with irrational actions never occurred to him. He just kept trying to tell himself that this was one crazy dream and that any minute he'd wake up with a stiff neck from sleeping cockeyed on the couch.

"Oh, I see," hissed the thing in front of him. "Now *you're* going to shoot me." With its legs dragging through the air behind it, the image of Pat O'Donnell raced forward, arms outstretched, fingers opening and closing in a clutching gesture. Billows of greenish mist spewed from its gaping mouth, and it issued a banshee-like scream that cut through Jack like nails on a chalkboard.

Without thought, without hesitation, Jack squeezed the trigger. The explosion was loud in the tiny hallway. It seemed to Jack that, at the moment he'd pulled the trigger, everything slowed down to an unreal crawl. He watched the bullet exit the barrel in a billow of smoke and powder. He watched it sail across the room, dipping slightly, punch through the forehead of the thing in front of him and dig itself into a cabinet on the back wall. When it struck the thing in the head, it was like poking your finger through a cloud of cigarette smoke. The entry point swirled in wispy circles and then condensed back into its original shape.

The image of Patty drew up to a complete stop, its trailing legs floating forward to hang beneath its body. The facial features softened, the snarl was replaced with a look of confusion and sorrow.

"Why would you do that, Jack? Why would you want to hurt me? Why weren't you there when I needed you?" Its voice was soft and pleading, barely audible. For a moment, it smiled, then dissipated, leaving behind a permeating smell of decomposition.

Jack's mind was reeling. None of this could be true. None of this could have happened. He walked forward, gun hanging at his side. He ran his finger over the hole in the cabinet door. There was a texture to it, the pad on his index finger sinking slightly into the opening. It hadn't been a dream. It couldn't have been unless he'd been sleepwalking – (sleepshooting?). *"But how could it have been real?"* he kept asking himself. As if he needed further confirmation, he popped the cylinder on the .357 and dumped the bullets into his palm. Five live rounds, one spent one. There was no escaping this nightmare. Something had just taken place that couldn't possibly have, and down in that psychic room we all have, the one where the lights are *off* most of the time, the light bulb was burning brightly – this was real, and it wasn't over. Not by a long shot. In fact, the light bulb illuminated the message that it was only beginning.

Jack walked to the sink, plucked the piece of glass out of his temple and dabbed off the area with a dish sponge. In the bathroom, he found a pack of old Band-Aids and stuck one over the cut. He then walked back into the living room. He felt like he should be reporting this, telling someone, but who'd believe it? He didn't even believe it. Ghosts aren't real. They don't snarl at you and throw beer bottles at your head. They don't come to ask you why you failed – not really. They come in your mind, haunting your failures, but they don't come in physical form and confront you in your kitchen.

Jack dropped onto the couch, set the Ruger on the coffee table and dropped the bullets beside it.

They rolled around, the empty shell dropping off the end onto the carpet. He left it there and sank back into the cushions. He sat there just staring at the gun and bullets until he could no longer keep his eyes open and dozed off.

CHAPTER 26

Arliss Peterson had been sitting in her office, working her way through the manifests when Bill Waters came in and told her that the shipment they had received that morning was, indeed, "a switcheroo." He told her he'd shipped the item they'd received back to its intended destination with a request to call and confirm that the other location had reciprocated.

Just before she left the museum that night at eight-thirty, Arliss had called info, got the number for Wedgemore Antiques in Banderman Falls, and left a message on the machine. She left the museum number as well as her home number. When no one had answered, she was pretty sure that the place was probably closed for the holiday already, but still held out hope that the owner would get in touch with her.

For the rest of the evening, something about this particular missing shipment kept nagging at her. She didn't know why, but there was a sense of danger associated with the missing parcel. There was also the faint, irrational sense that the item in question had been, somehow, deliberately rerouted, even though she consciously knew that that was an absurd notion.

Arliss stepped out of the shower, the bathroom totally fogged. She pulled a towel off the rack and wrapped it around her shoulder-length blonde hair, twisting it into a kind of turban. Sprinkling a liberal amount of baby powder into the palm of her hand, she began to dust herself, enjoying the fresh scent that puffed up. She placed the bottle of powder back onto the wire shelf and stepped over in front of the mirror. The top half was still steam-covered. Tiny droplets of moisture clung to the edges of the mirror-like early morning dew standing on the tips of grass blades.

Grabbing a second towel off the rack, she wrapped it around herself, tucking it in just under her arms in a way that only women can do without having it fall off ten seconds later. She turned back to the mirror and wiped a circular area clear with the flat of her hand. When she looked up, she screamed. There was a face in the mirror, hidden inside the fog, but it wasn't hers. In an automatic movement, she snapped her head around to check behind her. No one there. When she looked back, the face was still staring at her, its eyes following her every motion. She backed away until her back was against the warm glass of the shower, never taking her eyes off the image in front of her.

The face was that of an old man, a man who looked to be in his early seventies. His eyes scanned her up and down. It was the same look that all men give to women, sizing them up, drinking in the shape of their curves while wondering if they had a chance of getting into their pants. It smiled a lecherous smile, the lips curling back and deepening the age cracks that lined its face. A long tongue, longer than any human should have, darted out and licked its lips. It then shot out from the mirror, across the room and slid up Arliss' left cheek. She could feel the cold wet it left behind as it receded back into the glassy mouth, and it made her shiver.

"You taste good," the face said. "Very good indeed. I'll enjoy you, I promise."

Arliss stood there, frozen. Her analytical mind was not prepared to deal with this. Everything in her ordered life was rational and explainable. There was nothing in her professional, scholastic background that would permit her mind to grasp what was happening or accept its reality.

A bony hand eased out of the glass and pulled the towel off her. The eyes looked her up and down; the hand holding the towel hovered there in the air in front of her. The thing in the mirror licked its lips again, and then swiped the tip of its tongue up between her breasts to her chin and across her lips.

"Very yummy," it said. "I'll definitely be enjoying you. But, I have to go now. Have a pleasant evening, Arliss." It faded away as if someone had taken a hairdryer to the mirror and evaporated all the steam.

Arliss stood there pressed against the shower door. Her mind was in total shock and her body had followed by refusing to move. She looked down at the towel that was lying on the floor. As she did, the baby powder flew off the shelf and clunked down onto the tile. A cloud of powder sprayed across the floor and rearranged itself into squiggly white commands:

**KEEP AWAY FROM THE FALLS
KEEP AWAY FROM WEDGEMORE**

Arliss didn't bother with the towel, she ran to the bedroom, slammed the door and wished that she could lock it behind her, but there was no lock on it. Crawling into bed, she pulled the top sheet up around her neck and sat there shivering. She searched her mind for some kind of reasonable, scientific explanation – some form of rationality to what had just happened that would bring it into a sensible focus for her to deal with. She found none; all she could do was sit there with the feel of the thing's tongue on her body and shake.

CHAPTER 27

Ernie Johnson awoke to full darkness. He was still lying on the floor among the high shelves in the back, *Paradise Lost* lying open across his legs. He kicked, sending the book tumbling onto the floorboards. His stomach was churning; he rolled over and vomited. His body convulsed with the force of it, and when he'd finished he brought up a second round, mostly mucous and spittle.

Wiping his mouth with the back of his sleeve, he pushed himself up onto unsteady legs and leaned against the shelving for support. Just standing there, he let his head clear a bit. When he felt he could keep his legs under him, he worked his way along the bookcases to the doorway. The front of the shop was dark. All the lights had been turned off. He groped for the switch and then shielded his eyes from the flickering fluorescents as they blinked to life.

Halfway up the aisle he could see the shelving cart. The front door was closed and the OPEN side of the sign was facing him. He looked at the bird clock he had hanging in the front of the store. It was one of those with different birds for numerals that chirped when the hour struck. 9:45. Ernie had spent the entire day passed out in the back of the store, and no one had noticed. It was true that the store saw fewer people these days. But no one? Even if the sign read CLOSED, wouldn't there have been deliveries? Someone should have come and found him. At least, that's what he thought should have happened. But it didn't. No one came and he laid there, passed out, all day.

Ernie made his way to the front counter, worked himself in behind it and sat down on the little rolling desk chair he kept there. He was still feeling a bit nauseous, and he had a pounding headache. No matter how he tried, he couldn't seem to keep his eyes in focus. Everything kept fading in and out.

There was no doubt whatsoever in his mind that what had taken place that morning was real. What he couldn't figure out is how or why someone could have done such a thing. What kind of a sick joke had it been, and how did the blind man manage to pull it off?

A magician, thought Ernie, even though he didn't really believe it. *That's it. Must be! Some new magician in town going around playing stupid tricks on people to get them interested. Yeah. That's gotta be it. A fancy magician they brought in for the big picnic, a kind of Grand Finale, I'll bet.* But even as the words floated through his mind he knew it wasn't so.

By the time his eyes began to focus clearly, Ernie didn't much care what the reason was or how the whole thing had been accomplished; all he cared about was getting home and crawling into bed. He'd never had migraines in his life, but he was certain that what was pounding around inside his head at the moment was one of them. Even with better focus, his vision was still somewhat blurred and the lights from the overhead fluorescents seemed to burn right into his brain. He shuffled to the front door with an arm across his forehead to cut down on the glare. When he got to the door, he flipped the switch and the humming glow mercifully faded. He pulled the door open and staggered outside and locked it behind him. There was no way he was going to drive, not with the way he was seeing at present, so he made his way down to the bus station.

The bus system in the Falls was pretty good. There were a few places it didn't go, but it usually got you close enough to anywhere to be within walking distance. The only real problem with the system (if it could be called a problem) was that it stopped running after 10p.m.

Ernie was out of luck, he'd missed the last bus by ten minutes. He'd either have to call a cab or walk. Neither option appealed to him. For a moment, he stood at the stop, hoping that the bus was running just late enough tonight to be able to catch the last run. He peered through the darkness down the empty street. Nothing was moving; there wasn't even any of the usual trash lying around. He listened for a minute, but there was nothing to hear. Banderman Falls was dead silent.

Ernie dug into his pocket and pulled out his cell phone. He flipped it open and then stopped. He intended to call a cab, but something was staying his fingers from dialing. An unrecognized force from deep within his being was trying to keep him from calling. He struggled, pushing down on the digits one at a time with the stubby end of his index finger. He could hear the flat beeps the phone made every time a number had been pushed.

He had dialed eight out of the ten numbers for Loomis's Cab Service. Ernie didn't have to look it up, Max Loomis and he were bowling team buddies and Ernie knew both Max's work and home numbers by heart. But he still couldn't seem to complete the call. Every time he went to push another number, a chill would run up his spine and cause him to actually shiver. Something kept telling him that he would be safer walking home.

He'd made it as far as the last number when he decided not to make the call after all and flipped the phone closed. Ernie looked down the long, empty street. It was about a two-mile walk from the bookstore to his apartment on West Elm. He didn't relish the thoughts of such a long walk with such a bad headache. Then he had an idea. He scrounged in his pocket and pulled out the key to the shop. He didn't want to go back in, but it was better than walking all the way home.

When he opened the door, he stuck his head in first to see if anything or anyone was moving around. It was quiet, so he moved inside, leaving the door open so that the street light would provide all the illumination he'd need without having to turn on the overheads. He made his way around the counter (bumping his knee once and cursing), opened the register and pulled out all the twenties. He then scratched a quick IOU on the back of a paper bookmark (the kind you can take for free) and stuck it in the drawer. That way, it wouldn't look like he stole the money. He just wanted to borrow it until tomorrow. (Not that it really mattered, old man Pyle never came to the store. Ernie ran the place. Opened up and closed up. But he still felt he should leave the note anyway. It was the right thing to do.)

Ernie stepped back outside and into the night. The Motel 8 was just around the corner. He could spend the night there. If he was lucky, there'd be someone working the desk he didn't know. Someone he wouldn't have to explain to. Exhaling a long sigh in resignation, Ernie crossed the street, turned right and headed for the motel. Each shop he passed was locked up and dark. Even the security lights that usually cast their pale halo-glows out into the streets all night were out. The whole town seemed to be asleep, buildings and all, and the feel of it made Ernie pick up his pace. All he wanted to do now was get inside somewhere.

When he finally reached the driveway that led into the Motel, he let out a big sigh of relief. A few more yards and he'd be able to relax. He didn't know why, but he felt amazed that he'd made it. He felt as if he had anticipated being mugged – no, that wasn't it. That wasn't it at all. What he felt was that at any moment, the blind man would step out in front of him, and his terror would begin all over again. But he'd made it. He could see the light spilling out of the front sliding doors, and there was a woman standing off to one side smoking a cigarette. Another sixty seconds and he'd be inside and safe.

The woman in the corner stubbed out her butt and fished around inside her purse, finally pulling out another cigarette. As Ernie got to the front doors and they whooshed open, the woman looked up.

"'Scuse me, sir," she said, "but do you have a light?" Ernie stopped and looked at her. She was an older woman, yet still very attractive. She was wearing a black dress that stopped about two inches short of her knees and was pulled tight around her waist with a wide silver belt. Her hair was a soft brown and her lips painted a brilliant red. The eye shadow she was wearing lent an air of mystery to her, a soft bluish-purple. She was wearing the broadest, most inviting smile Ernie could ever recall having seen in his life.

Ernie wasn't a smoker but he always kept a pack of matches in his back pocket for emergencies. He reasoned that: You never know when you were going to need fire. He pulled them out, thought about handing her the book, and then decided he'd do the honors first. Stepping up to her, he pulled off a match and struck it. Its end flashed up and then settled back down to a constant wavering flame. He held it out, one hand cupped around it to keep it from being blown out, although there wasn't even a mild breeze at the time. The woman bent her head and drew in deeply until the end of the cigarette glowed to life, coloring the inside of Ernie's cupped hand in a reddish-orange tinge.

"Thank you so much." She smiled and Ernie smiled back. "It's nice to meet a gentleman in a strange town."

"You're very welcome, ma'am," was all Ernie could think to say.

"Maam? Do I look *that* old?"

"No, of-of course not," stammered Ernie. "That's no-not what I meant. I'm sorry if I-"

"Relax. I'm just teasing you. I didn't realize you'd get so flustered so easily."

Ernie looked down at his shoes. He could feel the warmth of a blush beginning at his neck and spreading upward across his face. He could see the woman's shapely legs, accented by the high heels she was wearing.

The woman laid a hand on Ernie's shoulder. "Look at you blushing. Aren't you just the cutest thing?" She put a hooked finger under his chin and lifted his head until their eyes met. "At the risk of sounding very forward, how'd you like to buy a lady a drink? I don't know about you, but I could use a little company tonight. You know, strange place ... don't know anyone."

Ernie couldn't pull his eyes away from her deep blues. They were enchantingly magnetic; he found himself wading in them. In his mind, he said that he didn't mean to be rude, but that he couldn't just now. But what came out of his mouth was: "Sure, I'd love to ... but I have to check in first."

The woman laughed. "Well sugar," she said, "if ya play your cards right, you just might not have to." She winked at him and he could actually feel his heart beating against his ribcage. A few moments later they were seated at the motel bar. Ernie had ordered a gin and tonic, and the woman a Margarita.

He sat on the edge of his stool, one forearm up against the bar rail and the other hand around his glass. He couldn't help staring at the woman's legs; her dress had ridden up high as she'd climbed up onto the stool. She was sitting sideways, facing him with her legs crossed, one knee touching his. His gaze shifted when she ran her tongue sensuously around the rim of the martini glass, her eyes half-closed and pouty.

"I'm ... well ... do names really matter?" she giggled.

"I'll have to call you something," said Ernie, trying to sound sophisticated in an imitation Bogart voice. "Sure won't do to be callin' ya, kid, all night."

"Then why don't you call me Peggy? Yes. I like that. Call me Peggy." She raised her glass in a toast. "To Peggy and-" She waited for Ernie to fill in his name.

"Ernie."

"To Peggy and Ernie - two lost souls stuck in a roadside motel for the night. May they both have some fun." Then she started laughing, a long, side-hurting laugh that came from deep down inside her.

"Finish your drink sugar and let's go upstairs for some fun."

Ernie was scared and exhilarated at the same time. Most of him objected ... didn't want to go ... knew he shouldn't. But the part that women can control didn't want anything else *but* to go upstairs – and right now – *it* was in charge. There was also something hypnotic in the way she spoke that relaxed Ernie - made him feel safe – even though another part of him was telling him that he was in great danger. And when Peggy leaned over and kissed him on the cheek, her hand sliding up the inside of his thigh, it was over. The only place Ernie was going was upstairs.

CHAPTER 28

It was eleven thirty-nine when Linda Killerman turned off the light in her tiny office at the B & B and made her way upstairs to her room. The guests all seemed to be tucked safely away for the night – all four of them.   She had Mr. Witherstone in 227, Mr. and Mrs. Hoffman in 109 and Ms. Willowbrand in 208. Tomorrow, the Killerman B & B was expecting another eight people to check-in.   With any luck, the Fourth celebration would bring in one or two more that would decide at the last minute that they'd had too much fun to leave. Linda referred to these guests as "the hangovers", partly because they were just hanging around an extra day or two, and partly because it described *why* they were hanging around that extra day.

It had been a long day, and Linda decided she was too tired for a full shower, so she just "bird-bathed", as she called it.   She slipped into her pajamas, which consisted of a black tank-top with the word, *Grumpy*, stitched across the front, and blue bottoms with fluffy white clouds on them. It was her favorite night-time ensemble.

Climbing into bed, she fluffed up a couple of pillows behind her back and picked up the *Tetris* game that lived on the bedside table. It was her relaxation reward to herself at the end of a hard day. She'd fight with the ever-faster falling shapes until she was too drowsy to continue. It was kind of ironic that Tetris was her favorite game. Linda had always been good with finances, able to take a small bit of money and make it grow. She would have been fascinated to learn that Tetris were a subunit of Georgian currency.

When Linda was finally too bleary-eyed to continue, she dropped the game back onto the nightstand –"To Be Continued" – in the morning. A few minutes with the game and a cup of coffee in bed was the usual start to her day. She readjusted the pillows and slid down beneath the light sheet, which would probably be kicked off at some point during the night. As tired as she was, sleep didn't come easily. Her mind kept racing, making mental lists of things that had to be done - things she hadn't accomplished today and should have, things that *could* be done – a kaleidoscope of To-Do's.

As the last To-Do faded away, the dreams took her. A succession of sexual fantasies, some of them romantic and pleasant, others darker and more violent. But all of them desired, needed, as if her inner will was being manipulated to accept what would never be accepted in the conscious light of reality.

The most vivid of the dreams, and one of the darkest, began with her asleep.

She could sense the man standing over her bed watching her, but couldn't open her eyes. Instinctively, she knew what he wanted and rolled over onto her back. On one level she was excited, on another deeper level, she just wanted him to go away, but her body was giving in to his desires. And, somehow, his desires were becoming hers.

She stretched her arms out, allowing him to handcuff her to the bedposts. Her breathing increased with the wanting to be touched, with the mystery of what was going to be done to her – what she wanted to be done to her. Goosebumps broke out across her body and she could feel her nipples stiffen as the figure above her slowly drew back the sheet. The silkiness of the blindfold that he tied tightly around her head made her moan with longing. Every fiber of her senses came alive at his touch. His fingers, sliding the strap of her tank-top down over her shoulder to expose her breast; the ripping sound as he tore the pajama bottoms open; the cold feel of his hand – every inch of her was awake to the sexual experience. It seemed as if it went on for hours, the dark figure taking her again and again.

Then, suddenly, the dream would dissolve into another. It was a sexual blizzard of encounters, each in a different setting and each one more intense than the last, but none as intense as the one in the bed with the dark figure, which came again at the end of them all.

When the faceless figure had taken her for the last time, the dreams dissolved and she slid back into the depths of her sleep.

CHAPTER 29

While the rest of Banderman Falls dreamt, Carlton Wedgemore remembered. His mind slid back in time, recalling all the indignities he had suffered - one at a time. Lying on the cool floor of his dimly lit basement, he reached back across the years and brought everything into focus – everything he would need to know to make them pay. He began with his parents, now beyond his reach. The grave had taken them, but it was the beginning of everything for him, so that's where he started.

"Place your hands on the table, boy." Gerald Wedgemore towered over his six-year-old son. His hair was a rusty brown, swept back over his head exposing a prominent forehead. He had already taken his suit jacket off and hung it neatly on the back of the kitchen chair. To Carlton, it wasn't a man standing over him, it was a giant; an angry giant, its face pulled tight into a scowl.

"Place your hands on the table," he repeated, "I'll not tell you again."

"But dad," squeaked Carlton, in an unsteady, pouting voice, "I didn't break it. I-"

"Enough," yelled the giant bending over and placing his wide forehead against the boy's. "I'll have no backtalk and no excuses. You erred, so now you must pay. It is the way of things, boy. Now place your hands upon the table."

Carlton closed his eyes and extended his tiny hands. Laying them palms down, he braced himself for the first sting of the strap. It was the customary punishment for anything that his father happened to think was caused by misguided hands.

Slap! Slap! Slap! The sound of the leather biting into flesh filled the kitchen. Behind Carlton, the cook and housemaid watched, feeling anguish and guilt for not being strong enough to put a stop to the abuse. They could only stand in silence and stare in horror as the boy's father brought the folded belt down across his hands, blow after blow, each one seeming to be delivered with more force than the last.

By the seventh slap, Carlton was in full tears, wailing and flinching. The wailing was acceptable, even desired by the giant, but the flinching was not. Each movement of the boy's hands added another swack, and each swack made it harder for the boy to remain still. A vicious circle that only the giant enjoyed.

"I do not enjoy this," rumbled his father, but he did, and his face showed it. "But discipline must be maintained. Young boys must learn to be disciplined in their actions, or disciplined *for* their actions."

Across the table from where Carlton was learning about discipline, Catherine Wedgemore sat, eyes down, swirling the olive around in her martini glass. It was her third, and she was sure that she would be next if she didn't perform her wifely duties, as would be expected. The lessons he administered to the boy enlivened her husband, and, without exception, Catherine was taken after each one, in a rough and aggressive manner, as if she were also being punished for the boy's transgressions. And she had learned long ago, the more martinis she could get into her beforehand, the better off she'd be.

When the boy's hands had been sufficiently cut open, he was dismissed to his room. And true to form, the giant now turned his attention to his wife. Grabbing her by the hair, he dragged her into his study and closed the oak pocket doors behind him.

The scene shifted; there was no retribution Carlton could pay to his parents, so he moved on to catalog those that still walked, those that could (and would) feel his wrath.

Carlton was sitting in the little lunchroom of the prep school he attended. He was eight years old and wore heavy rimmed glasses. He sat alone, for he had no friends. In front of him was the lunch the maid had prepared under strict supervision of the giant. It consisted of two pieces of bread, half an apple, two sardines and a Mason jar half full of water. As he sat there staring at the meager, unpalatable fare before him, he was flanked by the school bully and his cohort.

Anthony Blemmings was taller and heavier than any other boy in the school, including the upperclassmen, and everyone kept their distance as much as they could. No one crossed paths with Blemmings, and those that did became hapless victims of his malicious personality.

"So what's for lunch today, Carlton?" sneered Blemmings, wrapping his large chubby fingers around the back of Carlton's neck. "Doesn't look so appetizing to me. Not worth taking. So what should we do with it instead?" Blemmings would have laughed, but there was never any joy or mirth within him, not even when he was doing what he loved best – tormenting others (especially Carlton, his favorite target.)

"Hmmm ... Let me see." He had to stop and consider what he wanted to do. The lunch he was looking at didn't really provide him with material worthy enough of his sadistic talents. He glanced at the front of the room, ensuring that Mr. Allworth, the lunchroom proctor, was still dozing, arms folded across his chest.   Satisfied that no one of consequence was paying attention, he plucked up one of the sardines by the tail and whapped Carlton across the forehead with it.

Blemmings closed his fingers around Carlton's neck. His fingertips dug into the soft flesh on either side. The pressure was strong enough to slow the flow of blood through Carlton's carotid artery, and he could feel himself on the verge of passing out.

"What do you want?" stammered Carlton. "What do you want me to do so that you'll leave me alone? Tell me. Please tell me and I'll do it."

"Don't know what I want. Haven't decided. What say you and me just sit here and try to figure it out. Got any suggestions?" The fingers squeezed harder and Carlton began to see bouncing points of light flash across his eyes. The sensation made his stomach start to churn (like the time he'd hit his thumb with a hammer and then promptly threw up). He could feel it starting to pressurize in his stomach; a pot ready to boil over, its lid popping around the rim in a hectic dance.

Watching Carlton's face, Blemmings recognized what was happening and tightened his grip even more. He didn't have long to wait. Carlton gagged, then flooded the apple, bread and lone sardine with a thick, mucousy liquid. It shot from his mouth and dripped out of his nose.

Bradley Warren burst out laughing and had to cover his mouth with his hand so as not to disturb Mr. Allworth's slumber. Blemmings gave him an elbow in the ribs that instantly stopped the laughter.

"C'mon, Brad. Guess we're done here. Let's let Carlton finish his lunch." He then twisted Carlton around in his seat so that he was looking directly into his face, vomit still hanging from Carlton's nose. "I want you to eat every bit of it. I'll be watching. And if you don't ... well, I guess I'll just have to catch up with you after school, huh? He flicked Carlton's ear with the tip of his beefy finger, making it turn a brilliant scarlet. "Eat up! Every bit!"

The scene shifted again. Carlton was sitting at the laboratory bench in college. General Biology was a required course; otherwise, Carlton would have skipped it altogether. His real strength was in accounting and business, but graduation depended on passing other things that held no interest for him. So here he sat, dead cat stretched out in front of him in a metal pan that reminded him of one of the baking pans he'd seen the cook prepare capons in.

His lab partner was Audrey Archibald, one of the twins that would eventually become dispatcher for the Banderman Falls Sheriff's Department. Like Carlton, she was forced into the biology scene in order to complete her required credits in criminal justice.

Blemmings had disappeared from Carlton's life with graduation from the prep school. But there were plenty of others willing to take his place. Blemmings's successor was Randall Crusher. He was captain of the wrestling team and was known to all on campus as "*The* Crusher", and not because of his last name.

In keeping with Carlton's lack of good fortune, Crusher had the lab bench directly behind him. A never-ending stream of pencils, rubber erasers, pennies, or whatever else Crusher could find handy, was hurled at the back of Carlton's head. The bicycle that Carlton used to get around campus had suffered multiple flat tires, and had even been chained to a NO BIKES ALLOWED sign in front of the campus library. All Crusher's handiwork.

As Crusher eased his way around the lab bench and took up residence next to Carlton, Audrey leaned over and whispered, "Why don't you just leave him alone?"

"Shut up, cunt!" was the hissed reply, "or we'll catch you alone one day ... and I guarantee you won't like it." Crusher sniggered and reconsider his last statement before adding, "Well, maybe you will." He then turned his attention back to Carlton.

"Relax, little fellow," he chuckled, clapping Carlton on the shoulder with a massive paw, "I'm only here to help you out. I know how much you hate this class. So here ... let me ease your burden." He reached in front of Carlton, picked up the scalpel and shredded the cat. "There, now all the cutting's done for you. I'm sure you'll get an A for this one when Professor Martin sees what a fine job you did." Then, turning to Audrey, "You remember what I just said. If you open your mouth about this, you're next. Promise!"

Again, the scene started to shift, but this time the memory was interrupted by the hissing voice that now resided within Carlton's head.

"You can ssstop torturing your-ssself now, Carlton.   You don't have to remember each ssseparate incident. We know who we want to get ... who we need to get. You won't forget. But you mussst get some sssleep, now. Morning is not far off, and you will need your ressst to serve me ... serve usss in a manner that will please and satisss-fy."

Carlton pulled himself up off the floor, still clutching the broken sword handle to his chest. He didn't bother to brush his trousers off, or to collect his suit jacket. Only the treasure he clung on to was worth his time and attention.

"Yesss, Carlton," hissed the voice again, from somewhere deep in the bowels of his brain, "you will serve usss; you belong to usss, and you will do our bidding, for it is also your bidding. Now sssleep my little puppet, we will have much to accomplish tomorrow."

CHAPTER 30

The grandfather's clock in the corner chimed once, signaling the half-hour: 10:30. Father Jacobs rocked forward in his chair, placing his elbow on the desk in front of him and folding his hands together, his chin resting on the two index fingers. The expression on his face was somber and his eyes reflected the struggle that took place in his mind. All things reasonable and sane clashed with those of absurdity, tumbling around inside his head like children rolling around a basement floor. The banker's lamp on the desk spread a milky light across the blotter and wooden surface.

"I'm not sure exactly where to begin, Father," said Geoffrey leaning forward, drink in hand. "What just happened ... what you just witnessed is, I fear, just the tip of the iceberg."

The priest pulled his mind back into focus and shifted his gaze to Geoffrey. With a great deal of effort, he pushed the mental ramblings his mind was having into a temporary cerebral storage compartment, safe and sound and ready to be reexamined at a later time.

"Perhaps at the beginning would be the best place to start. Only, for the life of me, I can't imagine what kind of beginning that might be."

"I guess, then, I should start with me. We've been friends, albeit distant, for many years now, Father. And being an astute man I'm sure you realize just how little you actually know about me. Well, there's a reason for that. Or ... at least there was. I had always hoped that we would never cross paths professionally."

Geoffrey drained the last of his drink and set the glass up on the desk, pushing it forward with the tips of his fingers.

"Mind?"

Jacobs opened the drawer and refilled the glass, then set the bottle down in the center of the desk within easy reach of both of them.

Geoffrey took a big swallow. The *tic-tock* of the grandfather's clock, as its pendulum swayed to and fro marking the passing of minutes that mankind could never regain, was the only sound in the room. The two men looked at each other across the desk, neither of them really wanting to open the subject; both of them knowing they must.

"I guess," began Geoffrey, at last, "after what just happened, what I'm going to tell you won't seem quite as fantastic as I imagined it would. Still, it's probably not going to go down too easily." He took another big swallow of the amber liquid, swirled what remained around the bottom of the glass a few times, drained that and set it down. "I'm a member of ... shall we say ... a very secret society, for lack of a better term ... an organization, if you will. This ... *society* ... has been in existence for thousands and thousands of years. The members are few, and are-" he thought for a moment, considering his choice of word carefully "-*born* into it." He smiled, but it wasn't a joyous smile, it was the smile of someone who knew that they were about to say something so fantastic that their audience was going to think them mad.

"Relax Geoffrey," soothed the priest, "I'm not going to have you committed, no matter what you tell me. Not after the little drama that just played out on my front door. Take your time, by all means. Mind, I suspect that I'll have plenty of questions. Questions you, in all likelihood, won't, or can't, answer ... but I'm willing to hear you out from beginning to end without judging the validity of your tale."

Geoffrey gave a quick nod of his head and flashed a brief smile. He stood up and walked over to the window, lifted a corner of the drapes and peered out into the night and the empty parking lot.

A misty fog had descended, obscuring everything beyond the end of the Marquis. He strained his eyes, piercing a little further into the gloom. Nothing was moving. A sigh of relief escaped him as the curtain dropped back into place and he turned to face the priest – his friend.

"This society has but a single purpose in this world. It has nothing to do with feeding the hungry, ameliorating poverty or ignorance or any of that crap I told you so many years ago. Those activities ... that is ... we do those things as a way of getting close to what it is we really do.

"We are known, or were at one time, although probably only to ourselves now, as: Lumen contra Malum. The Eye against Evil. Our beginnings date back to times I cannot speak of, nor would you believe even if I did. We are the watchers and the waiters. We move through the ages, ever vigilant. As individuals, we are mortal, most of us. Yet our years extend beyond what you would consider a normal lifespan."

Geoffrey paused, studying Father Jacobs's face, searching for and expecting, any trace of incredulity. He found none. Rather, Jacobs was listening to every word, his expression was one of mixed acceptance and awe. It appeared to Geoffrey as though the priest could sense his sincerity, despite the outlandishness of the story and the situation.

"I'd be willing to bet," said Geoffrey, a bit lighter in tone, "that if I'd ask you now to estimate my age, you would come in a couple centuries short." Again, he paused, searching for a reaction, and again, the priest sat quietly listening, unchanged in facial expression or posture. Geoffrey idly walked over to the window again and looked out.

"Our job - our only purpose on this earth - is to stem the rising tide of evil. Now, I know how that sounds. I realize it's a bit melodramatic, but there's really no other way to phrase it. Every so often, man becomes the author of his own destruction. Again, melodramatic. But it's true. It's happened countless times over the millennium, in countless ways, but it all comes down to the same thing. Whether you choose to believe it or not, there is an inherent evil in this world. I suspect that, as a priest, you will grant me at least that much. But there's much more to it. It's not easily explainable, though I'll do the best I can.

"Every now and again-" Geoffrey let go of the curtain, walked around the desk and sat down, hunching forward with his elbows on his knees. "-mankind surpasses itself with avarice, debauchery, you name it. When it does, when it reaches what physicists would describe as critical mass ... that evil is transformed. Evil is an energy, an intense, malicious energy, and it's fueled by the transgressions of mankind. So when it reaches this stage, this critical mass – when man exceeds himself in ... let's call it nastiness-" Geoffrey took a deep breath and momentarily dropped his head into his hands. When he raised his head, he pursed his lips. Jacobs could read the frustration that Geoffrey was trying to control.

"Go ahead, Geoffrey," comforted the priest, "I believe in you ... and in what you're telling me, fantastic though it may be. You just get it out, and we'll debate its legitimacy at another time."

"Very well, then," Geoffrey went on. "When the level of cruelty, avarice ... all that, reaches a certain level, the evil energy is transmuted ... transmuted. In short, it gains the capacity of taking physical form. It's happened several times over the ages. I can cite its appearance in things like the Mongol hordes, the Roman Empire and its eventual sack, the Spanish Inquisition, Salem Witch Trials, and so on. We needn't get bogged down in the specifics of the past. What I need to impress upon you, what I need you to understand and accept is that, at certain times and under certain conditions, evil literally walks the earth. And I believe that we've just encountered its most recent form in the bar tonight."

The two men sat silently for the longest time, Geoffrey watching Jacobs's face, and Jacobs absorbing what he had just heard. Father Jacobs absently reached up and tugged at the white starched collar as though it had suddenly tightened. He closed his eyes, pinching them shut with his thumb and index finger, trying to visualize the whole thing on the screen behind his eyes. Geoffrey remained silent, allowing his friend time to wrestle with the impossibilities, improbabilities, and absurdities of the story he'd just been told.

Jacobs considered the fact that, sometimes, the most outlandish stories, those with the greatest potential of being impossible, were the ones that turned out to be true. Irrational and unbelievable as it seemed on the surface, Jacobs was inclined to accept Geoffrey's as one of those.

"Well," said Jacobs, unclenching his eyes, "assuming what you've told me is indeed the case, and I'm inclined to think so at this point, how do we proceed? Obviously, I'm curious to know more about you personally. Most particularly related to your connection with your society. But for now, I'll content myself with the history of this fellow we've just encountered and how you knew he was here. And why he's here, and how much power he has, and-? So many questions, not the least of which is, what can we do about this, and from the look on your face, there aren't going to be as many answers forthcoming as I would like, are there?"

"As to his history-" Geoffrey got up and began pacing, occasionally taking a quick peek out the window. "-he really doesn't have a history. Each ... incarnation, if you will, is a separate event. How much power he has remains to be seen, but it's definitely on a scale that I ... we ... haven't seen before. There's something that's drawn him here to this location, to Banderman Falls. What that is, I don't know. I *do* know, or should say, I feel, that whatever it is, it has the potential to be catastrophic. Maybe even more so than any of the previous events which have taken place over the course of the centuries. I don't know.

"I'm probably not making much sense. I feel like I'm rambling, and you'll have to forgive me. It's extremely difficult to articulate this situation to its fullest."

Geoffrey stopped pacing and sat down heavily in the chair. He ran his hands though his hair and shook his head. He suddenly looked older, more worn to Jacobs than he had at any other time he'd seen him. He looked as if he'd just completed a marathon and was considering taking on a decathlon. His face was strained, and the fingers he was running though his hair looked as if they could have belonged to an arthritic. But as Geoffrey pulled himself back together, his appearance seemed to follow.

"Tell me this much," said Jacobs, trying to take the strain off of Geoffrey's search for the right words, "is there a hope in hell that we're going to be able to defeat this... *thing* ... as you have in the past?"

"There's always a chance, but as you have probably already surmised, it's not going to be a bloody walk in the park. There's going to be a heavy cost involved, make no mistake."

Perhaps it was the resoluteness with which Geoffrey had spoken or maybe the British accent, but it had the effect of taking the edge off the tension that Father Jacobs was feeling. He felt as though there might truly be hope for the situation, even though he knew deep down inside him that what Geoffrey had just said about paying a price was probably an understatement.

"Well," said Jacobs, "as to paying a price for a victory over this thing ... I'm willing to ante up my share." Jacobs smiled, trying to keep things on the brightest side possible. "I'm just a pauper, myself, but whatever I have ... whatever I can do to help you send this thing back to the incorporeal hell from which it sprang ... I will."

"Make no mistake Father, this is going to cost lives. How many remains to be seen."

Father Jacobs rose to his feet. He placed his left hand over his breast and made the sign of the cross in the air with the other, saying: "Bless us O Lord, your humble servants, who will shortly be engaged in a battle for righteousness. Give us Your guidance and Your strength, and lead us in Your wisdom to victory, so that Your peace may once again dwell upon the earth. Amen."

"Amen," echoed Geoffrey. "Now, Father, I believe we should try to get some sleep. I'm fairly confident that we're safe within the sanctity of your rectory. Nevertheless, I'll keep watch for a few hours and then you can relieve me. What do you say?"

Trying to be as casual and unconcerned as he could, despite the fact that his nerves were still on end over the whole thing, Jacobs said, "I say ... goodnight, my friend. Wake me when you're ready, although I must confess, I doubt I'll sleep much."

Geoffrey smiled, "Well you give it a bloody good try. We're going to need to be at the top of our forms on this one, Father. Now go." He flipped his head back toward the door, gesturing to the priest that he should leave.

Jacobs nodded and turned to go and then stopped. Without turning around he said, "Sometimes, even paupers can find the means to accomplish what's needed." He then disappeared through the door without another word.

CHAPTER 31

Curtis Lattimore sat on his couch, next to the stranger who called himself Zach (Curtis' newly self-appointed –friend?), considering his options. Wondering if he *had* any options. The whole thing felt wrong to him, but at the same time, it somehow felt so right. He thought he sensed that he was about to be given a gift that he couldn't even have dreamed of. A gift of power beyond his imaginings.

"So what is it that you want from me, Zach?" There was an edge of anger in his voice. He wanted this guy to know that he wasn't accustomed to being bullied in his own home, or anywhere else for that matter. For a moment, he thought about reaching out and giving the guy a swift sucker punch to the side of the head.

"Now that wouldn't be very nice, would it?" said Zach, answering Curtis's thoughts. "And besides, you'll find that I can be quite a handful when I get upset. But I expect you know that, don't you, somewhere inside that concrete block you call a head?" He waged a finger in Curtis's face. "No denying it and no sense feeling self-conscious about it; you're basically an inept, bumbling wannabe. Oh, you'd like to think of yourself as a real tough guy, but consider this, my impetuous friend, you're really just a second rate thief. Sure, you've killed, but I ask you, how hard was it to take the life of a trembling little girl? I mean, c'mon, there was no threat to you was there? You, standing there gun in

hand, her cowering in front of you. A real
challenge, wasn't it?

"Well, fret not. I'm about to help you
graduate. I'm going to make you – hmmm ... what
am I going to make you? I know ... I'm going to
make you a pirate." Zach laughed and the large
beard he wore muffled and bassed the tone, making
it sound almost demonic.

"A pirate? Have you lost your mind? I ain't
getting on no boats."

"Please, please, remain quiet. There's really
no need to continually prove to me how dull and
dense you are. Now just sit still with your mouth
closed and I'll explain everything."

"Just one question first?" asked Curtis,
nervously, "Are you ... are you the-"

"The devil? Heaven's no. Hey, that's a good
one." He nudged Curtis in the ribs with his elbow.
"Heavens no! *Heavens* no ... that's a good one.
Anyway, no, I'm not the devil. Devils are so
overrated. Of course, I know you're speaking about
the devil. Alas, I'm just a humble servant of a
higher power. But don't let the beard and tubby
tummy fool ya. I got more power in me than a
nuclear ... or nucular, if you're Bush ... power
station. And believe me, son, you don't want to put
me to the test on a personal basis.

"Anyway, where was I? Oh yes, I'm going
to make you a pirate. You know, strictly speaking,
pirates don't always operate on the high seas. Think
about it. These days, in these times, anyone who
steals someone else's copyrighted works is called a
pirate. Am I right or am I right? The point is I have

something that you're going to steal. Actually, quite a few somethings, all of which could, I guess, strictly speaking, be considered copyrighted."

Curtis looked at him questioningly. It was obvious he wanted to speak, but wasn't sure whether or not it would be wise.

"Asking permission to speak. I think we're making progress. Go ahead, ask your question." Zach blew out a long tedious breath followed by a fake yawn, displaying his obvious exasperation and boredom with the whole situation.

"What's in it for me? Let's say I do decide to join up with you and your ... whatever it is ... what's in it for me?"

Zach laughed again, sonorously. "You decide? You decide? Oh my boy, you are a funny one. What makes you think you have any decision to make. But I'll tell you what. I *will* let you decide. How's that. I *will* give you a choice. How benevolent of me is that? Ok? Ready? Here goes."

Zach waved his hand. In front of Curtis, a large hunting knife hovered in the air, its point two inches from Curtis' throat. The blade waggled from side to side as if it had a consciousness all its own and could hardly stay itself from cutting the fleshy meat in front of it.

The color drained instantly from Curtis' face. He sat motionless, afraid that even the slightest movement would have dire consequences. He wanted to speak; he wanted to agree that he was in, but was afraid to even try.

Instantly, the knife disappeared.

"Now how about that?" snorted Zach. "You made a decision. And you did it all on your own." He clapped Curtis on the back of the shoulder. "I'm proud of you. My little pirate-to-be is learning the ropes." He laughed again and slapped his knee. "Learning the ropes, get it. Pirate? Ropes? Ah-" he wiped non-existent tears from his eyes, "you bring out the jokester in my, my boy. You really do. But we have serious business to discuss ... well, I'll discuss, you'll listen."

"Ok, I got it. I'm working for you. So what is it we'll be doing?"

Zach clapped his hands together like an excited child whose favorite TV program was about to come on. And then he stopped as suddenly as he began and stood up. Sweeping his hands in front of him from head down, his appearance changed. His beard receded into his face, growing in reverse, his skin wrinkled into a prune-like, leathery texture and his clothes went from jeans and T-shirt to three-piece suit. A polished ebony walking stick appeared in his right hand and an eye patch covered his left eye.

"Ahh, much better. Much more dignified, don't you think?" He whirled around in slow motion, like a model on a runway. When he was again facing Curtis, he said: "Now listen, my boy, here's how it's going to be. I will call on you when I choose. When I need you, and I *will* need you, *You* ... will drop whatever it is you're doing and answer my call." He scrunched up his face as though he'd just bitten into an onion. "I don't have to demonstrate again what will happen if you don't, do I? No, I'm sure I don't.

"At any rate, I'll have certain jobs for you to perform and you'll perform them to the best of your sorry, paltry, talents. But fear not, they'll all be within the limited scope of your abilities. And! And ... you'll be rewarded. Oh yes, you'll definitely be rewarded for your services. And in a manner which will make you very, very happy, I assure you."

Zach held up his hand and wiggled his nose like a rabbit. Nothing happened. Then he started laughing again. A boisterous, hearty laugh that Curtis felt was genuine. "Hmmm-" he said, placing his index finger on the tip of his nose, "I guess that only works for witches on TV. Let ... me ... see-" He folded his arms and blinked. Nothing happened. "-no, only works for genies, I guess. Oh well, how about this-" He stuck his right arm straight out and curled the fingers inward, rolling them up to his palms the way a paper new year's eve tickler would roll up. When he unrolled them, two pictures fell out of his hand.

"Here ya go. As promised. Two lovelies ... just waiting to take all the lovin you can give 'em. Whether they want to or not. Now, I'll tell you when and where you'll be able to have your little tryst. Until then, stay away from them. I don't even want you to be seen in the same store they're in ... alone or together. Am I-" He bent over and disappeared, and in his place was a large glass ball that rolled around the room in a circle and then reformed back into the suited body it had come from. "-crystal clear on that point?" He laughed again, and this time the whole room shook. In fact, Curtis was sure that the whole house was shaking.

"So, you're going to be a pirate. You're going to be happy working for me, and you're going to pay strict attention to detail when I give you an assignment, aren't you?"

Curtis just nodded, afraid that if he spoke he might say the wrong thing.

"Good. Very good. Now, I'll take my leave of you for this evening. But first-" He turned his back to Cutis and in a deeper voice, sounding like some TV game show announcer said: "-we have a lovely parting gift for you." He reached out and swept his hand across the wall where all Curtis's band posters were hanging. A greenish cloud of smoke momentarily obscured the wall from sight, and when it cleared, there were three very tall, very full pot plants with drooping buds.

"Enjoy, my boy! Enjoy!"

He bowed at the waist, turned and walked through the wall, leaving behind the faintest aroma of burnt flesh. An echo followed that seemed to come from every direction at once: "Adieu, mon pirate, adieu!"

***

At the B & B, Witherstone stood before the mirror in the bathroom. His eyes glowed a deep red, rimmed with a greenish haze. His face was contorted, as if the skin were being pulled in different directions. The flesh itself was a patchwork of colors; the colors of decay and rot -

flat gray in spots, greenish-yellow or black in others, and it clung tightly to the malformed bony structures of the skeleton beneath. In places, a black viscous slime oozed from pustules that had broken open and dripped, *plunk, plunk, plunk*, into the sink beneath. As one pustule drained and disappeared, another formed; they popped up and shrank away rapidly; great bulbous lumps rising and falling, as if his face were boiling.

"Oh really, Dorian," Witherstone said, leaning in close to the mirror, "you have nothing on me, old boy." His lips curled back revealing yellow, rotting teeth that were sharper than shark's teeth, and longer than a wolf's. The lips themselves were no more than a ribbon of putrefied skin that stretched across his mouth like a worn rubber band. "With all the evil, malicious people inhabiting this planet ... you ain't got a prayer of catching me, Mr. Gray." Witherstone sneered, then broke out in peels of rolling, stentorian laughter. "Yes, indeed, Mr. Gray; just look how hideous I can become. With each savage, uncaring act that gets perpetrated out there ... I grow more deliciously vile."

Witherstone turned sideways, admiring his decaying profile in the mirror. The rotting flesh on his chest was liberally sprinkled with crawling, chewing maggots; a greenish-blue puss dripped from exposed bone. Something that looked like a cross between a rat and a mole scrambled up his side, climbed through an open hole, skittered over top of a rib and disappeared inside him, sending a shower of dislodged maggots to the floor. Carefully collecting each one, Witherstone placed the little yellow-white writhing creatures back on his person. They wiggled off in various directions seeking out the tenderest morsels of rot.

When he'd finished admiring his state of decay, he strode over to the little writing-table by the window and sat down. Outside, the darkness was giving way to the pale gray light of morning. The rat thing that had crawled inside him popped out and jumped onto the table. In one swift motion, Witherstone snatched it up and held it in front of him. It scratched and bit, desperately trying to free itself from the bony fingers that clutched it tightly around its middle.

"Sorry my pet. I'll miss you, but ... alas ... all things have their service." A second later, Witherstone was chewing heartily on the things head, the *crunch, crunch, crunch* of the skull, and the smacking of lips (such as they were) as he chewed were the only sounds in the room. He sat there eating and looking out the window, watching the rising sun begin to spread its reds and pinks across the horizon.

"A great night's work, Witherstone," he said to himself. "Even if I must say so myself. But-" His mind shifted, and his face contorted into a pensive scowl. "-But, we've still to locate the object of our desire. It's close. Oh yes, it's very close.

"Yes, I *know* I know where it is," he said, acknowledging a voice within him. "I'm not stupid. What I meant was, gaining control of it is a very delicate matter. As the wicked witch observed in OZ: *'These things must be done del-i-cat-ly'.*"

Witherstone roared in laughter again, and then fell silent, considering what should be done next.

After a few moments, he got up and began to pace the room, dropping maggots on the carpet as he walked. He was tapping a finger to the bony outcropping that served as his forehead, every now and then popping a pustule that had arisen there and spraying the black ooze across the room.

"So many things to be done; so many plots to be hatched, so many lives to be disassembled, but where and with whom should I begin? This is going to require a bit of poetry and finesse, Mr. Witherstone. Can't go blundering through it like that idiot, Lattimore. Each line of destruction that you create must be carefully ... oh so carefully ... orchestrated. You must take great care to create a masterpiece of destruction. And once you have your hands on the object? ... Oh my, I can hardly allow myself to think about that yet. I'll get carried away for sure, and there's just so much to be done *first*.

"But how should you begin your epic poem of the demise of Banderman Falls and the subsequent-" He stopped. *Can't go that far yet*, he thought. *All things in their time and place.*

"Banderman Falls," he snorted. "What a little, insignificant, piss-ant place. It's almost not even worthy of my talents. I would greatly have preferred a larger city, where my achievements would be recognized. Ah well, it will be a challenge, won't it? I mean, a small town does not have the usual distractions of a big city, does it?

And therefore ... many more people to subvert in order to achieve your goal.

"I say, Witherstone, you may yet achieve the true glory you deserve."   He stopped smiling. "Enough levity.   It will soon be time to put all pawns into play; soon time to write the lines of my poetical destruction of this town, attain my prize and achieve permanent, corporeal existence."

Witherstone drew the drapes, lay on the bed and closed his eyes.   He fixed his mind – his energies – on reawakening.   It took a great deal of concentration for him to set an energy alarm clock, a mental imperative that would reform his body after his rest.   When he was certain he had achieved that goal, he let himself rest.   And as he began to slumber, his body crumbled to dust on the bed, the maggots crawling aimlessly across the sheets.

CHAPTER 32

Jasper Collins sat huddled up against the headboard of his bed.   Everything that had happened, everything that he'd been told tonight was just too much for him.   His mind couldn't grasp the fundamentals, couldn't accept that what had taken place was real; no more than he could understand or accept the incident in the cemetery earlier.   But the fact remained, like it or not, that it had taken place - it had happened.   He had been confronted, and spoken to by – the devil? – was that even possible?   His mind ran in circles and the confusion of all of it wore him down.   He sat in the bed with the torn dirty top sheet pulled up around his neck and he could still hear the thing's voice in his head.

"Jasper," the thing had said, "you'll be working for me now. Oh yes, full time ... with benefits. There'll be certain things I need from you that you'll provide. There'll be certain tasks I'll demand you perform. And you'll perform them. When I say jump, you'll already be climbing the ladder to ask how high."

Jasper could still hear the nasty, demonic laugh that roared out of the thing. The thing? Yes, that was what it was. It surely wasn't a man. And no matter what it had said, or how it had said it, Jasper understood that it wasn't the devil either, as he had at first assumed. No! It was something created by the devil possibly. Something the devil used like a hammer or a blow torch. A tool. *Yes*, thought Jasper, *that's what it was all right - a tool.* And it dawned on him, creeping into his mind as quietly as a mouse creeps across the counter at night to steal a cookie crumb, that he was a tool now, too. And there was no escaping *that* fact. It didn't matter anymore what Jasper wanted. All that mattered was what the thing wanted. And even though it hadn't been specific, Jasper was more than certain that any disobedience or resistance from him would result in something more horrible than he could probably imagine.

The small shadeless lamp with the 25W bulb cast a feeble light across the room. Jasper looked at the dresser that stood against the wall. It was now stacked with his presents – his bribe – his reward for cooperating in a situation in which he had no choice *but* to cooperate. He stared at the bottles of Old Crow, all lined up like revolutionary war soldiers across the top of the bureau and along the floor in front of it. No matter how much he would have liked to go grab one (and he *did* want to), he was too afraid. Too afraid that a single sip would seal his fate – even though he was fairly certain it had already been sealed.

Finally unable to resist anymore, he slipped out from beneath the sheet, tip-toed across the room as silently as he could and grabbed up a bottle. By the time he'd crawled back beneath the perceived safety of his sheets, he'd downed at least a quarter of it. The slow burn, as it slid down his throat, and the delayed burn in his stomach afterwards, felt like a visit from an old friend. Tipping the bottle up and tilting his head as far back as he could get it, he chugged down another large gulp. Some of it escaped at the corners of his mouth and dripped off his chin onto the stained sheets in which he was cocooned. He didn't care. He thought about his lot in life and decided that he didn't care about that either.

Despite his dedication to attendance in whatever job he held, Jasper never moved off the bottom rungs. He had no ambitions, and it occurred to him, now, sitting in his room, that he'd always been one of the disposable people. What he realized, drowning himself in Old Crow and fearing the return of his new boss, was that he was no more than a pawn – useful, but expendable. And now, in the shadow of his new employment, the idea of being expendable hit home with concrete reality.

Draining the last of the bottle, he tossed it on the floor, pulled the sheets up over his head and tried to go to sleep. But there would be no sleep for Jasper, the pawn, tonight.

CHAPTER 33

Jack came full awake; the dream had been more vivid and more terrifying than any he could ever recall. He rubbed heavily at his eyes as he swung his legs over the end of the couch. Thin slivers of rusty light edged across the floor through the partially open blinds. Morning. It seemed to have come more quickly than he'd hoped; but, then again, considering the dream he'd just awoken from, maybe just in time.

He sat on the couch pulling his hands through his hair and rubbing his face. He was awake, but the grogginess hung on like morning fog on a spring day. And the dream – the dream stayed tight in his mind, a piece of mental gum obstinately clinging to the sole of his memory.

Jack's mind swirled around the image he just awoke from. He'd been in the kitchen and Pat had been standing there chiding him for not saving her, her gaping head wound dripping clotted splotches of blood onto the floors. Every time she'd turn her head, splashes of the viscous fluid would splatter against the walls, leaving thick globular droplets that slid down like raspberry jelly.

He kept apologizing for not being there, but she refused to listen. Her tongue shot in and out of her mouth like a snake's as she spoke, and she kept a decaying, accusing finger pointed at him the whole time. At one point, her whole body transformed, it melted down to the floor and then reformed into the figure of an old man, who stood laughing and pointing at him. Then it changed again, melting and reforming. As it reassembled from the floor, it became a large wolf, its fangs bared in an evil, angry snarl. Before Jack could react, it was on him, ripping and tearing at his stomach. He laid on the kitchen floor, watching helplessly as the animal disemboweled him and dragged his intestines over to the corner by the refrigerator to eat them.

He tried in vain to scream, but nothing came out; he was frozen in place, unable to move in the slightest. He watched the thing devour his organs one by one, coming and going for each new morsel. When it had worked its way up to his chest, he was finally able to get out a scream, which he figured, sitting there on the couch now, is what had awakened him.

Recovering himself enough, and feeling a little more awake, he pushed himself to his feet and shuffled cautiously to the kitchen, wondering if he'd find Pat still there sifting through the beer bottles in the refrigerator. But the kitchen was empty. He stood there looking around, trying to bring everything back into some kind of focus and reality that he could deal with, but no answers or explanations sprang to mind.

After a moment of staring blankly around the room and coming to no real conclusions, Jack decided he should probably get something to eat, even though he wasn't at all hungry. He settled on a couple of pieces of toast and some coffee. Stepping around the kitchen table to get to the breadbox on the counter, he pulled up short. On the tile floor in front of the refrigerator were four large muddy paw prints. Hesitantly, Jack walked over and knelt down in front of them. What he had at first thought to be mud was actually dried blood. He pulled his hand away and stood up so quickly that he lost his balance and staggered backward into the wall.

"Geezuz, Jack. Get a grip," he said, following up with: "What the hell is going on here?" Taking a deep breath, he walked back over and bent down on one knee to reexamine the prints. As he reached out, they suddenly receded into the floor, leaving behind only the shiny, mosaic tile they had been sitting on.

Jack stood up, beginning to doubt his sanity, wondering if he should actually call Doc Robertson and schedule a brain scan. The feeling that things were out of control and slipping away from him settled over him like a heavy wool blanket. He slowly scanned the entire kitchen looking for anything else that might, but shouldn't, be there. There was nothing; only his kitchen, looking every bit the way it should. Whatever had, or had not, been here; whatever was, or was not only in his mind, had left no traces.

Somewhere off in the distance, a low buzzing sifted through the house. The sudden sound of it made Jack jump. At first, the sound was foreign, and he tried to figure out where it might be coming from. But then he realized that it was just his alarm clock in the bedroom, set to go off automatically every morning at 6:30. He could go turn it off, or just wait for it to stop on its own. He finally settled on letting it go while he brewed himself some coffee.

When the pot finally stopped gurgling and spitting, Jack poured a large mug of the black liquid for himself and sat down at the kitchen table. A sudden chill ran up the back of his neck and he had the distinct feeling of being watched. He also knew that there was no point in looking around because there was no one there.

Setting his coffee cup down, he got up and headed into the living room to get his Ruger. When he got there, it was neatly holstered, and there were no shells on the table or floor. He drew the pistol, popped the cylinder and gave it a quick spin. All the holes were filled – six shiny brass shells sat neatly in their respective chambers. He thought about dumping them into his hand to see if one was empty – the one he'd fired last night, but he knew it wouldn't be. He knew that all six shells were live.

Snapping the cylinder back into place, he slid the gun back into its leather holster, and buckled the belt around his waist. He considered a quick shower but opted instead to just wash up at the station and throw on some deodorant. He went back into the kitchen to shut off the coffee pot.

When he reached for the off switch, he caught sight of something on the kitchen table out of the corner of his eye. Turning slowly and lowering his gaze he saw a small piece of paper with writing on it.

Jack noticed two distinct sets of handwriting. The top part of the note read: *Please be careful, Jack. Things are worse than you can imagine. I am trying to forgive you and understand. I always liked you, Jack.* This part was written in a very flowing, gentle style. Beneath it, in broad, dark, shaky printing was: YOU MAY THINK YOU'RE KING OF THE REALM AS SHERIFF OF BANDERMAN FALLS – BUT THE REALM IS CHANGING AND YOUR SUBJECTS WILL SOON BE YOUR ENEMIES. LEAVE NOW AND SPARE YOURSELF THE IGNOMINY OF DEFEAT. GET OUT! – WHILE YOU CAN!

Jack could feel the anger welling up inside him. He never liked ultimatums and tolerated threats even less. He crumpled the note, squeezing his fist around it as tightly as he could. But before he threw it away, something stopped him. He unraveled it and smoothed it out on the table as best he could. *Better hold on to this, Jack; it may come in handy if you have to prove your sanity somewhere down the line.* He folded it as neatly as he could and stuck it in his shirt pocket.

Then and there, Jack decided that it was time he found out exactly what was going on in his town. Whatever was wrong had to be stopped – had to be put right. As he stepped outside, latching his door behind him, he could sense that the whole community had changed. He could feel that things were very different, and that beginning today, he would be looked at very differently by the townspeople. He knew, standing there looking out into the rising morning sun, that those who had been good friends would soon try to stop him from doing his job. What he didn't know was why, but he intended to find out.

Stepping around to the door of his cruiser he noticed that someone had written two lines on his windshield in soap. The first was comprised of just two words: GET OUT. The second of four: DEATH TO THE KING. He didn't bother wasting time washing it off. He slid in, turned over the engine, backed out of the driveway and headed toward the station. The tires squealed on the macadam as he bullied the car into a tight turn at the end of the block and sped down Main Street. Time was short, and he wasn't about to waste any of it.

It was Friday morning, July 3rd, and traffic should have been getting fairly heavy or at least as heavy as on any main street of a small town just before a holiday, but there wasn't a single car on the road, or a single pedestrian on the sidewalk. The change wasn't lost on Jack, and the realization that his gut feelings about the town were right gave him a very unsettled feeling.

"King!" he grumbled aloud, "I've *never* thought of myself as a king. Where the hell do people get off calling me *that*?" With each passing block, Jack's mood darkened; he could feel himself starting to boil inside, losing control. Anger was beginning to ripple through him, his fingers and knuckles blanched on the steering wheel.

Some part of him understood that what he was feeling was all wrong. But that understanding couldn't seem to break through to Jack's consciousness. It kept nagging at him as he sped along Main Street, blowing through stop signs with no warning.

"King!" he shouted out the window of the cruiser to no one. "I'll give you king, you bastards!"

CHAPTER 34

Morning dawned over Banderman Falls in a burst of reds and pinks. Shafts of white light poked through the leaves and tree branches, illuminating dancing particles of dust that swirled and floated in the pencil-thin rays. Crystalline drops of dew clung tenaciously to the tips of the leaves and grass as the morning's mist was slowly banished by the rising sun. Birds sat silently in the trees; on wires; in bushes – observing but not commenting - their usual chirping voices mute.

Two thousand, three hundred and thirty eight miles west, in Benderick Falls, Arizona, the sun was still two hours away from opening its great eye. It would rise as usual, bringing with it the stifling heat that was the trademark of the state. There, birds would sing, crickets would chirp, animals would begin their daily foraging routines, and the citizens would wake to a normal working day. There, the pall that had swallowed Banderman Falls would be unknown, unfelt and uncared about by everyone, except Arliss Peterson. For Arliss, the heaviness that had descended on Banderman Falls had also reached out its insidious hand and closed its malevolent, decaying fingers around her.

Her sleep was restless and fitful. Great black and green tongues lashed out at her from every side. She was imprisoned in a glass cage upon a stage that looked out over a vast sea of old and decrepit men, all staring back at her, all watching as she hung there, naked, being licked and fondled by a foul and slimy beast that couldn't possibly exist in real life.

Gagged, she hung there, her feet dangling above the floor, a cross bar at her ankles to keep her legs spread. The chants and hoots from the audience filtered through the glass in eerie, deadened tones. The whole time, she wiggled and struggled against the bonds that held her tight as the thing assaulted her body with its tongues and scaly fingers.

"Noooo," she screamed, awakening herself just as the unseen creature had grabbed her by the waist preparing to enter her. The sweat stood out in beads on her forehead and the hollow beneath her throat was puddled with it. Her breathing was short and labored, a gasping remnant of the nightmare's intensity.

Arliss glanced over at the luminous blue numerals which told her it was only 4:42 A. M. Going back to sleep was out of the question. And despite the vivid feeling of having been violated; the thoughts of another shower after the incident of last night were too repugnant to consider. Tossing the sheets back carelessly, she swung her legs out of bed, pulled her terrycloth robe from atop the dresser, used the downstairs powder room for nature's morning call, and ambled into the kitchen, turning on all the lights that she passed along the way.

The automatic Braun coffeemaker sat on the green marble countertop, waiting for its 5:15 A. M. call to duty; a ceramic *Star Trek* mug, depicting the *Enterprise* in flight, sat beside it. As she passed it, she hit the button that would bring the gurgling purveyor of her black, magic elixir of caffeine-laden life on line.

Arliss sat on the stool at the breakfast bar waiting for her coffee and trying to make some sense of what had happened in the bathroom. The dreams she chalked up to the incident itself, no more than a slumber's echo of the whole thing. No rational spin that she tried to put on it stuck. She knew she wasn't given to hallucinations (at least, she'd never had any before this) and things just don't randomly appear in your mirror and then lick you like a lost puppy dog who's found his way home. There was no way that she could turn it in her mind that made it fit into one of the neat scientific explanations that she was adept at coming up with.

The coughing and sputtering of the coffeemaker as it vainly tried to pass the last of its water over the grounds brought her back from her thoughts. Still semi-trapped within her search for an explanation, she poured her first morning cup. She sipped at it as she paced around the kitchen, absently wandering in circles around the breakfast island.

By the time she was finishing her third cup, the morning light was beginning to finger its way in through the blinds and lace curtains that decorated the double windows above her sink. She sat down on the stool again, frustrated and confused. Confused, because for some odd reason, she had the urge to fly east – to personally go find and retrieve her missing shipment. And yet, the very thought of it also sent a chill up her spine. The thought of going also lit up her memory and she could see the baby powder illuminated like an electronic highway warning sign with its message scrolling across the black panels of her mind: KEEP AWAY FROM THE FALLS.

Being able to sit idly was never one of her character traits and neither was bowing to threats. All her life Arliss had operated with the attitude that if you tell me not to or that I can't, I'm going to prove you wrong. Jumping up off the stool, knocking her mug over so that the Enterprise went tumbling through ceramic space across the countertop, Arliss grabbed up the phone and punched in the numbers for information. Ten minutes later she was booked on the next flight out to Philadelphia International.

Upstairs, Arliss hurriedly threw on some light travel clothes and a pair of Adidas. As she packed, toothbrush in, three pairs of jeans, hairbrush, underwear – all the necessities, it never occurred to her that she hadn't made any hotel reservations or that she really had no idea what she was going to do once she got there. All she knew was that she *had* to go.

Snapping the last latch on the suitcase, she suddenly stopped. An impulse struck her. She had the sudden urge to take something with her – something from the museum. She glanced over at the bedside clock; there'd be just enough time to get to the museum and still make her flight, but it would be close. Not pausing to figure out why she wanted the item – why she felt she *needed* the item – she picked up the suitcase and lugged it down the steps, dropping it by the front door. Stuffing her laptop into its travel bag and pulling the shoulder strap over her head, she opened the door, picked up her suitcase and headed into work.

***

The museum itself was not open yet, although it would be by 10:00. The curatorial staff had a long weekend and would not be in. Arliss pulled her Volvo into her reserved space in the enclosed garage, jumped out and ran to the elevators that would take her down to the bowels of the building, down to the work and storage rooms. When the doors slid open, she stepped in, swiped her card in the reader that would allow access to the lower floors and stood back, anxiously bidding the elevator to hurry up.

At the basement level, as soon as the doors began to slide open, she squeezed through and hurried down the long aisle that led to the back of the workroom. She had to swipe her card twice to get it to read. The mechanism clicked and the handle turned. Inside, Arliss didn't even bother turning on the lights; she knew exactly what she wanted and where it was.

Pulling the rolling ladder into place, she stamped down on the peddle break, climbed to the top and pulled a small wooden box off the uppermost shelf. She backed her way down, balancing the box on one hand, and raced back to the elevators.

Do you have any *idea what you're doing, Arliss*? she thought to herself. *You're going to fly to Philadelphia. Then what?* "I don't know. We'll see when we get there, won't we?" she answered herself, aloud, as she opened the trunk of the Volvo and gently placed the box underneath an old blanket she kept there. "We'll see when we get there, girl."

The tires squealed as the car wound its way down the concrete spiral exit ramp, the sound magnified in the hollow garage. It would take her the better part of an hour to make it to Sky Harbor International, the closest airport to Benderick Falls. That would only give her forty-five minutes for check-in. But since she only had one bag and one carry-on, she figured she'd be ok. Then she realized she had the box too. That could be a real problem. Without the proper paperwork, the antique, clearly marked as property of the museum, would never be able to board. She would have to come up with something to solve that problem, and quickly. She had less than an hour.

An idea struck her. She slammed on the breaks and swerved the car up against the curb. Flipping open her cell phone, she dialed information, then had them directly connect her to the number they'd given her -the Marriott in Banderman Falls. After booking her room, she pulled out and headed back to her office. Things were going to be close as far as making it to the airport for her flight, so she decided to switch flights. By the time she pulled back into her parking space, she had confirmed her seat on a later flight. She had some breathing room now, so she took her time getting inside.

Placing the box from the trunk inside another box, she filled out the FedEx label and attached it. Once that was done, all she had to do was to drive to the local office and send it on its way, overnight. It would arrive at her hotel tomorrow. On her way out, she decided that she now had time to grab something to eat, so once she sent her package on its way, she'd stop at the 5 & Diner on N. 16th Street in Phoenix, and scarf down some breakfast. She was beginning to think things just might work out after all, although she still wasn't quite sure *what* things.

Waiting for her eggs (over easy with hash browns and bacon), it occurred to her that she was not the kind of person who went off willy-nilly on some unknown, unfounded lark of an adventure. But here she was, doing just that. "Well," she said to herself, sipping on her coffee, "it's a good thing you're not a make-up, hair primping kinda gal, Arliss." *You barely took enough time to put clothes on*, she finished in her mind.

When the waiter set her plate in front of her and she smelled the still sizzling bacon, she realized just how hungry she'd been. Buttering her toast and splitting open one of the yolks, she thought about the package that was on its way to Pennsylvania. It was a strange item to want to bring and she still didn't know why she felt she needed it; she only felt that leaving it behind would be disastrous.

Arliss finished wiping up the last bit of yellow that remained on her plate with a tiny corner of toast and stuffed it in her mouth. There were not many things she enjoyed more than good eggs and greasy fried potatoes. She sat back, happy and satiated. She dug into her purse, looking for the little mirror she always kept to check things out. Searching blindly, her fingers closed around an odd-shaped object and she pulled it out. It was a clock; the hands were spinning backwards wildly. She didn't remember ever having a clock that looked like a miniature version of London's Big Ben.

As she stared at it, images began to flash across her mind, images of distant lands and long-ago times. Anyone looking at her from across the room would have thought she was having a petit mal seizure. In her head, voices bombarded her, coming in multiple languages. Greek to Latin, then to Russian, then back to Latin – a cacophony of discursive noise, none of which she consciously understood. But some part of her *did* understand. Some part of her seemed to be trying to awaken from a long slumber, or so it felt. There was a groggy sense of surrealistic recognition.

The hands on the clock stopped spinning, coming to rest on twelve o'clock. Arliss blinked twice, coming back to herself and placed the clock gently back into her purse. The action was almost mechanical, and when it was safely tucked away, she continued her search for the mirror, not even remembering that she'd found the timepiece. It was as if someone else, a different Arliss, had been looking at it, and that same someone had put it away.

Three and a half hours later, Arliss was rising above the Phoenix skyline on her way to Philadelphia and then on to Banderman Falls. The baby powder warning still flashed across the back of her mind, but it was too late for that now. In four hours and twenty minutes she'd be in Philadelphia. And for good or bad, she'd find out what awaited her there. And hopefully, what this was all about.

CHAPTER 35

All across Banderman Falls, people began to awaken from their restless slumbers, most of them feeling more exhausted than when they'd gone to bed, all of them vividly recalling the dreams they'd had. There weren't many that didn't welcome the morning sun, a burning symbol that the long night was over.

Rachel Parker climbed slowly out of bed. She ran a hand through her long dark hair that was tangled and matted with something thick and sticky. When she pulled her hand away, she knew instantly what it was. Horror surged through her, her heart starting to pound as she realized that her dreams had been much more than just dreams. They had somehow been real.

The mirror in the bathroom confirmed her realization. Her face was plastered with the shiny remnants of a man's (or men's) pleasures, and the same was true of her thighs. Sitting on the toilet, she could feel and hear the *plop, plop, plop* of the oozing cum as it dripped out of her. She sat there, her face buried in her hands crying, unable to get up – not wanting to get up. She just wanted to fade away into herself and pray the whole thing was still a dream.

Throughout Banderman Falls, the morning brought the same results for most of the town's women. For the men, it was completely different. They awoke to soreness, stiffness, welts, and bruises, depending on the particular torments their dreams had taken them through. But no one was willing to truly acknowledge it. Husbands and wives sat at breakfast discussing anything but the night before. No one mentioned the dreams, and if it looked like they might, the other person would get up and leave or instantly change the subject. They had been private dreams and they would remain buried.

Although initially horrified and disgusted, secretly, most of the women found themselves thinking about the night and the pleasures they'd felt. Most of them secretly desiring an encore. It was a double-edged sword - frightening and exhilarating at the same time – and most of them, at least subconsciously, wanted more, even against their better judgment. Not knowing exactly why or even recognizing the fact that they were, the women were looking at their husbands that morning wondering why the dream men could satisfy them more. A kernel of disappointment settled into them, a kernel that would eventually grow - rapidly.

Colleen Slater awoke to find that she no longer needed a boob job. Somehow, overnight, she'd gotten exactly what she'd wanted. All kinds of warnings and alarms should have sounded within her, but all she felt was gratification. Standing in front of her mirror, naked from the waist up, she lost herself in her new-found physique. Her breasts were not only larger, but firmer as well, with prominent nipples. Just the kind of thing that would put Rachel Parker in her place. There would be no bra for Colleen today and the tightest shirt she could find.

"Ok boys," she said, bouncing her breasts up and down, "you're in for some real eye candy today. By the time I'm done with you all, you'll be thinking that Rachel Parker looks like an adolescent in a training bra." She paused to admire her fullness, then added, "If the slut even *wears* one,"

Colleen sorted through her closet, looking for the shortest skirt she could find. The only two that seemed to fit the bill were a black one and a red one. Trying on both, she decided that neither of them was short enough. She could hem them, but that was too much trouble. In the end, she opted to wear the black one long enough to go buy a new one. The stockings were next. Buried underneath all her others was a pair of fishnets that she used to wear for her husband, but that had died out long ago. She examined them for wear and suitability. They seemed fine, so on they went. She chose a pair of white lace boy-cut panties, and then the hunt for the right heels began.

Like the other women of Banderman Falls on that July 3rd morning, Linda Killerman awoke exhausted with the feeling she'd been sexually used. Like Rachel Parker and Colleen Slaterman, Linda found that her dreams had been more real than she could have imagined. Like Rachel and Colleen, the remains of her night visitor's passions were all over her body. It was matted into her hair, it dripped out from between her legs and was crusted on her face and breasts.

She jumped in the shower and scrubbed herself as hard as she could, desperate to wash away any trace of the night's activities. Unlike most of the women in Banderman Falls, Linda was not having residual desires for further encounters. Instead, the feeling of violation and degradation that she felt brought her to a total breakdown. She stood in the shower, aggressively rubbing her body with the washcloth and sobbing uncontrollably. At some point she realized that the water that was collecting around her feet had a reddish tinge to it – she had scrubbed herself raw in places. Dropping the washcloth, she sat curled up in the tub crying, her knees pulled up to her chest and the water from the shower cascading down over her. It would be some time before she was able to pull herself together and get on with her day, all the time wondering just how a dream could have been so real and not understanding what really happened to her.

Most of the men in the Falls were able to dismiss the dreams of the previous night as just that. Any stiffness or soreness they felt from whatever tortured nightmare they'd had they chalked up to natural nocturnal tossing and turning – or "sleeping the wrong way." Most of them. For a few, the dreams were as real as those of the ladies.

Grady Peterson awoke to find that he could hardly hear and that his head was pounding. He had never had a migraine before, but he was sure that what he was feeling in his head at that moment would put any major migraine to shame.

Sam Twilling's nightmare revolved around his deceased customers. In his dreams, they had come back, two and three at a time to help him experience the pain of death. He had been repeatedly strapped to his own table and embalmed alive by the corpses of those he had administered to. In the morning, his whole body burned on the inside. He could hardly move, and the more he did, the more it burned. He was convinced that he was circulating the remnants of the embalming mixture, although he had no idea how he could still be alive if that were true.

Jack Dougherty had had his encounter with the deceased Patricia O'Donnell, and Antonio Ballario, the general contractor who'd been worked over pretty well by Father Jacobs, had spent the night being sawn apart, reassembled with a nail gun and then sawed apart again. When he awoke in the morning, large dimples indented the places in his skin where the nails had been shot in and all the joints had stitch marks.

The story was the same throughout the Falls. Everyone awoke to find some kind of physical reminder of the night before. Disbelief, horror, shock, pain, pleasure, longing and desire, loathing and disgust circulated throughout the population like a flyer for a Grand Opening. And in a sense, it *was* a Grand Opening – but not the kind anyone would want to attend. It was the Grand Opening of the darkest times the Falls would ever experience.

CHAPTER 36

When Carlton awoke, the sword handle was still clutched tightly to his breast with both hands. His eyes fluttered open and he instinctively squeezed his fingers around the handle. He sat up in bed, his legs splayed, bent at the knees, like someone trying to get into a yoga position but not quite being able to manage it. He wanted to rub the sleep from the corners of his eyes but couldn't bring himself to let go of his treasure.

Holding it out in front of him, the morning sunlight glinted off its polished silver surface, creating splashes of white that danced across the far wall. He turned it around and around, looking at it, absorbing it.

He clambered out of bed and went downstairs to the kitchen, not bothering to stop and change from the clothes he'd slept in. He could not be bothered with any of the mundane routines that usually started his morning. By the time he'd reached the kitchen he'd wet himself, but even that didn't shake him out of his trance. The treasure he embraced was the answer to all his prayers, and that was all his mind could focus on.

Carlton sat at the little round Broyhill table where he sat every morning. His fingers ran up and down the length of the handle and around the pommel, their movements almost dance-like. At times, he'd hold it up so the light would shine off it, then lay it back down on the table and caress it.

Carlton noticed the time on his antique 1820s Lenzkirch wall clock to be 8:23 A. M. The old timepiece ticked rhythmically along as its pendulum swayed back and forth. Staring at it, Carlton watched as each second ticked its way into the past. At ten after nine, he was sitting in the same place and in the same position, his hands mechanically polishing the sword handle. Pictures of the ways he'd get back at all the people who had humiliated him over the years played across the back of his mind.

Suddenly, all the pictures evaporated, replaced with a dark, faceless figure who told him that he must get moving. It told him that his shop must be opened precisely on time, as that fat bitch, Evelyn Ramsey would be waiting at the door and there should be no indication that anything was any different than any other day.

Gathering himself together, Carlton went back upstairs to prepare for his morning. He ran into a small roadblock when it came to bathing and dressing. The thought of relinquishing his hold on the sword, even for a few minutes, created a feeling of panic. But once again, the dark face and voice came through loud and clear, commanding him to put it down on the bed, assuring him that it would be safe there, and to do what he must to get to the shop – business as usual.

He finished dressing and found that, although very heavy, the handle sat nicely in the inner suit pocket of his jacket, if he placed it in pommel down. To keep himself from getting cut by the jagged blade, he slipped a length of plastic tubing that he'd cut from his vacuum cleaner hose over the end. When he arrived at the shop, Evelyn Ramsey was already standing at the front door. Carlton made his apologies, claiming that he'd overslept, which wasn't really far from the truth. He held the door open for Evelyn to go in, mentally thinking that the cow was going to ruin his entire day. But he smiled and was as charming as he could possibly be, which for Carlton, was out of the ordinary in itself.

Evelyn had no clue that anything was different today. She had not suffered any of the dreams. To her, it was just a normal, everyday Friday morning. She went about her business dusting the shelves and antiques and cleaning the glass cases. Carlton restocked the cash register with the usual three hundred and fifty dollar start of the day. The whole time he kept a keen eye on Evelyn, watching everything she did as covertly as he possibly could. If she turned suddenly he'd avert his gaze and mutter something unintelligible, just loud enough for her to hear, to make her believe that he was actively engaged in something that commanded his total interest and was in no way concerned with what she was doing.

When he felt satisfied that all was in order, he told her that he was going downstairs to finish the inventory and shipping receipts. Evelyn nodded, flipped the store sign from CLOSED to OPEN and continued with her chores.

"I guess I'll have to put up with that thing clumping around overhead all day," he said to himself as he reached for the light's pull chain. "Why in the world I ever hired her is beyond me."

Carlton walked to his corner desk mumbling obscenities the whole way and reached inside his suit jacket to caress the treasure in his pocket. "You're going to set me free from all this, though, aren't you? Oh yes. I know you are. And we'll have our day."

No more voices or instructions came to Carlton all that day, but he knew, as sure as he knew to breathe without being told, that he was only waiting for dark. And when it came – everything would change. The high and the mighty would fall and he, Carlton Wedgemore, would rise to take their place. But first, somehow, he had to get through this miserably slow day.

CHAPTER 37

Geoffrey sat at the small breakfast table across from Father Jacobs sipping on his tea. Neither of the men had yet broached the subject of the previous night. Jacobs worked, unenthusiastically, at a piece of dry (nearly burnt) toast, his eyes cast downward as if studying the pattern the dropping crumbs were making on his plate.

Geoffrey kept a surreptitious eye on the good Father. He knew that when he was ready, Jacobs would have more questions to ask and he felt it better to wait for them. From where he was sitting, the priest's mind was an open book, and he could have gone down the list, one, two, three, answering all his questions before they were posed.

For his part, Jacobs wanted to forget the whole thing. He'd like nothing more than to be able to dismiss it all as the result of some kind of shared hysteria between him and his friend. But he knew better. What he didn't know was what it all really meant and what was yet to come. His instinct told him that, whatever it was, it was going to be bad. He also felt that neither the authorities, local or otherwise, nor Rome were going to be of much help. Sitting there crunching on the blackened toast, he knew that the man sitting across the table from him would be the best he was going to get in the way of assistance. And he prayed to God that it would be enough.

"I'd ask you how you slept, Father," said Geoffrey, breaking the silence at last, "but I bloody well bet I already know the answer to that. So I'll just ask you what's on your mind and if you're willing to believe everything I've told you ... as well as whatever I might tell you?"

Jacobs cleared his throat, dropping the last corner of bread onto the plate and wiping the crumbs from his fingertips. He leaned forward, shoving the plate out of the way and folding his hands in front of him. For a moment, he didn't say anything; he just sat there studying Geoffrey's face. It was relaxed and genial. Genial, Jacobs could understand, relaxed he couldn't. Not for the first time, Jacobs realized just how little he really knew about the man in front of him.

"Well, first of all," said Jacobs, "you might as well stop with the 'Father' business and start calling me Gabe. I'm pretty damned sure that before this is all over titles aren't going to mean very much."

"Ok, then. Gabe it is. But I have to confess it feels a bit weird."

"No. Weird is finding a dead, talking cat stuck on the rectory door with a message on your front steps written in its entrails. *That's* weird. But ... be that as it may, what *exactly* is going on here?" Jacobs waved a hand in the air. "And please give me specifics. I believe this particular boat is far enough out to sea at this point to dispense with a soft sell. What's *really* going on?"

"I'd love to be able to lay it all out for you, Gabe, from beginning to end. But I don't have all the answers yet. In fact, I have more questions than answers at this point. But I'll tell you what I can." Geoffrey drained what was left of his tea and set the cup back in its saucer. He looked pensively at his lap for a brief second and then locked his clear blue eyes on Jacobs.

"Maybe we should start with ... this *thing*," suggested Jacobs. "What do you know, or suspect?

How bad, really, do you think it's going to get, and what can we do about it ... him ... whatever?"

Geoffrey cleared his thought and thought for a moment.

"As I already said, explaining it all is going to be a bit difficult. But what I know about this particular incarnation is very little. I know that it is seeking something. Something very old, very powerful. And if he manages to acquire it, things will get a whole lot worse. Maybe even unmanageable."

"So what is this thing it's looking for?"

"I don't know. I was working in a small village in the Ural Mountains when I first got the ... the ... sense, that-." Geoffrey broke off, squinting his eyes in concentration as he sought the right words. "-When I first felt that this thing had come to light."

"So," interjected Jacobs, "you get this feeling, or whatever it is ... and then what?"

"I can't tell you how, because I can't really articulate it myself, but I knew that my time - our time - had come to act. We have an inner sense, kind of like what you call intuition, only much stronger and much more accurate. I knew that this thing had managed to take physical form and that it was close by. I tried to locate it, and in doing so, I discovered that something had been found that was never meant to be found."

"What?"

"I'm not sure. As I said, it is something very ancient and something mortals were never meant to lay their hands on." Geoffrey gave a nervous cough. "I don't want to get into metaphysics here, or a discussion of heaven, hell, God, the devil, religion ... or any of that. Although I can say that these things are the expressions of your understanding of the way good and evil operate in the world. But the truth of it all goes way beyond that, and way beyond my ability to explain it. So, for the sake of argument, let's accept on face value mankind's interpretation of such.

"What is happening here is, what you might call, a collision of two great powers. I wouldn't quite classify it as a battle between your concept of God and the Devil, but it would come close to that ... as the simplest way of expressing it, I guess."

Jacobs held up a hand. "I think I know what you're getting at and the semantics of it are probably not very useful, although I must confess my curiosity is running amok. Still, I think we can move on to what you think is going to happen and what we can do about it."

"Right now, I don't know what we can do about it. What we *have* to do about it, first of all, is to find out exactly what it is that was found, where it is and why it's so important to our adversary."

"Do you have any idea at all what it might be?"

"No. All I know is that, whatever it is, it contains a lot of power. Power that this thing will be able to use to its advantage."

"Are you sure he doesn't already have it?"

"Yes. Of that, I'm positive. Things would already be a lot worse than they are if he did."

Jacobs sat back.   He understood what
Geoffrey couldn't put into words. Deep in his soul
he knew that what they were facing went beyond
any religious dogma, but, at the same time, lent
itself perfectly to such descriptions. At the heart of
it, it was an enigma. And as much as he would like
to be able to comprehend the full scope of it, he
knew he never would. All he could do would be to
accept it. That thought made him smile. Funnily
enough, religion or no religion, it was coming back
around to ... faith.

"Are you alone in all this? That is, are there
others out there like you that will help?" asked
Jacobs, hoping the answer would be yes.

"There are others, I can feel it. But I don't
know how many. One, maybe two at the most.
And I can also feel that this thing has already started
trying to put roadblocks in their way."

"Are they here? Are they in Banderman
Falls, now?"

"No. I don't think so. But they'll be coming
... if they can."

"That part about *if* they can is not very
reassuring." Jacobs laughed a bit. "I guess I'll just
have to content myself with the hopes that they're as
determined as you are."

"That much you can bloody well be certain
of, Fa-er-Gabe."

"Ok, you said that you were human but not
human. What does that mean? I assume it means
you're mortal, despite your implied longevity."

Geoffrey laughed out loud. It was the first
laugh that passed between them that wasn't

designed to alleviate their uneasiness. It was deep and genuine. Jacobs's face actually showed the first signs of relaxing since last night and Geoffrey looked as though he were having a casual breakfast with a friend. But that mood didn't last long.

"Yes. I'm very mortal. I might live a long time, but I bleed and die, just like you do."

Jacobs studied Geoffrey's face. "But there's more, isn't there? There's something you're not telling me. Am I right?"

"Yes, there's more. But I think that's best not discussed just yet. I have my reasons."

"I'm sure you do. And, as a friend, I won't press you. But I sure hope you're going to tell me that you're something of a superman, because I think we're going to need it."

Geoffrey shot Jacobs one of his uneasy, but totally charming smiles. It told Jacobs everything he wanted to know. There was, indeed, much more to his friend than he ever expected. And he hoped that it would be more than could be believed.

"Ok then, where do we start? What's first on our agenda of finding this ... whatever it is that he's looking for?"

"I'm not exactly sure. I know that it's here. It's been found; someone has possession of it. That much I know. But I don't know who. I can usually see things that give me clues or answers, but right now, I'm coming up pretty blank. And I think that's an indication of just how strong our friend is already. Trust me on this one, he's already set to work here and he's going to do everything he can to stop us. Not the least of which is-"

Jacobs cut him off in mid-sentence. "Kill us?"

Geoffrey didn't reply. The quickly flashed smile said all that needed to be said. "I can guess at this much. Whatever it is, it would have been found through an archeological dig, or by someone digging around by accident, something like that. It wouldn't have been easy to find and I'm betting its discovery was totally accidental."

Jacobs considered this for a few moments, unconsciously opening and closing his interlaced fingers. He had a hint of an idea that he should know where they should begin their search, but it just wasn't coming to him.

"Relax into it," said Geoffrey. "Don't try too hard. It'll just get further away."

"Are you reading my mind?"

"Not per se. At least, not in the way you'd interpret mind reading. I get images of what you're visualizing. Sometimes they're words, like when you're talking to yourself inside your head; sometimes they're just pictures of what you're seeing mentally."

"Well that's a damned handy trick to have up your sleeve."

"Perhaps, but I have to be careful."

"How so?"

"It can be used against me. If the mental images that are projected, let's say, by our nemesis, are strong enough, I can be misled. And I assure you, if he's able to do so, he will. There have been times in the past where I've been sent off on bloody wild goose chases because of the images."

"Are you telling me that this thing can plant whatever it wants into your mind ... into our minds?" For the first time, Jacobs looked horrified. Not even the cat on the door had elicited such a strong, visible response.

"Plant visions? No. Not really. At least, not in my mind. There is a good chance however, I'm sorry to say, that he probably can in yours ... or any other human's for that matter."

"Well, if he can't plant them in yours, how can he lead you on the wild goose chase?"

"He won't try to plant them directly. If the occasion arises where I'm close enough to read him, he mentally conjures up a false image in his own mind and hopes that I buy into it. Do you understand?"

"Yes, I think I do. If I have it correctly, it would be like me thinking of, say ... going to church when I was actually going to the hardware store. You'd read the image of the church in my mind and go there. Is that about right?

"That's absolutely right. That's why I have to be very careful in interpreting what I see ... read ... whatever. And it won't be limited to just him. Whoever he gets to do his bidding, and there will be many, will be instructed to control their thoughts as best as they possibly can." Geoffrey pushed back from the table and stood up. "The upside to *that* is, usually, the ones that fall in with him are pretty weak minded to begin with."

Geoffrey dropped another two teabags into his cup and filled it with hot water. He then turned, leaning back against the counter, saucer in one hand

and teacup in the other. "But not all of them are stupid or weak-minded. All they have to do is be in the right frame of mind, or too scared to fight back and he'll use them. So the upshot is, there will be a few people he's drawn in that will not be so easy to deal with."

Jacobs stood and moved over to the coffee pot, picked it up and then changed his mind. He set the cup on the counter and turned to face Geoffrey. His eyes locked on Geoffrey's as he conjured up a mental image of two headstones.

"Yes. There's a real good chance that neither one of us is going to survive this," Geoffrey answered his thought.

"Well I hope to God you're wrong about *that*," said Jacobs. "And," he added, "sorry about the little test just now. But you know us humans ... need to see for ourselves."

Geoffrey reached out and gave Jacobs a quick pat on the shoulder. When he touched him, Jacobs felt something. Something that reminded him of his childhood. He had fallen off his bike and cut his knees up pretty badly. His mother had comforted him and then washed the cuts out with peroxide. The sensation that quickly coursed through his body when Geoffrey touched him felt very much like the burn of that cleansing.

"I'm going to grab a quick shower and then-" Jacobs stopped, a gleam coming into his eyes as if he'd just answered Final Jeopardy correctly and won twenty thousand dollars. "You said that the mysterious object might have been found on some dig or, at the very least, be something very old. Is that correct?"

"Yes," Geoffrey replied. "What are you getting at?"

"I might be way off the mark, but there's only one place in Banderman Falls where things like that would go. Wedgemore's Antique Shoppe. Of course, it could be in a museum in Philadelphia. There's a few of them there. But if it's here ... if it's here in Banderman Falls, then Wedgemore's would be a good place to start."

"Capital! But we can't just go blundering in there. No matter where it is, you can bet that this thing is already extending enough control to have it protected. So, why don't you go take your shower and freshen up. I fully intend on doing the same. Then we'll see about this antique shop."

"Bloody sounds like a plan, mate."

"Stick to your American English, Gabe. You sound like a sick Australian when you talk like that."

"Got it," said Jacobs waving a finger in the air. "Got it."

CHAPTER 38

By nine-thirty, Banderman Falls had appeared to throw off its slumbers. The sidewalks were bustling with people doing their last-minute holiday shopping. Delivery trucks rumbled up and down the streets and pedestrians waited patiently for the yellow palms to disappear from the corner lights so that they could cross safely. Everything seemed normal, but the Falls was anything but.

Grady Peters walked down Main Street holding the business card he'd gotten last night from the stranger. He was about to walk past the Falls Diner when he got a sudden urge to have a cup of coffee. Digging in his pockets, he pulled out two dollars. He was immediately struck with conflict. The thoughts of spending two dollars on himself when his family was in dire need made him feel sick to his stomach. But a voice in the back of his head kept telling him that he was: *At least worth the price of a cup of coffee.*

He stood there in front of the diner's window turning the dollars over and over in his hand, as if he were going to find a secret message on them that would tell him what he should do. Finally deciding that his family needed it more, he moved forward, but when he got to the doors, he opened them and went in.

The place was packed. There was still one seat left at the far end of the counter so Grady made his way down the aisle, passing out good morning's as he went. Climbing up onto the stool, he waved to Sally Porter. When she got there, half-empty pot of coffee in one hand and her order pad in the other, Grady was already calling out his order.

Instead of the coffee (or rather, in addition to it), he ordered the breakfast special with everything. He could hardly believe what he was saying, but couldn't seem to stop himself. The conflict made him stutter a bit.

"What's wrong with all you guys this morning?" asked Sally, shaking her head. "This some kind of new club or something? Maybe some new holiday joke?"

"What? What are you talking about, Sally," asked Grady, perplexed.

"You all sashay in here, you all order the same thing and you all stutter. You tell *me*. What's the deal?"

Grady looked around. Every seat in the place was taken and everyone who had their order was eating the same thing. But what really struck Grady as odd was that it was all men. There wasn't a single woman in the place outside of Sally. He looked up at her and for a moment had the greatest urge to jump off the stool and run, but he didn't.

"I don't know about any clubs or jokes or any of that. All I know is I'm hungry. So why don't you just go fill my order."

Sally's mouth dropped open. She'd been spoken to unkindly before, by lots of customers, but never by Grady. Grady had always been gentlemanly. The surprise of it twisted her up inside and she couldn't even find the words to respond. When she finally did get control of her voice, she was horrified to hear the words that came out of her mouth: "Yes sir. Anything you want sir."

She was appalled. That was *not* what she wanted to say at all. What she wanted to say, what was on the tip of her tongue but wouldn't come out was: "I'll fill your order, just as soon as you kiss my ass." For the longest time, she just stood there staring. Not at Grady or anything else in particular, just kind of lost.

Grady poked the order pad with his index finger. "You planning on getting me my breakfast or waiting till I have to order dinner?"

"Why you arrogant-" she started, but was interrupted by the booming voice of her boss, Mike Alonzo.

"Get yer ass in gear, girl. Or start looking for new work somewhere else."

Sally could feel the rage building inside her. It was something she'd never felt before. If she'd had an Uzi, she'd have sprayed every man in the place. As it was, she settled for exchanging her half-empty coffee pot with one that had just finished brewing and slamming it against the side of Mike's head. The pot shattered, cutting into him deeply and the hot coffee turned his face red and then brought up large blisters.

Mike began screaming, clutched his face in his hands and staggered backwards. He kept back-peddling until he ran into the large butcher bloc cutting table, the corner of which jabbed into the small of his back. This made him lurch forward.

Sally was now in front of him. He could barely make out her form through his swelling eyes, and the pain of the scalding coffee kept his hands tightly on his face. He could just barely see she was holding something, but couldn't make out what it was. Inside, he was hoping it was a cold rag for his face. But deeper inside, he knew that it wasn't. A second later he was totally engulfed in flames.

With a single match, Sally ignited the boiling fry grease that she had just dumped on him.

Eating stopped. Talking stopped. Every man in the place turned his gaze on Sally. They all watched in silence as Mike Alonzo bounced off the stove, then the butcher block, then the far counter, then collapsed against the back door, burning like a Roman Candle. When the screaming and kicking finally stopped, the men, in unison, got up from their chairs and booths and walked calmly toward Sally.

Panic shot through her. There was nowhere to run. Mike's smoldering body was blocking the rear exit and there was no chance she was going to get past the men that were closing in on her. She grabbed a meat cleaver in desperation. As soon as she had it in hand, the panic and fear turned to rage. She held it out, pointing the blade at Fred Johansen and Gary Larch, the two closest of the men.

"C'mon! C'mon," she yelled, her face as red as Mike's had been after she'd doused him with the coffee. "C'mon you bastards. I'm gonna cut you up and be servin ya to the customers tomorra. C'mon!" She was screaming at them at the top of her lungs.

"You'd best just put that down and take what's commin to ya, bitch," said Fred in a calm and steady voice, something barely above a whisper. "It'll go a whole lot easier if ya don't fight it." He moved around the end of the counter. Charlie Dennis had taken the other side.

Sally looked from one to the other and then back again. This was bad. She knew she couldn't win this one, but she couldn't seem to make herself back down. With a good tug, she could have moved Mike's toasted body out of the way and escaped out the back. But the truth was, inside, she wanted this. She wanted to chop these men up – all of them – like so much lettuce for a dinner salad.

Fred was now only a couple of feet in front of her, the cleaver's blade waving wildly before his face. He didn't seem to care; he just kept coming forward, one step at a time.

"I'm not kiddin ya. I'm not kiddin any a-ya. I'll chop yer goddam heads off. One at a fucking time!"

"You ain't gonna hurt no one, bitch," was the last thing Fred Johansen said before she buried the blade in his forehead, splitting the skull right down the center. His entire head seemed to open up like a pistachio shell. He took another step forward then dropped to the floor, his weight and momentum pulling the handle of the cleaver out of her hand. Before she could bend down to retrieve it, the rest of the men were on her.

Charlie Dennis's meaty hands were wrapped tightly around her neck, squeezing her windpipe closed. The other men were holding her down, her arms and legs pinned. She tried to thrash her way out, but the men were too strong and there were too many of them. She was about to lose consciousness forever when Charlie suddenly released his grip.

She could hear them talking but couldn't make out what it was they were saying. She was wheezing too hard and her ears were ringing from the increased pressure the strangling had caused.

By the time she *could* hear, it didn't matter. She knew what they'd been discussing and what they'd decided to do.

Sally was dragged by her wrists and hair to the back of the diner and shoved into the walk-in freezer. Stunned, she lay there, still trying to get her breath back when she heard the banging. Looking up, she saw Elmore Wallace breaking the inside emergency release off the freezer door. Sally tried to get up, to get to the door before they closed it on her, but she didn't make it. The thick, latching clang rang in her ears as Grady Peterson pushed the heavy metal door over on it hinges and the lock caught.

Sally knew that the cold would take her soon and that there was no way out. She fumbled in her apron, searching for her cell phone and hoping it hadn't fallen out in the scuffle. It was still there. Flipping it open, hope turned to panic. There was no signal.

CHAPTER 39

Tom Kissling had been driving the Banderman Falls trolley bus for almost twenty-three years. Its main purpose was to give tourists a grand view of the Falls and its neighbors, Conshohocken and Philadelphia. Three times a week Tom would make the run around the circuit: pick up the tourists at the trolley stop on the corner of Main and Whitlow, shuttle them around the Falls pointing out the old mills and works built by old man Banderman in the way back when, glide through Conshy (a local name for Conshohocken), and then onto the Schuylkill Expressway (I-76) into Philadelphia. In twenty-two and three-quarter years he never missed a day.

It was a little past nine when Tom pulled out of the lot and onto Main Street. The stop was only five minutes away and he wasn't due there until nine-thirty. As was his custom on Friday mornings, he headed straight for the Starbucks. A nice latte and a couple of onion bagels would start his day. He smiled to himself as he thought about the three moves he'd come up with last night, and couldn't wait to see the look on old Roy Albertson's face when he laid the first one on him. Roy owned the Starbuck's franchise and he and Tom had an ongoing chess game. Every Friday they took turns exchanging moves. It wasn't a fast-moving game, to be sure. But it didn't have to be. The two were content to take their time and look forward to the next perplexing move at the end of the week.

At nine-o-seven, Tom suddenly felt like his head had caught fire. He could hardly breathe and his vision clouded over. He swerved the trolley left, corrected and then angled toward the curb. Bumping the passenger-side tire up onto the sidewalk he came to a jolting stop. A woman jumped out of the way, gave him the finger and went on about her business. Tom sat hunched over the steering wheel. He cradled his head in his hands as he tried to catch his breath and understand what had happened.

At first he thought he might be having a stroke. But as he sat there, the fire in his head began to abate and his vision cleared. He gently backed the trolley off the sidewalk and slipped it into PARK. Whatever had just happened wasn't good, and he thought that maybe he should just take the day off and go home, or maybe to the doctor. Maybe he *had* just had a small stroke.

He reached into his pocket for his cell phone to call the dispatcher and see if there was anyone who could take his place. Before he could dial, the phone lit up. The ID read: Not So Peaceful Haven.

Not really wanting to, but unable to stay his own hand, he flipped it open. "Hello?"

"Hello, Tom, my boy." The voice was that of his father, dead now some sixteen years. "I'll bet you're surprised to hear from me today."

Tom intended to ask who was making such a sick joke, but what he said was: "It's good to hear from you, dad. Are you calling from heaven?"

There was a hearty laugh on the other end that sounded hollow. It was what would have been heard if they were talking through tin cans and string instead of cell phones. "No son, I'm not. Would you like to come and see me? I sure would like that. It's been very lonely here these last years. I miss you terribly."

"Sure, dad; I'll come. I miss you, too. Where are you?"

"I'm waiting for you at the Starbucks, but I need your help. Can you help me? *Will* you help me?"

"Sure, dad. What do you want me to do?"

"I want you to save me. I'm surrounded by lots of folks who don't like me; they want to hurt me. Can you come now? I need you now?"

"Okay dad, I'm coming."

Without thinking, Tom threw the trolley into gear and pulled out into traffic, narrowly missing a Mercedes that was passing.

"Come quickly, son. I really need you. These people ... well ... they're not really people ... they're trying to get me. Please, come and run them all down. Save me. Drive right through the front window and run them all over."

"Okay, dad. You hang in there, I'm coming. I'm coming!"

Tom stomped on the accelerator. Three minutes later the Banderman Falls trolley made an unscheduled stop at the counter of Starbucks. It jumped the curb, sending two parking meters flying, and barreled through the plate glass window.

Tom's chess buddy, Roy, was pinned between the counter and the wall, the handle of the espresso maker buried in his back. His right arm was hanging by a thin strip of muscle at the shoulder and his legs were crushed. Tom was propelled halfway through the front windshield, his right leg ripped off at the hip. Half of his face had been sheared off on the way through the glass, like the peeled outer layers of an onion.

Judy and Michael Felton had had the misfortune of having a window seat. Both were plowed under the trolley and dragged along. Michael's head had been flattened by the front tire with a sickening *CRACK!* that was never heard, drowned out by the roaring motor and breaking glass. Judy lay pinned beneath the broken rear axle, her face pressed up against the dislodged muffler. Her screams of agony were mingled with the hissing, hamburger-cooking griddle sound of searing flesh.

Tammy Watson and Kim Albright had stopped in for their usual Irish mochas and were now misshapen human hood ornaments, Kim's dead eyes emotionlessly watching Roy Alberston slip away, the back of her head enmeshed in the trolley's grillwork and radiator.

The cell phone Tom had been using had flipped through the air and bounced off Roy's head. It landed on the floor at his feet, still open. From time to time, the soft click-whir of its camera taking snapshots could barely be discerned, and from it poured an unending peel of hideous laughter. Vibrating its way around the room, it took photos of the carnage. And when it had taken its last shot, it burst into flames and melted into a gray pile of goo, the laughter echoing away into silence.

CHAPTER 40

Jack pushed through the double glass doors of the station to find Audrey Archibald behind the desk. The short walk from the car did nothing to cool him down. The final glance he took at the soapy warning on his windshield only fueled the fire. Without a word he walked straight to his office and slammed the door behind him. He was still muttering to himself about being called a king when he plopped down into his leather chair. He rocked back as far as the chair would allow without tipping over and just sat there, palms on the armrests.

After a few moments Jack leaned forward and undid the top two buttons of his grey uniform shirt. He absently ran his hands through his hair and then let out a long cathartic sigh as he sat back. His mind began to clear and his rage subside.

Audrey had watched Jack go by and knew the look and demeanor. She had seen it before, but only a few times. Not much seemed to rattle Jack, but when something did, it was a 'clear the decks' situation. From experience, Audrey knew that he'd work through it and would eventually come out (somewhat sheepishly) and apologize. At least, that's the way it usually went down.

Shooting a final glace at the closed door, she turned back to her task at hand - finishing the article she'd been perusing in *Better Homes & Gardens*. She'd been trying to make up her mind whether to buy the rattan patio set or the wrought iron. Both were actually out of her price range; but all of a sudden, she was feeling like she owed herself something special and to hell with the finances.

When she heard the familiar creak of the door, about twenty minutes later, she just waved a hand in the air without looking around.

"Forget it. Want some coffee?" she asked. "It's relatively fresh."

"Yeah, sounds good," said Jack, in the expected apologetic tone. "Not quite sure what got into me."

"Oh, I dunno. Let's see ... Pat O'Donnell's dead; Charlie and Frank are missing; and ... oh yeah, Tyler hasn't checked in since last night and I can't raise him on the squawker. Why should you be *upset*?" Audrey was handing Jack his coffee by the time she'd finished her version of the morning report.

"Tyler hasn't checked in? Christ! What now? What's next?" Jack walked around behind the desk and bent over the radio console. Snapping the mic switch down he said: "Tyler? Twenty-seven two ... do you copy?" He waited, but there was no response. After several attempts, he gave up.

"I told you," said Audrey. "What do you think it means?"

"Damned if I know. All I know is that things around here are going haywire. And that's *not* a guess."

"So what's next, boss? Want me to bring in Bill Pinsky?"

"Yeah, get him in here, pronto. And give ... um ... give Ethan Kennedy a call and see if he still wants that temp deputy job. We could use some extra help."

"Right on it, boss." Audrey smiled. She flipped her magazine closed and pulled the pile of applications out of the in-basket. Rifling the corners, she quickly located the one she wanted, scanned it for Kennedy's number and dialed.

"I'm gonna start cruisin. As soon as you get Ethan, swear him in over the phone. We don't have time for formalities right now. We'll take care of the paperwork later."

"What if he doesn't want the job?"

"Beg him; sweet talk him. I don't care what you do, but get him down here and into a radio car. He's done this before, so he knows the drill."

Audrey gave a quick salute. "Aye-aye, captain." It was just what Jack needed to relieve a little tension. He smiled momentarily.

"Ri-ight," was all he said before leaving. Outside, he used his uniform sleeve to clean off the windshield as best he could before hitting it with the washer fluid. Frustrated and a little scared, he tried calling Tyler again as he backed the cruiser out. He got the same no-results results. A sickening feeling crept over him.

Jack slipped down Main Street doing the twenty-five miles per hour limit. He took note of the pedestrians and light traffic. In the back of his mind he kept wondering which of his fellow residents had decorated his cruiser, but the anger he'd felt earlier was gone. Now, he was only wondering who and why.

A fleeting image of Frank Mowery's jeep sitting by the water flashed across his mind. Without really thinking about it, he pointed the cruiser toward the end of town and headed down to the river. When he pulled into the lot, a brief surge of panic took him. Not the kind of panic you feel when you're in danger, but rather, the kind you feel when you know something is horribly wrong – a knot-in-your-stomach wrong.

Sitting behind Frank's jeep was Tyler's patrol car, the dome lights still flashing and the driver's side door hanging open. Jack pulled up behind it and parked. He took a careful look around before climbing out. There wasn't a soul in sight. But more than that, there wasn't a sound. There should have been. The surrounding woods should have been full of animal and bird noises, but it was dead still.

Before moving toward Tyler's cruiser, Jack took a good look at the gravel. There was something very odd about it, but he couldn't place what it was at first. And then it hit him. It was perfect. It was absolutely level. There were no tire tracks behind Tyler's cruiser or Frank's Jeep. He turned and looked behind his own. Small ruts in the stone led up to where his car was parked. And the same should have been true for Tyler's and Frank's vehicles.

Jack hunched down and cocked his head sideways examining the length of the lot. It looked as if a crew had come in and raked and leveled it. There wasn't a mark. He pulled himself up to his feet and rested his hands on his belt, looking around.

After examining the patrol car and Jeep, Jack made his way down to the edge of the water. It had been tough going; the brambles seemed to have grown thickest across the old path, which made no sense. He clawed his way through, tearing the sleeves of his uniform shirt and some forearm flesh in the process. If he didn't know better, he would have thought that the woods were actually trying to keep him from getting to the river bank.

At the water's edge, Jack looked up and down the creek and then scanned the thin dirt pathway that ran alongside it. There were no prints of any kind, animal or human. He noticed something else extremely odd, too. There were no insects buzzing about. This close to the water the mosquitoes and gnats should have been fierce. There weren't any water skimmers either, or a single dragonfly.

Taking the path to the left, Jack made his way along the creek looking for any signs of Frank, Charlie or Tyler. The air hung heavy with humidity, but there was a coolness by the water. Sweat was already running down his cheeks and staining the front of his shirt. His legs were starting to feel like lead in the heavy uniform trousers.

About a hundred and fifty yards from where he'd left the road, he started to smell it. The unmistakable stench of a corpse decaying in the heat. He pushed through a tangle of blueberry thickets and found the body. It was lying on the bank, the head and shoulders floating on top of the creek's surface.

There was no mistaking the sheriff's uniform. It was Tyler. He was lying face down in the water, one arm along his side, the other floating out in front of him as if he were waving. Jack knelt beside the body, wondering whether or not to turn him over. By rights, he should leave it alone until

Doc Robertson arrived, but this was Tyler, a colleague and friend.

Against his better judgment, Jack stepped into the creek, grabbed Tyler under the arms and pulled him up to the bank. The face of his friend no longer had the clownish smile he always wore. It was puffy and discolored from floating in the water, and the eyes were cloudy and vacant as they stared up, unseeing, into the sky.

"Christ, Tyler," intoned Jack, "what the hell happened?" He bent down and checked to see if Tyler's Beretta was still in the holster. It was. It had never been drawn. Whatever had happened had either happened too quickly for Tyler to react or it had happened at the hands of someone Tyler had trusted.

Not wanting to paw over the body too much before he could get Robertson out for an examination, Jack satisfied himself with a visual inspection. There were no obvious signs of trauma. His neck might have been broken, but Jack couldn't tell. From what he could see, there were no breaks in the skin.

Reaching for the mic on his shoulder, Jack called it in to Audrey and asked her to get Robertson out as quickly as he could make it.

"Did you get a-hold of Ethan, Audrey?" he asked, after explaining what he'd found.

"Yes, Jack. He said he'd be right in. In fact I'm expecting him any moment." There was a short pause, and Jack could hear Audrey's crying. "Geeze, Jack. What happened to Tyler?"

"I don't know yet, Audrey. But I sure as hell intend to find out. Things are getting out of hand around here and I'm about to start putting them straight." Jack closed his eyes for a moment, trying to bring everything into focus. "As soon as Ethan gets in," he continued, "have him start general patrol. Did you get in touch with Bill Pinsky yet?"

"Yes. Should I let him know about Tyler? He's cruising the upper end."

"No. Don't say anything about Tyler just yet. Have him meet me in the Bell's Mill creek parking lot."

"Ok. Anything else?"

"No. Not at the moment. Wait ... yes; have Doc Robertson give me a call on the radio on his way over here, will ya? You patch him through."

"Sure thing, Jack." There was a moment's silence, then: "Jack, what do you want to do about Amy?"

"I'll take care of that, Audrey. I'd like to know what to tell her about her husband's death before I go see her. I'll wait till after Doc's had a chance to look at the body."

"All right." There was another brief pause. "Jack ... let me know what you find out, will you?"

"Sure thing, Audrey."

While Jack waited for Doc Robertson to call, he began surveying the area. There was not much for him to find. The path was pristine; there were no broken ends on any of the surrounding foliage – no signs whatsoever that anything had taken place there. It didn't add up. If this was just a body dump, and the crime scene was elsewhere, then there should be heavy footprints from the one who'd carried Tyler in to dump him. If the crime had happened here, there should be signs of a struggle. The whole thing was beginning to give Jack a headache.

The sudden unexpected crackle of his radio brought him out of his thoughts. It was Audrey, and she sounded even more upset than when he'd just spoken to her.

"Jack, we have a couple more problems."

"What's up, Audrey? I'm waiting for Doc and my plate's a little full at the moment. What's so urgent?" Jack tried to hide the exasperation he was feeling. Wasn't it enough that he had a dead deputy and two missing men? What the hell could be more important that Audrey would think he'd drop what he was doing for another call?

"Jack," Audrey took a deep breath, "Tom Kissling's trolley just crashed through the window of Starbucks. Far as I know ... six dead, including Tom. And it gets worse. I just got a call from Linda Killerman. I think you better get out there as soon as you can. Linda said ... I mean ... she's claiming that-"

"What is it Audrey? Spit it out! I'm a bit busy here, for chrissake."

"Jack ... Linda's been raped."

"What! Oh hell. What the fuck is going on in this town?" Jack thought for a moment. His mind was swimming. Bad news fell on bad news, and it seemed Banderman Falls was coming apart like a continuous loop carpet thread caught on a dog's nail.

"Listen, have Ethan head over there and take the report. He'll know what has to be done. In the meantime, tell her not to wash and don't disturb the bed or scene. Also, tell Ethan to just take the report and then transport Linda to Doc's office for an exam. When Doc calls in, which I'm expecting any moment, I'll have him tell his office she's coming. When we're through here, we'll meet Linda there. Get Bill Pinsky on the trolley thing. You got all that?"

"Yeah! Jack, what's going on here?"

"Audrey, I wish I knew." Jack released the mic key and wiped the sweat off his brow with his sleeve. A moment later the radio crackled to life again. It was Doc Robertson. Jack filled him in and then told him to wait by his car when he got to the parking lot. He took a last look around and one final glance at Tyler, and then headed back out to the lot to meet Robertson.

***

When Ethan arrived at the Killerman B & B he knew exactly what had to be done. He was a decorated Special Forces veteran of Desert Strom. When he'd gotten discharged, he opened his security consulting firm. Most of his clients were big corporations in Philadelphia, although he was always happy to lend local businesses a hand with appraisals and recommendations.

Linda was waiting in the downstairs parlor when he arrived. When he walked in, he could see the frustration on her face. He had actually expected to see the glazed and ashamed look most rape victims wore. Instead, she was sitting in a chair in front of the fireplace with a clipboard in her hand.

"Hi Linda," Ethan said as he crossed the room.

The first thing she noticed was the star pinned above his left breast pocket. Without thinking about it, she stood up, walked over and put the clipboard on the reception counter and headed toward the staircase. Ethan took note of the fact that her steps were deliberate, not hesitant.

"I already washed," she told Ethan, as they climbed the stairs. "So you're not likely to get anything telling from me. I realized afterward that I shouldn't have. But at the time ... I really needed to. Sorry!"

"No need to apologize," he said.

"I didn't touch the bed or sheets though. Maybe they'll be of some help."

At the top of the stairs, Ethan took her by the arm and turned her to face him. He studied her face, looking for any signs that she was in shock. He couldn't find any.

"You're remarkably calm about this, Lin. Are you sure you're ok?"

"As ok as anyone in my situation could be. The thing about it is ... it wasn't real ... but it was."

"What does that mean?" asked Ethan as they walked down the hall toward the bedroom.

"I don't know. All I know is that it all seemed like a dream, but when I woke up I was covered in-." She let her voice trail off, allowing Ethan to finish the sentence in his mind.

When they got to the bedroom door, Ethan asked Linda to wait outside while he looked the room over and collected whatever he thought was appropriate. Before entering, he pulled out a pair of latex gloves from the kit he'd brought with him and struggled into them.

"I won't be too long, Linda. Then we'll head over to Doc Robertson's."

"Ethan," she grabbed him by the arm, "I know it's important, but I have guests. I just can't walk out and leave them while I'm sitting at the doctor's office."

Ethan considered this for a moment. He understood her position but, at the same time, understood the importance of having a medical exam. He carefully weighed the options.

"Ok. How about this? We'll stay and have the Doc come here. Since you've already washed, I don't think he's going to find much useful evidence on you. So I think that staying here, under the circumstances, probably makes as much sense as anything." His eyes were a deep brown and in them she saw compassion and understanding. "How many guests do you have? I'll want to talk to all of them."

Linda nodded. "There are four. Mister and Misses Hoffman; they're in room 109; there's a Miss Willowbrand in 208 and Mr. Witherstone in 227. I don't think any of them could have been responsible for this."

"Well, we can't rule anything out just yet. But even if they had nothing to do with it, they might have heard or seen something. I'll chat with them when I'm through in here."

"Well, I'm going back downstairs. I have a few things to get done while I wait. I'm expecting a few more check-ins this morning."

"Ok. Do what you have to do. I'll be down directly. If you need anything-" He didn't finish; he didn't have to.

Linda watched him disappear into her bedroom, stood there a moment, and then went back downstairs. She wasn't aware that, from time to time, she'd rub the side of her face, as if she were removing some unseen smudge. Ethan stood inside the bedroom doorway and listened to her descend the steps. When he could no longer hear her footsteps he turned to the task of collecting whatever evidence he could.

Using the small UV light, Ethan found several places on the sheets and pillowcase that looked like ejaculate. He bagged them all. He carefully inspected the bed, looking for any other physical signs, perhaps a knee impression or a palm impression, but didn't find any. Meticulously, he made his way around the room, but there was nothing else to be found.

"Sorry to butt in, folks," he said, "just need a quick word," he said as he reached the bottom of the steps and noticed the newcomers, then looked at Linda. "The emergency alarm on the stairwell is fixed, Mrs. Killerman. You shouldn't have any more false alarms." He then turned to the couple again. "You have a nice stay. I'm sure you'll love it here ... best B & B around." The made-up story was designed solely to keep the new guests from being unduly alarmed.

After he nodded and smiled, he looked at Linda again. "I'm gonna just put this stuff in the car. Mind if I grab some lunch while I'm here?"

"Not at all," answered Linda complacently. "We'll be serving in about forty minutes if you can wait that long."

"Not a problem. I'll sit in the cruiser and catch up on some paperwork while I wait."

Linda smiled, turning back to register the couple. Ethan took one last look at them and then went out to the cruiser. Sitting behind the wheel, he called Jack and let him know what was going on. Jack told him that he and Robertson were nearly through and that, after they'd transported the body they'd meet him at Killerman's.

CHAPTER 41

Standing in the parking lot in front of the creek, Robertson and Jack watched as the ambulance that held Tyler Berryman's body backed up and pulled out, headed for Twilling's. The gray dust kicked up by the tires drifted across the lot and faded into the bushes. Despite the shade of the surrounding woods and the coolness coming off the water, both men were drenched in sweat. Even with the help of the two ambulance attendants, it had been a struggle getting the waterlogged body back up to the lot.

For the longest time, Jack stood there with his hands in his trouser pockets staring off in the direction of the ambulance. Robertson placed his medical bag in the front seat and had just closed the door when Jack turned and faced him.

"So? Do you think he drowned?" was all that Jack could think to ask. At the creek bank, Robertson had gone over the body as thoroughly as he could but couldn't determine the cause of death. There were no marks whatsoever on the body, not even a bruise from falling.

"I don't know Jack," said Robertson. "I'll need a full post on this one. But I don't think he drowned."

"You don't think he drowned. No shit! I don't think so either. And I don't think he just decided it was a nice day to take a dip in the creek either. I need some answers Doc." Jack kicked a stone and sent it sailing into the woods. His face was tight with anger. He had his eyes pinched down to narrow slits and his jaw was set hard, the muscles rippling as he clenched and unclenched his teeth.

Robertson walked over and touched him on the shoulder. He was wearing a 'don't worry, Jack, we'll figure it out' smile. It was the kind of smile he would put on just before he told a patient the bad news that they were sporting the Big C. It was a practiced smile, but there was warmth and sincerity in it.

"So what do you want to do now, Jack? If you want me to head directly over to Twillings and get started on the autopsy, I'm already there. But I think we should probably swing by and check Linda out first. If nothing else, she's probably going to need some counseling."

Jack softened a bit and let his jaw go slack. He wiped at the sweat on his brow with his left hand then rubbed his face. He was doing his very best to keep his inner feelings from bubbling to the surface. The reminder of Linda Killerman's rape complaint was starting to boil inside him and he didn't want Robertson to see. He had to try and keep cool, professional. Otherwise, their secret might be discovered. And right now, with everything that was going on, he didn't think it would be a good thing to come out into the open with the romance he'd been having with Linda.

"I agree about Linda, and you're going to be very busy. Tom's trolley just went through six people at Starbucks," he said at last. "Let's go get Killerman settled and examined. Tyler and the others will wait. Leave your car and grab your bag, you can ride with me. We'll come back later. I'll want another look around here anyway."

The two of them drove in silence most of the way. Each had his own thoughts to deal with. Robertson was mentally ticking off causes of death that left no marks – coronary, stroke, embolism, but none of them seemed to fit. Almost all of them would have left some visible sign. A nose bleed or bleeding from the ears for stroke or aneurysm, cyanosis of the lips and sclera for coronary, something. There had been nothing. And there was the absence of trauma that would have occurred when he fell from any of these potential killers. Again - nothing. In between, he wondered what the hell could have caused Tom to have such an accident. Again, stroke, heart attack? Too many questions and no answers.

Jack was fighting his own mental battle. He was desperately trying to concentrate on what was going on in the Falls – in his town; on what had happened to Tyler, the two missing men and the disaster at Starbucks. Not to mention Patty O'Donnell's murder. But all he could think about was catching whoever raped Linda and working him over good. The thought of taking the barrel of his gun to the perp's joints, one at a time, made him smile. But the smile faded. No matter how much he wanted to, he knew he never would. He would do what he always did – uphold the law.

As they drove through town, Jack unconsciously took note of something odd. Although he was focused primarily on Linda, his mind took a mental snapshot of the street to show him later. As usual, on a day before a holiday, the main street was bustling with people, but what his mind noticed was that they seemed to be in distinct groups. Here and there three or four men were talking, over on the other side of the street, five or six women. It looked as if the town had divided itself. All the groups that he passed were single-sex groups. There wasn't a couple to be seen.

Jack eased the cruiser up behind Ethan's and threw it into PARK. They stepped out of the car and walked up the front steps. The screen door creaked as Robertson pulled it open. When he pushed the inner door open, the cool air-conditioned air from inside rushed out at them in a welcoming breeze. Inside, the front desk was empty and the place was quiet. The overhead fan was paddling around, circulating the centrally cooled air, and its whirr was the only audible sound.

Jack walked over and tapped the little silver bell on the counter. The *ding-ding* echoed briefly then died away. They waited, but no one answered. Jack moved in behind the counter and peeked in the little office. Empty. He looked at Robertson, his eyes asking the question that his lips didn't.

"Don't know," said Robertson. "Think they're all out back by the pool? It's hot enough."

"Maybe, but I don't think so. Let's check out the dining room."

That room was empty too. But the table was still set and there were plates of half-eaten food sitting around. A stack of sandwiches was sitting in the middle of the table and a bowl of mashed potatoes was still steaming. At one end, a bowl of salad lay upside-down, the lettuce spilled across the table and onto a chair.

Jack walked over and looked at it, and then at the chair. There was a dark stain on the back of the chair that ran down into a puddle on the seat. The spilled salad was sitting in a pool of blood. Overhead, a trail of blood spatter swept across the ceiling in an arc. The picture window was also broken out, as if someone had thrown something through it. Jack looked up at Robertson without saying anything. Robertson looked back. Jack nodded his head in the direction of the front door as he drew his .357. The message wasn't lost on Robertson and he quietly headed for the cruiser.

Jack thumbed the mic a few times and waited for Audrey to reply. He knew that Audrey would hear the radio burp and answer. It was their signal that an officer needed help but couldn't talk. A moment later, Jack's radio repeated the same sound, followed by a long pause and then another three bursts. Jack hit the mic button twice telling Audrey he got the message. Bill Pinsky would be on his way.

Leaving the dining room, Jack went back out into the foyer, looked around and then headed slowly up the stairs, keeping the gun up and cradled in both hands. At the top, he leaned around the corner and took a quick look down the hall. Nothing was moving and there were no sounds. He stepped out onto the landing and started down the hall, checking one room at a time.

CHAPTER 42

Colleen Slater pushed the double glass doors of Waterman's Boutique open and strode through. She was wearing a tight white blouse that was all but see-through, a mid-thigh black skirt, black fishnet stockings and four-inch stiletto heels. Without stopping, she walked to the back, her heels clicking loudly on the wooden floor. At the far end of the store, she turned and headed toward the skirts. Seeing exactly what she wanted as she approached, she snagged the tiny black skirt off its hanger, pulled the tag off, stripped off her skirt and put it on. She then strode to the counter and dropped the tag on the glass top.

Marjorie Larch was standing there, mouth agape. She'd never seen anyone strip in the aisle before.

"Ring me up and get me outta here," shot Colleen. "I've got places to go and boys to tease."

Marjorie had intended to tell Colleen that the kind of behavior she just displayed was not welcome in the store, but what she said was: "You go girl. Make em drool."

"I intend to do more than that honey. I'm gonna make em drip. And maybe ... just maybe, one of 'em'll get lucky. But I haven't decided about that yet." She smiled, but it was more of a sneer.

Marjorie smiled back, and then suddenly felt inspired. While looking Colleen right in the eyes, she took off her shirt, pulled off her bra and tossed it in the trash can. She then started giggling as she pulled the shirt back on and redid all but the top three buttons. "Maybe I'll join in the fun, too," she said, still giggling.

"Knock em dead," was all that Colleen said as she strode out of the store, leaving Marjorie standing there admiring herself in the mirror. There was something about the image that Marjorie was looking at that didn't sit quite right with her. She glanced around the store and then decided that she needed an entirely new outfit for her entirely new feeling.

When she was done, she was dressed in the shortest red skirt she could find, a red halter top; red stockings complete with red and white garter and red heels. Satisfied with her new killer looks, she walked over to the front of the store and stood at the display window looking out. Her rational mind told her that she shouldn't ... couldn't ... do what she was thinking. But deeper inside, she heard her own voice whisper: *Go for it!*

Flipping the sign on the door from OPEN to CLOSED, she stepped out into the sunshine of her new day. She glanced across the street and noticed a group of men having a conversation. The thought of becoming eye candy caused her to break out in goosebumps. She adjusted her breasts inside the halter, giving her nipples a little pinch to make them stand out and then crossed the street to parade herself past the target group.

Stupid idiots, she thought, *all a girl needs is a nice pair of tits and to show a little skin and their minds turn to peanut butter.* As she walked past them, she slowed her pace and started swinging her hips. The group parted to let her pass, and when she noticed one of the younger ones paying particular attention, she looked right at him and slowly licked her lips, something she *never* did for her husband Gary. At the end of the block, a few feet past the last of the men, she walked around the corner, leaving them behind to fantasize. An impulse to blow them all a kiss flashed across her mind, but she dismissed it as being just a little over the top. *Maybe next time.*

Meanwhile, Colleen had gone in the opposite direction. She had an entirely different agenda in mind. Oh, she was dead set on getting all the men in town worked up, that was for sure, but first, she had something else she wanted to do. Before she did anything else; before she let the fun really begin, she had to put that bitch, Rachel Parker in her place. Then, after that, it was no holds barred. Every man who lived in Banderman Falls was fair game – but especially the married ones.

I'll give 'em all a taste of something they never got from their dumpy wives, she thought. When she reached the park, she went in and sat on the bench. Before she could accomplish her goals, she had to figure out where the Parker woman might be. She might be home, but that probably wasn't the best place to confront her. The best place would be a place of Colleen's choosing. *Choose the right battleground – win the battle, girl.*

Colleen was too occupied with her personal motivations to notice how quiet the park was. There wasn't a child to be seen and not a bird was singing. In fact, there wasn't a bird or squirrel or any other animal around. But Colleen was totally oblivious to this. The only thing on *her* mind was what she was going to do with Rachel 'the whore' Parker.

CHAPTER 43

After the men had locked Sally away, Dave Grenemeyer started a fresh pot of coffee. When it finished brewing, he poured cups for everyone. The men sat there, lined up along the counter, drinking their coffee and listening to Sally bang frantically and uselessly on the freezer door. There was a new-found mental connection between them. They found that they didn't need to speak to communicate with each other. They all knew that none of them was going to leave until the bitch in freezer was dead, or, at least, close enough to death that it was a sure thing.

Grady was sitting at the far end of the counter. Part of him wanted to get up and let the girl out, but each time that urge came, a voice, Bill Palmerton's voice, came into his head from down the other end. "Just keep your seat, it'll be over soon. Then we'll get on with the business of teaching all the women in this miserable town to properly behave." And each time the voice came, all the rest of the men would turn and nod their heads in agreement.

The diner was 'pin-drop' quiet, yet conversations were being carried on. The men discussed how they thought the Phillies would do this year and the disappointment the Eagles had shown. Frank Watkins was talking to Earl Oprendick about the Sixers and Alvin Parris was discussing Arlen Specter's politics with Floyd Martin.

Each conversation was separate and distinct, but every man in the place was aware of every other's thoughts. The whole thing was starting to give Grady a headache. He was finding it difficult to shut out the voices of those he was not conversing with. They all jumbled together in his head. He felt as if he were trying to watch ten different movies at the same time and couldn't separate one from the other.

"Relax," said a voice. It was soft and soothing. "It won't be long before you get the hang of this." Grady didn't recognize the voice. It wasn't one of the men he was sitting with and he couldn't ever remember hearing anyone in town that sounded like that. It slipped into his mind, drowning out all the other voices, but was still softer, more pleasant. And then it came to him. It was the voice of the man who had visited him last night to offer him a job.

When Grady looked down the counter, he could tell by the looks on the faces of the others that they also were hearing the same voice and the same message. All the way along the counter, the men sat with both hands wrapped around their coffee cups and their chins resting on their chests. It looked to Grady as if they were listening to a sermon. And when he looked down, he noticed that his hands were also in the exact same position.

A part of him wanted to get up and run – to get up and shout that what they were doing and feeling and experiencing was all wrong. But there was another part of him that was exerting a will beyond that. It was a will that kept him sitting mum on the stool. It was a will that kept telling him that he was about to experience a great power and that he would no longer live on the bottom rung of life. It told him, as it told all men there, that he was about to become a very important force in Banderman Falls. It told him that he was about to meet someone who had all the answers, and that if he were smart, he'd listen to and follow this person.

When the voice faded, all the men turned and looked at one another. They all got the same message. In unison, they rose, ignoring the feeble pounding of the waitress in the freezer, and left. Together, they turned down Main Street and headed for their foretold destination. The group moved silently and slowly toward Wedgemore's Antique Shoppe.

At the corner of Main and Elm, the group stopped. They each nodded and then turned to their respective chores. The chores the soft voice had just placed in their heads. Two of them continued on to Wedgemore's while the other five moved off toward the park.

"A reckoning has come," said the voice in their heads. "You men will be the first in line and you must take the control you deserve. Your women have had way too much freedom for way too long. Go! Go and put them in their place. Their only true role is to serve you. Go see to it that they understand."

The men separated. The five that headed to the park, Charlie Dennis; Frank Watkins; Bill Palmerton; Earl Oprendick and Alvin Paris, had an image of Colleen Slater in their heads. It was an image of her providing the entertainment she owed them. The two on the way to Wedgemore's, Gary Larch and Grady Peters, had the image of Evelyn Ramsey doing the same for them. They all had the image of Carlton as someone who would have all the answers – as someone who would lead them.

CHAPTER 44

After he'd finished his shower, Geoffrey found Jacobs sitting in his study reading the bible. From across the room, it seemed to Geoffrey that his friend had aged since last night. His hair had silvered a bit on the sides, an unusual appearance for a man of thirty-nine. He'd also developed a few more worry lines in his face.

Geoffrey walked over and gently lifted the bible from Jacobs's hands. He turned it around and looked at the passage his friend had been reading and then set it face down on the desk.

"There's something we need to do before we start any of this," said Geoffrey. "I held off mentioning it until I was certain of what we were dealing with, *and* that you would be willing to help." His face was set; there was no mirth in it at all, and his eyes seemed as cold as an assassin's.

"What?" asked Jacobs.

"I don't think you're going to like this idea much. And to be totally honest, I don't either. But, from experience, I know it's something that should be done."

Jacobs sat back and rubbed lightly at his face. His instinct told him that he probably wasn't just 'not going to like it', but rather, loathe it. The expression on Geoffrey's face told him that much.

"What do you have in mind?"

"There's going to be a division. I'm not sure what kind, but it usually plays out that way. Most times it comes down to rich against poor or catholic against protestant ... something like that. What exactly the division here and now will be I can't say."

"Ok. So what can we do about it?"

"Actually, not much. At least, not much at the outset. We'll see about that as things get clearer. But there's a class of people that need protection. Those that are of the greatest risk of being deceived and used as pawns."

"And who would they be?" Jacobs sat forward. He could see that he had been right and that he definitely wasn't going to like what was going to be suggested.

Geoffrey stuck his hands in his pockets and walked over to look out the window. His eyes swept the parking lot, looking out beyond the far fence. He noticed the distinct absence of wildlife. He noticed that there were no children playing in the small park that belonged to the school. "The children," he said, turning back to face Jacobs. "We have to protect the children and keep them out of this as much as possible."

"The children? What in God's name would it want of the children?" Jacobs asked the question but really didn't need an answer. They were the most impressionable group around, willing to believe in the most outlandish things. Willing to believe in lies ... easily deceived. "What can we do to protect them, Geoffrey?"

"It won't be easy Fath-Gabe. What I want to do is-" Geoffrey let his voice fall off. He dropped his chin to his chest and bit his upper lip. Jacobs had no trouble reading the discomfort he was feeling at what he was about to propose. When he finally lifted his head, what Jacobs saw was pure resolve. What he saw was the will to do what was necessary despite how distasteful it might be.

"I want to put them to sleep. Into a coma, if you will. It will be much more difficult for him to reach them when they're that deep. And don't kid yourself, he *will* try to reach them."

"What if he's already done that?"

"I don't think he's gone that far. Although easily drawn in, children aren't his first line weapons. He'll need adults first. I think we have time. But not much."

"Well, pardon me for asking a silly question, but how in the world do you propose to put a whole town's worth of children into a coma? *And*, will you be able to bring them out again? Will they survive it?"

"Yes. It's been done before. Still, I must caution you, it's not easy to do and bringing them out of it is even harder. Of course, the only alternative is to take our chances and see if we can stop this thing before he gets to the children."

"Wait a minute," said Jacobs. "What if he does get to the children and we still defeat him. Will we be able to save them?"

"The problem is, Gabe, if he does convert the children, then, most likely we'll have to kill them, just as we may have to kill quite a few converted adults. They'll be his soldiers. Do you understand? He will own them. And anything short of stopping them cold will be dangerous. They will, children *and* adults, be lined up against us and they *will* be lethal." Geoffrey placed his hands on the table and looked directly into the depths of Jacobs's eyes. "Do you understand?" He said it one word at a time to emphasize the importance of the question.

Jacobs didn't like it, but he did understand. He sank back in his chair and closed his eyes, silently saying a prayer. When he sat forward, the soft look of an understanding priest was replaced with a firm resoluteness. There was no doubt that he'd see what was ahead of them to the end. Good or bad, win or lose. "Yes. I understand," he said in a tone that reminded Geoffrey of a line officer issuing a final command before taking on a hopeless mission.

"How do we put them in a coma, Geoffrey?"

Geoffrey bit his upper lip again and interlaced his fingers, rubbing the heels of his hands together. His brow was furrowed in concentration and Jacobs could see that he was mentally searching for something.

"I'm not sure we should do it now. It's best done at night when they're sleeping. If we succeed, there's a risk. If they're out playing they could be hurt or killed when they slip under. But ... I hesitate to wait until tonight. That might be too late."

"I see your point, but that doesn't answer how?"

"Well, that's another matter altogether. I'm not even sure if we can do it with only two. But I'm counting on the fact that your faith and resolve are strong enough to make up for the absent-" Geoffrey stopped short. He knew that he would have to tell the priest how, and he was pretty sure he'd have his complete cooperation, but it would also raise questions that he'd rather not have to deal with at present. He studied the priest for a moment, letting his mind reach out and capture the images the priest had in his head. He searched for anything that he might be able to use as a distraction if he needed one.

"For the absent what, Geoffrey? Where did you go? You look like a man whose thoughts are a thousand miles away."

"Sorry Gabe. Like I said, I just don't like the idea of this, but I think it has to be done. So, here's what I need from you."

Jacobs nodded. He knew that he didn't have to say anything further; he leaned back in his chair and steepled his fingers. His familiarity with the human psyche, and insight he'd gained from his chosen profession, told him that his friend would finish without any prompts ... as soon as he was ready.

CHAPTER 45

As Jack and Robertson were seeing Tyler's body off to the mortuary, Ethan Kennedy sat in the cruiser trying to get a handle on the couple checking in. There was something not quite right about them. They seemed affable enough, but there was something about the way they looked that just didn't sit well with him.

The man was wearing an old black suit that looked like it needed to be tailored and cleaned. The lapels were shiny with wear and covered in little spots. Most of the buttons were hanging by only a thread or two, except for the one that was missing completely, and his trousers looked like he'd slept on the ground in them. They hung on his body like poorly measured drapes over a small window. The woman's dress also looked in need of repair and a good cleaning. The lace around the collar hung down on one side and the right sleeve was torn at the shoulder. He also noticed that both their shoes were crusted with dirt and leaves, as if they'd just come back from a hike through the woods. And there was a pallor to both of them. They looked like people who avoided the sun at all costs. While he couldn't swear to it, he was certain that he hadn't heard their car arrive. As he looked around, he took note that there were no new additions in the parking lot. Even if they'd come by taxi, Ethan was sure he would have heard it. And then there was the luggage, or absence of it. They were checking in but neither of them had a single suitcase or bag of any kind. In fact, as he thought about it now, the woman wasn't even carrying a purse.

Ethan opened the door of the cruiser and stepped out. The July sun beat down raising shimmering waves off the car's hood. Stepping out of the air-conditioned car, the heat hit him as solidly as if he'd been punched. The unexpected intensity of it forced him to grab the door for momentary support. Sweat broke out instantly on his forehead and chest. It was not the usual heat associated with a summer day. It was as if he'd stepped into a blast furnace.

He took a few steps toward the front porch, but his legs began to feel rubbery. With every step, it felt as if the temperature rose another degree. Reaching the steps, he had to steady himself on the railing and catch his breath. He could feel and hear his chest wheezing. Something was definitely wrong. He was in top physical condition; he always made sure of that because of the nature of his job. He knew he should not be reacting to the heat like this.

By sheer force of will, he made it up the steps and into the lobby. The cool air brought goosebumps up on his overheated, sweaty arms and neck. His breathing eased. When he collected himself, he looked around. The lobby was empty. He assumed that Linda was showing her guests to their room. Deciding to check things out, he stepped over to the reception desk; the sign-in registry lay open. What he saw made him take a step backward. Instead of a name, the last entry read: GET OUT OF HERE OR DIE, RENT-A-COP!

Ethan pinched his eyes closed then opened them. The entry hadn't changed. It was also written in blood; he could smell the metallic odor coming off the page.

"What the hell?" he said.

"What the hell, what?" came Linda's voice from behind him. She was just coming down the steps. He turned and looked up at her.

"What the hell kind of sign-in is this?" he asked, his finger tapping the registry.

"What are you talking about?" Linda stepped down off the bottom step and walked around behind the desk. "Are you feeling alright, Ethan? You look pale."

Ethan swiveled the registry book around to face her, his finger still tapping on the page. "This is how you let your guests sign in?" He looked down at the page, ready to ask if Linda had lost her mind. His eyes widened. The line he was pointing to read: *Mr. & Mrs. Daniel Oppenheimer.* Ethan took a step back and blinked twice.

Linda reached out a hand and laid it on Ethan's. "Are you sure you're ok? You really *do* look a little pale. Can I get you some tea or water or something?"

Ethan shook his head and then looked down at the entry again. He was sure he hadn't been hallucinating, but the evidence before him said that he had. He took a deep breath.

"Must be hotter out there than I thought." He was still certain he had seen the warning. But since he had no proof and no explanation for it, he decided to drop it. At least, drop it outwardly. His mind still tried to figure out what was going on.

"Yeah," he said to Linda, "maybe some ice tea. That sounds pretty good."

"Well, why don't you come with me into the kitchen. I'm just getting ready to start making the sandwiches for lunch. Maybe you could give me a hand while you're drinking your tea." She stopped and looked at him, touching him lightly on the arm. "Keeping busy helps me keep my mind off last night," she said, as if she felt she needed to explain herself.

"I understand." He smiled, touching her hand lightly. "As to the help, sure thing. Love to help." Ethan took one last quick glance at the registry. Only the couple's names were on the last line – no blood-written warning.

In the kitchen, Linda poured him a large glass of tea from the pitcher she kept in the fridge. As he drank it, she asked him if he'd get the bread out while she got the cold cuts and salad ready. In less than ten minutes, lunch was ready to be served.

"Well, now what?" asked Linda.

"What?"

"Lunch is ready but we have another thirty minutes yet before it's time to be served."

"Umm ... we could eat it and then start over," laughed Ethan. He was trying to keep things on an even keel and not let on that he was still disturbed by the message. "Or ... we could just start yelling 'come-n-get it' at the top of our lungs."

Linda smiled. "How about if we just stack it in the fridge for a bit and go sit on the porch while you drink your tea."

"I'd love to. But it's nasty hot out there. It's as if there were a giant magnifying glass over the front of your quaint little B & B. Know anyone with a giant magnifying glass that wants to fry your customers?"

Linda put a finger to her lips and scrunched up her face in pretend thought. "Not that I can think of offhand. C'mon. Let's sit on the back porch for a bit." Linda held the screen door open. In the light that filtered through the open door, Ethan could see the places on Linda's face and arms where she'd rubbed the skin off in the shower. The abrasions on her cheeks made her look as if she suffered from Rosatia.

"Ok." Ethan hesitated before bringing up a subject that he knew would ruin the atmosphere. "Actually, I'd like to get a statement from you concerning last night." His eyes showed the compassion he was feeling. "If you think you're up to it."

"I think so. I don't know what I can tell you though. I mean, I really didn't see anyone. I only ... well ... I only kind of felt it."

"We'll just take it slow and you tell me what you remember. Try to give me as much detail as you can."

"If you promise you won't laugh at me or have me committed for being mentally unstable."

"You don't have to worry about that," Ethan reassured. "I got hard evidence from your bedroom. Nobody's gonna think you're crazy."

They stepped out onto the back porch and sat in the white metal glider. It seemed much cooler out back to Ethan than the front had and he didn't think it was because of the shade provided by the porch roof. He pulled a small pad and pen from his breast pocket. Linda sat with her hands folded on the blue apron that covered her lap. She kept her head down and was nervously rubbing her thumbs together. Ethan reached over and closed his hand over hers.

"We'll take it nice and slow."

When she'd finished explaining the dream and what she'd found when she woke up, she glanced at her watch. Ethan read in her face that she was relieved to have the story out.

"C'mon. Time for lunch. If you'll take the food into the table, I'll go collect the guests."

"Done deal," said Ethan, flipping the notebook closed and sliding it back into his breast pocket. "Don't be too long; I'm starving." His smile helped. He watched as she relaxed her shoulders.

"By the time you've got the table set, I'll have everyone assembled. Well ... at least notified." She giggled a bit. It was another nervous giggle that seemed to slip out on its own.

When Linda came back downstairs Ethan had everything set out on the table. He was standing behind one of the chairs, his hands on the back. The sandwiches, a mix of roast beef, chicken salad, egg salad, turkey and a few vegetarian, were stacked neatly on a serving plate covered by a large silver dome.

"Don't stand on ceremony ... or anything else for that matter," chided Linda as she entered the dining room. "Seating is first come – first served around here."

Ethan pulled out the chair next to the one he was standing behind and held it for her to sit down. When he'd taken his own seat, he asked: "So, how long do we wait before we get all rude on them and start eating?"

Linda laughed. "I think we can wait at least ... oh ... thirty or forty seconds before we faint from hunger, don't you?"

Ethan was about to give her a smart answer when the first guest arrived. It was Mrs. Oppenheimer. Ethan stood as she entered the room.

"No need to get up for me, young man," she said. When she smiled, Ethan noticed that she had several teeth missing and the ones she did have were turning black. He also took note of the fact that it seemed she had lost a good deal of hair between the time she checked in and now, and her dress looked even more disheveled than when he'd first seen her.

"Will your husband be joining us?" asked Linda.

"Oh yes. He's just a little slow, that's all." The old lady winked and flashed another tooth-decayed smile. The corners of her mouth turned upward as she did, giving her the same look that

Seuss's Grinch had when he *'thought up a lie and thought it up quick'.*

Ethan rounded the table in order to pull out a chair for her. As he got close he could smell an acrid odor coming off her body. It was much stronger than just normal body odor and there was something very familiar about it. It wasn't until he was seated again that he recognized it. It smelled like a mix of formaldehyde and decay. He was considering whether or not to mention it when her husband shuffled into the room and sat beside her.

They were sitting across from Linda and Ethan, one chair removed from the head of the table. When the old man seated himself, his jacket swayed open, briefly disclosing the mold that was embedded in his formerly white, now grayish, shirt. His eyes were glassy and vacant and the age lines on his face seemed to be flaking open, dropping sloughs of skin like dandruff.

"I hope I haven't kept everyone waiting too long," he said, apologetically, but his voice was flat and devoid of any emotion.

Linda was about to tell him that he was right on time when Miss Willowbrand came through the doorway. She was a young woman, in her late twenties Ethan estimated, and she walked with a flourish. The blue tank-top she was wearing was tucked neatly inside her jean shorts. Her legs were long and tanned and her blond hair hung down and fanned out across her shoulders.

"Hello everyone," she said as she entered. "I'm Kathy." She walked over to the head of the table and pulled out the chair. "Anyone sitting here?"

"Please," said Linda, motioning to the chair. "Wherever you like."

She sat down and adjusted her seat. Her tank-top was perfectly fitted; it exposed enough bosom to be inviting but not so much as to be slutty. Leaning forward she propped her elbows on the table and clasped her hands together underneath her chin. A broad, vivacious smile covered the lower half of her face, accenting her softly angled jawline.

"We're the Oppenheimers," said the old man, waving a finger back and forth between him and his wife. "We're old, but still kickin." He flashed a smile, exposing his lower gum line which was devoid of teeth.

Kathy did her best to try and hide the grimace that swept across her face, but failed miserably. She just couldn't hide the repulsion she felt.

Ethan intervened before the old man could say anything. "Hi Kathy, I'm Ethan Kennedy."

"Wow," she said, "a Sheriff. Are you staying here, too?"

"No. I just stopped by for the lunch. Believe me, Linda's cooking and sandwiches are much better than those at the diner. But please-" he held up a hand, "- Don't tell Mike Alonzo I said so." He let a small smile spread across his lips as he gave a quick wink.

"If I may ask my dear," said Mrs. Oppenheimer leaning in a little closer to her, "how old are you? I mean ... you're sooo pretty."

Kathy's face flushed instantly. She instinctively batted her eyelashes a few times the way young girls often do unconsciously when reveling in attention.

"I'm twenty-six." She grinned. "Actually, I'll be twenty-seven next month. This is my first vacation alone." She looked over at Linda. "I found this place in a vacation guide and it just looked so awfully cute that I had to come. In September I'll be starting on my graduate degree, so I was really looking forward to getting in a little sun and fun first."

"How lovely, my dear," said Mrs. Oppenheimer, "That's just wonderful. Don't you all think that's just wonderful?" She nodded her head all the way around the table, looking from one person to the other as if to confirm that they all thought it was wonderful. "And just where do you hail from, sweetie?"

"Oh, I'm from the great state of Georgia. Born and raised in Augusta. This is only my second time up north. Last year, my best friend, Jeannie DeCarlo, and I went up to New York to see a play. *Les Miserable.* It was wonderful. But I have to tell you, the people in New York are rude. I don't think I'll ever go back there."

"Well I'm sure you'll find the folks around here pleasant enough," broke in Mr. Oppenheimer. "It's the nicest town I think I've ever been in. Honestly."

"And where are you folks from," asked Ethan.

The old man laughed. "Is that an official question, officer? Are you gonna run a make on us and see if we're wanted. You know, ma and I are pretty dangerous folks." He let out a loud and hearty laugh. "Put that Capone feller and his assoichits t'shame, we would."

Kathy broke out in a peel of laughter, her whole body shaking. "I bet ... I bet ... I bet you're meaner than old Ma Barker and family." She slapped the table with her hand.

"Actually," said the old man, pushing to his feet, "we *are*!"

There was something in the way he had said it that brought Ethan's instincts on line. He slipped his hand down and flipped the snap open on his holster. A moment later everything spun out of control.

The lady burst from her chair, knocking it over behind her, and stood beside her husband. The skin peeled away from their faces like the hide off a baseball. The muscle and sinew that covered the skulls seemed to grow a grey leathery covering that reminded Ethan of the concrete statues in the park. Their mouths gaped open as they both hissed and snarled. The rotted teeth the old lady had displayed earlier were now longer and pointed.

Kathy screamed, as did Linda. Ethan drew his Glock 17 as he rose to his feet, but the old lady was faster than she looked. In the blink of an eye, her left hand shot out and grabbed Kathy by the throat while her right hand tugged Kathy's arm out of its socket.

Before Ethan could get off his first shot, the old man leaped across the table, grabbing him by his gun wrist and shirt collar. Instinctively, Ethan's free hand clamped down on the old man's face, finger's splayed, and pushed him back.

Linda jumped up and backed up against the wall trying to fight the shock that she felt setting in. At first, she just watched as Ethan and the old man struggled. She couldn't bring herself to look at the old lady and Kathy, who was slumped in her chair, passed out. The old lady looked at Linda and bared her teeth.

"You're next sweetie," she growled, "but I have to enjoy this tasty young thing first." She bent over and tore a hunk of flesh and muscle from Kathy's throat. Blood shot up to the ceiling in a red geyser, and Linda could hear the squishing sound of the lady chewing on Kathy's tissue.

The old man pushed his head forward with all his might, trying to break the face-hold Ethan had on him. Ethan could feel his mouth opening and closing, desperately trying to dig what teeth he had left into Ethan's palm. Dropping his hand from the old man's face and quickly grabbing him by the front of his suit jacket, Ethan stepped backwards, dropped his right leg out from under him and placed his left foot in the old man's midsection. As he rolled onto his back he pushed off with his left foot, sending the old man flying over his head and thumping against the wall. The moment he had released him, he rolled onto his stomach and fired four shots, all of them striking the old man in the forehead.

The old lady let out a long squeal, followed by a growling, hissing snarl. Her eyes were fiery red and her chin was dripping with the blood she'd been lapping from the young girl.

Ethan whirled and pulled the trigger three more times. The bullets slammed into the old lady's chest driving her backward a few steps. A thick blackish liquid oozed out of the 10mm holes.

"Ethan!" Linda shouted.

Ethan turned just in time to see the man struggle to his feet. Most of his head was gone. One eye hung loosely on his cheek and a black-green clump of brain matter dripped down the side of what was left of his face.

"C'mon," yelled Ethan, grabbing Linda by the hand. He dragged her out the door and through the kitchen. By the time they'd reached the screen door the old man was staggering through the kitchen doorway, still growling and snarling. Ethan hit him again, four shots to the chest, hoping it would slow him up enough for them to get clear. The old man staggered backwards, lost his balance and fell.

Outside, Ethan looked at Linda. Her face was white and there was a vacant look on it. He knew if he didn't do something quickly she was going to pass out.

Keeping his eye on the screen door, he reached out and grabbed her cheek between his thumb and forefinger and pinched it as hard as he could. She let out a little yelp, but the color started coming back into her face.

"Let's get to the radio car," he started to say but was interrupted by the sound of breaking glass. When he looked around the corner, he saw that the old lady had burst through the dining room window, cutting off their route to the front and his car. A few moments later he heard the kitchen screen door bang open.

Turning quickly, he fired again, and again he drove the old man backward.

"The woods. We can lose them in the woods, I think," cried Linda. She was pointing toward the left of the house where the upper edge of Fairmount Park encroached on her property.

Ethan grabbed her by the hand and they ran toward the tree line. As he pushed Linda through the stand of bushes that edged the property, he looked behind. The old man and lady were standing together looking at them. The old lady was trying to push what was left of the old man's brains back into what was left of his head. When she saw them looking she stopped and pointed a finger at them. Then she let out a long, bellowing hiss that was accompanied by a greenish cloud of foul-smelling smoke.

Ethan and Linda disappeared into the thickets. He had been tempted to take a few more shots but realized it would have been worthless. At that point, all that really mattered was getting away.

"C'mon, dear," said the old woman to her husband. "Let's go finish the young girl. That'll make you feel much better. Well finish her together. I'll let you have all you want." As she led her husband back into the house, she craned her head back over her shoulder towards the woods and shouted: "Y'all come back now, hea!"

CHAPTER 46

The first three rooms Jack searched were empty. At the end of the corridor, the hallway L-ed off to the right. The door to the room just before the hallway's break hung ajar. Jack eased up to it, his back against the wall. He swung the door open and dropped his center of gravity so that he was crouching. This room was empty, too.

He peered around the corner, keeping his body low to the floor. There was an odd sound coming from the far end. It sounded like the hum of a high-tension wire. The buzzing reverberated down the length of the hallway and Jack could feel its bass-like vibrations on the floorboards.

Out front, Robertson was leaning against the cruiser with his arms folded across his chest. He knew he was supposed to wait there until Jack's back-up arrived, but it aggravated him to be standing there doing nothing. After debating the issue with himself, he decided to take a look around the property from the outside, while Jack checked out the inside.

"Kill two birds with one stone, I believe the saying goes," he muttered to himself. The far right of the B & B was comprised primarily of a tiered rock garden. In the center stood a wooden, arched trellis that supported a fully grown Wisteria. On either side were three Lilac bushes. To the front of the garden, circles of marigolds were ringed in scalloped brick. Between them, rows of orange and red fire-bush plants blazed, giving the whole garden a staggered height look.

Robertson rounded the corner and stopped to look around. From where he stood it didn't look like anything was amiss. The sweet smell of the flowers wafted through the hot, choked air making it seem a bit more pleasant to be outside despite the heat. Robertson drew in a deep breath of the fresh scent.

At the back of the building, he paused to look cautiously around the corner. He knew that if Jack caught him back here away from the cruiser there'd be hell to pay. But he just couldn't stand the thoughts of waiting by the car like a useless hood ornament.

With nothing in sight, he stepped around the corner into the rear yard. Hedges of Forsythia lined one side, sweeping around to meet the edge of the woods. A small patio jutted off the back end of the building covered by an overhanging porch roof. A white glider stood silently on one side and on the other side of the entrance to the kitchen was a covered gas grill.

Robertson walked around toward the kitchen door and then stopped. On the grass in front of him was a gooey clump of soft material. He bent down to get a better look. He couldn't believe what he was looking at. As a doctor and medical examiner, it wasn't too difficult to identify the brain matter that was smeared on the back lawn.

"What the hell?"   His first impression was that someone had suffered a serious accident.   But closer examination led him to the conclusion that the brain material he was looking at had been embalmed.   It was part of the temporal lobe and most of the cells were crenated.   From the small amount available it was hard to tell if it were human or animal.   Instinctively, however, Robertson was sure it was human.   After all, how many animals get embalmed.   The real questions were: From whom did it come and what happened here?

Robertson stood up and wiped his hands together.   Now he had a decision to make.   Should he go inside and find Jack to let him know what he found; should he continue his investigation around the property, maybe finding more evidence, or should he just go back to the car and wait?   Being the inquisitive person he was, he opted for the first scenario.

He worked his way to the back door, ensuring that he wasn't corrupting any possible evidence – footprints, more tissue, anything.   Using a handkerchief, he pulled the screen door open just wide enough for him to squeeze through without touching it.   The inside didn't look any better than the outside.   There were more pieces of tissue spread across the kitchen floor leading into the other room.   Bits of bone and more brain matter dotted the tile; there was also some smearing, which told Robertson that someone had walked through the mess he was looking at.

Sidestepping the human debris, he made his way back through the dining room and into the lobby. He paused to listen, thinking or hoping that he might hear Jack. The place was totally quiet. He moved to the bottom of the stairs, placing a hand on the banister. A quick glance out the front window told him that Jack was probably still upstairs and that the back-up he'd requested hadn't arrived yet.

Robertson thought about following Jack upstairs but decided that he'd continue his search outside. He still had the other side of the building to scout out and, considering what he'd already found, who knew what might be out there. He took one last look up the steps and then turned to go. As he did, he thought he caught a glimpse of something dart across the upper landing. But when he turned back and looked, there was nothing there. For the briefest of moments, he could have sworn he saw an old lady peering through the banister spindles. A flash of grey hair and then nothing.

Craning his neck, with one foot on the bottom step, he tried to see a little further down the upper hallway. Nothing was moving. He climbed two more steps to get a better look but there was no one there to be seen. Satisfied that it had probably just been a floater he'd seen (he got them occasionally), he went back outside.

As Robertson was examining the brain matter in the back yard, Jack was crouched at the junction of the hallways upstairs. With the buzzing sound ringing in his ears, he eased himself around the corner and sidled down to the first doorway: Room 225. It was closed, and when he gently turned the handle, he discovered it was also locked. For the moment, he'd let this one go. The buzzing sound seemed to be coming from the next room: Room 227. He slid down next to it, his back planted firmly against the wall.

Jack turned the knob. It was unlocked. The slight click the latch made on opening was drowned out by the buzzing noise coming from inside. Steeling himself for the unknown, Jack flung open the door and swung around into the doorway, dropping down to one knee, his .357 out in front.

He was driven backward. The room was thick with huge, black flies. The cloud of them was so dense that Jack couldn't even see two feet into the room. They immediately swarmed him, entangling themselves in his hair; crawling up his nose and trying to get into his eyes and mouth. He could feel them filling up his ears. In the time it took him to get to his feet he was completely encased in them from head to toe.

They were horseflies, and their biting and stinging was already drawing blood on all Jack's exposed skin. The pain was substantial but not crippling, but worse than that, he couldn't breathe; his nose was clogged with them and he didn't dare open his mouth.

His hands pawed at his face, the .357 still clutched tightly, trying to pull them off. He wiped handful after handful off, only to have them replaced by new ones. Hundreds of thousands buzzed around him, landing on top of him – landing on top of the ones that were already on him – they were getting heavy and making it difficult to move.

Jack ran back down the hall and shouldered into the locked room. He could feel his chest tightening. Crashing into the bathroom, he jumped in the tub and turned the shower on. At first, it didn't seem to help much. But eventually, with the hot turned up, most of the flies flew off. Others ended up being washed down the drain. When he'd finally gotten them all off, the tub was an inch thick, at least, with fly carcasses, and the drain was solidly clogged with them.

Jack leaned back against the shower wall, the hot water still cascading down on him, and tried to catch his breath. A mix of blood and water ran down the shower walls and soaked into the pile of dead flies at his feet. His face and arms looked like someone had taken a belt sander to them and the pain from the hot water was almost unbearable.

After a few moments, when he was sure the flies were gone, he turned the hot off and the cold on. The pain was agonizing, but the cold felt much better on his raw nerves than the hot had.

Jack stepped out of the fly-filled tub and sat down on the toilet. His arm accidentally bumped up against the wall and he let out a sharp yell. His breathing was still labored and his strength was spent. He sat there, panting and gritting his teeth from the pain. He wanted to get up and look in the mirror to see just how much damage was done, but was afraid to. He could feel the blood dripping from his ears and running down his neck. *Damned good thing I have a doctor with me*, he thought, as he sat there recovering. The thought that followed on the heels of that one was: *What the fuck was that?*

CHAPTER 47

Ernie Johnson woke up and turned over expecting to find Peggy in bed next to him. The bed was empty. He sat up and arranged the pillows behind him before leaning back again. He could still smell her perfume clinging to his skin and his thoughts were awash with the passions of the previous night. All he wanted to think about was how her skin felt against his; how he felt when he was inside her and how she felt when she was on top of him. That was all he wanted to think about, but his mind had other plans. The book store. The bookstore and the horrid man with the copy of Milton's *Paradise Lost*.

He recalled, in vivid detail, waking up on the floor of the store, the book lying on his lap. He could still hear the man-thing's horrible laughter in his head. A chill ran up his spine and he tried harder to think of the woman. He closed his eyes and concentrated on her shape, how her breasts felt in his hands. He leaned over and pushed his nose into the pillow where she'd slept hoping to catch another whiff of her perfume or hair spray.

As soon as his nose touched the pillow he drew his head back. His stomach churned and he barely got his head over the side of the bed before throwing up. The smell in the pillow was putrid. It smelled to Ernie like the pillowcase had been saturated in rancid grease from rotted bacon. When that image came to him, he gagged again and hurled for a second time.

He crawled out of bed and staggered to the bathroom just in time to unload again in the sink. With his head buried in the marble bowl of the wash sink, he reached up and turned on the cold water, letting it wash away what he'd just emptied from his stomach. When he felt strong enough, he lifted his head and splashed it with a few handfuls of water. He looked in the mirror and staggered backward, bumped into the lip of the tub and would have fallen if it hadn't been for the glass doors of the shower.

Ernie raised his hand and gently probed his face with his fingertips while staring into the mirror. Huge reddish-brown welts had popped up all over his face. Some were turning black. As he looked, his arms also began to break out in them and then his chest. He could feel his stomach beginning to rumble again and knelt down in front of the toilet, throwing the seat up so hard that it banged off the tank and thumped back down onto his fingers.

He knelt there, waiting. His breathing was getting more shallow by the minute and he could feel his chest tightening like someone was sitting on it.

"Oh my god; oh my god; I'm having a heart attack," he yelled. He wanted to get to the phone but his stomach had other ideas. He let go again, filling the toilet with blood and chunks of tissue. He couldn't stop. As soon as one wave was over another began. In between, all he could do was to try to breathe before the next wave took him. Seven times he vomited, each time twisting his insides harder than the last, until he finally started to dry-heave. When it was through, the toilet was filled to the rim with water, blood and floating bits of, what Ernie took to be, his stomach.

Placing both hands on the lip of the toilet bowl he pushed himself upright. When he'd managed to stand, a wave of dizziness took him and he had to kneel back down. Not wanting to look at it anymore, he reached out and flushed. He could see his reflection in the refilling bowl. His face was now covered in blistering pustules and his eyes were swelling shut.

"Having a rough morning, honey?" came a voice from behind him. "Too much fun last night? Don't worry, you're probably just ... *dead* ... tired." Then the room filled with cackling, hissing laughter.

Ernie turned his head. It was the best he could manage; standing up was out of the question. Peggy was standing in the doorway. The only thing she had on was a pair of white lace panties. Her hands were on her hips and her soft brown hair hung down over one breast.

"And I thought you'd be up for a little fun this morning. But look at you. You look like a man that's spent the whole night drinking, not fucking!" She wagged a finger at him. "C'mere sugar. I think I want some more."

"I can't. I'm sick. What happened to me?" he stammered.

"Oh pasha. You're just fine. What are you going on about." She raised a hand and drew a circle in the air and then a star. "Now c'mon. The morning's wasting and I wanna fuck again."

Suddenly, Ernie felt better. In fact, he felt better than he ever had in his life. He stood up and turned to look at her.

"What happened to me? What'd you just do to make me feel better? What's going on?"

"Too many questions!" she shouted. "Get over here and fuck me!" She extended her arm and slowly drew her palm in toward herself as if beckoning someone far away. As she did, Ernie felt himself being pulled in her direction. He stumbled forward until he was right up against her. The minute their bodies connected, his arms went to her waist. She drew him in closer and they started kissing. She backed up and pulled him down on top of her.

"Fuck me, Ernie. Fuck me now! Fuck me hard!" She pulled his head down and pushed it against her right breast. She wrapped her legs around him and he slipped easily inside her.

After five minutes, she pushed him away and climbed up onto her knees. "Do me doggie style," she commanded.

The sweat rolled off Ernie's chest, arms, and back and dripped down into his eyes as he pumped her. When she'd had enough, she rolled over onto her back and pulled him back down on top of her. "Don't stop, Ernie. Don't you dare stop. You don't know how long it's been since I've been fucked good. It's been a long time."

Panting, Ernie said, "It was just last night."

"I know that. I meant before. I'm making up for lost time. I've been locked in that stupid casket for sooo long. Now I need what every woman needs. A really good fucking."

Ernie pushed himself up onto his hands. "What are you talking about? What do you mean, locked in a casket? Are you feeling ok?"

"I mean, Ernie, my dear ... that I've been dead for at least fifty years. Maybe longer, I'm not really sure of the date."

Ernie jumped up. "You're crazy."

"Maybe. But I'm a good fuck, aren't I? Now get back down here and finish me." She started laughing.

Ernie watched as the skin on her face started to shrivel and flake off. Beneath, the muscle too began to rot and peel away in shreds exposing black and moldy bone. Two and three at a time, her teeth dropped out and the bones of her fingers pushed through the receding flesh.

"C'mon Ernie. Hurry. Finish me. I want another orgasm." She kept cackling and laughing as she disintegrated. The laughter started to fade. Her chest caved inward, her ribs clacking together as they dropped to the mattress.

"You're a big disappointment," was the last thing she got out before everything dried into a pile of ash-colored dust.

Ernie stood there in shock. His eyes rolled back in his head and he passed out.

CHAPTER 48

It wasn't until a little past noon that Curtis Lattimore roused himself from sleep. He'd spent the better part of the night enjoying the pot he'd received from his new boss. Bleary-eyed, he pushed himself to a sitting position on the couch. The leaves of his pot plants dangled down in front of him and he thought about starting his day off with a quick kick-start. But a voice inside him told him he'd better not. So he forced himself to go take a shower.

He toweled himself off and thought about what he might want to do today. He also gave considerable consideration to his new partnership. It was somewhat distasteful, having always operated alone, to now be under someone else's thumb. But at the same time, he knew that there was going to be a great deal of power to be derived from his new association, and *that* he liked very much.

Throwing on an old pair of tattered jeans and a yellowed T-shirt he pulled from the hamper, he worked his last Marlboro from the pack and lit it. He let the cigarette dangle from his lips as he cinched up his belt and pulled on his boots. He had the feeling it was going to be a better day than he had at first thought. When he couldn't find his comb, he ran his fingers through his long brown hair and called it good.

He opened the front door; sunlight assaulted his eyes and he had to squint to keep from being blinded. He stood there on the stoop looking up and down the street. A quick glace to his right brought his eyes to his Harley, parked at an angle behind his primer-splotched Camry.

"Ahh. What to do today? What to do?" He unlocked the chain that secured his Harley to the bumper of his car and rolled it up. Then he took the padlock off the forks and turned the Sportster over. It rumbled to life, vibrating the windows of the nearest houses. He'd taken the baffles out and a quick twist of the accelerator filled the street with a thundering sound. Neighbors peered out from behind curtains, but no one wanted to challenge Curtis.

Curtis lived in a middle row house of faded red brick, called townhouses in better areas, but in this neighborhood it was just a row home. Trash blew freely up the streets and sidewalks, tumbling and swirling in the hot breeze. Windows were crusted with dirt, dust, and car exhaust and the air was thick and stifling. Empty trash cans lined the streets, some rolling back and forth on their sides like wounded soldiers.

The town's attempt at beautification took the form of emaciated Japanese Maples spaced out every fifty feet and encircled with angled sand-colored bricks. Aside from any plants that the neighbors might have in window boxes, it was the only natural color to be seen.

Cutis patted fruitlessly at his shirt, suddenly remembering that he was just finishing his last cigarette. First order of business then would be to go buy some more. There were a lot of things Curtis could do without, but a pack of smokes was not one of them.

Swinging his leg over the bike, Curtis knocked the kick-stand back, stepped on the shifter and roared down Cotton Street, leaving a trail of blue smoke behind him. At the end of the block, he came to a rolling stop. In his car, he would have just barreled right through the stop sign, but bikes were not as forgiving, so he begrudgingly semi-obeyed stop signs. Turning left he headed out toward Main Street and the EasyMart, the closest place to get smokes.

At the corner of Ash and Main, he had to wait while one of the Sheriff's cars shot by, lights flashing and sirens wailing. The passing patrol car made him wonder what the cops were doing about the EasyMart robbery he'd pulled off and the dead bitch he'd left behind. Since nobody had come knocking on his door, he figured he was in the clear. *And besides*, he thought, *I have my new friend to look out for me. If he needs shit from me, it's unlikely he'd let me take the fall for the EasyMart job.*

That thought made him wonder if he shouldn't just hold the place up again. Why pay for smokes when you can get 'em for free? But again, he had the feeling that his new boss wanted him to keep a low profile. *Oh well, it doesn't matter, even if I pay for 'em, they're kind of free. I'll just be paying the fools with their own money.* He laughed out loud. To Curtis, there wasn't a better feeling in the world than feeling that you were getting over on everyone.

He wheeled into the EasyMart and pulled up in front. A car pulled into the space beside him and he gave the driver a long hard stare, telling him without words that he'd better not even think about scratching his bike with his door. The man in the red Suzuki quickly averted his eyes, which told Curtis everything he needed to know about the guy.

Pussy, he thought as he cocked the front wheel to the left and climbed off the bike. *This whole shitty town is full of pussies.* He pushed past an old man struggling to get the door open while holding onto his walker. For a brief moment, he held the door as if he were going to let the guy in. But as soon as the old man took his hands off the door and went to move his walker, Curtis let the door slam shut, knocking the man backwards and the walker out of his hands.

Still laughing about it, Curtis walked up to the counter, asked for two packs of Marlboro and the most recent Playboy, which they kept behind and out of reach of the children. Curtis didn't bother with any of the standard accouterments of cycle riding like leather jackets and such, so he stuffed the magazine down the front of his shirt.

When he turned to leave, the old man whom he'd slammed the door on was standing behind him. He looked down at him and laughed. "Outta my way, grandpa, or I'll knock ya over again."

The old man gazed up at him and Curtis could see the fire in his eyes. He respected that, but also found it funny.

"Fuck you, asshole," the old man snorted.

Curtis's face grew red as anger swept over him. He reached out and palmed the old man's face, preparing to shove him backward. But before he could, a sharp pain shot through his body. The old man had swung the leg of the walker up into his testicles as hard as he could. Curtis doubled over clutching at his groin.

Looking down at him, the old man repeated, "Fuck you, asshole." He then stepped past him and made his purchase at the counter. The clerk said nothing, but smiled a big toothy grin at the old man.

Just before the old man made it out the door, Curtis recovered himself and shot forward intending to grab him by the back of the neck. He stretched his arm out and then suddenly found himself on the floor. When he looked up, two large men were standing over him. From their appearance, there was no mistaking that they were truckers. Their arms looked like swollen balloons and their muscles rippled as they each reached down and grabbed him by a shoulder.

"You're not a very nice person, are you?" one of them asked. "Maybe you need a lesson in manners that your mama never gave you."

"Please, please," yelled the clerk. "Not in the store. Not in the store."

The two men holding Curtis glanced over at the frail little man behind the counter and nodded. Then they dragged Curtis out to the parking lot. The bigger of the two took Curtis by the front of his shirt and lifted him up so that he was just barely standing on his toes.

"We'll give you a freebie this time, butthead. But if we catch you pulling any of that shit again, we'll kick your ass up around your ears.

You'll be wearing it as a hat for the rest of your fuckin life. Got it?"

Curtis wanted to fight, but there was no way he could win this one. "Yeah. I got it," he said, the indignation in his tone not hidden. "I got it."

"Good", said the other trucker. The one that had a grip on him gave him a quick shake then pushed him to the ground. Curtis was boiling and it took all his better judgment to remain quiet and sitting still until the truckers left.

He glanced around; the old man was just pulling out of the parking lot. Curtis shot him the finger, then quickly looked over his shoulder to see if the truckers had seen him. He was surprised when he turned around and the old man was giving him the finger back as he pulled into Main Street traffic and zipped away.

Before Curtis could make it to his bike, the old man disappeared around the corner. Curtis reasoned that he'd be gone before he could catch up to him, so the best thing to do right now would be to just let it go. "But I'll see you again, you old shit," he shouted. He revved up the bike and shot out onto the street, tires squealing as he laid the bike over to make the turn. Quickly righting the bike and laying it over to the other side, he shot around a lady pushing a baby coach across the intersection. He was so close that she could feel the breeze the bike created and its loud engine started the baby crying.

Three blocks down, Curtis pulled into the beer distributor's and bought a cold six-pack. He had enough room in his front fork-pouch for three of them and the other three he stuffed into his shirt along with the magazine. The cold bottles against his belly made him jump, but when he got used to the feel, it felt good on this hot July afternoon. He considered going back home to drink them but that idea didn't really appeal to him. He ended up heading for the park – the same park where Tyler Berryman had been found dead, and the same park where Frank and Charlie had gone missing.

As he shot down Bell's Mill Road doing seventy, the wind blew his hair back, his long bangs flapping wildly against his forehead. Pennsylvania did not have helmet laws and that pleased Curtis a lot. The only protection he ever wore was his sunglasses, and those, only because he needed to keep the bugs and sun out of his eyes.

At the bottom of the hill he turned into the parking lot and jammed on the breaks. The bike slid, kicking up dust and spraying gravel across the lot and into the bushes. He was a little disappointed when he found that there was no one there to see it. But it didn't really matter. It felt good doing it.

Once off the bike, he locked it up, snagged all the beer and headed down to the creek. At the water's edge he sat down and pried the top off the first one. It didn't take him more than three swallows before he was opening the second. Halfway through the third one he was starting to really relax. He pulled off his boots and socks and thrust his feet into the cool, muddy water.

A pair of Mallards swam by and he just couldn't resist chucking a handful of gravel at them. They squawked as the pellets rained down on them and then took to flight, sending ripples lapping across the creek. Curtis just laughed, kicking his feet and splashing.

By the time he'd made it to his fifth beer, he was starting to feel drowsy. It was fairly cool down by the water, despite the humidity, and a nice nap might feel really good. As he chugged down the last of the beer, he noticed an odd sound. It was a loud buzzing. It sounded like insects, maybe mosquitoes or bees or flies. He sat up and looked around but didn't see anything, but the sound kept growing in intensity.

A huge swarm of black flies came over the top of the bushes behind him. There were thousands of them and their black bulk momentarily blotted out the sun from overhead. They swarmed around his face in circles, but none of them touched him. He swatted at them, trying to get to his feet, but he kept slipping in the mud. When he finally did manage to stand, the flies made several more circles around him and then flew off. At least, the majority of them flew off. A dozen or so landed at his feet.

His first instinct was to try to squash them, but he knew he wouldn't be quick enough. He looked down.

"Psst. C'mere." The voice was tiny and weak, and Curtis turned around with a jerk. There was no one behind him.

"Psst! Idiot ... down here."

Curtis looked down. One of the flies was larger than all the rest and it had a face. It was the face he'd seen last night. There was something very comical about it. Curtis started to laugh. At his feet was a large fly with the face akin to a ZZ Top member. And it was calling to him.

CHAPTER 49

Unable to sleep, Jasper Collins had spent the night in an Old Crow bottle. It wasn't until a little after three that he'd passed out. There were no dreams for Jasper, only a sonorous, liquor-induced, temporary coma.

When he finally opened his eyes, the daylight was streaming in the open windows. His mouth tasted like he'd eaten rotten eggs and his head was throbbing. It was an effort to pull himself to a sitting position. A quick glance at the clock told him it was past 1 P.M. He'd missed work and was half wondering why his boss hadn't called him and half not caring in the least.

Dragging himself out of bed, he staggered to the shower, bouncing off the bathroom door jam on his way in. Now his shoulder hurt as much as his head. He'd had mornings like this before, although never on a workday and never quite this bad. Every fiber of his being was rebelling against movement.

Jasper sank down into the tub letting the warm water rain down on him. He didn't even have the strength to stand. Not bothering to wash, he just sat there until he ran out of hot water, fumbled his way out of the tub and dried himself off. When he pulled his work shirt on it clung to his body in the spots that were still wet. He didn't care.

In the kitchen, he poured himself a glass of orange juice, drank it down and was going to pour a second. It was too much trouble. He upended the plastic bottle and drained what was left of the yellow liquid and then tossed the empty jug into the sink. The three feet over to the trash can was too far to go.

By the time he had himself ready to go to work, it was after two. He considered just calling the day a loss, but he'd never missed a day's work before and the idea of it didn't sit well with him. Despite his condition, he still had his self-respect and work ethic. Blinking his eyes several times to bring them into focus, he dialed the cemetery office. When the secretary answered, he asked for his boss, Mark Hurlehey, and explained the situation. He told him he'd be in shortly and apologized profusely.

Mark wasn't wild about the no-call, no-show that Jasper had pulled; it was totally against company policy and grounds for immediate dismissal. But Jasper's perfect attendance record to this point made it a little easier to overlook. He told Jasper to just take the rest of the day and recover; and then he admonished him not to ever repeat it, emphasizing the fact that he would not be so tolerant the next time.

When Jasper hung up he was confused. He'd never had a day off during the week that wasn't a scheduled holiday and wasn't sure what he was going to do with himself. Despite the hangover, just sitting around wasn't Jasper's cup of tea. Besides, he didn't want to remain idle. That would give him too much time to think about yesterday, last night and his liquor benefactor.

"Please, please," he screamed, "get out of my head; get out of my head and leave me alone." He dropped into his worn-out easy chair, cradling his head in his hands. Fear, anguish, and despair flooded in and he burst into tears. For nearly an hour he sat there rocking back and forth sobbing and pleading to be left alone.

By three-thirty he'd run out of tears and just sat there rocking back and forth. His nose was running profusely and he had to keep wiping it with the back of his hand. At some point, he looked down and noticed the crusted snot that was smeared from his fingers to his wrists. More than anything else, this jolted him out of his sullenness. He stood up, went into the bathroom and took a proper shower.

When he stepped out he was feeling better. Redressing, he decided that he should go to the cemetery anyway. He didn't know why, but he felt that that was where he was supposed to be. If he hurried, he could get there before they locked the gates. There was a little access road in the back that was hardly ever used and he could hide there until everyone was gone.

On his way out the door he stopped and grabbed a couple of cans of Coke from the refrigerator. He'd thought about taking a few bottles of Crow but dismissed the idea almost as soon as he'd had it. His head was just starting to feel better and there was no sense in adding insult to injury. For Jasper, the hair of the dog shit didn't work. He'd been there before, done that and ended up only feeling worse. So off he went to the cemetery with his Coke.

Safely tucked away on the access road and obscured by the line of mausoleums that stood watch over the entrance, Jasper sat and waited for dark. He had no idea why he was there or what it was that he was waiting for. He only knew that he had to be there, that something had drawn him there and that something was going to happen tonight that he was supposed to – to what? He didn't know. But it didn't matter; he was here and here he'd stay for whatever might come.

Not adept at sitting still for any length of time, he fidgeted. He pawed at the stubble that covered his sharply angled jaw, turned the radio on, then off, on again, then off again, tapped his fingers on the steering wheel, wound the window down, then up, then down again and shifted from cheek to cheek in the seat. Nightfall was not coming fast enough to suit Jasper Collins.

CHAPTER 50

On the other side of town in a dark basement, Carlton Wedgemore was also waiting for night to fall. He'd filled his day to this point thinking about how he was going to get back at all the people in his life who had abused him and how satisfying it was going to be. Images of the bullies of his past suffering, dying and pleading for his mercy – a mercy he was not going to let them have – filled his morning and afternoon. From time to time he'd let out a short burst of laughter while chiding and tormenting his hapless victims, his voice echoing through the empty hollowness of the stone basement.

"Oh, you want me to stop do you?" he'd say, imagining one of his former tormenters in front of him. "Well I'm not going to. Oh no. Did you stop? Did you cut *me* a break way back when. I *doan theen* so. Now it's your turn, amigo. So just shut up and take what's coming to you." Then the image would shift to a different nemesis and he'd begin all over with a new, more sadistic scenario that would ensure their humiliation and death.

When Carlton heard the scuffling and banging about coming from upstairs, his first thought was that someone was coming to steal his prized possession. The noise brought him instantly out of his reveries. Clutching tightly to the sword handle that he'd been fondling the whole time, he scooted over to the darkest corner he could find and huddled down, hoping the noise above would soon stop. He waited in the darkness, not really hearing the screams and cries for help; only hearing the banging.

Dust from the rafters rained down on him every now and then. He didn't care. He clutched the sword to his breast, rubbing it, protecting it. His mind raced as he tried to come up with a plan as to what to do when they came for it. They wouldn't get it, of that much he was sure. He'd defend it with his life.

Anger started to well up inside him. It was the kind of anger that the meek and weak sometimes feel when they've finally had more than they could stand. It was the kind of anger that made them dangerous. It was a pure fury.

Forcing himself to get up, Carlton made his way over to the little tool bench in the far corner. He searched through the implements, looking for just the right tool. A large Phillips-head screwdriver went into his back pocket. *Not good enough*, he thought. He continued rummaging around until he found what he thought could do the most damage in the shortest amount of time. He found a battery-operated reciprocating saw. Flipping the switch, it buzzed to life, assuring him that the batteries were charged and ready to go.

With his weapon in hand, he thought about going upstairs to meet the thieves, to face them head-on. The idea fizzled when he reached the bottom of the steps.

"No. Not up there. Down here. Yes, down here in the dark. That's where I'll get them. They'll not get you. Oh no. I'll see them all cut to pieces first." He continued muttering and swearing curses at the unknown thieves above who'd come to take away his possession. "Too bright. It's too bright down here. They'll see me."

Taking the end of the saw he smashed the bulbs out of their overhead sockets. Pieces of glass flew out in all directions, some of them embedding themselves in Carlton's cheek and forehead. He didn't care. All that mattered was protecting what was rightfully his.

He closed his eyes, trying to help them adjust to the darkness faster. When the thieves came down, he'd be able to see and they wouldn't. And then he'd get them. It didn't matter how many, he'd chop them all to bits. Every last one of them. On opening his eyes, he found he could just barely make out the vague shapes that made up the items in his basement. An oblong shadow here, a dark patch of squares there. He was ready. By the time they found him down here he'd have the advantage.

Looking around, he settled on the stairs. He would hide underneath the stairs and when they came down the steps he'd saw their legs off at the ankles. Nobody was going to get *his* prize. *Nobody's going to rob Carlton Wedgemore and live to tell about it*, he thought. And then he said it out loud. In a low voice, just above a whisper, Carlton kept repeating that sentence to himself. "Nobody's going to rob Carlton Wedgemore and live to tell about it."

Carlton wedged himself underneath the dusty wooden stairs. He waited there, saw in hand and finger on the switch. Seven steps from the bottom, those who would come to take his sword would learn just what a mistake they were making. He flicked the switch and made a quick pass through the open riser of the step – a practice swipe. He was ready; now all he had to do was wait, and then get them – one ... by ... one

***

They entered the park, Alvin Paris in front. The men scanned the area looking for their target, looking for Colleen Slater. Alvin walked ahead with the rest trailing a few feet. He was licking his lips in anticipation of the fun they were going to have with this little bitch. He had one hand stuffed into his trouser pocket and was rubbing himself as he walked.

"Come out, come out wherever you are," was repeated over and over by Charlie Dennis.

"We have something for you," called Bill Palmerton, drawing out the word *for* in a sing-songy voice.

They passed the children's area: sandbox, swing set, monkey bars, not even realizing that there were no children in sight anywhere. All they had on their minds was what they were going to do with Colleen Slater and what *she* was going to do for them.

The five men walked slowly and steadily on, up to the pavilion, across its concrete pad and around the other side. They passed silently past the Men's and Women's bathrooms, pausing to look out over the ball field below. It was empty, so they moved on. Once around the back, they came to the open picnic area. It too was empty, which caused the men to come up short. There wasn't a soul to be seen.

Alvin looked at Frank Watkins who had moseyed up beside him. Confusion could be read on both their faces. When they left the diner they had all had a crystal clear picture of Colleen Slater sitting back here on a park bench just waiting to be used. All throughout their journey, the picture hadn't changed. She should have been here.

They stood together, not knowing exactly what to do. The disruption in the flow of events was giving their minds time to clear. Frank watched as the color drained from Alvin's face, and when he turned around he could see the same happening to the rest. He too started to feel sick in the stomach.

"What the fuck did we do?" asked Alvin of no one in particular.

"I'm gonna be sick," burped Frank, and then turned to vomit.

"We gotta get back there. We gotta let her out." Cried Bill.

"We can't. Oh, sweet Jesus, we can't," said Alvin. "Do you want to go to jail ... or worse? Do you think she's just gonna pop out of the freezer and say: 'hi boys, what a great joke that was?'"

"But we can't leave her in there to die," protested Bill. "We gotta do *something!*"

Alvin reached out and put a hand on Bill's shoulder. "What we gotta do is keep our heads and stick together. I mean, Christ, look what she done to Mike."

"Why the fuck did we do that in the first place?" asked Earl Oprendick. "Why the hell would we do something like that? And what about,

Sally? Why the hell would she wanna kill Mike and ... and-" Earl started to cry. "-and what she did to Fred-" He was sobbing so hard that the rest could hardly understand the words that were coming from his mouth. And they noticed something else – they were no longer in contact with each other mentally. Alvin was the first to realize this.

"Wait a minute," he said, firmly. "What happened to us? Why can't I hear what you're thinking?"

The question snapped the rest out of their remorse for Sally. At that moment, all they wanted to understand was why they lost the gift they had mysteriously been given. They all looked at each other, each trying to reach into the other's mind and failing.

Not really sure what to do, the five men milled around, determined to get their mental communication going again. Without it, they were feeling vulnerable and alone – not a group anymore – just individuals with a terrible secret.

Earl had collapsed onto one of the park benches, not even able to look at the rest. He'd never hurt anyone before. He was one of those good-hearted people who would go out of his way to help a friend – or even a stranger. Most of his free time was spent working with the kids of Special Olympics. He had never married, so that and volunteering at the Adult Learn-to-Read Center filled up his life. He sat on the bench, totally bewildered by what he found himself capable of.

The rest felt the same to one degree or another. Only Alvin, whose mother had always told him he had a mean streak in him, felt very little remorse. His major concern was how to avoid jail time for what he'd done. He *did* feel something for Sally, he wasn't a stone-cold killer, but his concern for himself outweighed everything else. While the others were being battered by their consciences, he spent his time trying to come up with an alibi that they all could use.

Then, as suddenly as it had gone, it was back. Each could hear the other's thoughts, and better yet, they knew exactly where Colleen was. They could all see her in their minds as she hiked up her skirt. She was in the Women's room, and they had passed right by her. In unison, they all turned and faced the pavilion.

"You ready for some fun, boys?" thought Alvin, and they all heard it. *"It's time to get our game on, as the younger folks say."*

In a group, they headed back up the hill toward the bathrooms. Again, Alvin began unconsciously playing with himself. Bill's sobbing turned to lustful panting. He could almost feel Colleen's mouth wrapped around him. By the time they were halfway to their destination, Bill could feel himself dripping into his pants. It was going to be a slam-bang afternoon.

CHAPTER 51

All morning, Willie Peters searched for a playmate but could find none. None of the other kids were at the park or at the ball field. He wanted to go into the woods to see if they were down by the creek fishing, only his mother wouldn't let him. So he hung around the house playing in the tiny front yard. He had his set of Matchbox construction vehicles (passed down from his father) all strung out as he built a miniature roadway.

"Brrruummmm-brummm," the bulldozer climbed the tiny hill pushing its load in front of it. Off to one side, a pair of police cars sat, making sure that passing traffic slowed to the appropriate speed. There was a red ambulance and fire truck parked on the other side of the construction site in case any of the workers got hurt or there was an explosion.

Willie maneuvered the bulldozer to the top of the dirt mound he'd built, raised its bucket and then backed the dump truck up to it so it could take on its payload. After the dozer emptied its bucket into the dump truck, Willie sat back and folded his legs under him Indian-style. He was bored. He wanted to play with someone. He rested his elbows on his knees and his chin in the heels of his hands while he pondered what he should do about it.

He was sitting there deciding when his mother came out. She had her purse strap nestled in the crook of her elbow and was wearing the uniform she wore when she went to work at the dry cleaners. She walked over to Willie and placed a hand on his head.

"Mama has to go to work for a while, honey," she said, rubbing his hair lightly. "Get up and give your mama some sugar."

Willie scrambled to his feet and gave his mother a hug and a kiss.

"Mrs. Washington 'cross the street's gonna keep an eye on ya till yer father gets home. You mind her good and don't be leavin the yard fer nothing. You understand me, young man?"

Willie nodded. "I'm just sittin here playing with m'turcks ma. There ain't nobody 'round to play with today."

Tamika smiled. "You mean ... there *isn't* ... *anybody* ... around to play with, don't you?" She laughed. "I know it's a pain, but it's important. You need to speak right to get yourself a good job, honey."

"Aww, mom! I c'n do that when I havta. Why can't I just talk reglar most o'the time?"

"Because, my little man, bad habits are hard to break. So just stay in the good ones." Tamika's cheeks widened with her smile. "Now give me another kiss, and be a good little man while I'm gone."

"K, mom."

"Yer daddy'll be home by six. So don't you stray outta the yard."

"I know, I know."

Tamika patted him lovingly on the head and then headed off to work. At the end of the block, she turned and waved once more before turning the corner.

Willie waited about ten minutes, kicking listlessly at the dirt road he'd just made. The great debate was on. He figured he had about two hours before his dad would get home. That would give him plenty of time to get to the woods. *Maybe I oughta just stay an hour and a half,* he reasoned, *give myself a safety zone. Yeah, that'll work.*

Willie took a quick look across the street to see if Mrs. Washington was peering out the blinds at him. She'd kept an eye on him before and he knew she was anything but attentive. She was always busy with her garden out back. When he didn't see any movement he figured the coast was clear. He left his trucks where they were and scooted around the back of the house, down the alley and across Mulberry Street. Two more streets and he'd be at the entrance to the old Peaceful Haven Cemetery. Cutting through it would shave five minutes off his travel time. It wasn't something that made Willie feel comfortable, but at least it was still daylight.

Standing in front of the arched gate, Willie stopped. He could feel his blood already running cold and goosebumps popping up on his arms. Nothing, except maybe ghost stories, freaked him out as much as the thoughts of being inside a cemetery. Still in all, though, a quick trot along the fence line and over the back gate and he'd be in the woods and in the clear. He took a deep breath and slowly edged a foot across the boundary between the living and the dead. The second foot followed. He stood there looking and listening, his breathing quickening as he tried to get control of his fears.

"Ok, Willie," he stammered, "just get to the other side and it'll be dope. Plenty of sunshine left to keep all the creepers in the ground." The distant sound of a machine engine, probably a backhoe refilling a grave, came floating through the air. It was a little after 4 P.M. They'd be closing the gates soon. He guessed that there were probably only a handful of people left, mostly just workers.

At a full trot, he started off across the first section, darting past the large headstones and jumping over the smaller ones. The fun of hurdling the stones almost made him forget where he was. He felt the wind on his face as he raced across the grass. Challenging himself, he angled toward the larger stones. Before he knew it, he'd reached the back of the cemetery.

In the shade of an old oak tree, he bent down, hands on his knees, to catch his breath. He was in the oldest section of the cemetery now. The headstones were cracked, some knocked over completely and most of the names on them had weathered away long ago. For a brief instant, Willie thought he heard music, but it faded as quickly as it had come. He stood up on tip-toes looking around. The last thing he wanted was to get caught by one of the workers. Kids weren't allowed in the cemetery unattended and he'd get in double-trouble when his mother and father found out.

He crept up to the oak and peered around it, his fingers digging into the bark so he wouldn't lose his balance. It came again. A faint blast of music, a few strains of a song he didn't recognize and then it faded away. It seemed to have been coming from the bushes behind him on his left.

Crawling on all fours he slipped from one stone to the next, making sure he stayed well below them. When he placed his hand on one to peek around it, the top broke off and thudded to the grass. He quickly twisted himself around and sank down below what was left of it, his back against the gritty sandstone. He waited and listened, hoping with all his might that no one had heard it fall ... or at least, couldn't place where the sound had come from.

After he waited what he thought to be long enough, he raised himself up to peek over the top again. The road the hearses used to get their guests to their new abodes curved around the bottom end of this section. On the far side of that, a line of bushes obscured the back fence. There was a small access road to the left that Willie could just barely make out. That was his target. It dead-ended at the back gate on Claremont Street, and right across Claremont was the park. At the other end of the park was the opening all the kids used to get into the woods.

Willie took a final look around before standing up, scanning left to right and back again. Nothing was moving. Taking a deep breath and holding it, he darted out from behind the stone, ran across the road and pushed into the bushes on the far side. Now all he had to do was get down to the access road and it was woods time. Of course, he'd have to be careful not to be spotted crossing the park, but that part didn't worry him too much.

Feeling safe, he began to breathe again. He stepped out of the bushes and casually made his way to the dirt road. At the mouth of the road, he turned to take a final look behind and make sure no one was watching. Satisfied, he forged ahead, secure in the knowledge that no one ever used it and he was now safe to take his time getting to the gate.

Drawing lines in the dirt with a stick he'd picked up, Willie followed the road, head down. He looked up barely in time to avoid walking into the back of the car that was parked there. He gasped, sinking to his knees, hoping the driver hadn't seen him in the rearview mirror. He held his breath for the second time today as he waited to hear the car door open. When nothing happened, he edged over to the passenger's side and peeked around. It was less than fifteen yards to the far gate, but that would mean running straight down the road past the driver. The only other option he had was to dart into the bushes and try to worm his way through, but that really wouldn't be much better. It would be much slower going for one thing and the driver was bound to hear him crash through the shrubbery in any event.

He took a few deep breaths then stood up and ran as fast as he could down the length of the car. Three feet from the gate he launched himself into the air, caught hold of the iron rails and scrambled over. Without looking back, he turned onto Claremont Street, ran down the sidewalk a few yards and then shot across the street, through the park and into the woods. He'd made it.

CHAPTER 52

At 4:25 P.M., Arliss Peterson checked into the Marriott, just outside of Banderman Falls. With any luck, the package she'd sent ahead would arrive tomorrow – if they didn't screw up the delivery because of the holiday. The bed and shower both looked extremely inviting. Arliss hated air travel. Not because she was afraid of flying; it was because she hated all the wasted time. Baggage lines, security lines, waiting to taxi, waiting to take off – and then the same thing on the arrival end. It all annoyed her. She was a doer and flying meant doing *nothing*.

Despite her last shower ordeal, she decided to take one anyway and then go down and get something to eat. Still being on Arizona time, she really wasn't that hungry, especially since she'd had a big breakfast, but thought a light sandwich might be nice. Before climbing into the shower she hung a couple of towels over the mirrors.

Feeling refreshed, Arliss slipped into her jeans, a khaki-colored short-sleeve shirt and a pair of sneakers. While she was getting dressed she opted to skip the sandwich and just grab a drink at the bar. As she was tying her laces an odd feeling crept over her. She had the sense that there was someone nearby whom she should know. She could almost see a face in her mind. Its features were blurry. It was the face of a middle-aged man, but the feel of it said that he was much older than he looked.

Completing the last bow on the sneaker, she sat up and tried to bring the face into focus. The harder she tried, the further away it seemed to get. It eventually evaporated, like bathroom steam off a mirror. There had been something so familiar about it, and yet, she was sure she hadn't seen it before.

Then again, she thought, *there have been so many people in and out of the museum. Maybe it was just one of those, kind of like a facial déjà vu.* She sat there on her bed, hands on her knees trying to figure out the puzzle. One thing Arliss never let go of was a puzzle. "But why should this surprise you," she said to herself, "after last night ... anything's possible."

She hefted herself off the bed, grabbed the key-card to her room off the bureau and headed down to the bar. The elevator was playing an instrumental version of "What's Goin On" by Marvin Gaye. Arliss unconsciously tapped her foot in time to the music as the elevator slid to a stop. When the doors opened she started forward, only to realize that it was the wrong floor. A man in an old army jacket stepped in, scanned the buttons. The G was already lit, so he stepped to the side, folded his hands in front of him and stared at the floor.

When the doors slid open again, he took a step back and motioned for her to go first. Arliss thanked him and then made her way down the hall and into the lounge. It was a little past five and the lounge was starting to fill up for Happy Hour. There was an open seat in the middle of the bar between what appeared to be two businessmen. They were dressed in suits, jackets open and ties loosened. When she sat down, the one on her right nodded a greeting and then went back to nursing his drink. The one on the left said nothing; he just eyed her from top to bottom, smiled and then raised his glass in salute.

"I'll have a Chivas-rocks," she told the bartender. Fishing out a ten from her purse, she laid it on the bar in front of her. The man on her left leaned over.

"Can I buy you a drink?" He winked.

"Thanks, but I'll pass," said Arliss, shooting him a quick, overtly fake smile that, hopefully, would put an end to whatever it was he was thinking.

"Suit yourself. Just trying to be friendly." He wrapped both hands around his glass and just stared at it.

The man on her right leaned in. "Don't pay ol' Larry, here, any mind," he said. "He's harmless."

"Oh what do you know?" said the other. "I got a right to ask a pretty lady if she wants a drink. No harm in that. If she doesn't ... she doesn't. No foul in askin."

Arliss really wasn't in the mood, so she looked around to see if she could find an empty table. They were all taken. Like it or not, unless she left, she was stuck between the business world's version of Kramden and Norton. Without a second thought, Arliss downed her drink in one large swallow and ordered a second.

"Don't let these two get to ya," said the bartender when she brought Arliss her scotch. "They're really ok guys. They like to flirt, but-" she shot them both a look, "if ya took either one of em up on their offer ... they'd run like rabbits."

Arliss laughed. She knew the type. She reached out and patted the hand of the one on her right. When he smiled, she tapped the wedding ring on his finger.

"You know, if you're going to try to pick up women, it might be a good idea to hide this," Arliss pointed out.

"Like I said," said the bartender, "all blow and no go."

"You cut me to the quick, my dear," snorted the one named Larry.

The bartender leaned in toward Arliss. "My name's Janet. If these two bozos give you any more trouble let me know."

"Why, what are you going to do about it, call the cops?" barked the man to the right of Arliss.

The bartender laughed. "Nope," she said dryly, "something much, much worse. I'll call your wife."

Larry laughed. "She got you on that one."

Janet turned a quick eye on Larry. "Oh, you don't get off free either, buster. Think I haven't seen you in here flirtin' with Anna Jones? How'd you like me to mention your googlie eyes to *your* wife next time she's in ... with or without you?"

Larry hung his head and the other man, whose name turned out to be Malcolm, paid his tab, bade everyone a goodnight, and left.

"Now see whutcha done, Janet? You went and chased him out. I'll have another, please." He slid his empty glass to the far side of the bar. Janet stuck her tongue out at him and got him another gin and tonic.

Arliss just shook her head and took another gulp of the scotch. She added two dollars to the ten that was already laying on the bar, said thanks and goodnight to the bartender, and patted Larry sympathetically on the back. Larry just gave her a shy smile and took another swallow of his gin.

Not quite sure what to do with herself for the rest of the night, Arliss walked through the lobby and out to the front of the hotel. There was a small concrete bench to the right of the doors. Wondering why she'd really even come here in the first place, she walked over and sat down.

The evening air was warm and the street in front of the hotel was jammed with traffic. Cars inched along, trying to squeeze through intersections before the lights changed, sometimes blocking them. Drivers honked and shouted at each other, each one trying to gain a marginal advantage.

Arliss watched in silence, wondering how mankind had managed to survive as long as it had. Even with the spirit of an approaching national holiday, there didn't seem to be much in the way of neighborly cooperation or simple courtesy. The swooshing of the gliding hotel doors opening snapped her out of her daydreaming. A man stepped out into the evening air, took in a deep breath and looked around. He tipped the Irish Jaunting cap he was wearing in her direction and gave a slight bow with his head.

"Good evening," he said. He had a thick German accent and his suit was a perfect fit on him. Arliss couldn't help thinking how proper he looked and that his accent should have been more English than German, judging solely by his looks and demeanor.

"Hello," she said, trying only to be polite.

"It seems to be kvite a lovely evnink, don't you think?"

"Yes, I suppose it does," said Arliss, hoping this guy wasn't trying to hit on her, too.

The man turned to face her and Arliss could see the dark crevice of a scar that ran the length of his left cheek. It made a zigzag curve from his temple to his chin. She couldn't tell if it was the shadowed-lighting or his actual skin color, but his face appeared a dull green color and his lips were almost black.

The man grinned down at her, his teeth a brilliant white. They stood in stark contrast to the rest of his features. He had a crooked, hooked-nose and his eyebrows were the bushiest that Arliss had ever seen – not counting the Neanderthal display at the museum. He had deep-set, blue eyes that flashed when he smiled and the left one twitched from time to time making it look like he was constantly winking.

"I see you've noticed my ... shall we say ... unfortunate features. I must apologize if they repulse you. I had an accident when I was a child, from which I never fully recovered." He made a slight bow at the waist and nodded his head as if he'd been formally introduced at a cotillion. It struck Arliss that the only thing he'd left out was the clicking together of his heels.

"I'm sorry," she said, "I really didn't mean to stare." She could feel her face flushing.

"It's kvite all right. It eez not an uncommon reaction." He shot her another toothy grin. "My name is Karl von Statheim." He bowed again.

"I'm Arliss Peterson." She stood up and offered her hand, half expecting him to kiss it. He didn't; he shook it gently, but firmly. "Are you here on business or vacation?"

"Vacation?" He squinted his eyes shut and furrowed his brow as if he were pondering the answer to a particularly difficult calculus problem. "Ah," he said at last, smiling. A holiday! Yes, dat's, it. You're asking if I'm on holiday. I'm afraid zat mine English eez not yet kvite perfect."

"I think you speak very well."

"Perhaps, perhaps. Yet, I still have a very heavy accent, voodn't you say?" He laughed. "But, in answer to your kvestion-" His eyes grew dark, seeming to fade all the way back into his skull until they were no more than tiny points of black. "-I am here on business. Just like you!"

As soon as he said that, the scar on his face widened, the edges peeling back like the skin of a sausage on a hot griddle. Arliss gasped. Beneath the scar, she could see movement. Something was crawling around under his skin. She back-peddled until the backs of her knees caught the edge of the bench she'd been sitting on and she dropped heavily onto its concrete seat. The impact sent a burst of pain all the way up her spine to the base of her skull. It was so intense that she was sure she'd fractured her tailbone; she'd also bitten down on her lip and could feel the blood dripping off her chin.

Momentarily dazed, Arliss watched in horror as the scar on the man's face peeled back and a great cloud of flies issued from the gaping wound. They crawled over the man's face and buzzed around his head. The noise they made was loud enough to drown out the sounds of the traffic. Arliss could hear nothing but the incessant, sonorous buzzing.

Beneath the cloud of swarming insects, the man's face was intermittently visible. He opened his mouth, much wider than any human possibly could, and small, whitish-yellow rods, like rice, came pouring out. As they piled up on the ground, they began to wriggle towards Arliss. Thousands of maggots wormed their way across the pavement, over her sneakers, and up her ankles.

Finding her voice and her strength, Arliss screamed and jumped to her feet. She tried stamping to get the crawlies off, but they clung tightly, inching their way up her legs. With both hands, she started brushing them away. As she did, the flies that surrounded the man's head enveloped her. They landed everywhere. She could feel them crawling down her shirt and into her bra; they were in her ears, eyes, and nose. She couldn't breathe.

Through it all, she could hear the man laughing. When she gasped for breath, they filled her mouth. She tried to spit them out, to pull them out, all to no avail. The more she removed, the more that came to take their place. Arliss staggered backwards and fell into the ornamental bushes the hotel had planted, kicking and clawing at herself. She could feel herself losing consciousness; she could feel the flies in her throat and the maggots in her panties.

Suddenly, she heard a loud snapping sound. A moment before she passed out, all the insects disappeared. She lay there in the bushes, panting heavily, tears streaming down her cheeks. The snapping sound she'd heard was the man snapping his fingers. He was recalling his pets.

He took a few steps toward her and leaned over, his hands on his knees. "You were told not to come, weren't you? I thought that I'd made myself clear about that. Apparently, some people just can't take a hint." The man broke out in a peel of laughter again and then vanished.

Arliss struggled to her feet, working her way out of the bushes. When she stood, she could feel something still moving across her thighs. Not worrying about impropriety, she undid her jeans and dropped them. Two maggots were still trying to work their way underneath the elastic leg band of her panties. She grabbed them and threw them to the ground. They wriggled away from her, moving faster than she'd ever seen maggots move.

She lifted her leg and stomped down on one, actually feeling it squish beneath her foot. The other turned, grew three times in size and had the face of the man she'd just seen, scar and all. It hissed at her, revealing long, pointed teeth.

"Go back while you can. This was only a taste of what you'll get if you stay. Next time ... I won't stop my lovelies. They'll enjoy every inch of your flesh and you'll feel every bite they inflict."

Before it could say anything else, Arliss charged forward and stepped on it. When she lifted her foot, there was nothing there, no flattened remains, no stain. Nothing!

Looking up, she noticed that a man sitting in traffic was staring at her and making kissing noises. She quickly turned around and pulled her pants up. She had just got the zipper pulled up when a couple came around the corner, walked past her and went into the hotel. The man in the car, who'd been kissing at her, lowered his window.

"C'mon baby. If you're so anxious to take your pants off, I'll take you for a nice ride."

Arliss didn't have the strength to shoot back a witty reply, so she just shot him the finger, turned and went back into the hotel. Without question, it was time for another shower.

CHAPTER 53

Father Gabriel Jacobs sat patiently waiting for his friend to explain how they were going to put a whole town's worth of children to sleep – into a coma. At any other time in his life, Jacobs would have thought the idea worthy of instant commitment to a psychiatric facility. As it was, considering recent events, he only wondered how it was going to be done. He watched as Geoffrey paced quietly back and forth, lost in thought, or perhaps, considering all the options. Jacobs wasn't sure which. He only knew that the man he was watching walk around the room like a caged lion was suffering under a very heavy weight.

When he glanced at the clock on the wall, Jacobs took note of the fact that he'd been sitting there in silence for over an hour and a half. It was getting on past noon. Finally giving in to temptation, Jacobs leaned forward in his chair.

"Ok, my friend. Are we going to do this or not? I hate to drag you out of your thoughts, but I'm not sure you realize just how much time has passed. The day is slipping away and we've done nothing so far."

Geoffrey stopped his pacing, shot a quick look at the clock and then turned to face Jacobs."

"Sorry, Gabe. I ... I just need to be sure we get this right. The fact that we don't have the third ... the third clock bothers me. A lot!"

"Clock?" asked Jacobs. "What clock are you talking about?"

Geoffrey plopped down in the chair in front of Jacobs's desk. Although it was barely past lunch, Geoffrey had the look of a man that hadn't slept in days. He rubbed heavily at his eyes and then shook his head. The stress he was feeling was clearly visible.

"Ok," he said, "that clock I gave you ... the one that looks like a small version of Big Ben ... well, it has certain abilities ... certain powers, if you will. If used correctly and under the right circumstances and at the right time, it's a formidable tool. When I first got to know you, I realized that you were someone I could trust – someone who had a strong moral compass. It was for that reason, more than anything else, that I decided to bestow it upon you. Initially, I was only thinking of giving it a safe place to stay until I might need it again ... if at all." Geoffrey reached in his pocket and pulled out his and set it on the desk. "Naturally, I hoped that that time would not come. Now we both know it has, although you don't fully understand what's going on. The bottom line is ... you were never meant to use it ... other than to let me track your whereabouts."

Jacobs leaned forward and looked at the clock and then up at Geoffrey. The look Geoffrey saw in his friend's face told him that he just might understand more than he was being given credit for.

"So what, exactly, can these things do?" question Jacobs. "I mean, other than act like some secret locator?"

"That's the million-dollar question, lad," said Geoffrey, sighing as he sat back in the chair. "To my knowledge, they've never been used by ... by-"

Jacobs broke in, "By a mere human?"

"Yes. I suppose that's the best way to put it. I-" Suddenly, Geoffrey rocked forward, cradling his head in his hands. "Ahhh!"

"What is it?" Jacobs jumped to his feet and ran around the desk. Geoffrey was rocking back and forth, his face red and contorted in pain.

"What's the matter, Geoffrey? What can I do?" Jacobs was holding Geoffrey by the shoulders. "Should I call 911?"

"No," Geoffrey managed to squeak out. "No ... I'll be ok. It's ... ahhhh! It's just the noise ... like millions of buzzing insects coming through an amplifier. He slid off the chair to his knees, his hands clasped tightly over his ears. "Something's happening. There's something going on ... not here ... not with me. I can hear it ... feel it."

His words were broken. It sounded to Jacobs as if Geoffrey were fighting just to get each syllable out. He could see the veins in his friend's temples pulsating and his eyes were clenched shut.

"Somebody's being attacked ... attacked by-" Geoffrey dropped forward, his elbows banging down onto the parquet flooring with a sharp thud. "Ahhhhh! It's ... ahhh ... it's deafening." He rolled onto his back and drew his knees up to his chest.

Jacobs didn't know what else to do, so he knelt beside his friend. "Dear Lord, whatever evil has reared its head in our town, please help us defeat it. Please bless and be with the soul who is now under attack. In your name, we beg salvation from these foul times. Please, oh Lord, hear my prayer and ease my companion's suffering. Amen."

Geoffrey rolled over on his stomach. He was breathing hard, his chest rising and falling in a heavy rhythm. Slowly, he drew his hands away from his head. Jacobs backed up a step. Geoffrey's face was full of tiny red marks. To Jacobs, it looked as if Geoffrey had come down with a case of the largest measles he'd ever seen.

"My God! What happened?" he said as he helped his friend to a sitting position. "You're coved in ... in-"

"Bites, Gabe. Insect bites." Geoffrey sat there, his arms wrapped around his knees as he regained his normal breathing. As he did, the red marks on his face faded away.

"Help me up, Gabe."

Jacobs helped him back into the chair and stood there with his hand on his shoulder. Again, he found himself playing the patient one, waiting for Geoffrey to recover enough to explain what had just happened.

Geoffrey took a deep breath, drawing it in to the capacity of his lungs and letting it out as slowly as he could. His color was starting to return to normal and the pulsing of the veins in his temples had subsided. He looked up at Jacobs.

"That was bloody fuckin awful," he said and then both men started to laugh. It was the kind of laugh men share when the situation is beyond belief and beyond their powers to do anything else *but* laugh. They both laughed until their sides hurt and tears were streaming from their eyes. They laughed, but neither of them thought it was funny.

"Somebody's in big trouble," Geoffrey finally managed to get out. "They've been attacked ... and not too bloody far from here. Insects, Gabe .. .flies ... hundreds of thousands of them. They were biting and suffocating this poor man."

"Do you know who it is ... or where he is?" asked Jacobs.

"No mate, sorry. I just got a glimpse in my mind. Then, I was feeling and seeing what he was. It was bloody horrific. The good news is he survived it. I know that for a fact."

"Do you have any idea where it happened? Did you see anything that I might recognize as a landmark?"

"A hallway. That's it, that's all I saw. And a bathtub ... a shower. That's how he got those nasties off of him ... in the shower." Geoffrey grabbed Jacobs by the arm. "And I'll tell you this, mate, he just barely managed before he died. Whoever it was ... is ... he was bloody fuckin lucky."

Jacobs patted Geoffrey on the shoulder. "Well, a hallway doesn't really help me much. I guess whoever it is is on his own."

"There's more too, Gabe. That wasn't the only thing I saw ... just the most intense. I can't be sure, but I think it was in the same place ... maybe earlier ... maybe later; there were two other people in deep too. A man and a woman, I think. There may also have been a third, but I can't be sure. The point is," Geoffrey sighed, "this thing is more powerful than I imagined. It's got abilities I've never seen before ... never even heard of. I can't go into histories right now, but I've never come across anything able to control insects. There's something more malevolent and powerful supporting it. This is a helluva lot worse than I thought. To put it mildly, in the vernacular of your country ... we're in deep shit!"

***

Two sharp raps on the door followed by a slight pause and the turning of the knob brought

both men to their feet.   When the nun's head
appeared through the opening, both men let out a
sigh of relief. Father Jacobs had his hand over his
heart as if he were experiencing the onset of a heart
attack.

"Come in, Sister Ellen. Geeze but you gave
us a start."

"Sorry to bother you both, Father, but Mr.
Ballario is here and he insists on speaking with
you."

"Please inform him that I'm extremely busy
at the moment, but would be willing to try to set
aside some time tomorrow.   Have him call first
thing in the morning and we'll see."

Geoffrey walked over and plopped down in
the leather chair in front of Jacobs's desk and
crossed his legs. With his eyes closed, he tried to
reach out into the images of the man waiting for an
audience.   What came through was a sense of
emptiness.   Ribbons of grays and blacks swirled
around in incoherent patterns.

"Father, he said for me to tell you, and I
don't quite know what this means-" She hesitated.
"-He said that if you didn't see him now, there'd be
darker things at your door than a cat." Sister Ellen
wrinkled her face and shook her head.

Jacobs turned to Geoffrey, the color visibly
absent from his cheeks.

"You'd better show him in, Gabe."

"Sister, if you will?" asked Jacobs.

"Yes, Father."

***

Sister Ellen ushered Ballario into the room and closed the door behind her on her way out. For a moment, she stood with her ear pressed against the door, blessed herself and asked the Lord to forgive her for eavesdropping and hurried off down the hall.

Antonio Ballario stood just inside the door. His head turned from side to side, taking in the room as if he'd never been there before. In stature, short, but in all other respects very reminiscent of Oliver Hardy, without the affable, if exasperated, expression. His eyes finally came to rest on Geoffrey Dunsmore, with only a passing glance at Jacobs. His lips curled into a snarl before settling down into a forced smile.

"What is it I can do for you?" asked Jacobs.

Ballario turned his head just the slightest bit, enough to see the priest yet still keep an eye on Dunsmore.

"You could die. But I doubt you'd be that obliging." His voice was hollow, mechanical, devoid of emotion. The words were spoken as if by a bad actor in a poorly written play. He dug into his pocket and pulled out what looked like a piece of melted plastic. "Yes, I doubt you'd be that obliging; so instead, perhaps you could take a call." He stretched out his arm, offering the lump in his hand to Jacobs, all the while his complete attention focused on Dunsmore.

Jacobs made no move toward Ballario or the proffered item. A moment later, the phone on his desk rang, the doorbell rang, the chimes on the church rang and the thing in Ballario's hand began vibrating, dancing erratically around on his palm.

"If you don't take it and answer, the ringing will just get louder and louder. Think of the poor nuns ... their residence just below the chime tower ... why, they'll all be deaf in a matter of minutes."

Geoffrey rushed forward and slapped the thing from Ballario's hand. It bounced on the carpet and began to shrink in on itself. Geoffrey and Jacobs watched as it reformed itself into a cell phone. As soon as it had, all the ringing stopped – all except the cell phone.

Ballario stood there with arm extended. There was no expression on his face. It was as if he didn't even realize the item – the phone – was no longer in his hand. "Please answer it," was all he said.

Cautiously, Geoffrey picked up the phone and slowly opened the cover. The moment he did, a bright flash enveloped the room, followed by five more. With each blinding burst of white, a new figure stood before them, each of them two-dimensional, like cardboard displays of characters at a movie theatre. After the final flash, a grating, stentorian voice broke the silence.

"I'm a bit indisposed at present," it bellowed, "and I apologize for not greeting you in person. Most especially since I've only had this dullard of a contractor to stand in for me. But I've dispatched some friends to keep you company. Actually, I've sent them to dispatch *you*."

***

The figures standing before them howled in anguish as their two-dimensional representations expanded to three, thinning and filling out at the same time. Each became a smoky representation of a human being – an afterimage of a digital photograph.

Father Jacobs recognized most of them, and a whistle of incredulity escaped him. Tom Kissling had no more than half a face and balanced himself on one leg. Roy Albertson's right arm dangled like a pennant from a single thread of muscle, and from the hips down his body was flat and fragmented. The two women standing side by side were unknown to Jacobs. One of them had what looked like the baffles of a car radiator stuck to the back of her misshapen head and her torso was twisted and partially flattened. Her companion was in no better shape. The top and left side of her head was missing and the right side had barely any flesh on it.

Behind this group, a young couple stood next to Ballario. The man's chest was concave; ribs poked through his torn and grease-smeared suit. The woman next to him looked as if she'd had one side of her face singed off on the burner of a stove. Her right eye hung on the blackened, crispy flesh of her cheek.

"This is not good," yelled Geoffrey, digging into his hip pocket for the pocket knife he always kept there and wondering just how effective it could be against creatures that looked like they were no more solid than the ghost images of poor television reception.

Jacobs backed up against his desk, his hand feeling its way across the surface for the letter opener he knew was there, somewhere.

In unison, the group of image-reconstituted trolley victims began edging forward. Their faces (those that had them) were contorted into a rictus of primordial rage. In the background, Ballario stood with his back against the door, barring any chance of a quick exit.

Geoffrey moved first, his arm no more than a blur. The knife blade slashed through Tom Kissling with a hissing sound that was accompanied by a bright blue flash. Swirls of what looked like oversized pixels spun out in all directions. Tom staggered back a few paces with a loud, but staticy roar.

As the blade had passed through Kissling, Geoffrey felt a stinging surge, like a low-voltage charge, run up the length of his arm. It took all his strength and concentration not to allow the muscles in his hand to spasm and drop the knife.

Roy Albertson advanced on Father Jacobs, along with the two women. Each girl broke to one side, keeping Jacobs from escaping around the desk. Just as Albertson reached out a luminous, picture-grainy hand towards Jacobs's throat, the priest's left wrist brushed up against the stem of the banker's lamp on his desk. With no more time to search for the letter opener, he snatched up the lamp. His arm arced in front of him, the green hood of the lamp slicing through the image-head of Alberston. A loud hissing sound announced the expulsion of photographic pixels from Albertson's head. He staggered backwards and went down on one flat knee with a popping *crack*!

Jacobs experienced the same electric-like charge, and the lamp was thrown from his hand. The bulb erupted into a shower of thin filaments and the lamp's socket burst into flames. Before he could recover himself, the two women, Tammy Watson and Kim Albright, each latched onto an arm and started pulling in opposite directions. Jacobs was now no more than a human wishbone. Their touch was the same feel as when the lamp had passed through Albertson's head, only magnified by a hundred. Jacobs's body jerked and contorted. His eyes rolled back in his head and he could feel his heart skipping beats. He was totally at their mercy, and they were showing none.

Geoffrey didn't hesitate; gripping the knife handle as tightly as possible, he hacked and slashed at Tom, not giving picture-man a chance to recover. Geoffrey was moving so fast that his motion was almost a continuous blur. Showers of blazing, blue pixels were flung out in all directions, sputtering and popping and fizzling, and making tiny burn marks in the carpet wherever they landed. But for all Geoffrey's effort, the picture-man kept coming.

Michael and Judy Felton had been working their way around behind Geoffrey as he flailed away at Tom Kissling. A split second before Michael wrapped his shimmering arm around Geoffrey's neck, the jacket sleeve on Jacobs's coat tore away and Tammy went heel-stepping backward into Michael.

When the two picture-people collided, a blinding explosion of colors filled the room. When it subsided, Michael and Tammy were one picture-person, their pixels merged haphazardly. Tammy's left eye sat on the bridge of Michael's flattened nose and her leg hung limply from his right shoulder. Michael's right hand was sticking out of Tammy's mouth and both of his legs were twisted together, dangling from Tammy's hip. Their arms had melded together back-to-front so that the back of Tammy's hand was also the back of Michaels. They were now a Photoshopped chimera, and in this state, useless. They lay on the floor moaning, sounding like a cross between a wounded cow and an angry raccoon.

"They can't touch each other," screamed Geoffrey, still working on Tom while trying to maneuver around so as to avoid Judy's clawing grasps. He stepped to his right, faded back and then stepped right again, forcing Tom to turn into Judy's path. The two nearly collided, but Judy stopped just short enough to let Tom pass in front of her. Geoffrey cursed, clutched the knife even tighter and rammed it forward into Tom's only eye. The charge he felt this time was enough to knock him back several steps. Dancing points of light shot across his field of vision and his legs went rubbery. With a thump, Geoffrey landed on his back at Jacobs's feet.

When Tammy had been hurtled into Michael with the tearing of Jacob's sleeve, the charges dancing through Jacobs's body had eased enough that his heart rate settled into its normal rhythm.

But Kim's grip tightened. Despite his best efforts, especially as weakened as he was, he couldn't shake her free.

As Geoffrey's vision cleared, he saw his friend standing over him, the picture woman drawing him closer to her gaping mouth as she reeled him in by his arm. Not thinking, Geoffrey reached out, grabbed her by the leg and yanked with all his might, hoping to knock her off balance. The moment his fingers touched her they went cold. It felt as if he'd thrust his hand into a pail of dry ice. With all the determination he could muster, he held on tight and pulled. It worked. She staggered sideways a step and lost her grip on the good Father.

Jacobs went down with a crash, his right elbow landing square in the middle of the open cell phone that was still vibrating in all directions across the floor. Its casing cracked beneath Jacobs's weight and then shattered. Sparks belched out from along its sides, setting Jacobs's shirt cuff on fire. He rolled off it just before it exploded in a shower of oranges and reds. As the pieces settled and melted down into individual particles of gray goo, the picture-people imploded. A horrid wailing, as if some wild animal was being sucked down a long tunnel, rose to a crescendo and then faded away.

Geoffrey rolled over onto his stomach and crawled over to Jacobs, who was lying on his side cradling his elbow. The priest's face was ashen gray and his breathing was that of a man who'd just finished a marathon.

"Still with us, Father?" asked Geoffrey.

"Stil-still here.   An-and what's with the-the
Father shit.   Thought we were up to-to first names
alread-already.

Geoffrey smiled.   Damaged but apparently
okay, his friend still had a sense of humor.   Puffing
a little himself, Geoffrey sat up on the carpet,
supporting himself with his left arm.   "I don't think
we're gonna get much bloodier lucky than we just
did, Gabe.   Thanks for hanging up on the son-of-a-
bitch."

Gabe laughed.   "You know, I'm usually not
that rude.   But in this case, I'm glad I made an
exception.   The smile he had been wearing as he
spoke faded.   "I think you were right, Geoffrey.
We're in deep shit."

Geoffrey nodded.   "Yep, deeper than I'd like
to be.   But-" He pointed toward the ceiling.
"Somebody up there likes us, and I'm hoping they
have a special liking for you, my friend."   He
pushed himself to a standing position and helped the
priest up.   "And if it's any consolation, I can feel
that our rather rude friend who sent the phone is
beginning to feel he actually has something to fear
from us."

"Well, that's good."

"Yes and no.   Now he knows we're a true
threat.   That's not going to make our job any easier."

Jacobs smiled.   "My British friend, when
have you *ever* done anything the easy way?"

The looked over at Ballario, still standing at
the door.   As Geoffrey started toward him, he threw
his hands up to the sides of his head and screamed.

Blood poured from his nose and ears and he slumped to the floor, dead.

CHAPTER 54

Across town at Killerman's B & B, maggots squirmed and flies buzzed. The evil conscience of the thing on the bed was enraged at its failure to stop the priest and meddling Brit. The maggots gnashed and gnawed on one another; the flies flew into the walls, bounced off and flew into them again. Thousands of them collided in midair, and the beating of their frenzied wings carried a horrid wail of frustration, disappointment, and rage.

Disintegrated for its rest period, the malicious Witherstone was impotent where Jacobs and Dunsmore were concerned. They were too strong for the parlor tricks he used on the weak and feeble-minded townspeople. Infuriated, he bent all his thought and remaining strength on bringing the town of Banderman Falls under his control, before Jacobs and Dunsmore could interfere.

He stretched out his thoughts, and with them would come darkness and destruction.

PART TWO

CARPE NOCTEM

CHAPTER 55

Up in Room 227 of the Killerman's B & B, the maggots began to recollect themselves into a cohesive group atop the outline of ashes that rested on the bed. It was a slow, drawn-out process. Once they were all in place, the dust and ashes began to envelop them and to reshape them, and itself, into a human form. It grew in both directions from the center out. First an abdomen and pelvis, then a chest and legs, feet and arms and finally, shoulders neck and head. It was a faceless being, lying on its back, its scalp devoid of hair.

The flies that had swarmed Sheriff Jack Dougherty settled down on the figure on the bed. They jumped or crawled to their required locations and then began their transformation. The ones on the figure's head sank into the skin of the skull, thinned and expanded, becoming its hair. Others did the same for his eyebrows and eyelashes, the hair on his arms and legs. Maggots dug their way to the outside of the flesh, forming the nose, eyes, and mouth. When its eyelids finally fluttered open, there were only vacant sockets. The thing on the bed, almost in human form, waited while the flies and maggots within it merged themselves together to create its eyes. Slowly and carefully, they rolled themselves into tangled balls and slipped into the empty sockets, all the facets of the flies' eyes to the front.

It rose up and sat on the edge of the bed, collecting itself. When it stood, it once again looked like the man who had checked in.

Stretching out his mind, Witherstone could see Jack and Robertson outside. But its mental vision was limited. Instantly, it realized that its rest had been disturbed; the attack it was forced to unleash on Jack had weakened it. Witherstone was not at full strength.

Concerned, but not in a panic, Witherstone tried to reach across Banderman Falls to the men he already had under his control. He could barely feel them, but could not complete the link. Although still very powerful, he was, for the moment, at a disadvantage. He would need help if he were going to get past the sheriff and nosy doctor.

Summoning all his strength, he called out for Curtis. It was time for his "pirate" to take arms. His mind stretched across the miles. It was a thin tendril of thought, much thinner than he could have normally generated, but it found its mark. Channeling all his energy, his mental thread took the form of a large fly. It gathered others and swarmed toward Curtis, who was sitting on the edge of the creek, feet in the water, downing his fifth beer.

With a face reminiscent of a member of ZZ Top, the fly crawled over to Curtis and called up to him.

"Psst. C'mere." The voice was tiny and weak, and Curtis turned around with a jerk. There was no one behind him. "Psst ... idiot ... down here."

When Curtis looked down, he couldn't believe what he was seeing, but he recognized the face from the other night.

"How did you-" began Curtis, but the fly cut him off.

"Never mind that now. Get your ass over to the Killerman's B & B. Be quick about it and bring a gun, you'll need it. There are two people there you need to take care of. Now, I'm sure I don't have to remind you what will happen if you fail me, do I?"

Curtis started shaking his head, "No, you don't. Who do I have to take care of?"

"You'll figure that out when you get here. Now stop wasting both our times."

The face on the fly seemed to start to drip like melting wax, but then it reformed itself. At first, Curtis thought he was seeing things from drinking too much. When it happened a second time, he figured it wasn't from the alcohol.

"Hey ... what's up with that face?" he asked, emboldened by the beers he'd downed. "Your face is running." When he said this, it almost made him laugh; he got control of himself just before he did. That laugh would have been a big mistake.

"Never mind about the particulars, just get your ass in gear." As soon as he said it, the fly took off and disappeared.

Curtis stood there staring at the spot where the fly had been sitting, wondering if what had happened really had, or if he'd imagined it. He finally came to the conclusion that it didn't matter. He'd better get himself to the B & B. If he had hallucinated, no harm done. If he hadn't, and he didn't show up where he was supposed to- (he didn't even want to think about the consequences.)

Forgetting about his socks, Curtis pulled his boots on, made his way back to his bike and headed home to get his gun. He couldn't imagine who in the world would be at the B & B that needed shooting. All he knew was that it wasn't for him to decide.

The Sportster thumped to life and Curtis shot across the cinders of the parking lot and out onto the street. It would take him a good fifteen minutes to get home and another ten or fifteen to get to Killerman's. He instinctively knew that he didn't have that much time. Opening the throttle, he shot up Bell's Mill Road doing eighty-five. At the top, he eased off the gas, laid the bike over and made the turn onto Ridge Pike, cutting off an oncoming car. Cranking the throttle around again, he sped off.

CHAPTER 56

When he felt he had enough strength to stand, Jack pulled himself to his feet. His mind was swimming. There was no way that what had just happened could have. The blood on his arms and cheeks and the bites from which it ran told him otherwise. He limped over to the sink and turned on the cold faucet. After cleaning out his wounds, he pulled open the medicine cabinet above the sink, hoping to find some kind of antibiotic ointment. It was empty. All he could do now was get downstairs and see if Robertson had anything in his kit.

He moved into the combination living room-bedroom and put his hand on the doorknob. Cautiously, he opened the door and took a quick look out into the hall. Everything was quiet. No buzzing. Raising his gun, he stepped onto the hallway carpet, facing the direction of the room of flies. Nothing was moving. He backed up, one cautious step at a time, making his way around the corner and back to the landing at the steps. The whole time he kept his .357 leveled out in front of him. Before turning away, he shot a glance down the steps to be sure it was clear, then turned and ran down, jumping the last several steps.

Outside, he saw Robertson leaning up against the front of the car, his arms folded across his chest and a pensive look on his face.

"Doc–"

"Jack-,"

Both men spoke at the same time.

"Go ahead, what is it?" said Jack, still standing on the porch, every now and then twisting his head around to look back inside.

"I've found something I think you should see." Robertson pushed off from the car and started toward the steps.

"Just wait right there, I'll be right down," admonished Jack, holding up a hand. "I'm gonna need a bit of your professionalism."

Robertson hadn't gotten very far before Jack had stopped him, but he'd made it far enough to see what shape Jack was in. "What the hell happened to you? C'mon, let's get something on these." He led

Jack down to the cruiser, dug out his bag from the back and started treating Jack's wounds.

"Doc, believe it or not, they're insect bites. Thousands of damned flies attacked me. They were all piled in a room in the back. 227. Have you ever heard of such a thing before ... professionally, I mean? Have you ever heard of flies attacking like a swarm of bees?"

Robertson shook his head no. "Never." Robertson patted Jack on the shoulder. "Here let me wrap those arms."

"Thanks, doc," said Jack. "Not necessary. A quick splash of iodine should do it. Now, you said there was something I should see."

"Yes. Out back I found what looks like brain matter. It looks human, except for the fact that it looks like it's been decaying for some time and it has the distinct odor of formaldehyde. So, unless someone's dragging corpses around, I'm not sure what to make of it."

Jack took a quick look down the driveway. "Pinsky never showed up?"

"No, at least, I haven't seen him. And except for my tour around the building, I've been out here the whole time."

"Yeah, well, we'll discuss you're tour later. I should kick your ass for leaving the car." Jack thumbed the microphone hanging from his shoulder. The usual crackling sound didn't come. "Audrey? Audrey, you there?"

Only silence answered him. He tried a few more times and then tried the radio in the cruiser with the same results. Both radios seemed to be dead. Jack checked the connections. Nothing.

"C'mon Doc, let's get out of here. Let's see if we can find Bill and maybe even get a-hold of Alex over at the State office. Then we'll come back and go over this place with the proverbial fine-toothed comb."

"What about Ethan and Linda?"

Jack looked around. "Well, it's for sure they're not here. So the best thing I think we can do is come back with some real help."

The two men got in the car. Jack turned the key, and like the radio, nothing happened – not even a grinding sound. The two exchanged glances.

"Ok, now what?" asked Robertson, "if you'll pardon my asking. This is your thing, Jack, not mine."

Jack slammed his palms on the steering wheel. "Dammit. What the fuck is going on around here? This shit ain't normal."

Robertson laughed. "That would appear to be an understatement, my friend." Robertson pointed out the windshield at the cruiser parked in front of them. "Think it'd do any good to try Ethan's car?"

"At this point, I'd bet not. But let's have at it anyway." After a moment's consideration, he added: "On second thought, you stay here ... *I'll* go give it a try." He opened the door and stepped out.

Jack turned the key a few times, then raised his hands and shrugged his shoulders. Robertson got out of the car and walked up to him. "Well, seems like we're stuck here for now. What's next on the protocol for this situation?"

"Wish I knew," Jack forced out a short laugh. "We're flying blind on this one, Doc."

CHAPTER 57

Carlton Wedgemore remained scrunched into the hollow beneath the basement steps, waiting. Above him, cries for help, banging, yelling and scuffling drifted down to him. He ignored them all, waiting in the dark to assail the would-be thieves.

Upstairs, Grady Peters and Gary Larch were struggling with Evelyn Ramsey. They had her stretched out across one of the antique dining room tables and were tearing at her clothes. Gary had ripped her dress from knees to waist and was struggling to tear her panties off. Grady was wrestling with her upper body, trying to keep her meaty hands from punching him in the face while, at the same time, working a hand into her bra.

When Evelyn realized that her screams were doing her no good and that no one was coming (or likely to come) she decided to fight back. And this she did with a vengeance. It was the one time in her life when she was thankful that she was not a small woman.

Bringing her left hand up in a fist, she caught Grady square on the jaw. She could feel her knuckles slam into the bone. Grady staggered backwards, losing his grip on her. When he did,

Evelyn reached down and grabbed Gary by his hair. Before he could react, she brought her knee up, driving it into his breast bone. He let out a yell and he fell back, clutching at his chest.

By the time Grady had recovered, Evelyn was off the table and headed right for him. There was no hiding the rage that boiled within her. Her eyes were wide and her lips curled in a snarl. Grady instinctively threw his hands up, but the blow she landed was so hard it drove his own fists into his face. The power of it knocked him back another step and before he had a chance to retaliate, Evelyn's knee found its mark between his legs. He sank to the floor clutching his testicles and moaning. His eyes rolled back in his head; the pain was so severe he lost consciousness and fell forward, slamming his forehead against the hard-wood flooring.

When Evelyn turned around, Gary was just reaching out for her neck. He missed, but managed to get a good grip on her hair. Screaming in pain, Evelyn was dragged across the room and slammed, head first up against the wall. The vibration of the impact jarred the shelves above. For the briefest of moments, a large brass bust of Muhammad Ali teetered on the edge. Gary looked up just in time to see it pitch forward. With a sickening thud, it caught him just above the ridge of his brow. Evelyn heard the crack of his skull as it splintered and watched as his eyes fluttered for a moment before he sank to the floor.

Still furious, Evelyn picked up the bust and struck Gary again and again. Each blow flattened the skull a little more; his eyes shot out of their sockets like a paper wad being blown out of a straw; the only thing that prevented them from being shot across the room was the ocular nerve they were each connected to.

When she'd finally run out of steam and couldn't manage to lift the heavy brass bust anymore, she spit on Gary's remains, flattened his eyes with her bare heel (her shoes had come off in the fight), and kicked him in the balls for good measure.

Panting, she stood there looking at her handy work. Gary's head was smashed beyond recognition and Grady lay on the floor face down.

"As soon as I catch my breath," she said in gasps, "you're next, you fuck," she growled at Grady. She pushed herself away from the wall, picked up the bust and walked over to him. She stood there looking down. "I'm gonna bash *your* skull in too, you stinking ni-" she caught herself before she said the word. Something inside her wouldn't allow her to use that word. Not even in anger. For a moment, the anger and fury she was feeling faded. The respite didn't last though. Only this time, when it came back, the anger wasn't directed at Gary or Grady. Now she set her sights on Carlton.

"You no-good bastard," she yelled at the top of her lungs. "I know you heard me hollering for help, you fuckin twit. Well, you'll be the one hollering next. I'm coming down there and smear your fuckin pansy skull all over the walls. Ignore me, will you!"

She stomped across the room, rounded the counter and headed for the back of the store to the basement door. Below, Carlton had heard every word. He had no idea what had happened upstairs. But it didn't matter. If that fat bitch came down and tried to take his prize, she'd get the same as the thieves.

"C'mon," he whispered. "C'mon down here, you cow. I'll chop you to bits too." Taking the reciprocating saw in both hands, Carlton flicked the switch on and felt it vibrate to life. He could feel the power of it in his palms, the blade dancing back and forth just waiting to cut through something.

When he heard the basement door creak open, he cut the motor and waited beneath the steps in the dark for his chance to start putting things right. He waited for his chance to start getting even – and he was going to start with that fat slut he let work in his classy store.

As Evelyn stood at the top of the steps, flicking the light switch and getting no results, Grady started to come too. His head was reeling and the pain between his legs told him that his testicles had already begun to swell. With every ounce of strength that was left in him, he struggled to his feet. Every movement made his head throb harder and his groin ache more. He had almost made it to an upright position when his legs gave out again and he found himself sprawled on the floor yet another time.

Grady squinted his eyes shut, pinching them with the thumb and forefinger of his right hand. His left hand was permanently plastered between his legs, supporting his damaged manhood. He thought about trying to stand but came to the conclusion that it would just be easier to crawl to the door. He didn't think he could defend himself from another attack, so the best course of action was to flee. On hand and knees, he inched his way to the front of the store, forced himself to stand and limped out onto the sidewalk. Once outside, he leaned up against the storefront and waited until he had enough strength to try to waddle home. He was pretty confident that Evelyn wouldn't try anything out in the open, though not completely sure of this, so he kept glancing in the window to be sure she wasn't coming.

"You down there, you little shit?" cried Evelyn from the head of the steps. "You down there hiding in the dark like the little cowardly turd you are? Well, I'm coming for you. Oh yes ... and when I find you, do you know what I'm gonna do? Huh? I'm gonna beat your worthless brains in."

Under the steps, Carlton closed his eyes, his finger on the ON switch. He didn't realize he was holding his breath, anticipating his big moment. He huddled in the darkness of the stairway waiting to strike his first "get-even" blow. His destiny was about to arrive and he was finally going to take control – real control – of his life.

Thump. Thump. Thump. Evelyn made her way down the steps, one at a time. She was bent over at the waist trying to peer down into the darkness, nine stairs from the bottom. Carlton wanted to giggle, he was so excited. Another three

steps and – *zziiipppp* – cut off at the ankles ...
literally.   A small whimper of a laugh escaped
before he got control of himself. He shrank back
further into the darkness.

"I hear yoooooou," bellowed Evelyn.   "I hear you
and I'm commm-ming! Don't you worry, mama's
gonna fix everything ... *shit-fer-brains*!"   She
descended another step and Carlton had to cover his
mouth to keep himself quiet. Two more steps to go.
Just two!

CHAPTER 58

Gwen Archibald had had no dreams other
than the ones she created for herself.   She had
covered the graveyard shift as dispatcher, relieving
her sister, Audrey. It had been a quiet night for her
and she'd spent it thinking about Ernie Johnson,
daydreaming of what it would be like to make love
to him.   At some point during her longings, she
came to the conclusion that she had to do something
about it ... good or bad. She decided to go over to
Pyle's Bookstore and tell Ernie how she felt. She
just had to do something; she hadn't been able to get
the thoughts of how good it felt when she'd rubbed
asses with him earlier that day out of her mind.   It
was time to act.

When she arrived at the bookstore, having
wandered around town most of the day working up
the courage, she found it was still closed. Not really
paying attention to the fact that the store being
closed was out of the ordinary, she walked across

the street to Dunkin Doughnuts and bought two large coffees. She sat outside at one of the bistro tables, keeping an eye on the bookstore. As soon as Ernie showed up she'd bring him his coffee and they'd talk.

"After all, girl," she said to herself, "no harm in trying. The worst that can happen is that he'll politely turn you down. Just be nice and ask him if he wants to go to the Fourth celebration with you." She sipped at her coffee, trying to make it last until Ernie showed.

Gwen was about halfway through it when she got a mental image of Ernie in a hotel bed with a strange woman. It swept over her like locusts over a cornfield. Her anger built. She could feel the backs of her eyes starting to burn. Without realizing it, she'd tightened her grip on Ernie's coffee, crushing it. Coffee dripped through the open lattice of the table and ran down onto her lap. She was so focused on Ernie and her anger that she didn't even feel it burning into her thighs.

When she couldn't stand it anymore, she jumped to her feet, knocking the table over, and stormed off down the street. Somehow, she knew exactly where to look to find the little bastard that was cheating on her. And when she did ... oh boy, would he pay.

"You don't cheat on me, you fuckin' prick," she yelled, as she crossed the street and headed for the Motel 8. "I'll show you just exactly what that expression about a woman scorned *really* means!" The angrier she got, the faster she walked. She strode across the street right into the middle of traffic, forcing two cars to come to a screeching halt, oblivious to the obscenities the drives yelled at her.

A block from the motel, Gwen heard a familiar voice. When she turned around, she was surprised to see Penny Bishop on the other side of the street calling to her. It struck Gwen odd that the old lady was wearing a big floppy hat. Gwen had known Penny for many years and could remember her saying over and over that: "Hats only make your hair look funny when you take em off. Never catch me wearing one. Not to mention how expensive they are." But there she was, waving from across the street and calling to her, a big black hat hanging down over her eyes.

When Gwen made it across the street, Penny grabbed her by the hand. "C'mon, c'mon. You don't want to miss this." She turned and headed off down the sidewalk, literally dragging Gwen along behind her.

"Wait a minute, where are we going?" Gwen was amazed at how fast the old woman was moving. If she picked up the pace just a little, they'd be running. "What's got into you, Penny? Slow down, I can hardly keep up."

"Mustn't slow down, dear ... gotta keep moving or you'll miss the whole thing." The hand that was dragging Gwen along was cold. Gwen tried to pull away but the grip was vice-like. She noticed, too, that Penny's hand was a peculiar shade of bluish-gray.

"Penny! Stop! Where the hell are you taking me?"

Penny pulled up short and turned around. She kept her head down so that Gwen couldn't see her face. "Why, just where you want to go to see just what you want to see. Your man ... your cheating, no good, stinkin man. I know where he is ... and what he's doin. Don't you want to know; don't you want to see; don't you want to catch the bastard in the act of cheating on you?" Penny laughed. "Now c'mon or you'll miss out." She started off again, yanking Gwen along.

Her words rang in Gwen's ears. She could see them – Ernie and that other woman – rolling around in bed, laughing, oohing and ahhing and having a grand old time. The anger surged through her. It should be her, Gwen Archibald, that Ernie was fucking, not some strange woman from the other side of town. He'd pay though, that's for sure.

At the end of the block, they turned down an alley that led to Baxter Street. Gwen should have been alarmed, or at least confused. Baxter Street dead-ended at the old Falls Chemical warehouse that went out of use twenty years ago. There was nothing else down there. The Motel 8 was on the other side of town. She should have had warning bells going off in her head; she didn't. All she had was anger and jealousy.

At the end of the ally, Penny stopped and pointed to the empty warehouse. "They're in there. Rolling around on the floor like a couple of in-heat mutts. Guess they figured no one 'ud find em in there. They were wrong though, weren't they? We found em. Oh yes we did. Now you go in there and give that cheatin fucker what for."

When Penny let go of Gwen's hand, Gwen stormed off toward the double sliding doors of the old warehouse. There was no rationality left in her, only pure hatred. At the doors, she stopped. There was a chain looped through the handles and padlocked. She tugged on it but it didn't budge.

"Oh, hang on honey. I can help," Penny's voice sounded reassuring, comforting. The old woman strode up to the doors and touched the lock with her blue hand. It began to steam, then to melt. With a ringing sound, the chain slid through the door handles and coiled up on the ground at Gwen's feet.

"Now get yerself in there and don't let him make no fool o'ya no more." Penny pointed at the doors. "Go, afore ya miss both of em."

Gwen pulled on the handle and the rusted door squealed and groaned as it rolled open. Gwen wasted no time; she charged in yelling: "Ernie! Ernie, you no good piece of shit! Where are you? I know you're in here so it's no use hidin. I'm gonna find ya, and when I do ... I'm gonna rip yer cheatin balls off and feed em to the bitch yer in here doin."

A dark peel of thunderous laughter rang through the building. It was coming from behind Gwen; it was coming from Penny Bishop. It was nearly deafening. Gwen didn't care. All she cared about was finding Ernie and making him pay for his transgression – making him pay for humiliating her – making him pay for the years he'd ignored her.

CHAPTER 59

Jasper Collins waited very impatiently in his hiding place on the access road. Every few minutes he checked his watch; the time was passing much slower than he would have liked. And beyond that, he had no idea why he was really here in the cemetery in the first place. He had the feeling he was waiting for something, yet couldn't imagine what it could be.

Nestled in the woods that ringed the edge of Peaceful Haven Cemetery, Jasper tried to think of anything that would keep his mind off the strange and imposing visitor he'd had last night. He watched the sun, what he could see of it through the thick canopy of trees, transit overhead. Here and there, thin rays managed to pierce through the leaves illuminating the dust and pollen that swirled through them.

Jasper sat back and closed his eyes, still mechanically drumming his fingers on the lower edge of the steering wheel. He was beginning to drift away, slipping into that ethereal border between wakefulness and sleep. His ears could still hear the slight rustling of the leaves when the breeze blew, but his mind was already skipping across the transient stages of thought we pass through on our way to full sleep.

It was his first rumbling snore that brought him up from the sleepy depths, or so he thought at first. He sat up and was rubbing at his eyes when he heard the sound again. It wasn't a snore; it was the sound of someone walking on a gravel road. He quickly looked in his review mirror, afraid that one of his co-workers had found him hiding here. He could see all the way back to where the first bushes obscured the main road. There was nothing there. He leaned over and listened out the window, waiting for the next crunch or crackle of paving stone. All was quiet.

Jasper was about to dismiss the whole thing as part of his having drifted off when a shape darted by. Out of the corner of his eye, he saw a small figure dash along the side of his car and emerge in the front. As quickly as he had come, he was gone, leaping onto the iron gate that stood at the end of the road and scrambling over. He vanished down the sidewalk on the other side.

A kid, he said inside his head, *damned kids; always using this place of rest as a cut-through.* He sat forward, hands gripping the steering wheel and stared out the windshield. He was gone. He thought about getting out and yelling after the kid that the cemetery was no place for children. He thought about it, but ended up just settling back, his head against the headrest. Jasper Collins had more important things to worry about than a kid. He just wasn't sure what they were.

CHAPTER 60

In the park, five men waited for Colleen Slater to come out of the bathroom. Each had a different idea of what he was going to do to her body once they had her on the ground. Bill

Palmerton had nearly cum in his pants with anticipation. The men stood there outside the pavilion and just around the corner of the WOMEN'S room.

As soon as she comes out, grab her, thought Alvin, sending that thought to all the others. They nodded. Charlie Dennis already had his belt undone and his zipper pulled down. Frank Watkins and Earl Oprendick stood with hands in their pockets, licking their lips. Alvin Parris had taken his belt off and looped the end through the buckle. Once they grabbed her, he'd slip the loop over her wrists behind her back and she'd be ready to go.

Once we get her down, sent out Alvin, *pull her arms behind her back Charlie, and I'll tie em up. Once that's done, she belongs to us for the afternoon.* The men started to giggle like school children. They passed their thoughts back and forth about who was going to do what. They were mentally arguing over who was going to hold her legs open and who was going to go first when they heard the bathroom door squeak open.

Colleen stepped outside and walked toward the park bench, her heels clicking on the concrete pad of the pavilion. She'd just made it to the edge of the grass before she was grabbed from behind, forced onto the ground and her hands cinched up tight behind her back. She tried to yell, but someone was pushing her face down into the dirt. Her nose was flattened against the ground and her attempts at yelling only filled her mouth with dry, dusty soil.

She could feel multiple hands on her body; she could feel and hear her clothes being torn off and she could feel fingers being pushed into her. She tried to kick and couldn't. Her legs were pinned firmly to the ground and spread as wide as her attackers could get them.

A pair of legs appeared in front of her as a man lifted her head out of the dirt. He slid himself in underneath her so that his legs were up on her shoulders and her face was in his crotch. She could feel the ooze on her cheek that dripped from his penis, as he tried to force it into her mouth.

Suddenly, there was a series of four loud popping sounds. The man who had been holding her by the head fell backward, his hands letting go of her hair and the back of his head slapping down onto the grass with a soft thud. Her legs were free now too, and no one seemed to be touching her at all. She rolled over onto her back but couldn't see too well. Her eyes were full of dirt and grass and she couldn't wipe them clean.

"Just what the hell do you think you're doing?" Colleen heard someone ask. It was a woman's voice. "If I were you, I'd get the hell outta here while I still could. There's plenty left in here for the rest of you. So if you don't want to look like your two friends there, I'd skedaddle." The voice paused for a moment, then added in a shout: "*Now!*"

"This ain't over by a long shot, slut," one of the men said. Colleen recognized his voice. It was Alvin Parris. "It ain't *nearly* over. And now ... you're on our list as well." He laughed.

"Is that so?" came the female voice. "Well then, guess I'd better take preemptive measures, huh?" Two more shots rang out. They echoed through the still air of the park and drifted away. Colleen could smell the cordite, heard the thud and felt the vibration of the body that hit the ground beside her. It kicked and twitched for a moment and then lay still. She could also hear the sound of feet scurrying across the pavilion floor as the two remaining men took off running.

Colleen struggled to sit up. A moment later, her hands were free and she was wiping the dirt from her eyes. When they were clear she looked up, surprised to see Rachel Parker standing there, a silver semi-automatic dangling from one hand.

"Never really liked you much," said Rachel, looking down at Colleen. "But damn if I'd let those buffoons think they could do whatever they wanted. To be honest with you, I have no idea why I even came out here, much less why I decided to bring my gun. Just had a feeling that this is where I should be."

Rachel reached down and helped Colleen to her feet. The two women looked at each other for a long time, neither of them speaking, both of them sizing up the other. Then they looked at the three bodies lying on the ground.

Never cared much for you either, thought Colleen, *but I'm glad you came along today.*

You're welcome, thought Rachel and Colleen heard it, just as Rachel had heard Colleen's thoughts.

"What the fuck is going on?" asked Colleen. "How the hell can I hear what you're thinking? How in all creation is that possible?"

"I don't know," replied Rachel, "any more than I know how I knew that I had to be here ... now ... at this very moment. I just knew."

Colleen looked down at the three men lying on the ground, large pools of blood welling up around their bodies. "What the hell are we going to do about them?"

Rachel looked at the .45 in her hand, opened her purse and pushed it in. She then spat on Alvin. "Don't know about you, but I'm not going to do anything about them. Already done as much for em as I can. Goodbye, Charlie, goodbye Earl and fuck you, Alvin!" She started laughing. It was a boisterous, infectious kind of laugh and Colleen found herself laughing too.

"So you're just going to leave them here?" Colleen asked after she got control of herself.

"Why not? What would you suggest we do with them? Have them stuffed and mounted?"

Colleen took a look at them. "Ok. So now what?"

"I dunno. Wanna go have a drink?"

"Never thought I'd even consider having a drink with you ... but yeah. I'm buying. As many rounds as you want."

"That'd be at least six. That's how many rounds *I* just served." They both laughed again as they turned and walked away.

CHAPTER 61

Pushing through a line of Rhododendrons, Ethan Kennedy and Linda Killerman stopped to rest. The B&B was now several hundred yards behind them, along with the things that had chased them out, hopefully.

"Do you think-" said Linda, panting, "do you think ... we ... lost them?"

"Not sure," answered Ethan, not panting at all. "I don't think they even followed us, but I can't be certain of that."

Ethan scanned the surrounding area. A few yards to their left was an outcropping of rocks and boulders, remnants of the glaciers that had formed the region some 17,000 to 22,000 years ago.

"Wait here a minute. I wanna take a look around."

Linda nodded, still trying to catch her breath. She rubbed lightly at the scratches on her arms and hoped that they'd been lucky enough to have avoided all the poison ivy.

"What the hell just happened?" she called after him, as he started towards the rocks. "I mean, Christ!" The aftermath nerves started to settle over her and she had to wipe the tears from her eyes. "What the hell were those things?"

Ethan stopped and turned to face her. "I don't know. I really don't know." He walked back over and sat down beside her, lightly placing his hand on her back. "It's gonna be ok. We'll figure this out."

"I'm ok. I'm ok," said Linda, straightening up and wiping at her face once more. Her hands were still shaking, but the look on her face told Ethan that she was getting it together. It was the look of a person determined to deal with circumstances. "I just can't believe it. You shot that guy; I saw it. And he just kept coming."

"Really Linda, I haven't got a clue as to what's going on. I've never even heard of anything like this before. But I do know one thing. We can't stay out here. We'll have to try and make it back to the car."

Linda stood up and brushed herself off. As she wiped the last of the dirt off her pants a thought struck her.

"What about the rest of the guests. There's Mr. Witherstone up in 227 and Mr. and Mrs. Hoffman in 109. We have to do something about them. We can't just leave them there."

Ethan rubbed at his mouth, his mind turning. He'd seen his share of combat, and of strange things. But until now, anyone he'd ever tagged with four or five 10 millimeter rounds usually stayed down – usually remained stone cold dead.

"I'm not sure what to do about them. I'm not even sure what we should do, except try to make it to the car and get out. Like you, I've never come across anything like this. And there's something else, too. You called in your ... your attack. Jack'll be on his way out here too. C'mon. Like it or not, we have to go back."

"I'm ready ... I think."

"I think if we stay inside the tree line when we get there we can work our way around to the front and the cars without being seen. But if it looks too risky, we'll probably have to wait until dark. That is, if Jack doesn't get there first."

"Dark? Hell, that's hours from now, Ethan." Suddenly, a concerned look washed across Linda's face. Her brow furrowed and then her eyes widened. "Ethan, what if Jack's already there. What if ... those people ... those ... things-"

Ethan cut her off, "Don't go there. Not yet. Let's just take one small step at a time until we can figure out exactly what it is that we're dealing with."

Linda settled herself. "Ok. Let's go. If we're going, let's go. Before I change my mind."

Ethan pulled the clip out of his Glock, reloaded it to capacity, slammed it back into the gun and then slipped it back in its holster. He then gave Linda a wink and started off in the direction from which they'd just come, his left hand in her right.

CHAPTER 62

Eric Baxter rocked back and forth on the old wooden swing that sat on the makeshift porch he'd built in front of his trailer. He'd been feeling uneasy all day – unsettled, unable to find anything to do with himself. He had the day off, the municipality closing for the long holiday weekend. All morning he had paced around, first inside the trailer, then out. Ruby, his dog, followed him faithfully until she got tired of walking in circles and just laid down in the grass out front.

Eric sat there remembering his conversation with Grady Peters at the diner. That had only been yesterday, but it felt like a month ago. He thought about how he begged Grady not to take any money and how he told him that something bad was going to happen in Banderman Falls, although he didn't know what. Now he was feeling that he'd been wrong. At least about the money part. It wasn't money that was going to trip Grady up ... going to draw him into something ... something wicked and evil. No ... Eric now felt it was something else, but again, couldn't figure out what, and that was what was eating away at him as he rocked.

He drew the pocket watch he'd shown Grady out of his coverall's bib pocket and looked at it. He turned it over in his hand and then back again. He thought about opening it, in fact, he had his thumb on the catch. He could feel the edge of it pushing lightly into the work-roughened skin. But for some reason, he felt it best to leave it closed.

"Dadblameit," he cried, getting to his feet. "Wutcha sittin here doin nothin fer, Eric Baxter. You know that sumpin's really wrong out there, don't ya? Oh yes ya do." He paced back and forth in front of the trailer, Ruby watching out of the tops of her eyes.

"Problem is ... t'ain't nothin t'be doin, is there?" He looked at the watch again and then pushed it back into his bib pocket. "There oughta be sumpin ya c'n be a-doin, though, shouldn't there?

Sure as spit blows in yer face on a windy day, there must be sumpin ya can be doin."

The sun overhead was riding high, telling Eric that it was some time past noon, maybe later. He'd never been one of those people who could tell time by the position of the sun. His cousin, Elmer, used to be able to do it within five minutes. All Eric could ever do was say if it was morning or afternoon. Now, he looked up at the bright, burning orange disc and felt it was much later than just afternoon. Later in the sense that time was running out for the good folks of Banderman Falls. A darkness was coming; he could feel it in his bones as surely as he could feel his arthritis.

Eric sat down and kicked listlessly at the dirt. Sitting back, he closed his eyes. He was nearly sixty-eight years old, born on December 7, 1941. His grandmother used to tell him that his life was going to be fraught with sadness because he was born on a day when treachery was made famous. She used to tell him that he had to be extra kind to people to help erase the bad luck he was born into. She had also told him that one day he'd have a great gift come to him. It would come because there was always a balance in the universe. It would come to offset the stigma of his birthday. She had seen it in a dream; he would accomplish something no one else could, and it would come at a time when it was needed most.

As he sat there thinking, the warm sun beating down on him, he drifted off to sleep. Sinking down, he began to dream, his left hand clamped over his bib pocket, his fingers clutching at the watch through the denim fabric.

It was dark, darker than anything Eric had ever known before. He was outside somewhere and it was quiet. A light breeze licked at his face, flapping the thin gray hair of his temples. The ground beneath his feet was soft and muddy, his work boots sinking in as he walked. Above him, a cloud slipped from in front of a fluorescently brilliant moon, its light cascading down through the surrounding trees. The air was ripe with the smell of Juniper and Balsam. There was an overpowering sweetness that hung there too, surrounding him, almost suffocating him. Flowers. Thousands and thousands of flowers, stacked ten feet high in all directions.

Standing in the center, he turned in circles eyeing the tower ring of decaying flowers. Funeral flowers. All pulled from graves that had been backfilled, locking their new occupants in forever. Keeping them safe – a larder for the worms, beetles, and bacteria that have the ultimate say over what becomes of us.

Eric watched as the flowers decayed at an unusual rate, turning black and shrinking into the nothingness that is the outcome of rot. As they shrank away, the air turned bitter, then acrid. He started to cough and couldn't clear his throat. He was drowning in the smell of death.

Then they were gone and he was standing in the middle of a row of headstones. All around him he could hear the voices of children. They were laughing and calling to one another. Some were counting as if playing hide and seek. Others were calling out rhymes used in skipping rope or yelling for Red-Rover to come over. And then the voices drifted away on the breeze.

Now crying. Eric stood there among the stones and he could hear the children crying. The sound rang in his ears and filled his head. He could actually feel the pressure of it in his temples – a balloon expanding in his head. He turned in circles, knowing there was nothing to see; the headstones orbiting past him as he spun faster and faster. He grabbed at his head and fell to his knees.

Silence.

He drew his hands away from his head and strained to listen. There was nothing to hear. Beneath him, the ground started to give way, his knees sinking into the grass. He jumped to his feet and back-peddled, stopping only when he bumped up against a headstone.

In horror, he watched as the ground around him began to undulate and crack open. Huge mounds of grass and soil shot up into the air. One by one, the cemetery plots began to break, the headstones toppling like a row of dominoes. A thick, foul ooze, the consistency of tar, bubbled up through the open graves and crept like molasses towards Eric's feet. The stench was overwhelming and he started to gag. His nostrils filled with the acrid smell of decay and a rancid taste filled his mouth. He spat, trying to clear the taste from his palate, and when he did, pieces of rotted flesh dripped from his lips, some clinging like spittle.

Frantically, he wiped at his mouth and nose as he watched headstone after headstone sink into the ground, only to be hurled back up again. They began to rain down on him from every direction, wedging themselves, upside-down, into the churned soil around him.

Gasping, Eric sat up. On the lawn in front of him, Ruby was watching him intently, her tail tucked tightly between her legs and her ears folded all the way back. Above, the sun had drifted further west and was hanging just above the tree line. How long, for certain, he didn't know, but it had to have been hours that he'd been dreaming there. He pulled the watch out of his pocket and looked at it again. This time, he did open it. Both hands were straight up on the **12**.

Not thinking about it, he wound the watch. When he let go, the hands began to spin in opposites directions. They circled the face at a furious rate, both of them coming to rest once more on the **12**. Closing the cover, he put the watch back in his pocket and went inside the trailer. There, the kitchen clock read: 4:47 P.M.

Eric took a beer from the refrigerator, twisted the cap off and leaned back against the counter. He had just taken his second sip when the radio in the other room snapped on. It was an old song ... a familiar song, but the words had been changed and the voice singing them sounded like it was coming straight from hell. It growled them rather than sang them.

Eric charged into the bedroom and pushed down on the OFF button. Nothing happened. The demented version of *"Young At Heart"* just kept blaring out, repeating the same strains over and over and promising Eric a heart attack. He plucked the radio off the nightstand, yanking its cord out of the wall and it still kept playing. Without hesitating, he hurled it against the wall. Pieces of plastic and strands of wire sprayed across the room, and the tiny speaker diaphragm rolled in circles on the floor, still issuing the corrupted melody.

Crushing the tiny disc under his heel was what came to mind next. As he lifted his foot, the music stopped and a voice, dark and sinister came rumbling out: "Keep out of all this old man. Keep out of this or your dreams *will* come true!"

Eric could feel his heart begin to pound in his chest. There was a tightness creeping down his left arm and he couldn't seem to catch his breath. Pulling the little dark brown bottle out of his hip pocket, he fumbled with the cap. When he finally managed to get it open it flew out of his hands and rolled across the carpet. He crawled after it on his hands and knees, digging the tiny yellow pills out of the nap and placing one under his tongue. A few moments later the pain in his arm had eased and he could breathe again.

Sinking down, he lay on the carpet, his right hand still clutching at his chest. Tears rolled from the corners of his eyes and the numbness in his lips told him just how close he'd gotten to becoming the newest resident of Peaceful Haven.

Eric rolled onto his back. He could hear Ruby outside scratching at the door to get in but he didn't have the strength to make it that far. In a feeble voice he called, to her: "It's ok, girl. Daddy's ok. You just be a good girl. I'll come and get you soon."

Still panting, he listened to the dog's soft whimpering, telling him she was upset, telling him she knew he needed her, telling him she couldn't get to him. He pulled himself across the carpet on his belly with both hands, reached up and pulled down on the screen door handle. A paw darted in, pulled on the door and a moment later he was having his face licked.

CHAPTER 63

"Come out, come out, wherever you are," Evelyn called into the blackness of the Antique shop's basement. "Come to mama, you fuckin creep." She took another step down and bent over, straining to see, one hand on the railing, the other cradling the bust of Muhammad Ali.

Carlton got ready. One more step. That's all he needed her to take, just one more step. He could feel the warm run down his leg as he relieved himself in anticipation and excitement. When he bent to look down, his finger accidentally triggered the saws-all and it buzzed to life.

"Ah-Ha," came Evelyn's voice. "I knew you were hiding down there. What have you got? Huh? What's buzzing?"

Carlton fumbled for the switch, the sudden noise and vibration in his hands had startled him and he almost dropped it. He ran his hand across the handle until he found the button and then switched it off. It was too late. Evelyn had located the source of the sound.

"Under the fuckin steps, are you? Hmmm. I'll have to think about this for a minute."

Carlton heard the heavy thumps as Evelyn backed up the steps to the top. He'd lost his chance and it infuriated him. His cheeks flushed with anger and the rage building inside him made his hands start to tremble. He wanted nothing more than to race up the steps with the saw and cut her fat head off her fat, mastodon shoulders. Stepping out from under the stairs he came around to the bottom and looked up at her. She was still bending over trying to see down into the dark.

She can't see me, he thought. *The moose can't see me down here. Why, I could just rush up these steps and cut her apart.* He was about to do just that when another thought occurred to him. *That could be dangerous. She'd definitely hear me coming, and even if she couldn't see me until the last minute, all she'd have to do is kick me down the steps and I could break my neck. No, I'm not being tricked into that. If she wants me, she'll have to come and get me. Down here. Right down here!*

"C'mon up here, you chicken shit! Don't you have any self-respect? I'm not gonna wait all day."

"You want me? You come down here and get me. We'll see who's a chicken shit."

"Actually, I have a better idea."

"Yeah, what's that, you moose? Gonna jump up and down until the building caves in on me, you female version of Frankenstein? Gonna crush me to death with your blubber?"

"No, you worm. I have a much better idea. A much better idea. Now don't you go nowhere! Mama'll be right back."

With a *wham*, Evelyn closed the basement door and locked it. "Sit tight," she yelled through the door. "Be right back."

Carlton debated climbing to the top of the steps as quietly as he could and then surprising her when she opened the door. And again, he passed on that idea as being just a bit too risky. *Since I have no idea what she's planning, probably best to stay hidden down here. Make her come and get me.*

A few minutes later, he heard the latch turn on the door and the familiar sound it made when it was pulled open.

"I'm back, pansy-ass. But don't worry. I won't be staying. However, I *do* have a lovely parting gift for you, dickhead!"

Glup, glup, glup, glup. Carlton recognized the sound immediately. It was a sound he heard often, the sound of liquid being poured out of a can. And the smell was familiar too. Paint thinner ... not the generic stuff you can buy at and Home Depot, this was the good stuff, the stuff only certain industries had access to.

The fumes started to build up immediately and Carlton had to cover his mouth and nose with his handkerchief to keep from gagging. It wouldn't help for long though and that wasn't even the worst of it. He was in serious trouble. If she was planning what he thought she was planning, he was in dire, life or death trouble.   A moment later, Evelyn confirmed his worst fears.

"Since you're obviously not too bright, shit-head, let me be of help and illuminate you're your worthless life."

At the top of the steps, Carlton saw a light flicker into view and cast its faint glow down the first few steps.   A second later the steps were aflame, the match igniting the fumes almost instantly.

"Bye-bye, asshole."

Carlton panicked.   With the steps ablaze, there was no getting upstairs to escape.   His fear was overriding his common sense.   He forgot about the freight elevator in the back.   Slowly, he backed up, watching the flames climb higher, watching them start to lick at the rafters, to char them and then to consume them.

Scared senseless, he rushed to the back of the basement to hide.   That's when he remembered the elevator.   He moved through the semi-dark to the far end of the cellar, flipped the switch that opened the mechanical doors in the alleyway and climbed onto the loading elevator.

Time slowed down.   It seemed to take forever for the elevator to make its way up to ground level.   When it did, Carlton bent down to take one last look at the basement and all the boxes he hadn't even opened yet.   When he stood up and turned around, the fist hit him right on the bridge of the nose.   He staggered back and fell against the small railing on the freight elevator.

"Thought I'd let you get out this way, did you? Well, guess again." Evelyn hit him again, driving him to the ground. "We're not nearly through."

Carlton was dazed and petrified. There was no way he could win this fight. She outweighed him and her blows were staggering. Then he heard it. A tiny voice in his head telling him exactly what he had to do.

"Do it, Carlton," hissed the voice in his head. "Do it now, before she hits you again."

CHAPTER 64

Whether it had been the maggot adventure, just plain exhaustion or something else, Arliss had slept through the night, not awaking until after noon. Her mind was a jumble. There was no way she could scientifically sort out, categorize and explain the things that had been happening. Given the series of recent, supernatural events, rationality seemed, to her, to have taken a vacation from her life. The concept of the irreconcilable had never before occupied a place in her thought processes. Anything of that nature that she'd come across in the past had always been something that only needed further investigation, study, and delineation. But this ... this was something completely different – something operating in a whole new order of reality.

Sitting on the edge of her bed she wondered what it was she should do next. It was a holiday. She felt it was highly unlikely that Wedgemore's Antique Shoppe would still be open. That was where she had to go, the point of her whole trip, and now she was at a loss as to what to do. To make matters even worse, she was worried that, even though she'd paid extra to ensure the delivery, her box might not arrive for the same reason. Although she really had no idea why she felt she needed it in the first place.

While she was pondering her situation, the cell phone rang. Looking first at the caller I.D., she was surprised to see Bill Waters's name. For a moment, she debated as to whether or not she really wanted to be bothered. At last, her inborn sense of curiosity got the better of her and she flipped the phone open.

"Hi Bill. What's up?"

"Hello Dr. Peterson. Sorry to bother you, but I thought you might want to hear this."

"It's not a problem, Bill. I wasn't doing much of anything anyway." *Except being attacked by maggots and flies that couldn't have been there in the first place*, she thought. "What have you got for me?"

"Well, wait till you hear this. I did some background checking ... you know me ... anyway, made some phone calls and then did some research, and you'll never guess what I found out about our missing shipment."

Arliss could hear the excitement in Bill's voice. He sounded like a kid about to describe what

he'd just found under the Christmas tree. The last
time he was like this, he'd found a rare fossil on
EBay. The seller had no idea what he had, thinking
it just another geode with the imprint of a plant on
it. He had no way of knowing that he was selling a
fossil of a Cycad, one of the first trees to appear on
earth. Bill had purchased it for a mere fifteen
dollars, and couldn't contain himself. On that
occasion, he'd called Arliss at home, too.

"Ok, Bill. What'd you find out? I'm
guessing from your level of excitement that it's
good news."

"Good news? Not sure about good, but
very, very interesting. If my research is correct, it
could actually be very scary news, but then, that
would depend on how you feel about myths and
legends and what you think about the supernatural
and what you think about the paranormal and-"

"I get it," said Arliss, breaking in. "What's
the scoop?"

"Ok. Ok. This is really cool. Are you
ready for this? I mean, this is really, really rad."

"Rad? Rad? Do people still use that
expression anymore?'

"Umm ... I dunno. I do ... and this is *rad!*"

"Well then, cool your jets Bill and tell me
about it."

"Ok, ok. Well, it turns out that the artifact
that we were supposed to get, the one that went to
that dinky little town in Pennsylvania ... well, it
seems that ... I mean, it turns out that no one has
been able to identify its origins. I mean, not

completely. And get this, when it was first found, they tried carbon dating it and couldn't."

"Couldn't? Why not?"

"Nobody knows for sure. I mean, Dr. Oliver Talbot couldn't even make sense of it. But that's not nearly the end. They couldn't x-ray it, they couldn't fluoresce it ... nothing. Nobody knows how old the thing is."

"Wait a minute Bill. Before you go on ... I'm assuming you know what the thing is by now. How about letting me in on that little secret."

"Well, Doc, it seems it's some kind of sword handle, complete with a big rounded pommel. And that's where it gets really interesting. There's a design on the pommel that's led Dr. Talbot to believe that this thing ... this sword is something out of religious legend. Now, he said he's not saying that it's a real ... um ... that it was *really* used by ... um ..." Bill fell silent for a moment.

"Bill, you still there?"

"Yeah. I'm here, just not sure how to tell you the next part."

"Ok. Just thought I'd lost you. You know how it is with cell phones."

"Yeah, I do. Anyway, here's the thing. It looks like ancient drawings ... I mean ... the sword handle looks like ancient drawings that depict the sword used by ... used by ... Lucifer, when he fought with Michael .. or is supposed to fight with Michael, however that goes ... and was expelled from heaven ... or *will* be expelled from heaven. Whatever."

From the other end of the phone, Bill could hear Arliss give out with a long sigh. He knew what was coming next.

"Oh, please, Bill. You're not seriously suggesting that this thing was actually used by the devil, are you? I mean, really."

"No, no. But look at it this way, if it was created way back when ... even as only a symbol of what the religious powers believed, then it's got to be worth ... I dunno ... you tell me. Probably more money than I can even imagine. And I can sure as hell imagine a lot. But even more important than that ... it'd be an artifact that we should have. I mean ... there'd really be only one of them wouldn't there?"

"Are you sure about all this?"

"C'mon, Doc, you know me. I get excited, sure, but when have you ever known me to come up with faulty info. I mean, really ... you *know* I always double and triple check my facts. Especially those that are so far off base they're in another field entirely."

"Alright. I'll check things out here."

"Here? Where's here? I thought you'd wanna come into the museum and see all my facts. Where are you?"

"Actually Bill, I'm in a little place called ... oh hell, I forget...but it's right outside of Banderman Falls. That is, I'm in Pennsylvania, trying to get a hand on our lost artifact."

"Wow, really? When'd you leave? I mean, why'd you go there? Why-"

"Never mind all that right now, Bill. I'll let you know what I find out. I'm going to personally pick up our missing item. With any luck, I'll be back after the weekend. See you on Monday morning."

"Ok, boss, see you then."

Arliss didn't say anything else, she just disconnected, sat back down on the bed and thought. She wondered what she really believed when it came to God and religion. Was the idea of corporeal demons and devils a possibility? Did the afterlife hold unspeakable horrors for those who transgressed and unimaginable beauty and peace for those who didn't? Could there really have been a Lucifer, cast down from a heaven in battle with another angel – an archangel named Michael? Or was it all just an invention by those who lacked scientific understanding in their time to create a means of keeping the public in line. A moral stick?

And what did she believe about life, death and beyond anyway? Most of her life she'd been confused about that. When she found science, it stabilized her, gave her a firm ground from which to work - a perspective that put the world and its workings in an ordered place. But inside, she still felt – knew - that there had to be something beyond the realms of science. There had to be some kind of force that man would never be able to fully comprehend. Was it a God? That, she didn't know. But ... if there was a God, then didn't it follow that there *had* to be some kind of antithesis ... some kind of devil. Can there be an understanding of light without an understanding of darkness?

It didn't take her long to realize that she was running around in mental circles. She needed to find a concrete place to start ... a jumping-off point from which she could rationally analyze the present situation.

"Ok, Arliss," she muttered, "let's assume for the moment that there is some kind of evil that operates in the world. Maybe it's corporeal, maybe it's not. But let's assume that the precepts from which the idea of God and the devil came have some basis in fact. If that's true, then it follows that, at some point in history, two great powers, whatever they were, came into being and into opposition. Now, assuming they're physical entities, then what remained of the battle would also be of a physical nature. So ... if this sword ... is representative of that battle or conflict, then perhaps ... just perhaps ... it does hold some power beyond our present scientific ability to analyze. Could the ancients have understood particle physics like we do now? No ... not because quantum theory wasn't viable back then, but rather because they lacked the tools to discover it. In the same vein, there must be things that we are inadequate to the task of understanding today. Things that future generations will have the tools to investigate."

Arliss rubbed at her temples. The whole thing was giving her a headache. She knew she could spend the rest of the evening, perhaps the rest of her life, trying to make sense of something that made no sense, or trying to put a rational spin on something that had no rationality. She came to the conclusion that the only thing she could do was to accept what was happening existentially and deal with it on that level.

"It doesn't matter where a rabid dog got its rabies when it's standing in front of you growling, snarling and preparing to attack. At that moment, all that matters is what you're going to do about it. That's where you are with this, Arliss, old girl. Just deal with it. Worry about the whys and wherefores later."

CHAPTER 65

Jack climbed out of Ethan's cruiser, hitched up his pants at the waist and looked around. The irritation he felt was mirrored on his face. He was wearing a deep scowl and his upper lip was clamped firmly down on the lower.

"What about the phones?" asked Robertson, stabbing a thumb over his shoulder in the direction of the B & B. "Think they're out of order too?"

"The way things are going today, I'd have to say yes. But you're right. Have to give em a try."

Jack started towards the steps and Robertson fell in behind him. Whirling around, Jack jabbed his index finger into Robertson's chest.

"You just cool your heels out here. I'll check it out. That's my job."

"Um, Jack?"

"What?"

"Considering how strange things are at the moment, don't you think it's a better idea if we just stick together? Harder to take out two than one."

Jack hated to admit it, but Robertson was probably right. "Ok, you win. C'mon. Let's see if we can't get old Ma Bell to give us a hand."

"Ma Bell? Geezuz, Jack, you're dating yourself. Ma Bell died years ago. Buried alive by Verizon, AT&T, Cingular, Sprint-"

"Yeah, I get it, Doc. I get it."

At the front door, Jack cupped his hands around his eyes and peered in the screen. The lobby was empty. He glanced at Robertson, then pulled the door open and stepped in, blocking it so Robertson couldn't get through. When he was certain no one was there, he moved aside and walked over to the front desk. Before he lifted the receiver, he looked at Robertson and gave him an "ok, here goes" look. A second later the receiver was back in its cradle and there was no need for further explanation.

Both men turned suddenly when they heard the sound of tires crunching up the gravel drive. They looked at each other and then Jack walked over to the screen door and looked out. Bill Pinsky's cruiser was just coming to a stop behind his.

Jack pushed through the door and jumped down the porch steps. He was beside the car before Bill even had a chance to open the door.

"Where the hell have you been?" shouted Jack.

"Flat. Damnedest thing, too. Soon as I got it fixed, another blew. Had to wait for Karpi's Truck and Tire t'bring me an extra spare.

"Why the hell didn't you try callin?"

"I did. Called you six times ... and Audrey four. Finally got her, never heard from you. So, soon as the tires were fixed, headed right here. Ran the lights all the way till I hit the driveway." Bill looked around. "Where's Ethan?"

"Gimme your radio mic."

"Won't help. Seems to have gone dead, just before I got here."

Jack grabbed the mic off Bill's shoulder and keyed it. As Bill had said, there wasn't even so much as a click or the hiss of static.

"Shit! Shit!" yelled Jack. "What the fuck is going on around here?"

"I think we covered that question already," said Robertson, as he joined the men on the driveway. "You'll probably get the same answer you did last time you asked it, too."

Jack smiled. "Yeah. Yeah, I guess you're right, Doc."

"How about-"

"Phones inside, Bill?" cut in Robertson. "Tried em already."

"Oh."

"C'mon," said Jack, "might as well get in out of the heat."

"Wait a minute," cried Robertson. "I think you've overlooked something."

"What's that, Doc?" asked Jack, his disgust for the situation showing.

Robertson thumbed over his shoulder. "The car. Bill's car."

"Shit, you're right. C'mon. Let's go."

Jack shot around the front of the cruiser and slid in behind the wheel. He was already cranking the key around when Robertson pulled the passenger's side door open. He froze in place and hung his head. The key turned, but the ignition didn't fire. Like the two cars that sat in front of it ... it was dead.

"Dammit, dammit, DAMMIT!" shouted Jack, pummeling the steering wheel with his fist. "Dammit!"

"But it was just working," protested Bill. "It was working just fine when I pulled in. 'Cept for the radio, that is." He took off his hat and wiped the sweat off his brow with his sleeve. "I just don't get it, boss. It was working perfectly."

CHAPTER 66

Father Jacobs looked out the window at the late afternoon sun. Geoffrey sat in the chair, the bite marks slowly fading from his skin. Jacobs turned to face him, his face grave, his eyes stern.

"I think that whatever it is we're going to do, we'd better get to doing it."

Geoffrey Dunsmore stood. It appeared to Jacobs that his friend looked younger, stronger than when he'd first arrived. Ordinarily, he'd have dismissed it as a trick of the light, but not today. Today, anything was possible, and inside him, a corner of him hoped that it was not just a trick of the light; a corner of him hoped that his friend had, indeed, somehow become stronger. Because deep inside, where all men keep their darkest secrets, Jacobs believed that they would need such a strength before this was all over.

"Give me your clock, Gabe," Geoffrey said, holding out his hand.

Jacobs produced the Big Ben miniature and placed it in Geoffrey's hand. His eyes were locked on Geoffrey's, studying him, watching his every movement and wondering if they had a chance in hell of defeating the ... the what? His conscious mind kept calling it a thing, but his subconscious kept pushing the word Devil to the forefront of his thoughts.

"Ok. Like I said, I'm not sure we can do this with only two of the three clocks. And I'm also uncomfortable about the timing. But we'll have to risk it. We need to eliminate the children from the scenario."

Jacobs had lots of questions but asked none of them. All things would be revealed, perhaps sooner than he'd like. He watched as Geoffrey slowly wound the hands on the clocks counterclockwise. With each passing of the midnight hour, the face of the clock grew brighter and brighter until Jacobs had to avert his eyes.

"I need you to concentrate very hard Gabe. I want you to picture in your mind every child in town sleeping. You need to see it in your head. They're beginning to get drowsy, then tired. I need you to see their eyes closing, their mouths opening in wide yawns."

Father Gabriel Jacobs closed his eyes and thought about the children. He watched them, willed them. Specific faces, faces of children he'd taught in catechism class, children who'd severed as altar boys for him, children whose parents he was familiar with – he saw them all and imagined them drifting off to a peaceful, quiet sleep. And even with his eyes pinched tightly shut the burning light from the clocks' dials reached in through his sealed eyelids.

The more he concentrated, the further into himself he felt he was falling. Always at the forefront were the drowsing and sleeping children, but behind them in a hazy silhouette of a movie he could see the phantoms of their darker sides. They danced and yelled, some torturing small animals, others tormenting the weaker children, still others committing more heinous acts. He tried to focus hard; he tried to keep his mind locked on the peacefully slumbering children, but it was becoming harder and harder to do. He wanted to open his eyes and see the dazzling light. A thought - an evil thought pushed through telling him to open his eyes and stare at the clocks and then to destroy them.

Suddenly, he felt a hand on his shoulder and a voice whispering in his ear. "Stand fast Father. Keep your eyes closed, keep your thoughts pure. Protect the children; help them to sleep."

The voice was soft and strong and female. He did not recognize it. Nonetheless, it was a comforting voice and the more it spoke, the hazier the dark silhouettes grew, fading into the background, disappearing like smoke on an evening breeze. Then came a stronger voice, a voice he *did* recognize.

"Don't open your eyes Father. Whatever else you do ... do *not* open your eyes." Geoffrey's voice was stern but reassuring in its tone. "Keep thinking, Gabe. Keep your mind on the children. See them sleeping in their beds."

Part of him wanted to laugh. The whole thing was almost sitcom ridiculous. Most of him did not find anything funny about it. Most of him was more frightened than he had ever been in his life. The room was beginning to get hotter, and it was becoming harder and harder for him to breath. He cupped both hands over his eyes, belying the weakness in himself, the weakness of all men – temptation. The temptation to do what he was told not to do. But his cupped hands were also an affirmation that he would not give in, no matter what he had to do to succeed.

Multi-colored fingers of sizzling hot light, like lightning bolts, shot forth from the face of the clocks. It sizzled and popped and Jacobs could smell the ozone and burnt air. He wanted desperately to see what was happening yet he kept his eyes firmly closed, concentrating on the children of Banderman Falls. At times, the temptation to look was overwhelming, as if someone were trying to pry his eyes open. A battle of voices thundered in his head. He could hear the pleas of mothers begging him to save their children and the growling threats of fathers, demanding that he leave their children alone, open his eyes and be done with this silly nonsense. But through it all came that same soft woman's voice telling him to hold his course. Encouraging him. And along with her voice came the images of placid lakes, snow-covered mountains, and pristine forests. Everything that Father Jacobs found relaxing and renewing was entwined in her speech. His respirations slowed and the heat of the room seemed to diminish. At the backs of his eyes, he could see the children - peacefully sleeping. And the cacophony of the parents' bellowings faded away.

The room began to shake as if taken by a sudden earthquake. Just barely above the rumble, Jacobs could hear Geoffrey telling him that everything was all right and to keep his eyes closed and keep concentrating. The shaking increased and he stumbled around, trying fruitlessly to keep his balance. His left shoulder slammed into something hard, the door jamb he thought, and it took all his will not to open his eyes. His hair was standing on end and his body tingled from electric charges that shot back and forth across the room.

"It's ok, Gabe. Keep your eyes shut. It's ok." Geoffrey's voice sounded like it was coming from a can at the bottom of a river. Jacobs wrapped himself around the door jamb to steady himself and slid down it so that he was sitting on the floor, one arm and one leg on each side of the frame.

As if in a dark dream, a face began to form in Jacobs's mind. It was a black, demonic face; its lips curled in a wolf's snarl. Rows of horns, each increasing in length and varying in texture and contour protruded from its head. They ran from front to back like shark's teeth. An accompanying smell of excrement and rancid garbage mixed with molten sulfur filled his nostrils and he could feel his stomach beginning to churn.

"Geoffrey," he called out, "Geoffrey, can you see it?" There would be no answer forthcoming that he could hear. At once his ears filled with the sound of buzzing, so loud and so intense that his temples began to throb and his nose to bleed. He tried to close his mind's eye, to ignore the image that was leering at him, but he couldn't. Its leathery and charred lips peeled back exposing a row of jagged fangs. A slimy green liquid dripped from their ends in long stings as it gnashed and chomped at him, and huge, orange, vacuous catlike eyes burned into him. And he knew what they were searching for. They sought his soul.

"Dear God, please spare me this horrid image. Help me to regain the solace and peace of the children-"

A booming laughter broke though, shaking Jacobs out of his prayer. The face in front of him hissed, and a great black tongue shot forth. It writhed in front of Jacobs's face, curling and uncurling. Deep within its maw the priest could see children, half-eaten, their faces contorted in soundless screams.

His eyes still closed tight, Jacobs tried to blot out the image. It would not go. And then another voice came to him over the rumbling laughter of the beast. It was a very familiar voice and it took the priest by surprise. It was a voice he would have never expected to hear, yet it came to him nonetheless. And when it did, the face of the beast shrank away into nothingness, its laughter echoing into oblivion.

CHAPTER 67

Jack, Robertson and Bill Pinsky stood on the porch of the B & B discussing their options. Their communication and transportation were shut down. There was no question about that. Walking back to town was also a moot point; it would take them nearly two hours.

"Well, we can't just stand around all day. Like it or not, it seems our only real choice at this point is to hoof it back to town. At least get on the main road and hope someone drives by." Jack mopped his brow with his sleeve. "It's a little after four-thirty. Assuming we don't catch a break, we could make it back to town by ... oh ... say, six-thirty or so."

"Unfortunately," said Robertson, "I concur. I think it's our only option."

"Well, one of us could go and then come back," suggested Bill.

"That's true. But there's no guarantee that when they got back we wouldn't end up with just another dead car. Things ain't right here. I don't know what's happening ... or why, but it seems clear that we can't assume that it's just going to blow over. I think we should all take the hike." Jack looked from one to the other. "What'd ya say?"

"Think you're right again, Jack," said Robertson. "Let's get going. *But* ... let's grab some water to take with us. It's going to be a long hot walk."

"Good idea, Doc," said Bill.

"All right," instructed Jack, "you go get the water, Bill. I'm gonna unlock the shotguns. Hope we won't need em, but as weird as things are now ... who knows."

Just before Bill pulled the screen door open, the familiar rumble of a Harley could be heard, the thumping sound of its V-Twin getting closer.

"Hey, I think someone's coming," shouted Bill. "Maybe if we're lucky-"

"Don't know why," broke in Robertson, "but for some reason I got a bad feeling about this."

"Me too, Doc," echoed Jack, a scowl spreading across his face. "C'mon, let's get inside before they get here. We'll be able to size things up better with a little cover."

The three went in, Jack moving over toward one of the windows and motioning Bill to take the one on the far side. Robertson instinctively knew where Jack wanted him and took a covered position in the office doorway behind the front desk.

"Now let's just keep things cool until we find out who we're dealing with. Whole thing could be harmless. Just want to be ready if it's not," commanded Jack.

Jack and Bill watched from behind the curtains as the Sportster rolled to a stop on the far side of Jack's car. The rider dropped the kickstand and then just sat there on the bike looking around.

Both Jack and Bill recognized him immediately. They'd each dealt with Curtis Lattimore on more than one occasion.

As Curtis twisted himself around on the bike, taking in his surroundings, Jack caught sight of the silver Taurus wedged into his waistband. He gave a quick nod to Bill, who indicated that he'd also seen it. Both men let their hands drop to the butts of their weapons, thumbing the safety straps open at almost the same time. They watched as Curtis dismounted his bike and then stood there looking at the front of the B & B.

Cautiously, Curtis moved forward, still on the far side of the cars. He checked them out first, making sure no one was hiding there. Then he moved around to the front of Ethan's cruiser and pulled the gun out of his pants, chambered a round and crouched down behind the fender. It was too bright outside for him to be able to see anything through the B & B's windows. It looked like the curtains were pulled back slightly, but he couldn't be sure. He thought it would be nice if his boss would tell him what to do, would tell him where his targets were. He waited, but no instructions were forthcoming.

Well at least I know who my targets are now, he thought. *Maybe not by name, but I sure as hell know they're cops. This ain't gonna be easy unless I get some help. Shit! There's three fuckin cars here. That means* at least *three oinkers.* He could feel the sweat begin to well up on his forehead and trickle down into his eyes. He blinked to clear it and then rubbed at them with his forearm.

The sting of the salt in his eyes started them tearing and rubbing them just made it worse. Forgetting his situation for the moment, he stood up. Had either Jack or Bill decided to, they could have ended things right then and there. Jack actually thought about it; he just didn't have any clear reason as yet to be able to declare it a clean shoot. So he waited to see what Curtis was going to do. Although he was pretty sure what that was going to be.

"Think he'll come in?" whispered Bill, his eyes searching Jack's. "Think he's here to pull some shit?"

Jack looked at him, almost puzzled. "No, he's here delivering pizza, Bill. What the hell do *you* think?" As soon as he'd said it, Jack wished he could take it back. No need to take his frustration out on Bill. Everyone was tense. "Sorry, Bill."

"Not a problem. It *was* a pretty stupid question. I'm just a bit nervous, that's all."

"You're not alone," replied Jack, sympathetically. "You're not alone."

Curtis stood looking at the building for almost five minutes. When he didn't see any movement, he sidled around the front of the car to the porch side. Cautiously, he inched his way to the bottom of the steps. With every step he took, his head swiveled from side to side seeking out any sign of danger or his quarry. The stillness and placidness of his surroundings unnerved him. He could feel his hands shaking and his mouth was as dry as the depression-era dustbowl.

At the bottom of the steps he paused, looking from left to right and then behind him. He wasn't sure whether he should go inside or not. It didn't feel safe to him, and right now, all he was concerned with was his safety. He finally settled on going around back to see what was out there, although the thoughts of being out in the open weren't any more settling than the thoughts of going inside. What he really wanted to do was just to get on his Harley and get the hell out of there. But he was certain that to do so would mean something far worse than what the cops could do to him.

Taking it one step at a time, the Taurus held out in front of him shaking unsteadily, he walked to the end of the B & B and stuck his head slowly around the corner. He could see all the way to the back where the edge of the woods stood as a fence line. Now he had to decide if he was going to run all the way to the back or make his way there inch by inch. Each method had its own set of built-in hazards.

"Where the fuck are you when I need you?" he asked, hoping the powers that drove him would give him some guidance. As an afterthought, he also hoped that it wouldn't take offense just because he asked and, most particularly, because he asked in what his new boss would consider a very rude fashion.

Bracing himself for the worst, he stepped out from the protection of the building's corner and started toward the back. His heart beat faster and faster with each step, thumping against the walls of his chest like some mad jungle drummer sending signals to his friends in the Tarzan movies he'd watched as a child. Before he was halfway down the side of the building he could feel his knees losing their solidity. The thought occurred to him that if he didn't hurry, he wasn't going to make it. He was going to pass out and the cops, or worse yet, his boss, were going to find him sprawled on the grass like a downed scarecrow.

"C'mon, Curtis, you can do this boy," he stammered, his hands shaking so badly that he couldn't even sight the gun. It waved back and forth in front of him like a flag blowing in the wind. "Come ... on ... man, you can do this. They're just no good pieces of shit cops. You can handle this." By the time he'd made it to the rear corner, Curtis was nearly in a state of full-blown panic. Even with two hands, he couldn't keep the Taurus steady. He pressed his back against the wall, wishing he could sink into it entirely. As quickly as he could, he thrust his head around the corner and drew it back again.

Summoning every ounce of courage he could find, he jumped out, arms outstretched, gun waving wildly and knees bent so that he was in a stooped position. If someone had been to his left, he would have never seen them because of the tunnel-vision his panic had created. All he could concentrate on was straight ahead. It took him a few minutes to be able to turn his head and survey the rest of the property. There was nothing to see. He wheeled and faced the kitchen door. From where he was he could only see a few feet inside, but there was nothing to see there. He took a deep breath, pulled the door open and jumped in. When it closed, it slapped him hard in the ass and a slight yelp escaped his trembling lips.

After Curtis had disappeared around the corner of the building, Jack sent Bill out front and then moved into the dining room. When Curtis hit himself with the door, Jack heard it and plastered himself up against the far wall beside the kitchen doorway. Bill made his way around the back, cautiously following Curtis' path, his Beretta leading the way. When he reached the corner, he stopped to listen, both hands steadying his weapon with the barrel pointed straight up. Bill took a deep breath, held it and stepped out, leveling his gun. The back was empty.

In the kitchen, Curtis had reached the breaking point. He was too afraid to go any further in and too afraid to go back. He could feel his knees beginning to buckle under him so he sat down. A moment later, Bill Pinsky tugged the screen door open.

Two rapid shots rang out, echoing through the kitchen. Jack immediately pivoted around into the doorway just in time to see Bill stagger backward. Bill slammed against the screen door, his Berretta discharging. The bullet whizzed past Jack's head and embedded itself in the door jamb.

Curtis spun around to face Jack, but he was too slow. Two .357 rounds burrowed into his left shoulder and upper chest, driving him to the floor. Jack crossed the room in two steps, kicked Curtis's gun across the floor and stood over him, the barrel of his gun pointed right at Curtis's forehead.

"Doc," Jack screamed. "Doc, get in here. Now!"

A moment later Robertson appeared at the kitchen door.

"Bill's been hit," said Jack, "see what you can do for him."

Robertson hadn't waited for Jack's command; he was already sidestepping him and Curtis on his way to the back. He'd heard the gunshots and when he'd got to the kitchen he could see Bill's legs sticking in through the screen door.

"You fuckin even sneeze and I'll ventilate your skull."

Curtis was rolling from side to side clutching at his shoulder and screaming. A large pool of blood was already beginning to surround Jack's boots.

Not lifting his eyes from the bleeding man on the floor, Jack yelled, "How is he Doc? How bad is it? Is he gonna make it?"

Robertson straightened up from examining Bill and came back inside. The look on his face told Jack everything he needed to know. Robertson just shook his head. A moment later he was kneeling beside Curtis examining his wounds.

"I'm gonna need some plastic," he said. "One of your slugs punctured the lung. I need to stop the air from leaking out."

"What kind of plastic, Doc?" asked Jack. "Not that I really wanna save the bastard, but..."

"A couple pieces of saran wrap should do it." Robertson was pressing down on the holes with both hands, trying to stem the bleeding. He could hear the distinctive whistle of the hemopneumothorax that Jack's bullets had created. Without the plastic wrap, Curtis's lung would completely collapse.

Jack dug through the kitchen drawers until he found what he needed. Curtis lay there moaning and rolling, but Jack kept an eye on him anyway.

"Here Doc, this do?" He handed the box of wrap to Robertson and then went over to Bill. There was a large hole in his left cheek and another at the base of his throat. For the second time in two days, Jack could hear the accusations in his head. "Where were you, Jack? Why didn't you have my back?" He looked down at Bill, who had the same glazed look that Pat O'Donnell had had. That same vacant stare that told Jack that he had failed.

"Ok, we're gonna need some gauze or bandages of some kind. You have a first aid kit in your car, right?"

"Yeah. You be ok in here with him while I go get it?"

"I think so. He's not in much shape for fighting. I'll also need my bag from the back seat."

"I still don't trust him. Watch yourself and keep alert." Jack handed him Bill's gun. "Know how to use this?"

"Yes, but I'd prefer not to. Not really my calling."

"Doc, I don't care about your calling right now. I just don't wanna come back in here and find you dead. Got it?"

"Crystal, Jack. Believe me, I have no great desire to depart this world just yet, but I still don't think I need the gun."

"I'd feel better if you took it."

Robertson reached down and pushed his index finger into Curtis's shoulder wound. Curtis let out a loud scream and his face went white. "See, just a touch is all it'll take. Funny how real gunshot wounds aren't like the ones you see on TV. They really hurt like hell. A bullet does a hell of a lot of damage. You see, torn muscle and a broken collar bone don't make for heroes."

Jack smiled. "I'll be right back."

"Jack," Robertson looked down at Curtis, "if we don't get him to a hospital soon-" He didn't finish the sentence.

"We'll try, Doc. I'd rather not, but we'll try."

Robertson just nodded.

***

When Jack returned to the kitchen with doc's medical bag and the first aid kit, Curtis was already starting to fade. His color was pallid and his lips were beginning to blue. Robertson was still kneeling beside him compressing the large holes that Jack's hollow points had dug into him.

"Gauze and ace wrap first," barked Robertson. "I have to close off this chest wound."

Jack handed Robertson a few gauze squares, a gauze wrap and the ace bandage. He waited while Robertson slipped the gauze pads underneath the saran wrap, wrapped his shoulder in the bandage and then cinched it tight with the ace wrap.

"Ok, I'll need some more pads for the other wound too." Robertson was panting as he supported Curtis' weight and figurge-eighted it with the ace. "I gotta tell ya, Jack, I don't think he's gonna make it. Luckily, you missed the subclavian artery, but I still can't stop the bleeding ... not completely. He needs surgery."

"You know, Doc ... it wouldn't be a bad thing for the world if he didn't make it."

Robertson looked up but said nothing. The look was enough. And he took note of the look on Jack's face and knew exactly what he was thinking – that he'd love to let him die but his professionalism wouldn't permit it.

"I'll go see if I can get one of those cars started. I have my doubts, but I'll give it the old college try.

Robertson nodded. "I know, Jack. I know you will."

Upstairs, Witherstone had completed his transformation. Once again he looked and felt like a man, yet he was still not at full strength. Things had happened much faster than he had anticipated and he'd had to stretch himself very thin in directing them. In his mind he could see what had happened downstairs. Things had spun out of control. What he needed now was an infusion of energy. The energy he drew from the malevolent natures of the citizenry.

Forgetting about Jack, Robertson, and Curtis, he stretched out his mind toward the center of Banderman Falls. With all the concentration he could muster, he began to chip away at every good belief that people held. Centering his thoughts on Wedgemore and his situation, he began to draw the dark nature of humanity out into the open. It was time to bring things to a head. It was time to set the good people of Banderman Falls against one another and draw his strength from the conflict. And then - then it would be time to claim his right - the prize that Wedgemore valued above all else - Lucifer's Pommel.

Witherstone closed his mind around Carlton's like a hand closing around a baseball.

"Do it, Carlton. Do it now, before she hits you again. Use it. It's your power, isn't it? Use it now to save your life."

CHAPTER 68

With one hand wrapped tightly around the exterior freight elevator railing and the other in front of his face, Carlton tried to shrink away from Evelyn's next blow. He had all but given up, realizing that he wasn't going to survive Evelyn Ramsey's wrath when a familiar voice began hissing in his head.

"Do it, Carlton. Do it now, before she hits you again. Use it. It's your power, isn't it? Use it now to save your life."

Carlton could feel the heat that rose from the flames in the basement. He could feel the anger welling up inside him; he could feel the pleasure he was going to have when he dispatched the fat bitch that was leaning over him, threatening him.

Evelyn reached down and grabbed Carlton by his lapels with one hand. In a single swift motion, she yanked him to his feet and drew back her other, balling it into a pudgy fist. Her mouth was agape with a sadistic grin, her puffy, lipstick-painted lips shrinking away from the edges of her white teeth.

"Time to eat knuckles, shit head," she bellowed. She pulled her punching arm as far back as she could get it (Newton's law of stored energy), aimed directly at Carlton's nose and started to uncoil it. She never got the chance. Halfway through her swing she let out an earsplitting cry and her arms clutched at her chest. She staggered backward, her eyes wide with surprise. When she reached the curb, she tumbled into the street onto her back, her head striking the macadam.

Carlton pulled himself to his feet. He was giggling and grinning.

"What? What did you say, you fuckin whore? You're gonna do what? Oh yeah, I remember ... you're gonna die!" Carlton was shouting at her as loudly as he could, enjoying the sight of her lying there, blood oozing from her mouth, her ears and the split in the back of her head that the street had so kindly donated to his cause. "Don't you ever fuck with Carlton Wedgemore. Ever!"

Carlton looked up and down the street. People had stopped and were staring at him. He didn't care.

"Do you hear me?" he shouted. "All of you. Don't fuck with Carlton Wedgemore or you'll all end up like this lump of worthless lard." His face was contorted in a sneer. Those watching stood silently, staring at the little man who had once been the butt of everyone's jokes and pranks. No one moved, they just stared.

Carlton wiped his hands together in a "there, that's that!" motion, walked over to Evelyn's twitching body, raised his leg and brought the heel of his shoe down onto her left breast. Blood spurted from her mouth and nose, and the air it forced from her lungs rattled away into the heat of the afternoon. He then casually reached down and pulled his prized possession out of her chest. He held it up, reveling in the sight of blood that dripped from its jagged edge. He thought about kicking her. He thought about stomping her face flat. But he did neither. Instead, he knelt down beside her, held his broken sword in both hands and proceeded to cut off her head, sawing at it like a carpenter with a two-by-four.

Picking it up by the hair and holding it out at arm's length, he stood and made a slow circle, the sword handle dangling from his other hand by his side. Evelyn's blood spray dripped from his chin and ran in rivulets down his cheeks.

"Do you see this?" he yelled as he turned. "Do you all see this? Get in my way ... say one thing I don't like ... look at me wrong ... and the same'll happen to you. Take a good look everybody. This is what happens when you mess with Carlton Wedgemore."

Suddenly, the head twisted round in his hand, the hair almost braiding itself. The eyes hadn't glazed over yet and they rolled from side to side as if they were trying to focus. Blood and snot dripped from the nose and the lips were quivering, opening and closing. It reminded Carlton of the goldfish imitation he used to do as a child. He gripped the hair tighter as the head swiveled from side to side, finally coming to rest facing him.

It opened its mouth and blood shot out, spraying Carlton in the face. Then flies, thousands of flies poured out of the mouth like bats from a cave on a summer's evening. And then it spoke.

"Carlton, you will listen to me very carefully and follow my orders to the letter. Do you understand?"

Carlton nodded. He wasn't afraid; he wasn't even surprised. Deep inside him, in his soul, he knew that his time was coming, and that the one speaking to him through Evelyn's head was the one that was going to set him free – to empower him.

"I want you to place me in the doorway of your shop. Do not try to stop the fire. Let it burn. In fact, I want you to start more fires. I want you to burn this town to the ground. They deserve it, you know. They all deserve it. When have they ever befriended you? When have they ever included you in their parties and get-togethers and picnics? Never. So now you can reward them. Burn their ignorant, uncaring town to the ground. Burn their lives. And when you are through ... when those who have wronged you know the scorching fury of your anger ... you will go to Peaceful Haven and await me there."

The disembodied head of Evelyn Ramsey began to laugh, a high-pitched cackling laugh. And Carlton began to laugh with it. He could feel the surge of adrenaline coursing through him. He licked at his lips, lips that were doused with the blood Evelyn's head had spewed upon him and he liked it. It tasted like revenge.

Carlton moved to the front door of his shop. Through the window, he could see the flames shooting up the cellar steps and engulfing the rear of the store. The orange light flickered and danced as it cast undulating shadows on the walls. Carefully, he placed the head on the front stoop, bent down and gave it a kiss. It kissed him back. He then turned away, fully prepared to honor his master's wishes.

CHAPTER 69

Gwen's heels echoed in the hollowness of the empty warehouse as she searched for Ernie and his whore. Her face was a brilliant red, flushed with anger and hatred. She was totally focused on the search and never heard the warehouse doors sliding shut behind her. She never heard the clinking of the chains and the echo of the lock snapping closed. She did hear the booming laughter coming from Penny Bishop, but she ignored it.

Rounding a corner made of old and rusting shelves, Gwen came to a dead end. Piled high in one corner was a conglomeration of oxidized chemical cans, a shredded, dingy canvas, and various bottles and jars, some half-empty, lying on their rounded sides like toppled bowling pins. Not finding the object of her ire, Gwen stomped over and kicked at the pile of cans, sending them bouncing off the wall.

A mix of powdery dust and dirt clouded up and settled back down. Gwen coughed, turned and headed for the other side of the immense structure. Half used shelving and old rotting crates created a maze through which she had to navigate. Turning this way, stopping and going back; turning that way only to have to go back again, her frustration built along with her fury.

In one corner of the building, well removed from the main floor, she came to a disintegrating office. Termite tubes stretched up its flaking wooden walls. What had once been a large window that looked out into the vastness of the plant was now just a gaping hole, its frame riddled with fissures and black mold. Inside, a torn, rusted-out metal and leather desk chair sat cobweb-covered behind its desk, waiting for a long-gone manager to come and take the company's helm.

Gwen Archibald, police officer and scorned lover, pushed through the silvery webs that spanned the doorway. She could hear the panting that drifted out from inside the office. She could smell the sweat of two people lusting for each other. She could hear the moans of the bitch that was letting her man penetrate her and the groaning of that two-timing fuck as he came inside her.

"All right you two, I'm here now. I've found you and you're both gonna pay." Gwen stormed around to the far side of the desk, rolling the chair aside with such force that the seat snapped off its rusted support and clunked to the floor. There on the floor, in the far corner of the office, a man was on top of a woman. Gwen watched for a moment as his ass undulated up and down. She looked around seeking something she could use as a weapon; her mind locked on a bloody revenge. Spinning around, she strode over to the broken window, pulled down a piece of splintered molding and charged back across the room.

The man and woman on the floor paid no attention to her. They kept moaning and clutching and pumping each other. Gwen stood over them, the molding pointed down, both hands wrapped firmly around its upper edge. She brought the make-shift spear down. It sank into the man's back with a soft squelch, went through him, went through the woman, and buried its point in the dilapidated flooring beneath them.

A ululating cry shattered the silence, followed by a peel of hideous laughter. The man and woman struggled to their feet, pinned together, front-to-front. They turned, their laughter booming through the empty warehouse, multiplying in the vastness of it and coming back to assault Gwen's ears. They stood there looking at her, their heads thrown back as they bellowed forth their thunderous mirth.

Gwen staggered backwards, her hands covering her face and her breath coming in short gasps as she let out a deafening scream. The two people in front of her were not Ernie and his play pal. They were corpses. As she watched, they disintegrated before her eyes, flesh falling from their emaciated and rotting bodies; their teeth dropping to the floor like Chiclets from a torn box. The man brought his head forward and his left eye dangled from its optic nerve for a moment and then dropped to the floor, bursting apart.

Gwen was horrified. Panic struck her and her legs gave way. She sank to the floor, unable to take her eyes from the two that stood before her, pinned together as if they were butterflies on a mounting board.

"Oh, my! You got us," the man said.

"Oh yes, you really stuck it to us, didn't you?" added the woman. The whole time, their lower bodies still engaged in the motions of carnal lust.

"I think we get her point, don't you dear?" asked the man.

"Could you possibly turn around, dear?" asked the woman, "I can't quite see the young lady's face from this position." The man and woman shuffled their feet as they twisted themselves so that both could see her. They stood over her, the window molding sticking though them – a corpsekabob.

"Oh, how nice. She's a law officer. Isn't that nice, dear?" said the woman, and then part of her cheek dropped off. "Oh my, I seem to be shedding," she cackled.

"That's all right dear; I've always thought you had such lovely cheekbones ... now I can really see their beauty."

Gwen felt herself slipping away. Her mind was shutting down and it was taking her body with it. She wanted to get up and run, but her legs wouldn't cooperate. Things were going gray.

"Oh no, you mustn't faint dear. You simply mustn't. That would ruin the whole thing. We have such a lovely surprise for you." The woman twisted her upper body, trying to see over the man's shoulder. When she did, one of the man's legs fell off and they tumbled to the floor, the man's head landing in Gwen's lap.

"Could you give us a push, please, dear? It's hard to see you like this," laughed the man, his head tilted back so that he could see her out of the top of his eye."

Things went totally black for Gwen. Her eyes rolled to the back of her head and she passed out, the sound of laughter ringing in her ears.

CHAPTER 70

Shortly before Evelyn had started the fire in the basement of Wedgemore's Antique Shoppe, Grady Peters had pulled what he could of himself together and hobbled off down the street, his hands cupping his swollen testicles. He had no idea where he should go. He knew he couldn't go home like this; there'd be no way of explaining it to Tamika or Willie. At the end of the block, he turned the corner and leaned back against the wall, catching his breath and mustering his strength to go on. He was trying to figure out a place where he could lay low for a while, at least until he felt better, when he heard Carlton's voice. He could hear the rantings and threats and wondered what it was all about. His curiosity was stemmed by his pain though, and he remained in place against the wall.

On the other side of the street, men were gathering in groups, all heading toward the sound of Carlton's voice. On his side of the street, a few blocks down, he could see a group of women coming his way. A clear division was evident. He watched as men crossed from the woman's side and women crossed from the men's side. In that instant, he knew that an awful battle of the sexes was coming. And he knew it was going to be bloody and brutal. He thought about Tamika and wondered what it meant for them as a family - wondered what it would mean for Willie. Tears welled up in his eyes as he thought about the loss of everything he held dear.

His mind began to clear a little and the memory of what had just happened in the antique shop came flooding back. His stomach began to rumble and churn as he remembered trying to rape Evelyn Ramsey. Why had he done that? he wondered. That was *not* who he was. What had come over him? And then more. The images of him and the boys in the diner. The sound of the freezer door clanking shut on Sally. A picture of Fred Johansen lying on the greasy diner floor with a cleaver buried in his forehead and Mike Alonzo, the owner, crisped like bacon against the back door. His stomach gave way and he sank to his knees on the pavement, vomit splashing down and soaking his pants legs. Stretching himself out when he was through, he lay there on the sidewalk crying.

The group of women he had seen down the street strode up to him. Most of them just stepped over him, ignoring him completely, their minds fixed on something else. One of them, however, stopped, looked down at him and then jammed the heel of her shoe into the middle of his back, grinding down on it with all her weight until she felt it sink in. Grady screamed.

With a snort, the woman yanked up her leg, ripping the heel out of his back. She had to twist it back and forth to free it. She was about to push it back in again when she realized she was falling behind. Drawing from deep down she leaned over and spat on the side of his face, then moved on down the street, trotting to catch up with her friends.

Not able to sit up yet, Grady turned his head and watched the women march around the corner. When they disappeared, he pushed himself up to a sitting position. Every movement of his right arm shot waves of searing heat and pain through his back. He pulled it across his chest and cradled it with his left. Using only his legs, he fought to a standing position and staggered off down the street in the direction from which his assailant had come and away from where she had gone.

At the end of the block, he crossed the street and turned down a small alleyway that ran behind

Cresson Street. Beyond the trash cans and dumpsters at the far end, he could see the old fence that bordered Peaceful Haven Cemetery on its easternmost side.

"That's it, Grady," he muttered. "That's the place to go and rest up a bit, undisturbed." He looked up in the sky, judging the time by the position of the sun. "Must be going on fer four or so, maybe later, maybe a little earlier. Should be pretty quiet in there now. Just go find yourself a nice shady spot out of the way and get yourself together."

He stumbled down the alleyway, knocking a trash can or two over as he went. At one point an old lady had come out carrying a large plastic bag, obviously intended for one of the cans. Grady kept his head down, but it looked to him like she was in her late eighties. When she saw him, she stopped and watched as he shuffled by. After he had passed, she hurled the bag as hard as she could. It just barely missed the back of his head, flopped to the paving in front of him and split open. Coffee grounds, crumpled paper, tin vegetable cans, and empty milk cartons went skidding across the driveway. Grady turned to look at her. She was standing by her back door glaring at him, her middle finger held high in the air. When she saw him looking, she raised it slightly higher, spit on the ground and then went back in the house.

Watching the woman's gesture and not looking where he was going, the flat of his foot caught a large mound of the wet coffee grounds and his leg shot out from under him. For the second time in less than ten minutes, he found himself face down on the concrete. A trickle of blood ran down his forehead and into his eyes from where he'd struck his head on a can of creamed corn.

"Ahhh," he screamed and the top of his lungs. It came more from anger and frustration than pain. Once again, he found himself struggling to get to his feet. When he had, he headed straight for the cemetery fence without stopping. It took a great deal of effort and caused a considerable amount of pain, but he managed to climb over the fence. At the top, he nearly caught his foot in one of the iron loops.

"Damn," he said, sitting in the overgrown grass on the other side, "that would have snapped my leg for sure. Ya got t'be more careful, Grady. Ya jus' gotta be."

He sat there for a bit, then crawled under the cover of a small line of shrubs. The bushes were thick enough to hide him from any prying eyes that happened to go by; so he pulled himself over to the base of a tree and leaned his back up against it. In keeping with the luck he'd been having so far, when he laid his head back against the bark, the shiny poison ivy leaves that had claimed that tree as a support settled down against his cheeks and arms. He didn't notice, he just closed his eyes wanting nothing more than to rest and ease the gnawing burning sensation from the hole in his back.

CHAPTER 71

Rachel Parker and Colleen Slater left by the opposite end of the park, leaving the three dead men behind. At the edge of town, they went into Crazy Verna's, a rundown taproom on the corner of Dilbert and Blythe Streets. It was the seedier part of Banderman Falls. A block over and two up was the house of Curtis Lattimore. Here, the buildings that hadn't been condemned and torn down were old stone and worn brick. Gaps between the still-standing buildings made the street look like a mouth full of missing teeth. Three clumped together here, a gap, another two after that, all the way to the end of the block.

"So what do you want to drink?" Colleen asked as they pulled out their stools and edged into the bar.

Rachel motioned to Verna who was washing out glasses at the other end. "Hey, Verna, lemme have a double scotch, no rocks."

Verna Middleton cocked her head in their direction, a cigarette burning in her mouth. She held a soapy glass in one hand and a dishrag in the other. "How 'bout you?" she asked of Colleen.

"Gimme a rum and coke with a wedge of lime," called Colleen.

"Two minutes," was all Verna said and went back to finishing her washing.

When she set the glasses down in front of the two women, she eyed them up and down. The cigarette in her mouth had gone out some time ago, but a long, gray, curved ash hung tenaciously on to the butt. "You gals celebrating something? You both look happier 'an Barney's broccoli rollin' in a basal sauce." The ash dropped off the cigarette as she was speaking, narrowly missing Rachel's glass. She plucked the butt from her mouth, tossed it over her shoulder and lit another.

Verna was a stout woman. Her hair was a fading blond color, the roots of which were much darker. It had the appearance of having been washed at some time or other this century, but no one would have been able to pinpoint exactly when. The blouse she was wearing had obviously been white at one time. Now it was a crusted yellow with a multitude of unidentifiable stains and splotches. Her beefy arms squeezed out of the short sleeves, making her look like a corrupted version of Popeye. She was wearing a pair of black pants that appeared to be at least a size too small for her, with large folds of skin spilling out over the top of the waistband.

Verna had taken over the taproom when her husband Karl died. That was almost twenty years ago. She made no pretense at being polite, partly because it wasn't necessary in this neighborhood but mostly because it just wasn't in her nature. She took things as they came and gave them as she saw fit. The bar had seen its share of troubles, but she never needed a bouncer. Anyone that stepped out of line got one of two things. A solid, fleshy punch to the nose or a swat in the head with a piece of pipe. Verna was not shy about using either (or both) if the situation warranted it. Most of the customers learned early on that it was much safer to behave oneself than have to deal with Verna's weight, strength, and temper.

"Actually," said Rachel, "yes, we are celebrating. We just educated a few yokels as to how to treat a woman."

"And more importantly, how not to," added Colleen.

"Well then, in that case," sneered Verna, "I'll have t'join ya." She pulled a bottle of bourbon off the top shelf, pulled the cork and took a big swallow.

"Here's t'education," she burped and took another long pull.

The three of them started laughing. They couldn't seem to help themselves and they couldn't seem to stop. Each time they did, one of them would start up again and the other two would join in. It was infectious. The whole time, Verna made sure they never saw the bottom of their glasses.

Rachel and Colleen spent most of the afternoon listening to Verna's stories about how she educated the men who stepped out of line in her bar. At one point, when she told them of how she'd sent Ray Copperfield home to his wife with a broken cheekbone and balls that would probably never work right again, they laughed so hard that Colleen actually fell off her stool. Of course, that made them laugh even harder.

"So then I grab 'im by his scruffy little neck, shoves him out the front door and kicks 'im in the balls again. Ain't never come in here after that," finished Verna.

"Well, ya think that's somthin," slurred Colleen, "*we-*" she waved her index finger back and forth between her and Rachel. "*We*...well, Rach here actually ... but *we* ... just put three no-good-stinkin men in the ground forever. I mean-" A series of hiccups interrupted her momentarily. "I mean we gave it to em good. *They* won't be botherin no women no time soon."

"In the ground?" questioned Verna, laughing. "Wudya do, bury em alive?" She slapped her hand on the bar, grabbed a fresh bottle of bourbon off the shelf and took another swallow. She then refilled Rachel's and Colleen's glasses. It was a while ago that Verna had switched their drinks to bourbon, but nobody seemed to care. They were having a wonderful afternoon, the three of them.

Around three o'clock or so, Albert Daniels and Clive Shillington pushed through the door. The laughing stopped and the three women turned and stared at them. They were so unnerved by it they just turned and left. This caused another breakout of infectious laughter.

Colleen looked at her watch but couldn't make out the time. Rachel was propping her head up on the palm of her hand, but it kept slipping off. Verna had hoisted herself up onto the bar and looked like she was riding it sidesaddle.

"Ya know," said Colleen, her words running together, "men are so stupid and so easily led. I mean, look-" She tugged at her shirt and three of the buttons went flying across the bar. "Show em some o'these ... and they'll do anything ya want. Anything!"

"Yeah, that's true," said Rachel, "butcha gotta be careful, too. Don't give em any then yer fightin. They all think they got the right t'take em if you won't give em. That's why I have this." She pulled the gun from her purse and waved it in the air. "Get too handy with me ... and you'll be goin home *wi'out* any hands."

"Yeah, but Col here's right. They're just plain dumber 'an swamp grass. Open yer shirt, just a little ... an' their brains fall out."

"Or show em a little leg," added Colleen. "That works too." Her smile faded and a sour look came over her face. "Course, some of em ... some of em don't act that way. Some of em are downright frustratin."

"Who? Who doesn't act that way?" asked Rachel and Verna, almost in unison. "I ain't never seen a man whose tongue didn't clean the floor for ya when ya shot him a little tittie."

"Doc Robertson," grumbled Colleen. "Tried to get him inta my skirt the other day and you know what ... I mean, I couldn't believe it. He just up an' left. I couldn't believe it. Who does he think he is? I'm a good lookin woman, ya know. Probably the best lay he'd ever have. Fucker!"

Both women turned and looked at Colleen. Verna belched. Rachel asked, amazed, "You tried to fuck the town doctor? And he didn't want any? I can't believe it. He really turned down a freebie?" The incredulity in her voice came through the slurred words in crystal clarity.

"Hey," broke in Verna, "maybe we should go over there and make him do all three of us. Bet that'd be fun ... and I bet we could *do* it to."

Colleen looked at Rachel and then at Verna and then back at Rachel. In her present state; in all their present states, it sounded like a swell idea. But when they tried to stand up, the booze anchor they'd been fastening to themselves all afternoon took over and they sat back down again. Verna fell off the bar and just lay on the floor behind it. No one laughed, no one moved.

"You ok?" called Rachel.

"I think so. Just gimme a minute or two," Verna called back. This was shortly followed by a sonorous snoring that crept up over the bar like fog over a mountain top.

CHAPTER 72

Eric Baxter's eyes fluttered open, but he couldn't see anything. Beside him, Ruby lay stretched out, her back up against him. As soon as he moved she was up and licking furiously at his face. He rolled over onto his back, the dog jumping over him from side to side.

"Ok, ok. Settle down, girl. Settle down," he told her. She paid no attention. His face was literally dripping with dog slobber as he pulled himself to a sitting position. He wrapped his arms around her neck and gave her a big hug, which she was not real enthusiastic about. Squirming and pulling, she backed out of his grip and then charged forward, licking at his face again, her tail swinging wildly.

The memory of his dreams and the strange music from the broken radio clock came back to him slowly. Instinctively, he reached for his chest, his hand flattening over his heart. There was no pain and his arm didn't hurt anymore either.

"Guess I skated on that one, old girl,"

Pushing Ruby away gently, he got to his feet, made his way across the room and turned on a light. His pupils contracted and he threw his hands up in front of his face. When his vision had adjusted sufficiently to the dark, he glanced at the wall clock. 8:37 P.M. He'd been passed out for hours. He stared at the clock for the longest time, watching its second hand sweep noiselessly around and around. Without realizing it, his left hand was on his chest, his fingers rubbing at the pocket watch inside his overalls.

He walked out to the tiny kitchen of the trailer, flicked on the light and sat down at the table. The memory of the dreams was vivid and he knew that there were things to be done, just as he knew that time was running out. He pulled the pocket watch out and placed on the table in front of him, leaving it closed. He then closed his eyes and ran his fingertips across its smooth metal surface.

"Clear yer mind, Eric Baxter; clear yer mind."

He sat there letting random thoughts skitter across his mind. They moved in waves, coming into focus then fading away. Eventually, they were all gone and it was quiet. A solitude settled over him and he waited for the void to be filled. He waited to know what it was he had to do.

Eric Baxter was not one for transcendentalism or meditation. He had always believed in God, though he was not outwardly religious. Now, in the silence of his tiny kitchen, he sat there, hoping against hope that his God would not forsake him, that his God would guide him, that he would learn what it was that he was supposed to do. For the first time in his life, Eric Baxter was waiting for a vision – the kind his grandmother had told him about – the kind she said she'd had, and that one day he would have. He waited, all the while knowing that something terrible was coming and there wasn't much time before it arrived.

Suddenly, he jumped up. He hadn't had a vision; he just instantly knew where he had to go. There was no hesitation or doubt in him. He needed to get to Peaceful Haven Cemetery. He needed to get there now, and he hoped that he wasn't already too late.

Grabbing the pocket watch off the table he charged through the living room and out the front door, pushing Ruby aside as he went. At the door, he stopped and petted the dog on the head.

"You have to stay here. Daddy'll be back in a while. You be a good girl and watch the trailer."

Ruby watched through the glass as Eric strode across the yard, climbed into his pickup and faded into the night. She stood there looking after him, her tail wagging and then curled up in a ball at the base of the door.

CHAPTER 73

Audrey Archibald was the older of the twins, Gwen being younger by a mere six and a half minutes. She was an optimist. Even dealing with the worst elements of society through her job with the Sheriff's Department couldn't jade her. She always had a kind word for people. She could be sarcastic at times, as evidenced by her attitude toward Rachel Parker, but even then it wasn't malicious. Audrey simply called things as she saw them, always trying to put a nice or humorous spin on them.

By 3:20, Audrey was beginning to become truly concerned at the state of things in Banderman Falls. She'd lost contact with Jack first and then with Bill Pinsky. Tyler had been found dead in the park and reports of fires, vandalism and fights had begun to pour in. On top of all that, her sister was due in to relieve her for the evening shift and she couldn't get in touch with her either.

Jillian Cunningham, Dr. Robertson's nurse, had called at two-thirty to say that the doc hadn't come back from examining Tyler's body and that Sam Twilling had called asking for him. Sam had told her that he was still waiting for Robertson to show up to do the post. She'd called again at three to say that she couldn't raise him on his cell either and that Twilling wanted to know what to do with Tyler's body.

The Banderman Falls fire department was housed four doors down from the sheriff's office. The engines had roared out of the garage at about two or so and hadn't come back yet. Normally, Audrey could hear everything that was going on over the radios, but they were dead. Nothing was coming in and nothing was going out. She'd tried to get in touch with the State Police with no luck. As to the phones, it seemed that only local calls were getting through and even they were sketchy.

Audrey sat at her desk tapping her fingernails on the blotter and wondering what she should do. There was an extra patrol car she could use to see if she could find Jack, but she didn't want to leave the office unmanned.

Through the window, she could see tall spires of smoke rising from various locations. She couldn't imagine what was going on out there. From time to time she'd walk to the front door, step out, and look up and down the street.

All across Banderman Falls, things were falling apart. Men and women gathered on street corners and alleyways in groups. When their paths crossed, vicious fights ensued. Marjorie Wilkins had been beaten and kicked to death by Floyd McCullough and Henry Dimmic. Tony DiDorio and Al Snodgrass had been dispatched by Margaret Tomlinson's shotgun, and Michael Mandrachi, the town's barber, sixty-nine years old and planning to retire next year, had had his face pounded flat with a sledgehammer and his genitals sawn off with a hacksaw by Alicia Tulblerone, Patty Burris, Elena Gorvoyovna and Mary Costello.

Marjorie Larch, who'd adopted a new and sultry look after Colleen Slater had left her store, had gone about teasing the men she passed. She had been reveling in how they had stopped and stared at her as she passed by. She had even entertained taking one or two of them to a secluded place to have some real fun. But by the afternoon, things had changed. She had narrowly escaped a trio of them who had chased her down the alley behind Pyle's bookstore. She'd had to climb into a dumpster to make her escape. When she was sure it was safe, she'd lifted the lid, looked around and crawled out. The incident had been enough to convince her that she should just go home. She never made it. Three blocks from her front door a group of five men cornered her. When they were done taking their pleasures, they held her down and strangled her to death. Shortly afterward on their way out of the alley, they came to their own deaths, gunned down by three women, one of whom was the wife of the strangler. Their bodies lay sprawled across the pavement in front of McKendrick's Pharmacy.

After Wedgemore's Antique Shoppe, Alderman's Tire & Battery was the next to be set ablaze. Frieda McIlvane and Carrie Simmons had done that. They were disappointed when they discovered that Frank Mowery and Charlie Maloney were not inside at the time. They'd had their hearts set on standing outside and listening to them plead for help – help that they would not allow – but they contented themselves with the fire. And when the batteries finally caught and exploded they were doubly thrilled and inspired to go find someplace else to torch.

By late afternoon chaos reigned. Guns, knives, clubs, anything that could be used as a weapon was put into service. Men and women clashed in the streets, in the stores and alleyways, in homes and apartments, and in the parks. Whenever and wherever they came in contact with each other, bodies were left behind. Husbands killed wives; wives killed husbands; everything that was dark and evil in a person's personality rose to the surface. Reason, compassion, and love were supplanted with hatred, jealousy, and rage. The primal instinct to kill and to survive ruled the hearts of all.

Fires raged throughout the town, the members of the fire department having moved off into their separate groups based on gender. Lisa Merryweather had barely escaped. A new member of the department, the first female in Banderman Falls's history, she had seen the stares her colleagues had been giving her and felt their anger building. Before they'd given up on controlling the blaze at Wedgemore's she'd slipped off, just before the blackness of malevolence overtook the men. It was a narrow escape. Two minutes after she'd disappeared around a corner the men dropped their hoses and began looking among themselves for their female newbie. They'd had to search person by person because of the anonymity their outfits gave them. It's what gave her the time needed to get away. Around the corner, she stripped out of the protective fire suit and headed off to find the comfort and solace of her own kind. When Calvin Heller finally found her empty jacket, he exploded. He wandered up and down the street searching the stores and shops looking for her, a fireman's axe dangling from his hand.

Calvin never found Lisa. Instead, he found Marsha Putnam, a thirty-two-year-old, mentally retarded woman. She'd been wandering around lost when her sister had gone off to join the battle. When he approached her, she was carrying an old, beat-up Raggedy Anne doll. He paused for a moment then raised the axe as high above his head as he could get it. He never got to strike the blow. In surprise and horror he looked down at the blade that had punched through his back and come ripping out of his chest – a thin, but long letter opener. He staggered, turning to see who had stabbed him, the axe dropping from his hand. When he dropped to his knees, Tamika Peters picked up the axe and delivered the blow that he had intended for Marsha. His head opened down the middle and he fell back dead.

"I can't find my sister," said Marsha, in a weak and trembling voice. "Do you want to play with my dolly?"

Tamika grabbed her by the hand and dragged her into the tailor shop.

"Come on, honey. Let's play hide and seek. We'll go down here and we'll win, because nobody will find us." She pulled open a door that led to a crawlspace beneath the building. "We'll go down here and we'll be safe and we'll win the game."

"But where's my sister?" asked Marsha.

"She's out looking for our next hiding place. She'll be back."

"Ok. Do you have any candy? I'm hungry."

"I don't have any, but I'll go get some. You have to stay here though if you want to win. You want to win don't you?"

"Is there a prize if I do?"

"You betcha. A whole basket of candy and dollies."

"Oh boy," cried Marsha. She slipped down into the crawlspace and Tamika closed the door, telling her not to come up or even look out until she got back.

"Do you understand?" she asked.

"Yes. I won't peek. Promise! My sister say's you should never cheat and never lie. Peeking is cheating. I won't do that."

"Ok, honey. You just stay here and pretty soon, you'll win all the candy."

"And the dollies too?"

"Yes, sweetie. The dollies too."

After she'd buttoned up the trapdoor, Tamika covered it with a piece of rug from the office and rolled a hanger rack of freshly cleaned suits and dresses over top of it. She was alone in the store, her boss having left hours ago to join the fray. When she'd seen Calvin confront Marsha, she knew she had to do something. Scared but resolved, she grabbed the sword-shaped letter opener from the counter and went out to stop him.

Now she stood at the window looking up and down the street, searching for any signs of men in the vicinity. She glanced at Calvin's body, blessed herself and asked the Lord to forgive her, then stepped out onto the sidewalk. She really didn't want to leave the safety of the store, but she knew that if she didn't get some kind of candy for Marsha it would be difficult keeping her there.

Cautiously, she eased down the street and around the corner. Two blocks up was McKendrick's Pharmacy. She'd be able to get what she needed there. If she could make it that far (and get back again.)

Back at the sheriff's office, Audrey paced back and forth battling with indecision and responsibility. Her main responsibility was to stay put and mind the office. Her gut kept telling her that she had to get out there; that she had to locate Jack and let him know what was going on ... if he didn't know already.

"Where are you Gwen?" She stopped her pacing long enough to look at her watch. 4:42 P.M. "You were supposed to be here an hour ago." She picked up the phone. No dial tone at all.

"Oh, that's just great," she barked as she slammed the phone back down. Audrey rarely lost her temper, but she found herself moving closer and closer to it today. Things were bad, although she didn't know how bad. Finally coming to the conclusion that there was no real reason to stay put – there was no incoming or outgoing communication anyway – she decided to take the last cruiser in the lot and try and find Jack. Her only problem was ... she didn't know where to start.

She'd almost made it to the front door when something made her stop and turn around. Moving over to the desk, she pulled out the keys to the gun cabinet, opened it and took out a pistol and a shotgun. After locking the cabinet again, she slid

the keys in her pocket, pulled a box of 9mm shells
out of the drawer, tucked the Glock in her belt and
loaded the shotgun. It was time to go find Jack;
time to go be a true police officer. It would be the
first time in her life that she'd ever carried a gun,
although she was trained in using them; and it
would be the first time she was out on the streets on
her own in an official capacity.

 Climbing into the cruiser she buckled herself
in, flipped on the rotators – she didn't bother with
the sirens – and pulled out.

 "Guess the first stop should be Twillings.
At least you can let him know you're going to hunt
for Jack." The idea of going to the mortuary didn't
sit well with her. She really didn't want to see
Tyler's body. "With any luck though, maybe Sam'll
have an idea where Jack might have gone."

 At the corner, she turned left. Now on Main
Street, through her rearview mirror, she could see
the flames of Alderman's spouting into the air.
From her perspective, they looked like overgrown
roman candles, belching their light and smoke
skyward. Ahead of her, she could see men and
women along the sidewalks struggling with each
other. Some were fighting hand to hand, others
were shooting at each other.

 "What the hell is going on here? Have they
all gone mad?" She maneuvered the cruiser around
a burning dump truck, turned down Dawson Street
and into the alley behind Twillings. Audrey
stopped the car just short of hitting the two bodies
that were lying in his driveway.

CHAPTER 74

Deep in the woods of Fairmount Park, Willie Peters was having a grand old time. He splashed and stomped through small streams, skimmed rocks across the Wissahickon, caught and released garter snakes, picked wild blackberries and ate them and tried, unsuccessfully, to catch fish with a bit of tangled line he'd found and a paperclip he'd had in his pocket. He never noticed the afternoon slipping away.

As the shadows of the trees lengthened and the sunlight began to fade, more and more creatures began to rustle around in the bushes. It was this that first brought his attention to the fact that he was going to be late getting back home and that dark would soon be upon him. When he looked up, the sun was already too low in the sky to be seen; only a faint band of orange and gold stretched across the sky.

He'd been trying to corner a wily crayfish that had, so far, managed to evade his grasp. Finally giving up, he scrambled up the small embankment and pushed through the bushes out into the horse path. On the other side of the path, two men were staring at him, both of them wearing funny looking grins. He recognized them, but they looked different somehow.

"Hello, Willie. How are you? What are you doing down here so late?" asked Charlie Maloney.

"Yes, shouldn't you be home with your mama, boy?" asked Frank Mowery, more sarcastically than questioningly.

Willie took a few steps backward. In the dusky light, he couldn't see them clearly, but what he did see frightened him. Both of them seemed to have been ripped apart. Loose flesh hung from Frank's arms and throat and the whole side of Charlie's face was missing, clear down to the bone. The only thing holding his jaw on was a thin piece of tendon.

"Where ya goin now, boy?" snarled Frank, as Willie backed up. "Don't ya wanna play with us? Don't ya wanna play with our friends?"

On the word, "friends," a pair of wolves appeared at his side. Their mouths were agape, their lips curled back and saliva dripped from their teeth. A third wolf pranced out of the bushes about one hundred yards up the road – the road Willie needed to take to get home. It walked calmly forward, sure of itself. It neither snarled nor growled; it just padded forward, a step at a time, blocking the path.

Willie turned and ran through the bushes back down to the little stream. In a single leap, he was across and fighting to climb up the other side. He wanted to look back; he wanted to see if they were chasing him, and if they were, how close they were. But he was too frightened for that. Hand over hand, clutching at roots and trunks, he pulled himself up the steeper side of the tributary. At the top he paused, still not looking back, but listening. He heard the splashing of the water. Something was crossing.

As fast as he could, he pushed deeper into the woods, the sounds of rustling branches behind him getting closer. His heart was beating hard in his chest and his legs were beginning to feel like Jell-O. Forcing his way through a thicket of brambles he emerged into a clearing. Halfway across, his heart sank as he realized there was no place to hide and he couldn't turn back.

He was looking around for anything that might serve as a hiding place when the wolves broke through the thickets. They stood in a line at the edge of the clearing, their fur standing on end, their eyes riveted on him. A few moments later, Charlie and Frank appeared behind them.

"Are ya ready, boys?" Willie heard Frank say.

"Are ya hungry? Look, tender meat ... just for you," said Charlie, pointing at Willie.

The wolves held their position, pawing at the ground, awaiting only the command that would send them ahead. Charlie stepped around in front of them, the whole time pointing at Willie. He was no more than a silhouette in this light, but Willie could see the grin he was wearing. It was an evil, malicious grin that seemed to engulf his entire face. Frank stuck his hands in his pockets and started to whistle. It was a song that Willie recognized. His father used to play it over and over again. A song by somebody named Frank Sinatra.

Frank stopped whistling and began to sing: *My Way*, emphasizing the opening phrase, "the end is near." When he stopped singing, he yelled across the field to Willie. "What I'm certain of black boy is ... you're dead!"

With that, the wolves began their charge. Willie turned and ran, knowing full well that there was no way he could outrun them. In a moment, they would be on him, and in a few moments after that ... he'd be dead. He was never going to make it to the other side of the clearing. He turned his head slightly over his shoulder to see how close they were. When he did, his foot caught in a loop of root and he went tumbling forward, arms outstretched to break his fall. He hit the ground hard with his chin. The force drove his teeth into his upper lip. He started crying; blood ran down his chin and formed a tiny pool around his face. He gave up. There was no more run left in him. He laid there, eyes closed, and waited for it to be over.

When nothing happened, he slowly opened his eyes, one at a time. He could hear the panting wolves, they were close. Turning over onto his back, he saw them. They stood around him in a semi-circle, watching him; staring at him; waiting, as if they were enjoying the moment.

Willie inched back away from them on the palms of his hands and seat of his pants. They didn't move. They just stood staring at him. Then one crouched and Willie knew his time was up. As it leaped into the air, he closed his eyes and covered his face with his arms.

A sound like snapping twigs followed by a loud yelp echoed across the field. Something struck Willie and he fell backwards, a heavy weight on his chest. He dropped his hands from his face. One of the wolves was lying across his chest and abdomen. It was dead. Its neck was broken. Willie pushed it off him and sat up. The sound of snapping teeth, howls and growls assaulted his ears. Darkness always seemed to make sounds seem louder. Willie strained his eyes, not believing what he was seeing.

In front of him, the two wolves were attacking a lone figure. It was a woman. She kept turning, trying to keep them in front of her. The wolves were trying to flank her. Willie watched as one sprang into the air. The woman caught it in one hand by the scruff of the neck and pitched it back at the other. Both wolves went tumbling across the field, kicking up clumps of grass and dirt.

"It's all right, Willie. I won't let them have you. You go. When I tell you ... you run. But not before I tell you."

She turned back in time to see them advancing again, keeping their bodies low. It was getting darker and Willie was having a hard time seeing what was happening. He sat forward, straining his eyes in the dark, waiting for the woman to tell him to run.

One of the wolves charged, then stopped and wheeled to its right. As the woman followed it, the second sprang forward and grabbed her by the leg. It twisted its head from side to side, ripping large pieces of flesh and muscle from the bone. The woman never let out a sound. Keeping an eye on the other one, she reached down and grabbed the one on her leg by the snout and hefted it into the air. When she did, the other attacked, leaping for her throat. She staggered backwards a few steps before she fell. The wolves were tearing at her, snapping at her face and neck and chest. Her arms thrashed wildly at them, but they were relentless.

Willie was sure it was over. He was never going to get out of there. The wolves would finish with her and then tear him into little shreds too.

In front of him, the woman and the wolves fought, rolling around, surrounded by the dust they were creating. A yelp rang out and one of the wolves went flying. When it hit the ground, it rolled over and charged back to help its partner who was still tearing merciless at the woman on the ground.

Willie started to cry. He hung his head and covered his eyes with both hands. It was then that he saw the light through his fingers. A bright glow that seemed to come from nowhere. Tentatively, he opened his fingers a bit wider.

Across the field, a hazy, bluish glow was moving toward him – toward the woman. As it got closer, it got brighter. It looked to Willie like a man made out of electricity. It crackled and hummed as it moved forward.

The wolves momentarily halted their attack and gazed at the approaching light. They let out a long howl and then their muzzles wrinkled back up into the snarls they'd been wearing. In that moment, when they looked up, the woman grabbed one, pulled it down to her chest and snapped its neck. In a fury, the second dove into the air, its mouth agape and aimed right at the woman's throat. It never made its mark.

As it slid through the air, the glowing figure reached out and grabbed it. It burst into flames and disintegrated. The smell of burnt flesh and hair settled over the field. It made Willie sick to his stomach.

The light-figure turned and helped the woman to her feet. In his glow, Willie could now see the woman clearly. Large amounts of her body had been ripped away by the wolves. There was a hole in the center of her forehead and most of the back of her skull was missing.

The glowing figure moved closer to Willie. His outline was familiar. He looked like he was wearing a police uniform – a sheriff's uniform.

"You can go home now, Willie. We've done all we can for you. We have to go."

"Who ... who are you?" stammered Willie, not really sure he wanted to know anyway.

"You know me, Willie," said the glowing figure, "don't you?"

Willie nodded. "Yes. I know you. But why are you glowing? How can you look like that."

"That doesn't matter, son. What matters is that you're safe."

"For now," added the woman. "This isn't over Willie, and I'm afraid Tyler and I have used up what energy was left of us. But we couldn't let you be hurt."

"Pat's right, Willie. It isn't over and it's going to get more dangerous and much scarier. You must go home. You must go home and stay there until this is all done and through with."

"But-" Willie started to say, but the figure's glow was already dying away. It shrank into itself and disappeared.

"I have to go, too, Willie. I was able to do something good with my life, something I hadn't been able to do because that man took my life too soon. But it's over now and I have to leave."

"Where are you going?" asked Willie with the wonder and curiosity of a child.

"I guess I'm going to what you would call heaven, but it's really not that. It's so much more."

Pat O'Donnell reached down and helped Willie to his feet. Her hand was cold and the flesh was loose and discolored. Willie wanted to pull his hand away, but at the same time, he wanted her to stay.

"Go home, Willie. Go right home and don't stop until you get there."

Without another word, she turned and started off across the field. Willie watched. Before she reached the other side she got thinner and thinner and then she was gone.

Willie stood there frozen, staring into the empty field. Then he turned and ran as fast as he could. All he wanted now was to get home where he'd be safe.

When the wolves died, Charlie and Frank faded into a shadowy smoke and drifted off across the field.

CHAPTER 75

As the evil and anger built across the Falls, mothers had left their children in search of revenge, vengeance or whatever else the darker side of them wanted. Most of the younger children continued to play with their toys or sat at the windows crying for their mothers. The older ones took advantage of their newly found freedom; some watching TV they normally were prevented from watching, others playing video games instead of finishing their chores and still others sneaking out to meet up with friends.

As dusk began to creep in, most of them found themselves growing drowsy. They were having difficulty keeping their eyes open and concentrating on what they were doing. A sudden wave of exhaustion seemed to crawl over them and they stretched themselves out wherever they were and drifted off to sleep. A few fought against it, struggling with all their might to keep awake and keep doing what they were doing. For those playing games, or watching TV, the consequences were minimal. A bumped head when they fell over or a dropped soda glass. For others, it was a bit more serious. Ralph Johansen fell off a swing and broke his arm. Martin McCullough split his lip on the corner of the dining room table he'd been running around and Janet Gruber suffered a concussion when she fell down the cellar steps and hit her head on the concrete floor.

Mary Anne Statler and Jennifer McGovern had been playing jump rope when the haze came over them. Mary Anne missed her jump and fell forward. Her head struck the sidewalk with a force that split her forehead open and fractured her skull. Blood ran out of her ears and mouth as she lay there helpless. Jennifer McGovern had tried to catch her, but had lost consciousness before she could and ended up lying on top of her. Mary Anne was the only fatality resulting from Geoffrey's and Father Jacobs's work.

Not all the children in Banderman Falls succumbed. A handful resisted and succeeded in remaining awake.

CHAPTER 76

Eric was thinking about Ruby when he turned on to the main road and his head began to pound. It was so sudden and so intense he pulled the pickup off to the side, skidding to a stop in the shoulder's gravel. He cradled his head in his hands, rubbing his forehead. The first thought he had was that he was having a stroke. His vision was blurry and he could feel the dull but prominent pain of his eardrums expanding.

He slumped over, lying sideways on the bench seat. For five minutes he lay there moaning and rocking in pain, his head pounding. It eventually began to ease. When he tried to open his eyes again, he found that he couldn't. He thought for a minute that he'd actually *had* the stroke he feared and that he'd damaged the nerves to his eyelids.

"No ... oh Christ no!" he moaned. "Not now. Not now!"

Slowly, a vision began to form. It was like watching a movie play on the backs of his eyelids. A face grew and expanded. It was a hideous face and Eric could see it - and see through *its* eyes. It was looking at Father Jacobs and he was looking at it. The face taunted the priest; it was trying to distract him from something.

Eric wanted to turn away; to open his eyes, drive home and hide inside with his dog. That's what he wanted to do. Instead, he found himself digging in his pocket for his watch. He pulled it out and clicked it open. He could see its dial, although he still had his eyes closed. The hands were spinning around and around in opposite directions. Watching the hands without seeing them, a flash of insight washed over him. All of a sudden he knew what he had to do. He didn't know *why*, but he knew *what*.

Forcing himself up, he placed one hand on the steering wheel to steady himself and closed the watch tightly in the other fist. He began to speak clearly and softly, knowing somehow that Father Jacobs would hear him.

"Darkness holds no sway over the powers of light and truth. Believe in what you are doing and abolish the beast in your mind. See it diminish; see it evaporate; see it dissolve into the nothingness from which it came. It is but a mirage, a picture of a picture. It cannot dissuade you from your purpose or keep you from your destiny. Believe it to be gone and it will be."

When he finished, Eric collapsed back onto the seat and for the second time today, he lost himself to darkness as everything turned gray, then black.

***

Father Jacobs could hear Eric Baxter's voice in his head. As he wrestled with the image of the thing before him, the voice of an old friend came through loud and clear. And with each passing word, Jacobs grew stronger and the vision of the beast thinner.

Jacobs opened his eyes. Geoffrey was standing there, the two Big Ben imitations sitting on the desk in front of him. Jacobs reached out an arm and Geoffrey clasped it in his hand.

"Are you all right, Gabe?"

"Yes. I believe so." He shook his head trying to clear the muddle. He felt like a man with a hangover trying to get ready to go to work. "How did we do? Did we put the children to sleep? Did it work?"

"No real way to know, mate. But I think so. At least, I think most of them. I can't really be sure and we were short-handed to begin with."

"So tell me, then," said Jacobs, pulling himself to his feet. "Who's got this other clock? And where the hell are they?"

"Again, I have to tell you I don't know. But on the bright side, I can feel that whoever it is ... is much closer. And that's a bloody good thing. It has to be one of us ... I mean ... one of me ... oh hell, you know what I mean."

"I hope you're right. And I hope to God they're very close. Because judging from what I just saw ... we're gonna need them. Badly!"

"Come on. We've done all we can here. We've got to get to that antique shop and see if we can find whatever it is this thing's looking for."

Jacobs held up a hand. His face was contorted in a scowl, his brow furrowed and his cheeks drawn in tight.

"You're not going to believe this one." He looked at Geoffrey, engaging his eyes as steadily as he could. "I know where we have to go. It just came to me and, for some reason, I know it's right. And ... it isn't the antique shop."

"All right then ... where?"

Jacobs grabbed Geoffrey tightly by the shoulders. "We've got to go to the cemetery. That's where we'll find it. I know it. I know it as surely as I know my own name."

Geoffrey studied his friend's face, but only for a brief moment.

"You know what, mate? I bloody well believe you. But we have to go someplace else first."

"Someplace else? Where? Why?"

"My hotel room. I have some things there we're going to need before this night's through."

Jacobs grabbed for his hat, thought better of it and just said: "So what are you waiting for?" and held the door open.

CHAPTER 77

Ernie Pyle awoke on the floor of the Motel 8. His eyes flickered open as he clumsily pulled himself up, using the mattress for leverage. When his head cleared the edge of the bed, everything that had happened fell upon him like an avalanche of boulders – the woman he'd spent the night with – the fucking – her laughter and the way she looked when she'd decomposed in front of him – it all came back to him and his stomach began to churn.

"No. Don't think about it, Ernie. Think about something else. Something nice." He crawled away from the bed on his hands and knees into the bathroom. He hadn't wanted to look at the bed, at the sheets where his lover had returned to ash, but he'd caught a glimpse of it just the same. Flipping the toilet seat up just in time, his stomach let go. The thoughts of having screwed a corpse, his tongue in its mouth, his arms cradling its putrid flesh and his... He brought up a violent second round, his stomach wringing itself out. Strands of vomit hung from his lips and chin and the foul taste of partially digested food and acid filled his mouth.

"I gotta get outta here," he murmured, wiping his mouth clean with a wad of toilet paper. "Gotta get out!"

Crawling over to the shower, he reached in and turned it on. Still kneeling beside the tub he let the water cascade down over his head, occasionally looking up to let it wash his face. When he was through, he cranked the faucet off and pushed himself up to his feet, using the side of the tub for leverage.

He dressed quickly, keeping his eyes averted from the bed as much as possible. As he buttoned his shirt he tried to convince himself, without much success, that everything that had happened had only been a bad dream.

"A bit of undigested beef," he snickered. "Dickens had it right. That's what it was ... a bit of undigested beef' and nothing more." He knew it wasn't, just as he knew it hadn't been a dream.

Not looking back, he left the room, left the motel and stepped out into the night air. It was only then that he realized that he'd lain on the floor passed out all day. He thought about the bookstore and wondered what people must have thought when he hadn't been there to open it. He thought about Gwen Archibald and wondered if he'd ever have a chance with her and what she would think if he ever told her about ... about...

"Don't go there Ernie. Don't go there."

Not knowing quite what to do or where to go, and still afraid to go back to the bookstore, he decided that he'd just walk a bit. Take a nice stroll, sample the summer evening air and relax. He drew in a deep breath and coughed it back out. The air was acrid and smoky.

He moved out from under the hotel's overhang and walked toward the street. As soon as he'd cleared the carport he could see the fires raging all over Banderman Falls.

"What the hell?" His mouth hung open as he took in the depraved scene before him. Numerous buildings illuminated the night sky with their towering flames. Burning cars and trucks clogged the streets as far as he could see. And there were other things too. He couldn't believe his eyes. Bodies! The street was dotted with bodies, male and female. Some were burned, that much he could see. The others – he couldn't tell what had happened to *them* from where he was, and he really didn't want to know anyway.

"What the fuck is going on here? What could have happened? Who could have done this?" In his head, he answered his own question. Somehow, whatever or whoever it was that had tormented him in the bookstore with the copy of Paradise Lost was responsible. He knew it as certainly as he knew where he had to go. He just didn't know why he had to go there.

Almost trance-like, Ernie started off down the street toward Peaceful Haven Cemetery. After the first block, he thought it best to keep to the back alleys and cut-throughs. Best to keep off the main streets. Not safe. He let his feet carry him along, not thinking, just walking. He paid only enough attention to where he was going to avoid stepping on a body or evade anyone he happened to see.

Ernie's head was a jumble. There was no way he could rationalize the events of last night. Things like that don't happen, except in maybe Stephen King's or Dean Koontz's novels. They just aren't possible. Knowing that made him start to question his own sanity and feelings. He wondered if he was having a mental breakdown. Fears about the possible closing of the bookstore because of the mall, which of course, would mean he'd lose his job; his desires for Gwen Archibald and his timid and shy ways that prevented him from asking her out; worries about his finances and what he'd done or hadn't done with his life so far; they all washed over him and he tried his best to use them as an excuse for what his mind seemed to be doing to him.

But the reality of the situation was all too clear. Each body he stepped over, each fire he could see, the man in the bookstore, all these things told him that something real and substantial was happening to him – to his town.

At the end of the alley behind Cresson Street, the same route Grady Peters had taken, Ernie came to the gate that bordered the cemetery. Hesitantly and unsure, he clambered over the fence. He looked back to see if anyone had been watching him. When he was sure he'd made it in unseen, he pushed through the bushes in front of him and started towards the center of the cemetery.

CHAPTER 78

From the back porch of the B & B, the sun looked like a gigantic orange ball balanced on the tops of the trees. Behind it, lines of pinks, reds, and oranges stretched across the sky as the blues of daylight faded into evening grays.

Sheriff Jack Dougherty and Doctor Michael Robertson stood on the porch watching the sunset. Neither of them spoke. There wasn't very much to say. In the kitchen behind them, Bill Pinsky lay covered with a tablecloth. Curtis Lattimore was slowly slipping away. There had just been too much damage and too little medical equipment to properly treat him.

At last, Jack turned and faced Robertson.

"Mike, I'm sorry, but I'm at a complete loss as to how to get the hell out of here. It'll be dark soon. I know we can't hang out here forever, but the thoughts of hoofing it all the way back to town in the dark doesn't make me feel comfortable."

"I know, Jack."

"But that's not all, Doc. There's still Ethan and Linda to consider. What the hell happened to them? Unless *they* hoofed it outta here ... and I doubt that, we didn't pass em on the way in ... they have to be here somewhere."

Robertson looked sternly at Jack. He hesitated saying what he was about to say, what he was about to suggest. Although he was pretty sure that Jack was thinking the same thing.

"Jack ... there's a possibility ... probably a strong one, that-"

"Yeah, I know, Doc. Let's not go there just yet, though. Ok?" Jack shot a look over his shoulder at the kitchen door. "One dead and one dying is enough for me at this point. Let's just hope they're out there somewhere."

"Well then, I guess there's really nothing else we can do. We either sit tight ... or start walking. What do you say? Which is it?"

The door to the kitchen suddenly burst open and Jack went flying forward off the porch, Curtis Lattimore wrapped around his back. Curtis had his arms around Jack's neck and was squeezing as tightly as he could. They rolled out into the yard, Jack ending up face down with Curtis on his back.

Training kicked in instantly and Jack reached up and grabbed Curtis's left hand, twisting it at the wrist. Curtis let out a long yell, his radius snapping clean. Jack rolled onto his back, pinning Curtis beneath him, still holding on to the broken left arm.

Curtis dropped his right hand and wrestled Jack's gun free from its holster. Immediately, Jack grabbed for Curtis's right wrist, but missed. He caught him on top of his elbow, driving the arm to the ground. The impact of Curtis's elbow on the hard dirt caused the gun to discharge. One loud *Bang!* rang out before Jack could get control of the arm. Using both hands, Jack forced the gun to the ground and rolled off Curtis.

Curtis lay on his back clutching frantically at the gun, blood gushing from his previous wounds. Jack could hear the wheezy breaths he was drawing and the hissing and gurgling sounds of air escaping through Curtis's chest. Jack pushed himself up on his knees, his hands wrapped around his assailant's right wrist. And then things got hazy.

As Jack struggled to control the gun; Curtis gritted his teeth, picked up a rock with his left hand and brought it up against the side of Jack's head as hard as he could. He knew he didn't have much time before his strength was gone, and he couldn't fail his master. Taking the pain, he gripped the rock as hard as he could and hit Jack a second time.

Blood oozed from the gash in Jack's temple and he released his grip on Curtis as he fell to the side. The second blow kept him from getting up. A moment later he was staring down the barrel of his own gun, Curtis kneeling over him grinning and laughing, blood dripping from his mouth, nose and chest wounds.

"I may go ... but you're going first, pig. Gonna kill ya with your own gun, too. That'll read good in a report, won't it?"

Jack watched, dazed, as Curtis placed the gun against his forehead.

Bang! *Bang! Bang*! The shots echoed through the woods that bordered the back of the Killerman's B& B. Curtis gave out one long laugh and then fell forward, landing directly on Jack.

Still shaken, Jack rolled Curtis off him and struggled to sit up. A hand reached down, took him by the arm and pulled him to his feet.

"You ok, Jack?" asked Ethan Kennedy, his gun barrel still smoking. "That was pretty close."

"Yeah ... I'm ok, Ethan. Thanks."

"No problem."

"Ethan, help!" yelled Linda. "Hurry, he's really bleeding bad."

Ethan and Jack turned to look at Linda. She was squatting beside Robertson, her hands pressing into his thigh. The bullet that had escaped during Jack's struggle with Curtis and had caught Robertson in the knee. His pants were soaked with blood and he was moaning and gritting his teeth. His face was strained and contorted and Jack could see the color running out of him.

Ethan and Jack were by his side in a flash. Ethan pulled off his belt and made a tourniquet that he cinched up just above the joint.

"How bad is it?" asked Linda. "It looks horrible."

Ethan looked at Robertson who was still conscious and grappling with the pain.

Ethan shook his head. "It's not good ... and, unfortunately ... he's the doc."

"What do you need, I'll get it. Anything!" cried Linda

"Right now ... just the tourniquet. The bullet's cut the popliteal artery. If we don't stem the bleeding he'll die in minutes. "Linda, see if the Doc has any clamps in his bag."

"Ok, this is gonna hurt, doc. A lot!" said Ethan. Then he reached down with both hands and yanked on the belt as hard as he could. "Hand me a stick or something."

Linda dashed in the kitchen, pulled the curtains off the window and came back with the rod. Ethan grabbed it, jammed it into the already tightened belt and twisted it around a couple times.

Robertson let out a long agonizing cry and then passed out. Ethan tied the rod in place around his thigh.

"There. That'll stop the bleeding. But we can't leave it like that forever or he'll lose his leg from lack of circulation. We gotta get him to the hospital. Now!"

"Sorry. No can do," said Jack. "None of the damned cars are working. None of em'll turn over."

"Ok ... ok. Let's just get him inside for now, then. Linda, why don't you go grab some blankets. He's gonna go into shock if we don't keep him warm. He's lost a lot of blood already."

Jack and Ethan carefully moved Robertson onto the leather sofa in the lobby and covered him up. They took his shoes and socks off to watch the color of his feet and toes. When they started to go blue, they'd have to release and retighten the tourniquet, a maneuver frowned upon in current medical circles, but it was all they could do if they wanted to try and save the doc and the leg.

Ethan set about clamping off the damaged artery. When he'd finished, he bandaged it up tightly and then called Jack and Linda over to the front desk away from Robertson.

"I've done everything I could here. But it's still pretty bad. Aside from the circulation problems, we'll have infection and hypovolemic shock to worry about. We're gonna have to find a way to get him out of here or we're gonna lose him."

"How will we know? I mean, what are the signs of that shock?" asked Linda.

"There's a few, but the worst will be the tachycardia ... fast heart rate. If that's left untreated ... he'll end up fibrillating and dying. And, there's not much we can do about it here." He turned to Jack, "He needs a hospital, Jack. I can't do anything else."

"Well, I'm open to suggestions. If we had a horse, I'd ride him out. But it seems we're stuck."

Ethan thought for a moment; he paced back and forth and the look on his face was strained as if he were worn out.

"What about the bike. I saw a motorcycle out there. That not running either?"

"I don't know. We didn't try that."

"Let's give it a shot. If it works ... if by some miracle it actually works, we can figure some way to fasten the doc on and I'll get him out. It's not the best option under ideal conditions, but I think it's the best one we have now."

"C'mon. Let's see if the fuckin thing works." Jack and Ethan went out to try the bike. Linda went back into the lobby. She was about to sit down when a horrible, banshee-like scream came thundering down the steps. The suddenness and intensity made her give out a yelp as she jumped.

Outside, Jack and Ethan heard it too. "What the hell was that?" asked Jack, not really expecting or wanting an answer. "What fuckin now?"

"You go. I'll see if I can get the bike started."

Jack raced up the steps and burst through the front door. He came to a dead stop. Linda was standing motionless by the couch. On the landing at the top of the steps stood a dark, solitary figure. From where he was standing, it appeared to Jack to be at least seven feet tall if not taller. It was featureless, almost a living silhouette and it was surrounded by what appeared to be a wall of moving smoke. It wasn't smoke, and Jack knew exactly what it was. Flies. Thousands and thousands of flies.

CHAPTER 79

After Carlton had deposited Evelyn's head on his doorstep, he set off in search of some matches and gasoline. He'd need them for the great work that was ahead of him. The idea of burning Banderman Falls to the ground titillated him. He walked along, giddy with excitement as he tried to think of a place where he could get what he needed. Of course, there was the EasyMart, but that was not within walking distance. He had to come up with a place that was close and had everything he needed.

The very last shop at the end of his block was Cerla's Ice Cream Parlor. He almost walked past it, his mind on greater things. He stood there looking in the window and wondering just what kind of damage a fire would do to an ice cream parlor. The image of all the ice cream melting and running into the streets tickled him. He actually giggled.

"Yes. Yes! This would be the perfect place to begin. But how do I start a fire in an ice cream place? That's the question." He thought about it for a few moments, then went inside. "Maybe they have a gas line ... maybe their water heater runs on gas ... I could use that ... that's for sure."

He walked around the end of the counter and then froze. In the back, Emma Cerla was trying to heft a large tub of freshly made chocolate ice cream into the freezer unit. Carlton hadn't expected anyone to be in the store. He'd thought they were all out fighting one another. He'd passed several groups engaged similarly on his way down the street. None of them had bothered him though. In fact, now that he thought about it, they had all stopped fighting and watched him pass. So he was surprised to see Emma still tending the store.

"Oh well, no matter." He pulled the pommel from his breast pocket, crept up behind her and plunged it through her back, twisting it around in semi-circles before he pulled it out. She dropped heavily to the floor, her eyes staring up at him, blood gushing from her mouth and the gaping hole between her breasts.

He smiled down at her, watching her die. He had a sudden urge to kick her and keep kicking her until that horrible gurgling sound she was making stopped. Instead, he knelt down and started tying her long blond hair in knots.

"How about that. The last thing that ever happened to you was the man you always made fun of messing up that hair you used to go around bragging about. Bitch! Bet that boosts your self-esteem, doesn't it?" Emma never heard the end of the sentence. Her head dropped to one side, her lungs gave out one final gasp and she was gone.

"Hmmm. Just like every other date I've ever had in my life. As soon as I start running my fingers through your hair ... off ya go. Oh well, time to melt some ice cream."

In the basement, he worked his way over behind all the boxes and broken ice cream churners and came to the water heater. It was run by gas and he was so thrilled he started dancing around, arms flying in every direction. Then, just as suddenly as he'd begun, he stopped. Bending down, he started following the pipeline ... up the side of the burner ... across the ceiling ... around the corner ... and there it was ... the main gas inlet.

"Ok ... now ... how to ignite this without blowing myself up in the process?   That's the question of the moment, Carlton.   That's the question of the moment."   He stroked his chin, considering the situation.   With a snap of his fingers, he had it. The perfect solution.

As fast as he could he ran back upstairs and searched all the drawers until he found what he wanted. Birthday candles. He knew the store had to have some for the stupid kids - and here they were. Boxes and boxes of them. Scooping up an armful, he raced back downstairs. At the foot of the steps, he dropped the boxes on the floor, then made his way back to the gas inlet. When he got there he realized that he needed something else.   A pipe wrench to loosen the fittings was what was called for here. So off he went in search of a pipe wrench or large pair of pliers, which he found in the front of the cellar in an old rusted toolbox.

It didn't take too many turns until he heard the familiar hiss of gas and smell the mercaptanol they put it in for leak recognition. Satisfied that it was going to do the trick, he ran back to the base of the steps, gathered the candles and candle boxes into a pile and lit them.   The boxes flared up immediately and he knew the wax would keep them burning. As soon as the gas from the other end reached the bottom of the steps...

Carlton laughed all the way up the steps and back out onto the street. He would have loved to stay around and watch things go *boom*, but he had more places to visit. And an appointment to keep in the cemetery.

Before he left the front of the store it occurred to him that he might find everything he needed at that stupid tire and battery place. That's where he would go next. A few cans of gas, the boxes of stick matches he'd found along with the candles and he was sure to have a blast - all afternoon and evening.

At Alderman's Tire & Battery, Carlton was disappointed to find that someone had already set the place ablaze. He stood and gazed at the flames shooting out the roof with mixed emotion. There were things in there he wanted, but the fire was so beautiful. He could hardly tear himself away. When he finally did, he came to the conclusion that the only option he had left was to drive all the way to the EasyMart.

"Guess I'll just have to blow that place up when I'm done, too. Their punishment for making me have to travel all that way. It'll serve em right. *And*, it'll make a great display in the process." Carlton patted his breast pocket for the billionth time that afternoon, reassuring himself that his precious prize was still there. Then he went off in search of a car.

Sauntering down the street, he noticed that more and more people were fighting and killing each other. He also noticed, for the first time, that it seemed to be the men against the women. As he walked along he wondered who would win in the end. Men were stronger, but women ... women were more ruthless, devious and, when pushed to it, more heartless and vindictive than men could ever hope to be.

"Glad I don't have to bet on this one," he said as he walked along, sometimes going around a fight, sometimes going right through the middle (the combatants parting long enough for him to pass.) He was magical. No one was going to touch him. He was invincible. And these thoughts made him smile the biggest smile he could ever remember smiling.

CHAPTER 80

Gwen swam back to consciousness slowly. She moaned as she struggled up from the depths of the blackness that surrounded her, her body stiff from lying on the cold concrete floor of the warehouse. On opening her eyes she found that she was still shrouded in black. Only a tiny shaft of weak, late afternoon light punched through the slats of the boarded-up window, the sole eye of the office to the outside world. She felt dizzy and disconnected, as if she were the embodiment of a blurred photograph, taken by an unsteady hand.

She wormed her way to a sitting position and tried to let her eyes adjust to graying surroundings. As her thoughts cleared, pictures of what had transpired earlier began to flip through her mind like a perverted kinescope: the couple skewered together, laughing at her, taunting her; pieces of their decomposing bodies dripping onto the floor and hanging off their bones like candle wax; Penny Bishop's morose and chilling laughter. It all rushed back and overtook her. It hit her hard and the impact fried her circuits. Her mind flipped the switch, cutting the juice to Gwen Archibald.

Dazed, confused and utterly blank, Gwen got to her feet. She looked around, taking in the scene as if for the first time. There was no recollection of how she'd got here, where *here* was, or for that matter, who *she* was. She stared blankly at the empty space of the office, turned a slow 360-degree circle and put a hand to her forehead. Nothing was coming.

Outside, the sun shifted its angle as it dropped below the horizon and the pencil-thin ray of light that had been stabbing through the rotting slats of the office window withdrew like a switched off lightsaber. Gwen stumbled toward the office door, not sure where she was going, but it seemed to be the only way out. She wandered through the darkness of the warehouse, bumping into shelves here, banging her knee against a metal drum there, searching for a way out. Panic was not an issue, she felt her way around, shuffling down one aisle and up the next in the same way a psychiatric patient on Thorazine might shuffle through hallways. Everything about her now was bland and colorless and her mind was as vacant as the warehouse through which she was wandering – perhaps even more so; the warehouse, at least, still held the memories of its former life, as evidenced by the boxes, tubs, drums, and shelves. Gwen was completely emptied.

Stumbling around a shelf at the end of an aisle, Gwen came to an open space. There was not enough light to see too far, although her eyes had adjusted. Arms outstretched and waving from side to side to protect her from any unseen obstacle, she maneuvered her way to the far wall, bumping into the edge of a rickety table. When her thigh caught its edge, it wobbled for a moment and then crashed to the floor. The corner of it slammed down hard on Gwen's instep and she screamed. The scream echoed around the building and came back at her in overlaid reverberations.

In an automatic response, she bent down to rub the injured joint, her hand brushing up against something soft and cold. Feeling around, another scream, much more intense and much more guttural rang out from her. The soft, cold object she felt was a hand. Her fingers followed it up the forearm to the shoulder, her eyes straining to see.

Another scream.

Something was moving – a lot of somethings.

Leaning in, she could make out a face. It was a woman's face, although it looked more like a caricature than a real person. The cheeks were puffed out and a thick, bulbous piece of flesh that had once been the tongue filled the cavity of her mouth completely occluding it, its rubbery-looking tip protruding from the gaping lips. The eyes stared blankly up through the darkness at an unknown point on the ceiling above them, one hand clutched tightly around its throat.

Gwen backed away, lost her balance and sat down hard on the floor. She shuffled backwards on her butt, her arms paddling behind her as if she were sculling. In her present state, she had no idea who the woman was. Several hours ago, however, she would have recognized the maggot-ridden body of Penny Bishop. Scrambling to her feet, she made her way to the wall and with one hand on it at all times, followed it around until she found an exit. Stepping out into the late evening light she looked around. Nothing was familiar to her. There wasn't a single landmark that made an impression.

Gwen looked left and then right and then left again. She had absolutely no idea which way to go or, for that matter, where she should go anyway. Turning right, she exited the gate at the far end of the warehouse lot, crossed the street and walked off into the dusk.

Two blocks down she came to a dead-end. On one side was an abandoned row of houses, on the other a thicket of woods. In front of her was a large, wrought iron fence. One of its joints was broken and a section tilted forward like a drunk hanging on a lamppost. Not wanting to retrace her steps, Gwen forced herself through the opening, catching her deputy's badge and tearing it off her shirt. She stooped, picked it up and stared at it. It meant nothing to her. She slipped it into her pocket and pushed through the brush that straddled a thin dirt path. The bushes clawed at her arms as she bulldozed through them in hopes of coming to a clearing. When she finally did, she stood motionless. As far as she could see, blocks of stone rose out of the ground in neat rows. The night air was still and the moon was just beginning to rise.

"A cemetery? I'm in a cemetery." She looked around, more confused than ever. She was totally lost. Finally giving in to the frustration, she sank to her knees, dropped her face into her hands and began to cry. Softly at first, and then, as her anguish grew, more loudly and more intensely. Her sobbing drifted off across the cemetery in an eerie wave.

CHAPTER 81

Jasper Collins sat in his car, still wondering what the hell it was he was doing in the cemetery, especially at night. He was bored and wanted to go home. Tucked away on a disused access road, he watched, bored to tears, as evening gave up its last light to night. He hated being in the cemetery at night. It gave him the creeps. It was ok working here during the day but at night, surrounded by hundreds of people who had departed this world, he found it chilling and unsettling.

He'd given up trying to listen to the radio; he'd drummed his fingers along to his own humming enough to have lost interest in that; he'd watched some crazy kid go streaking by the side of his car and over the back fence and now there was nothing left to do but sit there and wait.

He had just begun to doze off when the radio dial lit up. The light punched through his eyelids and he snapped them open. A voice came through the stereo speakers embedded in the door panels. It was staticy at first but cleared rapidly into a deep and growling timbre.

"Hello Jasper," it snarled. "Have you been waiting long? Are you enjoying your outing?" A deep laugh punched out from the speakers, rattling the windows. "I have work for you. And you're already behind schedule. Although, I guess I can't blame you for that."

More laughter.

"I want you to get on your digger. You have some people you need to set free. Don't worry, it's only about a half dozen or so. Shouldn't take you too long. Actually ... it better not take you too long or I'll be very upset."

A high pitched whine poured out from the speakers at a deranged volume. Jasper clapped his hands over his ears but it didn't help. His nose began to bleed and his eardrums began to swell. He screamed in pain, but the scream was swallowed by the whine coming from the radio. Then it stopped as suddenly as it had begun.

"Sorry about that," said the voice in a much softer tone. "Just wanted you to get the picture of how upset I might be and what would happen if you disappointed me. Now, to business. Here is a list of names whose graves I want you to open."

Jasper sat there listening intently, too afraid to do anything else, all the while hoping he'd be able to remember them as he had nothing to write them down with or on. Most of the names he didn't know. One or two he remembered because of how recently they'd been buried. The two he did recall made him shiver. They'd both died of natural causes, but he'd known both of them from his childhood. And both were the kind of people who gave humanity a bad name.

When he had the complete list and the radio turned itself off and fell silent again, Jasper climbed out of his car, looked around cautiously and then started off in the direction of the cemetery's equipment garage. Getting the backhoe running was no problem. He knew exactly where the keys were. Getting into the garage, however, would take some doing. He didn't have the keys to that and the doors and windows were alarmed. He'd have to be inventive. The last thing he needed, on top of everything else, was to have Jack Dougherty and his deputies show up. There was no way Jasper Collins would be able to explain opening graves in the middle of the damned night. Not to Jack; not to his deputies; not to anybody. He'd have to figure a way around the security system ... somehow.

Standing in front of the garage, Jasper rubbed at his brow, then at his chin, then at his brow again. What he really wished was that he had a drink to settle his nerves. A nice couple of shots of bourbon would be just the thing. He walked over and sat on a rock, resting his chin on his hands while he pondered the situation. Nothing was coming to him. And the warning for being tardy that kept playing through his head like a broken record wasn't helping much.

Absently, he picked up a handful of pebbles and started tossing them idly at the base of the garage doors. His mind kept slipping back and forth between the drink he wanted and the work he was supposed to be doing. He couldn't seem to concentrate on either.

Crackle. Snap. Crack. The noise brought him out of his thoughts. Someone was coming. Someone was pushing through the bushes to his left. He jumped to his feet, looking from side to side, trying desperately to find a place to hide. In his panic, it never occurred to him to scoot around the back of the garage. He stood there wringing his hands and feeling very much like a tree-cornered raccoon surrounded by a pack of braying hounds.

"Think, Jasper. Think! For Chrissake, *think*!"

It was too late. Before he had decided what he should do, a lone figure pushed through the bushes and came walking calmly toward him. In the dark, he couldn't make out who it was. He could turn and run, but he figured that wouldn't really do him any good. He'd still be in trouble with 'you-know-who'. There was really only one option open to him. Somehow ... he'd have to take this guy out. The thought of doing violence to another made his stomach ball up. But he felt he had no choice. He locked eyes on the approaching figure (hoping to hell they weren't carrying a gun), bent down and picked up the biggest rock he could find and hid it behind his back.

"Ok. Just stay calm. When he gets close enough, say hi ... then *wham* ... right on the noggin. That's what you have to do. That's what you have to do. That's what you have to do."

He kept repeating that phrase over and over, trying to convince himself that it would be the easiest thing in the world. One whack on the head and he could get back to doing what he was sent here to do. And ... *and* ... it occurred to him that it might just give him a fall guy to take the wrap for breaking in. As long as the cops didn't show while he was digging, that is.

The stranger was closer now, walking steadily forward, looking straight at Jasper. His path never deviated, his feet never faltered and his pace never changed. A Sunday afternoon stroll couldn't have been more leisurely.

CHAPTER 82

Billy Wurtz, Andy Johansen, and Cal Richards rolled the rusted-out drum up to the window of PARTY HAVEN. They'd filled it with every bit of trash they could find that would burn. The three boys had been fooling around behind Alderman's Tire & Battery when the sleepiness had hit them. Andy was the first to feel it. His legs had started getting wobbly and his eyelids felt like they were suddenly weighted down. It took him a few minutes before he could shake the feeling off. Billy and Cal were next with nearly identical symptoms, but they too were able to fend off sleep. Now they were all wide awake and had a burning urge to burn things.

"G'on, Billy, go siphon off some gas, we'll need it," demanded Andy, the oldest of the boys. He'd dropped out of high school last year and had since spent most of his time trying to get odd jobs: cutting lawns, cleaning out basements and attics, whatever he could find. Billy and Cal were both two years his junior and worshiped the ground he walked on. Mostly because he'd always treated them right and kept them from being picked on by any of the school bullies.

After they'd weathered their sudden and bizarre round of drowsiness, the three of them had had the same idea at the same time. For some reason, they all felt like setting fires, something none of them had ever considered before. The image of tall flames licking at the sky had slipped into their heads and expanded like the inflating of a balloon. They found themselves unable to resist, even though they had a greater feeling that it was wrong. Now they stood in front of the PARTY HAVEN, a place loaded with paper products and combustibles, planning to spark the biggest fire they could manage.

G'on, Billy," shouted Andy a second time. "Hurry up before somebody comes along and stops us."

"But I don't know how to siphon, Andy. You do it."

"Oh hell-in-a-hand basket, do I have to do everything for you two. Ok, I'll get the damned gas. You two shove this barrel through the window. Think ya can manage *that* or do I have t'do that, too?" He didn't wait for an answer; he grabbed the hose and the empty milk jug out of Billy's hand and marched across the street to the Mallman's Chevy. In no time at all, he siphoned off nearly a gallon of unleaded.

As he watched the pale amber liquid fill up the jug he heard the plate glass window behind him shatter, its broken pieces tinkling to the street like crystal rain. When he was sure he had enough for the job, he headed back across the street, the hose still dangling from the car and gas still pouring out of it onto the street.

"Ok. Watch out," he yelled and started dumping the gas on the trash inside the barrel and across the front of the window display. Taking aim, he tossed the milk jug, still containing a nice layer of gas in the bottom, into the store and landing it just where he wanted it - up against the pressurized helium tanks used to fill balloons.

"Who wants to light it?" Andy asked as he held out the book of matches.

Billy and Cal just stared at him blankly. They both wanted that honor, but they were both afraid to be the one to do it. Neither of them volunteered. Billy put his hands in his pockets and when Cal saw that, he clasped his hands behind his back.

Andy stared at them in disbelief. "Pussies!" He struck the match and watched as the head sprang to glowing life. Waiting long enough to be sure it wouldn't go out, he dropped it in the window. Before it hit the ground there was a loud *WUMPF* as the fumes ignited. The unexpected suddenness rattled the boys and they fled across the street for cover. In their haste to escape, they'd missed the fact that the car they were hiding behind to watch the spectacle was the very car that Andy had siphoned the gas from and was now still bleeding gas all over the street. It had run underneath the Chevy and was pooling up along the curb. Billy's sneakers were getting a good soaking, and it wasn't until he could feel his toes getting wet that he realized it.

A moment before the blaze inside ignited the gas on the street, which burned its way back to the Chevy and the boys, Cal Richards looked down.

"Oh shit!" he cried, but that turned into a horrid scream – a scream that was joined by two others. They ran into each other in their panic as the flames shot up their pants' legs and engulfed them. Billy tried to 'Stop-Drop-and Roll', but it was too late. His hair was already on fire and the skin was peeling off his face like the layers off an onion. Adam and Cal were suffering the same fate and in less than two minutes, the three boys lay randomly on the sidewalk, their bodies smoldering.

Half a block away, Carl Wedgemore stood reveling in the sight. He had his left arm high in the air, the sword handle and pommel held out. A hazy bluish-green glow surrounded it and him. A few seconds after the boys had dropped to the ground, the Chevy reached critical temperature and exploded. It was tossed into the air and came bouncing down in front of Carlton. Its nose hit first. He stood there and watched it coming, tumbling end-over-end. Just before it struck him, he pointed the pommel of the sword at it and it froze in space. Hanging there, it began to collapse in upon itself, as if some unseen compactor was hard at work. Its metal grumbled and groaned and it squeezed itself into nothingness, finally disappearing completely with a soft *pop*.

Carlton stood there admiring his handiwork and swimming in the glory of his newly found powers. He had discovered, quite by accident, that, with the pommel, he could do just about anything he wanted to do. And better ... he could make other people do *exactly* what he wanted them to do.

He had just turned a corner when he saw the three boys standing there tossing a ball back and forth. In his mind, he saw them setting fire to the store they were standing in front of. Immediately, they had dropped the ball and went in search of a large trash can, finally settling on the empty fifty-five-gallon drum.

Now they were nothing more than charred remains. Carlton collected himself and moved off down the street. He reminded himself that he had work to do and that some of this fun would have to wait for later. At the end of the block, he found an old Chevy Blazer with the keys still in it. He climbed in, cranked it over and headed off for his appointed rendezvous at *Chez EasyMart*, giggling the whole way.

*****

When he pulled into the lot, evening was almost at an end. He clambered out of the truck and stood there looking back at the Falls. The dusky sky was ablaze with orange and red. And where the fires were strongest, long black columns of smoke could be seen rising through them.

As he watched, a familiar voice came into his head. A comforting hiss that told him he was still in charge ... still *The Man*.

"Hurry Carlton. Do what you want with this station, but I need you to hurry and get to the cemetery. There is someone there that needs your help. Hurry, Carlton. Have your fun and then be on your way." The voice died away into the night like the last chord of a farewell concert.

Carlton went into the store, picked up two plastic gas cans from the automotive section, walked up front and paid for them, laughing the whole time. Lee Cho, Pat O'Donnell's replacement, rang up the sale and watched as Carlton went out and filled the cans, placed them inside his truck and then laid the gas hose on the ground, its handle lock still depressed. Lee wanted to kill the pumps, but he found that he could only watch with a sick, restrained fascination.

Carlton pulled his truck forward, stopped, pulled the pommel from his jacket pocket and held it out. He closed his eyes. In his mind, he saw Lee walk out of the store, sit down in the puddle of gas and strike a match.

Boom! Boom-boom!   Boom-boom-boom! Kablam!

Carlton opened his eyes but didn't look over. He didn't have to. He pulled out of the station, listening as the explosions continued, growing more aggressive with each pump in the line. Out of the corner of his eye, he saw the reflection of the flames and smoke in the side view mirror and, once again, he began giggling. He had one more stop to make and then it would be on to the cemetery. One more building to burn and then his work (and his new life) could really begin. He could feel it.

Less than five minutes after he'd parked in front of the house he was done. As he climbed back into the Chevy and tore off down the driveway his parent's home crackled and crumbled in the swarming flames. Never again would Carlton have to look at that place - that wretched place where he used to have to hide from his tormentors and depend on his father's reputation to keep them away. Never again would he have to lie in that bed, covers pulled over his head hearing his father call him 'A Loser' or walk down the hallway accosted by the ghosts of his past humiliations in that house.

CHAPTER 83

Rachel was the first to stir. She pulled her head up from the bar and looked around. Her eyes felt swollen and the heavy beating rhythm in her head rivaled any steel drum section imaginable. Beside her, Colleen was slumped to the side, her cheek resting on her right arm. She looked dangerously close to toppling to the floor. A small stream of spittle hung like a spider's thread from her mouth. Verna had disappeared completely, having fallen off the other side of the bar.

"Colleen," she called softly. "Colleen." Rachel shook her gently by the shoulder. It had absolutely no effect so she pushed a litter harder.

Still nothing, not even a grunt.

"Verna? Verna ... you still with us?

"Ahh. Huh? What? Who's that?" The voice rose thick and bassy from behind the bar. "Ahh. My fuckin head! That you, Rach?"

"Yes. Colleen's still out cold."

A few seconds later Verna's large paws appeared on the rim of the bar followed by a head and then a scrunched up face. Her eyes, bloodshot and half-hidden beneath puffed out lids, darted from side to side then squinched closed as she pulled herself to a standing position.

"What time is it?" Verna craned her neck around to see the Seth Thomas clock that hung between the two wall mirrors behind the bar. It took her several attempts at focusing before she came to the conclusion that it was either eight o'clock at night or eight in the morning. She wasn't sure which.

By this time, Rachel had slipped from the stool and was wobbling her way towards the ladies' room, her head cradled in both hands. Verna watched her bounce off the door jamb, a sharp *"ow"* shooting across the room. Verna started to laugh but the pain in her temples cut that short.

"Hair of the dog," she said. "That's what mama needs." She picked up the near-empty bottle of Jim Beam and guzzled it down, wiped her lips with her adipose-padded forearm, belched and then tossed the bottle into the waste can under the bar. "Much better. Much better, indeed."

In the bathroom, Rachel made her way to the sink, turned on the cold water and let it run. She splashed her face and dowsed the back of her neck.

The tingling sensation helped clear her mind but did nothing for the pounding inside her head. Snatching a handful of paper towels from the dispenser, she blotted her face dry.

"Good going, girl!" she barked at the haggard-looking image in the mirror that was staring blankly back at her. "You look *great*. Simply great!"

When she'd accomplished all she thought was possible at the sink, she turned and eyed the stalls. Peeing in a public restroom was nearly an Olympic event for most women. Difficult enough to manage sober, impossible drunk and intolerable with a hangover. It required a dexterity not demanded of men. Women rarely, if ever, actually placed their fannies on the seat. And when they did, it was only because there was absolutely no other choice. It was sort of a self-perpetuating problem, poor aim led to more squatting and more squatting led to poor aim.

Rachel braced herself, hoping her legs were up to the task at hand, stepped into the stall and clicked the latch over. Shortly after she began her acrobatic assault on the toilet, the muffled sounds of an argument drifted in from the bar. There was no mistaking the heavier voices of three or four men and the shouts of Verna.

She was about to hold off on nature's call and go see what was going on when the bathroom door burst open so hard it banged off the wall. Rachel held her breath. Something inside her told her to be quiet.

"Yoo-hoo. Anybody in here?" The call was followed by a few heavy steps. It was definitely male and he was well into the room. A second later, Rachel heard the slap of palms on the tile floor. Whoever it was, he was looking under the stalls. For the first time in her life, Rachel was glad about the contortions required for a simple pee, and the fact that she'd placed her high heels up on the toilet tank for safe-keeping.

"Go away ... go away. Don't check each stall ... just go away," she mouthed to herself. It was completely inaudible, but in her mind it was as loud as a church bell on Sunday morning. She clapped a hand over her mouth, immediately hoping that the soft slapping sound hadn't been heard. She waited, her heart beating so hard in her chest that she was sure that it could be heard as well.

A few moments later she heard the squeak of the door as it opened and the soft *whoosh* it made as it closed on its own. She remained statue-still, too frightened to move, straining to hear the slightest sound. Nothing! Not even from the bar area. But still she waited, crouched on top of the toilet seat like a catcher behind the plate.

Rachel was just about to climb down when she heard Verna cry out. There was a heavy thud, followed by two more. Then, for a moment, silence.

Laughter. The sound of men laughing, three, maybe four distinct voices. This was accompanied by another thump, somewhat softer than the first three, a muffled cry and then heavy panting and grunting as if someone were carrying an extremely heavy load up a flight of steps.

When the grunting stopped, maybe ten or twelve minutes later, a raspy gurgling sound ensued. Rachel searched her mind trying to identify the sounds ... all of them ... there was something familiar about them, especially the grunting ones. The gurgling sounds reminded her of someone gargling but that made no sense, unless, whoever it was had decided to freshen their breath with liquor.

Inside, she knew that whatever was happening wasn't good. Something terrible was happening to her friends. Shame and fear mingled together, stripping her of all will. Her heart wanted to go help; her mind told her to stay put or suffer whatever fate her friends were now suffering.

"We done here, boys?" came a booming voice. There was no answer, or, at least, none that Rachel could hear. A moment later she heard the front door slam shut, presumably behind the men as they left. But one couldn't be too careful, so she waited ... and waited.

Finally deciding that it was safe to come out and not really knowing whether she'd been on that seat for ten minutes or ten hours, Rachel climbed down, peered through the stall-door hinge gap, pushed it open a bit and cautiously stepped out into the room. She purposely left her shoes behind, not wanting to be clacking across the tile floor.

She placed her ear against the bathroom door before opening it and cocked her head around its edge, eyeing up the room. It appeared empty, but that was no guarantee that it was. She pushed the door open a bit further and took a step forward. Her legs were wobbly, but she'd completely forgotten about her headache and hangover. Her heart was beating so hard in her chest that she could feel it in her abdomen. Steeling herself for the worst, she stepped out into the barroom, the bathroom door closing softly behind her.

Her worst fears were confirmed. A shoeless foot and half a calf stuck out from behind the far end of the bar. From its shape, Rachel knew it belonged to Colleen. Verna was nowhere in sight.

The last light of day had withdrawn and the lights had not yet been turned on, so the only illumination came from the neon signs (Molson, Coors, Mike's Hard Lemonade) that hung in the windows and along the back wall next to the mirrors. It gave an added eeriness to a scene that was already disturbing.

Rachel raced over to see if she could help Colleen. When she rounded the end of the bar, she let out a high pitched, piercing shriek. Colleen lay on the floor, one leg bent up, her panties stuffed in her mouth. Her skirt was wrapped around her waist and her face spattered with the remnants of her attackers' pleasures. Her eyes were open but she was seeing nothing. Her blouse was tied tightly around her neck, heavily knotted at the base of her throat. Colleen Slater, former enemy, former drinking buddy, was dead ... strangled to death.

Rachel backed up, her hands over her face. Had it not been for the events of earlier, the events that had led her and Colleen here in the first place, she would not have believed this possible in this town. But reality, like death, comes on hard and cold and refutes disbelief in a way nothing else can.

Not really wanting to, Rachel placed her hands up on the bar, hoisted herself up and looked over. Verna was lying face down back there. Her head had been beaten open with her own steel pipe, which lay bloodied next to her. Rachel slid back down onto a bar stool, her legs too rubbery to support her. The horror that had taken her was dissipating ... transmuting into a rage that she could feel building in her very core. Reaching over without even looking, she snagged her purse off the bar, pulled out the gun and stood up. It was time for some good old, solid retribution. And she was just the one to deliver it.

She strode out of the bar, still only in stocking feet, gun held at the ready. It didn't matter to her that she had no idea who had done this. Something seized her, something that spoke to her: "If you've got a 'y' chromosome, you're a target."

Halfway down the block, on her way into the center of town, an old man stepped out of his doorway and lit a cigarette. One moment and two shots later he lay sprawled on the sidewalk. Rachel stepped over the body and scanned the street for her next target.

"If you fuckers wanna play rough ... I'm your girl. Time for a *real* manhunt."

CHAPTER 84

Jack stood at the bottom of the steps looking up. His mind was racing. There was no shower

down here. If those flies repeated their last
performance it was almost a sure thing that none of
them would survive.

The dark figure took a step forward. One at
a time he descended the steps, the flies buzzing
madly around him – enshrouding him in a living
black cocoon. A bony hand punched out of the
black cloud and gripped the banister. Immediately,
the flies extended their radius and re-covered the
hand.

Jack backed up slowly, grabbing Linda's
hand as he did.

"Get outside," he whispered.

"Jack, what are you going to do?"

"I'll be right behind you, believe me. Get
outside; get Ethan and get in one of the cruisers and
button it up tight." He motioned toward the couch.
"I'll grab Doc."

Holding on to Linda with one hand, he
pushed the screen door open a little, all the while
keeping his eye on the swirling blackness that was
coming down the steps.

When Linda was out and the screen door
shut, Jack stood for a moment. He had to decide
whether it would be better to move slowly toward
the doc to draw as little attention as possible, or
make a break for it and hope he could scoop him up
and get out the door before they were both
swallowed alive in a fog of biting horseflies.

He settled on the slow approach and moved
towards the couch sideways, his eyes never leaving
the stairs. He had made it as far as the sofa when
the attack began. En masse, the flies covered the

doctor, some breaking off to plague Jack. Jack swiped at them frantically, trying his best to clear the doctor's face and nose. When he did, the majority of them flew at him, driving him back. They kept coming, biting and crawling, stinging his ears and eyelids.

Jack was forced backwards. When he hit the wall, he rolled to his left, his hands working to clear enough flies from his nostrils so he could keep breathing. At the screen door, he tumbled out onto the porch and down the steps. His assailants flew off, gathering at the door and covering the screen, trying to get back inside to their master.

For the second time, Jack's face and arms began to swell with welts. He struggled to his feet and looked helplessly at the front door whose screen was now totally obliterated from view by the black horde. Anguish rose up inside him, followed by fury. There was nothing he could do. And feeling helpless and impotent was not one of his strong points. His anger caused him to draw his gun, but he knew the only outcome of that would be to waste ammunition punching holes in a screen door.

Cursing under his breath, he walked over to the cruiser. Linda pulled up the door latch and he got in, slamming it shut behind him.

"Doc?" asked Ethan.

Jack just shook his head.

Inside the B & B, the flies had so covered Robertson that you couldn't even tell there was a human on the couch, not even an outline remained. From a distance, it looked as if someone had dropped a large black tarp over it ... a moving tarp.

The dark figure, now unveiled, stood over the swarming flies. His face and head were ash-colored, his eyes an opaque green. The flesh that covered the skull was hairless and clung tightly to the underlying bone like shrink-wrap to a CD case. The cheeks were sharply edged, as if the zygomatic arch had been sharpened with a bench grinder. There was no nose, per se, only the opening one might associate with a fleshless skull and the eyebrow ridges were owlishly flattened and rounded. The ears were large and swept back against the side of the head, with the rear-most edge curled forward. Black, dry lips gaped open to reveal long, lupine-like teeth, the color of wet sawdust. His shoulders were thick and muscular, as were his arms, torso and legs, all the same ashen color as the skull. The fingers of his hands were inordinately long and thin, tapering to points at the ends. At the very tips, arched pieces of bone protruded upward about two inches like the curved thorns of a rose.

It stood there, looking down on the mass of flies that now encased Robertson, its radiant eyes giving the room a glowing, greenish tinge. It plunged its hand down through the undulating congregation of insects and hoisted Robertson up into the air. The flies scattered, buzzing wildly around the room.

"Did we have a boo-boo accident?" it asked, its free hand wrapping around Robertson's shattered knee. It curled its fingers inward, the sharp nails sinking into the thigh and wound like skewers through shish kabobs. Robertson let out a sharp, agonizing yell, which trailed off to a puling whisper.

"Is mommy not here to kiss it better?" Its voice was raspy, deep, and had a bubbling gurgle to it, as if it were speaking while gargling. Tiny drops of black liquid hung like dew from the tips of its teeth, reminding Robertson of venom on a snake's fangs. He clasped both hands around the thing's wrist, trying to wrest himself free. He didn't have the strength. His knee was bleeding freely again, the torn artery spurting what life he had left across the front of the creature that held him fast. Dangling in the air like a child's doll, Robertson began to feel cold and thirsty and his vision was starting to blur. Consciousness was slipping away; trying to focus was like trying to swim through peanut butter. His surroundings faded in and out, and it seemed to him as though he were looking through a paper towel tube.

In dreamlike slow motion, Robertson saw himself being drawn toward the gaping mouth and yellow, dripping teeth. His mind reeled, commanding his body to fight back. But all he could do was hang there and drift endlessly forward. A sudden pain shot through his system as his head hit the floor. The unbroken fall acted like a body slam and the air whooshed out of his lungs. Tiny points of light danced across the backs of his eyes and a warm, metallic taste filled his mouth, his teeth having been clamped down on his tongue by the jarring impact.

A bellowing roar filled the room, vibrating the pictures on the wall, the vases on the tables, and the plethora of knick-knacks that decorated the shelves.   Robertson strained to see what was happening but everything was fuzzy and indistinct. Something was thrashing around, screaming and doubling over ... something monstrous. Through the haze, just before he lost complete consciousness, Robertson saw the thing stumbling from side to side, clutching and clawing at its neck and abdomen as if it were suddenly seized by an intolerable agony. Small black specks began to rain down on him, pelting him like hail and bouncing off the floor with a hollow ticking sound.

"Nooo ... my babies ...not my babies," was the last thing the doctor heard before he slid into the gray depths of unconsciousness.

In his true form, Witherstone staggered around the room. His connection to his wolves was being severed, and as they died, so did a part of him. It was as if he'd been hooked to a high voltage line. His muscles were contracting violently and his organs felt as if they were being grilled. Through the wolves' eyes he could dimly see the outline of two shapes, but it was like looking through a thick fog. He collapsed to his knees, shrieking in pain and spewing forth obscenities and vows of retribution.

Outside, in the cruiser, Jack, Linda, and Ethan heard the hellish screams. They were looking at one another as the cruiser suddenly rumbled to life, its engine coughing and then catching. Not questioning how or why, Ethan, who was sitting in the driver's seat, slipped it into DRIVE and peeled out, tires kicking up dust and gravel behind it.

Linda and Jack stared out the back window at the B & B as it shrank into the darkness, both thinking about Doc Robertson and feeling guilty for having left him behind.

When they reached the end of the driveway Ethan cut a quick left and accelerated. A few miles further on, the Pike would once again turn into Main Street and they'd be back in town.

"Ok, so what the hell is happening, Jack?" asked Ethan. "I'd say things were strange, but I think it's way beyond that at this point?"

"I don't know Ethan. And, by the way, thanks for saving my life. I don't know where the hell you came from but you sure showed up at the right moment."

"A little late, *I'd* say. The right moment would have been *before* Robertson took a bullet."

Ethan filled Jack in on what had happened at the B & B and how he and Linda had made their escape to the woods. Jack told Ethan about the flies and his encounter with them upstairs. Not one of the three of them had an explanation for any of it, wanted to believe any of it could be real or could ignore any of it. For most of the rest of the trip they sat in silence, each occupied with their own fears and misgivings. And for Jack - another dose of guilt at having failed his friend and community.

CHAPTER 85

With the cruiser still idling, Audrey took a cautious look around. She swung the door open and got out, her hand on the butt of her gun. Whatever mania had taken the people of Banderman Falls hadn't seemed to catch up with her yet, and she couldn't for the life of her understand what was happening.

The back door to Twilling's Funeral Home was locked. She twisted the handle but it wouldn't budge. Now she was faced with a choice. To get in the front she'd have to go through the side parking lot, around ornamental bushes, and up under the alcove. A long walk when the whole town seemed to be having their own civil war. Or, she could get back in the cruiser and drive around. In the end, she opted to try to get there through the parking lot.

Moving to the corner of the building, she took a quick peek around. There was a small group in the front of the lot battling it out. Three women, all of whom she recognized, were struggling with two very large men. Velma McPherson was swinging at one them with a long piece of galvanized pipe. Denise Hoffman and Louise Caldera were struggling with the second. He had Louise in a choke-hold and was swinging wild punches at Denise every time she came within range. Denise, for her part, was lunging at his face with what looked to be a sharpened tree branch.

Audrey thought about trying to break it up but something inside told her it would be worse than a wasted effort. It would only result in her having to shoot someone ... maybe more than one someone. So she kept as close to the wall of Twillings as she could and made her way to the ornamental garden.

At the garden she stooped. So far, no one had taken notice of her. Rather than chance it by going around them, she pushed directly through the bushes and emerged on the other side under the carport. Two steps at a time, she bounded onto the porch. Taking a final look at the scene behind her, she was just in time to see Denise shove her homemade spear through the big man's throat. His hands clawed at it as he let go of Louise, took a couple of steps backward and fell down. Audrey didn't wait to see any more. She twisted the brass knob and slipped inside, closing and locking the door behind her.

"Sam?" she called. "Sam? It's Audrey Archibald. Are you here?"

The funeral home was broken up into five separate rooms, each merging into a central hallway. Audrey investigated each one, hoping to find Sam, hoping not to have to go downstairs to the embalming room. In the end, that was exactly where she had to go.

Somewhere off in the distance an explosion thundered through the air. The sounds of far off screams and yells also drifted across the Falls, fingered their way through closed doors and windows and into the funeral parlor.

Audrey shook her head in disbelief, drew in a deep breath and opened the door that led down to the room she dreaded. The lights were already on. She listened for any sound of Sam moving around down there, but the only thing she could hear was the chaos, rioting, and pitched battles going on outside.

"Sam? Sam ... you down there? It's Audrey."

Again, her only answer was silence. Summoning all her resolve, Audrey Archibald, Deputy Sheriff of Banderman Falls, proceeded down the steps. At the bottom, a hallway ran straight for about twenty-five feet and then turned left. There was only one door between the steps and the L. It was a thick metal door with a small, inset, wire-laced window. Audrey crept quietly up to it and peered in. There was a body on the table, but it wasn't Tyler's. Audrey absently blessed herself and mouthed a small prayer for the poor fellow lying in wait of his final manicure, facial, and hairstyling. Then she moved on down the hall and around the corner, gun drawn.

Halfway down the corridor ... *pop* ... an overhead light bulb blew out. Darkness swallowed her. The only light that could be seen was spilling from under a door at the end of the corridor. Audrey trotted down the hallway stopping just short of the door. As before, she stood silently, listening for any sound.

Whistling.

Spilling out from under the door along with the slice of white light was the sound of someone whistling *If I Had a Hammer*. Audrey recognized the off-tune whistle. Sam Twilling had never been able to carry a tune, although that never stopped him from singing or whistling as loudly as he could, no matter where he was or who was around.

Audrey opened the door and stepped in. The shock of what she saw caused her to drop her gun. She'd been totally unprepared for what was happening.

Sam Twilling was standing over a table, completely naked. On the table was a disarticulated body; Audrey assumed it was Tyler's although she couldn't be sure. Sam was leaning over it, whistling away, bone saw in one hand while the other repeatedly slammed down on the skull with the metal blade of a tissue grinder. He turned when he heard the gun clatter to the floor.

Audrey deftly retrieved the Beretta and aimed it steadily at Sam's head. "What in God's name are you doing, Sam?" she barked.

The whistling trailed off and he stood there looking at her dumbly as if she'd suddenly grown another head.

"Huh? Audrey? Audrey ... is that you?" There was a blank look on his face. It was like he didn't really see her.

"Sam ... I asked you what you're doing. I'm waiting for an answer." She'd bent her knees, lowering her center of gravity, and wrapped her left hand around her right on the butt of the gun. She was looking directly at Sam's forehead along the sight.

"Wha ... what did you say, Audrey?"

At any other time or in any other situation, Audrey would have thought he was sleepwalking. He didn't seem to have the slightest clue as to his surroundings. His head turned from side to side and then back to face her again.

"What are you doing here? Is Jack with you?"

"SAM!" she shouted.   "What were you doing to that body, and why?"

He turned and looked at the table. It was like he was seeing it for the first time. The bone saw and grinding blade clattered to the floor. When he turned back, his mouth was agape in horror, his eyes wide and blank.

"Sam ... who's on the table? Who is that?"

"It's ... it's-" He never finished. He took two steps backward and collapsed. His mouth was still moving but there was no sound coming out.

Very cautiously, Audrey moved over beside him. With the gun still trained on his head, she knelt down. He was definitely saying something but she couldn't make out what. Taking a big chance, she leaned in closer, pressing her ear almost directly onto his lips. A moment later, he was dead, his face contorted in a grimace and his eyes wide, as if he'd just seen the devil, himself.

The last words that Audrey got made absolutely no sense to her. She assumed that whatever had killed him had taken his mind first. (Which wasn't much of a stretch considering what was going on outside.) Standing up, she repeated his last words, hoping that maybe hearing them out loud would clear the matter up. It didn't.

"My babies. You killed my babies," had been his last words. Sam Twilling had no children.

Once again, Audrey was on her own with no idea where Jack was. But one thing was definitely clear to her. Something had to be done about what was happening. The question was ... what? Leaving Sam behind, she made her way to the back door, unlocked it and stepped out into the night. Thankfully, her cruiser was still there, lights flashing and door hanging open, just as she'd left it.

Buckling herself up, she slammed the door and locked it. She tried the radio again but it still wasn't working. She sat there thinking about what to do next. Her options were limited. What she really needed was some help. But that wasn't going to be easy to find.

Unless ...

Unless she got it from outside of Banderman Falls. With a kind of "Ah-Ha" insight, Alexander Kerrigan's name popped into her mind.

"That's it, Audrey. You win yourself the prize. Alex! Gotta get the Staties involved now. It's the only thing to do."

Audrey pulled the shift back locking it into R, backed out, slammed it down into drive, hit the sirens and sped off down the alleyway. Peeling out onto Clearfield, the tires squealed. She made a sharp left onto Main at the end of the block and ripped toward the Philadelphia line.

CHAPTER 86

Having settled on action as opposed to any further analysis, Arliss Peterson headed for the door. It was time to go find out where her missing artifact was and why she hadn't been notified that it had been erroneously received. She was certainly going to give that Wedgemore guy a piece of her mind concerning professionalism.

She'd just put her hand on the knob when the phone on the nightstand rang. Bill had just hung up and had used the cell phone. Nobody else knew she was here, so she was confused at who could be calling. Vacillating about whether or not to answer it, her inborn curiosity won out and she plucked up the receiver.

"Hello?"

"Miss Peterson? This is Shirley at the front desk." There was a sing-songy quality to her voice that put Arliss off immediately.

"Yes?"

"I have a package here that just arrived for you. It's a bit too large for our mail drop. Could you come down and pick it up?"

Surprised but happy, Arliss stammered out a yes. She hurried down to the elevators, waited as patiently as she could, tapping the toe of her foot the whole time and drumming her fingers on her arms. When the doors slid open on the first floor, she burst out at a trot.

"I'm Arliss Peterson. I believe you have a package for me," she said as she approached the front desk.

The girl behind it looked at her for a minute. Her head was tilted to one side and her eyes darted back and forth as if she had no idea what she was supposed to do. At last, she bent down and picked up a box and slid it across the counter.

When Arliss reached out for it, the girl slapped her hand down on the top. "I'll have to see some ident-ty-fi-cation first," she said, snapping the gum that she was chewing. "It's pro-seeder."

Arliss wondered how the hotel could ever have allowed someone of her obviously limited education to man the desk. But not wanting to have to talk with her any more than she had to, Arliss produced the necessary ID, signed for the package, and went over and sat down on one of the lobby sofas. She wanted in the worst way to open it immediately but knew that probably wasn't a very good idea. She could always cart it back up to her room, but something told her she should bring it along with her.

***

One hundred yards from the border that separated Banderman Falls from Conshohocken, Father Jacobs's car began to sputter and click, finally dying completely. It rolled to a stop, Jacobs maneuvering it to the side of the road.

"Bloody marvelous," said Geoffrey.

"I just had this thing serviced less than a month ago," complained Jacobs.

"I don't think it has anything to do with the car, old boy. I think our friend wants to keep the party exclusive. Nobody in or out."

"Well that's rather cheeky of him, isn't it?" said Jacobs in his best English accent.

Geoffrey just eyed him.

Jacobs thought back to when he'd hoped that he and Geoffrey wouldn't be alone in this ... and had come to the conclusion that they probably were, he still had hope that he was wrong. Now ... there was absolutely no doubt. Whatever was going to happen, there wasn't going to be any saving cavalry waiting over the hill to swoop in at the last moment.

"So what now? You're the expert in these matters."

"Don't know. Guess we'll bloody well have to walk."

"Do you need whatever it is we're going for? I mean ... *really* need it?"

Jacobs already knew the answer, and the look that Geoffrey shot him confirmed it. "Ok, then. Time for a nice stroll through the moonlight."

They got out of the car and started walking down the shoulder of the road. Despite the joke, there was very little moonlight. It had started to crest the horizon a while ago, but now it seemed stuck. Its dome hung just above the trees, suspended there as if it had been caught in the branches and couldn't free itself. Jacobs stared at it as they walked along.

"Geoffrey?" he said, at last. "Does the moon seem odd-"

Geoffrey cut him off. "You bet it does, mate. And I'll tell you something else. That-" he pointed at the hanging, inverted bowl of white light, "-*That* is not the oddest thing I suspect we'll see."

"Umm." Was all Jacobs said.

A signpost marked the spot between townships. It read:

WELCOME TO CONSHOHOCKEN
LITTERING TAKEN SERIOUSLY
SPEEDING TAKEN *MORE SERIOUSLY*

"Hold on a sec. I'd like to try something first if you don't mind." Geoffrey reached out his palm, pressing it into Jacobs's chest and stopping him short.

"By all means. Try away."

Geoffrey scanned the ground until he found a rock of suitable size. Taking a step back and dragging the good Father with him, he lobbed it forward. At the exact spot where Banderman Falls ends and Conshohocken begins, the rock sizzled, burst into a ball of blue flame and then disintegrated with a loud *Bang!*

"Well ... *that's* bloody inconvenient."

"Not to mention just plain rude," added Jacobs with a short hiccup of a nervous laugh. "Seems Conshy isn't taking in any visitors these days. Now what?"

"I'll let you in on another little secret too," said Geoffrey. "I don't think our friend had anything to do with our car. I think we're damned lucky it decided to quit on us. If we had driven though *that*-" He pointed a finger at where the rock had blown itself to dust.

"I get your point," sighed Jacobs. "Maybe someone upstairs *is* watching over us."

CHAPTER 87

Eric hoisted himself to an upright position, using the steering wheel as a handle. It turned slightly when he grabbed it and he almost fell over again. Sitting behind the wheel, his hands on top of it and his forehead resting against his hands, Eric started to gather himself together. He wished he could just turn around and go home; he wished he could ignore the feelings inside him; he wished he did not have to face what was ahead of him; he wished he knew what that was, and he wished he didn't feel as if, when it was all said and done, he would not be going home to his Ruby anymore.

Leaning back in his seat, he drew a deep sigh and let it out slowly, like a solder resigned to carry out a suicide mission. He thought once more of Ruby, waiting patiently at the front door, tail wagging, for a master that would never return. Then he slipped the old truck into gear, checked his rearview mirror, and pulled back out onto the highway. The pickup bounced back up over the shoulder of the road and sped down the macadam, headed for Peaceful Haven Cemetery

A loud *Boom!* of thunder broke the night's silence and dark clouds rolled swiftly across the sky swallowing the stars. Bluish-white fingers of lightning punched through the blackness, arcing and branching together like some bizarre electrical spider web. Black seemed to get blacker and even the Ford's high beams had trouble stabbing though it.

Eric rolled on towards the cemetery wondering what in the hell he thought he was doing. At his age, a man should be home resting and watching TV, not heading off to fight some unimaginable evil in the darkest of places on, what appeared to him to be, the darkest of night's he'd ever seen.

"Should have yer dadblamed head examined, Eric. I'll say this much though, you sure find unique ways a-screwin up an evening."

He was hunched over the top of the steering wheel, his chest just about resting on it. The headlights were casting hazy cones of white that ended about four yards ahead of the truck in overlapping circles on the asphalt. If anything happened to wander out in front of him he'd never see it in time to stop. Slowing down would have been the responsible thing to do – the common sense thing to do - but Eric suspected that it would also be the *wrong* thing to do. Whatever was coming ... whatever lay ahead for him tonight ... was already on its way. He just couldn't slow down. He'd have to take his chances and hope for the best.

"Dear Lord in Heaven, I been a simple man all m'life. Ain't never asked much a-nobody ... leastwise ... not often. And anything I *did* ever ask fer I always repaid ... and then some too, most of the time. I ain't been religious neither, but I guess I ain't gotta tell you that ... so I ain't never asked nothin a-you either. But I'm sure as hell askin t'night.

"Oh, I'm sure you got better n-more important things t'do than keep an eye on an old, foolish man, but if'n ya could spare the time, I'd really 'preciate it if'n ya'd just reach down a little finger an gimme a slight touch. I gotta stone cold feelin I'll be a-needin it afore this night gits t'the gold a-mornin. Thanks."

Eric drove on, his foot hard on the accelerator. The speedometer needle was stuck at 12; it had stopped going past that nearly two years ago and Eric thought it wasn't worth repairing as he rarely drove above 45. But tonight, he was sure he was well over 70. Dark shapes whizzed by on either side. He was sure most of them were trees and an occasional mailbox, but tonight, he really couldn't be sure of anything. He sometimes got the feeling, seeing the black silhouettes rush by, that they could just as well have been specters of people long dead, watching and waiting for him, ready to jump out in front of him and cause him to swerve off the road and roar headfirst into a pine tree. He drove on, trying not to pay too much attention to his peripheral vision or his mental one.

By the time he arrived at the front gates of the cemetery, the visibility had dropped to less than a foot. A thick fog had settled in and he had to keep flipping the wipers on and off. (Delayed wipers had only been an expensive *option* at the time Eric had bought his truck at Tiggleman's Ford.)

Looking around as best he could before getting out, Eric took a deep breath. Now he was faced with how to get into the cemetery. The gates were locked and he wasn't really much in the mood to start climbing at his age. Perhaps, he thought, if he followed the fence line around he just might find an easier way to get in. Leaving the truck parked in the middle of the drive, he started off to his right, running his hand along the bars of the fence as he went, his palm slapping along like a baseball card in the spokes of a bicycle tire.

CHAPTER 88

Tamika's heart was racing faster than she'd ever known it to. She'd never been this afraid before. The things she'd seen and was seeing, taking place in the streets of her home town panicked and confused her. Men killing women; women killing men, even children, the few that she'd seen on her way here to the pharmacy, didn't seem to be above it. And it was always male against female and female against male, no matter the age. If it weren't for the responsibility she felt for poor Marsha, stuffed in a hole beneath the dry cleaners for safe-keeping, she would have gone right home, locked the doors and hidden in the basement.

When she peeped around the corner of Ash and Main Streets, everything seemed to be clear. But she wasn't taking any chances. Things were wild and out of hand and unpredictability reigned supreme today. She waited a few more minutes, peeking and listening, listening and peeking. Finally feeling confident to brave it, she cut around the corner and rushed toward the pharmacy door. She had to hurdle four bodies on the way, one right around the corner and three lying in front of McKendrick's door.

In her haste to get in off the street, she pulled at the door five or six times before realizing that one of the bodies on the sidewalk was preventing it from opening. Grabbing it by the ankles with her eyes closed, she tugged it out of the way and pushed in through the door. While wrestling the body out of the way to get in, she never considered that the store might not be empty. Now, standing on the black and white checkered tile floor inside the door, *that* thought hit her like a hammer. She froze, too scared even to turn her head from side to side.

Her breathing was rapid and shallow and the salt from the sweat that was dripping down her forehead stung her eyes. She wiped at them like a dog pawing something off its nose. Except for wiping her face, she stood absolutely still, listening for the smallest of sounds.

At last, she felt it was ok to look around, as the only sounds she *could* hear were coming from the streets outside. She scanned the store using the big round mirrors that hung there to prevent shoplifting. It appeared as if she were the only one in there. She made a dash for the check-out counter where they kept all the impulse candy. Standing on tiptoe, she grabbed a couple of plastic bags from the cashier's side and started filling them with handfuls of candy. Mars Bars; Rolos; Three Musketeers; Almond Joy; Mounds; Pez (without the dispenser); M & M's; they all went into the bag by the handfuls. She was about to leave when she thought it might be a good idea to grab some milk and maybe some soda for Marsha.

The cold cases were on the other side of the store; she could see the end of them from where she stood. Tamika really didn't want to go over there; all she wanted was to get out and get back quickly and unharmed to Marsha, but if she wanted anything to drink ... across the room is where it was.

"Ok Tamika, girl. You can do this. It's just a few feet, a couple of bottles of this ... a carton of that ... and you're out. You ready?"

Twisting the bags of candy and wrapping the plastic loops around her hand, she charged off, slipped on the waxed tile, caught herself before she fell, and slammed up against the end case. The glass was thick and cold and it took the hit without breaking.

"Thank you, *LORD*, for that," she said. "Tamika Peters don't need no stitches in her face today."

She half walked, half ran, down to the end where the sodas, ice teas, and milk were kept. Not caring whether it was Whole, 2% or Skim, she grabbed a half-gallon and stuffed it into one of the three empty bags she had left. Ordinarily, she only bought Skim Milk for her family as she considered it much healthier. Today, she could have grabbed pure milk fat and it wouldn't have mattered as long as she could get it and get out. The same held true for the sodas. She snagged up two two-liter bottles of Coke and one of Ginger ale, and those, only because they'd been the easiest for her to reach. Now ... all she had to do was to get out of the store and back to the dry cleaners without getting killed.

"Prob'ly easier said than done, girl. But you gonna do it. That's for sure."

At the front door, she looked up and down the street through the picture glass, her cheek pressed against it this way and then that in order to see as far as possible. When she didn't see anyone, she closed her eyes and pushed the heavy glass doors open just wide enough for her to slip through sideways. She had to step over the bodies again, but went around the one on the corner this time instead of jumping over it.

By the time she was halfway back to the cleaners, full dark had set in. The sounds of distant and not-so-distant fighting and screaming seemed to be magnified by the dark. A chill ran up Tamika's spine. She was forced to slow down as visibility was severely reduced. Even more so a few moments later when the fog set it.

Rounding the last corner before the cleaners, Tamika's worst fear was realized. She came to a complete stop, grocery bags swinging in her hands and banging up against her thighs.

"Well, well, well," said a dark figure in front of her. "What in the world do we have here?"

Tamika couldn't make out the face in the dark, even though she was no more than ten feet away. But she sure as hell recognized the voice. It was Tobias Lewis, her next-door neighbor.

"Ummm ... um ... um," he said, stepping forward and licking his lips. "Lookie here what we got."

"That you Tobias?" barked Tamika, sounding sure, strong, and confident, and feeling anything but.

"Well, if it ain't Tamika hot legs Peterson. You know girl, I always wanted to do *you*. Guess me an m'pals here are fin'ly gonna get the chance. It's gonna be sweet, too, I bet. Sweet dark chocolate. Gonna lick all the sweetness right off-a ya."

He took a couple of steps forward and then stopped again. When he did, two other figures emerged from the dark behind him.

"So, tell me, Tamika ... you a moaner or a screamer? Not that it matters much ... me n-the boys are for sure gonna make ya a screamer."

Tamika instinctively took a few steps backward. She could see the two men behind Tobias, neither of which she knew, undoing their pants. She was bone scared but refused to show it.

"If I were y'all, I'd get my sorry butts outta here 'afore sumpin really bad happens t'ya. Ya never kno-"

Tobias raced forward and grabbed her by the throat, choking off her sentence. She tried to scream but all that came out was a hissing gurgle. A moment later, bags ripped from her hands, she could feel her dress being torn off while one of them pinned her arms behind her back.

They forced her down onto her knees on the sidewalk, Tobias still squeezing her throat. With his free hand, he reached down and pulled her bra up to her neck.

"Time for you to taste a *real* man," laughed Tobias.

"Time for you to kiss your ass goodbye, shit-for-brains," came the voice from behind him.

He never got to see who it was. The first shot took off the top of his skull and the second ripped through his throat and burrowed into the heart of the man holding Tamika by the shoulders.

The third assailant tried to run. Not an easy thing to do when your pants are down around your ankles. He'd made it about eight feet before he fell flat on his face. When he rolled over on his back, Rachel Parker was standing over him. Without another word, she bent down, placed the muzzle of the .45 against his forehead, and pulled the trigger.

She looked around at Tamika but said nothing. Then she scanned up and down the street looking for her next target. With no men readily in sight she walked on and disappeared around the corner.

Tamika resettled her bra and pulled what was left of her dress around her, holding it together with one hand; she grabbed up the candy bag, but couldn't manage the sodas and milk. Those she left lying there and hurried back to the cleaners, Marsha, and the little trap door of security.

Tamika had never liked Rachel Parker much. She'd always told her husband to stay away from her: "Cause she wasn't nothin but a cheap tramp." But tonight, whatever she'd been in the past, Rachel Parker was Tamika's savior, and that metamorphosis - tramp to savior -was hard for her to reconcile.

"You ripped your pretty dress," Marsha said, when Tamika came in. "Did you fall down? I fell down once and hurt my knees. They got 'fected and I had to see the white coat man. He made them all better."

Tamika smiled as best she could. She was still shaking and her heart hadn't slowed a bit, but she didn't want to upset Marsha, so she reached into the bag and handed her a couple of candy bars.

"Here honey, here's your candy. Just like I promised." Her voice was as shaky as she was. Marsha didn't seem to notice. She tore off the wrapper and started gobbling.

"id ooo et eye ollwees?" Marsha mumbled, her mouth full of chocolate and peanuts.

It took Tamika a minute or two to figure out that she'd asked if she'd gotten her dollies.

"No honey. That store was closed. We'll get them tomorrow, ok?"

"Ok," answered Marsha blankly, digging into the bag for another candy bar.

CHAPTER 89

Carlton pulled into the entranceway to the cemetery, bringing the Blazer to a stop behind an old pickup truck that was blocking the front gate. He sat there for a few moments, reliving the EasyMart explosions, the crackling sounds of his family home burning to the ground, and puzzling about what to do about getting inside the cemetery.

Backing out, he shot off down the street, taking the far corner almost on two wheels, finally skidding to a stop in front of the side gate, he jumped out and ran up to it. It was padlocked with a thick huge chain. He just laughed.

Drawing the sword from his breast pocket he touched it lightly to the padlock. Sparks shot out in all directions, igniting his left sleeve. Clamping a hand over his wrist, he extinguished the flame and watched as the YALE locked melted into a pile of molten goo on the ground.

Whipping the chain off and tossing it aside, he swung the massive iron gate open and walked inside, sticking the pommel delicately back into his breast pocket for safe-keeping. He made his way across the back lot towards the equipment garage, which he could just barely make out in the distance through the dark and the fog.

Drawing a little closer, he saw a lone figure sitting on a rock in front of the garage tossing pebbles across the driveway. When the figure caught sight of him, he stood up and danced nervously from one foot to the other. He picked up a large rock, which Carlton assumed he was going to try to hit him with. He wasn't worried at all. Carlton kept walking at a smooth and steady pace. He was in no rush. He was in charge.

**

Jasper Collins wanted to run but some force inside him kept him standing there. He considered the possibility that it could be a cop or one of the cemetery foremen and that made him extremely nervous. But he held his ground as if anchored.

A moment later, Carlton Wedgemore was standing in front of him, grinning like the proverbial cat that swallowed the canary. Jasper noticed immediately that there was something different, something commanding about him. He also, instantly, understood that whatever Carlton told him to do ... he would do, no matter what it was. He didn't know why, but he had the distinct feeling that his new boss fully endorsed Carlton Wedgemore and to disobey one would be to disobey the other. He dropped the rock he was holding, giving up all thoughts of bashing in Carlton's head.

Carlton suddenly knew exactly what he had to do. It flooded into his brain like stormwater down a drain. Without saying anything to Jasper he drew the sword from its resting place and proceeded to melt the alarm system and the lock on the garage door. He then turned back to face Jasper.

"Guess that takes care of *your* problem he said," and then started laughing. "Mine is elsewhere. But ... you'd better get started with your work. Wouldn't want to disappoint ... well, you know who."

He turned to leave, stopped, and turned back again, leveling the tip of the broken, glowing sword towards Jasper.

"Wouldn't want to disappoint me either, *would* you?" he asked, honestly seeking an answer.

"No! No, no, not at all, Mr. Wedgemore. Not at all."

"Good. That's all I wanted to know. Now ... hop to it ... dark's a-wastin.'"

Jasper didn't wait another second. He ran into the garage, grabbed up the keys off the hook over the workbench and fired up the backhoe. When he backed out of the garage, Carlton was nowhere to be seen. He sat there, engine idling in the dark, and wondered what was going to happen. Then, coming back to himself, he wheeled the hoe around and bounced off in the direction of the first grave he was supposed to open.

"Crap! I can't see three feet in front of me in this shit!" he complained. "More likely than not, I'm gonna run this thing into an open grave and that'll be the end of it ... and me. Shit!"

Suddenly, his headlights shot out a blinding blue light that covered a large swath of ground in front of him. It was like someone had kicked on super-sized floodlights.

"That better?" boomed a voice in his head and he recognized it immediately as Carlton's. But how had he known was the question running through Jasper's head. How could he have possibly known? He wasn't anywhere in sight.

"How could he have *known*? *That's* the question you're asking, you dumbshit? How could he have done anything about it would be a better one, don't you think?"

Great! was Jasper's next thought. *Now I'm fucking arguing with myself.*

At his first destination, Jasper maneuvered the hoe into position, dropped the stabilizers and started digging. As he got deeper, a chill ran up his spine as he heard the howling screams coming from the hole he was opening. He was now too frightened to keep digging ... but too frightened to stop. He had to think.

"That's it ... I just gotta take a minute and get myself together, that's all." He curled the bucket, swung it left and rested it on the ground. Then, his hands shaking furiously, he tried three times to light a cigarette before he managed it.

As he sat there smoking, refusing to look down into the hole he'd just opened, the wailing cries grew louder and more intense. A cracking and scraping sound accompanied them, punctuated by a heavy pounding.

A sudden impulse shot through Jasper, one he couldn't resist, although he would have preferred to be able to. Clamping the cigarette between his teeth, he lifted the bucket, swung it back over the hole and started pounding it down, lifting it up and pounding it down. After some three or four whacks, the distinct sound of concrete shattering rose from the hole. A moment after that, the wailing was closer. Another moment after that, a near skeletal corpse clawed its way to the surface. Its face was nothing more than decayed muscle and bone. Both eyes were missing and the jaw hung loosely from a single tendon on one side.

Jasper drew back, trying to hide in the darkness of the machine's cab. He couldn't breathe. What was left of the cigarette dropped from his mouth to the plate metal floor and rolled under the accelerator. He sat there frozen as the thing he'd just released scratched its way up and out of its grave and began shuffling unsteadily across the lawn.

Jasper watched as it struggled to get up a hill, slipping and falling several times before it made it. He watched as the rotting skull wobbled this way and that on an even more degenerated set of cervical bones. At last, to Jasper's relief, it disappeared over a far ridge.

Wishing the night were over; wishing it had never come in the first place, Jasper pulled up the bucket, lifted the stabilizers, and headed off to his next rendezvous.

CHAPTER 90

Willie hadn't realized how far into the woods he'd gone to play. Now, running back out, it became painfully clear. His side was beginning to stitch and he could feel his thigh muscles on the very edge of cramping. He didn't want to slow down, but the lactic acid build-up was going to have more to say about that than he did. Clutching his side with his right hand, he slowed to a trot and then came to a complete stop. He bent forward, one hand on his knee as he tried to catch his breath and waited for the pains to subside a bit. He glanced over his shoulder to see if the two men with the wolves had followed him somehow, but there was nothing there but the shrubs he'd just burst through.

Panting, he sat down on the ground. The only light now was a small sliver of white moon, but that would soon be gone too. Heavy dark clouds were sweeping in and the first crack of thunder rumbled through the treetops. It was the most intense boom of thunder Willie had ever experienced. The ground beneath him shook a bit and the trees swayed. When he looked up, a forked thread of blue light flashed across the sky followed by another strong slam of thunder. The smell of charged ozone instantly filled the air. Tight muscles or no, Willie knew he had to get home.

He dragged himself to his feet, took a couple of the deepest breaths he could manage and pushed on. He was sure the cemetery was pretty close. Not that that's where he really wanted to go, but it was the shortest way back home.

You're in big trouble, Willie Peters, he thought. *Ain't no way pop ain't home yet and boy are you gonna git it.* He tried to quicken his pace but he was already running full out. His foot caught the edge of a rock and he lost his balance, falling forward. His arms wind-milled wildly as he tried to stable himself and finally succeeded. A few yards before the boundary of the cemetery, things got worse. A heavy fog seemed to roll in from nowhere and his visibility dropped to near zero. Now he'd have to slow down. Running into a tree trunk head first would not be a good idea. He slowed to a quick walk.

As Willie slowed down, the thunder and lightning picked up. Huge arcs danced across the sky in rapid succession. The accompanying thunder roared and pounded, overlapping each other in a wall of terrifying sound. Willie was more scared than he'd ever been. The almost guaranteed punishment he was going to get when he got home was not half as frightening to him as the thoughts of being struck by lightning on the way. He had always been told to stay away from trees during a lightning storm. But if you're in the woods when it hits, there's just no way to do that.

Tears began to stream down his face as he picked his way along the dirt path. Every now and then a tree branch that he hadn't seen in the misty fog would slap him in the face or tug at his arms. The fog reflected the lightning; great inverted bowls of white flashed overhead causing long shadows to appear and disappear all around him. He walked on, shaking and crying, his clothes growing heavier as they soaked up the misty water vapor.

Finally coming to the cemetery fence, he stopped. He tried to see through the enveloping fog, looking for the car he had passed on his way out. His visible range was too short. Thinking he'd better not chance it, he began making his way along the fence line to his left. He knew there was an opening a little further down, but he wasn't sure just how far it was. He figured that, if he couldn't find it, he could always just climb over, scoot through the bushes, and then break for home from there. There was a good chance that once he was in the clear of the cemetery proper he'd be able to see better. At least, that's what he was hoping for.

Having gone along the fence to where he remembered the opening being and not finding it, he decided that up and over was the best thing to do. Willie went to grab hold of the iron rails to boost himself over when another flash of lightning peeled across the sky above. He drew his hand back sharply, imagining himself being sizzled while climbing over a metal fence that was under trees.

"Great! Now what?" he bawled. "You'll fry yourself."

He stood there in front of the fence crying, shaking, and confused as to what to do next. A moment later the rustling sound of bushes being forced apart came from the other side. Someone was coming. Someone was inside there and coming along the fence line. In a minute they'd be on top of him.

Willie tried to control his crying, trying to disappear quietly into the fog and hope that whoever was coming wouldn't notice him. He backed up, careful not to tread on any sticks that would snap and give his position away. He didn't manage it.

Crack! Crack-snap!

A loud gasp rushed out of him and he stood absolutely still, listening. On the other side of the fence, the rustling also stopped. In his mind, Willie saw a monster, crawling deftly through the bushes, its eyes glowing red and its teeth dripping with blood. It was searching for food; it was searching for young children; it was searching for *him.* It stopped and sniffed the air, its massive head twisting from side to side as it zeroed in on the scent of Willie Peters. It was coming for him. And when it found him ... it would gobble him up, chomping and chewing and gnawing at him until it swallowed the last of him in a great fiery belch.

A moment later, the rustling began again and Willie came back to himself. He waited, holding his breath, desperately trying to keep his knees from knocking together, his hands folded, palms together, between them. He waited. And the sound got closer and closer. His throat knotted up and his mouth was drier than the Sonora.

CHAPTER 91

Banderman Falls had taken on the look of a war-ravaged third-world country. Bodies lay in the streets, on the sidewalks, propped up in doorways, in the hallways of apartment houses, and in the back alleys. Fires raged uncontrolled across the town. The dark and the mist that had fallen over it had given the sounds of battle a muffled, dreamlike quality. Screams seemed to die out only feet away from the screamer; gunshots sounded like weak firecrackers, and the thumping and whacking sounds made by those using clubs or sticks could only be heard by those using them, or those on whom they were being used.

Alderman's Tire & Battery was now only ashes and half a skeleton of iron frame. The EasyMart on Ridge Pike was a large hole in the ground, fire spouting up out of it in fits and starts. Chew's Oriental Restaurant had stir-fried itself into oblivion along with Party Haven, Hildebrandt's Haberdashery and Merryweather Realty. Music City was currently producing a true *HOT 100* as the guitars, amps, keyboards, sheet music and everything else inside, including two dead saleswomen, charred, crackled, and burned in the inferno set by its owner just after he'd killed both of his female employees.

Cars and trucks burned outright or still smoked from earlier fires. The fog and mist did nothing to quell any of the raging flames. It only lent a surreal lighting to an already eerie backdrop of death and destruction as the electrical storm ravaged the blackness above.

Audrey had to slow down because of the dense fog. She kept a sharp eye on the road but her mind was trying to figure out what sort of explanation of current events she was going to give Alex. She was doing no more than fifteen when she approached the imaginary line that separated Banderman Falls from Philadelphia. Tonight, she learned that the boundary was anything but imaginary.

As the forward edge of the cruiser reached that line, huge sparks began to shoot out in every direction. The car stopped short in a jolt that slammed Audrey into the steering wheel. A moment later it began moving forward again at a snail's pace. If she hadn't been wearing her belt she'd have gone through the windshield like sand through a sieve. A lump bloomed into being just over her right eye.

When she looked up, the front of the car was rapidly disintegrating. It looked like it was being eaten by some unseen electrical monster. A sharp, blue line stretched across the hood from fender to fender like a moving chalk-line, creeping ever forward towards the windshield and her. Audrey fought to remove her seatbelt and get out of the car. The belt had held fast but the locking button had jammed. She tugged and pulled but it refused to let go.

Glancing back and forth between the approaching line of certain death and the seatbelt, she finally managed to beat it into cooperation with the butt of her gun. She threw open the door and fell to the ground, watching as the cruiser was slowly and inexorably drawn forward and consumed, leaving behind only the sharp smell of burnt metal and cloth. Why it hadn't exploded when the fiery blue line consumed the gas tank she didn't know but was grateful for it just the same.

Lying on the double yellow line of Ridge Pike in the black mist, she watched as the last of the car disappeared and the blue chalk-line-ripsaw with it. A final shower of sparks shot out through the mist like the end of some Fourth of July fireworks display. A sizzling sound, reminding Audrey of steaks on a grill, drifted away with the last of the sparks.

Standing up, she looked around. There was certainly no way she was going into Philadelphia now, there would be no State Police help, and the walk back to the Falls would be a considerable one. She figured that the first thing she should do should be to get her ass out of the road before someone came flying along in the fog and took her out.

"That'd be my luck," she chuckled. "Avoid being ... whatever that just was ... and end up as road pizza." She moved over to the shoulder of the road and began the long walk back to town. Drawing the flashlight out of her belt ring, she hit the rubber button, only to discover that the bulb had broken when she'd fallen out of the cruiser.

"Ter-*rif*!" was all she said as she slid it back into its circular holder. The long, black steel handle bounced against her leg as she trod down the side of the road, pebbles, and cinders grinding underneath her boots.

Nothing was making any sense anymore. The Falls was in chaos, this blue line-thingy shouldn't exist (whatever the hell it was), and people all just seemed to have gone stark raving mad overnight. On the drive out here all she could think about was Sam Twilling and what he had been doing and how he had been dressed, or undressed as the case had been, while doing it.

Now, with several miles walk ahead of her, she had plenty of time to think about everything that had been happening that day. She also had plenty of time to wonder and worry about what had become of her sister. She tried her best to shy away from thoughts of Gwen lying dead somewhere, beaten to death or shot by some crazed citizen. She tried, but she couldn't do it. She could feel the tears welling up in the corners of her eyes as the image of her sister, lying face down in some dirty alleyway with her head bashed in, forced itself relentlessly into her mind.

CHAPTER 92

Picking the package up off her lap, Arliss stood up and walked to the lobby doors. As soon as she approached, they whooshed open. She looked out, the last thing she needed was another attack of the maggots. The very thought made her shiver and give out an audible: "Ewww".

With no one readily in sight, she strode out into the night, cut around the side of the building and down into the parking garage to her rented Acura. Thumbing the trunk button on the key, she saw the taillights flash and the trunk door glide up. She walked over, deposited her box, slammed the trunk shut and got in behind the wheel. It took her a moment to dig the Garmin out of her handbag, punch in the address for Wedgemore's and attach it to the dash. The whole time, try as she might, she couldn't stop feeling as if things were still crawling on her. She wriggled a bit in the seat as she pulled out of the garage, made a right onto the bridge that crossed the Schuylkill River, and headed towards Banderman Falls.

At the corner of Ridge and Butler Pikes, she made a right onto Ridge. She began to notice that the closer she got to her destination (the Garman kept telling her how many miles or tenths of miles she had left before her next turn), the darker it seemed to be getting. About a mile out from the border between Conshohocken and Banderman Falls she drove into a thick, misty, fog and had to slow down considerably, the headlights barely penetrating the moist, drizzly soup.

***

At the opposite end of town from where Audrey's cruiser had been devoured, Father Jacobs and Geoffrey Dunsmore stood by the side of the road trying to figure out how they were going to get through the energy field barrier that they had run into. Geoffrey insisted that what he had in his room would be needed before the night was over, so there was no way they could just turn back.

They had been debating the puzzle when a weak glow appeared in the distance on the Conshohocken side. As they watched, the glow grew slowly and steadily in intensity. Suddenly, Geoffrey jumped out into the middle of the road and started waving his hands frantically. He'd moved forward, as close to the boundary line as he felt was safe.

Jacobs joined him. They realized that the light they were seeing was an approaching car. They also realized that if it hit the line, it would suffer the same fate as the rock Geoffrey had tossed at it. The best they could do was hope they'd get the driver to stop before it was too late.

"Stop! Stop!" They were both yelling and waving their arms over their heads. Jacobs was even jumping up and down like a man on an invisible pogo stick.

The car drew closer and closer, at first showing no signs whatsoever of intending to stop. But at last, it slowed and rolled to a stop just short of what Jacobs and Geoffrey suspected would have been the driver's death.

"Whoever they are," said Jacobs, "I'll bet they think we're maniacs and won't risk getting out."

"That's probably true. We look like a pretty ripe pair, I'm sure. But if they don't ... well then, I expect it'll be goodbye ol' chum for them."

After a few minutes, the driver's side door opened and a woman stuck her head out.

"What's the matter? Why are you in the middle of the road acting like idiots?" she hollered. "What do you want?"

"We want you to bloody stop. Just wait right there a minute and let me show you." Geoffrey picked up a rock.

As soon as Arliss saw him grab the rock, she slammed her door shut. She was about to throw the Acura into reverse when the man with the rock lobbed it gently forward. She watched, stunned and amazed as it seemed to digest itself in a shower of blue sparks and dancing electrical arcs.

She opened the door and got out. Cautiously, she moved forward a little. "What the hell was that?"

"We don't really know," said Jacobs. "But it would probably be a very bad idea for you to try to cross it."

"That's not good," said Arliss, holding her arms akimbo. "I have to get to Banderman Falls. Tonight!"

"Believe me," shot Geoffrey, "that's one place you really *don't* have to go. *Especially* tonight."

"And just why would that be?"

"Things here..." Geoffrey couldn't think of how he was going to describe what was happening, or come up with a good enough lie that would keep her away.

"Things here are going to hell," Jacobs finished for him. "Trust me. I'm a priest. And priests always know when things are going to hell."

There was silence for a moment. Geoffrey and Jacobs let out a little tension laugh while Arliss just stood there staring at them as if they'd both just managed to get out of their straight-jackets.

"Seriously though, Banderman Falls is one place you need to stay away from."

Arliss thought about this for a moment. It was hard to see in the fog, but she looked to Jacobs as someone who rarely abandoned a mission without a really good reason. Even the way she was standing told him that she was one serious gal.

Geoffrey had the same impression, especially since his vision was much better than Jacobs's. He could see her clearly through the fog. In fact, he had seen the car clearly a mile before it had arrived. He studied her now, taking in the resolve that shone in her blazing blue eyes.

"I don't know what your business is," Geoffrey said, "but I think it'll have to wait."

"It can't. It can't wait. I know this will sound crazy, but ... I have to get something and I have to get it tonight or something really bad's going to happen. Don't ask me what because I have no idea. I only know that I have to get what I have to get."

"Something bad's already happening in this town," said Jacobs. "Something that ... well ... if I tried to explain, you'd probably go running for the nearest psychiatrist for me."

Arliss bit her lip and rubbed pensively at her cheek.

"Ok ... here's the deal. If you won't laugh at me, I won't laugh at you," she said at last. "Deal?"

The two men nodded

"Does this have anything to do with ..." she broke off, still considering the possibility that they'd think *she* was crazy. Then, decided to go for broke. "with ... some weird guy?"

"Weird. How do you mean?" asked Jacobs

"I'm not really sure. But when I first got here ... I ... met this guy, except, he really wasn't a ..." she trailed off again, realizing how insane it was going to sound when she told them about the flies and the maggots.

"Except he's not really a man. Right?" finished Geoffrey. "The answer to your question, before you tie yourself into bloody knots is ... yes. It has to do with something extremely evil, corporeal - but not human and ... how the hell did you know that?"

"I've already met him. Couple of times, actually. Once in Arizona in my bathroom. If you can believe that."

A vague sense that he had seen this woman someplace before washed over Geoffrey as he stood there looking into her eyes. It was only a flash of a feeling, fleeting and ephemeral. He'd had feelings like this before about people and they usually turned out to be correct. But they were always much stronger and much clearer. He decided to dismiss it as one of those feelings that people sometimes get from time to time. A déjà vu of recognition.

"I think, at this point," Geoffrey said, taking a very cautious step forward, "that histories are not too important at this point. What we'll have to do, if we can, is try to figure some way around this barrier. Because ... in my mind, there's no doubt who put it here. It's obvious that he doesn't want to be disturbed by outside influences."

Arliss imitated Geoffrey and took a tentative step forward. "Any suggestions?" At that moment, she had the same feeling slip over her about Geoffrey as he had had about her.

"Unfortunately, bloody none. Damn!" Geoffrey clenched his teeth trying to control the anger he felt building. He was beginning to feel frustrated and frustration always led him to anger.

Behind him, Jacobs was kneeling, quietly and solemnly praying. Geoffrey hadn't noticed until Arliss pointed a finger in his direction. Geoffrey watched for a moment or two and then turned back to Arliss.

"Don't know if it'll help, but when you have a priest on your side ... no harm trying to get his Boss involved." Geoffrey shrugged.

Arliss suddenly slapped her forehead. "Listen, I have something that I brought along. I had no idea why I felt I needed it when I grabbed it, and I have no idea whether or not it'll do anything at all, let alone any good. But, to be honest with you, when I looked at the priest just now, the image of it flashed across my mind."

Geoffrey didn't laugh as she thought he might. He rubbed his chin thoughtfully and then winked at her.

"Don't think we have much to lose no matter what we try. So ... whatever it is you've got, and whatever you think it can do ... by all bloody means ... give it the Queen's try. At this point, I'm not disposed to sneer at anything."

"Be right back," said Arliss as she turned and headed for the trunk of her car.

CHAPTER 93

Grady awoke to full dark and a smothering mist. Sitting under the tree amidst the poison ivy, he'd dozed off. As soon as he tried to move everything that had led him to this point came rushing back in a series of searing waves of pain, both between his legs and in his back. He winced and groaned as he fought himself to an upright position, using the tree he'd been sleeping against as support. As soon as he was upright, he recognized the 'three-leaves-on-one-stem" monster that had surrounded his face.

"Ah shit!" he exclaimed. "As if everything else wasn't enough today." As soon as he said it, his mind flicked the memory switch and he became consumed in fright and shame for the things he'd done. Horrible things, things that only the worst criminals do – not things Grady Peters would ever do. But he had done them and he couldn't deny it. And he didn't know how he could live with it.

"I got t'put this right somehow. Grady, you got t'stand up like a man an' tell what you did. Ya got t'get to Sheriff Dougherty and turn yaseelf in. It's the right thing t'do. What ya done was bad ... real bad ... and there's no denyin that. Yer family's gonna take it real hard. But ya gotta try and make it right. Set an example fer Willy ... that when a man does somthin he shouldn't ... he has t'be a man and say he done it. And he's got to stand up and take the punishment fer it."

Grady pushed away from the tree and wobbled unsteadily through the brush searching for a path or a clearing that would lead him out to the cemetery proper and an exit gate. He thought about what had happened to him and what he'd done. The horror of it brought tears to his eyes and he walked shakily along sobbing and confused. He knew deep down that he was a good man, had always stood up for his ideals and lived up to the adage his mother had always imparted to him: "If ya ain't got time t'be nice to folks, ya ain't got time fer nothin." He had no idea how things could have gotten so far out of hand.

"Lord help me and fergive me. I don't know what came over me. I ain't sayin I ain't guilty ... 'cause sure as I'm here, I am. But I ask that ya c'n fergive me and help me stay on the right path. Amen"

He pushed through a large stand of blackberry brambles, his arms taking most of the beating but sharing some with his cheeks (which

were already starting to blister from the poison ivy.)
Once through, he found himself along the back
fence line.   He stopped and looked both ways,
trying to catch his breath. The pain in his back was
competing with that of his swollen testicles. He
didn't care. He considered it part of the punishment
he was owed, and guessed there'd be a lot more of it
to come before long. Looking left, then right, he
arbitrarily chose his left and started off, grabbing on
to the fence from time to time as support. Each step
was an agonizing reminder that his life had gone
from bad to terrible in the space of a single day.

He wound slowly around the fence until he
came to another stand of blackberry bushes. They
seemed to stretch out in almost every direction. He
only had three options, none of which he was
comfortable with. He could go back but that would
only lead him back into more brambles; he could try
to climb over but he didn't think he had the strength
for it, or he could grit his teeth and push through.
Sorting it out, he realized that he really only had
one option. He closed his eyes and pushed through.

Almost clear, Grady heard a sharp *crack!*
and pulled up to a stop. His heart raced, his back
ached, his face itched, and his testicles throbbed.
For a moment he thought he was going to pass out.
He stood stone-still listening.   When no other
sounds followed, he convinced himself that it had to
be some animal lumbering through the night in
search of its dinner. He gathered himself up, threw
his arms up in front of his face and drove himself
through the last three feet of sharp entanglement in
a single blast.

When he emerged, he froze, listening, straining to see through the dark and the fog. He scanned along the fence line as far as he could see. The mist collected on his face and arms and the cool moisture felt good. He rubbed lightly at his face, and then at his eyes. He still couldn't see more than a few feet in front of him but he could hear. Somewhere off in the distance a sound rose and fell in staggered waves.

Grady had worked enough construction jobs in his life to recognize the sound immediately. The intermittent whirring and grinding, the scraping of metal on stone, the squeaky hiss as the arm swung away and the bucket was emptied ... someone was digging a hole with a backhoe ... in the cemetery ... in the dead of night. It made no sense to him and scared him, too. If there were workers in the cemetery, how was he going to get out without being seen, and how would he explain why he was there in the first place? There was only one thing he could do. He turned to face the fence, willing himself to have enough energy to climb it. When he did, he jumped back.

A face.

There was a featureless face on the other side of the fence and it was staring at him. It was low to the ground, probably crouching, getting ready to spring. That was the first thought that ran through his mind. But as his anxiety settled a little, he looked closer and finally made out the features that went with the face's shape.

"What the hell are you doing here, boy?" he snapped.

"Pop? Pop, is that you?"

Willie rushed up to the fence and stuck his arms through. When he got close, Grady could see the fear in his son's eyes. He grabbed his arms and pulled him up close to the fence, hugging him as best he could through the ironwork. Admonishments could wait.

"Are you all right, Willie?" he asked, his voice as shaky as his son's.

"I dunno, pop. I'm scared. Things are happenin'. Bad things. Really bad things. I'm scared."

Overhead, a bolt of lightning lit up the sky and Grady could see clearly in the glowing flash just how sacred his son really was.

"Wait there, I'll climb over. Just back up in case yer old man falls. Don't wanna crush ya." He smiled and it worked. He could see the corners of Willies mouth turn up. But it faded quickly.

"No. Can't, pop. We gotta get out through the cemetery. It's the only way. There's ... there's ... behind me, there's ..."

"Never mind. You don't have to explain. You're right about the bad things."

"Pop, ya gotta believe me. We gotta go through the cemetery. It's the only way. The safest way."

"I'm not sure about that. There's people in here. Don't know what they're doin here this time a-night, but they're here."

"We can git around em. I know we can. We can't go back, pop. We can't."

"Ok. C'n ya climb over. I c'n give ya a boost and catch ya when ya get to the top."

Grady was far from happy about the situation, especially the "going through the cemetery" part, but some little voice inside his head kept telling him that the boy was right and that he'd better listen to him.

"It's ok, pop. I can do it. Just give me a little room."

Grady reluctantly took a couple of steps backward. He watched as Willie scrambled over the fence as easily as if he were climbing a set of steps. *Ah, to be young again*, he thought.

A moment later, Willie was in his arms, squeezing him so tight that it sent a bolt of pain up his spine. He ignored it and hugged him back with all his might. They remained that way until another flash of lightning warned them that they'd best get going.

"Come on, pop. I know the best way out. But we gotta be careful and quiet. There's a car parked near where we hafta go, so we'll hafta sneak by it."

Grady smiled, mostly for Willie's sake, and partly for his own. At least he wasn't alone anymore. "Ok, big man ... lead on. I'm right behind ya."

CHAPTER 94

The cruiser sped southeast on Ridge Pike barreling towards the center of town. Inside, Jack,

Linda, and Ethan rode in silence. Linda was in the front with Ethan, half turned and staring at Jack. Jack sat in the back, his chin on his chest. He wasn't a man often given to self-pity, and he sat there wondering how he could have let things in his town get so out of control. But he had no idea just how out of control they were.

About a mile and a half out, black clouds began to roll in and gobbled up the stars that had begun to appear in the night sky. Thick rumbles of thunder split the silence and flashes of stabbing blue lightning lanced through the sky. Beneath the heavy clouds, fog began to form and sink to ground level covering the car, road, and landscape like a gigantic wet carpet.

Linda and Jack were suddenly pitched forward as Ethan stood hard on the brakes. The cruiser skidded and fishtailed on the wet, oily road. The sound of tearing metal, like thick aluminum foil being ripped off a roll, screeched in their ears.

An overturned car sat in the middle of the road, obscured by the thick fog. Ethan didn't see it until it was too late. The fender of the cruiser caught the wreck's twisted rear bumper as Ethan tried to swerve around it. It opened the side of the cruiser like a key on a sardine can. The cruiser slipped sideways off the road and into the trees. When its passenger side slammed up against the oak, it bounced up onto two wheels and then thumped down with a jolt.

Jack banged his already cut forehead on the headrest in front of him. Linda just barely missed the dashboard, her seatbelt digging into her right breast and left hip. It jerked her back and a second after Jack's head had cleared the headrest, the back of her head imitated Jack's forehead. Ethan had braced himself with the steering wheel and the impact shattered his left wrist.

"Everybody ok?" asked Ethan through gritted teeth, his right hand cradling his left.

"I think so," said Linda with a slight falter in her voice.

"Yeah," added Jack. "What the hell happened?" He turned and looked out the window. He could barely make out the black, twisted hulk of the car that was lying on its side like a dead rhinoceros, its front bumper twisted up like a great silver horn.

"Shit that was close," exclaimed Ethan. "Sorry about that." He tried turning the engine over. It growled and moaned, choked, sputtered and coughed and then just clicked.

"Guess we're walking now for sure," said Jack. He popped the door open and climbed out. Ethan got out and gave Linda a hand scooting across the seat and out the driver's side.

Jack gave Linda a hug. "You sure you're ok?" he asked.

"Yep. Right as rain."

Ethan had walked over and was inspecting the wreck in the middle of the road. When he came back he was shaking his head.

"Not sure what happened, but Melissa Cartwright is deader than vaudeville."

"C'mon," said Jack. "Let's get outta here. I don't like this at all."

"I'd have to agree with you. What do you think? About thirty or forty minutes to town from here?"

"Less than that if we cut through Peaceful Haven. That way ... I'd make it about ten."

"Sounds like a plan," said Ethan.

"You up for it?" Jack asked Linda.

She nodded. "Not wild about the cemetery part, but I sure like the idea of less walking."

"C'mon then," said Jack. "Let's get back to the station and see if we can figure out just what the hell's goin on around here."

"Hold on a minute." Ethan went back to the cruiser, unlocked the shotgun, checked its load, and then turned around. "Ok ... I think we're ready now. Can't be too careful."

"Great idea, Ethan. C'mon everyone. Let's see if we can make up some time. We can cut through the woods here and be at the west end of the cemetery in about three to five minutes. It's not going to be easy though. Lots of sticker bushes."

"Wonderful," replied Linda. "I always wanted tattoos."

They made their way over to the shoulder of the road and into the brush. They had just disappeared behind a stand of rhododendrons when a large dark shape passed overhead, its black form sliding across the misty landscape beneath. As it passed, the wind from its huge, beating Chiropteran-shaped wings blew Melissa Cartwright and her car off the road and bent the cruiser around the tree it was up against.

The passing gust whipped through the trees, bringing down large branches that crashed and thundered like Thor's Hammer through the silent woods. A tall oak, long decayed and riddled with fungus, snapped in half, its skeletal spire hurtling down like a giant's spear. It buried itself in the ground three feet in front Jack, the resulting vibration knocking all three of them off their feet.

"What the fuck was that?" yelled Jack

"It's gonna be one helluva storm, brother," replied Ethan. "Maybe we better pick up our pace."

"Maybe we better pick ourselves up first," suggested Linda. Then they laughed, the same humorless laugh that passes between mourners at a funeral when a joke is made at the guest of honor's expense.

"C'mon," yelled Jack, pulling Linda to her feet. "Things seem to be getting worse by the minute. I can hardly wait to see what's waiting for us back at the station."

They brushed themselves off, worked their way around the newly planted dead tree and set off again into the brush. Fortunately, they didn't have far to go before they reached the old iron fence of Peaceful Haven. Then it was just a matter of getting everyone up and over. Ethan went first, slipping the shotgun in through the fence bars and then hefting himself over, ignoring the pain in his arm. Jack boosted Linda up and Ethan helped her down the other side. Then it was Jack's turn.

Reaching up, he grabbed hold of the crossbar and pulled himself up. His free hand wrapped around one of the large chevron-shaped spikes at the top. His boots slipped a bit on the wet iron but he managed to get his head and shoulders up above the spikes, mostly by using his upper body strength. He swung a leg up, hooking his right foot between two of the spikes and started to haul himself over when a bolt of lightning streaked through the sky and stabbed its hot, electrical finger into a tree behind him. The tree exploded in a flash of light and a shower of sparks. The concussion shook the ground and the fence wobbled. Jack lost his grip and slid down, narrowly missing being impaled through the armpit with one of the chevrons. Behind him, the tree crackled and blazed. Multi-sized chunks of bark flew off like bullets in all directions as the liquids and gases inside the tree expanded from the heat.

Jack, Linda, and Ethan went to ground at almost the same time, splinters of wood sailing over their heads and digging themselves into the dirt, grass, and surrounding trees. Jack crawled to the base of the fence and Ethan met him there.

"Go on, back off from this. I'll crawl down a little ways and climb over there. Let's get out of here before we all get skewered."

Ethan didn't waste any time talking. He just nodded, crawled back to Linda, and they both started moving away on their bellies. Jack followed suit along the fence. When he was pretty sure he was far enough out of range he stood up. The tree was still burning brightly and two others had already caught. He could smell the familiar and ugly odor of burnt hair and flesh. He felt the back of his neck, patting it gently with his hand. There weren't any blisters that he could feel but the back of his hair was coarse and stubby.

"Lucked out on that one, I'd say, Jack," he said to himself. "Just a quick haircut. Could have been a lot worse."

"You gonna stand there admiring your hairdo or what?" asked Ethan. He'd come up to the fence while Jack was busy checking his neckline.

"Right with ya, my friend." He hoisted himself up and over as quickly as possible, not wanting another repeat performance of nature's flashbulb. "You ok?" he asked Linda, once his feet were firmly planted on the ground.

"I'm as good as can be expected, considering today's events."

"Good." He gave her a hug and a quick peck on the cheek. He decided that secrets weren't worth keeping if you might not have enough time left for people to find them out anyway. And the way things were going, he thought that was a real possibility.

"Come on, love birds," said Ethan, a wry smile on his face. "Let's get our asses out of here."

Jack pointed to a thickening of the shrubbery. "That way, folks.

* * *

As Jack, Ethan, and Linda were speeding back to town, the dark gray shape at the B & B slammed against a wall and slid to the floor. All around Robertson flies crawled and hopped, trying unsuccessfully to get airborne again. Up against the wall, Witherstone pulled his knees up to his chest and bellowed and roared, then fell silent, sitting absolutely still.   Heavy breathing, like the low growl of a hunting lion, was the only sound in the room.   He sat there *–it* - sat there, gathering itself together, drawing its revitalization from the riots and panic that ran amok through Banderman Falls. It drew its strength from the hatred and violence the community was raining down upon itself.

Suddenly, all the flies took off, swirling up into two separate cones, each of which alighted on Witherstone's scaly back.   It closed its green eyes and stretched itself out.   Like a balloon being inflated, it grew to nearly eight feet in height.   The flies on its back burrowed into its leathery and rugose skin, forming two angled vertical lines.

"If they want devils, then devils I'll give them," it screamed.   The walls shook, widows blasted outward, and large hunks of plaster dropped off the ceiling.   It broke the fingernails, long, dagger-sharp shards of bone, from each of its index fingers and jammed them into its skull just above the eyebrow ridge.   He twisted them in deep, drilling them in with a sickly sound, like metal being scrapped across terracotta.   When they were in place, he scrunched himself up in knots, his fists clenched, straining all his muscles.   The nails grew thicker and longer, taking on the appearance of great rams horns.

"They shall have what they are afraid of. I give them ... their devil." It walked over to a mirror that was hanging on the wall behind the reception desk and turned side to side as if checking out a new suit. It then strode back, its large taloned feet clopping heavily on the floor. Stopping beside Robertson, it looked down.

"You probably can't hear me. You'll be gone soon anyway," it growled, "but I just can't resist a last bit of fun." It reached down with its massive clawed hand and plucked him up from the floor and shook him violently until his eyes fluttered open.

"As Roy Rodgers used to sing ... Happy *en*trails to you." He dug his fingers into Robertson's gut and made a long slit from the bottom of his breast bone to the top of his pelvis. Robertson's intestines spilled out like sausage from a casing machine. Robertson remained nearly silent with only a whispered gasp escaping his lips. He had already lost too much blood and most of his body was numb and cold. Disappointed, Witherstone tossed him aside like an empty candy wrapper.

"Hardly worth my effort, eh Doc?" It laughed a booming laugh and then turned and punched its way through the wall. It stood outside and watched the clouds, fog, and lightning roll in, its arms outstretched as if it were waiting to receive a gift from heaven. Hunching itself forward, the two lines on its back broke open and massive wings erupted. It folded and unfolded them several times and then leaped into the air.

Whomp.Whomp-whompwhompwhomp-whomp-whomp. Great gusts of air hurled the driveway stones in all directions as the gray beast rose into the air and flew off. It hovered above the road at the end of the driveway, sniffing. When it caught the scent it was looking for, the scent of death and destruction ... and the scent of the two prizes it sought, the pommel and its future bride, it flew off towards Banderman Falls.

As it sailed over the road, it cocked its head from left to right scanning the countryside for its runaway bride and the two men who had taken her. They were going to pay in a big way. Up ahead, it saw something in the road. As it drew nearer it saw it was an overturned vehicle, but not the one it was seeking. In a fury, it beat its wings harder and picked up speed. Had it looked to the left of the totaled auto it would have seen the sheriff's cruiser, the car it *was* searching for. Had it stopped to sniff the air it would have smelled the unwilling bride it sought, hidden in the brush a few yards away. It did neither of these things and flew on towards the town.

Its eyes pierced the black of night and the mask of fog. Ahead, it could see the raging fires of a town gone crazy. It laughed and snorted. And then it caught a whiff of what it wanted, what it needed. It smelled the pommel and the weakling who now possessed it. It pulled up and hung in the air, its legs dangling beneath it and its great wings flapping lightly. Divining the direction of the smell, it wheeled right and flew off in the direction of Peaceful Haven Cemetery, its great bat-wings beating furiously.

CHAPTER 95

Ernie Pyle stumbled blindly past the tree where Grady Peters was passed out. Had he been another two yards to his right he would have tripped over his legs. As it was, he walked right past him, pushing through bushes like a man lost in the jungle.

When he broke through to a clearing, the first crack of thunder rippled across the sky followed by a claw of lightning. A thick fog seemed to close around him like a glove from nowhere. His heart began to beat wildly in his chest and for a brief moment he thought he was going to have a heart attack and end up face down on some stranger's grave. He quickly moved further into the cemetery and away from the tree line. He made his way to a row of mausoleums that formed a semicircle at the edge of one of the sections. Hand over hand, he fumbled his way around the side, tripping once over a stone flowerpot at the sepulcher's corner.

He reached the front, squinting to see through the fog and dark. It was like trying to look through black muslin with sunglasses on. Cautiously, he stepped out from the safety of the mausoleum and padded across the driveway as quietly as he could. The whole time he kept wondering who he thought he was going to disturb if he made any noise. Certainly the residents wouldn't be overly put out by it. The thought made him chuckle, but it was weak and died away quickly.

Weaving his way through the headstones, one row at a time, he kept nervously glancing over his shoulder as if he expected the devil himself to be following him. With his head craned around, he walked right into the lone figure in front of him. The figure had been standing behind a headstone looking the other way. The impact sent both of them to the ground in a tangle of arms and legs and grunts and groans and one loud scream of surprise and terror. In the process, Ernie struck his head on the base of one of the monuments. His eyes rolled back in his head as stars danced across his field of vision. He slid down a long gray tunnel into unconsciousness.

CHAPTER 96

Eric followed the fence around until he found the same break in it that Gwen had used to slip in. He had thought about climbing over but dismissed that idea almost immediately. He was too old and way too short to even think he could manage it. So the only thing left was to find another way in.

Pulling on the rusted, hanging, wedge of a section, he squeezed himself through, catching his shirt and cursing at the ripping sound it made. The whole time he'd been wandering along he'd been asking himself exactly what he thought he was doing or was going to do. Monster hunting was best left to the younger set, although (and the thought made him laugh), most of the younger set couldn't find a monster unless it was one of them new-fangled video gamie things. That's how they spent all their time these days. To them, fresh air was only something that came in a spray can to clean off your computer keyboard.

Now that he was through the hole in the fence, he was faced with the challenge of getting through the not-so-inconsiderable underbrush to the open sections. He drew a heavy sigh and thought about Ruby, sitting at home, probably still right in front of the door. He thought about how he'd raised her, right here in this very cemetery, every Sunday afternoon, running, playing, and obedience training. Tears began to well up in his eyes and he fought them back.

"Come on ya ol'coot. Ya got stuff t'do t'night." And then, under his breath, "Although I have no frog-jumpin' idea what that is."

Bracing himself, he began his fight with the shrubs as a thick mist began to settle over the cemetery. Dark clouds had thundered in overhead and the first strikes of lightning flashed across the black sky.

"Guess no real monster hunt's right without the thunder, lightnin', and spooky dark t'go with it." He laughed out loud, a long and hearty laugh. Under ordinary conditions it would have carried all the way to the front of the cemetery, but the thick fog damped it out almost immediately, like a guitarist palming the strings. Finally managing to clear the last of the shrubs, he stood at the edge of the farthest section of the cemetery.

At his age, his vision was bad enough without having to deal with the dense fog he was now trying to see through. He picked his way between the headstones and around the flat markers.

He mentally apologized to those souls whose grave he trod upon and hoped they understood that he had no choice. A few times he was even forced to stop and rest, sitting uncomfortably upon one of their stones. It made him feel like an uncaring guest who plopped himself down on the arm of the best couch instead of on the seat cushion.

He'd made his way through three sections so far, still not knowing where he was headed, when he spotted a vague movement ahead. He came to a dead stop, straining his ears to listen as his eyes attempted to focus in on the dark shapes ahead. It was no more than a sudden splash of motion and then nothing. He lost it. For a moment, he'd thought he'd heard a scream, but with *his* hearing, it could just have well been the call of a passing barn owl. Waiting silently in the dark and mist of a lonely cemetery, Eric thought again of his dog and how he would probably never feel her licking him again.

"Stop it! Stop that right now," he whispered to himself. "Ain't no cause t'go gittin all sent'mental bout stuff like that tills ya knows fer sure the'nds really comin. Ya been a tuff'un all yer life. No need t'go 'soomin ya lost the fight 'afore it's even started."

Feeling stronger and more settled, he marched forward, confident that he was ready to deal with whatever it was he saw moving. At the spot where he thought he'd seen the movement, he was surprised to see two people sprawled out on the wet grass, crammed in between two closely spaced headstones. The man was lying face down and not moving. The woman was trying to roll him off of her.

When Eric walked up, it startled her and she screamed again. And again, like Eric's laugh, it died out almost instantly.

"Gwen? Gwen Archibald, is that you?"

Another groan.

Eric leaned down and grabbed the man by the shoulders and hefted him off to the side, laying him on his back. Eric recognized Ernie Johnson at once. He then reached out his hand and helped Gwen to her feet.

"What did you call me?" she asked. There was a blank look in her eyes.

"Gwen," said Eric, softly. "Gwen Archibald. That's yer name, ain't it?" He thought he was being glib, but the vacant look in her eyes told him that she wasn't fooling.

"I don't know. I can't remember. It sounds sort of familiar, but ..."

"What happened to you?" asked Eric, laying a hand lightly on her shoulder. She instantly drew away, shrinking back like a worm from the peck of a bird.

"It's ok. It's ok. I ain't a-gonna hurtcha. We're friends. Work t'gether ... sorta. At least, we both work fer the township."

"I don't ... I don't know you. I don't know anybody." Tears began to stream down over her cheeks, but the fine mist obscured them from Eric's vision. "I don't even know who *I* am ... or where I am. Except in a cemetery ... and I don't know why in God's name I should be in a cemetery."

"It's ok," smiled Eric. "We'll sort it all out. I promise. Fer now, just trust me; yer name's Gwen."

Gwen looked at him. His face was old and careworn but his eyes were soft and gentle. Some part of her knew that she could trust him, so she reached out her hand. He took it in both of his, patting the backs gently.

"It'll be ok. Now, let me take a look at Ernie here an' see what I c'n do fer him. He's out colder 'an these here monuments."

CHAPTER 97

Arliss slammed the trunk shut, balancing the box in one hand, and then walked back to the invisible vaporizing line. Jacobs and Geoffrey stood watching, wondering if what she might have in there might actually help them.

As she was unwrapping it, Geoffrey leaned in a bit. "By the way, I'm Geoffrey Dunsmore and this is Father Gabriel Jacobs."

"I'm Arliss Peterson," she said without looking up, "I'm the curator and general everything doer at the Antiquities Museum in Benderick Falls, Arizona. I'm here-" She broke off momentarily to wrestle with the packing tape and then began again. "I'm here because a shipment of mine was misdirected here and I've come to claim it."

"What sort of shipment, if I may ask?" inquired Geoffrey.

"Well, when I left Arizona I had no idea. But I've since learned that it is some kind of ancient sword handle. Purported to have belonged to Lucifer, if you can believe that."

She pulled open the box flaps and lifted out what appeared to be a rather heavy piece of ornate pottery. She held it up. "On the way out of the museum, at the last minute I might add, I had the strangest urge to bring this along. Had no idea why then, and I still don't. All I can tell you is that ... while we were discussing what to do ... I had an image of it flash across my mind and thought that, somehow, in some crazy way, it could help.

The piece she was holding was rounded, tapering from the top to the bottom, about two feet in height. It was painted in shades of bright gold, brilliant ocean-blue, and deep blacks. The top was shaped like an animal's head.

"It's a canopic jar," exclaimed Geoffrey. "I've seen a few of them before, but never one this ornately done. Could you turn it around so I could see the front, please, love?"

Arliss held it out turning it in her hands so Geoffrey could see the whole thing. "I'd prefer it if you'd call me Arliss or Dr. Peterson. I'm not your love, love." She smiled, but Geoffrey got the meaning.

He leaned forward a little more trying to see the detail. When he straightened up, he rubbed thoughtfully and his chin and then stuck his hands in his pockets.

"Ok, Doctor Peterson would you please just place it on the ground and then step back for a moment. Whatever you do, please don't take the lid off just yet."

Arliss placed it on the ground facing towards Geoffrey and Jacobs. Jacobs took a step forward to get a better look. When he leaned over, the edge of his scarf dangled into the barrier zone and began to sizzle. He tried to straighten up but the scarf was being drawn into the blue field and was tightening around his neck. He pulled and tugged, digging his heels in as if he were trying to stop a runaway sled.

Just before his face came in contact with the field there was a metallic click and he fell backwards violently, being saved from cracking his skull on the asphalt by Geoffrey's timely catch.

"There ya go, mate. Best be a bit more careful next time." Geoffrey closed the penknife he'd cut the scarf with and shoved it back into his pocket.

"Ok, so now what?" asked Arliss.

"One moment, lo ... er ... doctor. I just want to think about this before we blunder from one bad situation into a bloody worse one."

Jacobs was rubbing at his neck and staring at the jar on the ground in front of him. "I got it," he said suddenly. "I know where I've seen that before, and what it is. It's a jackal's head, isn't it? It's that Egyptian god of the dead or something. Anubis, I think he's called."

"Quite correct/That's right," said Geoffrey and Arliss at the same time.

"So how's it going to help us here? I mean, we aren't planning on storing any organs away for future use, are we?"

Geoffrey shot him an unpleasant look and Arliss looked to be as curious about that question as the priest.

"I'm not sure why, but I believe you're right, doctor. I *do* think this is going to help some, but I don't know how ... and ... I'm not quite sure how to go about using it. It could be as stupidly simple as removing the lid. Then again ..."

I bloody well wish I had a clue as to how to do this, Geoffrey thought, and instantly his mind heard: *You're not the only one.*

Geoffrey looked at Arliss and Arliss at him. Jacobs didn't know what was going on, but the looks that were passing between them told him something was definitely up.

You heard what I thought, didn't you? was the sentence Geoffrey formed in his mind.

Yes, I did. I don't know how, but I can hear everything you're thinking as if you were saying it aloud.

Jacobs touched Geoffrey on the arm. "Are you ok? You look like your miles away. *And,* while I'm on the subject of away ... don't you think that we should try doing something. Time's awastin, as they say, and I have the greatest feeling that time is the one thing we can't afford to waste."

The last half of Jacobs's sentence seemed to fade away as if being dragged off on some unfelt wind. An image was forming in Geoffrey's mind and he knew that the same image was forming in

Arliss's.   Almost in unison, Geoffrey drew the
miniature Big Ben from his pocket while Arliss dug
hers out of her purse.

"Gabe, if you please, would you fetch up
your clock?"

Jacobs looked surprised, but fished around
in his pocket and pulled it out.

"A triangle," said Geoffrey. "Place yours
about a foot directly behind the jar, doctor, clock
face facing toward the jar. Gabe, put yours down
over there and I'll put mine here. We're trying to
get them to form an equilateral triangle with the
canopic jar at the center."

When the clocks were in place, Geoffrey
motioned for everyone to move to the side of the
road for a moment. He stood there assessing the
situation. He had absolutely no idea what he was
doing or what he thought he was going to
accomplish, but something seemed right about it.

"Doctor," Geoffrey asked, still looking
extremely puzzled, "how old is that jar?"

Arliss got an excited look on her face but it
faded rapidly.   There was nothing she loved to
explain more than the origins of the artifacts she
worked with. But this was one of those questions
she couldn't fully answer.

"Well, that's kind of a conundrum. You see,
from what we've been able to establish through all
our testing of it, it seems older than it should be."

"How's that?"

"Based on current dating techniques, it
seems to be older than Egypt's Old Kingdom, the
period in which the first real canopic jars came in to

use ... at least, unquestionably into use. On top of that, this one is way too highly decorated for its period. Assuming that our information and assumptions are correct and that this is one of the earliest known, it should be quite plain and simple, fashioned from stone. As you can see, the inlay, painting, and shaping are all very intricate and detailed. More so than they should possibly be."

Geoffrey thought for a minute. "That's good. I think that works to our benefit, and I think you were right in bringing it along. Sometimes, going with your gut is what saves your ass. My only problem at this point is what to really do. I mean, how to activate what I think it's capable of."

"If I may offer a suggestion," said Jacobs, "perhaps we should just let the clocks do their own thing. I'm supposing of course, that you believe they have some vital role other than just providing a geometric outline of the jar. Of course, I'm no expert, you two seem to be that."

"What did you have in mind, Father?" asked Jacobs.

"Remember what you showed me in the rectory ... how you set the hands and then they moved on their own. Why don't we just try that? Just get them started and see what, if anything, happens."

Geoffrey smiled and clapped Jacobs on the shoulder.

"Capital. Simply fantastic. Leave it to a priest to come up with Occam's razor."

"Ok, everybody together. Let's set them for ... oh, I don't think it matters much ... let's say, one o'clock and then we'll release the hands at the same time and see what flies."

They each twisted the hands on their clocks to read one o'clock. Then, looking apprehensively at each other, Geoffrey said: "Ok, on zero. Three ... Two ... One ... Zero! They let the hands go and each clock face began to take on a brilliant blue glow with a greenish-yellow halo. It grew stronger and stronger, brighter and brighter, until they had to turn away from it, but not before they saw the hands start moving backwards, spinning wildly counter-clockwise. The blue light being given off by the clock faces cut through the dense fog like a lighthouse beam, expanding outward in all directions.

A thought occurred to Geoffrey and he yelled: "Cover. Everybody find some sort of cover as far away from the road as you can get." They all broke and ran.

Arliss tripped over a large stone at the bottom of an embankment and went sprawling forward. Geoffrey threw himself behind an old oak about thirty yards off the roadside and Jacobs behind a boulder a few feet further in.

"Hurry," Geoffrey yelled to Arliss as she scrambled back to her feet and dashed off, finally finding a large tree to duck behind.

Out in the roadway, the intense light from the clocks seemed to be growing outward like some electrically charged soap bubble. It expanded on both sides of the barrier field, looking like two halves of a beach ball trying to come together in the center. Everything it swallowed as it expanded began to crackle, as green and yellow colored charges danced across their surface. At the dividing line between Arliss's side and the men's side, the charges became more intense and burned in a rotating cascade of hues. Blue sparks mixed with orange and then faded into green and then back to blue and red. A black ooze rolled off the sides of the road as the asphalt began to melt, and the smell of hot tar was choking. As it reached the grass, the blades flared up and died out creating the illusion of Lilliputian torches being lit and extinguished. On the shoulder, pebbles, rocks, and gravel began to shoot into the air like bullets, exploding overhead, their powdery remains raining down in a dust-cloud blanket.

As the two sides of the fluorescent, sparking bubble pressed in against the edge of the barrier field, the field lit up, its outline stretched across the road like a gigantic plate glass window. Huge fissures began to form in it, cracks that spider-webbed in all directions. It warped, undulating like a snake on a hotplate. It began to fold in on itself, its wobbling corners rolling up and in toward its center. A howling screech broke the air, a blood-chilling sound like metal on metal, punctuated by rolling, thunderous explosions and hisses.

It shrank ever inward, becoming a blazing, distorted circle of energy. As the outer edges drew closer to the center, the lid on the canopic jar, Anubis's head, began to rotate. It spun around like a child's top. When the barrier had collapsed to a diameter of about a foot, the head rose into the air and the crackling, deformed field thinned to a smoke-like trail of sparks that was drawn into the jar. When the last thread had passed the rim, the lid settled back down in place, trapping the barrier inside. For a few minutes afterward, the jar tottered, wobbling unsteadily around on its base, finally coming to rest upright. Anubis's eyes glowed a fierce blue and the snout curled back and gave out a chilling howl. And then it fell silent, the glow in the eyes fading away.

Cautiously, Geoffrey stepped out from behind his tree, motioning to the others to stay put while he checked things out. He could hear Arliss thinking: *Be careful,* as he walked slowly toward the road, making a wide circle around the melted, lava-like asphalt. The air stank of burnt tar and sulfur and a light watery mist rained down as the fog tried to reclaim what had been cleared during the barrier's destruction. The ground sizzled as the mist settled on it.

Geoffrey walked to the edge of the melted roadway. He found that he had to go back to find an object to toss at the place where the barrier had been. Everything within the radius of the bubble they'd created had been powdered, melted or vaporized. Picking up a large rock, he walked forward again and pitched it at the barrier. It sailed through the air, crossed the spot where the previous one had disintegrated, and bounced off the hood of Arliss's rental car, putting a sizeable dent in it. Immediately, he heard Arliss curse him in his head. He just laughed.

"I think it worked," he yelled. Jacobs and Arliss came out of hiding and up to the road.

"Guess I'll be the first to test it." Geoffrey moved forward, closing his eyes and hoping he wasn't going to become a dust spot on the road. A moment later he was standing in front of Arliss.

Jacobs clapped and Geoffrey gave Arliss a big hug.

"You're a lifesaver," he said to her, hugging her a second time.

Jacobs ran up to them and gave both of them a hug. They whirled around as one, a rumbling vibration building behind them. The canopic jar began to wobble violently this way and that ... and then it exploded, sending shards of stone every which way. Geoffrey pulled everyone to the ground, but he'd been too slow. A quarter-sized piece of stone embedded itself in Arliss's left shoulder and she let out a sharp scream.

When the last of the projectiles dropped to the ground, Geoffrey pulled Arliss up to a sitting position.

"Here, let me have a look at that."

"It's ok, I think," stammered Arliss, a small river of blood running down the front of her and soaking her shirt in a widening splotch of red.

Her eyes seemed to glaze over as Geoffrey examined the wound. He thought she was going to faint. She didn't. Her face contorted into a tight ball, like a child throwing a temper tantrum. She stood up and seemed to be straining. Her eyes were pinched shut and her cheeks puffed out. Her whole body was shaking and the muscles in her neck and arms were rippling. A moment later the shard of stone shot out from the hole it had dug in her shoulder and embedded itself in a tree twenty yards away. The gash it left behind trickled blood, turned a reddish-orange and then sealed itself up, its edges coming together in perfect alignment.

At that moment, a door opened in Arliss Peterson's mind and a different Arliss stepped through. When she opened her eyes they were a shimmering fiery blue. Their light grew and then diminished rapidly, shrinking to the size of her pupils then fading into the light blue color her eyes had always been.

"I know where we have to go," she said. "And we don't have much time."

Jacobs looked at Geoffrey, not quite sure what to say. Had it not been for all the other events of the past two days he would have stood there astounded. As it was, it didn't seem all that strange.

"C'mon. Let's get going. We have to get to the cemetery. *Now!* There was not a doubt in anyone's mind that that was a command, not a suggestion.

You're the other, aren't you? thought Geoffrey to Arliss. *I should have bloody known. I should have sensed it. But I do now. I can feel your strength and I have no doubt we're going to need it before we're done tonight.*

You can count on it was her reply.

"Have to get to my hotel room first," admonished Geoffrey. "I have a bag of tricks there that I think we're going to need."

Arliss saw the image of the bag and its contents in Geoffrey's mind. "I *know* we're going to need them ... and so do you.   C'mon, let's get moving."

"Grab the clocks," yelled Geoffrey.   "Don't want to leave them behind."   He picked up his version of Big Ben and pushed it into his pocket. The others collected theirs.   They were all still very warm to the touch but had survived the barrier's destruction.

CHAPTER 98

By the time he'd opened the third grave, Jasper was numb. The corpses he'd freed scrambled out of the dirt and muck and walked off into the cemetery, their rotted stench filling his nostrils until he thought he was going to vomit. Even with the backhoe cab's doors closed it permeated the air and saturated his clothing. He didn't think he could do this anymore but he knew he didn't have a choice. One more grave to open. He rolled off into the misty night to find the last one, the hoe chugging and growling its way over the cemetery hills - an iron monster in search of not-so-fresh meat.

One of the things he'd freed from the ground had clawed and banged on the cab, biting at the glass with its decayed and partially missing teeth. It had finally given up and wandered away, but the ordeal had petrified Jasper and it had taken him some time before he could bring himself to repeat the procedure on the next one. Now, as he rumbled along he could see the bits of flesh and putrefied liquid it had smeared on the window, the free ends of the skin flapping in the air like a bizarre streamer from a child's tricycle handlebars.

As he crested the hill he immediately recognized where he was. Panic and terror sized him like a giant hand. He could hardly breathe and his heart was beating against his chest so furiously that he thought it might burst through. He was staring at the exact spot where Michael the Archangel had graciously roused himself from his stony slumbers to warn him of impending doom. The backhoe drifted to a stop and he just sat there gazing off into the blackness, not able to move.

Above him, the thunder was still pounding out its demonic drum rhythm but the lightning had dissipated, trailing off to intermittent blue splashes of light against the overhanging cloudbank. An acrid smell fingered its way into the cab of the backhoe. It reminded Jasper of the time his ninth-grade class had visited a chemical processing plant in Delaware. The tour guide, some ancient bald man whose shirt collar was too small for his neck, was explaining how they processed chlorine into household bleach. The smell had made him want to retch back then and this smell was having the same effect now.

He pulled a snot-spackled hanky from his back pocket and had to pry it open. It made a ticking sound, like a piece of duct tape being ripped off the arm of a leather sofa. He covered his nose with it, holding it there with one hand while he pulled the hoe forward. Ahead of him, at the far end of the section, he could see a blue flame stabbing upward into the sky. It lit the surrounding area and he saw, with an overwhelming sense of dread, the three things he had set free. They were standing in a semicircle in front of a large monument. At its base was Carlton, holding the sword handle that had miraculously opened the garage door lock and disarmed the alarm system. He was holding it straight up over his head with two hands wrapped around the blade. The pommel on the top burned with a hazy blue glow sending a tower of light skyward like a carnival spotlight.

Jasper pulled the backhoe over about halfway down the row and swung it into position to dig up the last of his appointed bodies. After the second bucketful of dirt, the ground began moving by itself; something was clawing its way to the surface. Great chunks of sod and rivers of dirt streamed into the grave as the thing pulled itself, hand over bony hand, out of the hole.

Most of its flesh was still attached and had gone a grayish-green color. One eyeball dangled loosely from its socket and the other was completely gone. A large flap of scalp and hair hung down off the side of its face like a sick beret and its muscles and joints cracked and wheezed as it moved. When it had broken the surface completely, it looked up at Jasper who shrank back. Its lower jaw dropped open and a wailing sound came bellowing out. It roared like a wounded lion and the windows of the cab rattled. It shot out an arm, grabbed the bucket, and twisted it. The hydraulic pump lines ruptured, spraying reddish liquid across the windshield and nearby stones. The arm of the bucket made a groaning sound as it bent upward and the backhoe began to tilt. A moment later it was lying on its side, several headstones crushed beneath it, and Jasper pressed up against the door.

When he'd started to open the grave, Jasper recognized the name on the stone above it. Leonard Carson. Jasper remembered *him*. He had always been afraid of him. Half the town had been afraid of Carson. He was the mental equivalent of Lenny in "Of Mice and Men". He stood six feet, six and one half inches tall and weighed in at almost three hundred pounds.

He ended up in Peaceful Haven because he murdered three children in Philadelphia. He'd used his bare hands to twist their necks until he heard a cracking sound and the heads fell limp against his arms. He had just grabbed for the fourth child when a Philadelphia Police Officer popped two 9mm rounds through his skull.

It had taken a lot of pleading on his parents' part to get him buried in a Catholic Cemetery, but they were persistent, arguing that he was retarded and didn't know what he was doing and should rest under God's care. They had gone so far as to quote scripture saying that we're all told that we can only enter heaven as children and that Leonard epitomized that. In the end, the church relented. Now, what was left of him, whatever he'd become as he'd fermented in the ground, was loose. And it scared the crap out of Jasper.

Lying inside the cab, helpless and terrified, Jasper began to pray and cry. He knew that if Lenny, that thing out there, wanted in at him there'd be no way of stopping him. His terror rose to panic

when it came around, leaned over the toppled hoe
and smashed the window in. Jasper shrieked and
closed his eyes, his lips mouthing a "Hail Mary."
He waited to be ripped apart.

A few moments later, when nothing had
happened, he chanced opening a single eye. He was
alone. Lenny had gone. He was down the end of
the row with Carlton and the rest of the
abominations. That was it. Jasper had had enough.
Bogeyman or no bogeyman, he was out of here. He
scrambled out of the top side of the cab and jumped
to the grass. When he landed, he twisted his ankle
and heard a sickening pop, followed by a river of
pain that shot up his leg. He didn't care. As best he
could, he started crawling away, digging into the
moist sod with his fingers and pulling himself
along.

CHAPTER 99

Witherstone, or Betorak as he now called
himself, swept over the countryside, his great wings
flapping in huge arcs. He could see his destination
clearly – a bright beacon of blue light blazing
skyward from the cemetery. A screeching,
growling howl burst from his throat as he slid
through the blackness. Oaks, maples, and pines
splintered and snapped at the sonorous cackle.

When it reached the cemetery border, its feet
curled, its wing flaps slowed and it lighted atop a
mausoleum. It stood and swept the cemetery with
its shimmering green eyes. Its vision punched

through the darkness like a spotlight at a Broadway opening. Nothing was hidden from its satanic view. Hunching down, it gathered itself, focusing its mind – its whole being – on the cemetery and its movements. But most of all, focusing on what it had come for ... the pommel, its key to permanent form.

***

Arliss gave the dent Geoffrey had placed in the hood of her rental car a sideways, exasperated glance. She climbed into the back with a slight grumble. Jacobs took the front and Geoffrey the wheel. He cranked over the ignition, slammed the Acura into reverse, and turned it back toward the hotel. The tires squealed as he whipped the car around and blasted off down the road. The car punched through the collapsing bubble of clear that the dismantling of the barrier had created and pushed its way back through the mist.

When they pulled up in front of the hotel, Geoffrey jumped out and went in to get his bag. Jacobs slid over to the driver's seat and kept the car idling.

"Might as well do the driving." He smiled at Arliss, "I'm the only one who knows my way around our not-so-quaint-anymore town."

When Geoffrey came out he tossed the bag on the back seat beside Arliss and just barely made it into the car before Jacobs pulled out. Most of the ride was done in silence, each wondering what lay ahead. Occasionally, Arliss and Geoffrey would interlock thoughts. Arliss reached back in her mind and found an attic full of half-forgotten memories, mental boxes filled with the remnants of another life. It was a life that had slipped from her consciousness long, long ago. It was a life that was coming back to her with savage fury.

Geoffrey was tapping into her reveries and, as best he could, guiding her. Her thoughts were stirring forgotten memories of his own, and Arliss was sharing those as well. They were coming together. They had always been together in the past; they had been, and were once again, a team.

When they reached the border of the two towns, Jacobs slowed the car and looked quizzically at Geoffrey. Geoffrey shrugged.

"Go for it Father. There's not much we'd be able to do now if it's back anyway, so we might as well just hold our breaths, close our eyes, and go for broke."

Jacobs didn't say anything; he stomped down on the accelerator and drove on. Three sighs filled the car as they crossed the dividing line and were still in one piece.

"Now that that's over with," Jacobs said, "mind if I ask what you've got in your bag of tricks back there on the seat?"

"Not at all," replied Geoffrey, his tone a bit stoic. "There are several very ancient, elaborately decorated, solid iron stakes, which had been blessed by one of your colleagues centuries ago. There is also a unique sword that was forged in the days that stretch back long before man was able to record his history. There are several very special darts that were hammered out of the same material and at the same time as the sword. There are a couple of discs, a pair of things you might identify as broaches and two ruby statuettes. And before you ask, that's all I can tell you about them. At least for now."

"You know," Jacobs said, shrugging his shoulders, "I don't think I'd ask anyway. Sometimes, ignorance really is bliss. And right now, I'm trying to stay as blissful as I possibly can. Here we are."

Jacobs turned the car into the entranceway to the cemetery, bringing it to a rolling stop behind an old pickup truck.

"Seems we definitely have company," observed Jacobs.

"There wouldn't happen to be a back gate to this place would there, Father?" Geoffrey asked.

"There is indeed, but it hasn't been used in ages. I'm sure it's completely overgrown and probably more rusted than the Titanic at this point."

Their conversation was interrupted by a loud bellowing roar that cut right through them. When it died out, a second split the night's silence adding to the deep eeriness the mist had already created.

Geoffrey looked up, craning his neck so he could get a better look through the foggy windshield. His eyes searched the misty darkness for the source of the cries. When he found it, he snapped back in his seat, sitting straight up and deadly still.

"I don't know if it'll do any good at this point," he whispered, "but let's try to be bloody quiet. It's up on the roof of a mausoleum just ahead of us. I don't think it's spotted us yet, but we'll know soon enough."

"What's *it*?" asked Jacobs. He knew about the thing they were looking for, or supposed he did. He'd seen it in the bar with Geoffrey. But the look on Geoffrey's face told him that something was radically different.

"It's changed its form, dear Father. I believe that what we're going to have to deal with now is a lot more menacing than what we ran into earlier."

"What *are* we dealing with, then?" asked Arliss, her head pressed up against the side window trying to see.

"It has taken a very ancient form from a time and space before man. A Betorak."

"A Betorak? I know those. This battle is not going to be easy to win," sighed Arliss.

"Well, *I* don't know what a Betorak is," Jacobs chimed in. "What *is* a Betorak?"

I don't think I'm going to like this answer much, was what he was thinking, even as he was still asking the question.

"And most of all," he continued, "can we kill it?"

Geoffrey and Arliss looked at each other. For a moment, it looked as if despair had crossed Geoffrey's face, an emotion that Jacobs had never seen in him before. Just the sight of it made the hairs on the back of his neck rise up in protest and goosebumps broke out down his arms.

"Betorak Omni Malum," said Geoffrey, still looking at Arliss. "It was ... it was an ... oh bloody hell, it's hard to describe. Let's just say that, at some point in time, this creature existed in a very different world than we know today. It's postulated that, occasionally, before they passed into total extinction, man had come across them. Their figure was eventually incorporated into man's artwork and architecture in the form of gargoyles. The evilness they embodied harnessed for the good, so to speak. Protection of sacred places and things. But make no mistake, this *thing* that we're facing now is *not* a true Betorak. It is no beast of some long-dead world. It can think and reason and it is very powerful. It has only chosen that form, I suppose, because it, in itself, is a frightening representation of all things evil."

Even as Geoffrey was explaining, its cry wailed through the darkness and the mist and sent shivers up the priest's spine. When he looked back at Arliss, he could see that she was no more comfortable with the sound than was he.

"Very carefully and quietly, open your doors and slide out. And I mean *slide*. Don't make any more movement than you absolutely have to. We don't want to draw its attention. Trust me, we'll meet it soon enough." Geoffrey clicked the handle of the door and winced at the sound. In the stillness, it might as well have been a firecracker as far as he was concerned. He waited, watching out the window for any sign that the thing had heard them. He could see it clearly, perched atop the mausoleum rooftop, scanning the cemetery. It seemed occupied by everything in front of it, ignoring what lay behind. That's a very good thing for us, was what Geoffrey was thinking as he eased his door open and slipped out onto the composition drive.   Sitting outside the car, he eased the door over but didn't latch it.   The others followed suit.

When they were all out, Geoffrey belly crawled around to the other side of the car.   Jacobs sat there in awe of how soundlessly Geoffrey had been able to move across the pebbled drive.

"I think our best bet," began Geoffrey, keeping his voice as low as possible, "will be to skirt along the fence here through those bushes.   It'll be a little noisier than I'd like, but I think it's worth a shot.   When we get around far enough, we'll have to climb over this God-awful fence without killing ourselves in the process.   Everybody up for it?"

Arliss and Jacobs just nodded in agreement. With his keen eyesight, Geoffrey could see the beads of sweat as they popped out onto Jacobs's forehead.   He could also see that the priest was visibly shaking, and he could see that, despite his fear, the priest's eyes held that same gleam of resolution that a soldier sometimes had just before they willingly gave their lives to save their friends'.

Following Geoffrey's lead, they inched their way across the concrete and onto the grass.   Now they were partially obscured by the taller monuments and mausoleums.   They could safely stand and pick their way through the brush.   It was difficult going, made more difficult by the fact that they had to do it slowly and quietly.   Thorns grabbed, pulled, and bit into their exposed skin. Jacobs wondered if this was what it would be like to crawl through barbed wire.

They had just cleared the last of the bushes when Jacobs grabbed Geoffrey by the shoulder and spun him around.

"You're not going to like what I'm going to say." Jacobs gritted his teeth and a grim look washed over his face.

"What's that, Gabe?" asked Geoffrey.

"Your bag. It's still in the car."

"No, it isn't," broke in Arliss, sticking her arm out. The bag dangled from her hand by its webbed strap. "Thought we might be needing it, so I dragged it along. Hope you don't mind."

Geoffrey slapped his forehead with his hand. "I can't believe I forgot it. It'd be a bit of a sticky wicket without it. Christ! I must be losing my mind."

Don't worry, thought Arliss so that Geoffrey could hear. *I'll help you find it later.* They smiled briefly at one another and then turned back to moving along the fence line.

The groans, bellows, shrieks and howls that had permeated the night had fallen silent. Crickets chirped in the grass and trees. They were all thankful for the sudden silence that fell behind them. Yet, at the same time, it meant that they no longer knew where their enemy was. He could, indeed, still be adorning the top of that mausoleum. But he could also be somewhere else by now. A disquieting image of some monstrous-looking gargoyle-like creature reaching out from behind and grabbing him by the throat made Father Jacobs wince.

"Here we go, mates," said Geoffrey, breaking the priest's vision of death. "Good a place as any to get in." He'd found a broken section of fencing and yanked it up and off its hinges. It made a groaning sound as the metal screws were torn out of the support post.

"That was good," quipped Arliss. "Maybe you'd like a kettle drum to announce our arrival as well."

"Sorry," apologized Geoffrey. "I hadn't meant to tear it completely off. Sometimes my adrenaline gets the better of me."

"Get down," commanded Arliss in a hushed tone.

As she said it, the tree branches above them and the bushes they'd just pushed through began to whip around. The strength of the wind knocked Geoffrey up against the fence. Arliss grabbed Jacobs by the shoulder and pulled him to the ground. He smacked his nose on a small rock and it began to bleed. The pain of impact immediately brought tears to his eyes.

Overhead, great wings beat the air as a dark shape sailed over them. It wheeled around in a great arc and then shot off towards the middle of the cemetery.

"That was a little too close for my tastes," Geoffrey said, getting to his feet. He helped Jacobs up. Arliss was already standing beside him by the time he'd reached out his hand for Jacobs. She handed him his bag and then cocked her head in the direction of the fence opening. "Let's go."

They moved through the opening. Arliss pushed past Geoffrey and took the lead. A new feeling had broken through to her; a new sense of authority. She reclaimed her complete memory and the position her station accorded. Geoffrey picked up the new-found knowledge that surged through her. They had not only been a team, but she had been his superior. And unlike Geoffrey, Arliss was an immortal. That was why her memory had been incomplete. To survive in a human world she was forced to regenerate, to become new again every three generations of man. Geoffrey understood everything in that instant. He was no more than a soldier, but she was something much more.

CHAPTER 100

Jasper dragged himself across the lawn, weaving carefully between headstones. Every now and again he'd glance behind him to be sure that none of the things he'd freed were following him. His ankle was on fire. In the dark, he couldn't see the damage he'd done, and he hadn't bothered to check too carefully. Arm over arm, he pulled himself along, occasionally stopping to rest against one of the cool stones. His goal had been to get as far away from the statue-decorated monuments as possible, but that was proving to be more difficult than he had expected. He was in the heart of the old cemetery where stone angels, demons, and gargoyles abounded. He tried to avoid looking at them, fearing they would come to life, jump off their pedestals, and crush him into oblivion or gnash him to death with their granite teeth.

The mist felt good on his face as he dragged himself up against the base of a monument to rest. His breath came in raspy gasps, his chest heaving heavily. He wanted to pull up his pants leg and see just how badly he'd hurt his ankle but he was too afraid of what he might find. A general weakness was creeping over him like an ivy vine creeps across a garden, and he was developing a consuming thirst. Neither of these was a very good sign. He knew from his experiences in Nam that a significant loss of blood was usually responsible.

Summoning all his courage, and with one eye squinted closed, he yanked on his pant leg. A fireball of pain shot up his leg as soon as he tugged. The pant leg was caught on the sliver of Tibia that had sliced through his skin like a stake through a tent rope. He let out a sharp yell that died out in the surrounding fog.

"Good goin, Jasper," he said to himself aloud, his voice bouncing back to him off the stones. "You really fixed yourself this time, you dope."

He bent himself as far forward as he could, as if he was trying to do sit-ups, but his reach was still too short. His fingers groped in vain for the cuff of his pants, trying to worm the end of his trousers off the spike of bone. When he accidentally touched it, the pain set off a cascade of flashing stars behind his eyes, ocular fireworks courtesy of raw nerve endings. He slumped back against the headstone, his arms dropping to his sides and his breathing more labored than before.

Jasper closed his eyes and let himself go. He could feel himself beginning to slip down that long dark tunnel from which there was no return. Flashes of the things he'd done; self-recriminations over his failing weaknesses; his inability to stand up for what was right rather than succumbing to his fears; all these fought for front and center in his brain. He was somewhere between consciousness and the peace of death when he heard the snapping sound. His eyes fluttered open as his heart began to run amok in his chest. As peaceful as death had seemed just a moment ago, its prospect did not seem so inviting with his eyes and ears open. Thoughts of being torn apart by some decaying corpse sent a chill of terror through him, and he found the strength to sit upright, listening for each little sound and probing the blackness to his eyes' extent.

Snap! Snap! Snap-snap!

The sound was coming from about two rows away. There was definitely someone or something coming in his direction and he really didn't want to hang around to find out what it was. But getting up and running was out of the question, and crawling just wasn't going to be fast enough. So he started probing the ground with his hands, desperately searching for a rock or stick or anything he could use as a weapon. His fingers clawed at his surroundings. He leaned this way and then that but could find nothing useful, only handfuls of dead grass.

The sound was getting louder now; closer. He could hear the panting breath that drifted across the soggy night air. It was almost rhythmical. He clutched his eyes shut, covered them with his hands and prepared himself for the worst. *Ya done it good* was what kept running through his mind as he sat there waiting for the end to come and hoping it would be fairly painless.

Now there was someone standing over him. He could feel it. He wanted to spread his fingers and peek up but he was too petrified. Tears ran down his cheeks and puddled up in his palms.

"Go ahead. Go ahead an' git it over with. Please God be merciful about it."

"What are you talking about?" asked Grady Peters. "Are you all right?"

"Look pop, his leg's busted," said Willie, pointing at the shard of bone protruding from Jasper's pants' leg.

"Christ, Mary, and all the Saints! How'd you manage that?" asked Grady as he knelt down beside Jasper.

Jasper looked into Grady's face and saw a savior. When he closed his eyes he had been sure that one of the things from the ground was what had been coming for him.

"C'n ya help me? My leg's broke good. I c'n hardly move anymore an' everything is kinda fuzzy."

"Just lay back a minute and I'll see what I can do. Ain't much light t'work by, though."

Grady ran his fingers gently down Jasper's leg trying to see if it was broken any place else. He was trying to put on a good front, but he was really scared. He had no idea what he was doing. He didn't know the first thing about *real* first aid, only what he'd seen on television doctor shows.

"Ya snapped it clean through, that's for sure," he told Jasper. "I'm not really sure what t'do with it."

"Here pop," cried Willy. He was carrying a long branch about three inches wide. "We can make a splint outta this, but first we gotta try and stop the bleeding. From what I can see it's only a trickle, so I don't think it's that bad. But I can't see too good either."

Grady wasn't sure whether or not he should be amazed or proud. He chose proud. The one thing in the world that he and Tamika were sure they wanted was for their son to end up more educated and more knowledgeable than they were. They didn't want another Peters struggling through life on minimum wage for maximum hours.

"Good son. That's real good. Do ya think we ought t'try t'straighten the leg. You know, get the bone back inside?"

"No. No, pop," shouted Willie. We can't do that. It'll make 'im really, really sick. I forget the word, but it's really, really, *really* bad. We just gotta wrap it tight so it don't move around none."

Out of habit, Grady shot Willie a sour look and started to correct his English. But at the last moment, with everything else that was happening, the thought of correcting grammar in the middle of a cemetery ... at night ... made him start laughing out loud.

"Wha ... what's so funny?" asked Jasper, scared and concerned. "You ain't thinkin a-leavin me, are ya? You ain't thinkin nothin like that and thinkin it's funny? You wouldn't? Would you?"

"Relax Mr. Collins. I ain't gonna leave ya. We're gonna patch ya up and help git ya outta here."

"Well ... it ain't gonna be as easy as all that. There's things runnin around in here. Awful things. Ungodly things. *I* know! I set em loose. They was buried and I set em loose."

Grady shot Willie a look that said: it's ok son, he's just rambling and hallucinating from the pain. Jasper saw it and snapped right back.

"I ain't a fool. And I ain't delirious or whatever ya call it. I'm tellin the God's awful truth." He looked from the man to the boy and back again, trying to see if he was going to be believed, or taken for an old idiot who had no idea what he was talking about.

"Well," said Grady after a long silence, "considering all the evil things I've seen today, I don't think I'm inclined to argue much with ya just at present." As he'd said the words: "things I've seen", in his mind he had added: *and done.*

The whole time he'd been talking, his hands had been wrapping the strips of cloth from Willie's shirt around Jasper's leg and the stick that now supported it.

As he worked in the dark he noticed that, from time to time, it seemed to get darker and then lighter and then darker again. Finally tying the last knot, the darkness deepened again and Grady, Willie, and Jasper looked up.

Overhead, a shadowy figure, like some giant misshapen bat, circled and dipped and circled and dipped. Each time it crossed above them the darkness of the cemetery deepened in thick shadow. They watched in silence, too scared to make any kind of sound as it wheeled above them and then disappeared into the mist.

"What was that?" asked Grady.

"I dunno pop. I ain't never seen nothin-"

Jasper cut the boy off in mid-sentence. "No ... you ain't! You ain't seen nothing like that before. An if ya see it again and up close ... you'll never see nothing again."

"Then what is it, Mr. Collins? Do you know?"

"Lord save us all, but I think it's the Devil come t'life." He blessed himself, and even as he was completing the sign of the cross, it crossed his mind that he might just be struck down dead for being a hypocrite. His arm trailed off before it reached his right shoulder as that thought seeped into his mind.

"C'mon. Let's get you up. Devil or no Devil, we gotta get outta here and get you to a real doctor. Gotta get ya to Doc Robertson." Grady shoveled his hands underneath Jasper's armpits and lifted him to a wobbly standing position on his good foot. "You git im on t'other side, Willie. We'll get im out t'gether."

They started to help Jasper hobble off, Willie on one side pointing the way and Grady on the other. Jasper rolled in and out of semi-consciousness as the throbbing in his leg got worse with each step. He kept mumbling about: *going back* and *not going this way* and *we can't go that way* ... all of which Grady ignored as ramblings and kept following Willie's directions.

The three came to a dead stop when Jasper finally yelled out at the top of his lungs: "Dear God, no! Not here. Not this way."

"C'mon. Help me set him down over there next to that big headstone," Grady said to Willie.

They shuffled Jasper over sideways and laid him up against the Langer's monument. When Jasper's head tilted back and he saw the two large stone gargoyles perched above him he gave out a sharp yell and then passed out.

Willie and Grady snapped straight up, both their heads turning in the same direction when they heard the ululating cry that was coming toward them from the end of the row of stones. A lone figure was approaching them. It looked to be no more than a dark shape. It wobbled unsteadily, knocking up against a stone, stumbling to its knees and then clawing its way back upright again using a headstone for support as it weaved its way toward them. Its wailing was both pitiful and frightening, a howling anguish that broke through the night like a tugboat's horn through the fog.

Grady grabbed Willie and drew him in close, his arms wrapped tightly around the boy's chest. He wanted to run but he knew he couldn't just leave Jasper lying there alone. As the thing staggered closer, Grady pulled Willie around behind him, his large frame completely shielding the boy from view.

"Don't you move son! Don't you move a muscle till I say so. And then, when I do ... you run like the wind an' git yerself t'home. Do you understand me?"

"But pop-"

"There's no buts on this one, Willie. You do as yer told. Ya hear?"

"Yessir," answered Willie dejectedly.

In front of them, the shape was taking a more recognizable form. To Grady, it looked as if it were coming apart. What he could see from where he stood just couldn't be alive and moving. Most of its flesh was gone from the bone, there was no visible jaw and the muscles were exposed and covered in a bile-colored ooze. It kept coming forward, wailing and waving its bony arms wildly, its fingers clutching at the air in front of it.

"Ok ... you ready, Willie?"

"Yes, pop."

"Now!" Grady rushed forward and tackled the thing. At the same moment, Willie turned to run in the opposite direction, but he came to a frozen stop. In front of him, the gargoyle statues on the Langer's monument were wrenching themselves free of their base. The grating sound of stone being torn apart cut through the darkness in thundering waves. As they freed themselves, they hopped to the ground blocking the boy's way. Their heavy wings opened and closed, their granite mouths gaped open and their stone tongues lashed in and out between the grimacing lips. They rocked their heads from side to side like a pair of inquisitive dogs as their fiery red eyes fixed on Willie.

CHAPTER 101

Jack, Linda, and Ethan emerged from the shrubbery in front of an old beat-up Chevy Nova. Spotted with rust and primer, it sat on the gravel road like a lethargic leopard. Jack and Ethan glanced at each other.

"Jasper Collins's car," said Jack. One of the benefits of being the sheriff in a small town was knowing who belonged to which car.

"What do you suppose it's doing here at this time of night?" Linda asked.

"I dunno," replied Jack. "Maybe he had it parked here today while he was working and then couldn't get it started. It sure doesn't look like it's in the best of conditions."

"Maybe," said Ethan, a skeptical look pasted on his face. "Maybe."

"Guess it doesn't matter, other than it's just another strange thing piled on top of everything else today. C'mon, we can cut straight up through the sections; it'll be quicker than following the road."

They had just made it through the farthest edge and were about to cross one of the main roads when a blazing blue light shot skyward somewhere in front of them. They stopped and looked up. It was a tall column of blue light and it punched up through the fog and dark clouds, giving the sky a hazy neon aura.

"What the hell is that?" asked Linda.

"Not a clue in the world," answered Jack. "But I guess we'll have to go find out. My bet is, based on the car we just passed, that Jasper Collins is in here doing something he shouldn't. He's most likely drunk again. Except ..."

"Except what?" Linda's face had scrunched up into one of those: "Please don't tell me things can possibly be any worse" looks.

"Except that, usually, Jasper just stays home in his own trailer when he drinks. I've only had one problem with him with that in public, and he had promised me that he'd never repeat it. And ... until now, he's kept that promise."

"Well whatever it is, it's very bright," Ethan pointed out. "I don't think we're talking about some ordinary flashlight here and I have no idea where he'd get the power for anything else. Unless he dragged a portable generator out here." Ethan just shook his head.

"Come on, let's go take a look." Jack had volunteered to carry the shotgun after Ethan had broken his arm. He now raised it, checked its load with a quick pump and then started forward. Linda fell in behind with Ethan bringing up the rear.

The blue fountain of light that stabbed upward in front of them reflected off the clouds and bathed part of the cemetery in a disc of hazy blue. Seeing was much easier and they now had a point of reference to aim for. Jack was moving quickly. He picked his way gingerly between stones and monuments, slaloming around them. Linda and Ethan followed. Ethan made sure to keep a careful, intermittent eye behind them as well.

The source of the light was still obscured by the stones, monuments and mausoleums, but it cast moving shadows that wavered in and out of view.

There was no question in Jack's mind that whoever was up ahead was not alone.

When he figured he'd gotten as close as he could without being seen, he stopped. In the dim, blue glow, his six-foot frame cast a large and menacing shadow on the stones around them. Linda found it extremely comforting. Although she showed no outward signs, her heart had been in her throat since they'd left the B & B. She was fighting with herself to keep focused and not think about any of the things that had occurred there, or of the events of last night. But being in a cemetery in the dark did not help much. Now, looking at Jack's imposing figure, she began to relax a bit. She moved into his shadow, wrapping it around her like a security blanket.

"Ok. Linda, you wait here. And keep yourself hidden, do you hear? We have no idea what we're dealing with here. Could just be some kids pulling a prank, but I doubt it." Jack's voice was stern, commanding, but the love he felt for her also came through.

"You don't have to worry about me," she said. "I'm good at a lot of things, but being a hero has never been on my resume'." She gave him a weak smile, glanced at Ethan, and then said: "What the hell." She grabbed Jack by the shoulders and gave him a long hard kiss. "Don't you be a hero either. I need you in one piece, mister. Do your job, but for Christ's sake, be careful."

Jack smiled. "Not a problem. My name's Jack Dougherty, not Jack Bauer. I'll leave that kind of hero stuff to you Special Forces guys." He jabbed a thumb at Ethan. "That's their thing, not mine."

A shrill, mournful scream suddenly broke the night's silence. It was high pitched and undulating. It rose and fell, reminding Jack of some mutant crow gone mad. When he looked up, a dark shape wheeled overhead. It seemed to be circling, and what it looked like sent a chill up Jack's spine.

Ethan put a hand on Jack's shoulder. "Are we seeing things?"

"I don't think so," said Jack as he dropped to the ground, pulling Linda down with him. "That ... that just can't be real?"

"It sure looks real enough to me," whispered Ethan.

They peered skyward, watching the thing above them make ever-widening circles like a vulture hunting for a meal. In the haze of the blue light, the huge, bat-like wings were silhouetted against the dark clouds. Beneath them, something in the shape of a man could be made out. The legs were long and trailed out behind the beating wings and the chest was broad. It circled a few times and then headed towards the tower of light.

"*Any* fucking idea what that was?" asked Ethan, not really expecting an answer.

"I've never seen anything like it before, but I'll bet we all know where it came from," answered Jack.

"The B & B. It was that thing in the B & B, wasn't it?" Linda's voice was shaking. Jack put his arm around her.

"If it was, it sure looks a lot different now."

"And a lot more dangerous," added Ethan.

The three of them lay crouched on the ground, their eyes riveted on the blue spire of light and the monstrous thing that was now circling it. It dipped and rose and flew around the column of light like a pole dancer. Then, suddenly, it folded its wings back and dove downward and out of their view.

"I think the eagle has landed," quipped Ethan

Jack just looked at him, then at the shotgun. He had serious doubts about how effective it was going to be against that thing. He felt like he was taking a cap gun to shoot an elephant.

"Come on," he said at last. "Before I change my mind completely."

"Right behind you," said Ethan. He turned, pulled his Glock 17 out and handed it to Linda, clicking the safety off. "It's ready to go. Just point and click ... think of it as a big computer mouse with a bigger bite."

Linda took it, turned it over in her hand, slid the slide partway back to see if there was a round in the chamber and then let it click forward.

"You've done this before, I see," smiled Ethan wryly.

"Yeah. Been to the range with Jack a few times ... after hours of course. But ... actually, I prefer a three-fifty-seven. Just more comfortable."

"Hollow points too, no doubt," said Ethan, still smiling.

"No doubt."

"Stay here," said Jack, and then he started crawling forward around the headstone they were behind. Ethan gave a final nod to Linda and then followed.

CHAPTER 102

After Carlton had improved on the backhoe's headlight design for Jasper, he swelled with the sense of power. He had heard Jasper's thoughts, his complaining. And with a simple thought of his own he had remedied the problem. What's more, he had actually seen the headlights flash to full brightness through Jasper's eyes. He was now, unquestionably, the most powerful man in Banderman Falls. With a single thought or wish, he could lay his enemies low and have them begging for mercy.

He turned the sword handle over and over, luxuriating in its radiance, bathing in its glow and reveling in the powers it had bestowed on him. He trudged across the cemetery not really knowing where he was headed or why; he just kept putting one foot in front of the other, trusting that they would lead him to where he needed to be. He couldn't concern himself anymore with mundane things like destinations or appointments. He was Carlton the All-Powerful, and by God, people were going to learn to respect him.

He gave no thought to what it was that Jasper was doing as he mounted a small hill, stopped and took a deep breath and raised the sword above his head like a general leading an attack. The damp mist felt good on his face and, for a moment, he wondered if he could control that too. He closed his eyes, holding the sword erect and said: "I command you to open a clear path for me." He waited, anticipating the shroud of mist to part before him as he walked on. But nothing happened. A puzzled and hurt look flashed across his face. And then an idea occurred to him. He took the sword and slowly leveled it in front of him. As he did, a wide swath of clearing opened up, the misty fog forming an alleyway. He walked on, sword held out and confident that his time had finally come.

As he started down the small slope that led to the next cemetery section, he began singing to himself, smiling at how apt he found the words to *Fire* by The Crazy World of Arthur Brown to be.

He had just crossed the road when a booming voice crashed into his brain. It was so loud and so powerful that he almost dropped the sword. He pressed his hands against his ears, the sword handle still gripped firmly in his right hand.

"You will go and command my children. They are waiting for you. They have slept long and now thirst for blood. There are others here ... others that would like to see you disgraced. You will set my children loose upon them and, in my name, you will be victorious."

The voice died away and Carlton had a clear picture in his mind where he was to go. He quickened his pace, bumping into stones as he passed between them. He was going to lead a great army to a great victory. He strode on, head held high, sword out in front of him opening his way, and the mental image of his tormentors bowed before him in his mind.

When he reached the Banderman mausoleum, the oldest in the cemetery, he stopped, climbed to the top of it and thrust the sword straight up in the air as if he were trying to impale the moon itself. A brilliant blue light shot forth, blazing up into the night sky. A beacon of power that would draw his army to him. Its brilliance was too much for him to look at, though he tried several times. He could feel the warmth in his hand that the broken blade created.

"I am here," he yelled. "I have come to command you, to lead you in battle to a great victory. Come to me. Come to me and we will crush our enemies together."

He waited, bathed in the blue aura that was reflected down from the thickened night sky. He waited and listened. And he heard what he needed to hear. They were coming. He could hear each shaky footstep. He could see through their eyes as they passed stone and tree and hillock on their way to him. They had come from the grave and they were his to command. An army of dead soldiers marching forth to serve him.

In his heightened state of exaltation, he forgot that he was no more than a puppet. He forgot that his true powers were coming from the voice that had invaded his head. He forgot that he was not the real bidder but only the one doing the bidding. He assumed the sword was his and never considered the possibility that it would be taken from him. Standing on top of the mausoleum, he waited like a lord for his troops to surround him and never gave a thought to what was coming for *him*.

He watched as those that Jasper had freed from their earthly interment gathered at his feet. He reveled in the awe that their disintegrating faces showed him. He stood there, the epitome of hubris, swallowed up by grand plans that were somehow not his own but felt like they were.

"Go forth now," he commanded, pointing an index finger down at the group of walking corpses before him. "Go forth and purge us of our enemies. They are here. Find them! Find them and kill them! One and all. Give them no mercy, for they surely gave you none in your lifetimes."

Carlton watched as they rambled off in different directions. He had no idea where the words he'd just spoken had come from. It was as if someone else was speaking through him. And now, the voice was gone and he found himself alone in the fog, the light from the sword dwindling, going cold, burning out. When the last of it faded, he stood atop the monument, cold and frightened and very confused.

CHAPTER 103

Eric was bent over Ernie, slowly and gently running his hands up and down his arms and legs looking for fractures. When he didn't find any, he carefully slipped a hand underneath his neck and probed with his fingers for any signs of a broken neck.

"I think he'll be all right. 'Course, we'd best be gittin 'im to a doctor soon. Lemme see if'n I c'n wake him." Eric tapped lightly on Ernie's cheek a few times. When he got no response from that, he pinched his neck, hard. That made Ernie give out a low moan.

"I think he'll be comin 'round soon nuff." He was about to tell Gwen to just sit tight when a blazing blue light jabbed an electric finger up into the sky. Eric and Gwen stared upward in awe. A chill crawled over Eric because he knew that this was the beginning of something big. And he was pretty sure that when it was all over he'd be taking up residence here in Peaceful Haven Cemetery permanently.

Standing up, Eric surveyed the nearby ground looking for a safe place for Ernie and Gwen to keep their heads down when the shit begins to rain down, as his father used to say. Spotting an old mausoleum with the front gate hanging open he dragged Ernie over and into it. Gwen followed.

"I wantcha t'stay in here and don't come out fer nothin. I ain't kiddin ya. Things is gonna get pret-ty dicey 'round here. You mark m'words. C'n ya do that till I git back? C'n ya stay put?"

His eyes were locked on Gwen's. Her face was still strained with confusion but she nodded that she understood. Eric slowly reached his hand out and held it there, waiting for her to feel comfortable enough to take it. When she finally did and he led her over to the mausoleum doorway, her face seemed to sag into relaxation, as if someone had just lifted an iron hat off her head.

"I know it's a bit spooky in here, but I think it's a place ya c'n be safe. When I leave, I'll shove this gate over a bit and ya c'n hide in the back there in the dark. I don't think no one'll find ya in here. Alright?"

Gwen didn't say anything. She nodded again, not quite sure what she should do or say. She looked over at Ernie lying on the floor and a half-remembered image of some kind of rack with books on it flashed across her mind. In desperation, she tried to hold on to it, to grab it with a mental hook and pull it out of the darkness where it hid, but it slipped away almost as quickly as it had come.

"All right, now," said Eric, "I gotta git t'gettin some business took care of. You just stay put and I'll be back fer ya before ya know it." He smiled, slid the gate to and walked off down the row of headstones, his hand on his bib pocket against the watch.

"Ya don't even know what it is ya think yer doin, ya ol' coot," he mumbled to himself. "Only thing that's prit'near sure is yer gonna end up growin grass fer Jasper Collins t'mow right on top a-yer thick head."

CHAPTER 104

The Betorak sat hunched on top of the mausoleum supporting itself on its knuckles like a lineman awaiting the snap of the ball, its great wings folded back. Luminous green eyes scanned the cemetery, blazing through the thick fog. Towards the back on the right, the beacon of the pommel shone upward, a blue column of intense light. The thing's eyes fixated on it for a moment and then swept back and forth, pinpointing the pockets of movement that dotted the grounds.

Extending its mind and will, it set things in motion. Stone gargoyles and demon shapes came to life, ripping themselves from their slag pediments. Through Carlton, the Betorak directed its army, still allowing Carlton to believe he was in control and all-powerful. But that would change soon enough.

Lifting its head, the Betorak sniffed the air like a bloodhound divining a quarry's scent. What it smelled sent it into a rage. It pushed off with its muscled legs and rose into the sky, a harsh, grating cry bellowing forth. It spiraled upwards and then began circling the cemetery, its fiery green eyes piercing the fog in search of the smell's origin. It was a smell it knew all too well, a smell that had thwarted it many times over the centuries. It was the smell of the guardians, a smell that had always foreshadowed its doom. But this time would be different. This time they would learn the full power and malevolence of evil. This time ... it would be they who perished.

A grin spread across its leathery face as it saw the boy (the one who had been responsible for the loss of his wolves) come to a dead stop, blocked by two stone gargoyles. Behind him, his father wrestled with one of the corpse soldiers, a battle he was sure to lose. The Betorak circled and circled, mentally directing his troops to the right spots, to the pockets of puny humans that dared defy him. And it searched. It searched for those whom it had real cause to fear. It searched for the guardians.

As it wheeled above the darkened land beneath, it began to feel the pull of the pommel. It needed it and now was the time for it to claim it. It bent its thoughts toward Carlton, standing alone atop the Banderman mausoleum with the blade burning furiously skyward.

"Your power is mine," commanded the Betorak of the sword. "You shall no longer give light to the human that holds you. You shall soon be in my possession and we shall control time itself."

Suddenly, the light from the sword began to fade, growing dimmer and dimmer until it blinked out, leaving only the darkness and fog to surround Carlton. The Betorak rose high into the air and then plunged downward, its eyes fixed on Carlton Wedgemore.

With a heavy thud, it landed on the ground in front of the Banderman mausoleum and folded its wings in behind it. It looked up. And as it roared and snarled, a foul black liquid dripped from the corners of its mouth. It raised a hand and pointed its sharp forefinger toward Carlton.

"I have come for what is mine. You will surrender it now." Its voice was deep and guttural. It growled the words more than spoke them. The horns protruding from its forehead waggled back and forth like antennae, and the tips of its wings curled and uncurled.

Carlton looked down, too petrified at first to speak. He looked at the thing below him and then at the sword in his hand. Something inside him told him that he must not relinquish his prize. It told him that it was his power and the obscene thing below was powerless to take it from him. It told him that he, Carlton Wedgemore, was the one in complete control and that the thing he was looking at could be bent to his will through the proper use of the sword. It told him that *he* was the master and that the thing below was here to serve him. His ego told him all that ... and it told him wrong.

"Stand back and prepare to do my will," Carlton yelled at it, pointing the tip of the sword directly at its face. "I am your master and you will serve my needs. You will be my slave and will perform the tasks I set before you."

A great peel of bellicose laughter burst forth from the Betorak. Its booming echo wafted through the mist-shrouded cemetery and bounced back again, assaulting Carlton's ears with a thumping harshness. In a single bound, the Betorak landed on the roof alongside Carlton, reached out and grabbed him by the shoulders lifting him up and drawing him in close. The sword handle dangled by his side and the grip that held him was tighter than any he could have imagined. He struggled, tried to lift the blade, tried to mentally command it to do his bidding and to again begin to burn. He tried to cut into the hideous thing that held him still, but the blade just slid along the leathery skin.

In that moment, Carlton's mind fractured. He couldn't understand how the sword could let him down; he couldn't accept that its power had deserted him. He couldn't go back to being plain old Carlton Wedgemore, antique dealer and unimportant little man. He retreated inside himself, his mind slinking back into the deepest of corners and locking the door behind it, never to come out again. He was broken and the light went out of his eyes like a flashlight's dying beam.

The Betorak laughed again and then pulled Carlton's arms out so that it held him up as if he were hung on a cross, the pommel clutched tightly in his outstretched hand. It looked into Carlton's eyes, then at the pommel and then back at Carlton.

"Have you enjoyed the power I have given you? The power I have allowed you to command? The power that is all mine? Like it, you belong to me and I may, and can, do as I wish with both of you."

The horns that he'd made from his fingernails began to grow, curling around one another in a great spiral, forming one large spike. It extended outward from its forehead and stopped just short of Carlton's right eye. Then, it shot forward, piercing the eye and pushing out though the back of his skull. Carlton jerked once and dropped the pommel from his hand. It clattered to the stone roof with a clinking metallic sound.

When the Betorak withdrew the great horn that had skewered Carlton's brain, it dropped him. Carlton lay there, slowly oozing life, waiting to die. The horn had stabbed right through his pons and his systems were slowly shutting down. The Betorak dug inside his mind, curious as to his puppet's final thoughts. Inside, Carlton lay curled up in a fetal position, his thumb stuck in his mouth and his unheard voice calling out: "Mommy, mommy, mommy."

The Betorak stepped over Carlton's body, it horns unwinding and sinking back into place above his eyes. It reached down and picked up the sword shard, turning it over in its clawed hand, feeling its leathery grip and staring into the center of the crystal pommel. Tilting its head back, it let out a long, shrill howl as it thrust the blade upward. Sparks shot out in all directions like fireworks and the blue light once again cut its way up through the fog. The blaze expanded and shrank as the blade's broken and jagged edge reformed itself and began to grow. The blue light fused with the steel and the blade was made whole. Standing atop the mausoleum, the blade held high above its head, the Betorak spat forth its fury. Blue, red and white flames belched from its gaping mouth, consuming Carlton's body in a ball of fire. It then turned its attention to the cemetery, and those who had come to stop it.

"I am coming for you, now. Can you hear me?" it roared. Its booming voice thudded through the dead land, splitting the darkness and shaking the headstones. "You cannot win now. I have the sword. It is once again complete. I am the commander of Lucifer's Pommel and that will herald your destruction."

It started to bellow a deep and sonorous laugh but was cut off when its mind was flooded. In its head, a powerful voice boomed out.

"It is you who will be destroyed. I have once again come into my own and I won't back down. Your entombment awaits you."

A vision of eternal solitude and imprisonment was forced into its head, a vision of its own anguish and torment, forever lived and relived. It screamed; and its scream split branches from trees and toppled headstones all across the cemetery.

In a full rage, it leaped into the air, its wings beating furiously. It soared straight upward and hovered, seeking the ones who dared to oppose it, seeking the one who had dared to threaten it, who dared to enter *its* mind. Seeking Terrenus Porta Custodis, the guardian of time's gate.

CHAPTER 105

Once they had gotten through the fence, Arliss leading, they pushed their way through the thickets, brambles and bushes that ringed the outer edge of the cemetery. When they finally broke through on the inner side, they stopped and knelt down. Geoffrey grabbed his bag and unzipped it as quietly as he could. Jacobs and Arliss kept watch while he dug through the bag, pulling out items the likes of which Jacobs had never seen before.

Geoffrey laid several different bundles on the ground. They were wrapped in an old cloth and made a clinking sound as he set them down. Then he drew out a set of statuettes; they looked to be cut from pure ruby and were carved in the shape of hornets. Behind these, Geoffrey took out two oval discs, each about the size of a half-dollar and studded with diamonds on the edges. Finally, he took from the bag two flattened, perfectly smooth and rounded onyx stones of Frisbee size, a nearly half-moon shaped object that appeared to be some kind of iron-diamond mix, pointed on the diamond end and rounded at the iron end, and a set of five things that looked like darts from a board game but were cut from pure marble.

"Quite a collection of goodies you have there," said Jacobs, eyeing the display on the wet grass.

Geoffrey turned to the priest. "If you wouldn't mind my old friend, how about a quick blessing for this lot?" He swept his hand over the pile he had laid out, his eyes never leaving the priest's.

Jacobs looked at Geoffrey and then at Arliss. The expression on her face almost made the Father's blood run cold. There seemed to be no emotion in her eyes and they looked like infinity mirrors. He could only see her in half profile as she scanned their surroundings, but the look was enough to convince him that, somehow, the woman who was kneeling across from him was not *quite* the same woman who had arrived with them.

Bending over the displayed objects, Jacobs folded his hands in front of him, closed his eyes and began to pray. His lips moved but the words were inaudible. As he finished, he raised his right hand, made the sign of the cross over the items in front of him, blessed himself and then opened his eyes.

"I hope that my blessing sticks," he said. "I also hope that the two of you don't think that that's going to be the extent of my participation in our little soirée tonight." He tried to smile, but it ended up looking as forced as it had been.

"Don't worry about that, Gabe." Geoffrey tried to sound as hopeful as he could. "There's plenty of work for you tonight. And I hope you're not opposed to getting your hands dirty. I have no doubt that this is going to get ugly and brutal pretty damned fast."

"Maybe the good Father *should* stay out of it," suggested Arliss. "The real work for him might begin when everything's over." She paused a moment and then added, "Assuming, of course, we survive it."

"I don't think so," chimed in the priest sarcastically. "I don't think that, at this point, I can just sit back and watch everything happen as if I were sitting in some movie theatre somewhere. And besides, what makes either of you think that I'll have a choice as to whether or not to participate. You said it yourself, things are going to get ugly and brutal, and it's been my experience that such things always spill over into unwanted areas. No! I'm in ... all the way in."

"Guess that settles that," Geoffrey said. "What do you think, Arliss?"

Arliss looked at the priest, studying his face. "I think you're probably right. Come on, Geoffrey. Let's get him set up as best we can. What do you think? The Kahnjal?"

"Yes," replied Geoffrey, stoically. "Probably best." He picked up one of the wrapped bundles and passed it over to Jacobs. "These," he tapped the bundle with his index finger, "are a very special kind of dagger. They were fashioned centuries ago by the first dabblers in what you would call Voodoo, although, strictly speaking, it was a more primitive and antecedent form of that. They're used to-" Geoffrey stopped. The concern in his face was evident.

Jacobs laid a hand on his shoulder and gave it a slight squeeze. "I think we're way past mincing words and worrying about what each other's reaction to what we're going to say will be. Don't you agree?"

Geoffrey smiled. "Yes. You're bloody well right about that, padre. Ok then, these things will send the dead back to being dead, if you will." He clenched his teeth together and smiled; it was the smile of a child who just got caught with his hand in the cookie jar for a second time.

Jacobs took the bundle, which was much heavier than it looked, balanced it in the palm of one hand and unwrapped it with the other. Inside there were eight long pieces of cast iron, each with a handle carved in the shape of a serpent's head. The diamond-shaped edges tapered downward from the gaping serpent's fanged mouth to a razor-fine point. Jacobs lifted one, feeling its weight. Geoffrey reached out and picked it out of his hand and laid it across his outstretched index finger. It wobbled there for a second and then sat still.

"Perfectly balanced, Father. Craftsmanship like this is a rare thing anymore, but ... the need for them, thank God, is even rarer."

"I wish *that* were true today," jibed the priest. "Apparently, the need for fine workmanship never goes out of style. No matter *how* much you'd like it to. So, what, *exactly*, do I do with these ... as if I didn't already have a pretty good idea?"

"It's simple," Arliss jumped in, "you stick it through their hearts or heads. Either way'll do the trick."

Geoffrey shot her a stern look. She just shrugged it off.

"I think it's a little late in the game to start worrying about feelings, don't you think?" was all she said. She stood up, lifting up the half-moon piece, one of the diamond-studded oval discs and the five darts. Geoffrey followed suit, picking up the flattened "Frisbee" stones, the two ruby wasps and the other oval disc.

"Both bundles are yours, Gabe. Can you manage them?"

The priest rose, stuck the first set of Kahnjal into his belt and then picked up the second set, unwrapped them and clutched them in his left hand.

"You know," Jacobs said with a half-smile that made his cheeks puff out. "I'm not sure whether I should be thankful I met you or downright pissed off. I mean really ... if I hadn't met you maybe this whole thing would have passed our sleepy little town right by." He grinned.

"It might have," said Geoffrey. "Then again-"

"C'mon," said Arliss.   "Time to set things right again."

"And let's hope we can," added Geoffrey under his breath.

CHAPTER 106

The gargoyles eyed Willie, their mouths opening and closing, their stony fangs gnashing together. Each took a lumbering step forward and unfolded its wings, effectively blocking the entire row. Their great muscled, stone arms stretched out in front of them, the granite fingers clutching at the empty space between them and the boy. Clutching at the boy.

Willie started to back-peddle, one step at a time. He had just passed the Richland monument when one of the stone figures leaped forward in a single hop and was standing within reach of him. It snarled a stony, grating snarl and then shot its clawed hand out towards Willie's face. As it did, a thunderous sound filled the hollow row of stones. It was the grinding sound of stone moving on stone and was immediately followed by a loud wailing sound as the arm that reached out for Willie was cleaved cleanly off.

Willie's mouth dropped open. He wanted to scream in both terror and delight, but the scream was lodged firmly in his throat, refusing to budge. In front of him, the statue of Michael the Archangel, which had been perched for time immemorial upon the Richland monument, had jumped down and in a single swipe of its granite blade, lopped off the extended arm of the groping gargoyle. The gargoyle, one arm short, hopped backwards, wailing and crying. The other leaped forward, landing just in front of its injured partner. They looked at each other briefly and then lifted off, their heavy stone wings paddling the air furiously.

In succession, they dipped and dove at Michael, their taloned feet trying to catch hold of him while they avoided his thrusting sword. They came in waves, one from the front while the other swung around to Michael's rear. Michael parried, whirling and slashing with his great sword. The sound of the battle was deafening, as if mountains were being blown apart, one after the other.

For their size and weight, the gargoyles were extremely agile, as if they were made of no more than flesh and bone. But Michael was just as agile and twice as cunning. As the one with the lost arm dove downward on him, he stepped back and began to flap his own immense wings. The resultant push of air sent his attacker tumbling through the air. It rolled backwards end over end, smashed into an oak and exploded into flying shards of rock.

At that instant, the second swooped in and grabbed Michael from behind by his wings, pinning them back like a child would pin a butterfly's. It howled with delight at having got a good hold on him and chomped down on the top curve of Michael's right wing with its fangs. A huge chunk of stone was ripped from the wing and spit out. The gargoyle cocked its head backward, preparing to swing it forward for another bite. It never got the chance.

As its head rocked forward, Michael swung his sword up and over his head, both hands firmly around the hilt, and brought the blade straight down behind his back. The gargoyle's head came in line at the same time as the blade came down between Michael's wings and he was impaled like a chicken on a rotisserie spit. It screamed a single agonizing scream and then dropped to the ground. It rolled this way and then that and then back again in searing agony.

Michael turned, strode over to it, pulled his sword out of its body and brought the blade down again. The head popped off as easily as if he were cutting a watermelon instead of granite. It rolled up against the base of the Richland monument and exploded. The rest of the body turned fiery red and melted away into the mist moistened grass with a sizzling, steamy sound.

Michael turned toward Willie who had been watching the battle in awe. With a raspy, gravely sound, Michael's lips drew back in a flash of a smile and then closed again. He lifted his arm and pointed in the direction behind Willie. The sound that came from his mouth when he spoke shook the ground and stones around them.

"Help your father. I have done all I can do for you right now."

When he finished speaking, he turned and jumped into the air, coming down once again atop the monument where he had stood sentinel for so many years. The damaged wing drooped forward a little as Michael solidified into the statue it had been – frozen again for all time above the Richlands.

Willie turned and saw his father grappling with the decaying thing on the ground. They rolled from side to side. Every now and then a sharp cry of pain rose up and the thing gouged out a hunk of his father's flesh with its sharp, bony fingers.

Not really thinking what he would do once he was there, Willie rushed forward and jumped on the corpse's back, wrapping his forearms around its neck as tightly as he could. The thing bellowed at the assault and tossed its head backwards, slamming it down on the bridge of Willie's nose. White spots instantly started dancing across the insides of Willie's eyes and his grip faltered. The thing shook itself violently as it clawed into Grady, and Willie went flying off its back into a nearby headstone. Grady lost his grip on the slimy torn flesh of the thing's chest and slipped to the ground. In a quick jab, the corpse shoved its entire skeletal hand into Grady's abdomen, leaving behind a huge tear as it withdrew it. Grady howled in pain and part of his intestines bubbled out of the gash in his stomach. He lay there clutching at them, trying to hold them in and remain conscious. He was helpless, and what was worse, he saw that the thing had now turned its attention to Willy. It wobbled forward toward the boy.

Willie was dazed. His nose was broken and a large lump had sprung up on the back of his head. He tried to force himself to focus his eyes but the pain and the tears would only permit a hazy, blurred vision of something moving in his direction. He rolled over and pulled himself along using the base of the stone. He couldn't seem to get his legs working, something was holding them back. When he turned and looked fuzzily down the length of his body, he saw with panicked horror that the corpse thing was gripping him by his ankle. Slowly, it drew him toward itself, its fingers stabbing through his jeans and into the flesh of his legs.

CHAPTER 107

Eric took a final look behind at the mausoleum where Gwen and Ernie were holed up. He said a silent prayer that they would be safe there, even though he wasn't a praying man. Still clutching at his pocket watch, he made his way through the darkness toward the fiery blue glow that pierced the sky. He kept telling himself that he was a fool to be out here in the cemetery preparing to do battle with God-knows-what at his age. But beneath that voice was another that told him that if he went home, everything he knew and cared about would be lost. So he trudged on, picking his way between the headstones and keeping his eye on the blazing blue that punched upwards ahead of him.

Rounding one of the rows he came to a sudden halt. The blue beacon dwindled away and died out. Something had happened and he was sure that it wasn't a good sign. Steeling himself, he picked up his pace and hurried forward.

***

In the mausoleum, Gwen sat on the cold stone floor next to Ernie. She was grappling with her thoughts, attempting to latch onto something that would mean something to her. Various images and ideas flitted across the screen of her mind like a disjointed trailer to some bizarre movie. Nothing seemed to be making any kind of sense. An office of some kind, with bars on the windows, flashed by and was replaced by a picture of herself ... but not herself. This was replaced with an image of stacks and stacks of dusty books ... and, for the briefest of moments, she was gazing longingly at some man's ass. But that faded too, dissolving into a picture of some woman with large, barely covered breasts, stiletto heels and a skirt hiked up to her butt sitting on a bench in the unknown office she'd seen before.

A growl of discontent and frustration ebbed out of her and echoed around the concrete chamber. The sound frightened her back into silence, but the frustration did not subside. She looked over at the man lying on the floor next to her. There was something so familiar about him and yet she had no idea who he might be. In an uncharacteristic gesture, she reached out and laid her hand upon his forehead. In that instant, her mind came flooding back. The suddenness of it made her head swim and she thought she was going to pass out. She leaned back against the cold concrete and block walls and waited for the dizziness to pass. When it had, Gwen Archibald was back and the events of the past two days flooded in on her like a tsunami. All except the last few hours.

A chill ran up her spine as she recalled the old, decaying couple that had been having sex in the warehouse and how she had been led there by ... by ... Penny Bishop. That in itself was odd because she and Penny Bishop had had only a nodding acquaintance. And what else? There was something that she was going there to see in the first place, but that was still a mystery. She shook her head, trying to clear more cobwebs and trying to figure out exactly how she'd ended up here. And by the way, she wondered, where the hell was here? She looked around at the dark room in which she was sitting. There was a dank musty smell to it and, from what she could see, it was just a concrete room, like some kind of bunker or something. When her eyes skidded across the floor they came to rest on Ernie. She recognized him immediately and knelt down beside him.

"Ernie? Ernie?" She tried to recall the last bits of forgotten time, but it just wasn't coming. Everything else seemed to have come back so clearly, but she just couldn't pin down the last two or three hours.

Ernie's eye rolled in his head, making his eyelids undulate, but he never opened them. There was definitely something seriously wrong with him. But what? She stood up and edged her way slowly to the opening. Some, but not much light was filtering in from outside, so that would probably be a good place to start. When she got to the doorway, she stopped dead in her tracks. She was in a cemetery. Of all places for God's sakes, she was in a cemetery. And at night. What the hell was going on? was the only thought that seemed to fit the situation.

There was a thick fog covering everything and the moon seemed to be frozen above the horizon, giving the whole place a dull, lusterless glow. She stepped outside and into the center of a row of stones. Looking from side to side, she couldn't pinpoint exactly where she was but at least she knew the cemetery. She was in Peaceful Haven. Christ! How the hell did I get here? was her next thought.

As she stood there gazing into the wet blackness, a shape lumbered into view at the end of the headstone row. It waddled like a drunken duck, teetering from side to side. At one point, it pitched forward and something rolled across the lawn and out of view behind one of the stones. Gwen couldn't quite make out what it was. A moment later, the drunk seemed to right himself and then it turned and began to fumble its way toward her.

Halfway up the row, the thing came into view. There was no mistaking the fact that it was a corpse. Even from a distance of fifty feet or so, Gwen could see it had no head. The bones that had once supported it jutted upward from its oozing neck, wagging back and forth as it trundled along.

Anyone else would probably have felt a shooting sense of panic. But Gwen was cut from a different stone. Unlike her sister Audrey, she had ridden patrol before, was certified in the use of deadly force and was not the least bit deterred by the thought of having to use it. Her first thought, then, was to go for her gun. Unfortunately, while working the desk, she never wore it. There was nothing but hip on her hip.

When she looked up again, the thing had made considerable progress, considering it had no head and its balance was worse than a toddler's. Gwen looked around for a good sturdy stick, but there seemed to be none available. The grounds around where she stood were totally pristine.

Just my fuckin luck, she thought. *I would end up in the place that old Jasper Collins had just freshly cut. Wait'll I get my hands on him. Who does he think he is, going around doing a good job?* The thought made her smile, but when she looked up, the smile slid off her face like eggs off a Teflon frying pan. An arm shot out and grabbed her by the collar and yanked her forward. She was surprised at how strong the thing was considering its condition.

In a quick self-defense move, Gwen snagged its right wrist (the one holding her collar) with her right hand and turned it over, rotating it around the axis of its arm toward its chest. The neck bones bobbed backward and then forward again as the brittle radius snapped apart like an overcooked chicken bone. Gwen guessed that the silly looking movement of its neck would have been accompanied by a scream of pain, had it had a head.

It dropped to its knees, temporarily cradling its broken wrist with the other arm. It was a comical sight, but Gwen quickly learned that there was nothing funny about its intent. Thrusting its arm forward, the broken end of the bone sank into Gwen's calf and she went down hard with a loud scream of pain. Before she could gather herself, the thing withdrew the arm and stabbed it down a second time, this time sinking into the flesh of her upper thigh.

Another scream of intense pain.

She kicked at it with her other leg, hitting it square in the chest with the ball of her foot and driving it backwards. It slammed down hard, making a squishy, hissing sound as its gas-bloated torso cracked open on the wet grass.

Gwen wrapped her hands around the upper wound in her leg. That was the deeper of the two and she could feel the blood flowing out freely. The whole time she kept an eye on the writhing thing on the ground as it tried to right itself and find her again. Fortunately, without a head, it had crawled in the wrong direction, but it was working hard at turning around.

Gwen tried to stand, but the gashed leg wouldn't support her. She had to pull herself up using a headstone and then hop and limp down the row. She hadn't gotten very far when she remembered that Ernie was lying helpless just inside the mausoleum – an easy target. A wave of anger shot through her as she envisioned the thing mauling him to death. She turned to face it, steeling herself for a battle that, by all intents and purposes, should have been easy to win, but would now be a contest of wills, considering she could only support herself on one leg. Nevertheless, whatever that thing was, it wasn't going to get Ernie. Not if Gwen Archibald had anything to say about it.

***

Eric trotted off down the row, his head swiveling from side to side to catch any sign of movement. At one point he thought he'd seen something walking along a few rows up and stopped to look, but whatever it might have been had already disappeared into the surrounding fog. He let out a long, low sigh and turned to continue his journey toward the now gone source of light.

He took three steps and then broke into a trot. He glanced over his shoulder and when he did he ran hard into something, lost his balance and fell. A split second later a hand was on his upper arm and pulling him up to his feet. The whole time, his hand never left the bib pocket or the watch. The fall jarred him hard and his consciousness wavered.

When his eyes cleared, he was being helped to his feet.

"Are you ok?" someone asked. The voice was familiar but it did not belong to the face of the person who had pulled him up to his feet. That face belonged to a woman. A rather beautiful woman, Eric thought. But the voice belonged to Father Jacobs. A second later he connected the face with the voice as Jacobs stepped around Arliss.

"What are you doing here, Eric?" asked Jacobs. "You need to leave. Now!"

"Can't leave, Father. I have business t'take care-a. Very dark business. It's you ... you're the one who should leave this place just as quick as ya c'n. It ain't safe here." He placed a hand on Jacobs's shoulder and drew him in closer, whispering in his ear. "Afore ya ski-daddle, liken ya should, ya gotta go fetch up Gwen Archibald and Ernie Johnson. I got em stashed in the old Hoffner's mausoleum. Gwen ain't 'memberin much; don't even know 'er own name. An' Ernie's e'en worse off. Banged his head or sumpin and is out colder 'an these here stones."

Eric looked over at the woman who was standing off to the side, next to another man he didn't know. Then he looked back at Jacobs. The concern in his face was as genuine as the urgency that was pasted there.

"C'mon Father. Ya ain't got time t'dillydally. Things is poppin an' if ya don't watch yerself, you'll get popped, too, I'll warrant."

"It's ok, Eric. My friends and I are here to take care of things. So why don't you just go back and hole up with Ernie and Gwen. Let us take care of this."

Eric's hand never left his bib pocket. Standing off to the side, Arliss had stretched her mind out and probed into his, seeking the identity of what it was he guarded so seriously. When the image of the watch came into her head through his thoughts, she immediately reached out an arm and laid it on Jacobs's shoulder.

"Never mind, Father. This man has a purpose here. He needs to come with us."

"Who *are* these people?" Eric asked, a concerned and skeptical look plastered across his face.

"Trust me, Eric. They're friends. Perhaps even saviors."

Eric looked at them a long time, studying their features. Then he looked back at Jacobs.

"Well, they got good faces, I'll say that much. An' if'n yer satisfied with their comp'ny ... then I guess ol' Eric Baxter is, too. But I'm tellin ya. There's evil afoot here an' it ain't no man we're dealin with. That much I'm sure of."

"You're right about that," said Geoffrey. "What we're dealing with here is pure evil ... of a kind I've never seen before, and trust me ... I've seen a lot. This is no game-"

"It doesn't matter," interrupted Arliss. "He's supposed to be here. He's the gateway lock."

"What?" asked Geoffrey, disbelief and surprise written across his face. "He's the gateway?"

"Show Mr. Dunsmore here what you have in your bib pocket, please, Mr. Baxter."

"How do you know what I got in m'pockets?"

"I saw it in your mind."

"In my mind? Are you crazy, girl. What're ya playin at?"

"Please," broke in Father Jacobs, "trust us, Eric. Show them what you've got in your pocket."

"Well, I don't like it much, but I trust *you*, Father."

He dipped into his pocket and pulled out the watch. He held it up by its chain. When he did, it began to spin, slowly at first, and then faster and faster until it was just a shiny blur. Then, blue light began to pulse out of it in waves. They widened and then collapsed in upon themselves and then repeated it again and again.

Geoffrey reached out and closed his fist around it and the light died out.

"I don't think we want to be doing that," he said. "Draws too much attention. Why don't you let me-"

Arliss interrupted him again. "NO! He's got to keep it. The whole thing is now going to rest with him."

"Are you sure about that?" questioned Geoffrey.

"Absolutely. He either succeeds ... or ... we all fail."

"Succeeds at what?" asked Eric.

"I'm afraid that you'll have to discover that for yourself. We each have a part to play, and no one of us can determine exactly what it is the other will do to either make things right or-"

"Yeah, I got the picture," coughed Eric. "Or make things so wrong nobody goes home. Ain't that it?"

Arliss just nodded.

"Come on," said Geoffrey. "I think we're all headed to the same place, so maybe we better get on with it."

"Yer goin t'the blue light that ain't there no more?"

"That's right."

"He's there, ain't he? Whatever that blue light was ... or is ... he's got control of it now, don't he?"

"I'm afraid so, mate. I'm afraid so."

"Then let's git t'gittin and get this here falderal over wi'."

CHAPTER 108

Jack and Ethan made their way through the headstones on their bellies. Four rows away from the mausoleum on which Carlton stood, they stopped and watched in awe and horror as the Betorak killed and toasted him.

"What the fuck are we dealing with here?" whispered Jack, his voice so low that Ethan could barely understand him.

Before Ethan could answer, the thing on top of the mausoleum turned and screamed out in a thundering bellow: "I am coming for you, now. Can you hear me? You cannot win now. I have the sword. It is once again complete and full. I am the commander of Lucifer's Pommel and that will herald your destruction."

The two men looked at each other. There was no need for words. Each was feeling the same thing. It was as if they'd fallen into some horribly real nightmare. Not fifty yards from them, some devil-like creature that could *only* exist in nightmares was screaming about destruction and retribution.

A cold shiver ran up Jack's spine and he got a sudden, disquieting feeling that he would not see home again and that any plans he had had concerning Linda Killerman would never come to fruition. An image of him being literally torn apart by the thing on the mausoleum roof filled his mind and he had to fight to bring his thoughts back around to the here and now.

"Come on, Ethan, I think we'd better make our way back to Linda. I don't think there's much we can do here. Unless you think you wanna stand up and take a few shots at that thing."

Ethan nodded, but then their attention was drawn back to the thing on the roof. It let out a long wail of consuming rage. Its voice boomed over their heads, bringing thick tree branches crashing down. The ground shook and headstones split and tumbled to the grass, embedding themselves upside down in the soft sod. One missed Ethan's leg by only a couple of inches. When they looked up, the thing launched itself into the sky, hovered there a few moments and then streaked off.

"C'mon," yelled Jack as he jumped to his feet. "I don't think we need to crawl around anymore. Any ideas how we're going to fight that thing?"

"Well," said Ethan a bit sarcastically, "I guess we *could* try walking up to it and blowing its ugly head into next week with the shotgun. But I'm also guessing it would be as effective as shooting spitballs at a crocodile."

"Yeah. Well, we better think of something. There has to be something we can do."

They started off back in the direction they'd come. The thing from the mausoleum circled over them twice. Jack thought that it had to have seen them but was apparently disinterested. That didn't make him feel any more comfortable though. He had seriously thought about taking a shot at it, and he thought that he just might the next time it came around, but then he thought that, perhaps, a better plan might be in order (although he had absolutely no idea what that plan might entail.)

He turned his head skyward, only for a moment, and ran straight into a man coming around the other end of the headstone row. The man had seen him in time and had grabbed him by the shoulders before they smacked into each other.

"Bloody hell," the man said, a stern look on his face. "If you're going to be charging around here willy-nilly you should at least look where you're going, mate."

Jack looked the man up and down and Ethan was standing ready, his good hand already balled into a fist. When Jack looked into the man's eyes they seemed to draw him in, like a hearth fire. He found himself staring into their crystal blueness, and as he did his whole body relaxed.

Ethan just watched and waited to see what was going to happen. At this point, he didn't trust anyone, especially someone who was skulking around a cemetery in the dead of night. When he thought of *that*, he smiled to himself, because, by that way of thinking, he shouldn't trust himself either.

"Who are you?" asked Jack. "And what the hell are you doing here?"

Geoffrey had sized Jack up almost instantly. The sheriff's uniform was a dead giveaway as to what his position in the town was, and when he had looked into his eyes he had seen only sincerity, kindness, and seriousness.

"Look, mate, I can see you're the sheriff, but I don't think there's bloody much you can do around here. Not in this situation. My best advice would be to leave now. Besides-" Geoffrey closed his eyes for a few moments and then opened them slowly. "-From what I can see, you're bloody well needed back in your town. The place is going to hell in a handbasket, as you chaps are fond of saying, and they could really use your help."

"First of all-" spat out Jack. He wasn't accustomed to taking orders from strangers, nor was he accustomed to people in his town ignoring his questions. "-I asked you who you are. And I want a straight answer. Second of all, what the hell are those things you're carrying and what EX-ACTLY do you plan on doing with them in our little cemetery?"

"My name is Geoffrey Dunsmore. I'm here with Father Gabriel Jacobs. As to the rest, if you haven't seen our friend yet ... you're in for an eyeful. It's not like anything you've ever dealt with. But it *is* right up *my* alley."

"And just what alley would that be?" asked Ethan, stepping up alongside Jack. "You think you're going to be able to tackle that ... that *thing* by yourself with ... what *are* those anyway? A couple of statuettes, a diamond broach and a couple of flat rocks?" Ethan was pointing at the things Geoffrey had dropped on the ground when he'd caught hold of Jack. Then he turned and faced Jack.

"I think our friend here just wormed his way out of a straightjacket."

"Don't be so bloody sure, mate," said Geoffrey, very sternly. "Trust me ...or don't. I don't really care. The bottom bloody line is ... if you stay here, you'll die. Is that clear enough?"

For a fleeting second, Jack thought about cuffing him and dragging him away with them. But before he could even reach for the cuffs, the trees around them began to sway, crack, and buckle. Huge splinters of wood flew in all directions and the last set of headstones in the row were blown over like dominoes as a dark shaped descended from the fog above and landed in front of them, and behind Geoffrey. Its black wings beat back and forth slowly as it snarled at them.

Jack and Ethan backed up a few steps and Geoffrey turned quickly to face it, bent down and snatched up the items he'd dropped. It took a heavy step forward, bringing up a large sword whose blade was burning with a blue fire. Jack and Ethan kept backing up one step at a time, Jack bringing the shotgun to the ready. He thought: If that Geoffrey guy would move out of the way, I'd have a clean shot at its head.

Geoffrey backed up, too, but more slowly than Jack or Ethan. His legs were bent, and Ethan recognized the stance from his years of Tae Kwon Do. Geoffrey was preparing to fight. Ethan admired his courage but questioned his sanity.

The Betorak took a large leap forward, landing only a few feet from Geoffrey. It raised the sword above its head, like a Native American would have raised a bow in triumph. Its smell, the smell of putrefied flesh, was smothering. A thick black liquid dripped from its large, pointed fangs. Tilting its head back, it bellowed out a roar that shook the ground.

Jack moved sideways through a pair of headstones into the next row hoping to get a clear shot. When he did, he noticed that the thing seemed to take no note of him whatsoever. Its whole concentration was bent on Geoffrey. Leveling the gun, Jack squeezed off both barrels at the same time, then quickly pumped it and squeezed off a second round of two.

All four barrel blasts found their mark, but for all the damage they did, Jack might just as well have been shooting an air rifle. The thing staggered back a few steps and let out a great roar of anger. Light filtered through the holes that had been punched in the things bat-like, leathery wings, but it soon faded as the thick webbing filled itself in again.

Now it turned its attention on Jack. Its green eyes fixed on him and it began to laugh. It was an insulting kind of laugh. It was the kind of laugh an older child laughs when a younger one can't quite reach the toy being held over his head.

"So you want to play, too?" it growled. "Very well. But I, myself, have no time to waste on your feeble attempts at bravery. Let's see how you do with my children." It swiveled its head from side to side, scanning the cemetery. Then, in a powerful, echoing voice it commanded: "Rise, my stone companions.   Rise and destroy those who would hinder your master."

The echo that wafted across the still cemetery sent chills down Jack's spine and caused the hairs on the back of his neck to stand on end instantly. The sounds of great masses of stone and slag being moved came thundering in from all directions. The ground shook in a series of jarring thuds.

"What the hell is that?" yelled Ethan above the thundering din.

Jack whirled around and couldn't believe what he was looking at. At the far end of the row, three stone gargoyles were lumbering towards them. Their strides were slow and heavy, their mouths agape, the lips curled back like rabid dogs'.

"Holy shit! What the hell?" cried Jack.

Keeping his attention focused on the Betorak, Geoffrey tossed the two ruby hornets to Ethan.

"Here," he yelled.

Ethan caught them both in his only functioning hand and looked at them questioningly.

"What the fuck? Do I look like your manservant? Hold your own damned toys."

"Toss em up in the air. As high as you possibly can."

"What the hell are you talking about?"

"Do it. Toss them up in the bloody fucking air over top of those gargoyles."

Ethan just stared at them for a moment, then, he turned and heaved them as high as he could in the direction of the stone things that were plodding toward them.

As the statuettes neared the height of their arc they began to glow. At first, it was no more than the glow a match would give off, then it grew. Bright red circles surrounded them as they climbed through the night fog. Just before they began to drop, the statues split and exploded; shards of ruby stone came raining downward in fiery points of light. From inside the stone, two large, ruby-red wasps came into being. They measured almost eight feet from head to stinger, their large lacy wings beating the air. They hovered there, side by side, then shot up and came plummeting downward. Each landed on one of the gargoyles, its abdomen thrusting forward. Their stingers lanced though the stone, right in the center of the two gargoyle bellies and they both split apart. It looked as if a diamond cutter had found exactly the right spot. The gargoyles split into equal halves, each dropping to the ground. The wasps immediately turned on the third. It was swatting furiously and ineffectively at them as they buzzed around it. They grabbed at it with their huge insect legs, picking it up in succession and dropping it to the ground. At one point, it tried to use its wings to fly. As soon as it had gotten airborne, the wasps attacked it from front and rear. Landing on its back and its belly, they jabbed their massive stingers through it. It exploded into a cloud of dust and stone debris.

Jack and Ethan could only watch in awe. Tree branches swayed and boughs bent in the great wind the wasp's wings created. And the buzzing sound they made was so loud that Jack thought it was going to split his eardrums. He had his hands plastered over them and the humming was still overpowering.

Behind Jack and Ethan, Geoffrey had taken out his two onyx discs and his diamond-edged, half dollar-sized oval. He tucked one of the onyx discs into his belt and then pressed down on the center of the oval. It began to expand in his hand, growing wider and wider. The diamonds along the edge began to fill in the growing plate, winding inwards in opposite concentric circles. When the oval had attained its full diameter (about two feet), the last of the diamonds slid into the center and expanded outward, forming a long spike. Geoffrey took a step backward, adjusting the newly formed shield on his arm. The flattened onyx disc he held tightly in the other hand as if he were preparing to toss a Frisbee.

The Betorak bellowed at the destruction of its gargoyle minions and then boomed out a long, raspy laugh. It fixed its glowing green eyes on Geoffrey, its tongue lashing in and out. Holding the sword high, it beat its black-gray leathery chest with its free hand and strode forward.

CHAPTER 109

When they'd made the decision to split up, Jacobs wasn't exactly comfortable with having Eric go with him. He would have much preferred to stay with Geoffrey. But he was a team player and if

Geoffrey and Arliss thought that the split was right, who was he to argue. They'd said their farewells, each hoping that when it was all said and done they'd all see one another again but seriously doubting that outcome. Arliss and Geoffrey had gone in separate directions as well, leaving Jacobs and Eric to hunt down the living corpses that roamed free, with the admonishment to avoid at all costs the Betorak itself. It was beyond anything they could do. That job would be left to Arliss and Geoffrey (although Arliss had mentioned something to Eric about being ready to come when called.)

Jacobs noticed that Eric never took his hand away from his bib pocket. Silently, he prayed that whatever power lay in that watch would be strong enough to do what was expected of it. He handed Eric one of the bundles of Kahnjal and explained their use.

At the edge of one of the sections, Eric, who had taken the lead (purely by accident), waved his hand behind him, signaling for Jacobs to stop. They waited there a moment, listening to the rustling bushes ahead. There was definitely someone or something up there, trying to make its way through the tangle of branches and brush.

Jacobs wrapped a hand around one of the daggers. As his fingers closed around the cold iron, he could feel the power in them. There had been two sets that Geoffrey had laid out on the ground. The second set had been given to Eric and Jacobs now saw that he too was clutching at one of the Kahnjal, waiting.

When the bushes parted in front of them (Jacobs was blessing himself at the time), a grotesque figure of a being pushed through. Its hair was hanging out in patches, clotted with mud and leaves and old roots. The skin on its face was a gray-green and had a waxy sheen to it. The eyes were glassy and opaque, like clouded marbles. Half of its nose was missing and clumps of dirt and grass hung from it moldy suit jacket and stuck out of its trouser cuffs. It was missing one shoe and the skinless toes of that foot poked through the socks.

When it spotted them, it turned and hissed. It tried to curl its lips back in a menacing snarl but the rotted skin just flapped loosely up and down. It moved toward them, steadily taking one step at a time, the legs shaking only slightly. It was in better shape than the one that had attacked Grady, having only been buried two and a half years ago. It came forward, stopping when it crunched down on a stick. It looked at the ground, stooped and picked up the broken stick, its point crudely sharpened in the snap. And then it came forward again, holding the stick above its head, point down.

Jacobs marveled at the level of cognition it was displaying, but never forgot what he had to do. He slowly withdrew one of the Kahnjal and held it against his leg, hoping the thing couldn't see it there in the dark. In front of him, Eric pulled out one of his as well and was holding it out in front of him like a foil.

When it was close enough, Eric lunged at it, aiming for the center of its chest. With surprising fluidity, the thing stepped sideways and Eric went right by it, losing his balance and falling flat on his face in the grass with a thud. The air rushed out of him in a gasping whoosh and he couldn't seem to get it back. The thing bore down on him as he lay there breathless and stunned.

The scream was ear-splitting. Its wailing cry cracking through the empty night like nails on a chalkboard, as Jacobs's dagger rammed through its back and came out the front, slicing like butter right through its breastbone. Its arms flailed wildly; the stick it was holding tumbled through the air and disappeared into the brush from where the thing had emerged. It grabbed at the point of the Kahnjal that stuck out of its chest, but each time its fingers came in contact with the pointed iron, sparks flew off it and the fingers burst into tiny flames. It staggered in circles for a few moments, crying in anguish, then it fell forward and stopped moving.

Jacobs helped Eric to his feet, asked him if he was ok, and when he was satisfied that he was, he walked over to the corpse and gave it a kick, just to be sure. When it didn't move, he reached down and pulled the Kahnjal out of it.

As soon as the point cleared the body, the thing began to stir. It pushed itself up on its hands and almost made it back to its feet before Jacobs reinserted the dagger, leaving it where it was this time. The thing dropped forward and didn't move again.

"Well," said Jacobs. "Guess we only get one use out of each of these things, huh?"

Eric picked up the one he'd dropped, looked at it and then at Jacobs.

"Sure hope we got 'nuff of em. I ain't too
happy 'bout the thoughts a runnin short. Just hope
there's more stickers here than there are things t'use
em on." He smiled.

***

After Jack and Ethan had crawled off, Linda
sat back against a headstone and checked the
Glock's load a second time. She didn't care for the
idea of sitting there alone in the dark, but what
bothered her more was just sitting there doing
nothing. She'd never been much for watching
without participating. Whether it was helping the
contractors lay the retaining wall or rewiring the
kitchen herself, she'd always been a doer. Now,
sitting still was really getting on her nerves. She
wasn't sure what, if anything, she could really do,
but she *was* sure that she had to do *something*.

Suddenly, things got darker. The blue light
that had cast its eerie glow across the cemetery had
faded away. Then, a thunderous wail split the
silence. Two of the headstones next to her fell over
and a tree branch broke free from its trunk and came
crashing down, missing her by only a few feet and
completely flattening a sandstone marker and the
empty brass flower vase that sat in front of it.

"Ok, that's it!" she said to no one but herself.
"Time to get your ass up and do something." She
heaved herself to a standing position and peered off
into the blackness. She could see the matted grass
path that Jack and Ethan had left behind them. She
thought about following them and then decided that

she'd go around in the opposite direction. That way, she figured, if anything was going on, she'd be able to come in from the other side to help out and not have everyone bunched up together.

It would have been better if she'd had a flashlight was the thought that crossed her mind next, but things were as they were and she'd have to make the best of it. Moving carefully and watchfully down the row of stones, she came to the composite roadway that snaked through the cemetery proper. Keeping to the edge, she walked along it, heading towards the heart of the cemetery and the place where the blue light had been. She figured that if there was going to be anything going on, that's where it would be.

Up ahead, the road curved gently around to the right like the handle of a cane. For an instant, Linda thought she saw someone step out, look up and down the road and then fade back around the corner. In the dark and fog, visibility was, at best, sketchy and she wasn't certain whether or not she had really seen anything at all. But to be on the safe side she moved over and crouched down behind one of the headstones and waited to see what, or who, would come down the road. She had gotten a fleeting feeling when she'd seen the – whatever it might have been – that it was not friendly. So down behind the stone she waited and listened.

Then it came, like a thousand overhead, high-powered electric lines all surging at once. The humming buzz ripped across the cemetery's dead night stillness, filling her ears and vibrating the ground on which she was crouched. She looked around but couldn't pinpoint exactly where the sound was coming from. It seemed to come from all directions at once. The thick fog did that, it pressed everything together, enhancing and muting sound at the same time.

Had she been looking in the opposite direction only a moment before, she would have seen the two circles of shimmering red in the sky, just before they exploded into the huge wasps that had been born of that explosion. But her concentration had been bent on the movement she spotted ahead. Now, all that was left was the tremendous buzzing sound that filled her head.

After waiting what she felt to be an appropriate length of time with nothing much happening, she stood up and peered over the stones that made their endless alleyways. From what she could see, nothing was moving. She strained her ears, hoping to hear the slightest rustle but all she could hear was the endless buzz that filled the skies. It was then that the cold, foul and dripping hand clamped down on her shoulder and dragged her backwards.

***

Arliss had not gone very far after leaving Geoffrey before she ran into one of the corpses. Lifting the half-moon object she carried above her head, she gave the shaft a twist. The end extended instantly, flattening, curving and elongating into a razor-sharp scimitar. With a single swipe, the corpse's head was instantly parted from its shoulders. It stumbled backward, its arms clawing frantically at the empty air in front of it. Arliss brought the sword down again and cleaved the thing in two from top to bottom. For a moment, it stood there, and then both halves peeled apart and fell to the ground.

"That was easy enough," muttered Arliss. "I don't guess it's all going to be this easy, is it?" she said to no one. Whipping the sword back and forth in front of her a few times, she admired its weight.

"Ok. On to bigger and nastier things." She hurried forward.

CHAPTER 110

Willie squirmed and kicked at the thing that was pulling him toward it by his leg. Several kicks had rocked it backwards but its grip held firm. He rolled over onto his back and started thrashing his legs wildly, like a toddler throwing a tantrum. The up and down motion was too fast for the thing to keep up with and it lost its grip. As soon as it did, Willie jumped to his feet. His head hurt and his leg and nose were still bleeding, but those things didn't concern him. What had his full attention was what he was going to do to save his father.

As the corpse recovered itself, pulling itself up to its knees, Willie charged it. With a howl of anger, he leaped into the air, wrapped his legs around its torso, and began clawing at its face and eyes, his fingernails sinking into the soft, squishy globes. Viscous yellow-green fluid ran down his fingers and the thing tumbled backward onto the ground.

Willie had experienced anger before, but never like this. This was pure rage. His fists were clenched so tightly that his fingernails bit into the flesh of his palms as he pummeled the thing beneath him. His balled fists pounded down on the corpse's skull. The sharp sound of cracking bone could barely be heard beneath Willie's bellows of fury as the thing's head was literally flattened to the ground. A black liquid oozed across the grass from the brain cavity and, eventually, the decayed arms and hands that clawed at Willie dropped limply down beside the battered body.

Willie kept pounding at the thing until his strength to continue was completely gone. Tears streamed down his cheeks and his breath came in ragged puffs and grunts. Forcing himself, he stood up and looked over at his father who had been trying to crawl over to help him.

"Pop," he cried and he knelt beside Grady. "Oh God, what am I going to do?"

Grady reached out an unsteady hand and grabbed Willie by the upper arm. Blood oozed from the corners of his mouth and dripped from his nose. His other hand was pressed firmly against the gash in his abdomen, his intestines bulging around it.

"You got t'git yerself home now, son. Do you hear me? There ain't nothin ya can do for me now. You and I both know that. Ya got t'get home and take care of your moth-"

Grady's arm dropped away from Willie's shoulder as his eyes rolled back and his head thumped to the ground. Willie caught him around the neck and hugged him to him.

"But you can't die, pop. You can't. Me and Ma need you."

"I'm sorry, boy. But you can't help yer pop now. He's gone. And we gotta find a way t'get outta here too." Jasper's voice was quiet but shaky. He had crawled over and laid a hand on Willie's shoulder. "It's hard a-septin what life throws atcha, but what's done is done. I ain't trying to be mean er without symp'thy, but the facts is the facts. And one fact is ... if we don't get movin, we're gonna end up just like your poor old pop here. And then where would your Ma be without both of you."

Jasper smiled as best he could. The pain in his leg was sending waves of fiery sparks up and down his entire body, but he knew he and the boy had to get out of there.

"But I can't just leave im here," cried Willie. "I can't."

Jasper's face took on a stern, parental hardness that even he didn't know he had. "You can leave 'im. You can and you will. Now come on, before more a-them things come along." He reached out, and with all his might, he tugged Willie back away from the body of his father. "Come on now; you got t'help me. I can't make it without you, son."

Willie was torn. He knew that what Jasper was telling him was right, but the thought of just leaving his father behind like discarded trash thrashed at his brain. The "what-to-do" was decided for him a moment later when another copse tottered into view at the far end of the row.

"C'mon, boy. Help me up. We gotta go. NOW!"

*   *   *

Its finger-stubs tightening around her throat, the corpse of Lenny Carson, all rotting three hundred pounds, pulled Linda back into the brush. His grip, even with rot-weakened fingers, was incredibly strong. No matter how she struggled, Linda could not break free. Reaching down, she pulled the Glock from the waist of her pants, but she had no target. Lenny had her back pressed up against his chest, his massive hand slowly closing her windpipe.

She tried to work the gun around to the side to get at least a shot at his leg, hoping that would loosen his grip. But by the time she had it in position, he'd noticed her arms moving and had grabbed her by the wrist. His fingers closed around the wrist and thumb and squeezed. The Glock dropped to the ground. A gurgling sound sputtered out of her throat as she felt herself beginning to lose consciousness.

Suddenly, just before everything went black, Lenny slammed her to the ground. He stood over her, watching as she wheezed and coughed, trying to catch her breath.

Linda tried to focus; everything was swimming. She stretched out her hand, probing the nearby ground for the dropped gun. She had just laid the tip of her fingers on the butt when Lenny stomped down hard on them. The cracking echoed through the dark, accompanied by the scream of pain she let out. Then, she felt his weight on the wrist of her other hand as he stamped down on that. She was pinned to the ground by her wrists and there was no way she was going to move three hundred pounds.

Linda looked up, tears streaming down the sides of her cheeks. What she saw sent her into a fit of screaming and thrashing around. Above her, Lenny was staring down, his blackened tongue licking at his rubbery lips. His face was contorted as if he were trying to come to a decision that was just beyond his mentally compromised capabilities (a trait carried over into death with him.) Then he grinned. It was a hideous and sinister grin, fashioned from the remains of long-dead facial muscles. But that wasn't what had sent the shock of terror through her. No! What did that was what he was doing. He was undoing his trousers, and there was no question as to what he intended to do next.

Linda kicked and screamed and thrashed. She could feel the broken fingers of her right hand wrenching themselves around inside the flesh as she pulled and twisted the hand in a vain attempt to free herself. She ignored the pain. It was nothing compared to what she envisioned was about to happen if she didn't free herself fast.

Lenny moved so that he was at her head and staring down the length of her body. He dropped his knees on her shoulders, his putrefying genitals hanging over her face. Under the weight, any movement above the waist was impossible. She tried to pull her hips up as far as she could and began kicking at his head. Lenny reached down, a slimy ooze dripping onto Linda's face, and ripped her shirt open. With his hands free now, pinning her solely with his knees, he grabbed the cuffs of her pants, twisting them so that they cinched her legs together. No matter how she tried, she could not move them, nor could she worm herself free. The unthinkable was about to happen and she was helpless to do anything about it.

Pinned on the ground, her legs held together straight up in the air, and Lenny's other hand struggling to free her breasts from her bra, she tried biting but couldn't bring her head forward enough.

A soft whistling sound broke through the air, just barely audible above Linda's screams. It was followed by another and then another. Two seconds later, Lenny Carson pitched forward, his immense, rotting frame falling squarely on Linda, knocking the wind completely out of her.

Everything was black and she was pinned even more tightly to the ground. Her chest tried to rise, tried to draw in the needed oxygen, but couldn't. She was certain that this was it. She pushed but couldn't budge him, her hands just sinking fruitlessly into the flabby flesh.

Not a moment too soon, the body was pulled up and off her and the damp night air rushed back into her deprived lungs. She gasped, drawing in each breath as deeply as she could. When she was finally able to look up, a woman she'd never seen before was standing over her. In her right hand was a long curved sword. In the other were two objects that looked like darts.

"That a little better?" asked the woman, her voice soft but firm.

"Yes," stammered Linda. "Thanks." A fit of coughing seized her and she just waved a hand.

"Don't mention it," said Arliss. "Here. Let me help you up." Arliss bent and pulled Linda to her feet in one sweeping motion. Her strength surprised Linda.

"I won't ask what it is you're doing here," said Arliss, "I assume that we're, for one reason or another, all in this together now. How many more of you are in here?"

Linda held up a hand. "Hold on a minute," and then walked over and gave Lenny a few good kicks in the head. "Sorry, I needed to do that."

Arliss laughed. "Can't say I much blame you for that."

"Before I answer your question, how about telling me who you are? My name's Linda." She would have extended a hand to shake, but she was busy cradling the one with the broken fingers.

"I'm Arliss," came the reply as she walked over to Lenny's body to retrieve the three darts she'd downed him with.

"I'm here with the Sheriff and a friend." She coughed, her throat still burning from Lenny's grip. "I could say that there's been some strange goings on, but I'm sure you already know that." She shot a nod at Lenny's body.

Arliss explained in brief who she was and who she was with while Linda picked up her dropped Glock, checked the action and stuck it back in her waistband.

"You know how to use that thing?" asked Arliss, gesturing at the gun.

"Yeah," snapped Linda. "If I get the shot, I guarantee you ... I won't miss."

"Good. I'm sure you'll have a chance to prove it before we're through. But right now, come on. Things are already happening and my friend, Geoffrey, could use some help."

CHAPTER 111

Gwen's eyes narrowed as she focused her hatred and determination on the thing crawling along the ground toward the mausoleum where Ernie was laying. She instantly dismissed the gash in her thigh; the only thing of importance to her was stopping that hideous creature from hurting her Ernie. Adrenaline began to surge through her system and mixed with her rage creating a perfect cocktail of destruction.

Gwen charged and tackled the headless corpse just as it had managed to work itself upright. The snapping of its fragile bones as her weight drove it into the ground beneath her sounded like firecrackers. Straddling it, she wrapped her fingers around its swaying neck bones with one hand and dug furiously at its back with the other. Its putrid flesh was soft and easy to penetrate, but the cartilage was a different matter. She tugged and pulled, trying to wrench free one of its ribs.

It squirmed and kicked and tried to reach up to grab her. But each time its hand got close, Gwen would give a sharp tug on the neck, forcing its hands back down to the ground to support itself. A couple of times it attempted to stab at her knees with the shard of bone that had been so effective on her thigh. But her legs were just out of reach.

Finally giving up on the upper ribs, Gwen punched through its lower back and tore out one of the floaters. It was much easier to dislodge. As soon as she had it free, she let go of the thing's neck, wrapped both hands around the thickest part of the rib and brought it down fiercely between the writhing corpse's shoulder blades and through its non-beating heart. Its legs and arms jerked a few times and its naked cervical vertebrae waggled back and forth, and then it lay still.

Breathing heavily, Gwen sat up straight and rested on the thing. She felt woozy, and it was hard to catch a breath. She was unaware of just how much blood she'd lost during the fight. But now that it was over, her body was shutting down. She tried to stand, to push herself up off the corpse, but all she could do was slump over sideways. When she reached down to check her thigh, her hand came away soaked in the life-giving liquid that had gushed out of her. Her eyes rolled up in her head and she toppled over.

***

Eric and Father Jacobs took a final look at the corpse lying on the ground with the Kahnjal stuck through its back and then headed off. Rounding the end of a set of headstones, almost dead-center in the cemetery, they pulled up short. Ahead of them, with its back turned, a stone gargoyle was crawling along sniffing the ground. From their angle, it looked like a bloated bulldog with wings.

"How d'ya s'pose we're gonna handle this thing?" whispered Eric.

"Not a blessed clue."

"I don't think these sticky things 'ud do much good. Do you?"

Suddenly, the gargoyle stopped crawling and sniffing and sat up on it haunches. It tilted its head back and drew in deep breaths. Then it let out a low, rumbling growl, jumped to its feet and turned to face the two men. It started toward them, lumbering forward and snapping its jaws open and closed.

"Guess we'd better figure out a plan now, wouldn't you say?" asked Jacobs, a bit sarcastically.

"I vote on runnin."

"Good plan."

The men turned and began to run. But before they could reach the next line of headstones, the thing landed in front of them, its heavy wings folding up behind it and its mouth agape.

"Guess that wasn't a good plan," said Eric.

Inside his bib pocket, the watch began to glow. Eric could feel the warmth it was generating and plucked it out. As soon as it was free of the pocket it began to spin. Waves of bright, blue-white light radiated outward. When the first of these struck the gargoyle, the thing came to a dead stop. Eric held the watch by its fob at arm's length.

The gargoyle tilted its head from side to side, staring blankly into the glow of the rotating watch. Jacobs thought the thing looked like a hapless volunteer at a hypnotist's show.

The waves of light began to encircle the stone beast. They covered it from bottom to top like a stack of old tires. When the last bright wave settled into place on top, the rings began to shrink inward. The look of it reminded Eric of the small white dot that appeared on the screen of old TVs after you turned it off ... shrinking away into blackness. As soon as the outer edges met in the center there was a bright and sudden flash ... and then the light faded. A moment later, the gargoyle fell over, sliced into layers.

"Well," said Jacobs, "That was rather handy of you."

"Not my doin, Father. I never take credit when I ain't done nothin. The watch knew what to do. Not me."

"Come on," prodded the priest. "I got a feeling that everything's coming to a head in the middle of this place. Let's hurry up and get there." He paused, then added, "And don't even think about losing that thing."

"Not a chance, Father. I'd rather lose my nuts first." Eric blushed for a moment, but the darkness obscured it. "Sorry, Father. I fergit m'self sometimes."

Father Jacobs just laughed, the first real laugh he'd had in a long time.

CHAPTER 112

The Betorak leaped forward bringing the blazing sword down hard. Geoffrey pitched to his right, dipping and rolling as he tucked his shoulder underneath him. The sword tip sliced into the ground where he'd just stood. Instantly, the grass went black, the ground began to shudder and split open and clumps of earth flew everywhere.

As Geoffrey rolled to his feet, he tossed the disc he'd been holding into the air at an angle that carried it out behind the Betorak. It hovered there for a few moments, the top and bottom halves separating slightly. Along the edge, razor sharp saw-teeth sprang out. The disc started to whirl and as it picked up speed it shot forward toward the Betorak. At the same moment, Ethan rushed forward and slammed himself headfirst into the Betorak's stomach.

"No!" Geoffrey yelled, but it was already too late. The force of Ethan's impact drove the Betorak backwards a few steps and the disc came whizzing by, missing it by inches. Unfortunately, it didn't miss Ethan. A sharp cry of pain split the battlefield as the disc ripped across Ethan's chest. He pitched forward, clutching at the open wound that was gushing blood.

The Betorak wasted no time; it brought the sword up and was about to finish Ethan for good.

Two loud explosions ripped through the air as the Betorak's sword reached the top of its swing. Jack's shotgun blasts pushed it back and the fiery blue blade missed its mark.

Rage surged through it and it focused its glowing green eyes on Jack. In a bound, it cleared the headstones and landed directly in front of him. Before he could reload, it grabbed him by the throat and lifted him up. Jack's hands immediately tried to break the vice-like grip that was cutting off his air supply, and the gun dropped to the ground.

The Betorak hissed its foul breath into Jack's face and drew back its gray, leathery lips. Then its head rocked backwards and a great cry of pain rose from deep inside it. The disc had arced around, clipping off a large chunk of the Betorak's right wing. It loosened its grip just enough for Jack to worm free and fall to the ground.

Geoffrey rushed over to Ethan. The gash in his chest was deep but not life-threatening. Turning his attention back to the Betorak just in time to see its wingtip go flying, Geoffrey pulled the second disc from his belt and sent it on its way, just barely above the surface of the ground.

The first disc had circled and was coming at the thing from above, its saw-teeth racing around its circumference. In a single motion, the Betorak raised his sword and deflected it, while jumping just high enough for the second to pass underneath him. When he came back down, both discs were headed straight for him.

Clang. K-clang. The sound of metal on metal echoed across the emptiness as the two discs

were sent flying in different directions off the tip of
the Betorak's sword. Both discs started to wobble
and then buried themselves in the ground. The
Betorak let out a great roar of victory and turned
toward Geoffrey.

"Now you shall perish, foolish one. Did you
really think you had it in you to defeat *me*? I
promise-," it said as it bore down on him, "-I'll
make this as painful as possible." And then it
laughed. A long, sonorous and malicious laugh.

The sword came down hard. It clanged off
the edge of Geoffrey's shield with a loud, hollow
ringing. With both clawed hands wrapped tightly
around the hilt, the Betorak beat down on Geoffrey,
whose only defense was the shield he held above
him.

Two more shotgun blasts rang out and the
Betorak staggered sideways. When it did, Geoffrey
grabbed the edges of his shield, and with all his
might, rammed the diamond, spear-like tip upward.
It sank into the Betorak's upper thigh and he went
down hard. The wailing that issued from inside it
was earsplitting, to the point where Geoffrey was
forced to drop the shield and cover his ears.

Swinging wildly, the thing brought the
sword across its chest while still lying there. The
blazing edge hacked through Geoffrey's left
shoulder. A large flap of skin and muscle fell away,
exposing the upper part of his humerus. Geoffrey's
eyes rolled back in his head and he slumped
forward.

Ethan rushed the Betorak a second time as it
struggled to its feet. In a sweeping motion, the

leathery, muscular arm connected with Ethan's chest and sent him tumbling through the air. He smashed up against one of the headstones and flipped over it backwards, landing on his neck. There was an awful cracking sound, like moist sticks in a hot fire.

The Betorak strode toward Geoffrey, stood over top of him and raised the sword with both hands. He held it aloft, point down, directly over Geoffrey's head. With a great, guttural yell, it brought the sword straight down.

***

Arliss and Linda had made it to the edge of the center section when a dazzling light flashed into existence and then disappeared again somewhere off to their left.

"C'mon. Let's find out what that's all about," commanded Arliss. She turned and headed off in the direction of the flash, leaving Linda to try and catch up.

When they rounded a corner of markers they found Father Jacobs and Eric Baxter standing over the sliced gargoyle. Father Jacobs was laughing heartily.

"Having fun?" asked Arliss as she closed the distance between them.

"Not really. No," said Jacobs, a tinge of anger in his voice.

Arliss looked at the gargoyle, then at the two men.

"How'd you manage that?" she said, nodding toward the pile of disc-shaped stones.

Eric just smiled and tapped his bib pocket.

"I see.   Well, apparently, there's more to your watch than even I know.   Come on.   The battle's already begun."

The four of them turned and trotted off toward the heart of the cemetery and the battle that was raging there.

"C'mon. We've got to hur-" Arliss's words were cut off as she let out a piercing yell, grabbed her shoulder and fell forward.

Jacobs was kneeling beside her instantly, his hand resting lightly on her back.

"What's the matter?   Are you all right? What happened?"

Arliss rolled over on her back, still rubbing at her shoulder.   Her eyes were glassy at first but cleared quickly.

"Not me. Geoffrey. Come ON. He's in real trouble. And if we don't get there quickly-" she left the last part to their imaginations.   She scrambled to her feet and took off at a dead run.

Jacobs, Eric, and Linda looked at each other for a moment.

"You two git goin. I'm too old t'run. But I'll catch up. Don't you worry 'bout that none."

Jacobs and Linda took off running.   Eric shook his head and started forward at his own pace.

"Sure wish this shit woulda happened when I was young 'nuff t'handle it all. There's gotta be sumpin' wrong wi' me. Draggin my old ass around a cemetery at night.   Tryin t'fight demons and whatnot. Geez-uz!"

CHAPTER 113

With his leg in a splint, a broken tree limb to lean on and Willie's support, Jasper managed to hobble along. He and the boy weren't moving nearly as fast as he'd like, but at least he was moving. He blamed himself for most of what had happened to him so far. If he had been stronger; if he had resisted; if he had just stayed home, his leg would be fine and the boy's father would probably still be alive. And it was that thought that nagged at him the most. He'd vowed to never again hurt a human being after he returned home safely from Vietnam ... and now ... here he was: responsible for the death of a young boy's father, and who knew what else.

"C'mon, son," he said through gritted teeth, "we gotta keep movin. We gotta get outta here."

Willie hadn't stopped crying, although the sobbing had dwindled to soft moans and lots of sniffles. Jasper was leaning on him heavily. His shoulder felt like it was going to break any minute, but he kept going. He kept going because he knew that that's what his father would want of him. He knew that that's what would make his pop proud of him. And above everything else, his pop's approval was utmost.

When they reached the gravel road between sections, Jasper hobbled over and leaned against a stone. He was winded and his leg was sheer misery. He absently fished around in his shirt pocket for his pack of cigarettes, keeping a wary eye on his surroundings. He had no desire to have to battle any more zombies ... or anything else, for that matter. All he wanted now was a quick smoke and safe passage out of the cemetery.

Willie sat down on the ground in front of Jasper with his knees pulled up to his chest and his arms wrapped tightly around them. At any other time he would have been the first to hear their approach. Now, all he could hear was his father's voice telling him to get home and take care of his mother.

Jasper jumped and let out a little squeal, his cigarette falling out of his mouth, when the hand closed around his shoulder. He landed on his bad leg, screamed louder and collapsed forward, narrowly missing a serious encounter between his forehead and the roadway. Willie was on his feet instantly, mentally preparing himself for another battle.

"Sorry. Didn't mean to scare you," said Father Jacobs. "Guess I should know better, huh?" He bent down and was helping Jasper to an upright position. A few rows over, Arliss was peering off into the night's blackness, almost oblivious to the others in the group, or to the newly found strangers.

"Jumpin Christ but ya sceered the hell outta me, Father. What the ... er ... I mean, what are you doing here, anyway?" Jasper was wincing and speaking through clenched teeth. And even in the pale light, Jacobs could see the fear in his face.

"My guess is that we're here doing what you're doing."

"Huh?"

"Dealing with ... well, dealing with whatever awaits us, I guess."

Jasper blushed and was thankful for the dark to cover it (at least he hoped it covered it.) When the priest said that they were there doing what he was, Jasper thought of how he'd set the abominations loose and shame swallowed his heart.

"Father. Believe me. You're not here doing what I did tonight. And if I could undo it, I would in a second. But there ain't no goin back. And I expect I'll be payin for it in a big way. Bigger even than this." He rubbed his hand lightly up and down the splint on his leg.

"Let's go," broke in Arliss. "We're wasting time. And we don't have any to waste." She started off across the road, not really caring if any of them were following her. She was concentrating on Geoffrey. And on Eric. She knew he was still behind them, and she *knew* that they'd be needing him before long.

On the other side of the road she stopped and turned around, calling to the others.

"Father, go back and hurry Eric along. Don't leave him alone. But please ... hurry. We're out of time." With that, she turned and vanished into the misty blackness, leaving them all to make their way.

Linda had immediately gone to Willie. She cradled him in her arms as he told her of his father and what had happened.

"Perhaps it'd be best if you waited here until I catch up with Eric," said Jacobs. "Much more strength in numbers for all of us."

"Will you be ok going back by yourself?" asked Linda

Jacobs patted the remaining Kahnjals that were tucked in his belt. "I expect so. Besides, I don't think Eric is *that* far behind. Probably be back in a minute or two."

Linda nodded and the priest hurried off back the way they'd come.

CHAPTER 114

Ernie's eyes fluttered open but everything was black except for a small sliver of muted moonlight slipping through the grated door of the mausoleum. He had no idea where he was and his head was throbbing. When he reached up, he could feel the caked blood that had matted his hair to his head. He tried to bring things into focus but everything remained hazy as if he were looking through a thick curtain.

Using the wall for support, he worked himself to his feet, which only caused him to acknowledge the nausea that was now churning his stomach. He wanted to sit back down again but forced himself upright. For a moment, he thought he was going to vomit and the room seemed to be swimming. He clung to the wall and waited. Slowly, the feeling passed and his vision cleared a bit.

At the gate, he cautiously peered outside. He had a vague memory of running into someone and falling, but the pieces were disjointed and he couldn't put a face to the person. He stepped through the doorway and out into the mist, still hanging on to the gate's cold bars for support. Standing there, looking through the drizzle at the cemetery, his mind flashed back to the motel. He shuddered and then staggered out onto the grass, resting up against the first headstone he came to.

As his vision began to clear he could make out a dark shape laying on the ground further up the row. From where he was he couldn't tell exactly what it was but it looked to be someone lying on the ground.   With a great deal of effort and determination, he pushed off from the stone and made his way up the row. Each step made his stomach churn harder and his head throb more steadily. When he reached the shape he'd seen from the headstone he was surprised to see that it was two people, not one. A woman and ... And what? It looked to be a man ... but... He knelt down beside the two; the woman was face down and the other ... *thing?* ... was ... rotted.

That did it. Ernie quickly turned to the side and threw up. He couldn't stop. Even after his stomach was emptied (which was after the first bout) he continued to heave, his stomach twisting and contracting until he could hardly breathe.

When he finally stopped, he knelt there, one hand supporting him and the other on his stomach. He couldn't bear to look at that thing again so he crawled around it on his hands and knees, his head constantly turned in the other direction, until he got to the woman. There was just enough moonlight to see that she was wearing a uniform and Ernie recognized it immediately.

Forgetting his stomach, and in a panic, he grabbed her by the shoulders and turned her face-up.

"Gwen? Gwen!" He shook her by the shoulders. Gently at first, then more vigorously, but she didn't stir.

He began checking her out from head to toe. When he got to her legs he could see that one of them was covered in a dark fluid. And without having to check any further, he knew it was blood. He could smell it, and when he drew his hand away from the wound it was covered in it. He held his hand out in front of him and in the pale light he could see (and feel) that it was already beginning to coagulate. If he'd been able to see better, if he'd had more light, he would have noticed the color. It wasn't dark red venous blood. It was arterial blood, and Gwen was already cold.

Ernie felt for a pulse, first at the wrist and then the carotid. Neither was there.

"No!" he screamed. "No. This can't be. What the hell happened here?"

He looked over at the corpse thing lying partially underneath her. "You did this didn't you?" Tears were freely rolling down his face mixing with the mist that was slowly saturating him. The woman he'd always wanted was lying in his arms at last, but it was not the way he had always envisioned it. He pulled her in close to his chest and sat there rocking back and forth and crying, still not comprehending what was going on or how this could have happened.

***

In the far corner of the cemetery, the ruby hornets were battling a mass of gargoyles. Six of them had gathered at the utility garage and were planning their assault when the hornets swooped in. The first two went quickly, taken completely by surprise, but the remaining four were led by the largest in the cemetery and were much more agile than the ones the hornets had dispatched when they were first released from their stone housings.

Through guttural grunts and clicks, the largest (standing nearly eight feet tall) was directing his army. As the hornets approached, he had them gather back to back with him in the center, making it nearly impossible for either of the large Vespas to find a suitable target. Twice, the leader had nearly beheaded one of them with his marble sword. When they'd retreat to the sky for another dive, the lead gargoyle would dart up after them, its powerful wings beating the murky air. If they turned, he'd retreat to the ground, curling into a ball and covering himself with his stone wings.

The buzz of the wasp's wings as they parried with the gargoyles reverberated throughout the cemetery, cutting through the damp stillness. From a distance, it sounded like someone was busy sawing lumber. Like the gargoyles, the wasps communicated too. But their communication was chemical and inaudible.

In unison, they streaked skyward. At the top of their climb, they hovered a few moments and then shot straight down, side-by-side, aiming directly for the center of the stone warriors and their leader. At the last minute, only a few feet above the reach of the giant gargoyle's sword tip, they split and began to circle the group in opposite directions. With each pass, they increased their speed until they were no more than a loud, buzzing blur.

As the intensity of the buzzing rose, the gargoyles that ringed the leader began to clutch at their recurved ears, covering them, protecting them from the damaging vibrations the wasps were creating. One at a time they began to double over, all except the leader. He stood upright, flailing wildly at the circling blurs with his great stone sword.

The hunched-over gargoyles began to break and run. Their leader bellowed for them to return and hold their positions, but they did not hear him. Tiny cracks had begun to form in the stone carvings of their ears. They ran helter-skelter, some falling down and rolling from side to side.

In anger, the leader, now the only one being circled, began slashing up and down, keeping the sword in the same location. The new tactic worked. He felt the blade rip through something solid and one of the wasps fell to the ground, wings still flailing. It was cut neatly in two, the stinger pumping uselessly from the severed abdomen. He lunged forward and brought the blade down again, separating the wasps head from the pedicle. The antennae twitched and the jaws opened and closed in spastic jerks.

His triumph, however, was short-lived. Staring at his helpless victim, he'd almost forgotten the other wasp. He whirled around, but not in time. The wasp's forelimbs settled on his shoulders as its stiletto-like stinger punched through his back and came out the center of his chest. He threw his arms up into the air and rocked his head back to scream out but never got the chance. In a shower of stone, he exploded.

Immediately, the wasp took off and continued its attack on the hapless gargoyles that were still struggling to regain their senses, most earless by now, with large fissures opening in the stonework of their carved heads.

***

The Betorak stood over Geoffrey, savoring the moment, the tip of his blazing sword dangling inches above Geoffrey's lips. Slowly, with both hands wrapped tightly around its leather grip, the Betorak raised the sword above his head and thrust it downward.

In a diving leap, Arliss cleared the headstone, rolled forward and caught the edge of the Betorak's blade with the tip of her scimitar knocking it just far enough out of position to cause it to bury itself in the ground beside Geoffrey's right ear. As soon as it struck the ground, the whole section began to vibrate. Sparks flew upward, along with chunks of dirt, grass, and stone. The shaking became more violent. Headstones toppled over and fissures began to form in the ground, spider-webbing their way across the lawn.

Arliss rolled sideways and was up on her feet before the Betorak could pull his sword from the sod. She lunged, not giving it any time to regain itself. It had to lean way back to avoid the gleaming blade that sliced through the air only millimeters from its chest. It lost its balance and staggered backward a few steps, leaving its sword sticking out of the ground. Extending its hand, it called the sword to it and was able to grasp it just in time to deflect Arliss's next blow.

All around them, graves were breaking open. Each time a fissure line crossed a grave it would split, like a sausage casing on a hot grill. Where it did, the corpses beneath began to stir, banging and scratching at their coffins, and bellowing horrible noises of agony and rage.

The Betorak bore down on Arliss, wielding its sword with all its might. It slashed at her in a relentless series of blows, and each time Arliss countered them. The blades clashed together in a cacophonous ringing as the Betorak drove Arliss slowly backward.

She was completely on the defensive, trying to avoid both the blows and the opening graves. She knew that if she didn't take control soon her chances of winning this fight would dwindle to almost nothing. Planting her feet firmly, she parried. Their swords were moving faster than most eyes could see, creating a glowing blur between them.

***

Geoffrey struggled to his feet. His left arm was a pulpy, bloody mess. A great flap of muscle and skin dangled from the bone. He had to force himself to remain conscious. Concentrating all his will on regaining his strength, he made his way over to where the discs had buried themselves in the ground. He picked them up and heaved them into the air. With a soft whoosh, they shot off into the night and disappeared into its blackness. At the top of their arc, they split away from each other in parabolas, zipping downward towards the Betorak.

Geoffrey fell to his knees after letting them go. He began to crawl toward his shield, which was lying on the ground where the Betorak had beaten it out of his hands. His vision was clouded and he was consciously fighting the urge to just lie down and pass out. The pain in his left arm was excruciating, and every movement he made exacerbated it. Inches felt like miles. But at last, he was within reach.

Extending his right arm he grabbed the edge of the shield and began pulling it toward him. It was almost in hand when a foot came down on it, stopping its progress and momentarily pinning his fingers between it and the ground. What used to be a human being was standing over him, one foot planted heavily on top of the shield. Its leather shoe was disintegrating and the cuff of its pants was covered in a think mold. Most of its facial flesh had long since peeled away and what was left hung in tattered strands. A dark fluid dripped from its gaping mouth, which was almost completely devoid of teeth, the lower jaw being held on by a single strand of rotted tendon.

Geoffrey pulled his fingers back and rolled to one side. The thing standing on the shield bent down. Its head tilted from side to side as it studied the object on which it stood. Then it reached down and picked it up, the diamonds that made up its outer layer shining brilliantly in the dusky moonlight. The corpse tilted the shield from side to side, making the light play across its surface. It stood there, trance-like, watching the diamonds gleam.

Geoffrey pushed himself up. As soon as he did, the creature's fascination with the shield was broken and it turned its attention on him. But it was too late. In a single, swift lunge, Geoffrey grabbed the edges of the shield and impaled the thing with the long, diamond spike that extended from its center. It gave out a wailing moan and then burst into flames. He pulled back, yanking the spike from its chest, and it waddled off a few yards and fell to the ground, wriggling helplessly until it was no more than a pile of burnt ash.

Geoffrey took a deep breath, closed his eyes and concentrated on ignoring his pain and regaining his strength. Ahead of him, Arliss was slowly driving the Betorak backwards. Their swords sparked and clanged together as they attacked and defended. Taking himself deep inside himself, Geoffrey concentrated on healing his wound. In his mind, he saw the tissues begin to knit together. The sounds of the battle began to fade as he sank deeper and deeper. Eventually, he was alone in a great void. No sound or sense entered. There was only Geoffrey Dunsmore and his damaged shoulder.

CHAPTER 115

As Arliss's blade made contact with the Betorak's, stopping it from shearing through Geoffrey's face, Jack picked himself up, rubbing at his throat. He wasted no time getting the shotgun up and reloaded, but there really wasn't a shot he could take. Arliss had moved in close, and she and the Betorak were engaged in a furious sword battle. Nevertheless, Jack kept the shotgun trained in their direction, hoping for a clear shot. He didn't believe he could do the thing any real harm, but hoped that he could knock it off balance long enough for Arliss to get a clear kill with her sword.

He watched intently, following every movement, adjusting his position, wondering if he could just walk up to it while it was busy with Arliss and shoot it in the head. The whole time the butt of the shotgun lay cradled against his shoulder, the barrels held steady on his intended target.

At last, his moment came; Arliss brought her sword dangerously close to the thing's throat and it leaped backwards. There was now enough distance between them to take the shot. His fingers squeezed the triggers, but his shot went into the air. A hand had grabbed him by the shoulder from behind and pulled him away from his aim.

When he turned, Jack's mouth dropped open. In front of him, wearing a minatory grin, stood Doc Robertson. His intestines were trailing along behind him like Jacob Marley's chains.

"Thought you were rid of me, didn't you?" croaked Robertson. "Just up and left me to die. Right? Well, now it's your turn to be left behind for dead. Only I guarantee ... you really *will* be dead."

Robertson's voice seemed to be empty and hollow. It didn't sound at all like a person's voice. To Jack, it sounded like a voice that was made in China for some poorly made doll. It was somehow raspy and squeaky at the same time.

Jack took a step back and the thing that used to be his friend and doctor limped forward. The grin on its face disappeared and it snapped its mouth wide open. A foul-smelling, green fog came billowing outward and Jack back-peddled to avoid it. His heart was pounding in his chest and his mind reeled at the thoughts of having to shoot his long-time friend.

"Come-*On*, Jack," he said to himself aloud. "This ... whatever it is ... is no longer Doc. Come on and shoot it already." His fingers rested up against the triggers but he found he could not pull them.

Robertson advanced on him slowly, his left leg occasionally giving out on him. He'd stumble, right himself and then continue forward, the whole time keeping his arms outstretched and his vacant, black eyes on Jack. It reminded Jack of the old Frankenstein movies with Boris Karloff, only this was no movie, and what was coming for him was no longer anything close to human or friend.

Summoning all his willpower and closing his eyes, Jack let loose with the shotgun. At close range, the blast tore the upper part of Robertson's body to shreds. The upper third of his torso disappeared, and for a sick moment, the lower half kept lurching forward toward Jack, the fragmented right arm still grasping blindly in front of it. Then it pitched forward, jerked a couple of times and laid still.

Jack mopped the sweat off his brow with his sleeve and stared down at what was left of Robertson. His temples were throbbing and his heart felt like it was going to explode at any minute. He could feel the warm tears rolling down the sides of his face, and the emptiness that comes from losing a long-time friend began to churn in his stomach.

No time for this now. Sorry Doc, he thought. Jack turned and raced over to Ethan. Not too far ahead, Arliss and the Betorak were moving back and forth, flailing away at each other, almost too quickly to see. Jack cleared the headstone that Ethan had tumbled over in a single bound and almost landed square on his friend's chest. It was just a matter of luck that he missed him wide.

Ethan lay on the ground, unmoving. His eyes followed Jacks and his lips quivered but no sound came out. Jack knelt beside him and took his hand.

"Can you sit up?"

Ethan mumbled something that Jack couldn't quite make out. He leaned in closer.

"Can't feel my legs or arms," whispered Ethan in a breathy voice. "Think my neck's a goner."

Jack gently reached around behind Ethan's head, his fingers lightly probing the back of his neck. He could feel the misshapen bones just below the skin.

"Just lie still. I'll get you out of here just as soon as I can."

Ethan smiled a feeble smile. "Don't think I can do much else. Do you? If I were you, I think I'd be trying to find a way to help end this. I can't see shit from here, but it sure sounds like a lot of fighting going on."

"Yeah. That guy Dunsmore and some woman who showed up. Actually, she's doing most of the fighting. Dunsmore was down for a while ... lost half his damn arm. Now he's standing absolutely still like some kind of human statue while the woman battles it out, sword to sword. You wouldn't believe how fast she and that ... thing ... are moving."

"I can believe it. Just from the sound of it. Go on, Jack. I'll be fine right here."

Jack nodded, picked up the shotgun and pumped two shells into the chamber.

"Time to take care of things. I'll be back."

"Jack! Don't go getting yourself killed. I'm gonna need you to lug my lazy ass outta here."

"Count on it." Jack smiled then moved off.

Ethan closed his eyes and wondered if he'd ever walk again. He seriously doubted it, and if that were truly to be the case, he wished he had been killed outright. A life of virtual inactivity was never in *his* game plan.

***

Jacobs hadn't had to go far before running into Eric. He was slowly making his way up a row of headstones muttering to himself about dadblamed adventures in a dadblamed cemetery in the dadblamed middle of the night with dadblamed monsters and ghouls. When he caught sight of Jacobs coming toward him, he didn't recognize him at first and his hand instinctively closed around one of the Kahnjals. He stood stone still, waiting to be attacked. When he saw it was the priest, a wave of relief swept through him and he could feel the muscles in his face relax.

"Dang-it-all, Father. Don't be sneakin up on a body like that."

Jacobs laughed. "That's the second time in less than five minutes that I've been told that, Eric. Guess I'd better start taking the advice to heart. Come on. We have to catch up to the others."

"I know it! I know. I'm old. Ain't deaf."

The sounds of the clashing swords filled the cemetery. Anyone even close to the grounds would have heard it.

"We ran into some other folks just up ahead. They're all waiting for us."

"What other folks?" asked Eric. "Seems to me there's a lot-a crazy people runnin 'round this dadblamed cem'tery tonight."

"Come on," insisted Jacobs. "I have a feeling we're needed."

"Yeah. But that ain't the *only* feelin I got. And the other feelin ain't so good."

Eric and Jacobs worked their way back to where Linda and the others were waiting. When they arrived, Willie was sitting on the base of a monument, his chin resting on the heels of his hands. Linda was pacing back and forth, wearing a small dirt rut into the grass, and Jasper was propped up against a stone smoking a cigarette.

"Finally!" cried Linda when she saw them come into view. To her, it seemed like the priest had been gone for hours when in reality it had been less than ten minutes.

"Come on.   There's something big happening and I think we're supposed to be part of it. Jack and Ethan are out there and I'll bet they could use our help." Linda looked over at Willie and Jasper. "Maybe it'd be better if you two stay here. I don't think you'd be much good in a fight, Mr. Collins." She turned her gaze on Willie. "I don't think you should be anywhere close to it."

Willie was already on his feet.

"I gotta come. I know I do. "

"I think it's best if the boy comes along," said Jacobs.

"You really think that's wise?" asked Eric, looking at Willie. "Besides, I think he'd be the perfect choice to stay here with old Jasper there.

Don't think he'll be doin much fightin in his condition. The boy can have my sticker thingies. I don't think they'll be doin me no good."

"No!" Jasper piped up. "The boy'd be safer with all-a you than he would be here with me. I agree; don't think I'll be much good in a fight. So if'n sumpin *does* come along, the boy should be with people that c'n help 'im."

Jacobs broke in. "It's all irrelevant. I believe that everyone here is here because they have to be, and because they have a part to play. And that, unfortunately, includes Willie. And I also don't think that he's here just to babysit Mr. Collins, here. No offense."

"Well, I say ... if we're gittin inta the fray, we best be gittin inta the fray, stead a jus yappin 'bout it," barked Eric. "I kint stan' here no longer or I'll lose m'nerve complete and skedaddle. Let's git t'gittin. No more falderal." Without another word he turned and started off across the divider, his hand pressed firmly against the watch in his bib pocket.

"Guess that settles that. Come on, son. And stick close to me." Jacobs took a few steps forward, stopped at the road that Eric had just crossed and swept his arm out in front of him in a gentlemanly gesture and waited for Linda to reluctantly cross.

When she got to the other side, she looked back at Jasper. He was lighting another cigarette and waving her to move on ahead. She nodded and turned.

"Lead the way, Father. Like Eric said: if we're gittin to it, let's git to it." She tried to smile but it came out more like the grin of someone with an upset stomach.

They made their way across the cemetery, zigzagging through the headstones and around the ornamental trees that dotted the rolling grounds. The smell of Jasmine and Honeysuckle blended together, hanging heavy in the mist-laden night air. Above, the moon seemed to have risen higher but still seemed much lower than it should have been.

As they rounded the last row of stones in the section, they could see the dazzling light show the sword fight ahead was creating. Linda's mouth actually dropped open as she stood gazing into the distance watching the swirling light move back and forth. Jacobs felt a deep sense of dread, deeper than anything he'd ever felt before and blessed himself. Willy stared in awe for a moment. He'd been holding on to the priest's hand but now he let it go. He rubbed at his eyes in disbelief. It looked like something out of a sci-fi movie to him and its allure was overpowering. He broke and ran forward, scared but excited.

"Willie! Wait," cried Jacobs. "Don't go up there alone. Wait for us." But it was too late. The boy raced ahead into the blackness, his outline growing dimmer until it vanished completely. Jacobs looked at Linda and Eric. No one said anything. No one had to. Almost in unison, they started off at a trot and broke into a run. Even Eric was running, his hand still clutching at the pocket watch.

"We'll never cetch 'im," panted Eric, bringing up the rear but keeping up just the same. "He's too dang spry."

A sudden flash of the boy running straight into that horrible thing they'd seen flying overhead shot through Linda's mind and she quickened her pace. In only a few seconds she was well out in front of the others and close enough to see Willie cutting around a mausoleum in the distance. Her heart was beating wildly, and a warm cascade of anger washed over her. *Nothing* was going to happen to that boy if she could help it. She stretched her legs to their maximum length with each stride, closing the distance between her and the boy. She rounded the mausoleum and ran smack into him and they both tumbled to the grass in a tangle of arms and legs.

Just ahead of them, Arliss and the creature were slashing and hacking at each other. With the speed they were moving, it was hard to tell who was where. Neither Linda nor Willie had ever seen anything like it before: in real life or in film.

Jacobs and Eric caught up to them as they were standing there, mesmerized by the action in front of them. Jacobs looked at the scene and then at Linda and Eric. He knew they were all thinking the same thing. *God help us!*

CHAPTER 116

Ernie lay huddled next to Gwen's body. He no longer had the will to get up. All he wanted to do was to be with the woman he loved. And all he could think about was how cowardly he'd been: too afraid to ask her out and how it was now too late. It was the sudden clanging that brought him back to himself. From nowhere, a loud ringing began to fill the night. He looked up slowly but from where he was he could see nothing. He got to his feet and then climbed onto a headstone. Off in the distance, he could see a flashing of light. He had no idea what it could be or what it meant. He watched as the light moved forward then backward, then to one side then to the other. His curiosity finally got the better of him and he jumped down, gave his Gwen a kiss and promised to come back, and then marched off toward the light.

Something was drawing him there, he could feel that. He turned and gave a final look at Gwen and then broke into a fast trot. Whatever was happening, he was sure it had something to do with his love's death. And if that was true, by God, he'd make them pay, whoever they were. Now in a total rage, his trot turned into a dead run and his face was contorted in rage and revenge.

CHAPTER 117

The Betorak's sword moved left, right, up and down, each time glancing off the defensive movements of Arliss's. It struck in a never-ending series of blows in all directions but could gain no advantage against her. Anger welled up inside it. It bellowed and screamed as it moved in and then was forced backward.

Arliss was moving faster than even she had thought possible. She could sense the creature's mind. It was only a loose thread of connection but it was enough to foretell its next strike; it was enough for her to bring her curved blade into position before the blow fell.

Without warning, the Betorak jumped backwards and launched itself into the air. Its damaged wing struggled to create the lift required and the creature listed to one side before plummeting back down two rows to Arliss's left. It drew in a great breath, threw open its arms and belched forth a searing ball of flame.

Arliss was defenseless. The flames washed over her, catching her hair and clothing on fire. She stumbled backwards and fell, a loud scream of pain bellowing out from deep inside her.

The scream brought Geoffrey out of his trance. His arm had stopped bleeding and the muscle had re-adhered to the bone, but there was no strength in it. In two large bounds, Geoffrey was at Arliss's side, smothering the flames. The flesh on the left side of her face was completely burned away and her left eye was nothing more than a dark, misshapen ball. The skin on that hand was also burnt and blistered, black in places and absent in others. The tendons of her fingers were clearly visible.

The Betorak wasted no time in taking advantage. It leaped over the rows of stones and landed right behind Geoffrey. He turned, but not quickly enough. With a single, powerful swipe of its arm, Geoffrey found himself tumbling through the air. He slammed up against the wall of a mausoleum and slid down the side like an egg off a tilted frying pan.

The Betorak let out a loud roar of laughter and reached its clawed hand down towards Arliss's face. But the hand never made contact. Inches before the grotesque fingers closed on their target, the Betorak let out a loud yell, stood bolt upright and then fell forward, its massive body sprawling across Arliss. One of the discs that had still been circling in search of a target buried itself deep in the Betorak's back, grinding away.

In a fury and in great agony, the Betorak crawled forward, clawing at the object digging into its back. Each time his fingers came in contact with it, the spinning blades hacked at them and he drew them away. Finally, ignoring the pain and working as quickly as he could he grabbed the disc, yanked it out of his back and hurled it against a headstone. Its blades cut through the stone as easily as they'd cut through the Betorak's flesh and the disc came to a grinding halt, lodged firmly in the granite marker.

Arliss had managed to regain her feet. The Betorak whirled on her as she approached, scimitar gleaming in the rising moonlight. For a brief moment, she thought she saw panic flash across its face as it realized that it had dropped its sword. It scrambled across the ground in an effort to retrieve it before Arliss struck.

Diving headfirst out of the way of her first swing, the Betorak closed its clawed hand around the blade of its own sword and rolled on to its back. It barely had enough time to get it in front of its face as Arliss's scimitar sliced through the air. There was a muffled ring as Arliss's blade cut into the leather handle and stopped short of the Betorak's face. The Betorak rolled to its left and then to its right. Arliss's blade followed it, giving it no time to change its grip. It was now warding off her blows with the handle, not the blade.

Using all the force it could muster, the Betorak kicked at Arliss. Its heel caught her just below her right knee and she went down hard. It was the opportunity the creature had been looking for. It scrambled to its feet and turned the blade in its hand. But before it could grab the handle, the second disc came humming in.

***

At the sites of contact with the Betorak's sword, the ground had broken open. Now, corpses, those that hadn't been buried in concrete vaults, had clawed and scratched their way to the surface. Dirt- and mud-covered, partially rotted, or completely rotted, they struggled their way out of the open soil. Once above ground, they turned, snarling and hissing and clawing at the air.

The first one to spot the group of onlookers, Jacobs and the others, made a moaning howl which rose above the sounds of the battle and called the others. There were six that had worked their way up through the surface and another four that were still struggling and grabbing at the mist-laden grass and dirt, their waists and legs still held captive by the ground in which they'd been entombed. Each of their heads swiveled, their attention focused on the group.

Those that were already standing fell in behind the caller. In life, he had been Adam Dahl. He was thirty-five at the time of his planting, a casualty of the Iraq war, returned home for honorable burial. He was in better physical shape than most of the others, with very little postmortem damage. The left side of his head and his left eye were missing, the reason for his demise in the first place: a sniper's round. He strode forward, lifting his arm and pointing directly at Father Jacobs.

"Kill," he drawled. "Kill all."

The others fell in behind him, as did the stragglers that had finally managed to extricate themselves from the ground. Most of them lumbered along, the decay impeding their ability to maneuver easily. But Dahl moved at a much quicker pace. His steps were deliberate and his gait steady.

Jacobs and Eric quickly pulled out the Kahnjals and passed them out as far as they would go. Between the two of them, Jacobs and Eric, there were fifteen daggers left. Jacobs kept three of his own and passed out the other four, giving two to Linda and two to Willie. Eric kept three, gave one to Jacobs and two each to both Linda and Willie.

Speaking quickly, Jacobs said, "You only get one use out of each of these. Stick it in their hearts or head and leave it there."

There was no time for further explanation. Adam was only a yard away and the others a few feet beyond that. Jacobs looked at the boy and wished he could somehow keep him out of all this. But that was impossible now.

"Try to stay behind us Willie, you hear? Let us do the fighting."

Willie hadn't heard a thing. All he could think about was what one of those things had done to his father. His stomach was in knots with fear but his anger was much stronger. Yelling at the top of his lungs he rushed forward.

Adam instantly turned on him, but Willie was faster, dipping his shoulder to the right and then going left. Adam lunged and missed. He went sliding across the grass on his belly, arms clutching at a boy who'd already passed him, gathering in nothing but empty air. He snarled, his lips drawn back like a rabid wolve's, and hoisted himself to his feet.

Jacobs and Linda followed Willie's lead and charged forward, each picking a target. Eric just ambled into the fray, remaining calm and collected. He had already reasoned that there was no real need to hurry. The fight would come to him quick 'nuff. And he was right. He'd only gone a few steps before he got the chance to use up one of the Kahnjals.

The thing had lumbered up from his left and swiped at him with its ragged excuse for a hand. It only caught the edge of his shirt, its fingernail getting stuck in the fabric. When Eric wheeled on it, it was dragged sideways and toppled over, its index finger pulled off and hanging from Eric's shirt. Eric stomped down hard on the thing's throat, pinning it to the ground and plunged the dagger through its heart. It went instantly still.

Linda attacked her target head-on. She leaped at it, wrapping her legs around its waist and sinking the iron dagger through the center of its forehead. It staggered backwards and then fell, temporarily pinning her legs beneath it. The impact and the angle at which her legs had been when it fell twisted her knee and she let out a sharp chirp of pain.

Jacobs had run completely around his target, grabbed it around the face from behind like a commando, and buried the Kahnjal in its chest. When he let go, it walked forward a few paces and then flopped to the ground with a dull, moist thud.

Willie had wormed his way in and out of the main group of them and fixed his sights on the last. He put his head down and ran his shoulder into its knee, the force bouncing him backwards. The things knee came apart and it went flying through the air, its arms pin-wheeling as it cart-wheeled backwards. It landed with a hard thump, most of its ribs being driven up through the skin of its chest. One had bent inward from the side and pierced its heart. It laid there like a broken doll, smashed to bits by an angry child.

Willie picked himself up, turned and chose another zombie victim. This time, he held one of the heavy iron spikes out in front of him as he charged, again, yelling at the top of his lungs.

CHAPTER 118

Not too far across the cemetery, Ernie heard the howling cry of anger that Willie had let loose when he'd charged. He stopped and listened a minute, then turned and headed in that direction. He had no real idea what was going on or who might be involved. All he knew is that he wanted revenge for his Gwen. His mind was a wasp's nest of anger and rage. He stopped at a Maple and snapped one of the thinner branches off. After sharpening the jagged end on a headstone, he set off in a dead run. He weaved in and out of the stones and rows, the whole time his mind racing with a line from a movie he liked: Tombstone.

"You tell em I'm comin. And hell's comin with me."

As he reached the section where the battle raged, he came to a dead stop. He could hardly believe what he was seeing. A grotesque bat-man-like creature was sword fighting with a woman. The sheriff was, apparently, waiting for the right moment to unleash his shotgun; another group was fighting with what looked like corpses, just like the one he'd found lying next to his Gwen.

Tightening his grip on his homemade spear, he bolted forward into the fray, screaming at the top of his lungs.

"Hell's arrived. And I'm takin' you all with me."

A moment later he was dead. In his haste, his left foot had caught on a root and he was pitched forward. He landed on his own home-made spear.

His last thought was that he and Gwen could finally be together.

CHAPTER 119

The drone of the incoming disc burned into the Betorak's ears and it wheeled just in time. The deadly Frisbee was headed straight for its face and it was close. Instinctively, it raised the handle of the sword to eye level, still clutching it by the blade. The disc careened in and sliced off the rounded, crystalline pommel. The impact sent the disc and pommel in opposite directions.

Wobbling heavily, the disc ground itself into an oak. The pommel thumped to the ground and rolled away. The Betorak threw back its head and began to howl, the broken sword still clutched in its spiny, clawed fingers. It peddled backwards like a drunk, weaving from side to side and bellowing horrible screams, and then belched forth its fire, incinerating the tree and the disc that had robbed it of its power. The blue light that had illuminated the thing's blade shrank to a single point at the center and then disappeared.

The thunderclap of Jack's shotgun blast rose above the things screams. The pellets tore into its chest and it was pushed back by the blast. It stutter-stepped and toppled over.

Arliss was struggling to get to her feet. The kick the Betorak had landed had shattered the upper portion of her tibia, just below the kneecap. She had to lean on her scimitar to finally get her balance. She looked at the creature. A dark liquid was flowing from the holes the shotgun pellets had created. A slow smile crept across Arliss's face. In that instant, seeing those wounds, everything became clear; she understood.

Geoffrey! She locked her mind on his. *Geoffrey! It's the pommel. We need to destroy the pommel.*

Arliss's voice in his head was loud and strong, like thundering drums. He pushed himself up, still shaken by his abrupt meeting with the mausoleum. It took some effort but he finally regained his feet. He could see what was in Arliss's mind. And what was in Arliss's mind was the location of the pommel, lying on the ground behind her.

Get the pommel, she commanded. *I'll stay on top of the Betorak.*

Geoffrey could see the pommel through Arliss's thoughts, but its exact location was unknown. It would take some searching in the dark.

Arliss moved toward the Betorak. It seemed to be in agony and was shrinking away from her, its hand wrapped defensively around the hilt of the decapitated sword. It flapped its wings, trying to gain some lift but remained steadfastly on the ground.

Using its still powerful legs, it leaped into the air and scrambled up a tall poplar. It was moaning and writhing, clinging desperately to the branches as it struggled to climb higher.

And there was something else happening. Something had fallen from the tree and landed a few feet behind Arliss. She had to hobble over to get a clear look at it. It was one of the thing's great wings. Without the power of the pommel, it was coming apart. When she looked up, focusing all her power and strength into piercing the darkness, she could see the Betorak beginning to shrivel up, like a plumb left sitting too long. It was slowly reverting to its humanoid form.

***

After seeing his pellets rip through the thing, Jack pumped the shotgun again, only to find he was out of shells. He watched as the thing scrambled backwards away from Arliss. He thought about drawing his pistol but decided, instead, to leave the thing to Arliss. When he turned to go back to Ethan, he froze. Across the lawn, Linda, Jacobs, another man he couldn't identify from where he was, and Willie Peters were under attack. There was absolutely no need to think on this one. He drew his .357 and broke into a run.

The first shot he squeezed off ripped through the collar bone of one of the things towering over Willie. The shot entered from the back and pushed the thing forward. Willie scrambled out of its way and as soon as it dropped to the ground, he was on it. The dagger made a loud cracking sound as it sliced through the thing's sternum.

By the time Jack got there, Willie was already moving off, Kahnjal raised above his head as he raced toward another corpse.

***

Linda finally managed to get her legs out from underneath the thing. But it hadn't been quick enough. Something had her by the hair and was dragging her along the ground on her back. With one hand still clutching her daggers, she reached up behind her and tried to break the grip. It laughed, a sour and spiteful laugh.

"You're mine. And I'm going to break your scrawny neck, lady," it belched. Its voice was raspy but the words came out crystal clear.

A few feet away, wrestling with his own adversary, Jacobs turned his head at the sound of the voice. His attention wavered momentarily and that was enough for the corpse he fought to gain an advantage. It struck him hard on the cheek and sent him reeling sideways. He jigged a bit, tried to regain his balance and then fell, his head missing the base of a monument by mere inches; the Kahnjal he was carrying tumbled to the ground in a metallic clatter. The thing was on him before he could get up. He lay there, face down in the grass, the zombie sitting on his back and the Kahnjal just out of reach. He tried to twist around, to throw it off, but it was firmly entrenched. The next thing he felt was its fingers closing off his windpipe, the ragged bones digging into the flesh of his neck.

Adam Dahl dragged Linda over to one of the open holes and tossed her in like a bag of trash into a dumpster. She landed hard and the breath went out of her in loud *humph*. Adam jumped in on top of her, his knee landing in her mid-section, effectively removing any air that hadn't already been squeezed out of her lungs by the fall. His hands clutched at her hair on either side of her head and he began banging the back of her head on the hard ground beneath her. She clawed at him as best she could but could reach no higher than the collar of his shirt. Her world started to go gray.

For Jacob's, too, things began to swim. His face was pressed solidly into the wet grass and the hands around his throat felt as if they were gaining strength. He kicked his legs and squirmed as much as he could, hoping to dislodge his malevolent passenger. It would not be long before things went into the black for him, too.

Willie had reached his third target, a tottery remnant of a human. He slid in underneath its legs on his knees, driving one of the daggers straight up into what used to be its genitals. It let out a sharp yell and pitched forward, its head striking a headstone almost dead center. There was a loud *crrr-aak*; its skull shattered. Its ragged cheek slid down the side of the marker and its jaw broke in two when it slammed into the base.

Willie quickly pulled the dagger from between its legs and stuck it through its back, piercing its heart and spiking it to the ground.

CHAPTER 120

The Betorak, now almost completely reduced to Witherstone again, clung tightly to the uppermost branches. It concentrated. It needed power; it needed to draw more power from the evil it had released in the town. It closed its eyes and started to inhale as deeply as it could.

Arliss had no hope of scrambling up the tree after it with her leg in the shape it was in. She could also sense that it was up to something; she could feel it stretching out its mind and will. To what exact end she had no idea, but she knew she had to think of something.

Behind her, Geoffrey was desperately searching for the pommel. Usually, his night vision was much better than that of ordinary humans. But he was depleted. The energy he used to partially heal himself left him weakened. He was on all fours, slowly combing the grass for the crystalline object.

Ahead and to his left was a stand of hyacinths that someone had planted in memory of a loved one. He edged closer, sweeping his right hand along the ground. When it slipped beneath the overhanging leaves of the hyacinth, he felt a quick, sharp pain and yanked his hand back. There were two small holes just above the knuckle. He'd been bitten by a snake. And from the instant burning sensation it was causing, he knew it had to be poisonous.

He leaned back, searching the ground for a stick or something with which to lift one of the branches. As he did, two viper heads reared up from under the bush in front of him. They were both hissing, their fangs exposed and dripping venom. Behind them, beneath the bush, he could see a blue glow with two red centers.

Slowly, he pulled himself backwards, trying not to make any sudden moves, his hand a hot tangle of screaming nerves. Both snakes slithered forward, side-by-side, keeping pace with him. Then, one slipped around to his left and the other to his right. They were tightly coiled and ready to strike. And Geoffrey had no way to defend himself.

I believe I've found the Pommel was the thought he sent to Arliss. *But I don't think I'm going to be able to get it. You'll have to.* He concentrated on closing down the blood vessels in his arms to slow the poison's ascent.

Geoffrey knew he'd be fast enough to catch one of the damned things with his right hand if it struck, despite the bite. His left, however, was too damaged at the shoulder to be fast enough. The snakes hissed, arching their heads forward and then drawing them back as if they were testing him. He waited, his attention focused primarily on the one to his right, the one he actually had a chance of grabbing.

A soft whistle broke the stillness and something shot by his left ear. At the same time, the snake on the right lunged forward. Its momentum stopped abruptly as Geoffrey's hand shot out and grabbed it just below the angle of its head. It squirmed and hissed and flailed its tail, snapping its jaws open and closed.

Geoffrey looked at it for a moment, stared directly into its empty, black eyes and then crushed it in his hand. He was already wondering why the other hadn't attacked at the same time. When he turned around, he found the answer. The soft whistle he'd heard was one of Arliss's darts and it was stuck in the throat of the other snake, its feathers sticking out of its open mouth between its fangs. It lay on the ground, its tail swishing back and forth in a slow death dance. And then it laid still.

Arliss was now beside Geoffrey, helping him to his feet as best she could.

"Thanks for that," he said. He looked her up and down. "Well, you've looked better."

"You should talk?" she quipped.

Geoffrey pointed to the hyacinths. *It's under there.*

Do you think? The sarcasm was not lost on Geoffrey and he smiled.

"What about ... it?" He jabbed an already blackening thumb in the direction of the Betorak.

"In the tree for now. But not for long, I'm sure. We'll have to act quickly."

The glow beneath the plants was growing brighter. The leaves that were covering the pommel began to wilt, then crisp, then burn.

"Any suggestions?" Geoffrey studied Arliss's face. Her brow was contorted in thought.

"Reach in and grab it?"

"I don't think so," answered Geoffrey. "I doubt it'll be that easy. Besides, in a moment or two, my right hand will be more useless than my left. But don't worry, didn't get enough venom to kill me. That much I *do* know."

"Well, we'll have to try *something*."

Geoffrey laughed. "Ok. What the hell. Might as well get *some* kind of use out of this thing." He raised his left arm.

He walked over, knelt down and reached out. The pommel was burning in plain view now, the relief skull's eyes blazing red. There was no doubt about it; it was watching every movement that he and Arliss made. Just as his fingers were about to close around it, it rolled backward, just out of reach. The skull in the center seemed to be grinning.

When he tried to grab it a second time, it rolled to its left, then to its right, always staying just out of reach. The eyes burned like hot coals, shifting in the skull to follow Geoffrey's hand.

"Hmm ... this isn't going to be easy."

Arliss snorted. "Humph. Well, I'll leave this to you. I've got to do something about the Betorak. It's lost a lot of its power but not all of it. And it's planning something."

Without waiting for a response, she limped off in the direction of the tree, her mind racing to find a solution before it was too late.

CHAPTER 121

All across Banderman Falls, the fighting raged on. Longtime friends and neighbors had suddenly found themselves at odds for no real reason. Husbands and wives, brothers and sisters, all fighting for the sake of fighting. Anything the least malevolent in their natures was brought to the surface and magnified. Those that *were* able to resist found themselves either hiding or fighting for their lives in pure defense. Buildings burned to the ground, unattended by squabbling firefighters.

It had taken Audrey Archibald the better part of the evening to hike back to town from where her car had disintegrated. And although she should have been able to see the fires rising into the night sky from quite some distance, it was not until she was almost back in the heart of town that she could see the flames. It was as if something was shielding the chaos that raged from the outside world.

Standing on the corner of Main and Arch streets, hands on her hips and her feet aching, she took in the carnage and destruction. Overturned cars dotted the thoroughfare. Some were no more than charred hulls, others still smoldering or aflame. More disturbing were the pockets of fighting. Small groups of men and women apparently trying to kill each other.

Audrey couldn't get a grasp on the situation. She knew most of these people. Very few of them had ever had run-ins with the law, so what could have brought out such anger in them? She had no idea. Nor did she have any idea how she was going to put a stop to it. On top of that, she hadn't heard from Jack or her sister, Gwen, all day.

On the opposite corner, the nearest combatants were Selma and Irving Rothman. Both of them were in their eighties. The last time Audrey had seen them out and about, Irving was using a cane. Now he was choking and being choked by his wife. Audrey calmly walked over and pushed the two apart. It didn't take much of a push and it sat Irving down hard on his bottom.

"What the hell's the matter with you two?" she asked. Then hollered at the top of her lungs down the street.

"What the hell's the matter with *all* of you."

For a moment, the fighting stopped as everyone turned to look at her. But it started up again just as quickly as it had stopped. Audrey had the greatest urge to start using her nightstick on everyone. Her hand actually gripped its handle before she consciously pulled it away.

She stood there trying to decide what to do. All at once, the fighting stopped. People stumbled backwards, some falling, some leaning up against the nearest wall for support. Audrey suddenly felt dizzy herself and had to squat to keep from falling over. She rubbed her forehead and the back of her neck. When she felt a little better, she looked up. Her mouth dropped open at what she saw.

All along the street, everyone had their heads tilted back as if they were going to start howling at the moon like wolves. A thick green cloud seemed to be coming out of their mouths. It drifted up into the night sky. Threads of it came from every direction of the town. They strung themselves together and coalesced into a long, comet-tail cloud that drifted across the town.

When the last of the green filament exited a body, the body slumped over and lay where it fell. Most of the people were muttering incoherently or just moaning. Audrey had a sudden onslaught of nausea but it passed quickly. She watched, dumbfounded, as the green cloud drifted along and disappeared over the horizon in the direction of Peaceful Haven cemetery.

The streets had gone silent, except for the moaning. In the dead air it sounded, and felt to Audrey, like some scene out of a B horror movie. She shook her head in disbelief, then started down the street toward the station, carefully stepping over the near-dormant bodies.

CHAPTER 122

Witherstone clung to the top of the tree, his elbow hooked over one of its bulbous and knotted branches, the still formidable, but less powerful, sword held firmly by its grip. His chest had grown to near barrel proportions as he drew the evil from the townspeople to himself. It snaked its way across the dark, hazy sky: a green, luminescent ribbon of amalgamated hatred. And he sucked it in as desperately and greedily as an asthma sufferer pulls on his inhaler.

He absorbed it, and with each assimilated molecule he could feel his strength and power grow again. His muscles began to re-solidify; his legs and torso thickened and grew. It was a potent admixture of greed, immorality, hatred, envy – everything that typified humanity's worst qualities – and it fueled his rejuvenation. But it was not the pommel and it would not sustain him forever. For that permanence, he would have to get the pommel back. And his mind centered itself on that task.

Below him, Geoffrey struggled to capture the very same object, while Arliss searched for the headstone that held the disc that had wounded the Betorak. Not much further off behind her and Geoffrey, Linda, Jacobs, Eric, and Willie grappled with the lifeless but animated bodies that the Betorak's blade had released.

When it had assimilated the last of the town's malevolence, it sprang from the tree, thudding to the ground behind Arliss. It now had the appearance of the gargoyle that had cleaved one of the wasps in two. It strode toward Arliss, growling, snarling and slashing at the air. It covered the distance between them quickly and Arliss had to shoulder-roll to her left to avoid the swipe of its blade.

It reached down and plucked a marble marker from its base and tossed it at Arliss.

"Catch," it growled, its voice deep and gravelly.

Arliss rolled right and the marker dug itself into the ground where she had just been. Her broken leg was shooting white-hot ribbons of pain up her leg as she worked herself to a standing position. She eyed the thing, her eyes no more than narrow slits. Then she bent over, plucked the marble marker out of its depression, and hurled it back. It caught the Betorak square in the chest and sent him reeling, his arms paddling the empty air. As he fell, she could see the look of surprise and fear that spread across its face. It hadn't expected her to be able to lift the marker, let alone throw it back.

Arliss closed her eyes and drew on all her powers. She could hear the thing as it pushed the stone off its chest and lumbered to its feet, but she still kept her eyes closed, concentrating. She could hear its heavy steps as it plodded toward her, and could hear the whistling its sword made as it cut the air ahead of it. And still, she kept her eyes closed, concentrating.

Then the footsteps stopped and the thing let out a booming roar. She opened her eyes. It stood in front of her, no more than three feet away, its sword dangling by its side. Its face was contorted and she knew it was afraid. The bone in her leg had fused and she stared into its eyes with a determination that withered its resolve. It took a tentative step back, no longer so sure of itself. The light breeze billowed Arliss's hair out behind her and she walked slowly and steadily toward it.

The Betorak took a giant leap backwards. Without the pommel attached to the head of the sword, its confidence, despite its appearance, had faded. Then, resolving itself anew to reclaim its possession it jumped forward, sword slashing.

Arliss leaped backwards and held out her scimitar, and when the two blades connected, great sparks burst out in all directions. As before, their movements were almost too fast for the human eye to see. Strike after strike, blow after ringing blow, they parried, jumping and lunging at each other.

Arliss drove at it with a fury and pushed it back. The backs of its knees caught against a stone and it tumbled over it onto its back. It scurried backward on his elbows, pushing itself along with the heels of its taloned feet. It tried to belch forth another burst of flame but nothing more than a roar came from within.

Arliss sprang onto the headstone that had toppled the beast, raised her sword and launched herself at its retreating form. She landed astride it and brought the scimitar down swiftly and firmly. The tip of the curved blade made contact with the leathery skin of its throat and sank through to the ground. A huge green cloud poured from its mouth and its body began to sizzle and shrivel up. The green cloud drifted down the row of stones, inches above the ground. When it reached the far end it stopped, folded in on itself and reformed as Witherstone.

***

Geoffrey was scrambling around under the burnt hyacinths, trying to corral the uncooperative crystal. So far, it had managed to elude every attempt he'd made at grasping it. At one point, it actually hopped over the top of his hand and rolled around him in a circle and then back into the deepest recesses of the bush. Occasionally, it would roll forward and wobble from side to side, testing him – teasing him. As soon as the muscles in his arm gave the slightest sign of movement, it would skitter away, the whole time, its glowing red eyes seeming to laugh at him.

Geoffrey had had enough of this dance. He stood up, grabbed a handful of the scorched hyacinth stems and yanked them up out of the ground. As soon as they came free, clumps of dirt still clinging to their tattered roots, he dove forward, trapping the pommel beneath his chest. He could feel it trying to roll, trying to escape. He also felt something else. It was an odd sensation, like someone had just given him a large shot of morphine. His eyelids felt like they were made of lead sinkers and his arms seemed to be going numb. He fought to keep focused on capturing the elusive pommel; he fought to remain conscious.

Keeping the thing pinned between his chest and the ground, he slowly brought his arms in underneath him and grabbed it with both hands. The minute it was firmly in his grasp a storm of impulses swept over him. His mind translated the impulses to images. He saw men battering women, women stabbing their husbands, somebody set somebody else on fire using gasoline and a fireworks sparkler. The scenes shifted rapidly and he could feel the anger in himself begin to build. Suddenly, all he wanted was to vent his rage.

He clambered to his feet, the pommel secure within his palms and turned toward Arliss. Looking around, he found a large rock, shoved the pommel into his pocket, picked up the rock and headed toward her.

By this time, Arliss had drawn her blade out of the ground and was staring down the row at Witherstone. He was wearing a grin, and as she moved toward him, he bowed at the waist, touched his hand to his forehead as if he were doffing his hat and smiled. Very slowly, he raised his hand and poked out a bony finger. At first, Arliss thought he was pointing at her, challenging her, but then, a sudden burst of rage filled her mind. It was Geoffrey's rage and she could feel it burning inside him. Confused, she turned her head to see what was happening with him.

K-thunk. The rock opened a large gash on the side of her head, just above her cheek. Her eyes blinked rapidly as she tried to steady herself, but to no avail; she could feel her knees folding underneath her and she went down.

Blood covered the side of her face and ran into her good eye. Above her, a very blurry Geoffrey was leaning over her, his face knotted with rage.

"You bitch! Did you really think I was going to jump at your every command for the rest of my life. Do you really think I need *you* as a boss, you silly slut!

She felt the tip of his foot slam into her belly. The breath whooshed out of her. He kicked her again and again. She tried to crawl away. There was a sudden pain in the middle of her lower back. He was grinding his heel in circles just above her buttocks and she could feel her legs going numb. She tried to reach into his mind with hers, but there was nothing there to reach, only a solid wall of hatred that she couldn't seem to penetrate.

Geoffrey raised the rock above his head and brought it down savagely. The blow never landed. His wrist had been trapped in mid-swing by a thick, strong hand.

"What the hell are you doing?" asked Jack, an angry and puzzled look on his face.

Geoffrey whirled around and drove his fist into Jack's stomach. Jack doubled but did not let go of Geoffrey's wrist. He came up with a rocking uppercut that sent Geoffrey stumbling. He trundled two steps backward, tripped over Arliss, who had managed to get to her hands and knees, and fell flat on his back.

Arliss lunged at him, pinning him flat.

"Get the pommel away from him," she yelled to Jack. "But don't touch it."

"How the hell do you expect me to get it then?"

"Never mind. You hold him. I'll get it."

Geoffrey was still a bit dazed from the punch. By the time his head cleared, Jack Dougherty was straddling him, pinning his arms to the ground over his head by his wrists.

Arliss retrieved her scimitar and was about to use it to cut the pommel from Geoffrey's pants pocket when a firm hand grabbed her by the hair and pulled her away.

CHAPTER 123

The whole time the battle had raged, Jasper Collins had kept himself quiet. He sat with his back up against a stone, smoking cigarette after cigarette, trying the best he could to ignore the relentless throbbing in his broken and splinted leg. A few times he had almost talked himself into going to help; he couldn't help but feel that most, if not all, of what was happening was his fault. But each time

he made a move to get up, the furnace of pain in his
leg would send white-hot tendrils of flame all the
way up to his spine and he'd abandon the idea.

He lit the last Marlboro he had, crumpled
the red and white carton into a tight ball and tossed
it over his shoulder. A moment later, it landed in
front of him.

"You really shouldn't be tossin yer trash all
over, you know." The voice came from behind and
was both familiar and unfamiliar.

Jasper twisted at the waist, leaning over to
peer around the stone he was leaning against. From
that angle, all he could see was a pair of muddy
shoes and pants cuffs that seemed to have gone
through a shredder. He craned his head upward, but
the way he was sitting kept him from seeing any
higher than the man's waist.

"Who is it? Who's there?" he shouted.

There was a short burst of laughter followed
by a long sigh.

"Geeze. Times surely ain't what they usta be
is they, when one goes an fergits their very own
neighbors." The man stepped forward, his legs
struggling to support him. With each step, Jasper
could see more clearly and what he saw made his
jaw drop. Tottering toward him, his legs, arms and
torso as shredded as his pants, was his next door
neighbor, Wilcox.

"Lord a-mighty," yelled Jasper. "I thought
fer sure you was a goner ... that them wolves had
tore you apart."

Wilcox laughed again as he stepped around
the headstone and looked down at Jasper. "They

did. They did. And now ... I'm gonna do the same t'you."

Wilcox lunged forward, grabbed Jasper by the collar and yanked him to his feet. Jasper tried to fight back, but as soon as he raised his arm, Wilcox kicked him hard in his bad leg. Stars burst forth behind his eyes and he whimpered. Another kick and he screamed.

Wilcox shook him from side to side then dumped him on the ground and stood on his broken leg. The louder Jasper yelled, the more he twisted his weight down on the leg.

"I know whutcha been thinkin," hissed Wilcox. "I could hear yer pathetic thoughts in my head. And frankly, I'm sick a-hearin ya bellyache about whutcha done. Ya done it. Live with it. Or ... in this case ... die with it."

Wilcox stepped off of Jasper's leg and watched as he tried to crawl away. He waited until Jasper had almost made it to the macadam roadway before seizing him again. He lifted him up by his hair, took his chin in one hand, the back of his head in the other and snapped his neck in one jerking motion. The crack echoed off the closest stone and then was swallowed by the night.

He unceremoniously dropped the limp form of his former neighbor to the ground, stepped over him and headed toward the heart of the cemetery. On the other side of the road, he turned and waved at Jasper's body.

CHAPTER 124

Thump, thud, thump. The pain was like exploding fireballs in the back of her head. Linda clawed and scratched at the thing that was trying to pound her brains out, the former Adam Dahl. Her fingers tore through the grayed flesh of his chest, tearing long ribbons of dead skin away. She kicked and rocked but she couldn't budge him, and each blow brought her closer to blacking out. Her arms felt like lead and she could hardly breathe from the weight of his body pressing down on her. Her flailing began to falter as she lost strength.

Above her, she could see Adam's face grinning. He was drooling and it splashed down into her eyes, mixing with the tears that were rolling down her cheeks.

Then, the pounding stopped. Adam sat bolt upright, his eyes rolling back in his head, his mouth dropping open and his arms clawing at his back. Her vision was blurred, the tears and drool making everything look cloudy, but she could see the tip of the Kahnjal poking out of the front of his chest. The weight on top of her eased as her attacker was dragged up and out of the hole in which she'd been pinned.

A hand reached down, grabbed her by the wrist and pulled her up. She expected to see Jack standing there smiling, but when her vision cleared she saw it was Eric who had saved her life.

"I think you dropped these," he said, smiling. He handed her back the Kahnjal that had been knocked from her hand when Adam attacked her.

"I used one. Sorry." He smiled again and nodded at the dagger sticking out of Adam's back. "Hope ya don't mind too much."

Linda coughed heavily and pointed in a direction behind and to the left of him. When Eric turned, he saw the thing on top of Jacobs.

"Wait here, pretty Lady. I'll be right back." He pulled a Kahnjal from the hip pocket of his overalls and strode across the lawn.

Linda watched, catching her breath and trying to clear her head, as Eric freed Jacobs from his captor and certain death. She swept the graveyard looking for Jack. It was still hard to see, not quite total darkness, but close. There was only a faint glow from the moon.

Way over to her right, a few rows down, she saw what looked like shadows dancing. Their movements were almost convulsive. She strained to narrow her focus. It was definitely two people, but she couldn't quite make out what was happening. It looked like one was being dragged backwards by the other. There was no way to see who it was from this distance and in this lighting.

"I'll be over there," she choked out to Eric, who was still tending to Jacobs.

She started off in that direction but someone shot by her. Instinctively, she reached out a hand and tried to grab him. She missed, and Willie was halfway down the row before she could get her feet under her enough to start running.

"Willie, no! Wait. Wait for me. Wait for help."

Willie ignored her calls, shrinking to no more than a moving shadow in the darkness ahead of her.

***

Witherstone dragged Arliss back away from Geoffrey and the pommel. She started to bring her arm up, hoping to plunge the point of her scimitar into his chest, but as soon as he caught sight of the movement he stomped down hard on it. He was now semi-straddling her, one leg across her shoulder and a foot on her forearm. He had a firm grasp on her long hair with both hands, thick strands of it wrapped through his fingers. Each time she tried to reach up with her free hand to disentangle herself, he'd give a sharp tug, jerking her body backward.

Witherstone twisted around, grinding the ball of his foot down on her forearm. He was now facing her and he planted his other foot solidly in the crook of her other elbow. He stared down at her, still pulling and jerking on her hair with all his might. Some of it had already torn loose and he'd had to adjust his hold. He knew the pain of it was intense and he was enjoying her agony.

"Did you really think you could win? What a ridiculous thought. But ... I guess when you're a ridiculous little person all you have are ridiculous little thoughts."

"This is far from over," she panted, the words coming out in broken syllables as Witherstone continued to pull and tug.

"Trust me, my dear. It would take someone far bigger and stronger than you to topple me. You should have stayed at your stupid, quiet little museum."

He laughed, loud and long.

Arliss tried to gain some leverage with her feet and legs. She dug her heels into the soft earth and tried to arch herself up. But as soon as she got her feet into position, Witherstone yanked her backward.

"I'd so love to continue our little waltz here," he said through the laughter, "but I'm afraid the time has come to end all this nonsense. Really though-" an artificially puzzled look played across his face, "-I just can't believe that a puny human could think they could stop *me.*"

He let go of her hair, jumped into the air and came down on her sword arm with both heels. Arliss screamed. Her fingers splayed open and the sword slipped from her grasp. Witherstone immediately dragged her away from it. He let go of her hair, after one final tug that nearly cracked her collarbone, and dropped his hands around her throat. He plucked her up and held her out in front of him, squeezing as hard as he could.

Arliss pulled at his wrists but couldn't break his hold. She could feel his thumbs closing off her windpipe. She kicked at him, but he ignored the blows, which were becoming steadily weaker.

"I told you, my dear," he snarled, "it'd take someone much bigger and stronger than you to defeat me. Now just keep still and this will all be over soon."

***

Jack could hear what was going on behind him, but his concentration was focused on containing Geoffrey. He realized that he couldn't keep him in this hold, pinned beneath him, forever and that he'd have to do something fast. Temporarily letting go of one of Geoffrey's wrists, he reached for his gun.

"Sorry pal," he said, and brought the butt of the gun down on Geoffrey's forehead.

Geoffrey's eyes rolled back in his head and he went limp. Jack holstered his gun, sat up and took a deep breath, and then dug in his pocket. When he found what he was searching for he drew it out, pulled open the blade and climbed off of Geoffrey.

"Swiss Army Knife ... don't leave home without it."

Jack tugged on the corner of Geoffrey's pocket and began slicing around the edges. When he finished, he picked up the pommel, still wrapped up inside the pocket material. He wasn't sure what to do next. He could feel it vibrating in his hands and it seemed to be getting hotter. He knew he didn't have much time before the thing burned through the fabric and was free to absorb him. He thought about dropping it on the ground and then bashing it or shooting it, but was afraid that neither would have any effect and it might be able to roll free.

He looked over to see how Arliss was doing and was shocked to see that she was slowly being choked to death. Now he really had to do something. But what? He didn't dare take the pommel near Witherstone. That's exactly what he wanted. And it was taking all his strength and both hands to control the thing as it was. He felt helpless and a little lost, a feeling he'd only had once before, when he kept hearing Patty O'Donnell asking him: "Why didn't you save me, Jack?"

***

Over Arliss's shoulder, Witherstone could see a small shape coming toward him out of the darkness. It was moving fast. It darted deftly in and out of the headstones, jumping over some. It was coming straight at him. And there was another shape several yards behind it, much bigger but less agile.

Willie shot past Witherstone to his right, wheeled and dove on his back, pushing off as hard as he could with his legs to get height. He hit him square in the small of his back, wrapped his legs around him piggyback style, and plunged both of his remaining Kahnjals between his shoulder blades.

Witherstone shrieked, dropped Arliss, threw his arms up over his head and clawed at the iron daggers stuck in his back. Each time one of his hands got near one Willie would slap it away. Witherstone lurched forward, staggering, clawing and screaming. When he came to a mausoleum, he turned and rammed his back against it in a series of hard jerks, each time slamming Willie's back against the cold hard stone until his grip faltered and he dropped off.

Once free of the boy, he dashed forward and pulled the spikes from his back. He was seriously wounded by them, most of his strength gone, but not fatally wounded. He turned on the boy, hatred and revenge sweeping over his face.

Willie picked himself up and ran off into the darkness before Witherstone could reach him. He was trying to figure a way to get around behind him again, grab the Kahnjals and repeat his last attack when an idea came to him. It was no more than a light butterfly of a thought, but it froze him in his tracks. Where it had come from, he had no idea. He stood there, completely immobilized while the thought took shape in his mind. And it was accompanied by words, words spoken in a voice that was semi-familiar.

"You're the one," the voice said. "You have the power to change the course of everything. Use it."

Willie blinked. All of a sudden he felt warm as if he'd developed a sudden fever. The heat seemed to be swallowing him, devouring him. He felt as if he were going to burst into flames at any moment. He let out a long, bellowing scream.

Linda arrived in time to see Witherstone pull the Kahnjals from his back and Willie to dash off into the darkness. It was a few steps too late. By the time she got control of her run, she came to a stop no more than three feet away from Witherstone.

He turned slowly to face her. A minatory smile slid across his face as he slowly walked forward. His eyes glowed a deep green that seemed to draw her in. Linda's hands dropped limply to her sides as she stared into the emptiness of those green orbs.

Witherstone reached out a hand as if he were inviting her to dance.

"Don't be shy, my dear, come ... come see what I have for you." He opened his mouth and it looked to be full of shark's teeth, rows and rows of pointed, black shark's teeth.

As soon as their hands touched, Linda snapped back to reality, but it was too late. Witherstone had a firm grasp on her wrist and was pulling her toward him, mouth agape.

CHAPTER 125

Willie started back towards Witherstone, not really knowing what he was going to do. Somehow, he felt different, stronger, more aware. The heat inside him began to push outward, surrounding him in a bluish-white glowing bubble. He rounded the corner of the mausoleum where Witherstone had dislodged him from his back, walked calmly over to the Kahnjal and picked them up. He looked for a long moment at Linda and

Witherstone, then turned and walked slowly and deliberately down the row of stones toward Jack.

Witherstone cocked his head over his shoulder when Willie appeared and watched as he picked up the spikes and walked off. A flash of fear chilled him when he saw the hot white glow that surrounded the boy. He let go of Linda and turned to watch as the boy walked away from him. He didn't realize that he was trembling, that somewhere deep inside him he knew that this boy could somehow be his downfall, but consciously, he dismissed it. He started off in Willie's direction.

Linda shook her head. Everything seemed a little dream-like, and her wrist, where Witherstone had held her, began to swell. She wanted to move, to go after Willie and Witherstone but her legs wouldn't cooperate. She felt as if they had suddenly been turned to stone.

***

By this time, Arliss had regained her breath and retrieved her sword. She strode over to Jack, who was bouncing the pommel between hands like a hot potato.

"So what the hell am I supposed to do with this thing now that I've got it?" he asked.

Arliss tore one of the sleeves from her shirt, wrapped it around the already pants-confined pommel and took it from Jack.

On the ground behind Jack, Geoffrey began to stir, moaning loudly. There was a terrible throbbing in his head and he felt like he was swimming up from the bottom of a cold, dark lake. He sat up slowly and tried to focus. Everything was blurry.

"Go help Geoffrey," commanded Arliss. "He's ok now, we have the pommel."

Jack just stared at her for a minute. This was all getting to be a bit much for him. Criminals and waywards were more his speed. Dealing with the damned, dead, and devils was best left to the heroes of motion pictures.

He helped Geoffrey to his feet, apologizing for having had to crack him.

"It's ok," stammered Geoffrey. "Believe me, I completely understand. I can't believe that thing infected me so quickly."

CHAPTER 126

Eric and Jacobs had just finished dispatching the last two corpses that seemed to be wandering aimlessly when a third figure stepped out of the bushes. It lunged at Jacobs, its fingers digging into his upper shoulder. It drew him backward and sank its teeth into his neck, whipping its head from side to side like a wolf with its prey. A large hunk of flesh was ripped out just at the angle where the neck meets the shoulder. Jacobs screamed.

Eric reached for a Kahnjal. His hands came away from his waistband empty. He'd just used his last. A fleeting sense of panic slipped through him but dissipated. Kahnjal or no Kahnjal, he had to do something.

Jacobs dropped to his knees writhing in pain, blood spurting rhythmically in huge arcs from the wound. Eric recognized the figure standing over Jacobs, a hunk of Jacobs's flesh hanging from its mouth, its one hand still firmly grasping the priest's collar. Wilcox turned and looked at Eric, pointed a finger at him and winked.

Infuriated, Eric prepared to charge the thing when the bushes behind it parted again. Jasper Collins lurched forward, his head bobbing loosely on his chest with every step. Looking out of the tops of his eyes, his gaze fell first on Wilcox, then on Eric. He stopped and half turned toward Eric. There was a sorrowful expression plastered on his face that Eric could just make out in the moonlight. The corners of Jasper's mouth turned up. It was more of a grimace than a smile, but its meaning was not lost on Eric. It was the face of someone trying to do what couldn't be done. It was the half-smile of a person trying to atone for actions that could never be atoned for.

The corners of his mouth drooping back down, Jasper turned, struggled forward and grabbed Wilcox around the neck. Wilcox had been watching, and the expression that swept across his face when Jasper grabbed *him* was one of shock and surprise. He had assumed that Jasper Collins was here to do the same bidding he was. He had assumed that Jasper was under the same mandate and the same control. He was wrong. Whatever good was left in Jasper Collins had taken control and it now set about destroying his killer.

Eric watched, mouth agape, as the two zombies battled. For a while, it looked as though Jasper was going to lose the fight. But at the last minute, as they wrestled on the ground, rolling and clawing at one another, Jasper finished it for both of them.

Straddling his opponent at the base of a tall headstone, Jasper reached up and used all his might to topple the stone down on top of both of them. There was a heavy thud and the sound of breaking bone, accompanied by a sickeningly loud squishing as both corpses were crushed beneath the granite marker.

**

When Geoffrey got over to Jacobs, Eric was kneeling beside him, his hand pressed firmly against the gushing wound. Jacobs was lying face down, his upper body already saturated in his own blood.

"I'll take it from here." Geoffrey nudged Eric out of the way. Reaching into the wound, he pinched off the severed artery with his fingers. "This isn't going to hold him for long, I'm afraid."

"What else can we do?" asked Eric.

"I don't-" Geoffrey's words were cut off as his head shot up, his eyes riveted on the glow that was coming from the bushes ahead, the same ones from which Wilcox and Jasper had emerged. It illuminated the leaves and ground in an approaching bubble of blue-white, giving everything a surreal look.

"What now?" asked Geoffrey.

The bubble of light grew larger and the branches parted.

Willie stepped out, surrounded by the bubble, looked around and then walked over to Geoffrey.

"He's coming. Not far behind me. You should get ready. I can fix this."

Willie gently pulled Geoffrey's hand away from Jacobs. Eric and Geoffrey glanced at each other, an expression of total amazement on both their faces.

Willie touched his index finger to the wound. A ring of blue-white light chased itself in circles around Jacobs's neck, then seemed to sink in, be absorbed. After it faded, Willie drew his hand back. There was still a large fissure where the flesh had been torn away, but the artery was no longer spouting fountains. In fact, there was no bleeding at all, just a deep, raw depression.

"You're going to need your clocks," said Willie as he bent down and took another Kahnjal from the priest and added it to the two already in his hand.

"The clocks? Yes, of course," mumbled Geoffrey. "How the hell could I have been so stupid?"

Willie smiled at him and then turned and walked over to Arliss who was still wrestling with the wrapped pommel. When he got there, he jammed the Kahnjals, one at a time, into the ground forming a triangle.

"Place it in the center," he said.

Arliss stared at him for a moment. She wondered how it was that she hadn't foreseen this. How she hadn't felt, hadn't known, that Willie Peterson was the true third and not Eric Baxter. She wondered how she hadn't been able to recognize, even in this form, her rejuvenated brother.

She dropped the pommel into the center of the triangle. It rolled and tumbled around but could not cross any of the boundaries between the Kahnjals. It vibrated and bounced and glowed. Eventually, it burned through its wrappings, the skull's dark, red eyes glowing and its jaws snapping open and closed. Each time it tried to pass between two of the spikes sparks would fly in all directions and fingers of blue electricity would dance across its surface. When it did, its jaw would drop open wide in a silent, but evident, scream.

Geoffrey got to his feet and dug in his pocket for the Big Ben replica. He drew it out and stared at it for a moment, not believing that he'd forgotten all about it – forgotten all about them. He started off towards Arliss and Willie, shaking his head at his own stupidity and leaving Eric to tend to Jacobs.

Jack had gone back to check on Ethan who was bouncing back and forth between consciousness and unconsciousness. He had just knelt down beside Ethan when he heard the bushes stirring to his left. He whirled around on one knee, bringing his gun up at the same time.

Linda pushed through the tangle of leaves and vines. There was a vacant look on her face, as if she weren't sure where she was. She looked at

Jack and then grinned. But there was something hollow in it, something not quite right.

A moment later, Witherstone stepped out from behind the bush, the fingers of his left hand buried in Linda's back. He turned his head and looked at Jack and then over at Eric and Jacobs. Linda's head mimicked his.

"Do you like my puppet?" he asked. "I can make her do anything I like. And probably will." He laughed. "You know, it's all your fault. All of you, actually. You left her behind. I thought that she must be a present, a wonderful gift for livening up your dead town."

Jack jumped to his feet, as did Eric. They both advanced on Witherstone.

"Un-uh," he said, wagging a finger at them. "Don't forget who's in control." He pushed his hand deeper into Linda's back, through the ribs and wrapped his fingers around her heart.

"Watch this." He squeezed and Linda went limp. Her lips began to turn blue and all the color drained from her face.

"Amazing, isn't it?" Witherstone released his grip on her heart and made her stand upright again. "My own living doll. What fun.

"Now, knowing that you two are kind of a thing, I'm willing to make you a trade. Isn't that just magnanimous of me? I mean really, considering I don't really need your puny help at all ... I think it's outstandingly generous of me to make such an offer. What do you think?"

Jack was seething. His face was twisted into a knot of anger, his jaw clenched and his eyes narrowed. He held the gun out in front of him, the barrel pointed directly at Witherstone's face, his finger tight around the trigger.

At that moment, Eric stepped in front of him and lowered his arm.

"I don't think you'd really wanna try that," Eric said to Jack. "I'd be willin t'bet our friend here'd move the pretty lady right inta yer way."

Eric took another step forward, moving directly between Jack and Linda and Witherstone, one hand pressed firmly on his bib pocket.

"I'm prit'sure," he said, looking directly at Witherstone, "that we can't afford t'trade ya fer what ya want. That'd be that dadblamed bally thing, wouldn't it?" He stared directly into Witherstone's eyes and didn't blink once. "Well, truth-a the matter is, no matter how much we value this pretty lady ... an' we do a'course ... we just wouldn't b'able t'make such a trade."

Witherstone moved his fingers in Linda's back and she began to speak.

"Ah, Jack, you aren't going to let this old coot tell you what you can and can't do, are you? Really! Who's sheriff around here? Him or you? Besides, I thought you loved me. Aren't I worth the crummy top of a sword?"

Eric spun around to face Jack.

"Ya know ya c'nt listen t'this, don't ya? Ya *do* know that? Jus' think about it and y'll see. That thing-" he shot a thumb over his shoulder at Witherstone, "-it'ain't trestwerthy, and you know it. It's gonna kill all-a us anyway, whether ya do what it wants er not."

CHAPTER 127

Eric was still standing in front of Witherstone when Arliss walked up. Her scimitar dangled loosely from her hand at her side, her other hand tucked inside her belt. Her face was relaxed but her eyes focused. She stepped up and stood beside Eric.

"Your time is nearly done here," she said, her voice flat and even. "You can't win. Not now; not without the pommel."

Witherstone manipulated his fingers inside Linda's back. She turned her head and stared blankly at Arliss.

"We'll get it back momentarily," said Linda. The words came from her mouth but the voice was Witherstone's. "Certainly you don't think that you've defeated me simply by corralling my ... my toy. You can't tell me that you honestly believe that that is the sole source of my powers. You couldn't possibly be that dense ... could you?" He smiled again and cocked his head a half twist over his shoulder.

"You might as well come out, Dunsmore. I know you're there behind me," he called over his shoulder. "I don't think there's much you can do to me without these, is there?" He held up the two remaining Kahnjal that he'd taken from Linda.

Geoffrey said nothing. He was looking past Witherstone at Arliss. His mind was blank and so was hers. They were each concentrating on the emptiness of space. They were each shielding their thoughts from Witherstone.

"Jack," Geoffrey called, "why don't you go check on Father Jacobs. Make sure he's still ok."

Jack hesitated. There was no way he was going to leave while that thing had control of Linda. He would wait, and as soon as he got a clear shot, he'd take it. But as he stood there, an image began to form in his mind. A clock. He could see the face of a clock. And it kept getting bigger and bigger.

Everything around him seemed to dissolve. Sounds dwindled to the roar of pure silence. He began to feel dizzy and slightly sick at his stomach. He tottered on his feet, stumbling back a couple of steps. Arliss reached out and grabbed him. The touch of her hand on his arm was like an electric shock. It ran all the way through his body; his hands jerked and he dropped his gun. His legs momentarily gave out, but he caught himself before he fell. In his mind, a slow movie was playing over and over again. And somehow, he knew he had to imitate what he was seeing in his head.

"Yes," he said. His words were slightly slurred, as if his jaw had been pumped full of Novocain. "Yes, I'll check on Jacobs."

"What's going on?" asked Witherstone. "I can feel it. You're up to something." He was looking at Arliss, sparing intermittent turns of his head to keep track of Geoffrey. A nervous look spread across his face like a shadow across a sidewalk.

"We're not up to anything," said Arliss. "We're just waiting to see what your next move is going to be. You're the one holding all the cards, aren't you? You're the one with the girl's life in your hands. What's next?"

Jack knelt down beside Jacobs, leaned in and examined the wound on his neck. With his back to Witherstone, he mimicked what he was seeing in his mind. He reached into Jacobs's pocket and pulled out an object. As he stood up, he pushed it into his own pocket before he turned around.

"How is he?" asked Geoffrey. "Still ticking?"

"Yes, still ticking," answered Jack, his voice sounding almost mechanical.

Witherstone raised the sword that hung in his right hand. He jabbed it into the air. A flash of blue ran up the length of the blade from the hilt and shot off the tip. Like an arc of lightning, it struck a tree behind Arliss, splitting it in half and engulfing it in flames.

"You see," he said, grinning. "There's still more power left than you might have imagined." He stepped forward, Linda preceding him. They moved slowly and cautiously around Arliss toward the captive pommel.

Arliss gave way, just barely moving to one side to let them pass. Like Geoffrey, she waited.

"Lucifer's Pommel. That's what they're calling it isn't it?" asked Witherstone. "Well, I don't know if it was really his. For that matter, I don't know if there is a Lucifer. But I *do* know that that crystal is an ancient conglomeration of collective-" He paused. "Shall we say, unpleasantries. It was cast by an ancient society that wanted to rid itself of all its evils ... to contain them if you will.

Consequently, over the centuries, like a good wine, it's aged ... festered, grown heavy with a restless idleness of malevolence. And I know exactly how to put such a lush treasure to good use. It will sustain me. It will nourish me. And in so doing, it will drain the life from you. From you and all mankind."

***

Witherstone and Linda, his chosen bride, were now only a few yards away from the pommel. Arliss and Geoffrey had kept pace with them, Eric slightly behind and Jack behind him. Geoffrey and Arliss kept sending inconsequential thoughts back and forth, creating a kind of mindless chatter that served only to add a bit of distraction. They knew that Witherstone would be following those thoughts, that he couldn't afford not to.

Witherstone stopped. Just ahead of him he could see the pommel rolling madly around, a shiny blur of motion. He slowly withdrew his hand from Linda's back and she collapsed. Jack sprang forward but Arliss grabbed him and held him back.

"Not yet," she said, just barely breathing the words.

Jack's arms dropped to his sides and his head dropped to his chest. He felt like a puppet. His mind and heart wanted to do something, but his body didn't want to cooperate. He stood there looking at his girlfriend stretched out on the damp cemetery lawn.

Geoffrey moved to his left, circling to the other side of Witherstone. Witherstone immediately jerked his head in his direction.

"I don't think I'd try anything fancy if I were you, mate," said Witherstone, placing the point of his sword down on Linda's chest. "Not if you'd like to see this young lady keep breathing." He laughed, then turned back to Arliss.

"You, my dear, can just drop your silly-looking sword on the ground. No! Wait. Better yet, I want you to stick it in the old man there. Kill Mr. Baxter for me, would you dear? I'd be so appreciative. And so would Mrs. Killerman here." He pushed down slightly on the sword and a point of red oozed up from the broken skin.

Jack was furious. He wanted to lunge forward and take his chances. He didn't care whether he survived or not. But his feet seemed glued to the ground, unwilling to do his bidding. He felt as if someone had severed the connection between his nerves and his muscles.

With no warning, Arliss reached out and shoved Jack. She shoved him hard and he staggered several feet to his right, almost fell and then regained his balance. Now he was stuck in a new spot, still wanting only to wring Witherstone's neck.

"I'm waiting," chuckled Witherstone. "I'm usually a very patient individual, but not now. You kill Baxter there, or I kill the girl. Your choice."

Arliss slowly raised her blade and half turned toward Eric. As she did, her other hand slipped into her pocket, the fingers closing around the timepiece.

Eric stepped forward, his left hand still snug against his chest over top of the pocket watch.

"I guess if someone's gotta git it, it oughta be me. I lived a long and fruitful life. It's a fair trade fer the girl." He drew the watch from his pocket and extended both arms out to his sides, offering Arliss a clear target to his heart. "I just ask that ya make it quick."

"No. Oh no, no, no," shouted Witherstone. "I want you to push it into his heart very slowly. I want to watch each expression as it crosses his face and he begins to realize that he has only seconds to live. Don't you dare make it fast and painless."

"Kneel down," Arliss commanded, the tip of her blade pushing against Eric's chest.

"Oh my," cooed Witherstone. "That's a marvelous idea. All of you ... kneel down. All except you of course, my dear. You should definitely be standing. Much better sticking leverage, don't you agree."

A sound began to rise. It started as a low hum, grew to a drone and then climbed to a loud buzzing. Witherstone looked up just in time to see the giant ruby wasp come plummeting out of the sky toward him. He didn't flinch. He waited. He watched. He could see its abdomen flexing as it prepared to impale him with its stinger. He stood there looking skyward and waited.

It swooped down, circled the group once and then headed straight for Witherstone. Witherstone winked at Geoffrey and then raised his blade and pointed it at the incoming wasp. Again, a blue light shot along its length and jumped off the tip. It stretched out into a ribbon of electric-blue fire and plowed into the center of the wasp's head, just between the antennae. It coursed straight through its body and shot out the other end. The wasp turned a glowing blue, burst into flames and dropped to the ground.

"Well, said Witherstone, "that was exciting, wasn't it?" He rubbed the nails of one hand on his lapel and then blew on them. "Very exciting, indeed. But a little anticlimactic, eh? Now, where were we? Oh yes, you were about to dispatch Mr. Baxter for me. Please, by all means, continue."

Still a few paces behind Witherstone, Geoffrey sank to his knees. As he did, he slipped his hand in his pocket and pulled out the clock. He set it on the ground next to him. The action was unobserved by Witherstone, whose attention was centered on Arliss and Eric.

Jack also knelt down. His face was still crumpled into barely controlled rage. He kept Linda in the periphery of his vision while staring at Witherstone.

Arliss flashed a thought at Geoffrey and immediately turned her concentration back to Eric. She hoped it had been clear enough for Geoffrey to have received and, at the same time, fleeting enough to have escaped Witherstone's grasp. It had.

Geoffrey started to get to his feet. Witherstone whirled on him. At the same time, Arliss pulled the darts from her waistband and sent them whizzing at Witherstone. Two of them dug into the back of his neck and the third between his shoulder blades. They continued to spin and dig, to tunnel their way through him.

The sword dropped from his hand as he lurched forward, his hands clutching at the burrowing darts. He managed to grab one by the feathers, but they tore loose when he pulled on them. He screamed and dropped to the ground.

Arliss pulled her clock from her pocket and placed it on the ground, yelling to Jack to do the same thing. When he had, Witherstone was centered in the triangle of clocks, just like the pommel was centered in the triangle of Kahnjals.

Almost in unison, Arliss and Geoffrey began winding the hands of their Big Ben replicas in a counterclockwise direction. When they let go, the hands began to swing forward, increasing in speed with each pass of 12.

"Wind your clock backwards," Geoffrey hollered to Jack. "Wind the hands and then let go. Quickly!"

Jack obeyed. As soon as he released the hands, all three clock faces began to glow a soft blue. The glow intensified as the hands spun faster and faster and spread into a beam. The beam narrowed and shot from one clock to the other, creating a pencil-thin line of dancing electricity that formed a glowing fence around Witherstone.

Inside the fence, Witherstone was on his back, rolling from side to side, his legs kicking and his arms thrashing wildly. The two darts had dug in, the point of one already beginning to show through the saggy pale skin of his throat. A hazy aura could be seen beneath the flesh where the darts burned.

"We need you now," said Arliss as she helped Eric to his feet. "The watch. Your pocket watch is the final element, the lock to his prison."

Eric held the watch out in front of him. It was warm and glowing a bright red.

"Don't open it," commanded Arliss. "Not yet. Come on."

She grabbed Eric by the strap of his overalls and dragged him forward.

"I'm comin," he protested, trying to get his feet under him before he toppled over. "No need t'be a-draggin me like a dadblamed doll."

Witherstone was still writhing in agony, but something else was also happening. His body seemed to be shrinking, drawing in on itself. It reminded Eric of the time he'd used the heat gun on the shrink-wrap to send a chocolate Easter Bunny to his niece. As the body shriveled, green smoke began to billow from the mouth, nose, and eyes.

"Oh Christ!" yelled Geoffrey. "That shit's gonna slip through the barrier. He's going to get out."

Arliss grabbed the pocket watch out of Eric's hand and snapped it open. But it was too late. The green filament had already begun to drift out underneath the clocks' hissing, blue electric boundary.

"So what does that mean? We're fucked? Are you saying we're fucked?" demanded Jack, kneeling beside Linda and cradling her head.

The green smoke snaked its way over to the pommel. It circled the perimeter the Kahnjals formed. One thread tried to cross between them. As soon as it did, a bright flash erupted. The smell of ozone and burned flesh filled the air and the smoke retreated.

"We've got to try and figure some way to contain it," said Arliss.

Geoffrey was standing beside her. "We have to get it back inside the clocks' perimeter. Somehow."

Behind the Kahnjal barricade, a hazy light began to break through the thickets. It grew stronger and more brilliant, and the bushes began to part.

A bubble of blue-white light pushed out into the open. Inside was a dark silhouette, no more than a wispy shadow of a figure. The bubble-figure moved toward the Kahnjals and the pommel, seeming more to float than to walk. It stopped just at the border.

The green smoke moved away, slithering around to the opposite side. It curled into a tight coil with one slender thread sticking up, like a cobra head.

The figure in the bubble reached down into the center of the Kahnjals and picked up the jittering pommel.

The raised thread of green smoke shot forward, taking the shape of a snake's head with gaping mouth and curved fags. It pierced through the bubble of light, closing its filamentous jaws on the outline of the shadow-figure's arm.

As soon as its fangs embedded themselves in the dark arm, the rest of the green ribbon was drawn in, sucked inside the bubble-like a string into a vacuum.

The figure inside held up the pommel in one hand, turning it so that the skull was facing him. The green ribbon began to thin, the snake-shaped head dissolving into a powdery mist. It swirled around inside the bubble of light, circling the figure. And then it was drawn into the gaping mouth of the pommel's skull.

The skull started to lose its shape; it started to bend and warp. Its hollow jaw dropped open and a loud, chilling scream filled the night. Tiny fissures began to form in the crystal, running in all directions.

The figure inside the bubble moved toward the clocks, and when it was standing directly over them, dropped the crystal into the center, and then stepped back.

The electric boundary the clocks had formed started to sizzle and spark, shooting thin lines of hot blue into the center. They surrounded the crystal pommel in an electric web, squeezing in on it, dancing across its surface and widening the fissures.

Arliss moved in, holding the pocket watch out. It was still glowing a fiery red but the hands weren't moving.

"I don't understand," she yelled to Geoffrey. "Nothing's happening. It should have started to collapse by now."

In desperation, she thrust her arm into the glow of the clocks. Fingers of electricity rebounded off the pommel's circumference and wrapped themselves around her arm. The pain was excruciating. The flesh on her forearm began to blister then turn black. Instinctively, she jerked her arm back out.

"Now what?" she asked. She was puzzled. The watch should have been the capstone on the whole thing. It should have worked. And she had no idea why it hadn't.

The figure in the bubble took a few steps backward, then swayed and fell. The bubble began to lose its glow and shrink in on the figure. As it collapsed around the shape inside, it dissipated, leaving behind the dazed and spent body of Willie Peters.

"Maybe I should give it a go," suggested Geoffrey.

"No! That would be my job. That would be the dadblamed reason I'm here in the first place."

Eric walked up to Arliss, and without saying another word, plucked the pocket watch out of her hand. He looked at Jack and Linda and smiled. He then turned to Geoffrey and winked.

"What, exactly, do you think you're going to do?" asked Arliss.

"What I was meant t'do. We all have a reason, a perpis. Thisun's mine."

Eric nodded his head, a so-long-see-ya-later gesture. He then turned and stepped into the middle of the clocks, holding the pocket watch above his head, its numerals facing the pommel.

The red glow of the watch intensified and expanded. It grew so brilliant that all had to avert their eyes and shield them with their arms. It expanded until it encompassed everything on the inside of the Big Ben replicas, and then swallowed them, too.

There was a momentary hissing and a barely audible *pop*, followed by a baleful wailing. Then the glow began to diminish. It collapsed in on itself, pulling everything in with it. The clocks were lifted and sucked inward, as was Witherstone's sword. Everything condensed in the center to a small, brilliant dot of red.

The dot hovered there above the ground, pulsating as if it were breathing. Then ... it exploded outward in concentric rings of hot red and disappeared, leaving behind burnt grass and a deep imprint.

A putrid, fetid smell hung in the air. The mist began to clear, and the moon slid across the sky above the trees to its appointed place in the night.

CHAPTER 128

Arliss walked over and lifted Willie up. His eyes fluttered and then opened. She sat him up against one of the headstones.

"You ok?" she asked.

He tried to answer but was too drained. He just bobbed his head up and down in a slow yes. His insides felt like they were bound in hot chicken wire and his arms and legs felt like rubber.

Jack helped Linda to a sitting position. He ran his hand down her back searching for the wound Witherstone had inflicted but found none. She raised a hand and laid it on his cheek. When she spoke, her voice sounded as dry as autumn leaves and a trifle distant.

"Jack? Is that you? Everything seems dark and fuzzy."

"It's me, babe. I'm here. Just sit still. You'll be ok." He shot a look at Geoffrey, hoping that he'd confirm that statement.

Geoffrey nodded. "She'll be fine. Just give her some time. I'm going to go check on Father Jacobs." He turned and walked off.

"Can you sit here for a few minutes?" Jack asked Linda. "I have to go check on Ethan."

Linda gave him a weak smile and kissed his hand. "Go on. I'll be ok."

Jack kissed her on the forehead and then headed over to Ethan.

"Willie, can you hear me," asked Arliss. "You did good. You did real good."

Willie coughed and then looked up at her. "I'm not done yet. There's something else I have to do. Please, help me get up."

There was more man in his voice than boy. A fixed determination that stretched beyond his age. Arliss helped him up and steadied him while he got his legs back.

"What, Willie? What else do you have to do?"

"The other man, the man that the sheriff went to help. I can help him. Please, help me get over there."

Arliss bent down and scooped him up. "I'll do better than help you; I'll take you."

When they got over to Ethan, Jack was kneeling beside him holding his hand.

"He's in bad shape. I can't wake him."

Arliss set Willie down and helped him to kneel next to Jack.

"Why don't you move back a minute. I think Willie, here, can do something for him," said Arliss.

Jack pushed up to a standing position and took a step back. Doubt flooded his mind, but hope was stronger. He didn't even realize he was holding his breath.

Willie leaned in over Ethan and slipped his hand beneath his neck. A warm glow circled Ethan's throat, a blue ring of dancing light. It chased itself in circles around his neck and then soaked in and disappeared, just like it had for Father Jacobs. A few minutes later, Ethan opened his eyes.

Willie slumped over and Arliss and Jack caught him before he hit the ground.

"Is he ok?" asked Jack.

"He will be," Arliss assured him.

"What happened?" asked Ethan as he sat up. "I remember feeling like I couldn't move a muscle, but then everything went blank."

"I'll fill you in later," said Jack, a big smile plastered on his face. "I'll tell you all about it over a couple beers."

Ethan rubbed his head.   "How about a couple hundred?   Man, I feel like I just finished a marathon."

Arliss smiled and Jack laughed.   Jack stuck out his hand and helped Ethan to his feet. Arliss bent to pick up Willie.

"I got 'im," said Jack, and lifted the boy into his arms.

When they got back over to Linda, she was sitting up talking with Geoffrey and Jacobs. Geoffrey was explaining what had happened and what Eric had done.

Father Jacobs said a small prayer of thanks and gave Eric Baxter absolution in-absentia.

"I don't believe that Eric was a Catholic, but then again, I don't think it matters.   We all deserve forgiveness ... and when we do, does it really matter where it comes from?"

"No, I guess it doesn't Gabe," agreed Geoffrey. "I guess it doesn't."

CHAPTER 129

THREE MONTHS LATER

They sat at the dining room table at Killerman's B & B. It was the first time they'd all been together since Peaceful Haven. Geoffrey and Jacobs sat on the far side of the table, across from Linda and Jack. Ethan was at the head. Geoffrey had flown in from London that morning and Ethan had just returned from New York where he was now the head of security for a large Wall Street firm.

"Well," said Geoffrey, looking up from his tea. "It looks like everything is pretty much back to normal here."

Jack nodded. "Yeah. For the most part, anyway. I don't think this town'll ever really be the same again, but most of the people seem to have forgotten just about everything. Kind of strange, really."

"Oh, I don't think it's that strange at all," said Jacobs. "I think there's an inherent safety switch in all of us that trips when things get too much to handle. Besides, I think that on some level-" He looked over at Jack, "-that you might label as mystical - it was somehow supposed to be this way. Without the ability to forget, I don't think most of these folks could go on with any semblance of normality if they had to relive what they had done, what was done to them, or what they'd seen. I believe that forgetting is nature's way of purifying and reestablishing a sense of order."

Ethan set his coffee cup down on its saucer and looked at Jacobs.

"I don't know about any of that. Maybe you're right. Maybe it's just that people don't want to remember. Either way you cut it, I wish I had the same good fortune."

"Oh no," said Linda. "I think you're wrong, Ethan. I think, we, we *have* to remember. I think that as easy as forgetting might make things for us, if we forget, we just open the box for some other ... I don't know ... evilness ... to creep in."

"Well," broke in Jack, "I'm just glad the thing was disposed of. Not sure I'd be able to go through all that again. Not and remain sane, anyway."

Jacobs laughed. It was long and deep, and when he finally stopped an expression of serious concern slid over his face.

"You know, of course," he said, "that we didn't really destroy it. We eliminated its form, but evil still lives and walks in the world. Maybe not like Witherstone - probably and hopefully not. But it walks around every day. It's in all of us, whether or not we want to admit it. I just pray to God that it never gets so strong as to seep out into our world again the way it did here."

"The good Father here is right," said Geoffrey. "This was only one battle in an infinite war. They'll be others, I assure you. But for now, the only evil I think we're likely to encounter is the day-to-day stuff. The things we read about in the papers or hear on the evening news."

"I think we've talked about this long enough," said Linda. "I'd really like to change the subject to something more pleasant."

"I second that motion," said Jacobs with a smile. "So tell me, Jack, how do you like being part owner of a B & B? And when the hell are you two gonna get married?"

"What?" asked Ethan, completely startled. "When did this happen?"

Jack smiled. "Last month. I tendered my resignation as sheriff. They brought in a new guy from Texas. He actually seems like a pretty fair fella. As to *your* question-" he looked over at Jacobs, "-when we feel the time is right."

"And that'll be soon," assured Linda.

"You seem to have recovered nicely," Geoffrey said to Ethan.

"Yeah. Good as new. But it was nothing I had anything to do with. It was all Willie. Whatever happened to him, anyway?"

Geoffrey smiled. "He and his mother have moved to Arizona. He's now training under Arliss's supervision. I think he's going to be the strongest ... iteration, for lack of a better term ... of our kind, yet."

Jack got up and went into the kitchen. He came back carrying a tray with five shots of Wild Turkey. Ruby trotted along behind him, his tail wagging furiously as Jack passed out the drinks. They each took one and raised it.

Jack looked from face to face, his shot glass held high. "To friends who are no longer with us. To Doc Robertson, Ernie Johnson, Gwen Archibald, and most of all, to Eric Baxter."

At the sound of his former master's name, Ruby gave up two barks.

ALSO BY **THOMAS A. BRADLEY**

THE SHADOW DEMON

THE COVENANT OF WICKERSHAM HOLLOW

BLOOD TRACKS

SUNDOWN RISING – Also available in Audiobook

PRIMORDIA

13 ECHOES – 13 Short stories

ABOUT THE AUTHOR

Born in Philadelphia, Pennsylvania, I live in Drexel
Hill, PA with my wife, Linda, and two German
shepherds, Georgia and Morgana. I served with the
Army Medical Corps during Vietnam as a Clinical
Specialist. I hold a Bachelor's Degree in
Microbiology, my Master's work done in Virology.
I have worked for a number of biotech companies
as a virologist (a great platform for cultivating the
weird and terrifying).

My short stories have appeared in several
magazines, both print and online.

When it comes to writing horror, I prefer to stick to the old school style rather than the slash and hack. "Allow the imagination to fill in the gaps...the mind can conjure "scary" better than words.

A Gentle Request: Dear Reader, please be kind and post a review. A few words are all it takes. Reviews are helpful to the author, and also to other readers. Thank you.

Tom

Please visit me at:
www.thomasabradley.com